THOSE WE LEAVE BEHIND

GEORGE D. SCHULTZ

ISBN: 978-1-4669-3432-0 (sc)
ISBN: 978-1-4669-3433-7 (e)

Trafford rev. 07/24/2012

www.trafford.com

North America & international
toll-free: 1 888 232 4444 (USA & Canada)
phone: 250 383 6864 ♦ fax: 812 355 4082

ONE

TRUST ME! BECOMING A SCHMUCK is <u>not</u> easy!

Schmuckdom ("Schmuckification"?) is not easily attained. Not by most people, anyway. I've never come across a situation—where a subject such as "Becoming A Total Schmuck" was being taught in any authorized classroom. No "How To" books on the subject—that I know of.

On the other hand, I'd not seemed to have worked too terribly hard—in actually attaining that "lofty" status. "Achieving" that classification hadn't, in truth, been all that difficult. Maybe it just comes/came naturally—to someone like me. Simply a matter of reaching my potential, in that highly specialized area, you might say.

"I'm sorry," came the voice—seemingly overcome with grief and sorrow—from the other end of the phone, "but, *Braniff Airlines* does not serve New York City. Not on our present schedule."

The "Present schedule"—to which she referred—encompassed the period, smack dab, in the middle of

April, 1965. I was living in San Antonio, Texas, at the time. "The Big Apple" was a far piece down the road. Well, up the road.

Good, I remember thinking—almost smiling. Almost. Just as well, I reflected. At least I can put THAT crappy temptation behind me.

Or could I? My eyes shot back down—taking in the cluttered surface of what had, laughingly, passed for my desk.

In truth, the old baby-blues had seldom wandered very far from the inescapable—the riveting, the captivating—center of attraction, lying on the ragged hunk of furniture (so called). The center of attraction was simply lying there! Almost in flames! The focus—the sum total—of my attention seemed to have sprouted red-and-blue flashing lights!

My concentration was—continually and, mercilessly, without let up—nailed to that one intoxicating, overwhelming, focal point! Riveted to the epicenter of all this mind-warping activity! There the intoxicant had lain! That single, dazzling, item! The one completely inescapable object! The one unavoidable object! The item that, relentlessly, encapsulated—each and every one of my devastating, mind-numbing, never-ending, mind-clouding, inner struggles! It was not an exaggeration to state that my whole, entire, life—was wrapped up in that one stupid piece of paper!

Listen, those damnable internal conflicts—truly were overwhelming! And these battles-from-within were witheringly many—and unimaginably varied. (Well, maybe not all that varied. In point of fact—

definitely not all that varied. But, many! Yes—a massive, staggering, wearying, scary, total of them!)

There was an enormous—an uncountable—multitude of these mind-warping, mental and emotional, entanglements! An overwhelming number of raging, interior, battles! So damn many! Too damn many to even begin to tabulate! To/for me, anyway.

Yep—there it had lain! There it—spectacularly—still laid! The exceedingly-generous "helping" of money! Coin of the realm! The real thing! Nothing phony about this monetary cache! The dazzling parcel of dough! The "prize"! That piece of American currency, which would not allow me to crowbar my eyes away from its entrancing—its intoxicating—presence! Yes, the damn silver certificate was still there! In spades! Lying there—atop the freshly-written rental contract!

Staring at me! Sneering at me! Probably laughing out loud—at me! The thing—that single, monetary, note—had, without a doubt, a mind of its own. A very warped mind of its own! It had taken on its own very real—it's own bona fide—personality! Seemingly dwarfing mine! (Well, more than "seemingly"! And more than "dwarfing".)

The cash! The damn cash! Isn't it always the cash? The money? Isn't that what always corrupts? This particular, almost-unheard-of, sum was threatening to set the stupid rental agreement—and probably everything else, in the seedy, badly-in-need-of-a-paint-job, office—afire!

I could just about smell the smoke! It would not have surprised me—to see the damn currency simply combust! On the spot! The emotional heat—already coming from all directions—was tremendously intense! And, to that point in time, "nobody had done nuthin'"! As you might imagine, my overheated brain was a definite—a positive—contributor to the overwhelming amount of this all-consuming combustibility.

I blinked my eyes closed! Then, snapped them open—and looked again! Yeah—there it still was! There it remained! Thumbing its nose at me! There it continued to lie! In my bleary eyes, it was performing some kind of spectacular kabuki dance! That stupid damn thousand-dollar bill!

I'd never actually seen one of those before! Never been in the same room with anything even close! Never before! Let alone ever having actually held one of these intoxicating, mind-blowing, little devils—in my own greedy, sweaty, little hands!

This particular benevolent issuance from the Secretary of The Treasury—this damnable silver certificate—continued to stare me in the face! Smiling at me—grinning at me—it still was! Could it be laughing out loud? Consuming what was left of my fevered brain, is what it was doing! That thing had succeeded in taking over—usurping entire possession of—my badly-warped-by-then consciousness!

I'd already sent Bonifacio—the devoted, efficient, enterprising, Latin-American, service agent—home. Had dismissed him early. The move had, quite understandingly, surprised him. Had actually shaken him—mightily. Quite possibly, it had utterly shocked him!

Shocked the hell out of him—the way my eyes were burning two ever-widening holes in that stupid thousand-dollar note!

Or, hell—maybe it <u>didn't</u>! Maybe, by that time, in his terribly-difficult life, nothing could ever really shake him. A hard-working man—in his late-fifties, I'm guessing—it could very well have been that he'd pretty much "seen it all".

Just listening to this almost-saintly man, as he'd—from time to time—related some of his life's story, had always been out and out <u>fascinating</u>! For me, anyway.

I could never have imagined the far-reaching, the raging, poverty, and the out-of-control lawlessness, in the tiny village—in Central Mexico—where he'd grown up. This was, of course, before the drug cartels had—so ruthlessly—taken over the country! Still, even back then, there had been more than enough poverty—and viciousness—to have frightened me! And I'd never been involved in <u>any</u> of it!

How Bonifacio had <u>ever</u> dealt with all these survival-of-the—fittest circumstances—and had, so valiantly, come through them—has always been beyond me. This was one great man!

I'd considered him a friend—from the moment I'd first "come aboard" at "the truck rental joint". We'd had many frank conversations—over the preceding months.

Maybe—(possibly? probably?)—he was patently aware of the evil little plan that I was hatching, in my twisted, demented, warped, little brain. I found myself fervently hoping—almost praying (almost)—that he wouldn't make any kind of a big thing, as relates to my "strange" manner, since that damnable $1000 had come into play.

Especially whenever he would get together with Red—our glorious, sainted, always-lovable, manager—on the following Monday morning. On the other hand, it probably wouldn't matter—by then—how much he would say. Or <u>what</u>! Or <u>when</u>! The die might very well have already been cast! Who knew? Who the hell <u>knew</u>? At that crucial point, I certainly didn't.

Upon reflection, I guessed that, if I were to actually submit to—give in to—the incredible temptation, which, by then, had become my constant companion, anything and everything (obviously) would wind up being a "big thing", come Monday morning. To quote an old, and tired, cliché: "All hell would break loose." Not original—but, certainly apt.

Everything that would've gone on—on this particular, this fateful, Saturday morning—well, It would all be thrashed out! On Monday! Totally rehashed! Countless times! By Red—and the cast-of-thousands law enforcement people! <u>All</u> would be poured over—relentlessly—by all concerned! Of course it would!

As soon as "Bonny" had left—as soon as his battered old pickup truck was out of sight—I'd hurried out of the "palatial" *Laswell Truck Rental* office. Had made the long, exhausting, on-the-double, trek—all the way down to the double gate, at the far end of the immense, dusty, gravel-and-pot-hole-laden, lot. Once there, I'd chained both sides of the huge, cyclone-fence opening together! Site closed! Well, it was no longer open to the public—once I'd snapped the stupid-looking, gigantic, padlock into place! Closed!

This was at 11:50 AM! An hour-and-ten-minutes earlier than our cast-in-stone Saturday schedule called for. I'd deliberately locked those massive, chain-link, gates—with me inside.

Fortunately (or, maybe, unfortunately) we'd had no further truck rental reservations for the day. But, devotion to duty was—as you can imagine—the last thing on my steam-filled, greedy, little mind.

Given the situation with which I was grappling, I didn't need anyone walking in on me. I'd had sufficient—more than enough—companionship: In the form of—temptation! Incredible temptation! Or, quite possibly, the presence of Ol' Satan! The Devil! Diablo—personally! His-own-self1 He was, without a doubt (I'd decided) definitely, present! Lurking there— I'd become positive—in every nook and cranny of the grungy facility! I could actually feel him! Hear him— breathing! I could smell the sulfur!

Without exaggeration, my entire life was, literally, hanging! Was dangling—precariously— over an enormous precipice! At that precise moment! Suspended—slippery-slope-wise—in the middle of a damnably perilous crossroad. My very existence, I was positive, was at stake. (This all may sound a good bit overdramatic to you—but, I was absolutely convinced that it was true! In fact, I'm still convinced!)

Having no further rental reservations, I'd found that I simply couldn't wait any longer to attempt to "get all of my ducks in a row" Another clammy cliché. But, sadly, it was the definite truth. In my case, anyway.

I strongly believed that I simply had to try—at that point—to get what was laughingly referred to as my affairs in order.

"Affairs"! Unfortunate choice of words. For me, anyway. At that time, anyway. That seemed to be my sad forte of late. Everything I did (or said—or even thought) back then always appeared to evolve around some unfortunate choice of words. No matter how innocent they might have been intended. (Yes—innocent!)

I'd hurried—I'd, literally, actually run—back to the run-down rental office! Yes! IT was still there! That stupid-assed thousand-dollar bill! There it laid! Almost as though a thousand high-intensity spotlights had been trained on it! Emphasizing the spectacular presence of the stupid thing—to the exclusion of everything else in the whole damn place! In the whole damn world! All I'd have needed, at that juncture—for any more heightened-drama—would've been a 32-piece orchestra! And someone like Henry Mancini as the leader! (Drum roll, please!)

As stated, I'd never seen one of those before. (The currency—not the spotlights, or orchestra. Or Mister Mancini.) And—as you can tell—the coin of the realm continued to completely usurp my undivided attention! Undivided! Completely! Ever since the greenback had been so casually placed there!

My celebrated boss—the sainted Adrian (Red) Boyle—had set up the pivotal rental. Well, what could—what probably would—turn out to be the most pivotal rental. Three weeks before all of these moral struggles had descended upon me—had out and out consumed me—my "Peerless Leader" had arranged, over the phone, for one Mr. Asa Phillips to rent one of our three huge *International Load Star* semi tractors, along with our only trailer. Compiled quite a latch-up—those heavy-duty semis. Well, of course, they still do.

The gentleman had, apparently, advised our lovable, epitome-of-warmth, manager that he'd be driving the behemoth rig out to the Pacific Northwest and back.

Since—according to our reliable mileage table, Seattle was almost 3,000 miles from San Antonio—Red had put a pencil to what the rental would realize, in revenue. Something just under nine-hundred bucks!

So, he'd advised Mr. Phillips—that he could pick up the rig on that crucial, that fateful, Saturday morning. He would, however, be required to leave $1000 deposit! A thousand bucks—in <u>cash</u>! The old coin of the realm!

Sure enough, the true-to-his-word customer had come in—right on time—and had picked up the tractor/trailer rig. That dazzling transaction had taken place—two full, long, laborious, torturous, hours before I'd finally ventured out to lock the stupid gate (the "Gates Of Hell"?) those 70 minutes before closing time. We'd had two additional reservations—after Mr. Phillips. Both of these gentlemen had come and gone—within an hour-or-so of the Phillips' departure.

I had, by then, reached a point—where I simply could not wait! Well, in my warped, overheated, little mind, I'd waited long e-damn-nuff! The room-full-of-temptation was tearing me from stem to stern!

So? So *Braniff* did not serve "The Big Apple"? Well, that was a bit of a downer. Becoming more and more of a disappointment—as I'd sat there, pondering what might lie ahead for me. New York was really the place I'd <u>always</u> wanted to be. I'd been fascinated by "The Big City"—from the time I was a little kid!

Johnny Carson had once said, "Outside of New York . . . it's all Bridgeport". I'd always believed that. Rosemary Clooney had responded to that statement, one time, by observing, "Well, you know, when you're out of town . . . you're out of town". And, regrettably, I'd spent my whole, entire, life—"Out Of Town"! And Mr. Carson was right on! It <u>was</u> "all Bridgeport"!

From the time I was a kid—growing up in Detroit—I'd clung to the ambition, of eventually "making it" to New York City! And even in the highly-troubled years that I'd come to know in Texas, I'd always wanted to live in New York! For that long a period (literally, a <u>lifetime</u>), I'd always felt that each and every day—every day that I was forced to be situated elsewhere—I believed that this was a totally wasted day. In my heart, I "knew" that to be true. An actual fact.

The *Tonight Show's* host's "Outside of New York," line had always haunted me. Literally—<u>haunted</u> me. So had the hackneyed old saying, having to do with: "New York . . . I'll lick you yet!" How often had I heard <u>that</u>? For that matter, how often had I heard <u>myself</u>—actually <u>saying</u> it?

It was, to most of the population, simply, "The Big City"! To me, it was "The Only City"! The most-desired place, where—what else?—everything was happening! As stated, I'd come to staunchly believe one undeniable "fact": If you did not live—or at least work—in "The Big Apple", why, you were simply, "socially out to lunch"! "Out to lunch"—in every aspect of your obviously-humdrum, certainly-uneventful, life! You were—tragically—missing out on life itself. You poor soul. (And I was, spectacularly, one of them! I'd always hated that "fact"!)

"There's a broken heart for every light on Broadway". That's what another rather-overworked saying had always proclaimed. The broken-down bromide was apt—in the extreme—I'd always guessed! The overused line had always appeared as unquestionable "gospel" to me. Unquestionable logic! Over the previous year—or-so, this particular "legend" was, consistently, hitting awfully close to home. (And I had never been anywhere close to Broadway! More's the sorrow.)

All those bromides had been long cast in stone! They were truthful—unquestionable, in every way— when it came to good ol' Paul Marchildon! (That's me—in case you'd had any doubts.)

Look! My heart was already broken! In eleven-trillion pieces! Had been broken—positively shattered—for the better part of the damnable, aforementioned, year. Maybe even longer. Probably longer.

At that extremely-tense point, though—on that terribly-bleak, dismal, Saturday—the trauma had engulfed me. For a damn century (or two).

Obviously (to me, anyway) I'd be able to fit right in—up there, in good old NYC. Fit in—right fine. I'd be another luminous bulb—on The Great White Way! That's me! That'd be ol' Paul! And possibly—quite possibly—this fantasized-to-death bit of wonderment would soon/<u>could</u> soon come to pass! Might be! Could be! May be! Again, who the hell really knew?

I picked up the phone again. It took me four fumbling attempts to connect.

American Airlines—the kind lady, with the sexy voice, advised me—<u>did</u> service Gotham. Just not on Saturday! Not on any Saturday! Hmmm. She went above and beyond the call of duty—informing me that <u>no</u> airline served New York City, from San Antonio, on Saturdays. Or—for my further information—on any Sunday, either. The airline business was substantially different—as you can see—that many years ago. (Well, so was San Antonio. And, hell—just about everything else!)

The next flight, this kind lady informed me, would be *United's* Flight 777—on Monday morning. <u>Early</u> on Monday morning. Like 5:30AM.

<u>Thanks a batch</u>!

Well now, stop and think, Paul! Stop and think!

Mr. Phillips had gone on and on and on— just a mere couple hours previous to my call to *American*! The man couldn't stop <u>raving</u>—about how staggeringly-beautiful the entire Pacific Northwest was! How majestic the green, hill-laden, scenery! How clean—and fresh—the water! And the air!

<u>You have always wanted to see the Pacific Ocean, Paul</u>! <u>It would be</u>, <u>you'd always speculated</u>, <u>almost a</u>

religious experience! Almost as soul-stirring as "The Big Apple"! (Almost.)

Why should that be? This "hallowed" Pacific thing, I mean. Hell, I'd most certainly seen the Atlantic. Many times. Had sailed the Atlantic, countless times—when I'd served in the Navy, in the early-fifties. Had even swum in it.

There hadn't seemed to have been any sort of religious sensation—connected to any of that. Why should the Pacific be so overwhelmingly "sacramental"? Everything was so confusing! Everything!

Vis-a-vis my service in the Navy: Can you picture me—protecting you?

Maybe—just maybe—the Pacific Northwest would be the answer. Sure! Why not? It might not be the lifetime goal—the Holy Grail—that New York has always promised to be! But think, Paul! Think!

New York would be one of the first places that the cops—or anyone else—would go looking for a fugitive! Especially this fugitive! This one—who'd always (so loudly) proclaimed his love for "The Big Apple"!

And that's exactly what you'd be, Paul! A damn—a damnable—fugitive! A crook! You are also someone who'd always expounded—to anyone who'd listen— upon the wonderful qualities that could be found only in "Gotham"! Yeah! That's the kind of fugitive/crook you'd be!

A fugitive? A crook? Me? Lovable old Paul Marchildon? A despicable fugitive? Some kind of crook? Me? An on-the-run, damned, fugitive? A cowering crook?

A fugitive! A common—well, maybe, <u>not</u> so common—fugitive! But, no doubt, a totally common <u>crook</u>! That's what I'd be! <u>Exactly</u> what I'd be! <u>Precisely</u> what I'd be! A total <u>schmuck</u>! No sense trying to gloss it over!

If I went ahead and actually <u>took</u>—actually (gulp!) <u>stole</u>—that overwhelming thousand bucks, that's precisely what I'd be! If I were to abscond with that damnable "C-note"—the little item that was still staring me in the face—I'd be a damn fugitive from justice! A common, ordinary, garden-variety, run-of-the-mill, crook! And <u>deservedly</u> so! Obviously!

God! That was <u>heavy</u>! <u>This</u> was heavy! This whole, demented, tear-myself-apart, internal, battle was so damn heavy! I'd always called myself a person who'd hate <u>anyone</u> who would deign to operate outside the law! I mean—to me, the law had always been sacrosanct!

I'd always believed that there could <u>never</u> be <u>any</u> logical excuse for <u>ever</u> breaking the law! <u>Any</u> law! Especially breaking it—in such a spectacular, cowardly, way! (Obviously, to me, a thousand bucks <u>was</u> pretty spectacular. As I've indicated, I'd never had the two proverbial "nickels to, proverbially, rub together". At any time in my life!)

And there I was—"principled" old me—on the brink of becoming a common <u>thief</u>! A damnable lawbreaker! A hated lawbreaker! In spades! And a "common" lawbreaker, at that! Dear Lord! It felt as though my brain was on fire!

To make matters worse, all of a sudden, my alleged mind was flooded with—<u>bombarded</u> with— shadowy images of those almost cartoon-like, hard-boiled, detectives! Mike Hammer-type "dicks"! The kind you would always see—all over television! Or in those glorious old black-and-white, "noir", movies!

Flint-jawed guys like Phillip Marlowe! Like Michael Shane (who'd been my hero during my illustrious naval career)! Like, even, Mr. & Mrs. North! (Well, that was a bit of a stretch.) But, even—God help me—like the aforementioned Mike Hammer! That was pretty scary!

Him—Mr. Hammer—I really did not want to deal with. I'd always remember how *I The Jury* had turned out. I'd read the book, in 11th grade. And I'd wound up getting an "F"—in English! A failing mark—because I'd picked such a "trashy" book, on which to report.

The teacher had to have read the at-the-time-totally-outrageous tome. It was the "hottest" novel on the market, in 1948. By far! But, in my book report, I had made the cover-to-cover racy text out to be completely innocent. As though the work had been written by Louisa May Alcott, maybe. Possibly by Elizabeth Barrett Browning. Maybe even by The Apostle Paul. My submission was that clean and innocent.

Back to my current—extremely-troubling—situation: By indulging in such a dastardly deed of thievery, undoubtedly I would activate—a whole, entire, army of clever-but-ruthless, brilliant, experienced, almost-genius, lawmen! And who-knew-how-many private detectives! (All Mike Hammer-types, of course!) All of them—each of them—dedicated to tracking me down! All those pros! Every one of them—lined up against one poor, single, confused, muddle-headed, little, amateur. What kind of odds were those?

Let's face it! I'd be on the run! Constantly! Continually! Would have to—constantly, unfailingly—look over my shoulder! Both shoulders! Every damn day! Every single minute! I'd never know if this man—or that woman—would be the one who'd cave in my tremulous house of cards. My exceptionally-precarious, totally-illicit, house of cards!

You never really recognize the Paul Drakes of the world! None of the real gumshoes look like Dick Tracy. Nothing close! Well, they could resemble Rip Kirby, maybe. Or Kerry Drake. But, certainly not Dick Tracy. Or Sherlock Holmes. So, you never knew!

The bank teller? Could it be—would it be—him or her? The guy selling papers, at the stand, on the corner? The person running the elevator—in any one of the hundreds of buildings? The cabbie eating at that hot dog cart—parked at the curb of Seventh Avenue and 47th Street? The guy downing a powder-sugared doughnut—across the counter from me—at Chock Full O' Nuts? Any of them? All of them? Could he/she/they be the one(s) who would—without fail—swoop down on me? Eventually, anyway? Bring me "to justice"? No matter how long it would take?

I shuddered! An involuntary spasm! But, it was almost a convulsion! One which, instantly, rattled me—from head to toe! Totally shattered me! In my precarious condition, that didn't take much! Involuntarily, I shook my head—violently!

Stop this! Stop this, Paul! Stop it! This is all bullshit! Then another voice, from a little deeper inside me, chimed in—much more melodically: No it's not! It ain't bullshit! <u>Go ahead, Paul</u>! <u>Take the damn thing</u>! Dear Lord!

Back to formulating my nefarious little plan—or, possibly, not: "It's probably just as well that I actually cannot <u>get</u> to New York." I said that to myself—probably too loudly. And numerous times. "At least not on a Saturday," I groused. "Or even a damn Sunday. At least not from San Antonio". Again, I sighed—and muttered, "Probably just as well, dammit".

Surely, the undeniable fact is, that they'd look for me in "The Big City"! Right from the top! First thing! No matter what! Especially as many times as I'd rattled off my big mouth. Had proclaimed—especially to Joanne, my spouse (and her parents)—the many reasons why I'd <u>love</u> to live up there. Wanted nothing more—than to move up there! To be gloriously able to <u>live</u> up there! "I'll lick you yet!" (Listen, my spouse was <u>not</u> thrilled with that prospect—to say the least. In fact, the shadow of such an "incredibly stupid" move scared the hell out of her!)

Joanne! My wife! Probably my loving wife. Well, <u>possibly</u> my loving wife. I was certain—absolutely positive—that, in her own mind, she'd always loved me. That, at least, her sincerest mindset would be—that she'd <u>always</u> loved me! Would always <u>continue</u> to love me! Despite my telling her of Elena! <u>Elena</u>! Of the beautiful Elena <u>Barrientos</u>!

Joanne had always had a bit of a martyr complex. Well, <u>more</u> than "a bit" of a martyr complex. And my "affair" with Elena would fit in—<u>did</u> fit in, fit in perfectly—with that major portion of her highly-emotional makeup! In fact, it already—undoubtedly—had taken its toll! Of that, I was certain. For her, it redounded to the old "It figures" concept. The one that she'd unfailingly nourished—throughout her entire life. Especially whenever it had come to me.

If/as/when push ever came to shove, she'd probably even forgive me for deserting her—which was what I seemed to be doing! Despite the fact that I'd be saddling her with "all those kids", she'd probably forgive me. Of that I was fairly certain. It would've all fit in. ("It figures"!) That was, simply, Joanne.

She'd do her best to overlook my heinous crime— If I actually did give in to the incredible temptation! (There was that screaming, flashing-neon, thousand-dollar, bill, y'know. And it was still, noisily, tap-dancing, all over the surface of my desk, y'know.)

My wife would, I was positive, absolutely forgive me for leaving her! Eventually, she would, anyway! "Wipe the slate clean" even for running out! For deserting her—and leaving her with four kids! Four little kids! For leaving her—high and dry! And broke!

Broke? Hell, we were always broke! We'd always been broke! That had—forever—been our natural state! Undoubtedly, we would always be broke! Your friendly neighborhood paupers!

Well, truth to tell, Joanne wouldn't be left totally high and for-sure-dry. Not completely. In fact, probably not nearly, It could/should, very well, turn out to be just the opposite, for her. From a financial point of view anyway.

It would—I'd convinced myself—turn out to be a situation that would be 180 degrees opposite from the consistent—the never-ending—stupid poverty! The constant, pauper-for-life, life! The miserable, highly-stressful, lean years that she'd <u>always</u> known—during the entire eleven-year duration of our marriage! Of that I was sure. Well, at least I'd, by then, <u>convinced</u> myself that such would be the case.

Her parents—who, for years, had been living in Brownsville, down on the southern-most tip of "The Lone Star State", about 350 miles south of "The Alamo City"—were extremely well off. Loaded, in fact! They could—they <u>would</u>, I was positive—support Joanne and the kids! Support them—in <u>style</u>!

The Yorks would take care of them—in a manner which was far superior to any level I could ever <u>hope</u> to attain. Far better than I, most assuredly, had <u>ever</u>—in my entire life—come even close to achieving.

"Support 'em! Joanne and the kids! Take care of 'em—far better than I ever have." I kept mumbling that to myself. "A helluva lot better . . . than I ever <u>could</u>! A <u>helluva</u> lot better!" Was I breaking apart altogether? "Far better than I ever <u>could</u>," I continued murmuring, under my breath. Finally, I acknowledged—once again, "Hell, that wouldn't be much of a damn accomplishment."

I'd <u>never</u> been able to turn a buck. I mean <u>ever</u>! Anybody who'd ever known me has, forever, been <u>aware</u> of that inescapable fact. That would, of course, include the parents of my wife. <u>Especially</u> does it include Joanne's folks.

The previously cited cliché—pertaining to the "two nickels"—certainly applied. <u>Always</u>! It was a constant. Only, in my case, this wasn't just some stupid, stale, old bromide. It was an indisputable—universally known—absolute, fact. It was so true. So true! So damn true! So spectacularly true! So consistently true!

"Yeah," I kept murmuring. Maybe, by then, the unending declaration was coming out a shade louder—than merely muttering. "Definitely" I added. "Joanne and the kids! God! How much better off would they be . . . with her folks. So much better off."

Ahhhh! Come off it, Paul! That's all conjecture. All rationalization. All . . . let's face it . . . it's all bullshit. All this thinking and planning. All this plotting.

Hell, I wasn't going anywhere! That goddam thousand bucks was safe! It had to be!

For one thing, I'd have to think—much more deeply—of my kids. Stop and really consider them! Their feelings! Their emotions! Their reaction! How would they respond to such a sacrilege? My kids! My wonderful kids! What would my kids ever think of me—if I were to turn my back on them? If I was to turn tail—and run? Especially after having swiped—having stolen—a thousand bucks—and having become a damn thief?

Mary Jane! Dear Lord! Especially little Mary Jane! She was only three! After a few years, she'd have absolutely no memory of me! Of her father! None! None whatever! No memory of me! Of me—of her father! Except, of course, that I was a crook! And, obviously, a coward! Dear Lord! This cannot be! The very thought—the God-awful images the horror produced—brought on another series of violent, head-to-toe shudders!

Even Cynthia—age five. She wouldn't remember, either! Not after awhile, anyway! It might take a few years! Probably would! But, I could just see myself! Could actually picture myself—also fading from her consciousness! Steadily evaporating, in her memory!. Eventually, my image would completely disappear! Vanish! altogether! Slowly—but, eventually—I'd be completely gone! Banished from the kids' memories!

Even the boys! Even Stephen and Randy! All of them! Every kid! Every one of them! POOF! Gone! No father! None! Dear Lord!

My two sons! Steve, age 10, and Randy, age 8. What kind of lesson would my running out teach them? That it's okay to churn out kids? Just crank 'em on out? In wholesale lots? Shrug then—and say, "Pish-Tosh"? Figure, "What the hell"? If, as, and when things get a little bit too hairy—it's fine to just simply go ahead, and split? Simply "green the scene"? Abandon those—the ones who should be—closest to you? The helpless ones? The vulnerable ones? The ones who are counting on you—to protect them? To support them? (Oh, I've been doing wonderfully at that!) Desert the ones who have depended on you? Have had their care entrusted to you? For their entire lives? Those who have every right to expect you—to take care of them? Those people? Those kids? You're going to just go ahead—and leave them behind? Leave them dangling?

"Support them?" I found myself muttering, aloud. "Yeah, right! Take care of them? Not hardly!"

Just turn tail—and run? Is that your brilliant, well-thought-out, plan, Paul? Run? Absolutely desert? Abandon them? Flat run out on your responsibilities? Isn't that a wee bit cowardly? A wee bit? And, with the boys—especially whenever they get older, and can see how their buddies (and their buddies' <u>fathers</u>)—how <u>they</u> respond to rough times?

Would my running out not be a devastating consideration for <u>them</u>? A horrible <u>load</u>—a God-awful <u>burden</u>—for them? One which would <u>remain</u> with them—<u>haunt</u> them—probably for all of their <u>lives</u>? Isn't that a <u>horrible</u> thing—for them to have to <u>contend</u> with? An <u>unpardonable</u> yoke—with which to <u>saddle</u> them? The worse <u>possible</u> legacy? You <u>have</u> to consider <u>those you would leave behind</u>! You can <u>not</u> consider only yourself!

"<u>NO!</u>" I'd shouted it. I'm sure that every dog in the neighborhood heard it. Might even have scared the multitude of cat-sized rats—that had been homesteading the ramshackle building for years.

I couldn't <u>do</u> it! <u>Can't</u> do it! Can't just turn tail—and run <u>out</u> on them! Joanne was one thing. (And, obviously, I'd still have no business deserting <u>her</u>!) But, consider the <u>tads</u>! <u>They</u> were something else! Four beautiful <u>children</u>! Abandon <u>them</u>? Remove <u>them</u>? Blot <u>them</u>—completely—from my <u>life</u>? <u>Despite</u> all the rationalization—as to how many <u>problems</u> such a cowardly act would seem to solve?

<u>NO</u>! No, I couldn't <u>do</u> that! Simply could <u>not</u>!

Stop and think, Paul! You're being <u>selfish</u>! You're being <u>damn</u> selfish! Joanne's folks . . . and you know this . . . <u>they</u> can support those kids! <u>Would</u> support those kids! Would <u>provide</u> for them! Provide for them—far better than <u>you</u> could ever hope to do. Why subject them to never-ending poverty? Just so that you can keep your stupid, your precious, self-image intact? You're <u>far</u> from being so damn <u>noble</u>—

continuing to <u>force</u> them to live like they've always had to! Like they've <u>had</u> to! For all their <u>lives</u>!

Dammit, we were back to square freaking-one! Why could I not put the unforgivable—completely <u>mercenary</u>—temptation out of my mind?

Out of my mind? Out of my mind—indeed!

The truth—the inescapable truth (yes, I was back to <u>that</u>)—was that the kids would be <u>far</u> better off, with their grandparents. <u>Financially</u>, anyway. <u>Much</u> more advantageous—with my wife's parents! In Brownsville. They'd be <u>infinitely</u> better off—when all is said and done. When all the smoke clears away. Far better off. They'd have so many neat <u>things</u>. Stuff that I could <u>never</u> even <u>dream</u> of providing for them.

<u>That's bullshit! It's rationalization, Paul! Pure and simple! Nothing but a damn copout! A copout . . . to simply cover the fact that you don't have any balls! You don't have balls enough . . . to face up to things! Balls enough to face up to your shit-assed situation! A situation that you . . . you yourself . . . created! In case you haven't noticed! Balls enough to cope! To deal with your responsibilities!</u>

<u>Well, I'm not totally responsible! Yes you are!</u>

Man! Was I going completely off the proverbial deep end? There I was—arguing with myself! And out loud! That was—most definitely—a sign of <u>something</u>! <u>Had</u> to be! And it could <u>not</u> be good! Not at <u>all</u>! Man! You talk about a <u>split personality</u>! And that was probably only the <u>tip</u> of my totally-irrational—my all-too-emotional—iceberg!

I was totally <u>overcome</u>, by this black—this terribly bleak, this damnable inescapable—feeling! This out and out <u>hopelessness</u>! The perception—that I was, in reality, completely <u>losing</u> it! <u>Unraveling</u>—with a rush! Possibly going completely <u>insane</u>! And really <u>fast</u>! <u>Really</u> fast! A real live emotional <u>basket</u> case!

To say that I was being torn apart—torn between two (or, probably, far <u>more</u> than two) terribly hairy and conflicting situations—would be a gross understatement. Almost like saying that Marie Antoinette "died from a sore throat", or something. Or something.

All this ruminating! And I'd not even <u>thought</u> of Elena! Maybe that was just as well. <u>Should</u> have been just as well! After all, she <u>was</u> the always-hated, universally-reviled, "<u>other woman</u>"! The sinister "<u>Jezebel</u>"—in this whole sordid mess!

<u>Elena</u>! <u>She</u> was the "shameless hussy"—as they used to say. Were they not <u>all</u> shameless hussies? Morally—and ethically—Elena shouldn't even be a <u>consideration</u>, in my plight! Not at <u>all</u>! Not any <u>part</u> of the equation! Not even the <u>remotest</u> of considerations! And yet, and yet . . .

How could Elena <u>not</u> be a consideration! All right—I was being <u>selfish</u>! And I <u>knew</u> it! God <u>damn</u> selfish! A <u>schmuck</u>, you might say!

But, had that not <u>always</u> been the case? At least, over the past ten-or-so damn, tear-producing, soul-wrenching, months? Had I not turned into a total—a complete—<u>schmuck</u>? I'd always done my best to convince myself that I was <u>not</u> being inconsiderate—when it came to Elena. Or <u>irresponsible</u>. The old "Love Always Makes It Right" trick. Another hackneyed bromide! And yet, and yet . . .

I plopped myself down into the creaky old chair by the battered desk. The chair—with the one caster that never rolled properly. Story of my life. The desk—which must've been manufactured during the Millard Fillmore administration. (Maybe, in its former life, it had been an orange crate, or something.) Yep—the very, self-same, overwhelmingly-frustrating, venue! The one—which featured the constantly-staring-at-me thousand-bucks! Yeah—that desk!

Well, at least the battle-weary, venerable, antique was propping up my arms—as I rested my elbows on top of all the clutter. The crappy piece of "furniture" was, at last, serving some useful purpose. Probably the only entity—in the whole damn office—that was at least somewhat productive.

I tried to ignore (HAH!) that cursed (that crackling) sheet of currency—as I'd rested my kind-of-flushed face in my suddenly-moist hands! I even scrunched my eyes closed—and tried to sort everything out. (Yeah—right!) Sort everything out? Was that not what I'd been trying to do? Constantly? Ever since Red made that stupid reservation? (Well, ever since that spectacular thousand-dollar bill showed up?)

Actually—truth to tell—for months before that? Had I not been making a 'valiant" attempt to actually sort things out? Constantly? Continually? And what exactly—precisely—had I ever solved? What had I ever solved? In my whole damn life? What had I ever solved—ever resolved—intelligently? Nothing! Absolutely nothing! Never! Not one damn thing! Ever! And my mental faculties—what was left of them—were rapidly deteriorating! I could feel them evaporating! Deserting me! With a damn rush! Of that, I was lead-pipe certain!

And still, amid all of these, ever-constant, always-exhausting, mind-warping, mental calisthenics—during all these highly-frustrating, emotionally-draining, months—I'd not accomplished one damn thing! Not one single thing! And now—with that damnable thousand dollars sitting there—I was further behind than ever! Was this progress—or what?

I opened my eyes! Couldn't see anything! Nothing except the blackness of the palms of my clammy hands—still clapped tightly, as they were, around my fatigued baby-blues!

Well, that wasn't true! Was definitely not true! I could see! I could see—Elena! Dear Lord! Elena! When could I not see her? When would I ever not see her? She was always there! Without fail! Constantly! Always!

TWO

I THOUGHT BACK TO THE spring of 1964—a year or so, before that mind-warping Saturday, at the "Truck Rental Joint"! My marriage—I'd been sure, at that point—was over. It sure was <u>getting</u> that way! Of <u>that</u>, I was absolutely positive

Joanne had always been a wonderful woman. A wonderful mother. Probably as good a mother as had ever been created. Anywhere! Certainly the most altruistic human being—man or woman—that I'd ever met. Totally selfless. Always thinking of someone else.

Her only problem was that she could be easily led. If someone sold her on an idea—and she was always susceptible to buy into it—she'd jump at (or jump into) the project! With both feet! <u>Immediately</u>!

We'd married more than eleven years before— September 12, 1953. A date, that I would learn— seven or eight years later—happened to be the same day on which a young senator from Massachusetts, named John F. Kennedy, had married the lovely and beautiful, the gracious, Jacqueline Bouvier.

Our marriage, on that "magical" date, was, I was convinced, to be the fulfillment my idea what would become the "Greatest Love Story Ever Written". I'm talking about Joanne and me. (I'd never <u>heard</u> of JFK. Not in 1954.)

Sadly, the "Greatest Love Story", it was <u>not</u>! Regrettably, nothing close to being the embodiment of the much-celebrated "Classic Love". As much my fault as Joanne's. Maybe more so. Probably more so. Certainly more so!

But, not <u>entirely</u>!

I'd known from the time she'd been pregnant with Mary Jane (our youngest), that the marriage was in trouble! Bad trouble! We were living in Detroit, at the time. "Muh ol' home town"! Both of us had lived there—since birth.

In 1958, her parents had moved from the little town in which they'd lived, for all of three years. Had departed from the town—a few miles northwest of Detroit—called Novi, Michigan. (My uncle had always called it "November The First".)

My parents-in-law had moved 1500 or 1600 miles—all the way down to Brownsville, deep in South Texas. Joanne's father—an accountant—had been transferred there by his employer. He'd said, at the time, that he couldn't understand why. (I was to—much later—find this to be untrue.)

"Whoever heard of Brownsville?" he'd asked—incredulously—when the move got made. As things would turn out—in the years ahead—it developed that <u>he</u> would've heard of the town. No one <u>else</u>, in the family had knowledge of the place—but, my father-in-law had, most assuredly, known of it. <u>Most</u> assuredly!

How <u>anyone</u>, back then, could <u>ever</u> have foreseen the way in which Brownsville—as well as most of the rest of "The Lone Star State"—would boom, has always been beyond me. This was fully five years before LBJ would ascend to the presidency—and, of course, begin to slather the state with, literally, billions of federal dollars. (For openers? Hello *NASA*!)

Joanne and I had each grown up in northwest Detroit. We'd lived three or four miles from one another. Would never have met—had not both of us attended the illustrious (the sainted) Cooley High School.

I'd met her in Bookkeeping One—which I'd flunked (on merit) the year before. She'd been dazzled by my residual "knowledge" of the subject—which is probably the only reason I'd ever passed the course, that second semester. I began walking her home—and then, of course, coming inside, to help her with her homework. (Of course!) Actually, it never really amounted to much more than our pouring over the bookkeeping stuff—four or five afternoons a week.

After I'd joined the Navy, in 1949, our relationship—suddenly—<u>really</u> "blossomed"! This "great love story" had grown—mostly through an immense (and constant) exchange of letters. As it happened, we were—both of us—inveterate letter writers.

I seldom came home. (Due, mostly, to ongoing problems I'd been having with my mother.) My father was not a factor. He had, long-since, split! Left us! (Sound like something you might've heard discussed?)

His absence—his being gone, for over eight or nine years, at that point—was, I'm sure, the basis of so very many troubling, in-and-out, imponderables, when it came to the God-awful prospect of my "running out" on my own kids. In any case, outside of my kid sister, there wasn't all that much appeal—that much motivation—for any great number of nostalgic trips, back to Detroit.

Once—sometimes twice—a year, when I did make it to "The Motor City", Joanne was always there. Always available. And I'd always made it a point to come home with a bountiful number of dollars, in my pocket. (Numerous bucks, for me—and for the times. There'd not been a multiple number of things, on which to spend my generous $150.00-a-month salary, in Norfolk.) So, I was able to save—and take my future wife to some of the better restaurants in town. And a live-theater production or two. (Which she'd always seemed to enjoy.) And there were numerous first-run movies—in "Beautiful Downtown Detroit". Even took a cab on a couple or three occasions. Pretty impressive, hah? (An obvious invitation—for her to, eventually, experience "The Good Life"? *La Dolce Vita*—by God!)

The problem was: She and I—we really didn't know one another well enough, when we married. Not really! Of course, we'd thought that we did. The whole "romance" had evolved through the multitude of what turned out to be probably-overdone-but-from-the-heart "love letters".

Listen, the whole arrangement was fine with me. The situation was just <u>hokey</u> enough for me. Well, and for Joanne too. Or so I'd <u>thought</u>. Obviously, the letter-writing campaign would prove <u>not</u> to have been sufficient. The massive number of missives—as we were, sadly, to find out, eventually—did <u>not</u> provide the storied, fabled, complete "personality profile". For either of us. It turned out that there had been an infinite area of misunderstanding—on <u>both</u> of our parts. Not at <u>all</u> intentional. Well, <u>none</u> of it intentional. But, sadly, it <u>was</u> there!

Once 1962—our ninth year of "wedded bliss"— had rolled around, I'd reached a critical decision:

I'd become convinced, by then—that the only way to possibly salvage my marriage to Joanne would be to move my spouse down South! Preferably to South Texas. Set her down, as near to her parents' home— in Brownsville—as I could get her.

By that time, Joanne had become positive— absolutely convinced—that <u>everyone</u> in Detroit absolutely hated her. Four million people up there, at the time—and each and every one of them <u>hated</u> Joanne Marchildon.

She'd always maintained that my family had merely "tolerated" her. Right from the git-go! "You, they <u>love</u>," she'd repeatedly contended, virtually from the start. "You're funny . . . and you're outgoing," she claimed. "<u>You</u>, they love. <u>Me</u>? Me, they merely <u>tolerate</u>."

Not true! But, there had been absolutely no convincing her of anything other than that concept.

Believe me—I'd <u>tried</u>! <u>Endlessly</u>! Didn't work! <u>Nothing</u> worked! <u>None</u> of it!

So, I'd reached a point, where I'd deemed it downright <u>critical</u>—an absolute <u>necessity</u>—to get her as close as possible, to her parents. At least get her down to the South. Hopefully, the Southwest. Hopefully, even, to Texas.

But, even if we should wind up in, say, some town in Alabama—or, maybe, in some place in Mississippi—neither one of those locations was Detroit. Probably nothing close. Hopefully, everyone <u>there</u> would not wind up "hating" Joanne.

At the time, I'd been working for one of the national finance company chains. I'd started in January, of 1961—for 325 glorious dollars a month. Each and <u>every</u> month! As you might guess, the wage was a complete and utter pittance—even in those Neanderthal days.

In the summer of 1962, the firm had bought a string of small loan offices—all of them in "The Lone Star State". I'd put in for a transfer to Texas—not knowing exactly <u>where</u> I'd be sent, if, indeed, the company would, in its corporate generosity, see fit to ship me down south.

I didn't realize this at the time, but the adventure had been a rather large crap-shoot! I <u>could</u> have been sent to El Paso! That was almost as far away from Brownsville—and from Joanne's folks—as Detroit.

On the other hand, it <u>would</u> have been Texas. Hopefully, as indicated above, the people there wouldn't "hate" Joanne. At least, not universally.

Certainly not like they all did in "Wheel Burg" (as it was sometimes known in those pre-*MoTown* days).

Turned out, that the company decided to ship me to San Marcos, Texas. I'd never even heard of the town. Not till my employer told that the hamlet of 12,790 (at that time) would be the place where I would light.

That was fine with me. Seemed like the ideal spot for a "New Beginning" for our marriage. I was, honestly, deeply committed. Really! I was! Otherwise, I would certainly not have pulled up the old tent stakes—and made such a significant move. An overwhelming move—for me! At that time!

I'd really loved "The Motor City". Probably one of the most faithful fans that The Detroit Red Wings had ever had. (The hockey team had been a member of the *National Hockey League* since the 1920s.) But, I believed that picking everyone up—and setting 'em down in San Marcos—was vital! Was positively critical! Was—most certainly—the "thing to do"!

It turns out that Lyndon Baines Johnson's alma mater—known then as *Southwest Texas State Teachers College*—is located in San Marcos. The school has now grown to be the immense *Texas State University*.

The present-day town is six or eight times the size that it was in the early-sixties. (At least.) And, believe me, it's still growing. Gorgeous town—at the rim of the breathtaking "Texas Hill Country".

I was, as stated, really and truly committed, at that time, to the rebirth of the marriage. It was my Number-One Priority! This mind-bending relocation would be a major contribution! A brand new <u>start</u>, for us!

My wife would now be in a small town. Far preferable—to Joanne's way of thinking—than a bustling big city.

And, as it turned out, San Marcos was an extremely friendly town. Most importantly, she'd be in Texas. Maybe 350 or 375 miles from her parents. It could only turn out well for us.

I was up early—each and every morning—promptly, at six-thirty. Briskly walked the dog at seven o'clock. <u>Every</u> morning! <u>Loved</u> hearing them blow reveille—at the *San Marcos Academy*, a Baptist military school institution, nearby, back then.

I was working in an office—located in the center of town. Two blocks from our really-small apartment. I came home for lunch every day. We went to the movies—at least once—every week. Mostly, to one of the two movie "palaces" in town. Sometimes, though, we'd venture down to San Antonio (55 miles south)—or up to Austin (35 miles north). Joanne didn't drive then, so I was always the chauffeur—which was, also, fine with me.

I <u>swear</u> to you: I did my <u>best</u> to see that my wife would enjoy herself there. Did my <u>damndest</u>—to assure that she would be happy, in "Small Town Texas". It simply didn't work out that way. Well, she liked the town—<u>loved</u> the town! Plainly, It was <u>me</u>—that was making her so unhappy!

When Joanne—fine woman that she is—found herself under the considerable thumb of her mother, there turned out to be nothing that I could do right! Nothing! I cannot think of one thing—that I ever did right! Ever! As a result, it became evident to me—eventually—that there would be nothing I could ever do, to save the marriage! And I'd tried! Please believe me! I did try! Tried hard! Tried damn hard! Tried continually! Tried my damndest! Tried, in vain—as it turned out! Frustratingly in vain!

I could never overcome the constant barrage from "The Old Girl". Could never compete with the constant, consistent, never-ending, "Pastoral Message", from on high: The verbal "encyclicals"! The never-ending drumbeat: The poverty—that we'd always experienced—was, obviously, all my fault. (Well, it probably was! It undoubtedly was! But, I was trying! And you weren't helping, Ma!)

Joanne had—when all was said and done—completely bought in to what her mother was consistently preaching! Bought in to it—whole cloth!

The old "War Horse" did everything she could to feed my spouse's martyr complex—and successfully managed to, spectacularly, nourish it! In abundance! Listen, as indicated previously, it didn't take much.

Joanne's having to put up with me—and my "ridiculous" love of schmaltzy music, and, of course, my unforgivable "hang-up" with the "stupid theater"— was more than any human should have to ever endure. All of that—in addition to our being constantly broke. No one should have to put up with all of that!

With any of that! Pure unadulterated, condensed, martyrdom—stoked, heavily, by Eva York, my old "War Horse" of a mother-in-law!

Ultimately, I realized (finally) that there was simply no way—none—in which I could ever combat the repetitive, negative, destructive, never-say-die, din that continually flowed up from Brownsville.

On those weekends—when her folks had so generously deigned to journey up to San Marcos—I got double (and triple) the repetitive rotten ration! No way could I ever combat the incessant martyr-producing rhetoric! Especially—when constantly being spewed from "The Old Girl"!

But, Luther, my father-in-law, never failed to take his occasional "shot across my bow" too! Just not as often—nor as vociferous—as his "War Horse" of a wife! The deck was clearly stacked against me! As indicated, eventually, even I managed to figure out "the lay of the land"! The marriage had reached the point, where—in my eyes—it had become no longer salvageable! A frightening prospect! For me, anyway!

But, I did continue to try! Really! Listen—I kept giving it my best shot! It's just the fact that—no matter what I'd attempted, no matter what I did—it was simply never good enough! None of it! Ever! Everything always fell short! Always! These almost-daily evaluations were virtually all specimens of my mother-in-law's judgment, originally. But, they wound up—always—being roundly seconded by her spouse! And enacted by my spouse! Without fail!

Well, eventually, Joanne <u>did</u> reach a point—more or less, on her own—where she'd finally "outgrown" the need for her mother's constant "coaching".

She'd, ultimately, figured out that—truly—she <u>was</u> a martyr! <u>Had</u> been a martyr—for most of ten years, by then. And she was positive that my staggeringly-numerous <u>shortcomings</u>—especially in the field of finances—were <u>overpowering</u>! <u>No</u> marriage partner should have to <u>endure</u> such a pauper's fate! This, simply, was too much for <u>anyone</u> to overcome! The financial circumstances—in which we'd found ourselves drowning—were simply too <u>enormous</u>! For <u>anyone</u> to have to cope with!

As stated—over and over—I'd really <u>tried</u>! I <u>swear</u> it! I tried! <u>Hard</u>! Damn hard! I really <u>had</u>! Did everything—everything/anything I could think of—to assure my wife's happiness.

Honestly, I strove—mightily—to prove my devotion to her. I'll go to my grave—<u>believing</u> that I did everything humanly possible to salvage the marriage. I'm convinced—to this day—that I'd done everything I <u>could</u>, to assure the rebirth. Maybe not wisely—<u>probably</u> not wisely—but, I <u>did</u> make the honest-to-God attempt! I <u>swear</u> to it!

<u>Nothing</u> worked! <u>Nothing</u>! Not one damn <u>thing</u>! And <u>that</u> situation held for my job, too! A double-barreled shellacking I was taking!

After having moved up the "corporate stepladder"—in just three short months (this was after being promoted to manager of the San Marcos branch)—I was given manager-ship of the "highly-coveted" Austin office.

It was then—while I was "prestigiously" ensconced in the State Capital—that the company began screwing me around! Royally! To the point that—on one dark and frightening day—I was positively convinced that I was in the midst of a bona fide heart attack. (It probably didn't happen—but, you could never have convinced me of that fact, at the time! I was afraid of losing consciousness. For days/weeks/months thereafter. These days—I'm still not sure. But, it was touch-and-go there for awhile!)

No sense going into all of the crappy corporate details here—but, suffice to say that I'd reached a point, where I was convinced that I could never continue to work for these people!

The powers that be—the ones that operated out of Houston—had been (how shall I say?) a bunch of total bastards. Completely and utterly different—than those who'd populated the "Ivory Tower", in Detroit. Like night and day—as they say. I have no idea how the difference from one division to another—in the same corporation—could be so pronounced. To this day, I do not understand the stark contrast. But it was there! In spades!

On the bleak, the tragic, the horrendous, day—November 22,1963—that President Kennedy was assassinated in Dallas (he was slated to come to Austin that evening; there was bunting festooned all around the city), the corporate grinches decided—in all their glowing saintliness—to finally "let me the hell up".

They'd discovered an "irregularity" in the Monthly Delinquency Summary, that—as it turned out—had way preceded my taking over the office.

These cretins, though, had kept me hanging—they'd kept me in utter, terrifying, limbo—for three endless, cardiac-threatening, days! I had stewed—big time—till they could determine that the nefarious "accounting trick" had not continued "on my watch"! (I'd not even been aware that I'd "solved" anything, when I'd taken over making up the stupid damn report!)

But they had called in every auditor in Texas and Louisiana. And these leeches spent three spooky days—crawling over every report—in the entire office—for 14 or 15 or 16 months! A multitude of hurried, whispered, conferences!

The two guys and the two ladies—who'd worked for me—could, obviously, see my consistent, troubled, just-this-side-of-cardiac-arrest, condition. And the seemingly-endless duration over which it continued. One of the women—a beautiful, China-doll-looking, 18-year-old girl—was almost constantly in tears! Especially—whenever she could bring herself to look in my direction.

I was positive that I would be fired! This was a month before Christmas, for heaven's sake. Where would Santa Claus ever come from? More to the point: Who the hell would ever hire me—if I were fired, and had some kind of questionable-honesty cloud handing over my head? I wouldn't hire me! I sweated that reeking-of-suspicion situation out—dealt with it (and not very well)—till midmorning of the assassination! Then, in their infinite charity, the lynch mob finally decided that I could be let off the damn hook. (Oh THANK you! THANK you! THANK you!)

The supervisor eventually told me, "We either kill . . . or clear."

"Yeah?" I'd groused. "Well, I think you did a little of both, here."

I'd never "lipped-off" at "The Great Man" before. It took him quite aback—that I'd ever deign to question the pure, the saintly, motives of sanctified old him! And, of course, his charitable, vampire-like, cohorts! He made some unintelligible remark—mostly under his breath—as he was turning his back on me! Turning away—and (thank God) making his way out of the office.

Don't let the door hit you in the ass . . . on the way out, I remember thinking. (Maybe aloud!) Young, 18-year-old, "Emmy Lou"—as I'd always called her (from a popular comic strip of the day)—suddenly had her tears dry up! She gave me the warmest smile imaginable. And then—a hug! The only really good things that had happened to me almost all week. (Well, except for all the corporate "hounds" dragging their dismal butts the hell out of there!)

I'd made up my mind—on that very day—that I could no longer work for such an uncaring bunch of sons of bitches (as we say)! They'd really put me through the emotional wringer.

It was also a week when Steve—my oldest son—had broken his collarbone, on Monday. And, of course, the "Week From Hell" was topped off by the terribly-tragic happenings—in Dealey Plaza. Not one of the better periods, in my young life.

In 1964—after a considerable amount of looking, and interviewing—I'd finally managed to discombobulate myself from that loving, caring, firm! I took a position with a small-loan chain—headquartered in Tyler. They operated out of East Texas. I would open a brand new office for them—in San Antonio. This would be their most-western branch. A <u>pioneer</u>, I was!

By then, I'd become convinced that there was absolutely no hope—where it came to my relationship with Joanne. Not a chance—not one shot in the everlovin', blue-eyed, world—to salvage the marriage. I'd even stopped trying. Hadn't bothered even putting on a husband-like front—beginning just shortly into my Austin career.

I would, of course, continue in the marital situation. Would remain with my wife, until "my responsibilities"—toward the kids—were satisfied. But, then—once <u>those</u> were discharged—I was going to <u>divorce</u> Joanne! I'd actually made that decision—while still managing the San Marcos office. I'd just not "solidified" it—in my "worthless" mind—until a month or two into my celebrated stint in Austin.

When all was said and done, I needed to <u>know</u> that—eventually—I'd be able to get <u>out</u>! <u>That</u> was critical! The old "Light At The End Of The Tunnel" dirge, don't you see. (As with the others, it was <u>very</u> hackneyed. But, also very <u>apt</u>! In my case, <u>very</u> apt!)

I'd really had no idea—as to how many years I would be "hogtied", in my unhappy—my dismal, my highly-frustrating—marriage. How-ever-many years (decades?) that it would take—well, I would "put them in"! I would gladly—if not happily—"serve them out"! But, then! Then—once I'd discharged all of my responsibilities—I would be freaking gone! Conspicuous by my absence!

Also, by the time I'd managed to change employers, I was bound and determined—that I was going to cheat on Joanne! Not the best of character traits. Maybe that was the launch pad—to "schmuckdom"!

I'd done my best to be a good—to be an excellent, a devoted, a faithful—husband. (Finances to the side.) And I'd been shot down—at every point! Constantly! Continually! I was, by then, of course, making all sorts of excuses to myself—for myself—to justify the coming, the impending, infidelity! There was—I was absolutely convinced, by then—nothing left of the marriage! Ashes! It was all ashes!

"In effect, it's over . . . all over," I kept telling myself. "So I wouldn't really be cheating! Would I?" I knew the answer, of course. I just refused to acknowledge it! Rationality was very big, with me, during that period!

Starting work at the new company—which operated under a completely different loan system, regulated by a totally foreign (to me) set of laws—I would be required to train at their office in Victoria, Texas, about 150 miles from San Marcos.

As you might have determined, my wondrous previous employer had never (ah) bothered to move me, residentially, to Austin, once they'd bestowed—

upon my unworthy countenance—the "honor" of managing their glorious office in the "critical" State Capital. So, it had always been a 70-mile round trip from San Marcos to Austin and back—just to go to work! Every damn day! For the first month or so, they gave me a nickel-a-mile for the drive! Then, that stopped! Great crowd for which to work!

While in training, I'd struck up somewhat of an acquaintance with the manager of the Victoria office of my sainted former employer. I'd previously spoken with him a few tunes, on the phone. Our paths didn't cross all that often—but, I knew him a little bit.

Victoria, in those days, was also a small town. Not unlike San Marcos. And, as in most small East Texas towns of those days, not too much ever got past most of the population.

One of those things that didn't get by anybody (including me)—was this manager's relationship with his head bookkeeper. Her name was "Laura"—and she was absolutely gorgeous! A lovely, a dazzlingly-beautiful—exceptionally well-built—too-die-for blonde. She could say "Hello"—and you could just about feel her tongue in your ear! I'd seen sexy women before—but, "Laura" abused the privilege! You couldn't look at her without thinking "Serta Perfect Sleeper"! Bedposts automatically appeared!

Everyone in town knew that she was sleeping with her boss! They were the only finance company (of five or six), in Victoria, that always closed—at one o'clock on Wednesdays. Every Wednesday! (How they'd ever gotten those sainted people, in Houston, to go along with such a "sacrilege", I'll never know.) Each Wednesday—immediately after the assistant manager and the two cashiers would have left the office—down would come the venetian blinds! Hmmmm!

The envious employees, toiling in the rest of the finance company world, in town, would sit around—ensconced, as we were, in our usual get-together, at *The Copper Kettle* café, at two o'clock, every afternoon—and make book, as to the exact desk (or maybe even the counter?) on which this couple would be frenetically coupling!

Their weekly (at <u>least</u> weekly) trysts had been almost a joke. Almost? A source of humor—to all my confreres. But, to me? Not really! It had a <u>most</u> profound effect on moi! A really <u>profound</u> effect!

In a few week's time, I would hire some woman to assist me—once I'd open that brand spanking new San Antonio office! And <u>then</u>, I'd <u>spring</u>! Like a damn <u>cobra</u>—or something! I was going to hire <u>me</u>—a "Laura"!

I'd had this picture—this overblown image—of suave, debonair, continental, old <u>me</u>! There I would be! In a silken, maroon, robe! With graying temples! And a pure-white, silken, what-ever-they-call-it around my neck! Probably holding (seductively) a long cigarette-holder—although I smoked a pipe in those days. (Indeed, in San Marcos, I'd been known by my many friends, in the Mexican-American population, as "The Gringo With The Pipe".)

I would be the complete—the utter—virtuoso, in seduction! I would say, to this as yet unknown woman, "Ah . . . my dar-<u>leeng</u>"—in the most sexual of voices (probably with a not-so-slight, Charles Boyerlike, French inflection)! This was gonna be great! I'd spend my life—getting laid!

The "biggie", of course, was that I'd have my own "Laura"! And, exactly like the guy in Victoria, I would do some serious boffing with her! And not just on Wednesdays either! (How I was going to do all that—on $450.00 a month—was something I chose not to think of. Handling money—in case you've not surmised as much—was never my strong suit.)

This was not a lot of money! Even in those prehistoric times! In fact, it was the exact same "overly-generous" salary that my wondrous former employer had—in their infinite charity—bestowed upon insignificant little old me. And that munificent stipend came—only once I'd taken over their sanctified Austin office. Up from a glorious $425.00, in San Marcos.

But, of course—as noted numerous times before—I'd never had a whole lot of money! Ever! My mind couldn't comport with the idea of not constantly struggling—financially! Could never envision living in any other manner—than from paycheck-to-paycheck! I was positively convinced, that I'd be a poor man—a bona fide pauper—throughout my entire life!

Hopefully, I could keep the paychecks—as modest as they'd always been (and as "pauperish" as they would, undoubtedly, always be)—coming in. I'd always had this constant fear, this never-ending phobia—of being unemployed. Of not having some sort of paycheck coming in. No matter how piddling the amount thereon might be. Something had to be coming in. Always!

I just could not imagine what it would be like to—ever—receive a really tidy paycheck! One with lots of zeros on it! To not have to scratch for every lousy, damn, stupid, shittin', nickel—that I could ever lay my grubby little hands on! In my heart, I knew that I'd always be poor! As stated—your friendly, neighborhood, pauper. In perpetuity!

But, still—despite my lifelong history, pertaining to consistent lack of funds—I was gonna get me my own "Laura", by nab! And I was gonna boff her— continually! Constantly! Consistently! Endlessly!

Well, I went through all the corporate training, with my new employer. After which I'd screened out a dozen locations in "The Alamo City". I must've walked every inch of "Beautiful Downtown San Antonio".

I'd had to get the district supervisor—the guy who'd trained me in Victoria—to approve the extremely-narrow (and extremely cheap) storefront location that I'd ultimately chosen. He did. He was, in fact, exceptionally happy with the location—on Main Street (which was not, really, the "main drag"). And he was ecstatic—when it came to the small amount of rent involved. I was—fast—becoming a "star"!

Then, I bought furniture. Even (can you imagine?) built the stupid counter myself. (Listen, if you knew how un-mechanically inclined I was—and still am— you'd know what an adventure that turned out to be! To me, a rubber band is a machine! But—VOILA!— the stupid counter was presentable. Probably just barely! Still, it's creation was a distinct upset.)

Then? Then, the big—the never-to-be-ignored—lecherous move! To hire my own (ta-DAH!) "Laura"! (Hee Hee!) You'd, of course, never know from the ad that I'd run in *The San Antonio Light* that I was looking to book in some well-constructed, nymphomaniac-oriented, sex machine! (Especially would you never know that esoteric motive—because I'd be paying the "lucky" woman a massive $250.00 a month. Be still, her heart!)

Well, wouldn't you know? This one lady answered. This lady named—Elena Barrientos.

She was the third applicant that I'd interviewed. And not a potential "Laura" among them. All very ordinary-looking. As you might imagine, $250.00 a month didn't draw all that many "Lauras". Not even in 1964.

I remember thinking—when Elena first walked into the office—that, "Holy mackerel . . . this one surely is ugly as a mud fence"! She had a really serious overbite. Like, from here to North Dakota. Her gums, in fact, looked almost purple. I'd figured that—underneath all that lipstick—her lips might very well take on some shade of purple also. Definitely not "Laura" material.

But, hell! The woman really needed a job. Needed the two-hundred-and-fifty bountiful dollars—that I was authorized to pay. As indicated above, If $450.00 was a pittance, back then (and it was) can you imagine in what category $250.00 would find itself?

This lady was freshly-divorced—and still emotionally devastated by what had been the abrupt termination of her marriage. She had two kids. Boys.

Ten and eight. In, both cases, those boys were just a few months older than my own two sons.

Having always had to struggle for a stinking buck—and being able to relate to children the ages of Alton and Albert, her sons—I decided: <u>What the hell?</u> <u>This lady needs a job. I'll hire me a "Laura"</u> . . . <u>the next time</u>!

So, I employed Elena Barrientos! The one with the almost-grotesque overbite. The one with the "purple" gums. (And who <u>knew</u> about her lips?) The one who was "ugly as a mud fence"! Yeah! <u>Her</u>! <u>That</u> one! She went to work for me. Went to work <u>with</u> me! Like <u>immediately</u>!

During those first three or four weeks, there really wasn't much to do, in the office. I'd brought Steve and Randy in from San Marcos, on one Saturday, to hand out flyers over on Elizabeth Street—the main drag, downtown, about three blocks from my dinky new office.

Joanne and I had always gone house hunting on the weekends, during those days. But, on Monday-through-Friday, Elena and I were pretty much "stuck" with each other.

She'd suffered—had really <u>suffered</u>—through a <u>terrible</u> marriage! For one thing, her husband had cheated on her—repeatedly. ("You'd never do <u>that</u> . . . <u>would</u> you Paul?" she'd asked—after a couple of weeks into my employ.) In addition, this son of a bitch had beaten her! Badly, on a couple occasions. Was mean to Albert, the younger son.

Alton—his firstborn—was aces for the guy! The apple of his father's eye! Go figure!

Elena and I—we did a lot of talking! A whole bunch of talking!

As fine a woman as Joanne was, I could never talk to her! Not without scaring hell out of her! As stated, I was always saying, "New York, I'll lick you yet"! Also as stated, those "outbursts" really frightened her!

She'd already hated Detroit! And, of course, New York, she knew, was even bigger! Twice as many people to hate her, up there. Double the number of reasons—to not want to live in "The Big Apple". Believe me, she was far from being thrilled by the prospect of even moving to San Antonio. "The Alamo City" was far smaller in those days. Still, the 1964 largeness of its population was most threatening to Joanne!

She'd been extremely happy in San Marcos. (Well, with everything/everybody—but me. Thanks, Ma! Thanks a helluva lot!) Everyone in town knew her. That was very important to her. And they liked her! That was absolutely critical! Not one "hater" within the city limits!

As indicated, it really took some sly doing—to convince her that we "might should ought" to move to San Antonio!

I still had not, of course, brought up the well-nurtured idea of our eventually divorcing! That would really have rattled her foundation! And there was no sense in stirring up any further emotions—creating any more tumult—than her mother had already churned up inside (and outside) her!

A parting—<u>any</u> parting, no matter how far "down the road"—would, I knew, affect the kids!

Especially my girls! I've always felt that there was something special between daddies and daughters. I most assuredly didn't want to screw <u>that</u> up!

(The "Laura" element was not a consideration—in <u>any</u> of this, of course. Such a "mythical creature"— once she would enter my world—would, by necessity, be "on the side". And, therefore, many times <u>removed</u> from the actual family situation. Or from any <u>sense</u> of morality. I'd <u>already</u> rationalized that part away.)

I had most <u>certainly</u> never let Joanne in on my devious little plan to hire—and to thoroughly bed, early and often—that potential, sex-crazed, ravishing, "Laura"!

How I actually managed to convince my spouse that we <u>should</u> move to "San Antone" is still beyond me. To this day. Smooth-talker that I am.

As previously indicated, in the mid-sixties, "The Alamo City" was not <u>nearly</u> the immense metropolis that it is now. Had anyone spoken of such things as the *NBA's* San Antonio Spurs, in the mid-sixties, they'd have been laughed out of town! Still, it sure <u>wasn't</u> San Marcos—and Joanne was, from head to toe, suspicious of <u>any</u> town larger than 12,790!

But, she <u>did</u>—finally—condescend to go house hunting with me. And we <u>did</u>, eventually, find a really nifty house (for our price range)—out across from *Lackland Air Force Base*. And, thankfully, my spouse <u>did</u> relent—and sanction the purchase, and the move. Saved me a daily round-trip drive of some 110 miles. Half again the round-trip mileage—that I'd been logging, on my once-new Valiant—while at my old, vaunted, State Capital, job.

During all these rather disquieting weekends, and evenings—in both towns—I was discovering that my one, lone, island of calm and serenity was turning out to be my daily, weekday, <u>escape</u>! My highly-anticipated flight—to my cherished Shangri La! To the sanctuary—of my brand spanking new office! In "Beautiful Downtown San Antonio"!

And, of course, the major element abounding in that "Veritable Paradise" was turning out (<u>most</u> unexpectedly—honestly!) to be Elena!

Yep—the original "mud fence" lady! (Although I honestly didn't realize <u>any</u> of this! Stupidly, none of this was getting through to me! I recognized <u>none</u> of these slowly-overtaking-me feelings! These beginning-to-become <u>emotions</u>! Not at <u>first</u>, anyway.)

<u>Her</u>, I could talk to. And, more importantly, she'd talk to <u>me</u>. She was not only exceptionally compelling in some of the stuff she'd tell me—mostly about her God-awful, abusive, marriage—but, in addition, this woman didn't question everything (literally everything) that I ever said and/or did. The stark opposite of Joanne! Completely 180 degrees from where Joanne had been! Ever since my wife had come under the corrosive influence of her "War Horse" mother.

"Oh, Paul," Elena would say—on numerous occasions, "You talk so beautifully."

It was almost a throw-away line. But, <u>no</u> one had <u>ever</u> told me that I talked "beautifully" before! <u>Never</u>! <u>Ever</u>! Not in my whole, entire, <u>life</u>!

As you might have determined by now, for all of my above-mentioned life, I've been totally hung-up on schmaltzy music. (Still am—in spades.)

I could always be (<u>can</u> always be) moved, to tears in so many cases—moved very easily—by the lyric of a song. (Probably by even the words to *Goodnight Irene* or maybe even *Mairzy Doats*. Well, maybe not. <u>Those</u> two might be a bit of a stretch.)

Try, though, as I would, (as I had)—for, literally, years—to relate to Joanne, through the lyric of this song, or that song (just about any song), it had just never <u>worked</u>! Schmaltzy music was simply not in her DNA. Has never been. Same for hokey old *MGM* musicals. (Her many letters—while I'd been in the Navy—had always seemed to suggest something entirely different.)

In San Antonio, I'd had a little stereo in the office. And the first time Elena ever heard Eddie Fisher's recording of *With These Hands*, she—literally— teared up! Well, so did I! But, then, I always <u>had</u>. (Listen, I cry at baseball games.)

"Oh, Paul," she'd exclaimed. "That's the most beautiful thing I've ever heard."

I informed her that—if I were to ever get married again—I would want that song (along with *I Hear The Music Now* and *My Concerto*) played at the wedding. I went on to quote the entire to-me-stirring lyric of both songs. She was <u>moved</u>—<u>totally</u> moved—by the words. And I was merely reciting them. (And—believe me—I'm not <u>that</u> much of a "smooth talker".)

These heart-warming exchanges—started a whole new ball to rolling! I wrote down for her—on my stupid, well-worn, yellow legal pad (was that class, or what?)—lyrics to all the many (really many) songs that I'd always treasured. The multitude of tunes. The music which had always—for virtually all of my life— meant so much to me. That I'd always felt so deeply. The ones—that never ceased to move me.

She wept openly—as she'd read the words to Frank Loesser's *My Heart Is So Full Of You* and Sigmund Romberg's *Close As Pages In A Book*! These were real tears. I'd never seen such a thing. (Except for my-own-self, obviously. And I didn't look in the mirror all that often.)

I advised her that I'd probably also want *My Heart Is So Full Of You* played and sung, at any future wedding. She thought that was a wonderful idea! (Funny! My sentiments exactly!)

I wasn't realizing this at the time, of course, but she was looking less and less like a stupid damn "mud fence". Well, maybe I was realizing it—and simply couldn't (or didn't want to) acknowledge that fact! Or any of the other highly-emotional feelings! Those completely unexpected—those sneaking-up-on-me, beginning-to-be-heartwarming—emotions. I was, basically, ignoring them! (Consciously or subconsciously.) Who the hell knew? My mind was becoming so outrageously muddled—as time was going on!

Elena told me, at one point, that I was the most brilliant man she'd ever known. No one had ever told me that, before—either! Nothing close!

And she wasn't <u>angling</u> for anything! I mean, how much could I <u>offer</u> her? Look Ma—no silken robe, no cigarette holder, no silken whatever around my neck. She had to have known that I was earning approximately the spectacularly-moderate salary that I was taking home. The company certainly was anything but the epitome of generosity. (It was mostly my hope, when I went to work for them, that they simply wouldn't continually screw me around—as my former employer had.)

The relationship, with Elena—whether either of us realized it or not—was just simply growing! ("Blossoming", you might say.) Becoming more and more nourished! And all of this—out of an attitude (on both of our parts) of truly complete and utter innocence! (<u>Truly</u>! I <u>swear</u> it!)

As stupid as this may sound, I <u>put</u> these words— "complete and utter innocence"—before you! I do so—after all these years! And I set them before you—after all I, presumably, would have learned in all these ensuing years! I put them before you—and, to this day, I <u>believe</u> them! Every <u>one</u> of them! <u>None</u> of what was to transpire was <u>ever</u> intended! <u>None</u> of it!

For starters, I began taking Elena home at night. It was about 12 or 15 miles out of the way—to San Marcos—but, it was the least I could do! Was it not? I mean, bus fare—even one-way—was a significant expense! Was it not? Especially for a lady—who was earning that majestic two-five-oh a month! (Each and every month!) Was it not? With two kids to support! Was it not?

Finally, the moment that neither of us could ignore came about three-and-a-half months into her employment with our grand and glorious company. (I guess you could say, "It sure took you long enough"!)

On this one startling evening, we'd been walking to my getting-tired 1961 Valiant—parked in a paid-monthly lot. The facility was located about three blocks from the office. As we'd started to cross the street—a half-block from our corporate bailiwick—a car swung into our paths! It was making a high-speed right turn, from Main Street! Careening onto the little side street—at the end of which was located my paid-by-the-month parking slot. This oncoming vehicle was, as indicated, traveling pretty fast!

I'd reached out—and grabbed <u>hold</u> of Elena! <u>Grabbed</u> her—by her arm! (By her <u>arm</u>—I swear it!)

People talk about "The Lightning Bolt"! (Well, <u>some</u> people do.) This overwhelming force was supposed to have hit "Michael Corleone", in *The Godfather*—when he was hiding out, in Sicily.

He was "struck"—by "The Lightning Bolt"—the moment he'd first encountered the woman that he would soon marry, in that country. (The marriage wound up in a car-bomb tragedy—but, that's another story.)

I've always been moved by the possibility of such an out-of-the-blue occurrence! Even before I'd ever seen the flick! A situation like that has always been just hokey enough—just schmaltzy enough—for me to warmly embrace!

On the other hand, I'd doubted—seriously doubted—that such a glorious phenomenon actually existed! That it <u>could</u> exist, within the human element! I fervently <u>wished</u> that it would—that it could—but, doubted the possibility that it <u>did</u>! (Even if it existed—there was <u>zero</u> chance of something like that ever hitting <u>me</u>!)

Listen to me! Such a miracle <u>does</u> exist! It hit <u>me</u>—on that very evening! That "enchanted" evening!

What's more it also hit <u>Elena</u>—with every bit as much force! The whole experience was about as subtle as a tidal wave!

Neither one of us came close to mentioning it in the car! I guess each of us thought that the other had probably not experienced the all-the-way-to-the-bone—the head-to-toe, the all-consuming—shock wave!

I advised her—before she shakily stepped out of the car—that I would begin picking her up in the mornings! A new wrinkle! That, of course, would mean leaving home a lot earlier. We were still a week or two away from moving from San Marcos.

The trip to Elena's house, in northwest San Antonio would mean my having to come in from the northeast quadrant, drive across town, pick my fellow employee up—then, fight the traffic all the way downtown. Of <u>course</u> I would do it! It would be illogical to <u>not</u> do it! I never gave it a second thought! (Well, I <u>tried</u> not to give it a second thought.)

Driving in to the office, with her—the following morning—I'd finally tried to relate to her, what I'd felt, the night before. Tried to inform her—of the phenomenon that I had experienced.

Of course—compelling speaker that I am—I stumbled all over myself. Stuttered and sputtered—consistently! Couldn't finish a sentence! Not even if my life had depended upon it! Could, maybe, put together 3 or 4 totally-inane words! Tops! All this, of course, from a guy who could quote lyrics—decades-old lyrics—literally by the hundreds! All this from a man—who "talks so beautifully".

She reached over—and put two fingers over my lips.

"I felt it too," she said softly.

So softly did she speak, that I was almost unable to hear what she'd just said! Add that—to the fact that I couldn't <u>believe</u> what I was hearing. I'd <u>never</u> thought any of this was even remotely <u>possible</u>. Or, at the very least, I'd always believed that such glorious things could <u>never</u> happen to me. <u>Ever!</u> In my entire lifetime!

I cannot tell you of the emotion that rampaged through me—when the earth-shaking significance of her words finally penetrated! I'd never experienced anything like my all-consuming reaction to this incredible woman's tender declaration before! <u>Never!</u> Not in my entire life! Have never experienced it since! Nothing even close!

So! Here we <u>are</u>! We're back to that fateful (???) Saturday morning! That crestfallen Saturday morning! Sitting in the *Laswell Truck Leasing* office! "The Truck Rental Joint"! With that damned thousand-dollar bill staring a burn-hole in my forehead!

How, I asked myself again, was it impossible <u>not</u> to think of Elaina?

<u>Joanne!</u> <u>Her</u> I had to think of! Steve and Randy—my sons! Had to think of <u>them</u>, too! Of <u>course</u>!

Cynthia! Mary Jane! My two little girls! All of them! But, most especially, I'd guessed, were my little girls! As noted before, there is that very special "thing" between daddies and daughters, y'know! The kids though! They were all souls—ones that I had to think of.

Even my mother and my sister—up in Detroit! I'd have to consider their feelings. Their reaction. Probably even my best friend—my very best friend— in Chicago. We'd served in the Navy together. What would he think of me—if I was to desert? Another head-to-toe shudder!

What would any of them think? What would all of them think?

But, damn me, foremost in my alleged mind, there was Elena!

There even was Alton and Albert. Alton had been having a terrible time trying to cope with the absence of his father! The kid had been the hands-down favorite! It would break your heart. I'd only met the lad once—in the weeks before the "lightning bolt" had bowled me/us over! And It broke my heart!

What was I to do? What the hell was I going to do?

THREE

S O THERE I WAS! STROLLING through this kind of seedy-looking used car lot on The Military Highway—in south San Antonio. This further adventure, into the possibly-total-unraveling of one Paul Marchildon, was occurring on that very same Saturday! That <u>fateful</u> Saturday? Yeah—I was guessing—<u>that</u> fateful Saturday! (On the other hand, it was <u>only</u> a guess. Pertaining to the "fateful" part, that is. Who could actually <u>know</u>? Certainly not me! Even that many hours later in the day.)

There was, for one thing, that stupid thousand-dollar bill! It was now burning a flaming, flagrant, never-ending, hole in the breast pocket of my robin's-egg-blue, slightly-sweaty, pretty-well-wilted, cotton sport shirt.

I'd not left the *Laswell* facility—not until about 1:25PM! Almost a half-hour after the posted one o'clock closing time. That was because I <u>still</u> could not make up my mind. Could not decide <u>what</u>—if anything—I wanted to do! Long Marchildon tradition, y'know. Well, to be truthful, I knew what I'd <u>wanted</u>

to do! Knew <u>exactly</u> what I'd wanted to do. Hell, I just hadn't <u>done</u> it! Not <u>yet</u>, anyway! Would I <u>ever</u>? At that point, your guess would've been just about as good as mine.

Of course, I <u>also</u> knew what it was that I <u>should</u> do: <u>That</u> was the looming, lurking, celebrated, no-brainer! Long before I'd finally closed up "The Truck Rental Joint", I was perfectly well aware of what it was that I <u>ought</u> to do. The proper course, obviously, was: Put that stupid piece of currency in the stupid safe, close the stupid joint—and go home to my wife and kids.

Only a bona fide <u>schmuck</u> would consider any other option. Was that not true? It was apparent that I was fast qualifying for that reviled classification. In spades! Probably with an oak leaf cluster!

So! So, what was I doing? I was wandering around, on this cheap-o used car lot! With that damn bill smoldering, in my pocket! In point of fact, I was looking at (seriously looking at)—would you believe?—a huge, old, iron tank of a 1948 Chrysler New Yorker. (How apropos was <u>that</u>? How completely apropos—to <u>anything</u>?)

For one thing, I was caught up in some kind of nostalgic reflection. The well-known "blast from the past". (I've always been very big—on nostalgia. <u>Always</u>! Probably to my detriment.)

Constantly—from the time I was a <u>child</u>—my mother had never failed to admonish me about such "flight of fancy" things. She had, consistently, out and out <u>warned</u> me—some times at the top of her <u>lungs</u>—that I was "altogether too nostalgic". She never ceased to blather—that I was spending <u>way</u> too much time—"living in the past". This, despite the fact that—starting at eleven, or twelve-years-of-age—there'd not been all that much "past", in which to have spent all that overwhelming an amount of time.

This particular trip down memory lane—on that particular Saturday—can only be explained as follows:

My first car—when I'd gotten myself honorably discombobulated from the United States Navy—had been (guess what!) a 1948 Chrysler That one had been a Saratoga. Still, it was a four-door. Just like this one! Only this dandy was a top-of-the-line New Yorker. Well, I could never really tell the difference.

This "classic"—the one that was currently dazzling me—was a kind of royal blue. Mine had been a shiny black one. Had been absolutely gorgeous—despite the fact that the auto had registered something like 57,000 miles, when I'd gotten her.

This blue one? Well, it was pretty good-looking too. Actually, to me, it was damn good-looking! That imagery wasn't helping! I was doing my best to ignore the fact that she'd had over 87,000 miles on her. Complicated? Throughout my anything-but-humdrum life, I'd seldom gotten myself involved in anything that was not entangled—and, usually, pretty knotty.

Now, why was I even looking at that car? Scoping out any used car? Any cheap used car? Well, my wonderful 1961 Valiant—the only new car I'd ever owned—in my entire life—was just this side, I knew, of being repossessed.

Over the previous couple of years, I'd wound up paying a fortune to keep the car. The vehicle had lived up to its name. Without fail, it had, truly, been Valiant. Always. But, I'd had to refinance the vehicle twice. The second transaction found agreeable old me signing up, to pay an extremely outrageous—actually, a usurious—amount of interest! It was a note, which I'd known—down deep—would be impossible for me to ever honor. Of course, I was never one—to let a piddling little detail like that bother me. "Living for the moment"—some would call it. In my overheated little mind, I was "covering my fanny". (At least, for the moment!)

And now—as I was painfully aware—I was still going to lose the car. After all that—and I was still going to be forced to forfeit the unit! I was on the verge of having the valiant Valiant—which I'd always loved—repo'd!

Like everything else, on that totally-screwed-up Saturday, I really didn't know what I was going to do! Had not the foggiest idea how I'd act—when the traditional "push" would come to the proverbial "shove". The blue Chrysler was priced at $295.00. I "knew" that I could probably get the guy down to $250.00—maybe even to $225.00. (Despite the fact that some kind of "smooth-talking" salesguy I was not. Was definitely not!)

I was painfully aware that, if I did do that—did buy the Chrysler—the unprincipled, schmuck-like, action would mean that I'd actually have gone ahead! Gone over the damn cliff! That I had irretrievably cut the umbilical cord! Severed any connection with "The Honorable World". If I went ahead with the purchase, of this aircraft carrier of a Chrysler, there would be (there could be) no turning back! I would have—for good and all—become a documented schmuck! A card-carrying schmuck! Certified!

This reprehensible action would—for openers—signal that I was, indeed, a common thief! A bona fide, documented, crook! More importantly, it meant that, surely, I was going to desert! Going to run out! Going to actually turn-tail, and—damn me—run!

The desertion/abandonment factor was, of course, infinitely more important—infinitely more critical—than any "mere" thievery! In any case, once the dastardly deed would be done—if it were to be done—there would be, as stated, no turning back! Could be no possible turning back! The "bona fide schmuck" die would be cast! Irretrievably forged—in pig iron! In pig iron! For everybody to see! Including my kids!

I'd be—essentially—giving up my kids! More than "essentially:! I'd be abandoning them! Deserting them! Forever! Dear Lord!

Of course I'd be abandoning them! Otherwise, what would be the sense? The "logic" in buying some stupid, damn, car? An antique? Especially one with 87,000 miles on it? In point of fact, where was the sense in anything? In anything I was even thinking about? Anything I'd even considered? Anything I would have done? Or would almost have done? Or not-quite-have done? Where was the "logic" in anything?

It would, obviously, be sheer folly to go blindly ahead—and to buy the iron hunk of a Chrysler—and then to not split! I would have spent a full quarter of the embezzled—the stolen—thousand dollars! Maybe more than a quarter of the ill-gotten booty! Probably nearer a third of the loot! And for what? A 17-year-old Sherman Tank? One that would probably use twice the amount of gas—maybe three or four times the amount of gas—as my beloved "Slant Six" Valiant? Are we being brilliant here—or what?

When the dedicated leaches from the finance company would—eventually—descend, to "repo" my Valiant (as I knew that—eventually—they would) I'd simply have to deal with that happening.

On the other hand, the "positive" side was—that I'd not have to cope with that highly-unpleasant, stomach-churning, situation. Not until that dreaded, in-the-near-future, occasion actually arose. I didn't have to be a college professor to know that a junky, gas-guzzling, old Chrysler really didn't seem to be much of a "preemptive strike". Certainly not an extremely-urgent one. Not totally—inescapably— panic-urgent, anyway. (It all depended on the powers that be—at the finance company. Isn't that always the case? "There, But For The Finance Company, Go I", as the saying goes. My unfailing, ill-fated, financial history—in a nutshell!)

Nothing—nothing having to do with the (for want of a better word) "plan" (the "strategy", which had been formulating in my evil, twisted, demented, schmuck-like, little brain)—was making any sense! Nothing had ever shown a lick of logic! None at all! Especially, when such a patently stupid—such an out and out goofy—purchase would, most assuredly, result in my eventually winding up in jail! Sooner or later! (Probably the former!)

So, if I was going to go ahead and do the nefarious deed—if I was actually going to buy the stupid '48 Chrysler—I'd have to keep the other $700.00 or $750.00 (or whatever), "for expenses", as they say! And—obviously—do what I could, to get away! Get out! Get away! Abandon! Run! Scoot! Ditch! Get the hell out! Run! What a melancholy array of choices!

This whole rigmarole would—obviously—mean actually running away! Running—from Joanne! Running away from Stephen and Randolph! And, Lord help me, even more tragically—running away from my Cynthia and my little Mary Jane! Dear Lord! Away, even, from—from Elena! Hell, running away from (would you believe?) Alton and Albert! Even her kids were a consideration!

A ghastly realization hit me! Overcame me! Said realization: If I did pull this caper off "right"—if I turned out to be that clever—I'd never see them again! Any of them! All of them! Never again! Ever! Dear Lord! Dear, dear Lord! You do have to concern yourself with *those you leave behind*!

And how far would that stupid Chrysler even get me, anyway? Halfway to Houston? Maybe! A distinct possibility—that it could give up the ghost in that short a distance! ORG! If that happened, it would leave me a mere 100 miles due east! In the middle of nowhere! And fanny-deep in moral—and economical—quicksand! Probably in that order! Then, what? What would I do then?

All of these moral/economic considerations to the side, east seemed to be the only reasonable way in which to head. South would only lead me to Brownsville—where Joanne's parents would be waiting! Anxiously waiting! With an abundant amount of tar and feathers! And that would be the occasion—only if they were in a really charitable mood! Luther had never been bashful—when it came to talking about his shotgun!

Certainly, I couldn't head north. San Marcos was only 55 miles away—and everyone up there <u>knew</u> me! "The Gringo With The Pipe"—remember? To head west—and try and forge my way across all those desolate, barren hills, and overpowering mountains, in a car like this "hunk of iron"—would be, I was positive, the height of stupidity! Same with landing in Austin. As the comedian used to say, "I usta woik in that town"!

Well, maybe it was actually time to <u>reconsider</u> the West! Hell, I was spending virtually all of my whirling-dervish life doing little—<u>other</u> than reconsidering! Especially lately. On that haunted Saturday—as you can see—I was, consistently, abusing the privilege!

El Paso was, perhaps, 500 miles away! Maybe 600! Hell, maybe 700! What did <u>I</u> know? Well, I knew that the town was "forever" away from "San Antone"! If that blue pile of cast iron didn't/couldn't/wouldn't make it <u>that</u> far, then, I'd <u>really</u> be in the middle of nowhere! A goodly portion of West Texas is terribly desolate! Was <u>especially</u> so, back then! Plus, for one thing, I would not have "crossed state lines". (I'd had not the <u>foggiest</u> idea—as to whether that would've been an advantage, or not.)

I had heard that most people—deadbeat fathers (like I was on the verge of becoming)—always seem to head for Phoenix. Sometimes Albuquerque. With a car like that 1948 Chrysler, such an ambitious destination would—undoubtedly—be out of the question. Well. it positively <u>should</u> be out of the question. <u>Everything</u> I was pondering should have been out of the question. (But, with ol' Paul Marchildon, one never knew—did one?)

Look! Why not go back to the stupid *Laswell* office? Put that stupid thousand-dollar note in the stupid safe? Restore it—to where it <u>should</u> be? Then, drag my stupid, amoral, butt—back to the stupid house? And "put in" another drab, bleak, endless, colorless, weekend? Good question!

What I did—was to take the Chrysler for a "test drive"! Y'know? It didn't run bad! Not half bad! Not as smoothly as my beloved black one had—so many years before—of course. But, really <u>much</u> better than I'd suspected. On the other hand, I've always been about as mechanically inclined as that newspaper you might, as we speak, have lying on your coffee table. Or, hell, it might be in the trash can, by now—out in the kitchen. What did I know about cars? About <u>anything</u> mechanical?

Answer: Nothing! Absolutely zilch! To me, as noted previously, a rubber band has always been a machine. And a complicated one at that.

When I got back from my silly test run, I got into a semi-serious "discussion" with the salesguy. He—adamantly—was refusing to come down from the $295.00 figure. Not one dollar less! Probably just as well. I simply could <u>not</u> do three-hundred bucks! Decision <u>made</u>! (Well, decision made <u>for</u> me!)

I turned and left! Got three or four blocks away—and <u>almost</u> made a stunning U-turn. Came <u>this</u> close—to heading back to the lot! But, I didn't! The three-hundred <u>was</u> too much! Too damn <u>much</u>!

Next big decision: Do I now go back to the office? Put that flaming "G-note" in the damn safe? Where it belonged? Executive Decision <u>made</u>: Of <u>course</u>! Of course I do! What else? Finally dedicated to "Doing The Right Thing", I headed the Valiant in that direction!

And drove right on <u>past</u> the *Laswell* complex! Missed it—by the proverbial mile! But, why? Why <u>anything</u>?

<u>This whole damn thing is stupid! It's goddam stupid!</u>

I was headed out Bandera Road! Out, damn me, toward Elena's house! <u>That</u> was also stupid! Even <u>more</u> than merely dopey! The last place I should be going—at that critical moment—was to Elena's house, for heaven's sakes! Well, I wasn't—necessarily—going <u>there</u>! Yeah. Right.

This wonderful woman and I had vowed—almost two long, grief-filled, months before—that we'd stop seeing one another! Would <u>never</u> see one another! Ever again! A dagger through my heart! Through <u>both</u> of our hearts, actually! Of that, I'm <u>convinced</u>! It had been a terribly-tearful parting! At her house!

I'd told Joanne, on that night, that I was going over there—to say "goodbye" to Elena! And <u>that's</u> exactly what I did!

I'd finally summoned up enough courage—enough class—to tell this "other woman" (this "other woman"—whom I'd truly, deeply, loved) that we couldn't go on as we were! As we had been!

What an upset <u>that</u> had been! For me to have finally acted even halfway responsibly! But, I actually did! (It may never fall that way again!)

We'd wound up, both agreeing—tearfully, but willingly—that we were only heading toward certain desolation! Toward unavoidable heartbreak! Toward unmitigated disaster! Only sheer, utter, destruction could lay ahead, for us! We were doomed! The damned! An inescapable fact! All of this! A tragic truth! One that we'd both broken-heartedly acknowledged!

It took some doing—for each of us! But, we had finally come to grips—with the damnable, poison-tipped, dagger! The one that had been hanging over both of our heads! A veritable *Sword of Damocles*! An instrument of utter doom! Of inescapable catastrophe! A bludgeon—that had been looming there! For what seemed to have been forever!

Yet, damn me, I'd still call her at the office. Two or three times a week. (Sometimes two or three times a day.) Just to hear her voice, at the other end. She'd answer—and I'd hang up. I doubt that she'd ever had all that much trouble—when it came to guessing who that was.

From time to time—not nearly as often—the phone at *Laswell* would ring. I'd answer—and, whoever-it-was would hang up. Three guesses!

In the mid-sixties, there were still a goodly number of drive-in restaurants operating in San Antonio. They were, for the most part, individually-owned—non-roller skating—operations. I never was much of a drive-in kind of a guy.

Three blocks from Elena's house, the semi-operating, multi-colored—wildly-pretentious, aged, noisily-crackling—neon sign flickered away. This antiquated tribute-to-something-or-other—had (for years, in its own, kind-of-charming, totally-unique, way) denoted the location of *The Rainbow Drive-In*!

On that Saturday-to-end-all-Saturdays, I'd found myself wondering if she was still working there— part time! Two-five-oh a month, even back in the mid-sixties, didn't go far! (Or had I mentioned that before?)

She'd begun moonlighting, at this joint, about a month before I'd left the employ of the small-loan company, in whose vineyards she was still toiling.

Back then, I'd usually spent one or two nights a week—chasing deadbeat borrowers (of which there were many). Sometimes, I'd spend three or four nights pursuing them—in a particularly bad week. "Calling upon them" at their residences. Such a practice today—in those same neighborhoods—would be the height of foolishness! Utter nincompoopery! Progress! Ya can't beat it!

Inevitably, on those "chasing deadbeats" nights, I'd stop at the ol' *Rainbow*! This, despite the fact that the joint was, most usually, <u>miles</u> from where I'd been on the prowl.

I would wait—impatiently—to hear her voice ask, "May I help you?". Hers was a delightful vocal tone. Even over one of those stupid, crackly, just-this-side-of-garbled, speakers—which were in only slightly better condition than the crackling, buzzing, neon sign, out in front of the place.

I would come up with some deathless, vibrant, poetic, pure-classical, reply. Something like, "I would like a plain hamburger . . . just the meat and bun, please . . . and a cup of coffee. You are a beautiful woman. This is a recording."

The "mud fence" days had, obviously, long since been assigned to the garbage can—consigned to the dim red mists of the ancient past! And deservedly so! By then, she'd become the most beautiful woman I'd ever met! Ever seen! In my entire life! ("Laura"? EH!)

I could always hear the hamburger-flippers (although that was a term I'd never heard back then) giggle and chortle and guffaw—at my humorous order! Yessir! Ol' Paul Marchildon—the last of the red-hot comedians!

Sometimes, I'd change that classical monologue to "This is a beautiful woman. You are a recording." (Was that brilliant—or what?) I'd had a million of 'em!

Elena had always sprouted the broadest of smiles—when she'd bring out my order. Always! (She was not a designated carhop—but, always, she'd managed to deliver the above-mentioned "humorously-placed" order.) Which was always an answer to a prayer! A fervent prayer! Always!

The over-bite had been reduced from "gigunda" to "it ain't hardly there, no more". ("Who'd ever notice?") And the purple gums? I'd been totally mistaken about them! Never even thought about the color of her lips, anymore! She truly was a beautiful woman! Truly beautiful!

On that particularly goofy Saturday, I swung the Valiant into the parking lot, of the *Rainbow*—and pulled up next to one of those "high-tech" speakers!

Big decision coming: When she would ask for my order, would I pull off the tired old "beautiful woman/ this is a recording" schtick? Would that be good? Would <u>anything</u> be good? Would Elena be glad to hear that sanctified "blast from the past"? Or would such an opening—simply make the precarious-at-best situation even worse? Hell, could things even <u>get</u> much worse? (Well, yeah, I guessed. Probably!)

As it turned out, "schtick"—use or non-use of same—was a moot point. When the "May I help you?" call came—it was from a voice that was totally unfamiliar! Damnably different! It gave me the blackest—the most foreboding—of feelings! <u>Everything</u> was unraveling!

"Isn't . . . doesn't . . . is Elena there?"

"No, Sir. She doesn't work here anymore."

Dear Lord!

"Okay, thanks. Never mind. I mean . . . uh . . . goodnight. Thank you."

Was that a brilliant response—or what? Was I the epitome of rock-solid—or what? I backed out of the stall! And squealed my way—further out Bandera!

"You!" Elena practically screeched it! From inside her door! She'd looked out through one of those stupid convex (or concave—or whatever the hell they are) "peep holes"!

I'd hate to think that my eyes were <u>that</u> screwed up—and had been for all these years—but, I've <u>never</u> been able to recognize <u>anyone</u> through one of those idiotic little holes. Elena did, though! Maybe it was more of a guess—a feeling—than anything else. Could've been, I suppose. Possibly her "peasant cunning" kicking in. Who knows?

"Go 'way," she shouted. "Just . . . please, Paul! Just . . . just . . . just go! Please . . . just go away! Please! Please? It's . . . it's . . ."

"I . . . I can't, dammit! I can't, Elena! God help me . . . but, I just simply can't! Cannot! I need to see you! God . . . how I need to see you! Stopped off at the damn drive-in! They told me that you'd . . . that you weren't . . . that you didn't work there anymore. I don't know that I knew how much I really needed to see you! Not till . . . not till then! Till that moment! That God-awful moment! That God damn moment! Look! Listen, I guess that I'd really must've just turned in there . . . turned in there, on a . . . maybe on a damn lark."

"A lark? On a lark? On a lark, for God's sakes? On a damn lark?"

"No! As usual, I'm screwing up what I meant to say! I've got my tongue wrapped around my eye teeth . . . and can't see a damn thing!"

She'd heard that corny line before. Many times. Still, I could hear her laugh! Even through the thick wooden door! I could hear it! Despite—I was certain—every effort that had been made to stifle it!

The door—thankfully (I guess)—opened! At long last! She rushed out—and into my arms! She was wearing a bathrobe, and (I was certain) nothing underneath the thin, floral-print, cotton, wrapping

"Oh, Paul! Paul, Paul, Paul! Paul, what're we . . . what can we . . . ?"

"I don't freaking <u>know</u>," I rasped—my lips just above her left ear. "I simply don't freaking <u>know</u>. I don't even know why I started <u>out</u> here this afternoon. This evening. Or maybe I <u>do</u>. I <u>guess</u> I do. I was just . . . ! And then, I pulled into the damn drive-in! And . . . dear Lord . . . they said you . . . that you . . . that you don't <u>work</u> there any longer! And then I . . ."

She put those two enchanted fingers over my lips! Those same two spellbinding fingers! Just as she'd done in the car—on that unforgettable morning! The day after "The Lightning Bolt" had struck!

"I know," she soothed. A tear trickled down—one from each of those lovely, fawn-like, brown eyes. "I know."

On the way back over to the other side of town—the damn south side—to put that damn thousand-dollar note in the damn safe, where it damn should've been in the first damn place, I must've been a prime candidate for the "Funny Farm". You talk about "Malfunction Junction"!

To this day—this many years later—I don't really know how close I might've come to driving the ol'—the repossess-able—Valiant off the highway! Off of the overpass—which transcends the stock yards. At least the road did <u>then</u>! I have no idea whether it does <u>now</u>! Today, I don't even know <u>where</u> the damn thoroughfare was located! Don't even know if they've even <u>got</u> damn stock yards in the city, anymore. I'd unquestionably attained—at that point—the well-known status of "basket case"! Could "The Men In The White Coats" be far behind?

I've never—ever—had the gumption to go back there! Have never—ever—been close to approaching that horrible locale! Never an attempt to seek out that spooky venue! Have never driven on that overpass again! I don't even know if it still exists! The thought of doing so? Of revisiting that God-forsaken, macabre, area? To this day, the chilling thought scares the hell out of me! Still sends shudders rattling through me! Decades later!

My memory is that there was no guardrail—on the overpass! But, that cannot be true! Can it? I mean, doesn't every overpass—everywhere—does it not need a guardrail? Isn't that the law, for heaven's sakes? A universal law?

My mind was in such overwhelming turmoil, on that twisted Saturday, that—to this very moment in time—I can still envision myself driving closer! Ever closer! Closer to the edge! Dangerously closer! Closer yet! Then, "pulling out of it"! "Just in the nick of time!" Swirling away from the edge! Is that melodramatic—or what?

But, that was what I was "seeing"! (Probably deranged! Undoubtedly deranged!) But that was what I was "seeing"! The still-stark vision is the overheated, honest-to-God, memory—that has always haunted me! That still haunts me! The ensuing years have done nothing to cause that memory to "mellow out"!)

How close did I actually come to "ending it all"? Hell, I'll never really know! The very thought of that little adventure has always sent all kinds of shock waves through me! Did then! Does now! In all honesty, I don't really know <u>what</u> happened—what <u>really</u> happened—on that night! Don't know what <u>could</u> have happened—guardrail or no guardrail! But, it still scares the hell out of me!

"How can you possibly do this to your kids?" I found myself asking the question aloud, as I—badly shaken—drove away from the "suicide site". Then, I'd <u>shouted</u> it! Six times! Eight times! Ten times! Maybe twelve times! Who the hell <u>knew</u>? Who the hell <u>knows</u>? All I <u>do</u> know is that my throat was sore! Raw as hell! Simply from screaming!

What I also knew—is that I'd fare-thee-well better straighten myself out! Welcome, Paul. Welcome, Mr. Marchildon, to the <u>real</u> world! Climb aboard! Climb aboard—if you can!

<u>Straighten myself out! Yes! I must pull out of this nosedive! But how? How in the hell . . . at this point in time . . . how the hell do I do that?</u>

What was I going to do? What was I <u>ever</u> going to do? I'd found myself more confused—more muddled—than ever! (A condition I'd thought to have been <u>impossible</u>!)

Well, for one thing, seeing—and holding Elena— had <u>truly</u> opened my eyes! I <u>guessed</u> it had, anyway!

Even though I'd not ventured inside her house. Not on that screwed-up, totally-disjointed, Saturday! We'd simply stood there! The two of us! Holding each other—<u>tightly</u>! For fully five or six minutes! An eternity! Neither of us saying a word! Must've been a thrilling spectacle—for all her neighbors to have beheld.

Then, as though someone had dropped a hanky—or blown a whistle or something—she and I had released one another! Simultaneously! Tenderly—but, simultaneously! It was not as though an electric shock had engulfed us. The fairly-brief encounter, I'm thinking, had simply drained the pair of us. Had left both Elena and me—had left us both—totally emotionless.

To this day, that explanation sounds terribly, terribly, stilted. And horribly oversimplified. But, I believe it to be true. As I sit here—recalling what, to me, was an amazingly sacred moment—I still believe that!

Seeing—and holding—this beautiful woman had sure "opened my eyes"! Yeah. Right. That new-found vision, of course, was why I'd come within how-ever-many-inches (or feet, or yards or whatever) of driving off the stupid overpass—or whatever-in-hell I'd done! Or not done! The tender encounter had really opened the ol' baby-blues, all right!

Actually, upon leaving Elena's house, I really was heading back for the office! (I know—about damn time!) Whether I'd ever get there, of course, was still open to question! How many times, on that disjointed day, had I started out to do something? And then, had not come close to actually doing it?

In fact, as I was looking back over the previous few months, how many times had I started out—heading to a specific place? And had never gotten there? Resolved to do some specific thing? And failed to perform? Failed to accomplish the goal? To say nothing of all those other—those added, those latest—surreal occurrences, on that particular, from-another-planet, Saturday alone!

So, while the latest plan-of-the-day was to put that goddam piece of currency—that white-hot, still-smoldering, piece of currency—place it where it freaking belonged, who knew if I'd actually get there? The office was still miles away! So, apparently, was what is laughingly referred to as my mind!

And—if I actually did go to the office (what an upset that would be)—would I actually unlock the gate? Actually schlep all the way to the office? Actually unlock the door? Actually open the safe? And, if I did all that, would I have enough class—enough strength, enough principle—to actually put the stupid money in there? Enough strength of character? All of that—I was positive—was up for grabs! Schmuckdom was never far away! My constant companion!

It was ten o'clock when I'd gotten home! Where had the highly-disjointed day gone? The whole, entire, damn day? Where had it gone?

Well, on the last stop—before coming home—I had pulled in, at a restaurant (not the *Rainbow*). Had downed a hamburger and a few cups of coffee.

I'd always had the poorest conception of time! The worst notion of hours passing! It just so happened—that, on that terribly-strange Saturday-from-hell—it was simply another situation, where I was abusing the privilege!

"Well," began Joanne. She was trying hard—to show outrage. But, as outraged as she might've been—as outraged as she'd probably have had a right to be—she could never quite bring it off. Not to that point in our lives, anyway.

Being hurt? Now, that she could do! Did do! Did it—exceptionally well! Even on those occasions—when she'd had no business being hurt. Emotional pain, yes! Constantly! Outrage, no! Never!

"You did decide to come home, did you?" Sarcasm was a whole 'nother thing, for her. She was pretty good at sarcasm. Truth to tell, she'd become awfully deft at sarcasm—thanks to her "War Horse" mother. "You did remember the address . . . did you?" she pressed on. "Decided to favor us with your presence? To what do we owe this overwhelming privilege? That you should favor insignificant old us . . . with your exalted presence?"

Her tone really wasn't as confrontational as I'm undoubtedly making it sound. She was, as indicated above, more hurt, I guess. More sad—than mad. Upset. And hurt! But, mostly hurt.

"Are the kids in bed? We need to talk."

"What difference does it make whether the kids are in bed? You're never home to see them, anyway! Not these days anyway. I don't even know if they'd recognize you! Like I said, I'm really surprised . . . shocked, you might say . . . that you even remembered the damn address! I've been waiting for . . ."

She broke down! Rushed into my arms! Began crying—hysterically!

I did my best to comfort her. Began patting her on the fanny. (I'm an inveterate fanny-patter. A consistent part of my being.) The "therapy", though, wasn't working, on this occasion. Actually, it seldom had—from the beginning of our ill-fated little "marriage-saving" excursion from Detroit. The "never home" accusation was no longer a fact—since I was no longer seeing Elena.

"Listen. Joanne, listen. Listen to me. We have to talk. We've got to get the hell <u>out</u>! Get the hell <u>out</u> of here! We've got to get the hell <u>out</u> . . . out of San Antonio! Soon! Like <u>yesterday</u>! We've <u>got</u> to! Simply <u>have</u> to leave! We can't . . . we just can't continue this way! At least, I can't! We've <u>got</u> to get the hell out! Simply <u>got</u> to!"

FOUR

TWO DAYS LATER, ON MONDAY, I listened— intently—as the phone rang at the other end. And rang and rang!

Yes, I was back "on duty"—at *Laswell*. (I had actually done <u>right</u>! Difficult as it may be for you to believe, I <u>had</u> gone ahead—and had put the damn thousand bucks in the damn <u>safe</u>! On Saturday damn night.) Before stopping for that damn hamburger— and those damn cups of coffee.

Now, here I was: Listening for—fervently hoping for—an immediate answer, to the call I'd so hurriedly (and urgently) placed.

<u>Elena</u>! She would've been—<u>should've</u> been— at the office, by now. The sanctified locale of my former employer. The firm—for which I'd toiled, so many pain-laden months before! I sincerely hoped— fervently hoped—that this woman would <u>be</u> there!

It was ten-fifteen in the morning—and the sainted, revered, Adrian (Red) Boyle had stepped into the restroom. With a newspaper. As he did virtually every morning, at precisely ten-fifteen. (If nothing else, he was consistent. "Regular", you might say.) I knew (we all did) that he was good for 25 or 30 minutes, in the can. The standing joke around the office was that—once Red came out of the john—you should never light a match! Not within 200 feet!

The phone, on the other end, was ringing! And ringing! Continued to ring! For the fifth time, it rang! Six! Seven! Eight, even!

Please, Elena! Please, please . . . PLEASE! Please answer! Don't let it be that asshole, Tony! Please don't let it be him . . . let him not be the one . . . who picks up the damn phone!

I didn't actually know whether my replacement, as manager, really was an "asshole" or not. Just goes to show you—to illustrate—the state of what was left of my mental capacity, in 1965. He may well have had the "milk of human kindness . . . by the quart . . . in every vein"—as "Professor Henry Higgins" had once, so self-effacingly, described himself in My Fair Lady.

Elena seemed to like him. That, of course, was something else I didn't want to deal with, in those distressingly-troubled days. But, because he now had the job—the one that was once going to be a marvelous springboard to new and wonderful triumphs for yours truly (and because of the fact that the whole sorry situation had wound up being the exact opposite of those lofty expectations)—he was automatically, ipso facto, classified as an "asshole". In my vastly-disturbed, convoluted, mind, that made all kinds of sense.

"Hello? I mean, L and M Finance" She sounded like a pillar of strength. (Not really.)

"Elena? Elena! Please! Please don't hang up! I've got something to . . . something to . . . to tell you."

"Listen Paul, we can't . . . I mean, Tony'll be back in . . . I mean we . . ."

"Elena . . . I've got something to tell you."

"Like . . . like you love me?" Then, her tone softened. There was almost a sob, as she rasped, "I . . . I know."

"Yeah . . . and what I'm gonna tell you will make it sound like I don't!"

"Now what?" Her voice had hardened, with the first word—and then assumed a mind-boggling element of dejection, with the second.

"Listen, Elena. Listen. I'm . . . I'm leaving!"

"What? Laswell? It's a wonder you didn't leave before . . . leave well before . . . before this! With Red . . . or whatever his name is . . . being such a prick and all, I thought that you'd have, long since . . ."

"No!" I interrupted. "No! I'm moving! Moving away! Moving out of here! Probably up to New York! Well, possibly up to New York. Hell, I don't know!"

"Are you . . . are you leaving Joanne? Leaving Joanne? Leaving her . . . and the kids? Are you going to . . ."

"No! We're all . . . uh . . . we're all going."

"Oh! I see."

I'd just gotten hit by an iceberg! One that would have, efficiently, done in the Titanic! And the entire Seventh Fleet! In half the time! And even I could understand her reasoning. I'd have had no legitimate reason to expect any other reaction.

"Elena! Listen! We can't . . . we can't go on like this!"

"I know," she bristled. "You've said that before." Her voice was still cold! Stiff, even. She was struggling to maintain that distant tone. I could tell. But, it was a struggle!

"Yeah," I murmured. "I'm not sure, though, that the total impact of what I was just saying . . . what I'm telling you . . . I don't know that it's ever really hit me! Whether it's . . . truly . . . struck home! Not before this moment, anyway. Not till now! As hackneyed . . . as overworked, and as overdramatic . . . as that line is, we really and truly can't! Can not! Can't go on like this, I mean. I've always thought that that stupid-assed line actually was an overdramatic . . . a God-awful, melodramatic . . . totally-schlock, line."

"I never got that impression." Then, her tone softened, once again. "Not from the way you've always said it."

"Well, it was there. Hidden, probably. Or maybe it was obvious. Or whatever. Hell, I don't know. But, it's true! Too damn true . . . especially in our situation."

"You . . . you're telling me?"

"Listen, Elena! Look. Listen to me. You've got to listen to me! We've never been to bed! But, how much longer do you think we could ever hold out? Hold out on that end? I mean . . . eventually . . . we're gonna wind up in the sack! If I don't know anything, I know that!"

I'd found myself fervently hoping that I'd not just insulted—or even shocked—her.

"I . . . I know." Her voice being even <u>more</u> soft. The way I'd always <u>liked</u> it. The way I'd always <u>loved</u> it. The way that—forever—I'd hoped I'd always <u>hear</u> it.

"I'm not that <u>strong</u>, Elena," I blurted. "I'm not that <u>honorable</u>! I'm not that <u>principled</u>! In fact . . . somewhere in my inglorious make-up . . . there's a real <u>schmuck</u> factor. I'm <u>positive</u> that . . . at some point, . . . we'd have wound up in the sack! We <u>would</u> have, my darling Elena! I just . . . for sure . . . <u>know</u> it! And, listen, I just can't . . ."

"For awhile," she interrupted, "I thought <u>that</u> was going to be last Saturday. I was <u>sure</u> that it would be last Saturday . . . when that was going to <u>happen</u>. Figured for sure that . . . once I'd opened the damn <u>door</u> . . . figured, for sure, it was gonna be Saturday <u>night</u>, when we'd . . . when we'd finally . . . you know . . . when we'd . . ."

"Saturday <u>night</u>? But . . . but, we never got inside the <u>house</u>. Never even got off the damn <u>porch</u>!"

"I know."

Her voice was a bit stronger—yet, it held a heart-rending degree of sadness. Despair—that I'd not heard before. An entirely different tone.

"But, if we <u>had</u>, Paul," she continued, her voice the epitome of sadness, "if we <u>had</u> . . . we <u>never</u> would have stopped! Not in the living room! We'd have headed straight for . . . headed right straight for . . . for the <u>bedroom</u>! You know that as well as I do!"

"Elena, look . . ."

"The boys were already in bed, you know. And I'm <u>convinced</u> of this, Paul! Sure as I can <u>be</u>! We would've . . . I'm absolutely <u>positively</u>

convinced . . . we'd have gone on, and we'd have wound up in bed. I was thinking . . . was deathly afraid . . . that one of the boys would've, maybe, walked in on us. And do you know what? At that point, I don't think I'd have <u>cared</u>! Don't think I'd have been <u>that</u> upset! Don't think I'd have . . ."

"But, Elena, we only . . ."

"Yeah. We '<u>only</u>'! I <u>know</u> what we 'only'. You were holding me so <u>close</u>! So very, very, <u>close</u>! Here's another silly-assed line for you: I was melting in your arms! Another hackneyed line! Hackneyed, as hell! But, that's what . . . really and truly . . . that's what <u>happened</u>! What was <u>happening</u>! I felt you so . . . so excruciatingly close! And so . . . so . . . so <u>hard</u>! So incredibly <u>hard</u>! And, of course, there <u>you</u> were! There you <u>were</u> . . . <u>continually</u> patting me on my bum! And patting me and patting me and patting me! And I was . . ."

"I was <u>patting</u> you? On your <u>bum</u>? <u>Really</u>? I don't remember <u>that</u>!"

"Shows you what a total <u>wreck</u> you were! Well, so was <u>I</u>! I was exactly the same! Except that I <u>was</u> aware . . . I was <u>spectacularly</u> aware . . . that you were patting me! The fact that <u>you</u> don't remember . . . that should tell us <u>something</u>! You being such a pat-on-the-<u>fanny</u> man, and all."

"You're probably right," I sighed. "Undoubtedly right. If we'd have made it in . . . made it in, off the porch, y'know . . . I'm sure that we'd have . . ."

"But, we <u>didn't</u>! We damn well <u>didn't</u>! Did <u>not</u>!"

"No. But, the next time we damn well <u>might</u>!"

"Do you think I've not <u>thought</u> of that? Look Paul, Tony's going to be back . . . any second. Tell me what you were going to <u>tell</u> me. You're all <u>moving</u>? To New York? New <u>York</u> . . . of all places? Dear <u>God</u>! <u>Why</u>? I mean, why <u>there</u>? Why New damn <u>York</u>? I know you've always <u>talked</u> about wanting to live up there and all. But, for heaven's <u>sakes</u>! Do you <u>realize</u> how far that is? How far <u>away</u>? What a move like that would <u>entail</u>? To . . . my God . . . to move all the way up <u>there</u>! Move <u>way</u> up to . . ."

"It's . . . look, it's . . . it's <u>neutral</u> territory. I guess it's <u>that</u>! That fact . . . more than anything else. Joanne would <u>never</u> want to move back up to Detroit. Like <u>ever</u>! Everyone up there <u>hates</u> her, y'know."

"I know. You told me." The hardness had returned—although I'd had the distinct impression that she was, once again, fighting it. In any case, the coldness—which was completely overcoming her natural tone—was, once again, a factor.

"Listen," I pressed on, "I can't <u>stay</u> down here. For obvious reasons. But, <u>another</u> reason is that . . . is that I've got to . . . got to get Joanne away. Away from her mother's shit-assed <u>influence</u>. I can't . . . I'm tired of . . . tired as hell . . . goddam <u>sick</u> of it! Sick as <u>hell</u> . . . fighting the <u>both</u> of 'em! Every goddam <u>minute</u>! So, New York is, I guess, what you'd call . . . call neutral <u>turf</u>."

"Do you . . . I mean can you . . . I mean what'll you do for a <u>job</u>, up there? I mean, you can't just . . ."

"Oh, I've got a couple connections . . . I sincerely hope. A few connections. Up on Long Island, y'know. One guy who was a supervisor . . . up in Detroit . . . he's a big mucky-muck, these days, with *Reprise Finance*. At their national headquarters. He could, maybe . . ."

"I'm impressed." I couldn't tell if that was sarcasm—or not.

"Don't be. Listen, Elena. There's another possibility."

"Another . . . another possibility? What in heaven's name do you mean by that? What kind of possibility? I flat-out don't understand. If you've got your mind set on moving . . . moving all the way up to New York, then . . ."

"No. I'm talking about, maybe, another move. A possible one. My moving . . . at least a move as far away as New York . . . well, it isn't an absolutely, sure-fire, definite, thing. At least, at this point. There's an outside chance . . . a fairly remote one, I'll admit . . . that I can maybe get back on with my old company. You know . . . the one I used to work for. Worked for them . . . up in Austin."

"Them? You'd go back to work for them? I clearly don't understand you, Paul! Don't understand you at all! You've always said that they were a bunch of sons of bitches. You said you'd never . . . and I'm quoting here . . . that you never work for those miserable bastards again."

"Yeah, I know. And I meant it. Always meant it . . . whenever I said it. But, I couldn't possibly have imagined the situation. The one I'm fanny-deep in . . . at this moment in time. Look . . . I'm supposed to drive out to Houston. Drive out there . . . tomorrow. I've made an appointment . . . to talk to Mister Heddon. He's the division supervisor, up there. The head gazink, y'know . . . for all of Texas and Louisiana. The stupid company even has an office . . . a lone office . . . way out in Albuquerque, of all places. Shows you their corporate thinking. And that one . . . I kid you not . . . falls under Mister Heddon's command also."

"That's a helluva of a surprise. That you're even considering going back to work . . . for them! A shocker! To me, anyway. Isn't that a bit of a surprise . . . for anyone? For everyone? I mean, you once said . . . you once told me . . . that you'd never . . ."

"Yeah, I know. I know what I told you. I said the same thing . . . to anybody who'd listen! Elena look, I'm certainly not thrilled with the prospect. But, you know what they say . . . about any port in a storm. Strange bedfellows . . . and all that."

"That would be awfully strange . . . bedfellows-wise."

"I know. Listen, the company . . . they might even pay to move me to Houston. Well, probably not. I moved from Detroit to San Marcos, you know. Moved all that way . . . on my own damn dime. But . . . whatever . . . that'd be only two-hundred miles. And, God help me, I'd still have to withstand a whole hell of a lot of temptation. A hell of a lot! Just to keep from getting in my car . . . and driving back here! Driving back here . . . seven thousand times! Just to see you. To see you, Elena. To even just see you merely walk by . . . if for only all of ten or fifteen damn seconds. Just for . . ."

"Somehow, I can believe it. Can believe that! Can believe that you'd move heaven and earth . . . just to get a glimpse of me!" She began to cry. "Somehow, I know the truth of that."

"Yeah. It gets so . . . so damn <u>complicated</u>. I'm sure that you can <u>understand</u>. You've <u>always</u> understood me. I'm even positive that you understand <u>completely</u> . . . the entire all-hell-breaks-loose depth, of what I <u>feel</u> for you! <u>That</u> . . . for sure . . . makes the Houston thing a really <u>iffy</u> situation. Hopefully, the whole thing would be different . . . in Houston."

"Why should it be any different <u>there</u>? It's the same damn company."

"Well . . . for one thing . . . I'd had all kinds of troubles with the asshole <u>supervisor</u>, when I was working there. The son of a bitch, in Austin . . . and in San Marcos. This guy was a world-class asshole!"

"Seems like the world is <u>filled</u> with assholes."

"That it does. But <u>hah</u>! On <u>my</u> last day in Austin . . . <u>that</u> turned out to be <u>his</u> last day. The asshole supervisor, I mean. His last <u>day</u> . . . in the damn division. He's <u>gone</u>! At least, I wouldn't have to dick with <u>him</u> anymore. They transferred <u>his</u> sorry ass . . . on out to Seattle or someplace. So, chances are, I'd wind up with a lot better supervisor. Let's face it. Whoever it might turn out to be . . . the guy couldn't be a helluva lot <u>worse</u>."

"I . . . I suppose so." Her sigh probably registered halfway up—on the *Seismograph*, out at the university. "I suppose."

"And," I added, "Mister Heddon, in Houston . . . the head honcho, in the division . . . he'd always <u>seemed</u> to be a fairly nice guy. The few times that I'd ever met him, anyway. And the few times that I'd ever talked with him on the phone. A helluva lot nicer than the damn supervisor. So, maybe . . . just maybe . . ."

"And just what does Joanne think of that? Well, what does she think? How is she handling the whole damn thing? The thing . . . about moving? To Houston? Or . . . dear God . . . up to New York? You've always loved that house, and all."

"Always is a long, long time. I liked the house, yes. But, it's not as though it's the old ancestral homestead. Not like the old 'little bit of heaven', or anything. In fact, in a way . . . in so damn many ways . . . it's kind of a bloody symbol. A symbol . . . of all the crap. All the out and out crap! All the shit . . . that has come down, over the past year or so! That house? Well, it's gotten to where it seems to embody . . ."

"And I'm . . . I'm part of that . . . of that . . . all that crap? Part of all that shit?"

"NO! No! Dear Lord! NO! Hell no! You were the most wonderful thing . . . the most glorious thing . . . that could ever have happened to me! That did happen to me! That has ever happened to me! Ever! In my entire lifetime! Elena, I can't just . . ."

"Yeah. Wonderful!" She'd stopped crying. Or, at least, slowed it down—substantially. "It's all been a veritable paradise," she said, at length. "A damn Garden of Eden . . . a paradise . . . that we're living in."

"Well, it damn well could be! Damn well would be! If we were living in another time! In another place! In different circumstances. In a whole shit-load of different circumstances! If we were only . . ."

"Paul, listen to me! If your aunt had balls . . . she'd be your uncle."

"This isn't getting us anywhere."

"You expected it to?" She was beginning to sob again.

"Listen, Elena. I don't know . . . had no idea . . . as to what the hell I expected. I just know that I really can't leave Joanne. Not now! Not with four kids to care for."

This was the first time I'd ever said that—even to my-own-self. Out loud, anyway.

"No! God forbid!" After that rather explosive exclamation, her voice softened, once more. Softened—measurably. "No," she sighed—after an excruciatingly long pause. "You . . . you really can't! You certainly can't! For heaven's sakes, don't even think of leaving Joanne! Not with the . . . I mean . . ."

"It's my kids, Elena! You know that! Can you imagine what they'd think? What they'd think of me? If I went and . . . and, and, and . . . and deserted them? I can't! I can't possibly imagine what they'd think of me."

"I can." She signed heavily. Then, she sighed again. "Look." Her voice was barely audible. "Look, Paul. I actually do understand. I really . . . and truly . . . do. I may sound like I don't . . . but, I really do. I actually do."

"Well, that puts you one-up on me. I don't understand shit! Not anymore, I don't."

"Yes you do. Look, I know that I'd never be able to respect you . . . could never bring myself to genuinely respect you, no matter how hard I tried . . . if you did! If you did go . . . go ahead, and desert your family! And listen, when all was said and done, I could never really remain in a relationship . . . not in any kind of relationship . . . not with a man who I didn't respect.

A man that I <u>wouldn't</u> respect. How's <u>that</u> . . . for a mind-warping round robin?"

"Thank you. Thank you, Elena."

I'd had no idea what my muted response had intended. Had implied. I simply couldn't think—could not think—of anything else to say. <u>Nothing</u> seemed to fit. (Including what I'd just said!)

"Look, Paul." Her voice was assuming yet <u>another</u> tone. One that I'd never <u>heard</u> before. "I know . . . know that this is just as difficult for <u>you</u> as it is for <u>me</u>. But . . . please <u>know</u> this . . . it <u>is</u> difficult for me. It <u>is</u>! God <u>knows</u> it's so difficult! So damn <u>difficult</u>!"

"Elena, listen! I <u>know</u> that it's . . ."

"I <u>also</u> know," she broke in. "I'm aware that . . . <u>painfully</u> aware of the fact that . . . I don't have anywhere <u>near</u> the complications that you do. I'm divorced. And, of course, I'm thankful for <u>that</u>. But . . . now . . . how do I tell my <u>son</u>? The one, who's having such a really piss-poor <u>time</u> . . . trying to adjust to the fact that his father <u>never</u> shows his miserable ass around there? What do I say to <u>him</u>? What do I say . . . to <u>both</u> of them? To <u>either</u> of them?"

"Elena, I <u>love</u> your kids! <u>Both</u> of them!"

"I know. I know you do. But, how do I inform . . . especially this one little boy? Tell him . . . tell him . . . inform him that a <u>second</u> father figure is <u>also</u> abandoning him? This may <u>surprise</u> you . . . but, a father figure that he's become kind of <u>attached</u> to? Well, <u>more</u> than just simply 'kind of'! That's <u>you</u>, Paul."

That last statement <u>did</u> come as a surprise! A <u>shock</u>, actually. I'd not thought that I'd spent all that much time with the lad.

"I really wish you'd not have used that <u>word</u>," I winced. "I mean, 'abandoning'! It's such a . . . such a . . . . a . . . a . . ."

"What <u>are</u> you doing, Paul?" Iceberg time again. "Just what the hell <u>are</u> you doing?" Then, the softening—thankfully—once again. "Look, in <u>either</u> scenario . . . in <u>any</u> damn scenario . . . you'd be abandoning <u>someone</u>! Abandoning <u>some</u> kid or another. Plural, actually. I <u>understand</u> that, Honey. I <u>do</u>. It's just . . ."

"It's been a long <u>time</u> . . . such a <u>damnably</u> long time . . . since you've ever called me '<u>Honey</u>'!"

"Oh," she sighed, "not so long. Saturday night. Remember? Or is that filed in the same abstract file? The same goofy kind of cloud? The same one . . . as forgetting about your continually patting me on my bum?"

"That <u>too</u>? You called me '<u>Honey</u>'? On <u>Saturday</u>? You actually <u>did</u>? <u>Honey</u>? I didn't know that . . ."

"You weren't <u>wrapped</u> too tight, Saturday. Well . . . truth be told . . . neither was <u>I</u>. We were some kind of <u>couple</u> . . . at that point! Some kind of <u>pair</u>, we were."

"Listen, I understand . . . at least I <u>think</u> I do. Understand your reaction to all of this. This whole bundle of . . . of . . . of whatever-it-is. I don't really know how to act, Elena. Haven't the foggiest clue . . . as to how to act. But, then, I haven't <u>known</u> how to act . . . not for <u>months</u> now. Maybe <u>years</u>."

She began to completely break down. The sobs were larger—louder—and much longer! Much, <u>much</u> longer!

"Look," she rasped. She was just this side of what was almost a convulsion, "Tony's coming. I need to <u>go</u>! I <u>really</u> need to go! Whatever you <u>do</u>, Paul . . . wherever it is that you wind <u>up</u> . . . I want you to know that I <u>understand</u>. God <u>bless</u> you! God <u>bless</u> you, Paul. God bless <u>you</u> . . . and may He bless <u>everything</u>! Everything you <u>do</u>! <u>Everything</u>!"

And then, she <u>really</u> broke down! Went completely to pieces! Overwhelmingly emotional pieces! I don't think I'd ever been so—so dumbstruck! Never before—in my entire life!

<u>God bless me</u>? That's the first time she'd ever said that to me! <u>God bless me</u>? <u>And everything I do</u>? <u>Everything I freaking do</u>? Does one <u>say</u> such things—to a certified schmuck? I was even more rattled than before! And that took some doing!

The phone, of course, went dead in my hand! I could barely see the stupid instrument—through all my tears!

When thinking about *those we leave behind*—no matter <u>where</u> I was going to wind up—there were two <u>more</u> names to be added to the list: Alton and Albert!

FIVE

ON WEDNESDAY EVENING—FOUR DAYS after that tortured, tormented, tumultuous, Saturday (you do remember Saturday—do you not?) I found myself approaching that same stupid, seedy, used car lot.

Many things—many consequential things—as well you might have imagined, had taken place, since the continual, unending, emotional-rollercoaster, upheaval of the previous weekend had submerged me, in all manner of chaos. The Saturday upheaval? HAH! That had been only the beginning. The problem was: I hadn't known things would get worse. That events could—or would—become even more hairy! (What else was new?)

First of all, I'd spent all day Sunday, at home. Like any good husband should. Joanne had made a really major concession—during a tense, hour-long, discussion on Saturday night. She'd ultimately agreed—to our making a move. A big one! The big one!

We would "pull up the old tent stakes"—and move (with everything we would be able to cram into the still-available Valiant, and a prospective *U-Haul* trailer)! We would relocate—to New York! Onward—to "The Big Apple"!

Still, although she'd not said anything further—about the gigantic, mind-blowing, move—by late Sunday evening, I could tell that she was rethinking her "hasty decision". Mulling it over—thoroughly. I could "smell the wood burning" from way across the room—which is where I'd spent most of Sunday. Way across the room! (I'd not quite spent that endless period, in a fetal position. But, I'm sure, I'd not been all that far removed.)

On Monday, I'd engaged in that lengthy—that highly emotional—phone conversation with Elena. The poignant "goodbye" exchange—that had left me totally drained!

Emotionally bankrupt! To the point that even my sainted—my loving, caring—redhead of a manager had stayed off my case! Had kept well out of my way—for the entire day! A distinct upset! But, a good move—on his part.

Monday night, at home, was still tension-filled! To the brim! As had been the case the day before. Joanne was, definitely, still "reviewing the situation"— when it came to the big move.

She'd ultimately agreed—substantially more readily—to an alternative: A possible closer—much closer—relocation. A move to Houston was much more to her liking—were I able to make a connection with my former employer.

I'd advised her—earlier that Monday forenoon—that I'd put in a call to the head meatball, in Houston. Informed her that I'd set up a meeting, with Mr. Heddon, for the following day, Tuesday, in "The Bayou City".

In truth, the plan had been a good deal more than simply a "Cover My Fanny" move—since I knew that my wife was fast bailing on the rather far-fetched (and getting more so by the second) "Gotham Relocation Plan".

By the morning of that fateful Tuesday, I—my-own-self—had even begun to suffer a good many second thoughts. I'd started to experience some pretty immense reservations of my own—once such a gargantuan move was looming closer and closer.

Obviously, what I'd been planning—my life-long desired move to Shangri La (i.e. New York)—would be a gigantic undertaking! Until Monday, I'd not even begun to actually analyze—to start to realize—the many and varied complications that such a mind-bending journey would portend! I was coming to grips with this actuality—more and more—as the time had so painfully ground past.

This, obviously, would be a gargantuan undertaking—one that I was becoming less and less enamored with. Reality was setting in! The old cold-feet thing was creeping up on me. Well, more than merely creeping! What an earth-shaking adventure, I would be undertaking! A major migration—one that I was becoming less and less sure that I could pull off.

Alternatively, a move to Houston would seem more logical. ("Logical" had never been a typical thought pattern for me.) Such a situation as Houston, I was beginning to realize, just might get Joanne and me— off from a substantial hook! Possibly a multitude of hooks!

The prospect of reconnecting with my old employer—and moving to Houston—would, not unexpectedly, lead to even further adventure:

On Tuesday: I'd called in sick, at "The Truck Rental Joint". Then, I'd taken off for Houston. For better—or for worse!

As mentioned, I'd set up that appointment to be interviewed by none other than the omnipotent Mr. T.O. Heddon. Had set it up—early Monday morning. As also previously stated, I'd never actually "interfaced" all that much with Mr. Heddon. Not personally. Not during my wondrous tenure in San Marcos. Or even after I'd been granted the lofty management position, in Austin.

On those rare occasions—when we had been in touch—he'd always seemed to be a very nice man. Mr. Heddon had always treated me well. Had never failed to show me much more respect than my sainted former supervisor. (Well, that had never required much effort.)

The job interview, in Houston, was—surprisingly— moving right along. Going fairly well, actually. At least that was my perception. (Not usually all that reliable.)

Obviously, I'd had no idea—as to where I was going to dig up the money to move to Houston. That, of course, would be a consideration—of major import—were the great man to make me an offer. But, then, I didn't really know how I was ever going to finance the even-more-mind-warping move to "The Big Apple". Logic—as has been noted previously—has never been my strong suit!

Mr. Heddon was in the process of offering me an unheard-of $500.00 a month! Five hundred bucks! Could I believe that? More than I'd ever earned—in my entire, celebrated, life. I'd been stuck on a monthly stipend of $450.00—ever since I'd last been in his employ. As mentioned, I'd pulled down the same tired old salary—at the small loan outfit, in San Antonio. And that was, precisely, the generous remuneration that I was being paid in my wondrous, current, truck-rental-agent position.

Five hundred bucks! Each and every month! Sounded good! Really good! Almost too good! Such a move, I was delighted to acknowledge, might well be a way out of my seemingly-doomed situation, in "The Alamo City"! I might even get to keep my Valiant! Great! That would be one of the sweetest things of all! A true blessing!

Of course, Elena would remain—would loom, would be lurking—a mere three-and-a-half hours away. But, at least, Joanne would be happier with the less complicated relocation. (So, undoubtedly, would her mother.) You've gotta take whatever small victories you can claim—when the claiming is good. Is that profound—or what?

Besides, the pay increase was not small. Not to me, anyway. Not at that turbulent time in my life. Helluva step forward—pay grade-wise

Still, dammit, as the afternoon wore on—and it really <u>wore</u> on—the many phone calls from the various supervisors, in the far-flung reaches of Mr. Heddon's vast empire, began to filter in.

I kept hearing him. Kept listening to him—as he was giving those (poor?) supervisors as much unending, disparaging, grief, as those men were, undoubtedly, handing out to their underling branch managers.

Did I want to go back to being one of <u>them</u>? <u>Again</u>? Always on the receiving end of never-ending, unceasing, criticism? Consistently second-guessed? Every movement? Every decision "reviewed"—no matter how insignificant? Day in and day out? Day after day? Week after week? And all of this sort of stuff—all this <u>crap</u>—apparently, was coming from the top. From Mr. Heddon, himself! <u>He</u>, obviously, was the source of all the BS!

Time and time again, I sat there—and listened to this small, heavy-set, dynamo! Witnessed each <u>unrelenting</u> diatribe—as he continually belittled these guys! This "dynamo" never <u>ceased</u> to berate them! Without exception! Without let-up! Time after time after time, he consistently put these men down! (There were no women supervisors—at least not in Texas or Louisiana. Another corporate message there, I suppose.)

I'd finally decided—sadly—"The hell with it"! I just simply could <u>not</u> work for these people. Not again. Not anymore. (I'd been right—the <u>first</u> time! There was, really, no <u>way</u> that I could go back to work for these abusive, uncaring, "clear-or-kill", cretins.)

They'd pulled that awfully dirty deal on me in Austin—to the point that, as noted before, I was convinced that I was going to be fired! Would they play the same kind of heartless—totally unprofessional—game with me again? Once I'd sign on, in Houston? Sounded like it! I simply could not put in any more time with them! Not on their ever-present, stupid-assed, unstoppable, bar-b-q spit! If I'd never learned anything else, in my young life, I'd learned that!

So, there I'd sat! On that stupid Tuesday! In Mr. Heddon's lavish office! In Houston! And I'd finally awakened to the true—the unending, the inescapable—harassment quotient of the job that was being offered to me.

I couldn't help but be overwhelmed by the self-preservation impulse—that suddenly took over! The hell with it, I finally decided. I ain't gonna do it!

I arose—and thanked the exultant high poobah, for the generous amount of time that he'd spent with insignificant little old me. Advised him that I'd appreciated the audience he'd granted me. But, I did turn down the offer! Five-hundred bucks! More money than I'd ever earned! In my entire lifetime! Gone! Right out the old window! Up the flu!

I'd had to go and be disgustingly truthful—in reporting back to my spouse. (Even when I was actually being somewhat "principled", it still wasn't working out. None of it was!) I'd had to go ahead and give Joanne an honest—a completely accurate—

play-by-play accounting, of the way the interview had gone. Advise her of my horror—at what I'd sat and listened to! Had—to my horror—witnessed, for 40 or 45 long, drawn-out, unending, minutes. And, of course, I advised her of my ultimate turning down the "generous" offer! (I'd even told her of the "unbelievable" five-hundred bucks, that had been proffered!)

Joanne, then, simply exploded! (Simply?) For the very first time in all our years of marriage, she'd totally lost it! No sadness—nor heartbreak—here! No martyrdom! It was all undiluted anger! Pure, unadulterated, rage!

"I can't believe this," she ranted—and continued to rant—at the top of her lungs. "I cannot imagine . . . could never imagine . . . that you, in your right mind, would've ever turned that down, Paul! Simply can't believe it! Can not believe it! Five hundred dollars? And that's not good enough for you?" She continued communicating—at the highest decibel level imaginable. "Five hundred goddam dollars! You turned down . . . five hundred goddam dollars! We don't have a pot to piss in . . . or a goddam window to throw it out of! And you turn up your shit-assed nose . . . at five-hundred goddam dollars? Five hundred dollars?"

"Yeah, but Joanne, listen! It was just . . ."

She was not to be denied. "Well, screw you" she snarled. Her voice lowered to where she was merely seething! "I'm leaving you, Paul! I'm goddam well leaving you! Something I should have done . . . months ago! Years ago! I've had it! Damn well <u>had</u> it! For good and <u>all</u>! I'm <u>gone</u>! No more of this <u>bullshit</u>!"

"<u>Joanne</u>! It's <u>not</u> bullshit! <u>None</u> of it is bullshit! <u>Listen</u>, you can't . . ."

"Yes it <u>is</u>! It's <u>all</u> bullshit! <u>All</u> of it! Every <u>bit</u> of it! <u>Everything</u>! Everything . . . over all these <u>years</u>! All of these goddam <u>years</u>, Paul! I'm all <u>through</u> putting up with . . . with, with, with . . . with all this <u>bullshit</u>! <u>Enough</u>, already!"

"Joanne, you can't just . . ."

"<u>I</u> <u>can</u> . . . and I <u>will</u>! I <u>am</u>! Being so damn <u>poor</u>! Being so <u>goddam</u> poor! <u>Always</u>! Scraping for every goddam <u>nickel</u>! Having no damn <u>money</u>! <u>Never</u> having any money! <u>Ever</u>! I'm <u>sick</u> of having to scrimp and save, for every lousy, pissy-assed, damn nickel . . . the few of 'em you've ever brought into this house! And <u>you</u>! You having some <u>slut</u>! Screwing some <u>bitch</u>, of a . . . of a goddam floozy-assed whore-girlfriend!"

"Now, <u>wait</u>! Wait just a goddam <u>minute</u>! Elena's <u>not</u> . . ."

"She's a <u>slut</u>! A goddam <u>slut</u>! I could probably even have put up with <u>her</u> . . . if we'd only had two nickels to rub together. What-ever-little money we've ever had . . . there's <u>got</u> to have been <u>some</u> spent on <u>her</u>! On that <u>bitch</u>!"

"Listen, Joanne! I never spend all that much on . . ."

"I don't care if it was a quarter . . . for a goddam candy bar! It was <u>too</u> much! Don't you <u>understand</u>, Paul? There's <u>always</u> been the fact of the <u>money</u>! The goddam <u>money</u>! The fact that there was <u>no</u> money . . . that there has never <u>been</u> any money . . .

that was bad enough! But . . . added to that . . . you've got this floozy! This goddam bimbo! You're screwing this . . . this bitch! Screwing her . . . screwing her . . . on the side! That's too damn much! It's all just too damn much! No more! No mas! I'm goddam out of here!"

"Now wait just a damn minute! Elena and I have never . . ."

"Bullshit! Like I said, Paul . . . it's all bullshit! And I'm all through! Up to here . . . with all the bullshit! With not having the pot to piss in! I'm taking the kids! Taking 'em . . . down to Brownsville!"

"Come on, Joanne! You can't just . . ."

"Oh, yes I can! I goddam well can! Mom and Dad . . . they've said that I can come down there! Live with them! Any time! Any goddam time! Any shittin' time I want to! They'd just love to have the kids, down there, with them! Listen . . . unlike you . . . they'll be a little free with a dollar. The kids will have a few nice things . . . for a goddam change! Courtesy Mom and Dad! That's not like someone I know!"

"That's not fair, Joanne. I've always done the best I can."

"Bullshit! Now, if you want to move your cheating ass on down to Brownsville, go ahead! That's fine! Go ahead! Nothing I can jolly well do about that! No way I can stop you! But, you're going to have to find your own damn quarters. And your own damn employment. Get your own job . . . if you can! One where, hopefully, the meanies won't pile any grief . . . on your poor, sensitive, little ass! We're ka-poot, Paul . . . you and me! So, don't look for Daddy to go ahead . . . and to hire your worthless, cheating, ass!

Or even get you a goddam job! Anywhere in town! Never happen!

"Joanne! Look! I haven't . . ."

"I'm . . . for certain . . . not going to New York, Paul! Not now! Probably not ever! Never in a million years! I don't even know . . . why I went ahead and agreed to that whole stupid-assed, outrageous, numb-skulled, dimwitted, asinine, shit-assed, plan, in the first goddam place! It was stupid! Right from the start!"

"It was . . . look . . . it was, maybe, the only way we could've salvaged our marriage."

"Our marriage? Salvage it? Salvage that? Our goddam marriage!" She spat the word—twice. "Our marriage . . . it's a goddam farce! It's been a farce! Forever! Pure and simple . . . a damn farce! And it's all over! Done! Hell, it's been done! It's been over! Over . . . for goddam years!"

"Joanne, look . . ."

"Why don't you just go ahead . . . and stay here in San Antonio? That way, you can continue to . . . to shack up . . . to shack up, with that bitch! With your precious goddam Elena! You can go ahead and plank her now! Out in the open! Whenever you goddam want to! You won't have to worry about me . . . about whether I'm good with you screwing the ass off her, or not!"

In all the years that I'd known Joanne, I'd never heard such venom pour forth from her! Nothing even close! Not in decibel level! Not in long-windedness! Not in four-letter words! Never in profanity like she was using that evening! But, mostly, never with such pure, undiluted, venom! Ever!

"Now, wait a minute," I half-shouted. "Just a damn minute, Joanne! Elena and I . . . we have never been to bed! Like . . . in ever! I've told you that! Many times . . . I've told you that! And it's true!"

"Yeah! You've told me all that before! To which I say . . . bullshit! You expect me to believe that? You actually expect me to believe that? That you haven't screwed her? That you don't screw her?"

"Yes! No! I don't know! I don't know what to . . ."

"It's all bullshit, Paul! Every bit of it! Everything you're telling me! Probably everything you've ever told me! And it's all bullshit! Utter bullshit! Total, condensed, bullshit! I don't believe any of it! Not for a minute! Not for one lousy, damn, minute! Not any more . . . do I believe it! Not one damn thing! Not one damn word! Not one! So, save your goddam breath!"

"Out of all our problems, Joanne, I would hope that you'd believe this! Trust me . . . that we've not been intimate, Elena and I. Never been to bed! Ever!"

She stood there—hands clenched! She pounded the bottom parts of her fists—into the front of her thighs! Her face flushed! It turned—horribly, frightfully—deep-crimson!

"Again, I say bullshit," she hissed. "Total bullshit! Pure bullshit! Look, I'd have considered the move . . . the one to Houston. Would really have considered it! Favorably . . . as a matter of fact. Really favorably . . . especially if I'd have known that the job was going pay you five bills! But, you? You can't be bothered! Noooo! Not sensitive . . . fragile . . . old Paul Marchildon! He can't be bothered . . . with putting up with a little static!"

"Joanne, it's <u>more</u> than that. It's not <u>just</u> a little static. It's the whole damn . . ."

"You keep telling me what a bastard <u>Red</u> is," she interrupted. "I'm sure that's true. To a <u>point</u>, anyway. But then, <u>here</u> it was . . . here it <u>was</u>, Paul . . . your chance to get the hell <u>out</u>! To get the hell <u>away</u> from him! To get <u>way</u> away from him!"

"That . . . that's not <u>fair</u>, Joanne! Not fair at <u>all</u>!"

"But, <u>no</u>! Not <u>you</u>! Not fragile old <u>Paul</u>! Not sensitive old <u>you</u>! <u>You</u> can't take . . . can't put up with . . . a little <u>heat</u>! Not from Mister Heddon! Not from some stupid-assed supervisor! Some <u>unknown</u> stupid-assed supervisor! You don't even know who the hell he'd <u>be</u>! Sensitive old you, though, can't put up . . . with <u>whoever</u> it might turn out to be! Not even for fifty-dollars more a month! Fifty goddam <u>dollars</u>, Paul! Fifty <u>dollars</u>! That's two-thirds of our mortgage payment, y'know! Which is no big deal to <u>you</u>! Mainly, because we haven't . . . <u>you</u> haven't . . . been able to <u>pay</u> the goddam thing! So, <u>hell</u> on it! <u>Screw</u> it! Screw <u>you</u>! <u>Enough</u>! <u>Enough</u>, already! The kids and I . . . we're <u>off</u>! We're goddam <u>gone</u>! We're off to <u>Brownsville</u>!"

"Joanne! You <u>can't</u>! <u>Really</u>! You <u>can't</u> just . . ."

"I <u>can't</u>? I <u>am</u>! I just <u>did</u>! You just <u>watch</u> me! I'm going to call Daddy <u>tomorrow</u> . . . first thing <u>tomorrow</u> . . . and I'm gonna ask him to come up here! Come up . . . and pick us all <u>up</u>! I hope you'll be happy . . . up in your precious New <u>York</u>! Or banging that <u>broad</u>! That <u>bimbo</u>! The one you used to work with!"

"Joanne . . . <u>stop</u>! Stop all this . . ."

"Maybe she'll go with you," interrupted my wife. "Then you'll have everything! Everything you've ever wanted! New York . . . and your own private floozy! Bang her . . . whenever you damn please! And in wonderful old New York! A roll in the hay . . . for every light on Broadway! What more could anyone want? You'll be in heaven, Paul! In frigging heaven!"

So saying, she stormed off! Off—to bed! How the bedroom door ever survived that ultimate slamming, I'll never know. It should have wound up resembling a toothpick factory!

The kids were still up! They'd kind of huddled in the kitchen. The room was no help! Joanne and I had been exchanging our pleasantries in the living room—a mere eight or ten feet away!

The tads had—naturally—become totally petrified! Every one of them! By what had just unfolded—before, more or less, their very eyes!

I was trying—trying my damndest—to calm them down. To reassure them. And, of course, I was meeting with abject failure! No matter what I tried to do. No matter what I tried to say, it wasn't enough! It wasn't—obviously—what needed to have been said! Obviously!

At nine-thirty, I put them all to bed! Kissed them—much more fervently than I had, in a long time! Watched Cynthia—as she struggled to close her eyes (and keep them closed, for my benefit).

I—spectacularly—couldn't stop the tears from rolling down Mary Jane's cheeks.

The boys? They were a much more difficult "read"! They were trying—making a heroic attempt to be as macho as possible (although I'm not sure I'd ever heard that term, back then). They were not all that successful—at the charade. But, it <u>was</u> a valiant attempt!

I did my best to see that all of them would be as comfortable as possible. I could not <u>let</u> them see how the impending break up was affecting me.

I waited till I got out into the living room—before I broke down! I don't remember ever having cried like that! Nor for that long! Never that <u>deeply</u>! Then, after about a half-hour, I bunked in—on the couch!

On Wednesday morning, I called Elena—at home. Early! Before she would've left for work. She didn't want to talk. Was <u>almost</u> going to hang up on me!

When I'd, hurriedly, told her of Joanne's rant—how my soon-to-be-ex-wife had become completely unhinged—and the extremely-troubling situation, vis-a-vis my spouse absconding to Brownsville, with the kids, Elena expressed all kinds of sympathy. Great amounts of empathy. But, she maintained, the situation between the two of us was—sadly—utterly <u>untenable</u>!

"You need to move to Brownsville, Paul," she admonished. "That's where your <u>kids</u> are. Well, that's where they're gonna be."

"Yes, but . . ."

"Look, Paul, If you were to stay up here, you'd <u>miss</u> your kids. Miss 'em . . . . <u>terribly</u>. You <u>know</u> you would.

Miss 'em . . . like nobody's business. That's only natural. Look, before long, the situation . . . your being separated from your kids . . . would wind up being a real tragedy! A real damper! A permanent . . . an impregnable . . . damper! It wouldn't take long . . . to screw up anything! Everything! Anything we'd ever have between us! Screw up the whole thing! Whatever would be between us. Screw it up . . . horribly! It would have to! Positively have to! No way out of it! It'd just be a matter of time. And . . . please. Paul . . . I've got enough problems as it is."

"Elena? Couldn't we just . . . ?"

"No! No . . . we couldn't! We can't! Let's face it, Paul. I love you! Love you . . . very much. More than anyone I've ever known! I never knew what it would feel like . . . what it'd be like . . . to love someone, as deeply as I love you. And I'm convinced that you love me. Love me . . . just as deeply."

"I do, Elena! If you don't believe anything else, please know that I do!"

"I do believe it, Paul. I know that to be true! That . . . well, it would seem to be the answer! The answer . . . to all of my prayers. To all of your prayers. To all of everyone's prayers. But, Paul, our loving one another . . . even as much as we do, as deeply as we do . . . it's simply not enough! Nowhere near enough! Not by a long shot! Face it . . . we've got to face it . . . it's an impossible situation! A completely impossible situation . . . you and me! It is, Paul! You have to realize that! Completely impossible! Totally impossible!"

"No it's not, Elena! It's not! It wouldn't be easy. I know that. If I don't know anything else, I know that! But, we could, Elena! We could make a go of it! Others couldn't! But, we could! A love as deep as ours? We could make it work, Elena! We could! And . . . we jolly well would!"

"No, Paul. There's no way out! For either of us! Nothing good . . . can possibly come from anything between us! No matter how we tried! No matter what we'd ever do! It would never work out. Could never work out! Not in a million years! Paul, look! I'm sorry! Just as sorry as I can be! But, I just can't take on anything like this! Could never handle it! It'd be impossible! My life is (she sighed—deeply) complicated enough! Complicated enough . . . as it is!"

"But . . . but, Elena! You can't just . . ."

"Goodbye, Paul!"

And she hung up! Wednesday! What a day! What a helluva day!

I went back to work—at that God-awful truck rental place. I was, as you can imagine, totally overwhelmed—completely bemused—by the damnably destructive double-whammy! By the twin gut-shots—that I'd taken over the previous 12 or 14 hours.

My mind—the moopie remnant of same—was totally swamped! Completely snowed under—by the situation! Both with Joanne—as well as with Elena! It certainly wasn't helping—that Red was particularly on the muscle! Irascible—for the whole damn day! The entire day!

My hokey little world was collapsing! Hell, it already <u>had</u> collapsed! Had completely turned! To bitter <u>ashes</u>! <u>Dust</u>! Nothing but <u>dust</u>! All around me! I'd never really known what "wormwoods" were. What the term actually <u>meant</u>. Whether they were living, breathing, organisms. But, I knew that they were always supposed to be "bitter". I was positive that I was fanny-deep in damn wormwoods!

Looking back, I'd only <u>thought</u> that I'd been having a bad day—on that previous, disjointed, Saturday! It was to laugh! (Except for the fact that I was, at that point, emotionally—and physically—incapable of even a weak smile. Would've been unable to have produced even the slightest smirk.)

As that bleak, black, God-awful, never-ending, Wednesday dragged itself on (and on and on and on), I found myself <u>regretting</u>—regretting in <u>spades</u>—not having signed up for another hitch with the big, the foreboding, national finance company. Mr. Heddon's offer would've, at least, kept me with my kids—and would've gotten me out of my present manager's sadistic clutches! Plus, it <u>would</u> have paid me a scintillating $50.00 a month more! What had I been <u>thinking</u>? What <u>could</u> I have been thinking?

<u>Well Paul, you've done it again! You've gone</u> . . . <u>and blown another one! It's become a tradition!</u>

Red finally decided to call it a day—denks God—at about four-thirty Wednesday afternoon. And so there I was! Back to being terminally tempted—

overwhelmingly tempted—by that damn thousand dollar bill! I could <u>hear</u> the damn thing—pulsating! Through all those layers of metal! It was still in the safe. (I'd looked.) Why Red had never deposited the damn thing, by <u>that</u> late date, I'll never know.

This guy—ol' Asa, the renter of the tractor and trailer—was due to be returning Friday or Saturday. But, he'd advised me—as he was signing the rental contract—that there was a distinct possibility that he could, possibly, be getting back on Thursday. He'd also advised that the chances of completing his little jaunt by then were slim.

But, the possibility <u>was</u> there. I found myself admitting that It would be better for me—significantly better for me, infinitely better for me—once the stupid transaction would (at long last) be <u>completed</u>! <u>Done</u>! <u>Finished</u>! And that damn thousand-dollar bill would, finally, be "outta here"—for good and all! (It <u>should</u>—really—have been in the stupid <u>bank</u>, by then!)

On the other hand, if I <u>was</u> going to "do something rash", the "caper" was going to—by necessity—have to be <u>soon</u>! <u>Really</u> soon! Like, <u>immediately</u>! The ever-consuming, heat-laden, criminal scenario was fast evolving! Reconstructing itself—into a "Now Or Never" situation! Push <u>was</u> coming to shove!

Well, truth to tell, it had already <u>evolved</u>! If I was going to <u>do</u> the dastardly deed—it was going to wind up being the former! The "Now" part!

After Bonafacio left, I went ahead—and <u>did</u> it! I <u>filched</u> the G-Note! I drove the faithful Valiant <u>way</u>

over to a run-down section on the far east side—and abandoned my faithful old friend. Maybe the repo guys would find it—and maybe they wouldn't. Quite possibly, they'd decide that the car had been stolen, from me. I certainly was not going to lose any sleep over what-ever-muddle I may have caused them. It didn't matter to me—what they thought. Least of my worries!

It took two buses—for me to get back to get to my side of town. And to that goofy used car lot.

It was getting late. Almost seven-thirty. The lot may have already closed down—at six o'clock—for all I knew. That might turn out to be a blessing in disguise, although—at that point—I couldn't see how. It turned out that they were, ploddingly, still open for business—though the place was almost deserted.

I'd not thought of it—till I'd finally told the guy that I'd buy the Chrysler—but, it suddenly occurred to me that he might not have enough cash on hand, to give me change for the thousand-dollar bill. (Another "blessing"?)

Hell, he might not even consider accepting a bill that large. Not from a total stranger. Not at eight o'clock at night! Probably not from someone who could barely peel off $300.00 for a pile of scrap iron.

But, surprisingly, he did the deal! Took the large bill—and gave me cash back! And in nothing larger than $20.00 bills. (He must've had a pretty good day! Actually, he must've had a helluva day! I was glad that someone had.)

I drove my new blue "treasure" out to the house. Joanne and the kids were already gone! Had already gone! Dear Lord! That was quick! Her father must've gotten himself right into his snooty, brand-spanking-new, Mercury Park Lane station wagon—and headed, immediately, for "The Alamo City"!. Must've done that—bright and early, that morning. Didn't know that he was that fond of the kids!

My spouse didn't leave with much. Hell, there wasn't all that much to leave with! Not a great deal of stuff—that would be worthwhile transporting over such a distance.

At her parents' home, of course, she'd have access to an infinitely higher-grade assortment of furniture. Far grander—than our woebegone "sticks". Everything—for her, and for the kids—would be of much higher quality. And far more—quantity-wise. Much more opulent! Everything would be infinitely more opulent! (I sighed—expelling just about every ounce of breath that been left inside me!) That wouldn't take much either.

I'm sure that you can believe that our house was, probably, just a matter of weeks from being foreclosed on. I guess Joanne had figured to let the mortgage company worry about disposing of our less-than-elegant belongings.

Apparently, the bulk of the scant cargo that had gone south in the sumptuous Park Lane had been—almost 100%, I'm guessing—clothes. Well, clothing—along with what little jewelry my spouse had managed to come by over the years. (Which was damn little!) And, probably, a few toiletry items. Well, a number of the kids' toys had to have been included.

Sighing heavily, I'd had to acknowledge that they never <u>did</u> have the benefit of a multitude of the more desirable toys. <u>Far</u> too expensive—most of them—for what was, laughingly, referred to, as the Marchildon budget.

I guessed that this was probably a fitting end for the bare-bones marriage. Joanne <u>had</u> had to grapple with being poor—for the entire time we'd been together! The <u>entire</u> time! And things were <u>far</u> from "looking up". <u>Always</u> far from "looking up"! <u>Always</u>!

In addition to constantly fighting those damn disconnect notices—virtually every damn month—from the damn electric company and the damn phone company, I'd had a loan from the large bank—with which *L&M Finance* dealt. I'm sure that the only reason the suits there had given me the loot, in the first damn place—was the fact that I was the damn manager of the local damn *L&M* office.

Plus, I'd taken out numerous <u>small</u> loans! <u>Numerous</u>! From <u>five</u> or <u>six</u> of my close-by competitors. Again, I'm <u>positive</u> that they were extending me small, "neighborly" services. They <u>were</u> a nice bunch—with <u>one</u> exception.

I'd especially <u>hated</u> to impose on one of them. A middle-aged woman named Dolly. She'd managed a small loan office—two doors away from me—for <u>years</u>! We'd struck up an unusual friendship—built mostly on our common love of schmaltzy music.

Down deep, I <u>knew</u> that it would be a monumental struggle—to ever pay her back. Well, actually the same went for the other five or six small loans that I'd managed to float. (But, if I was—<u>ever</u>—going to pay back <u>anyone</u>, it would be my friend Dolly!) Needless to say, I was about to leave them all holding the bag! Every one of them!

I looked around the house. It was probably a blessing—albeit a hollow, highly-emotional, one—to finally leave "This Vale Of Tears". The place had come to symbolize everything that was closing in on me.

I found myself guessing that a goodly portion of my recent dedication to the prospect of moving to New York, had been to put as much of this upheaval-producing symbolism—as well as the strangling financial burden—behind me. Leave it! Leave literally everything! Leave it—miles behind.

But, now—now that I'd lost my kids—well, the money stuff all seemed so damned insignificant. My head was swimming! Obviously!

Just when you think that things couldn't possibly get any worse, they jolly well get worse. My kids! My kids, for heaven's sakes. Gone! Forever?

Well, they were gone—unless I were to follow them, down to Brownsville. My father-in-law—who'd, by then, owned his own, thriving, accounting business would, I was positive, have me blackballed!

I'd be *Persona Non Grata*—throughout the entire city! The old saying, "You'll Never Work In This Town Again" kept bobbing up and down throughout my overheated mind! How was I ever going to fight that? How could I fight that? The answer kept coming back: You can't!

Moving to Brownsville? Hah! I was picturing that projection as a situation—where I would be not unlike some prizefighter! One who is forever shadow-boxing—with some unknown opponent! One he cannot see! Countless jabs and roundhouses—all aimed at some ethereal mass of flames, or smoke, or steam, or <u>some</u> damn thing. I'd <u>never</u> land a punch!

Moving to a town 350 miles away! <u>That</u> seemed to present an even more impenetrable, "irresistible" force—than moving to a city 2000 miles in the opposite direction. Go figure! (No! Don't!)

What was I to <u>do</u>? What <u>could</u> I do? Quite frankly—even at that late (and critical) point in my life—I didn't <u>know</u>! Flat did <u>not</u> know! Had no <u>idea</u>! Not <u>one</u>! I just knew—that I <u>had</u> to get out! Had to get the hell <u>out</u>! Get <u>away</u>! Get <u>far</u> away! Put a <u>lot</u> of distance, between me and that damn <u>house</u>—and the damn <u>city</u>—and all they represented!

I turned back to the task at hand. Almost with renewed energy! (Almost!) <u>I must pack! I must leave! I must get the hell out! Get the hell out of here!</u>

Fortunately, my soon-to-be-ex-spouse had, graciously, left my rather large, table-model, *Olympic* stereo for me. That was nice of her. That little dandy had been my pride and joy.

It had also presented a <u>major</u> crisis—earlier in our marriage! <u>Major</u>! A <u>real</u> problem! That had been in 1959—when we were still in Detroit.

My treasured phonograph! This <u>glorious</u> *Olympic*! It had been a floor model—a "demo"—at one of the larger appliance stores in the *Northland Shopping Mall*. The bottom part of the hinge—on the full-opening top—had come loose. Also, blond wood was fast becoming "out to lunch"—style-wise. The glorious unit had been marked down from about $250.00—to something like $165.00. And—on the spot—I'd upped and <u>bought</u> it! On payments, of course. Ten bucks a month.

I'd known (also of course) that we really couldn't afford it. Not even the piddling ten monthly bucks. This wasn't rocket science-type stuff. As always, we'd been fanny-deep in debt. The record player merely added another layer.

But, you see? My beloved, my poor, overworked, old *Columbia 360* "HiFi" unit—which I'd bought new, before we'd gotten married (and which had served well above and beyond the call)—had, finally, given up the ghost. A situation of pure hell for me!

Now, I'd never imbibed alcohol, and—though I did smoke a pipe, a pouch of *Kentucky Club* tobacco (in the plaid pouch) cost something like 32-cents, in those days. And one of those "fixes" lasted me about a week. So, I hadn't been in the habit of blowing a lot of cash on what I'd considered foolish, frivolous, stuff. (Well, actually, there'd never been much cash to blow! On anything! Frivolous—or "un"!)

I also was never a great fan of buying flowers. They'd always cost a good deal more than most LP records. And, in a week? They were gone. Records— on the other hand—always lived on! (Forever—in my mind.)

On the real other hand, I was addicted! Still am! I'm a schmaltzy—music junkie. A hokey music nut! I simply could not face life! Not without a phonograph! A machine on which to play my treasured, cherished, Mantovani, Frank Sinatra, Jo Stafford, Perry Como, Percy Faith. et.al. LPs.

A couple of years later—when the movie, *Days Of Wine And Roses*, came out—I could identify with Lee Remick's character, when she'd told Jack Lemmon's character, "I couldn't face life . . . knowing that I could never have another drink". Like that poor woman, I couldn't face life, either—knowing that I couldn't listen to Margaret Whiting or Nat Cole, or Paul Weston, whenever I damn well <u>wanted</u> to! Whenever I damn well <u>needed</u> to! An <u>addict</u>! <u>Truly</u>!

I don't have to tell you: When I'd come home with my wonderful new *Olympic*, Joanne had flipped! Well, nothing like her reaction to my "disgraceful, irresponsible" little pilgrimage to Houston—on that fateful Tuesday. But her reaction—"The Old Silent Treatment"—<u>had</u> been substantial! And sustained—for <u>weeks</u>! Joanne had, pretty well, <u>perfected</u> it! The whole situation came as a shock to me—although it should <u>not</u> have been. (I guess.)

My wife, in fact, <u>did</u> threaten to leave me then. The threat had been issued, however—in a tone that had been multiple decibels lower, than those she'd employed upon my return from Houston!

It took—literally—a month or so, before she'd even begun to "come down" Till then, it was "The Old Silent Treatment'. In <u>spades</u>!

To be honest, she never <u>was</u> completely accepting of the machine. Not at all! She <u>did</u> put up with it—I guess—over the ensuing years.

Actually, she'd never really much cared for schmaltz. Not that deeply, anyway. Unlike what I'd "determined" from her many letters—when I was in the Navy.

It took me <u>years</u> to figure out that she'd always, pretty much, <u>tolerated</u> Tony Bennett and Bing Crosby and Vic Damone and Rosemary Clooney and Jo Stafford and Ella Fitzgerald, <u>et.al</u>. But, she was never really "in" to such stuff. Tolerated—in many areas—is the key word. Apt. Apt as hell!

Her "War Horse" mother had always referred to my music as "trash". (And don't even get her started on the cost of live-theater tickets!) To the "The Old Girl", the amount of money that I'd always spent—that I'd (what else?) consistently "wasted"—on those "stupid damn records", was absolutely, positively, "outrageous"! But those "stupid theater tickets?! Those expenditures were sinful! Outrageous! (Well, given the circumstances, I suppose that maybe they were. Maybe!)

As you might imagine, that cherished stereo was the first item to be loaded into the "new" blue Chrysler. Well, the glorious machine—which was followed, immediately, by about 85 or 90 LPs. (Those vinyl wonders represented an about 10—or 12-year collection—and included a surprising number of those old, smaller, 10-inch 33rpm dandies. Remember them?) Those latter discs held some of my all-time— to this day—very favorite recordings.)

I was able to throw all my clothes, shoes, etc. etc. etc. into the car. Filled up the backseat area— surprisingly. But, truthfully, I'd had room to spare. More space than I'd expected.

The car, itself, is huge! It had always seemed to me—that half of the vehicle had been located ahead of the front wheels. But, let me assure you: The trunk, on that dandy, was very small—and the jack and the huge spare tire (both of which appeared to be in pretty good shape) practically filled the compartment up.

I wasn't thrilled with the fact that, even at that hour, a number of my soon-to-be former neighbors were witnessing my loading of all that gear—such as it was. Stowing it—into some strange (really strange) old car. But, there wasn't much that I could do about it. Of course, there wasn't much that <u>they</u> could do about the situation, either.

After about an hour-and-a-half, I finally cranked the not-quite-filled-to-the-gills Chrysler to life! Sighing heavily, I took one last, highly-troubled, look at "our house"! Then, I eased myself off into the night.

SIX

IT WOULD, OBVIOUSLY, HAVE MADE much more sense (an inclination which was, as you've no doubt noted, totally, completely, foreign to me) to have just simply remained in my former residence—for the night. How far was I ever going to get—before I'd need to "flop"?

But, <u>man</u>! There <u>was</u> that God-awful "vestige", about the place. A more-or-less "haunting"! A disparaging shroud, enveloping the almost-haunted joint! An ungodly vestige—that had come to represent everything that I'd <u>ever</u> found unpleasant. Unpleasantness—from even before the stupid bungalow had ever <u>existed</u>!

The place simply seemed to encapsulate every rotten experience—in my whole, entire, life. Every crappy occurrence that I'd ever had to deal with. <u>Ever</u>! Well, I guess, that my being so totally spooked, by the joint, was, maybe, little more that a macabre justification for me. To "cover" my inane splitting—running away, that late in the evening. More of a rationalization—than I was willing to admit. Ahhhh—who knew? Who the hell knew?

Whatever! In my convoluted mind, I really and truly needed to get the hell out of there! And so I did! Logic be damned!

There was one redeeming factor. One which made my "get away" not completely ridiculous: A small matter of that troublesome—that soon-to-turn-up-missing—$1000 bill. It would be discovered to be AWOL early on Thursday morning—a matter of a few hours—I was sure! And, of course, so would I! So, maybe—just maybe—it might not be such a bad idea to split! As soon as possible! Quite probably, not totally idiotic—to, pronto, put some serious mileage between myself and "The Alamo City". Having become a bona fide criminal—a certified schmuck—it would probably behoove me to begin to actually be thinking like one.

One aspect: A "process" that I did have going for me—once the track-me-down authorities would put out an APB on me—was the fact that they'd most certainly have me fleeing, in (Hee-Hee!) a black '61 Valiant. Not some "Blast From The Past" clunker of an old battlewagon of a '48 Chrysler. Pretty astute, Paul-Baby! My compliments—to the crook!

You may find this difficult to believe (not really) but, I actually didn't know exactly where I was headed. Probably—well, possibly, anyway—percolating, in the back of my demented little mind, was some kind of "master plan". No matter how "remote" that stroke-of-genius campaign might be from the surface.

Somewhere—tucked away in the old gray matter—there <u>must</u> be a positively-brilliant scheme! One which—more than likely—would have me heading toward New York. I pulled my "vintage" beauty onto the still-under-substantial-construction Interstate 10. I was heading east. Toward Houston. I was, I had discovered, <u>already</u> ultimately headed toward Gotham! "The Big Apple"! Whether I'd <u>wanted</u> to—or not! Whether I'd even <u>realized</u> it—or not!

The venerable, (well, the old) car was, actually, handling beautifully—especially considering the "Neanderthal" suspension systems of that era. In addition, none of the products out of Detroit, back then, were particularly aerodynamic.

Of course, the old "Straight-Eight" motor would probably wind up producing a glorious three—or four-miles-to-the-gallon—something that I, most assuredly, should've paid more attention to, when I'd bought her.

On the other hand—as I'd continued tooling, fairly slowly, eastward—I'd remembered having seen only one or two true "economy' units, on the car lot.

One of these "classics"—was a faded-maroon old Simca. Didn't <u>look</u> all that dependable. And—I'd thought—maybe there was also one of those teeny little Opel Kadetts. That model that they'd tried to make look like a miniature Corvette. An orange one. (It seemed to me that they'd <u>all</u> been orange. Every last <u>one</u> of them.)

Would've been—either one of 'em—<u>much</u> more cost-efficient to operate. Cheaper—no doubt. But, possibly (probably?) not nearly as dependable as the comfy old vehicle—in which I was ensconced. Sifting through the ruins of my memory, it had always seemed to me that those dinky little cars had been deemed not very staunch. Rather fragile, in fact. Some people—<u>many</u> people—had, I'd thought, even referred to them as "<u>toys</u>". Besides, neither of those worthies—was <u>close</u> to being a '48 Chrysler! For openers, they'd <u>both</u> lacked a beautiful blue dashboard!

I was approaching the little town of Seguin—about 55 miles to the east—and the my new/old car's AM radio (which, till then, had been doing fine) was beginning to fade. I glanced down at the thing. Then glowered at it. Probably, I was believing that a substantial scowl—properly placed—would fix the problem.

That model Chrysler—as referred to above—featured one of the most beautiful plastic dashboards I'd ever known to exist. Virtually every one—each one that I'd ever seen, anyway—was a shiny symphony, in glorious ultra-bright-blue. To this day, I've always loved the instrument panels in those cars. (But, that's just me.)

The speaker, in that gorgeous console, took up the entire center of the kind-of-narrow (but, still exceptionally beautiful) instrument panel. That better-quality-than-I'd-expected speaker was located right next to the vertical (yes, the vertical) radio dial. The well-illuminated dial run up and down—rather than sideways. Don't hardly see vertical radios these days.

Obviously, I'd found myself wishing that this particular set would've turned out to be somewhat stronger—reception-wise. A good bit more efficient. I guess that I'd hoped—from the git-go—that it would've provided me quite a lot more range.

This trip was, I now feared, going to be a good deal more lonely. At least more desolate—than I'd found myself wishing. It would turn out to be depressingly-quiet—between major cities. Especially if I was headed toward "The (far away) Big Apple"!

Listen, that—more and more—seemed to be the ultimate destination! As conditions were shaping up, anyway. I believe—that I really didn't know. Well, safe to say that—at that point—I wasn't quite sure! I think that was probably the reason that I was driving so slowly. (Of course, it might have been in deference to the "Iron Lady's" age—although she seemed to be chugging along quite efficiently.) The main reason, though, was I'd not truly known where it was—that I was headed.

Then—a shocking development! A shattering experience! I almost lost control of the car! Came within an ace—of piling up!

All of a sudden, I heard this loud, almost-deafening, crackle—coming from the speaker, in the adored dash!

Oh, don't tell me! The damn thing's giving out! Crapping right out! Already it's going south? Shit!

Not quite! The weirdest—most penetrating—voice I'd ever heard blasted into the automobile! This highly-disturbing voice was coming from the dash!

From the radio's not-deceased speaker! The strange voice filled the entire car! Overflowed it! In higher-fidelity than could _ever_ have existed, in 1948!

"Paul!" the voice beckoned. "Paul! Pull off the highway, Paul! Pull up . . . pull over, into that _Enco_ station! Up ahead!"

"Wh . . . WHAT? What _is_ this? Who _are_ you?"

"I'll tell you in a minute! Once you get yourself off the road . . . and away from the traffic. Now, pull off, up there! Pull into that darkened _Enco_ station! Yeah . . . _that_ one!"

Making a panic-type, extremely hard, right turn (without benefit of power steering), I managed to pull in to the stupid gas station—and came to a complete stop. Don't ask me why! Don't ask me about _anything_!

"Good," announced the chilling, surreal, voice! Still coming from out of the stupid radio speaker. As indicated, he was coming to me—in _far_ higher quality, than the disc jockey show to which I'd been listening.

Needing to conserve on gas, I'd also killed the engine—which _should_, also, have shut the radio off. (I'd not thought of that—but, turning the ignition key wound up making absolutely no difference.) The spooky voice continued to drone on: Well, it wasn't a drone. He/it had a voice—like a rusty file!

"So . . . Paul! Paul? Where . . . in heaven's name . . . _where_ do you think you're headed? Exactly where are you _going_? Do you even _know_? Do you have even the _slightest_ . . . even the _foggiest_ . . . _idea_? Any clue at _all_?"

"I'm . . . I dunno . . . I guess I'm . . . no. No . . . dammit! NO! Not . . . not really. I'm just . . . !

Look . . . who the hell are you? What the hell are you? How the hell can you be . . . be in the damn speaker?"

"Actually, I'm from the other way. Direct opposite direction of hell . . . truth be known. Listen, Paul. Does my voice sound familiar? The least bit familiar?"

"Yeah." I sighed—heavily. What else was going to happen tonight?

"I guess it is," I muttered—completely perplexed. "It probably is . . . I guess. I . . . I think so. But, I just can't . . . uh . . . can't really place it. Look! This is . . ."

"I'm sure that you'll remember this one picture, Paul. A movie. From out of the early-fifties. Nineteen fifty-one, to be exact. *Angels In The Outfield*? Remember that movie? Old black-and-white flick. One of your favorites, it was. I'm sure you'll recall it . . . since you saw it six or seven times, back then. Starred Paul Douglas and Janet Leigh. He was 'Guffy McGovern' . . . the manager of the sad-sack Pittsburgh Pirates. That was before the actual team got to be really good, of course. Remember that?"

"Yes. Yes, of course. I most certainly remember the movie. You're right. It was one of my favorites But, how did you know? I mean, how do you know? How do you know that? How would you know? Know anything about that picture? Let alone how much I've always loved it? I mean . . . what's an old flick got to do with all this . . . with this . . . all this . . . all this . . . ?"

"You'll recall that there was an . . . are you ready? . . . an actual angel in the picture. There'd been this little girl . . . this little girl, named

'Bridget White'. She'd always given her name and age . . . whenever she was asked what her name was. She'd always answer 'Bridget White . . . eight-years-old.' Played by a little girl . . . named Donna Corcoran. Beautiful little girl . . . she was in the movie. Kind of stole the show, actually. I'd always thought so, anyway. Remember?

"Of course I remember. She'd always torn out . . . from me . . . the heart. In a way, I can still hear her, saying that. Saying, 'Bridget White . . . eight-years-old'. I can still remember that."

"Then, you'll remember that she was praying for hardened, obscene, ol' 'Guffy'. Little orphan girl, she was. And this angel, he was sent down to earth . . . to answer her prayers. To help ol' 'Guffy' out. Help him. And that miserable team of his. Help them to finally win a few games. But, only if he'd change his obscene ways. Only if he'd clean up his act. This angel . . . he was in charge of straightening the guy out. Putting 'Guffy' on the straight and narrow, as it were. So that God could answer little 'Bridget's' prayers. Remember?"

"Yeah. Of course I remember. I remember the whole . . . ! Wait a minute! Are you telling me that you . . . that you . . . that you are an . . . an . . . an angel?"

"Bingo! That's precisely what I'm telling you. Glad that I finally got through to you . . . at long last. Look, does my voice not sound the same? The same as that angel's voice? The one . . . in the movie?"

"Yeah, I suppose. Yeah, I guess so. Yeah, you do. Yeah, it does. I guess so, anyway. But, look! I mean . . . an, an, an . . . an angel? An angel . . . for God's sakes?"

"Funny you should mention that. The 'for God's sakes' part. Very apropos. You see, just like little 'Bridget White . . . eight-years-old', two little girls are praying for you. Actually praying for you! Your two daughters."

"Cynthia? Cynthia . . . and Mary Jane? They're praying for me?"

"Yep. Your two little girls. They've been praying for you . . . for some time, now. Since the older one, I guess, was first able to figure out . . . that you and Joanne were having your problems. A whole slew of serious problems. She picked up on that. Picked up on it . . . a pretty good while ago. We think that, maybe, your sons might have too. They probably have been sending up a number of prayers too. But, us mere angels . . . we can't actually determine that. Not for sure, anyway. We're on orders, you see. Well, at the moment, I'm the one that's on orders. I'm saddled with the duty . . . of answering the prayers of little Cynthia . . . and little Mary Jane!"

"Aw come on! What kind of hogwash is this? Angels! Sheeeee!"

Suddenly, there was a deafening sound! An all-encompassing thunderclap! And an accompanying—almost blinding—lightning bolt! The latter flared up the length of that elongated 1948 hood!

I'd thought (read feared) that the overwhelming charge was coming inside! Coming the whole way in! Straight for me! To out and out "torch" me! To—undoubtedly—disintegrate me! I was positive that the frightening electrical charge was coming right across that work-of-art, glorious-blue, dash! Coming to get me! Fortunately, the thing veered upward—at the last possible second! Then, I lost sight of it! Good thing that I was not driving! The angel might've thought of that!

"Do you remember, Paul?"

It was, of course, that same voice. Coming from the same place. The babble was—as even I could figure out—not going to stop. Not anytime soon.

"Do you recall?" the voice pressed, "Do you remember what happened, Paul? What happened . . . when 'Guffy' was questioning his angel? He wound up on the wrong end . . . of a little thunder and lightning! Pretty much like what you just experienced! And . . . if you'll recall . . . the angel admonished him. The angel said, 'Don't rile me, Boy'. Said it . . . ah . . . rather forcefully. And, in like manner, I'm telling you, Paul . . . hopefully, equally as forcefully . . . I'm telling you, 'Don't rile me, Boy'!"

This entire—this true, bona fide, lightning-bolt-festooned, mind-boggling, episode—was the maraschino cherry, atop a God-awful, brain-warping, emotionally-staggering, sundae! A "confection" which was, I knew, only a tiny portion of what had been a totally-devastating week or so!

The mind-numbing results of the previous few days had left me totally drained! Or, at least, that's what I'd believed. Actually, I'd only thought that I'd been bled dry—when I'd pulled away from my former home!

It was to laugh! That mindset was minimal—given my present, totally mind-numbing, just-this-side-of-the-booby-hatch, condition!

I sat there, crouched over! In kind of a lump! And <u>shivering</u>! Shaking! <u>Badly</u> shaking! <u>Violently</u> shuddering! For a couple or three never-ending minutes! An eternity!

What could possibly be <u>happening</u> to me? What was <u>going</u> to happen to me? What was going to happen—<u>next</u>? Had I gone—completely—around the bend? Totally off the old <u>trolley</u>?

"Look," I finally muttered, "I've . . . I've had a rough day! A <u>really</u> rough day . . . already! All day! Okay? I mean, the whole damn . . . the whole darn . . . day. Okay?"

Merely the utterance—saying just those few words—was totally exhausting, And—believe it— barely audible. I'd become a lifeless glob of—of ectoplasm!

"Yeah, we know," came the answer. "Oh, and by the way . . . for your information, and gratification . . . we <u>replaced</u> that G-Note! The thousand-dollar note? Remember <u>that</u>? The one that you'd stolen . . . from your esteemed employer? It's <u>back</u>! Back in good ol' Red's safe! Where it jolly well <u>belongs</u>! The same exact bill, as a matter of fact. We got the used car dealer to swap it out with us . . . for twenty fifties."

"<u>What</u>? How could you . . . ? I mean . . . ! Look! This is . . . I can't . . . I mean . . . this is . . . this whole thing . . . it's . . . well, it's <u>incredible</u>! This whole furschlugginer <u>thing</u>! For one thing . . . even if I <u>believed</u> you . . . why would you even <u>think</u> of putting that stupid thousand-dollar bill back? Even if you . . . I don't know . . . even if you . . . well, even if you possessed the <u>power</u>? How could you even <u>know</u> about it? About <u>any</u> of this?"

<u>Another</u> thunder-and-lightning display! This one not quite so violent! Or, maybe, some part of me was—subconsciously—expecting it! Had halfway prepared myself for it. Again, who knew?

"Oh, we've <u>got</u> the power all right!" The grille—on the speaker in the dash—seemed to almost "mouth" those words! Not unlike a scene out of some stupid *Loony Tunes* cartoon! My whole life seemed to be becoming a caricature of that of *Daffy Duck*! Or someone! I mean—I <u>was</u> going over the cliff! Right <u>over</u>! <u>Had</u> to be totally off the pasture! Right?

"Now," snarled the voice, "<u>you</u> listen to <u>me</u>, Paul. And you listen <u>good</u>! (I had a <u>choice</u>?) We understand the extremely low image you have, of yourself. The terrible self-image that you harbor. The horrible self-image . . . that you've, pretty much, always had to contend with. Especially has that been true . . . your problem with your self-image . . . over the past few months. Listen, we understand . . ."

"I don't think so." That seemed to have been the first time I'd been able to put together a full sentence—since this whole, bone-rattling, scenario had been launched. "I don't think you <u>do</u>! I don't think <u>anyone</u> understands," I muttered. "<u>No</u> one really gives a damn . . . not one tinker's damn . . . about me. Excuse the language. But, <u>really</u>, no one <u>does</u> give a damn about me! Or anything that . . ."

"Oh, come <u>off</u> it, Paul! Quit wallowing in all that stupid self-pity! We <u>do</u> understand. And we <u>also</u> understand the pity potty that you're on. <u>Been</u> on! And for far too <u>long</u>!"

"Oh, sure," I muttered—with as much sarcasm as I could scare up.

"You can disbelieve all you want, Paul. But, we can . . . we can actually fathom why it was, that you stole that thousand dollars. Not that we condone any sort of crookedness up here. I mean . . . let's face it . . . thievery is thievery. But, in your case, we've seen fit to make an exception."

"An exception? What the hell are you talking about?"

"Just what I said. An exception! A highly-precarious exception, to be sure. But, we've kind of closed our eyes . . . to the conventional thinking, up here. We're looking the other way . . . you might say. Something we actually can do . . . even on our level, which is not the highest."

"Well, excuse me for questioning some kind of an angel, but . . ."

"Actually, I'm not 'some kind of an angel'. I happen to be an archangel. Truth in advertising. Full disclosure . . . and all that."

"Okay. Questioning an archangel. But, if you're answering my little girls' prayers, you sure have a funny way of showing it. I mean, my house is about to be under foreclosure . . . in case you didn't know. Well, if it's not . . . it soon will be. My car's about to be repo'd! My wife has just taken my four kids from me! Has removed them . . . three-hundred-and-fifty miles to the south! They're now going to be living with their glorious grandparents . . . both of whom cannot stand me. Well . . . to be honest . . . the feeling's kind of mutual."

"Kind of? Merely kind of?

"*Touché*! But, let me tell you! In addition to the aforementioned little bumps in the road, <u>Elena</u>, the woman . . . the only woman I truly <u>love</u> . . . <u>she</u> has shut me out too! She's shut me <u>completely</u> out! Out of her entire life. Just one more little kick you-know-where! And now? Now, here I am! Wandering! Wandering! Wandering . . . freaking aimlessly. In a car that could blow up any second now. And probably <u>will</u>! Why am I not seeing any kind of <u>evidence</u> . . . <u>any</u> kind of evidence . . . that <u>any</u> prayers are being . . . are being <u>answered</u>? Prayers . . . of <u>any</u> kind? No matter <u>who</u> is sending 'em up?"

"One of your more famous Men of The Cloth . . . down there, on earth . . . once said that <u>all</u> prayers are answered. He was correct. It's just that . . . you see . . . sometimes you people, down there, you people wind up not being particularly <u>happy</u> with the answer. And I don't have the wherewithal to explain to you why <u>that</u> should be. Above my pay grade." (It would be some 40 <u>years</u>—before I'd hear anyone <u>else</u> mutter <u>that</u> line.)

"Yeah," I groused—completely unmoved by the oral witticism. "Why does <u>that</u> not surprise me?"

"Well, suffice to say that . . . in this particular case . . . there are other people involved. Like Joanne . . . and like Elena. As well as your kids. Well, and even Elena's boys. You ramble on. You ramble on and on and on. Jaw away . . . endlessly. And you don't even know what it is . . . what it might be . . . that your girls are praying for. You'd had no idea that they were even <u>mentioning</u> you in their prayers! Or . . . for that matter . . . that they were even praying! For anyone! Or anything! Not till just now. Not till I just advised you . . . of that more-important-than-you-think fact."

"Yeah, but . . ."

"No! Don't be giving me, 'yeah, but'! Now you listen to me, Paul! For once, shut up! Shut your face . . . and listen!"

"I thought I was listening pretty good. I don't see where I've ever had much choice . . . but, to listen."

"You may be listening. With one ear, maybe. But, you're sure not hearing! Clearly not understanding! Now, one way or another . . . whether any prayers are involved or not . . . you're pretty well wiped out! I know that. We know that. Us guys, up here . . . we know all about you. As things stand right now, you're in terrible shape! You're at a complete . . . and utter . . . dead end! As things stand now, you've hit a brick wall."

"Yeah," I muttered. "You've sure got that right. And the wall's hittin' back! Clobbering me . . . pretty good."

"Of course I've got it right. Look, there's something else we don't . . . as a rule . . . go along with, up here. Not as a rule. An almost-cardinal rule. And that is unfaithfulness. As I'm sure you know, Joanne is a nice lady. Whether or not you'll acknowledge it, she is a nice lady. And she didn't . . . she doesn't . . . deserve to be cheated upon."

"I didn't! I haven't! Did not cheat on her! Elena and I have never been . . . uh . . . been involved. Never been . . . ! Look, I don't feel right talking about things like this. Not with an angel. Most especially not with some archangel. But, we've never been . . . Elena and I . . . we've never been . . . uh . . . never been . . . ah . . . what you'd call intimate."

"You think we don't know that? On the other hand, you . . . you, yourself . . . you admitted that it wouldn't have taken much for you guys to . . . quote/unquote . . . 'wind up in the sack'. Look, Paul. There are levels of unfaithfulness. And . . . so far . . . you've not gotten really bad. But . . ."

"Oh, thanks a lot! That's really complimentary."

"Will you shut up . . . and listen? Look, we're getting nowhere . . . and fast! Let me explain . . . to stubborn old you . . . the reason for all this angel skullduggery. For my . . . ah . . . visit. Maybe that'll provide you with . . ."

"Yeah. Please do. Please . . . explain something! Someone explain something! Give me something! Something that makes even a little bit of sense! Because, so far it hasn't been . . ."

"Y'see? There's a bunch of us guys . . ."

"Wait a minute! 'Us Guys'? 'Us Guys'? Now, what the hell does that mean?"

"Oh, there's a group of us guys . . . us angels and archangels . . . up here, you know. And we, pretty much, tend to hang out together. And, we've been looking down at you . . . for quite a good while now."

"Why not? Why should anything be any different . . . up in heaven? Everybody looks down on me."

"Oh, stop it! Stop it, already! Will you come off it . . . for once? You want another shot? Another dose . . . of thunder and lightning? Us guys . . . us guys up here . . . we figure that you're pretty much a case unto yourself. Just a few feet shy of becoming a bona fide <u>basket</u> case."

"A few feet <u>shy</u>? I think I'm <u>there</u>, already!"

"Listen. Listen to me . . . for once in your life! Now, <u>everybody</u> down there is . . . ah . . . <u>unique</u>. Every earthly creature. Totally unique. <u>You</u> just happen to take 'unique' to the nth degree, is all. You abuse the privilege, you might say. And so, in our warped little minds, us guys have come up with a sort of a . . . well, sort of a game. One we figure that . . . given your situation . . . you might be interested in playing!"

"A . . . game? A sort of a game? What kind of angel stuff is <u>that</u>?"

"Well, to be brutally frank, it's quite un-angelic. It's actually a game of . . . a game of chance. A real live <u>bet</u>, you might say. More than a <u>few</u> wagers, truth to tell. A <u>multitude</u> of kind-of-earthly bets. Now, I came down here . . . to see if you'd want to involve yourself, Find out, if you wish to let yourself get involved . . . in this whole goofy contest."

"Aw, look! This is . . ."

"The entire thing is <u>voluntary</u>, Paul. <u>Totally</u> voluntary . . . on your part. The return of the thousand-bucks was . . . as I believe I've already advised you . . . it was simply a kind of a token of our . . . ah . . . of our sincerity. Our good faith, you might say. Our good will. A genuine show of . . ."

"Now, you've <u>really</u> got me confused. Which doesn't take a helluva lot of doing. Excuse me! Doesn't take a heck of a lot of doing. I can't even believe that I'm sitting here . . . in my stupid car, in some stupid deserted gas station . . . talking to my stupid dashboard."

"Yeah." The voice laughed. "It is a little strange, isn't it? Listen, Paul. Us guys, we have devised . . . have come up with . . . a hokey little proposition, for you. Something we'd like you to consider."

"Oh, please! Look, everything is screwed up enough! Without a bunch of gobbledygook about angels . . . and stupid-assed games!"

"A proposition," the voice droned on, "that we've fashioned. That we've put together . . . just for you! Trust me, you're one of the few people . . . one of the very few people, on your whole, entire, planet . . . who's absolutely hokey enough. Who'd be hokey enough . . . to even consider . . . even give thought to . . . going along with something like this. Something this . . . well, this . . . this wild!"

"I wish," I sighed, "I wish I knew what you're talking about."

"Paul, listen! Listen to me! All your life . . . you've been broke. You've worked hard. But, you've had nothing . . . nothing, but really menial jobs. Terribly menial jobs. Yeah . . . you've gotten to mid-management, on a few occasions. But, you've never really made any serious money."

"You're telling me? You're advising me . . . of all this? Like I don't already know all of this? Like I don't already know that . . . ?"

"Plus," the voice went on, totally unfazed by my obviously-failed attempt at sarcasm, "you've never considered yourself to be especially good-looking. Certainly not handsome," the angel observed.

"Tell me something else I didn't know. What the hell does that have to do with anything?"

"Well, for one thing, you'd never really gotten anywhere with the girls."

"You think I don't know <u>that</u> too? Look, what do <u>angels</u> have to do with all this? With <u>any</u> of this?"

"You'd had girl trouble," the voice was ignoring me, once again, "mainly because you didn't think you were good-looking. Didn't have 'the looks' to 'score with the babes'. Always struck out . . . because of your <u>looks</u>. So, you seldom tried. Why leave yourself open . . . for rejection?"

"That's true. I didn't believe that I'd <u>ever</u> had 'the looks'. The only woman who'd ever told me I was handsome . . . the <u>only</u> one, in my whole <u>life</u> . . . was <u>Elena</u>."

"Stop and <u>think</u>, though! You never gave that many 'babes' the chance. Seldom ventured out . . . in search of a woman. That . . . more than anything . . . explains why you were a virgin, when you got married. And you'd . . . whether you've ever wanted to acknowledge it or not . . . you'd married Joanne, because you'd thought that you'd be unable to do <u>better</u>. Be unable to do any better . . . than Joanne."

"Oh, come <u>on</u>, now. Look! This isn't . . ."

"Might be hard . . . <u>must</u> be hard . . . to face. In fact, it <u>is</u> hard for you to accept that fact. But, that <u>was</u> the case, Paul. It really <u>was</u>. Truth to tell . . . and this may <u>surprise</u> you . . . that's also the reason why <u>she'd</u> married <u>you</u>."

"Why <u>she</u> married <u>me</u>? Listen, this is . . ."

"This is <u>true</u> . . . is what it is. She didn't think she was, at all, attractive. Thought <u>you</u> were, probably, the best <u>she'd</u> ever be able to do."

"That's . . . why that's ridiculous! The whole thing is . . . is ridiculous!"

"Not so. She felt that she might as well latch on to you. You were, undoubtedly, the best she could hope for! You'd be surprised: Lot of that going around. Has been . . . for years. Centuries, actually. People who . . . whether they realize it or not . . . decide that they're gonna have to settle for second-best. Sometimes even third-best! Believe they have no other choice. 'Take what you can get . . . while you can still get it!' That was you, Paul! But, it was also Joanne! It was! Believe me! Believe it!"

"But, that's . . . that's crazy! This whole thing is crazy! This whole thing is . . . why, it's nuts! Of course she was attractive. Of course she was! She still is!"

"Right. You know it . . . and I know it. But, Joanne doesn't know it. To this day, she doesn't know it. Never has. To this day, she really doesn't know that."

"Oh, please!"

"Listen, I could be having this same . . . this exact same . . . conversation with her, Obviously, I'm not. But, believe me, I could! Only the personalities . . . they would be reversed. Well, there'd have to be a few other slight alterations. But, basically, it'd be the same conversation. Trust me, on this."

"Believe you? Believe you?" Then, I sighed (again)! Deeply (again)! Finally, I muttered, "Why not? Why the hell not believe you? Everything is so screwed up! So, why the hell not believe some angel . . . in my radio?"

"On the other hand," I was still being ignored, by my dashboard friend. "Let me assure you . . . I've never had this discussion with her. Nothing even close. Don't ever intend to. But, believe me, it would be essentially the same dialogue. From self-image to beauty . . . or to handsomeness. To money. And on to . . . to everything else. I could cover all the exact same subjects . . . the exact same details . . . with her. The very same!"

"I suppose," I groused. "I guess we are a bit alike. At least we were. At one time, anyway. But, since we got married, she's . . . she's changed."

"And you haven't?"

"Not really. I really don't think so. I don't believe that there's been all that much change in me. I've never much deviated. I mean, I still like . . . still love . . . to listen to my music. Love old movie musicals. Fred Astaire. Gene Kelly. Judy Garland. Rita Hayworth. And I will always love the live theater. *My Fair Lady*, *Brigadoon* . . . those things, y'know. Joanne doesn't seem to be all that interested in them. Not anymore, anyway. She used to be. I think she was, anyway. Years ago. But, not any more! Especially since her 'War Horse' of a mother . . . since she got her rear end involved."

"Did you ever stop to think, Paul? Ever stop to think that nobody is as wrapped up in that stuff as you are? People wear out . . . on certain things . . . Paul. Just get tired of them. Joanne just plain wore out."

"I'd never thought of that! Makes sense . . . I guess."

"And it didn't help . . . that you'd spend five or six bucks for an album. Her first reaction, to that, was that the money you'd just spent . . . that the money you just wasted . . . that money could've been put to better use. On little <u>luxuries</u> . . . like <u>food</u> and <u>rent</u>! Maybe even pay the electric light bill, on time! <u>That'd</u> be novel."

"Okay! <u>Okay</u>, dammit! All <u>right</u>! So, I'm a <u>schmuck</u>!"

"I didn't <u>say</u> that! Just like <u>you</u> can't understand her lack of <u>interest</u> . . . her not being 'in' to all the schmaltzy stuff . . . <u>she</u> can't understand <u>your</u> being completely enraptured with it. You're both earthly humans, y'know."

"Well, it's not like I never gave her a clue, y'know. She's known . . . since we were kids, in high school . . . how I've always been wrapped up in this stuff. Most of my letters, when I was in the Navy, y'know, they were <u>filled</u> with . . ."

"Yes. But, I don't think <u>anyone</u> could understand . . . could ever <u>realize</u> . . . how <u>completely</u> immersed you were. How totally immersed you <u>are</u>! How deeply immersed you continue to <u>be</u>. How immersed you've always <u>been</u>. To the veritable exclusion . . . be honest now . . . of practically anything <u>else</u>!"

"Well, I dunno. I <u>can't</u> be . . . it can't be . . . not <u>that</u> much of a shock to her. To <u>anyone</u> who knows me."

"Look, Paul. You've <u>always</u> been wrapped up with Axel Stordahl."

"Of <u>course</u> I have! He was the most brilliant arranger/conductor <u>ever</u> to walk the planet. Did all that wonderful work with Frank Sinatra . . . for over those ten or twelve years. All those recordings. And so many radio shows. And even tee-vee shows. Ever since he'd gone ahead . . . and left Tommy Dorsey's band. Even before that. Axel was . . . he was . . . he was a positive genius. So was Paul Weston."

"I'm not going to argue the point with you. I know how wrapped up you used to get with Dolly . . . your neighbor on Main Street. She was always touting Paul Weston . . . and you were always yapping on about Axel Stordahl. Do you think anyone else would be interested in any of those conversations? You were simply fortunate enough . . . to have found her! She truly loves you. Not in love with you. But, she does love you."

"Yeah, I guess you're right," I finally acknowledged—at length. For the first time, I was not jumping, at the sight or sound, of anything! Of everything!. "We really did have some really interesting conversations. Dolly and I. Dolly and me. She was a neat lady. Still is a neat lady."

"Right. But, stop a hundred people . . . on any street corner in America. Ask 'em who Axel Stordahl is. Ninety-eight of them won't know! Maybe none of the hundred would know. Most people have no idea who he is. Who he was. Yet, to you he was a positive genius! Irreplaceable! I know how upset you were . . . when he died, just a couple of years ago."

"That's another thing that got the old 'War Horse' going. The day I learned that he'd died, I'd . . ."

I know. Joanne's folks were up that weekend. Had come up to San Marcos. They had . . . they still have . . . no idea who Axel Stordahl is. Who he was. And here you go . . . raising all kinds of sand about his dying."

"Well, I just caught the last few words of the . . . of the . . . of the damn bulletin. Or whatever it was. It was nothing more than a throw-away line . . . at the top of the hour . . . in one of those stupid disc jockey shows. I couldn't <u>believe</u> it! Couldn't believe what I'd just <u>heard</u>! Flat-out couldn't <u>believe</u> it!"

"Well, you <u>were</u> causing so much commotion about it! That's what really <u>did</u> it . . . for your mother-in-law. She'd <u>always</u> thought that you were <u>way</u> too hung up on that stuff. They couldn't even talk to you, that day! <u>Nobody</u> could! Not for an <u>hour</u>! <u>Longer</u> than an hour! Not after you'd heard that <u>announcement</u>! You were <u>that</u> upset!"

"Damn <u>right</u> I was," I grumped. "They never did <u>repeat</u> the line . . . on the three o'clock news . . . an hour later. Or on any of the <u>later</u> newscasts . . . so <u>called</u>! I <u>tried</u> to call the damn station. Had no damn <u>luck</u>!"

"I know. It <u>was</u> Saturday . . . and the switchboard <u>was</u> closed."

"Well, it took me three stinking <u>days</u> . . . to learn, what I'd been <u>fearing</u>. What I'd been <u>afraid</u> of . . . all weekend long!"

"And you can't <u>understand</u> people . . . <u>any</u> people . . . not being <u>that</u> 'in'? That '<u>in</u>' . . . to Axel Stordahl? To Axel <u>Stordahl</u> . . . of all people?"

"Aw, it wasn't just that. She's been on my butt . . . my mother-in-law has! She's been all <u>over</u> me! Ever since we got down here! They can't understand . . . or they <u>won't</u> understand . . . that I <u>moved</u> their daughter <u>down</u> here. Moved her <u>down</u> here . . . so she'd be closer to <u>them</u>! Fat lot of good <u>that</u> ever did me! Now, here I am. On the lam . . . and talking to some stupid damn dashboard, in a stupid car, in a stupid closed gas station!"

"Let me <u>tell</u> you a few things about that 'Old War Horse' . . . as you call her. Have you ever wondered <u>why</u> . . . why Joanne was their <u>only</u> child?"

"No. Not really. Not especially. Never gave it much thought."

"Well, you <u>might</u> take some time . . . and ponder that question. You see, her father . . . Joanne's father, Luther . . . <u>he</u> didn't <u>want</u> any kids! <u>Any</u> kids! <u>None!</u> <u>Zero</u> kids . . . did that man want. <u>Ever!</u>"

"<u>Really</u>?"

"Really. Her mother . . . ah . . . kind of <u>tricked</u> him. Told him . . . a year or two after they'd gotten married . . . told him that it was a 'safe' part of the month, for her, fertility-wise! This was, of course, <u>way</u> before anyone even <u>thought</u> of 'The Pill'. The Yorks were using 'The Rhythm Method'. Also known . . . by many . . . as 'Vatican Roulette'. Now, her menstrual cycle, you have to understand, was exceptionally regular. So, she just <u>knew</u> when she was fertile! <u>Always</u>! And she talked Luther into going ahead and . . ."

"She . . . she <u>tricked</u> him? <u>That's</u> . . . that's how Joanne was . . . ?"

"<u>Precisely</u>! And, <u>listen</u>! He never really <u>forgave</u> her. You'll note that there have <u>never</u> been any more kids. You're always fond of saying that there's something special between daddies and daughters. Look back, Paul. <u>Think</u>! Would you say that this was the case, with Joanne and her father? Were they <u>ever</u> what you'd call really <u>close</u>? <u>Really</u> close?"

"Well, I dunno. No. Not that I remember. No . . . I guess not."

"Your mother-in-law . . . Eva, the 'War Horse' . . . she didn't want to leave the Detroit area. Never wanted to move from Novi. Especially to some tiny . . . some dinky, little . . . place! Like Brownsville. A town she'd never even heard of."

"But, she moved there . . . moved there, anyway?"

"Yes. Your father-in-law was making life miserable for her . . . up there. Seemed to tie the fact that Joanne was conceived . . . tie that in, with Detroit. It took some years, actually, for him to come up with that mindset. But, he jolly well did. Eventually."

"He equated the fact of Joanne's birth with . . . with Detroit?"

"He most certainly did! Then his company . . . his employer . . . had this gigantic opportunity! A chance to take on a giant refining company. Accounting . . . the whole works . . . with them! For them! Listen . . . they had an immense operation, in the Rio Grande Valley. And Luther's company had landed them . . . as a client. Meant opening an office down there. Once your father-in-law got involved with overseeing that event, he decided on Brownsville. Wanted Brownsville . . . as the site for their office down there."

"This was . . . this was all his doing? He wanted to move . . . specifically move . . . to Brownsville? He always told anyone who'd listen . . . that he'd never even heard of the burg."

"No, he had his choice. It was all up to him! His decision . . . where he wanted to open the corporate office. It could have been Harlingen or McAllen. Or even Raymondville. Brownsville is right smack-dab on the Mexican border. Your dad-in-law was figuring . . . how he was going to start his <u>own</u> business. His own accounting business."

"In <u>Brownsville</u>?"

"In <u>Brownsville</u>! He began the whole thing . . . part time . . . once he got down there. Worked out of his house . . . for the first few years. Let me tell you: After almost four of those years . . . he was able to tell his employer to take a flying leap. He was doing exceptionally <u>well</u>, by then. Still is! <u>Exceptionally</u> well. But, all this . . . this relocation scam was all cleverly calculated! All part of a gigantic . . . a really well-thought-out . . . master plan he'd hatched."

"But . . . but, if he doesn't like <u>kids</u>! And <u>my</u> four kids are . . ."

"I really don't know, Paul. As I'd told you before. We can't see into the future. Maybe, by now, he's mellowed out. I certainly <u>hope</u> so. We <u>all</u> do. <u>All</u> us 'guys' . . . up here."

"Listen, this is all leaving me . . . with a gargantuan headache."

"I know. I realize that. But, listen! Here it <u>is</u>! As <u>promised</u>! The celebrated master <u>plan</u>! <u>Our</u> angelic master plan! The one that we . . . that us 'guys', up here . . . have conjured <u>up</u>! One we'd like you to simply consider. Hopefully, you'll <u>accept</u>!"

"Oh" I rasped. "I'd forgotten. Completely forgotten about that. About any deal."

"I can believe that. Listen, Paul. We're prepared . . . us 'guys', up here . . . we're prepared to set you up in <u>an entirely brand new life</u>. Completely <u>different</u>! Unlike anything you've ever <u>known</u>! Unlike anything you've ever known! Or could even imagine! Completely . . . and utterly . . . different!"

"WHAT? What is this? What kind of . . . ? Look, I'm . . . Are you kidding me? Because . . . let me tell you . . . ! If you are . . ."

"Nope. Real deal! Of course, you're going to have to get yourself to the destination. To where all this can take place. A little town. Different kind of little town."

"Wait a minute! Destination? A town? A different town? Different . . . from what? From where? From San Antonio? I'm already headed to a . . ."

"This one . . . this town . . . is completely different! Far from where you're headed! Both in direction . . . and in culture! Way different tradition! This is a neat little town! Beautiful little town! Absolutely gorgeous! Right on the Pacific Ocean. Called Newport. In the State of Oregon."

"The . . . the State of . . . of Oregon? What're you . . . ? God! It's true! It's true! I have! I' have, y'know! I've gone off the deep end!"

"Not really! That's the deal, Paul. You'll have to get yourself out there! To begin your new life! Face it! Tell me . . . is your old life anything to write home about? This is a beautiful place . . . Newport . . . where you'd be. And it'd be a whole . . . an entirely different . . . lifestyle for you. One that, I think, you'd be overjoyed with!"

"ME? Overjoyed with anything! Boy . . . have you got the wrong number!"

"Listen, Paul! Listen to me! You'd have money . . . a goodly amount of money . . . for one thing! And a really wonderful place for you to live! Pretty luxurious, don't you see. All . . . a whole lot of stuff . . . things that you've never experienced before! Have never even come close to experiencing! I figure that . . . if you'll just look closely, if you'll simply be fair, in your thinking . . . I believe that this is something you should jump at. Especially given your present situation."

"Money? Luxury? Luxurious stuff? I can't imagine . . ."

"Well, if you'll listen to the proposition, I truly feel it's something you'll accept! You should accept it, anyway! Still, we've got a few . . . well, a couple of the 'guys' up here . . . a few of us think otherwise. That, maybe, you'd not be all that thrilled. I'm not one of those. It is the breathtaking Pacific Northwest. And listen! Listen to me! You'd be set up! Set up . . . in a really nice life! In a really nice place! A wonderful place! Can you think of any situation . . . one that wouldn't be eons better than where you are now? Where you're headed? Eons better?"

"Well, you know," I'd admitted, having calmed down—measurably, "I guess that I always have kind of wondered about it. About what it'd be like . . . up there. Up in the Pacific Northwest. In fact, the guy that rented that semi rig, from me . . . he went on and on, about how gorgeous it is up there."

"We know. And he's right! Absolutely correct!"

I sighed—deeply, and finally muttered, "It's supposed to be simply magnificent out there. Up there. Fresh air! Clear water!" I couldn't believe that I was actually saying this. Any of this. And to the stupid dashboard!

"You'll love it! Well, you would love it. I think so, anyway. Paul, it's picturesque as it can be. Big beautiful hills . . . just to the south of town. Well, nice ones to the north, as well. There's a gorgeous . . . a gleaming-white . . . lighthouse. Just off shore. It's out and out beautiful! Breathtaking, actually. Like I say . . . I sincerely believe that you'll <u>love</u> it. Well, you <u>would</u> love it. You really and truly <u>would</u>. Trust me on this. You'd positively fall in love with it. That's <u>my</u> take, anyway."

"But, dear Lord! Getting all the way out to the Pacific Coast! I . . ."

"Well, all of us . . . we actually believe that this old bucket of bolts will, in point of fact, actually <u>make</u> it out that far. But, of course, we can't <u>know</u> that. Not for sure, anyway. Unlike what some of you Earthlings might think, we really can't . . . absolutely can <u>not</u> . . . see into the future. For instance, we . . . honestly . . . don't really know whether you're even going to accept our hokey little gig or not. Don't even know if you'll <u>consider</u> it."

"You're not the only one. Not the only ones . . . you and 'The Guys'."

"Well, let me <u>tell</u> you something, Paul: If you <u>don't</u> . . . if you don't go <u>along</u> with us . . . then, you're strictly on your own. Do whatever it is that you're determined you're going to do. Go wherever it is . . . that you decide to go. But, you'll strictly be on your own. The thousand-bucks? That's our <u>gift</u>! Our <u>gift</u> to you! <u>That</u> still stands! It's <u>yours</u>! You're officially <u>off</u> that hook. No grand theft charges for <u>you</u>! Good faith <u>reigns</u> . . . and all that."

"A brand new <u>life</u>, though? A <u>really</u> brand new life? For <u>me</u>? <u>Me</u>? For <u>me</u>? Look! This is so . . . ! I simply don't understand . . ."

"Of <u>course</u> you don't. How <u>could</u> you? For one thing, you've been thrown a lateral pass! None of us know . . . if you're going to catch it! Or if you're going to pull away . . . and let it fall to the ground."

"You've got <u>that</u> right. I don't know whether . . ."

"Let me explain, Paul. Let me draw the thing out for you: First off, you'll be getting a complete <u>physical</u> makeover. A total body <u>makeover</u>! This would mean a complete new <u>you</u>! From head to toe! And everything in <u>between</u>! Totally <u>new</u>! <u>No</u> one would <u>ever</u> recognize you. You'd be a whole new <u>person</u>. In the physical sense, anyway."

"<u>Me</u>? A . . . a complete . . . a total body <u>makeover</u>? A total <u>physical</u> makeover? How does <u>that</u> happen? I mean, I can't even <u>imagine</u> . . ."

"Well, let me modify that . . . slightly. You'll still be thirty-three. That's another reason . . . a fairly significant reason . . . that we're all interested. Because of your <u>age</u>! Pretty famous age, dont'cha know . . . in our precincts, up here. Sanctified age . . . up here . . . don't you see. But, listen. Getting back to our proposition . . . you're going to look totally different! I mean . . . <u>totally</u>!"

"<u>Different</u>? <u>Totally</u>? Different? <u>How</u>? I mean, how would I . . . ?"

"You'll wind up looking, pretty much, like a sort of cross between Robert Taylor and Robert Young. You've seen enough of their schmaltzy old movies . . . to know what they look like. Well, what they <u>did</u> look like . . . in the forties, and early-fifties. <u>Handsome</u> blokes they were. Well, you won't be blessed with Mister Taylor's pencil-thin moustache. However, if you really wanted to <u>grow</u> one . . . we wouldn't care. Go right <u>ahead</u>! You could grow a cookie-duster . . . or a handlebar. Or even a beard. A goatee, maybe. And <u>none</u> of it would bother us. Duck's rear end? Mutton chops? Whatever. Be our guest. Look as dorky as you want."

"Let me <u>understand</u> this! You . . . you mean . . . what you're saying . . . you're telling me that I'll be . . . that I'll be . . . I'll actually be kind of <u>handsome</u>? Is <u>that</u> what you're saying?"

"Yessir! <u>More</u> than 'kind of'! You'll actually <u>be</u> handsome! And <u>then</u> some! What's more, you'll also be <u>successful</u>!"

"<u>Successful</u>? How? What do you mean . . . by successful?"

"Just what I said! <u>Successful</u>! Financially . . . and artistically! You'll be a published <u>author</u>! You'll be a <u>writer</u> . . . of fiction. All kinds of fiction. You'll, no doubt, want to <u>read</u> the books . . . the 'masterpieces' that you've 'written' . . . so that you can discuss them intelligently with others. In fact, I'd <u>recommend</u> that you make that dandy little task . . . make it a certain, etched-in-stone, priority. Just a <u>suggestion</u>, of course. You can <u>do</u> whatever it is you darn please. But, if I were you, I'd certainly make it a point to . . ."

"This . . . this is . . . it's <u>incredible</u>! Where . . . where am I going to <u>find</u> all these . . . all these books? The ones that I've . . . supposedly . . . written?"

"Oh, they'll be in your bookcase."

"My . . . my bookcase? In my <u>bookcase</u>! And where might <u>that</u> be?"

"In <u>Newport</u>! Up in <u>Oregon</u>! Have you not been <u>listening</u>? That's what I've already <u>told</u> you! The only thing is: It's up to you . . . to <u>get</u> there. The whole project is totally in <u>your</u> hands! How . . . and when . . . . you get there, well, that's completely up to you."

"Sheeeee! <u>Oregon</u>! I don't know. That's such a long . . ."

"<u>Listen</u> to me, Paul. You'll have . . . you <u>will</u> have . . . many <u>benefits</u>! A paid-in-full <u>condo</u> . . . for one thing! A really <u>beautiful</u> one! And <u>that's</u> just for openers. <u>Paid</u> this thing will be! Paid . . . In <u>full</u>! <u>Nifty</u> place . . . right on the <u>beach</u>, as a matter of fact! <u>Beautiful</u> beach . . . simply <u>gorgeous</u> beach . . . let me tell you! Like I said, there's this exquisite, tall, white lighthouse . . . one with a bright-red tiled roof . . . and it's just south of where you'd be."

"This . . . this is all a <u>dream</u>! <u>Isn't</u> it? A <u>pipe</u> dream? I can't believe . . ."

"<u>No</u>! It's <u>real</u>, all right. This is all <u>real</u>! You'll <u>see</u> how real . . . when you get there. Simply look for 'Beacher's Delight'. That's the name of the complex. Easy to spot. Right off the Pacific Coast Highway. You'll be in unit B-eleven-twenty."

"I can't . . . I'm not <u>believing</u> this!"

"Building B is the northern-most of the two front buildings." I was being ignored, once again. "The ones that are right on the beach. This is a really big complex . . . six or eight buildings. But, <u>you'll</u> be right on the beach. Remember the condo number . . . B-eleven-twenty. You can go right into the apartment. It'll be locked, of course. To everyone but you. On the other hand, that's a first-time . . . a one-time . . . thing."

"Now, what the hell does <u>that</u> mean?"

"It means that . . . as we speak . . . it's locked! <u>You</u> merely have to touch the knob . . . to open it! After that, you're going to need to use the key . . . just like everyone else. The key . . . by the way . . . you'll find on the dinette table."

"I'm not believing this."

"Yeah, I know. You've already said that. Numerous times. Well, you'll have, probably, a couple or three more days of non-belief. But, once you're there . . . once you're up there . . . you'll totally believe it."

"Yeah, but . . ."

"I don't think you'll want to push this old clunker too harshly. Of course, you've got that sneaky six-hundred-and-sixty-dollars-or-so, in your pocket. So . . . for most repairs . . . you shouldn't be in too bad-a shape. A car of this vintage . . . well, it shouldn't be too hard to fix. The mechanics isn't that complicated. Beautiful in its simplicity . . . and all that."

"I . . . I don't know what to . . . what to . . . what to say."

"Don't say anything. Look, your new name . . . remember this, now . . . is going to be 'Taylor Young'. Combination, don't you see, of the two guys you'll be resembling. Is <u>that</u> apt . . . or what?" (I could just picture him—smirking. I <u>swear</u>! I could <u>see</u> him—even through that glorious blue instrument panel. In my still-smoldering mind, anyway.)

"This whole new life," I responded, at length. I think my voice was barely audible. (I really don't believe that angels need all that much help—with amplification.) "This . . . this new life. I mean . . . being a total schmuck, the way I've been . . . ? I mean you're talking about a . . . well, a . . . some kind of a . . . a dream life! Uh . . . isn't that kind of against everything I'd been brought up to believe? I mean . . . isn't something like this actually rewarding schmuckdom? I mean, with my having a girlfriend . . . and stealing the thousand bucks? And honestly considering running out on my family? Well, isn't that . . . ?

"Truth to tell, we don't think that you've quite attained the rank of schmuck. Not yet, anyway. I guess you might've come close on a few occasions. But, there are very few people, down there, who do not come close . . . have not come close . . . . from time to time. Quite often . . . in many cases. Truth to tell, we simply picked you . . . because of where you are in your life. Your situation offers many intriguing possibilities. Selfishly, we simply wanted to see how . . . and if . . . you would work your way through a completely different lifestyle. How you'd deal with events . . . that come with that different lifestyle. We're more than a little interested, given that . . . well, given all those things . . . with which you've already had to deal. All the stuff you've had to jack with . . . to this point in your life. It's inescapably curious!"

"Well, it's nice to hear you say that I didn't make 'Schmuck First Class'. That helps. This whole thing, though, is . . . well, it's so . . . it's so . . . so . . . just so . . ."

"So bizarre? Amen! Well, actually it's more hokey . . . than bizarre. That fact alone . . . should make it right up your alley! Listen, there'll be a wallet out there . . . with a few bucks in it! Well, more than a few! Substantially more than a few! We all figured that your financial status shouldn't be one where you go from starvation-to-starvation. It will be lying on top of one of your books . . . will the wallet be. You'll find all this ensconced . . . in the shelving on the south wall of the living room. Driver's license . . . and all-important voter registration card . . . all will be inside the billfold. Social Security card too. All on the up and up . . . thanks to our unparalleled ingenuity, up here."

"But . . . but, how am I . . . ? I mean . . . what I mean is . . . when is this really major <u>transformation</u> going to take place? <u>How</u> is it going to take place? This big <u>physical</u> change? I mean, I <u>do</u> look . . . like I <u>look</u>! At least I <u>think</u> I still do! Of course, at this moment in time, I'm not sure of <u>anything</u>!"

"You <u>do</u>!" An angelic chortle. "You do look the <u>same</u>, I mean! And you <u>will</u>! But . . . just not for <u>long</u>! Tomorrow <u>night</u>! <u>That</u> is when comes the big transformation! Listen, you've been through enough <u>today</u>, Kiddo. Through enough <u>tonight</u>. <u>More</u> than enough."

"You're telling <u>me</u>?"

The angel's voice took on a demeanor I could never have imagined.

"Wherever it is that you stop . . . <u>where</u> you stop . . . <u>tomorrow night</u>," he advised, "you'll go to <u>sleep</u> as Paul Marchildon. You'll wake <u>up</u> Friday morning, as . . . ta-DAH! . . . the dynamic <u>Mister Taylor Young</u>!"

"Taylor Young!" I cannot describe my tone of voice. I'd never heard anything like that come out of me before. "Taylor Young! Taylor Young! Taylor Young!" I kept on <u>repeating</u> the name! Don't ask me how many times.

"Right! Taylor Young. Now, I'd suggest that you stop soon. Like <u>immediately</u>. And get yourself a room. Like the song says . . . 'Little Man, you've had a busy day'. Selfishly, none of us guys wants to see you crack yourself up tonight. As I've told you . . . we've got a few bets going up here. A <u>lot</u> of celestial currency! But, the wagers will come to life . . . only if, as, and when, you ever make it out to The Left Coast."

"<u>Bets</u>? Angels . . . they <u>gamble</u>?"

"What have I been <u>telling</u> you? Yeah, a little wager here . . . and a little wager there. Every now and then. As I've indicated, the currency's a little different, up here. But, the idea is pretty much the same . . . as down there. Same theory."

"This is all . . . well, it's all . . . it's all beyond belief."

"I'm sure. But, you'll get used to it . . . eventually. In the meantime, we'll all be curious . . . we <u>are</u> curious . . . as to what you'll do, in a given situation. <u>How</u> you'll do. How you'll <u>react</u>. And . . . pretty much . . . how you'll adapt. How you'll cope with . . . for instance . . . the exceptionally good looks. And with a little money. To say nothing of a more relaxed . . . more opulent . . . professional, lifestyle. It'll be interesting . . . to all of us . . . to see how you cope. How you'll go about your life . . . without having to scrounge for each and every single, solitary, dollar. We're interested in what you'll be like . . . with all the drag-you-down burdens completely off your back. How you'll navigate . . . how you'll operate . . . as a free, blithe, spirit."

"This is . . . this is . . . I don't believe this! It can't be <u>happening</u>! With the day I've just had . . . with the couple months or so, that I've just had . . . I'm just . . . I feel like I must've just . . . just flipped out! Feel like I've totally damn <u>lost</u> it!"

"Oh! I almost forgot," came the voice from the dash. Once again my little tirade was being ignored. "You're also signed up . . . to write a column. A column . . . on politics, if you can believe it . . . for a small, local, paper out there. You might remind yourself . . . that they're pretty liberal out there. You'll probably be the most conservative person in the whole durn complex. Maybe in the whole entire town. But then, you never know."

"Really? They're <u>that</u> liberal?"

"It <u>is</u> the West Coast, you know. The contract . . . the one, with the paper . . . is for three months. After that, you're on your own. But, we all think that you're talented enough to . . . that you'll be able to . . . keep the thing going. It's going to be all up to <u>you</u>. You'll have to adapt some . . . well, probably <u>more</u> than 'some' . . . but, we're confident that you can do it."

"Sheeeee! Writing a column." I guess I must've become a believer by that point. A true <u>believer</u>! I was, at least, <u>heading</u> that way. <u>Undoubtedly</u>! "I dunno." I ruminated, almost beneath my breath. "I mean, I can't . . ."

"Oh, come <u>on</u>, Paul. You can <u>do</u> it! You <u>can</u>! There are a number of books . . . books on the writer's craft. Some of them are . . . you'll find 'em, on those shelves. You'd be well advised to be devoting some time . . . to, maybe even, writing another book or two. Or three or four. Listen, as long as they're even moderately interesting . . . your current publisher will buy them from you! You can be <u>assured</u> of that! Look . . . they're <u>not</u> going to take pure garbage! You can also hang your hat on that! The books cannot be just simply pure blathering. They're not going to pay good money . . . for drivel. That goes for the column too. There has to be some substance to them. To all of them. The more substance the better, of course. But, I'm convinced that you've got talent enough . . . to succeed."

"This is . . . this is . . . why, it's <u>incredible!</u>"

"Yeah. You've already said that. Truth to tell, <u>we</u> think so too. Us 'guys'. And . . . listen to me, Paul . . . we'll do <u>nothing</u> to restrict you. Absolutely nothing . . . to <u>hamper</u> you in any way. We'll simply <u>not</u> interfere with your life. We're not going to send anyone <u>in</u> to your life. Not going to put up any <u>barricades!</u> No <u>tests!</u> Not from <u>us</u>, anyway! We're all <u>dying</u> . . . to quote an expression . . . to see how <u>you</u> handle all these things. How you deal with <u>whatever</u> comes your way."

"All these <u>things?</u> With '<u>whatever</u>'?"

"Yes. Listen, if we were to interfere . . . in any way . . . then, we wouldn't be getting the real <u>thing!</u> Would miss out . . . on the <u>genuine</u> reaction. The genuine <u>product.</u> Wouldn't be observing the genuine, new, <u>you</u>."

"Hmmm. 'Observing'! You'd be <u>watching</u> me? <u>That</u> bothers me."

"We're <u>not</u> going to be 'Big Brother'. I <u>encourage</u> you to go where you want to <u>go</u>. Do whatever it <u>is</u> . . . that you want to <u>do</u>. Interact with anyone you choose. We're not going to interfere. Not going to push you, in any way."

"Not going to 'push' me? Now, what the hell does that mean?"

"It means that we're not going to shove you . . . in the direction of this person. Or the direction of that person. If you see some lady, for instance, who you think is kind of . . . you know . . . ethereal, she will not have been sent by us. She'll simply be, more or less, ethereal-like. And all on her own. You're just hokey enough . . . to think that, in some relationship or another . . . that there's certain to be an inevitable heavenly connection. Not true! Definitely not so! Definitely! Not in this arrangement! You'll be flying solo. Definitely on your own. Now . . . do you think you have everything?"

"Everything? What do you mean, everything? All I know . . . all I know, for sure . . . is that I'm sitting here. In a closed-up gas station. Talking to my stupid dashboard. Do you mean . . . do I have all the instructions? All the data?"

"Yes. Listen carefully . . . once more. The complex is on the beach . . . in Newport, Oregon. It's called 'Beacher's Delight'. You're in Building B. B-eleven-twenty is your condo. You're Taylor Young. Most of the other information that you'll need, it'll all be available to you . . . completely obvious to you . . . all included in the stuff, in your fency-schmency bachelor pad."

I must—finally—have come around. For I asked, "I . . . how can I ever thank you?"

"No thanks necessary. Just be the guy that you are. The guy you can be. We all . . . all of us 'guys' . . . we all have a more-or-less stake in some of the things you'll probably wind up being engaged in. Although we don't really know . . . have no idea of . . . any of the specifics. The currency up here's a little different . . . as I'd said. The earthly game-of-chance theory? That's pretty much in order . . . in this little enterprise."

"But my little girls! Their prayers."

"I think that . . . basically . . . they're praying for you to be happy. Where you were heading . . . I believe that you'd have, undoubtedly, found everything. Everything . . . but happiness! I can just about guarantee that. In fact, I will guarantee that. Now, listen to me, Paul. I hate to say this, but you've got virtually no chance . . . literally no chance, I believe . . . to resume a father-daughter relationship with them. With your little girls! Not anytime soon, anyway. I could be wrong, y'know, but I really feel that . . ."

That declaration was a "knife through my heart"! The angel picked up on the overwhelming dejection, that had . . . instantaneously, and completely . . . overtaken me! Without my having said a word.

"Not at this particular juncture, in any case," he hastened to add. "In the future? Who knows what the future would hold? Will hold? Where it could lead? We sure don't. That's the reason for all the betting. Maybe you can reenter their lives . . . somewhere down the road. Only it will . . . by necessity . . . have to be as someone else. Heaven knows . . . I feel safe in saying that . . . heaven knows, they won't be able to recognize you. You'll be Taylor Young. Remember? A completely different man! Their father will be <u>dead</u>!"

"<u>Dead</u>?" <u>Another</u> shocker! "I'll be <u>dead</u>?"

"Not you . . . <u>personally</u>! Paul <u>Marchildon</u> will be 'dead'. He will have 'died' on Interstate Ten. <u>Tonight</u>, as a matter of fact. It'll fit in with the time line. We'll make sure that Paul Marchildon will have 'passed away'! You'll be a <u>new</u> man! Fresh <u>start</u>! <u>Remember</u>?"

"Yeah," I responded—sighing heavily. "I remember."

"Oh! And there's one other thing, Paul."

"What's that?", I asked—trying to stave off weariness that I'd never before experienced. "What's that?"

"This is <u>vital</u> that you keep this in mind! A <u>critical</u> part in all of this! You have entered into a <u>permanent</u> . . . no <u>strings</u> . . . arrangement. But, it's no strings . . . on <u>both</u> sides."

"Yeah. I <u>guess</u> I realize it. But, maybe you'd better <u>explain</u> it to me. Part of me has <u>no</u> understanding . . . of <u>anything</u> that's gone on here! My mind . . . what's <u>left</u> of it . . . is so damn <u>numb</u>! So that <u>anything</u> is . . ."

"Well, just so you're <u>aware</u>, Paul: <u>There's no going back</u>! There'll be no way of <u>undoing</u> it! Undoing <u>any</u> of it! Once you wake up . . . when you wake up on Friday morning, as Taylor Young . . . you'll <u>BE</u> Taylor Young! Forevermore! For good or ill! Taylor Young! Hear what I say! There'll be <u>NO</u> turning back. In fact . . . from this moment <u>on</u> . . . there'll be <u>no</u> turning back! This whole thing . . . this whole agreement . . . is set in stone! The entire arrangement is set in stone. There's no turning back."

"I know," I answered—with another monumental sigh. "I guess I've known . . . for quite awhile. For quite awhile."

"Excellent! Now, go get yourself a room . . . and good luck! Good luck, to you . . . Mister Taylor Young!"

SEVEN

NEWPORT, OREGON! WHAT A REMARKABLY beautiful town! Sits—so picturesquely—between two sets of majestic, lush, green, hills. (To me, they actually seemed like mountains—but, what do I know?) Clean, massive, beach—as promised! Right, smack-dab, on the majestic Pacific Ocean!

I'd been right, all those many, many, times, when—on my way out—I'd pretty much envisioned, in my tattered mind, the original sighting of the Pacific. (In truth, it would be my initial beholding of that magnificent body of water.)

That first time—once I'd actually laid eyes on this overwhelming body of water—it was as though I was kind of floating above the massive-yet-soothing waves!

I'd been driving—just north of Coos Bay. And there was this clearing! And I could actually see the ocean! It laid about three-quarters-of-a-mile away. There was that much distance—between me (standing alongside the highway) and the ocean. And it was still a dazzling experience!

Listen, I found myself in the middle of some kind of soul-stirring—overwhelmingly-religious, highly-spiritual, probably-even-holy—experience. More than a few absolutely-sanctified minutes, I spent! Just standing there! Looking out—at the Pacific! I was actually moved to tears! Real ones!

Don't ask me why. But, I'd remained there—totally transfixed—by the absolute splendor, that I was (as mentioned) beholding! The incredible, out and out, magnificence! As mentioned, I'd actually gotten out of the car—and had walked across the road (dodging a speeding car or six, while crossing). I'd remained— simply standing there! Like some kind of bump on a log. Staring—in utter awe—at the ocean.

On the other hand, I cry at baseball games. (I think I might've mentioned that before.) Or at flagpoles. Or even parking meters. My mother—always—used to tell me that my bladder was awfully close to my eyes. (I suppose.)

Fortunately, a few hours after that stirring first sighting, I'd gotten a second—much more satisfying, close-up—opportunity to look out upon this "sanctified" ocean. This equally-as-moving, encore, experience occurred—once I'd gotten to where I was merely a few miles south of Newport. That second "beholding" was—if that could ever be possible— even more soul-inspiring! None of this may make sense to you. But, it—most assuredly—made sense to me. (Still does.)

I'd been in this most providential—most opportune—observation place. It was a pull-off spot. On the left side of the highway—substantially north of Coos Bay.

This was a spot—where one could actually <u>see</u> that gleaming white lighthouse. Behold it—rather close up! The very one that the angel had spoken about. It had seemed almost like a throw-away line, when he'd mentioned it. But, looking out at the out and out <u>majesty</u> of that tall, spectacularly-white, circular, building—topped by the bright-red tile roof—was yet <u>another</u> staggering, highly-emotional, moment for me! I was going to <u>like</u> it here! <u>Love</u> it here! I just <u>knew</u> it!

There had been two other cars parked there. Both with three or four passengers. Each vehicle sported out-of-state license plates. Let me tell you: Those people, I'm certain, had been every bit as moved as I was—simply by the massive <u>splendor</u> of such an overwhelming, dazzlingly-picturesque, scene. How could they—how could <u>anybody</u>—be otherwise?

Let me fill you in: This long, arduous—this filled-with-wonderment—pilgrimage had, as one might imagine, turned out to be quite a trip! <u>Quite</u> a trip! A voyage to remember!

I'd left Seguin, Texas—still as good ol' Paul Marchildon—on Thursday morning. I hadn't really pushed my old "hunk of iron". Well, not that hard, anyway. Not at first, anyhow.

I was growing to like the venerable car—maybe even <u>love</u> the venerable car. Was becoming more attached to it, than ever. As much as—maybe even a bit more than—had been my "relationship" with my late, great, Valiant. As we'd rolled along, that clunky old Chrysler and I were becoming—more and more—"joined at the hip".

Actually, "upon further review", maybe I'd not been all _that_ easy on the old bird, on that first, disjointed, day.

As pooped as I'd been Wednesday night—that was when I'd pulled into the first motel I'd seen, after I'd gotten possession of my radio back from the angel—I still could _not_ sleep. (Would _you_ have been able to?) I was simply too bedazzled—completely pumped—at the prospect of what would (or, hell, what would _not_) await me! At what—if anything— would be my future! Over what might lie in front of me—a couple thousand miles away! In the opposite direction—from where I'd been headed! (Would there _be_ a future—any _kind_ of future—a couple thousand miles away? Was this all a pipe dream? Or _worse_, some dastardly trick—from above—to punish my descent into schmuckdom?)

For one thing, I couldn't help but wonder what I'd _look_ like (or what I'd _act_ like) as—tah-DAH!—"Taylor Young". I'd never _seen_ him before! Had never _been_ him before! Only ol' Paul Marchildon. Kinda late in life—to be becoming a brand new human being. Undoubtedly, that was a substantial part of the (truly) out-of-this-world equation! The formula—which would, undoubtedly, cause a lot of "currency" to (presumably) change celestial hands.

The prospect of possibly entering into some sort of mind-warping adventure—one that I could never, possibly, have imagined, even in _my_ demented, twisted, overheated, little, mind—had left me simply too psyched! Too "amped"! Too wound up! Would I ever be able to "come down"? Return from whatever ethereal world that I was, at that point, populating? The one to which my dashboard-based angel had—seemingly wittingly—dispatched me?

The inescapable thought continued to haunt my tortured, overheated, little mind: Maybe this was all part of some grand—some heavenly—scheme! The perfect way, possibly—with which to deal with a card-carrying schmuck! Who knew? Who could possibly know?

I finally did manage to doze off—along about three-thirty or, maybe, quarter-to-four. But, I was only able to sleep for about three—well, possibly three-and-a-half—hours. Can you believe that I was up—bright and early? (Neither can I—but, I was! And do not put all that much faith—in the word "bright".)

Anxiously, I'd bolted down a very light breakfast—sweet-roll and coffee—and was on my way! Off to my destination! To my destiny! To wherever—and whatever—this bizarre expedition was going to take me!

By nightfall, that first day—Thursday—I'd covered almost 600 miles. I was, at that point, really tired. Exhausted! Totally pooped! And so—I'm sure—was my poor, dutiful, overworked, ever-faithful, Chrysler.

We'd, sadly, come "only" as far as El Paso. To be sure, the miles I'd covered had represented a tidy day's travel. But, dammit, I was <u>still</u> in the State of Texas.

I'd wanted to—had <u>intended</u> to—have "progressed" further. A <u>lot</u> further. Had wanted—at the very least—to have simply gotten into another state. But, there I was—still remaining in the far reaches of West Texas. For better or for worse.

On the other hand, I'm not a total idiot. (It only <u>seems</u> that way, sometimes.) I knew that neither I—nor, probably, my cherished "Old Iron Horse"—should make an attempt to go any further. Not on that exhausting Thursday. I think that we were <u>both</u> fighting overwhelming fatigue. And—speaking for myself—I sure was <u>not</u> winning that battle. The Chrysler—as it would turn out—was made of much sterner stuff!

In a fit of unprecedented logic, I checked in to a small, locally-owned, motel. It had been the first one I'd seen—once I'd made my "executive decision", to conk out for the night. Once ensconced in my rustic little room, I found that I would have absolutely <u>no</u> trouble dropping off to sleep! Like at nine-thirty! I don't even remember my back hitting the sheet. And a deep sleep it was! <u>Very</u> deep! <u>Immensely</u> deep!

As anxious as I'd been to see morning come, that anxiety was absolutely <u>smothered</u> by the urgent need to—immediately—get some sleep. Morning would come soon enough, I remember thinking—as I'd begun to lay my head down. From that point on—it was "Blackout City"!

I'd apparently contented myself, by then. Come to peace with myself. I would—sooner or later, I was convinced—find out what this "Taylor Young" would actually <u>look</u> like! That astounding revelation would come to pass—<u>only</u> if, of course, that encounter, with my beautiful dashboard, had not been some kind of, entirely-possible, fatigued, stinking-as-hell, absolutely-tragic, form of ultimately-masochistic, pipe dream.

In any case, I'd dropped right off into the Arms of Morpheus! (I think I <u>might</u> possibly have had a little celestial help, in that procedure.)

Early Friday morning—precisely at 4:35AM—my eyes snapped open! (You could just about <u>hear</u> the overwhelming "CLICK"!)

I bolted out of bed! (Hadn't done <u>that</u>—in <u>years</u>!) Practically <u>vaulted</u> my way into the bathroom!

And there he <u>was</u>! There <u>I</u> was! Yessir! <u>Mister Taylor Young</u>! (May I present?)

I blinked my eyes open and closed—harshly— many, many, times! (Countless more highly-audible CLICKS!) I couldn't believe what I was <u>seeing</u>! (Hackneyed old cliché, but—in this case—very <u>apt</u>! <u>Most</u> apt! <u>Dazzlingly</u> apt! I actually <u>couldn't</u>! <u>Couldn't</u> believe the reflection staring—staring so wide-eyed— back at me!)

The image blinking—harshly (and noisily)—back at me was (can you <u>believe</u> it?) positively <u>handsome</u>! Body was even a little muscular-looking. Well— comparatively speaking—<u>quite</u> muscular-looking!

And I'd become substantially "better endowed"! <u>Much</u> more well-endowed! <u>Amazing</u>! (I could <u>see</u> all these "improvements"—right <u>away</u>! Mainly because

I've always slept in the nude. Well, most often—
through my life. Obviously, having kids sometimes—
ah—"complicates" such practices.)

My hair had remained the same length and color.
But, the old mane was about the only thing that had
remained unchanged. It was the only "feature"—that
was even close to its former "self". Well, that's not
quite true. My shoe size seemed to have remained
the same—once I'd worked my way down (with great
attention to detail) and had finally analyzed the old
hooves.

Not surprisingly—once I'd gone ahead and
actually shaved (having, finally, brought myself to
the point, where I could, in fact, stop staring at that
glorious image, in the huge mirror)—I discovered that
my clothes did hang a little loosely on me. Nothing
scandalous, you understand, but, I'd definitely need a
whole new wardrobe. My first (and last) thought was:
The old collection, of cheaply-priced clothes, turned
out to have been sacrificed! But, in a glorious cause!

It took me—as previously noted—a good while to
break loose from that "handsome-dog" reflection in
the mirror. But, ultimately, I did make my way down
to the coffee shop—to grab some breakfast. No one
who had been on duty the night before—in any area
of the hotel—seemed to be around. That, to me, was
a distinct relief!

I'd had this worry—far-fetched as it might've
been—that one of the personnel (someone seeing
me, that morning) would not have recognized me.
It was, as noted, a small hotel—with, presumably, a
limited number of employees. But, still . . .

I'd worried that, possibly, one of the workers—seeing some "stranger" on the premises—might panic. (Who could—possibly—be "stranger" than me?) Was afraid someone would call the law! Get me into some manner of trouble! Maybe real trouble! Probably real trouble! A situation—which I was positive I'd not be able to handle! I could picture myself winding up in jail! Like, forever!

Apparently, a new driver's license awaited me—on the far-away Pacific Coast. However, the one I'd possessed featured a photo! One that did not—in the least way—resemble what I'd, so recently, come to look like. If I were to be stopped by someone in some local constabulary, along the way, that could present a serious problem! Most certainly would present a serious problem!

Would such an occurrence have been part of the angels' ("The Guys'") plan? Would angels ever be part of such a reprehensible adventure? Under some kind of "Justice For Schmucks" program? Who knew?

Of course, nothing untoward, in that area, happened. (Of course?)

Thankfully, remaining—for the moment—a non-jailbird (no matter how temporarily), I went ahead and bought a morning paper—then, seated myself in the rather tiny coffee shop. The waitress—an attractive blonde, probably in her early-thirties—seemed awfully friendly. Really attentive! This was a reaction, which was one—that had (for always and ever) been extremely "foreign" to the likes of Good Ol' Paul Marchildon.

Her "interest" in serving me! Could it be my new "handsomeness"? Could the just-acquired "good looks" factor be kicking in? Attracting the ladies? (At least this one?) This—surprisingly enough (to me, anyway)—would become a real question. A genuine "puzzlement"—as the "King", in Rodgers & Hammerstein's *The King And I* had termed it.

This was a bona fide concern. For the likes of me, anyway. One that would follow me, I was sure—well into the future. Like so many other "advantages", having "good looks" was something I'd never counted on. Had never had to "deal" with. Had, in fact, never encountered such a situation. Not as far as I'd ever been aware. Had never even considered such a condition. Never—in my lifetime. Ever!

It was close to noon, before I'd finally checked out. I felt as though I was getting the fisheye from the hotel clerk. I think that it was more that she was upset—because check-out was supposed to be eleven o'clock. I doubt that it was some far-fetched "realization" thing. I really don't think the "handsome" factor had entered into the highly-uncomfortable discussion.

Back on the road, I found myself becoming quite fatigued—and at mid-afternoon. That was a bit of a surprise—given that I was this ultra-new, young, masculine, handsome-devil, "hunk". All this new-found "machoness" was now—supposedly—"in command"! In charge of my entire physical being! In every dimension! Or so I'd thought! Nevertheless, I was, un-mistakenly, "slowing down"—substantially dragging—by early-evening.

So we—this old gas-guzzling "rattletrap", that I'd really come to love, and I—finally stopped. We called a halt to that second day—in Las Cruses, New Mexico. As stated, I was pooped. But, "upon further review" it turned out, that I was, in point of fact, a good deal more hungry—than fatigued.

I checked myself into a handy *Ramada*. Then, found a truck stop—whose restaurant offered a delicious t-bone steak for something like six bucks! I couldn't imagine such a place—or such a steak—even existing! What a day that glorious (if abbreviated) Friday had turned out to be

I made up for the dearth of mileage the following day. Driving—dedicatedly—over a long, terribly-hot, Saturday, I'd finally managed to make it to the eastern Los Angeles suburbs. Quite an accomplishment! For me—and for my cherished, old, "Iron Horse"!

My faithful Chrysler was performing heroically. An inescapable fact: My dear, antiqued, friend had really been required to labor—labor mightily—in coping with an unending ration of immense (and intense) heat! The inferno simply would not let up—not at all—during the never-ending afternoon. Especially in the area in and around Phoenix. We could barely breathe! Both of us!

So, despite the fact that it was still rather-early evening, I'd decided to show some mercy to the venerable, blue "Iron Lady"—and checked into a much-more-expensive-than-I'd expected *Holiday Inn*.

After a nice dinner in the posher-than-I'd-imagined hotel restaurant, I decided to spend the balance of the evening/night in my room.

The management—thoughtfully or otherwise—had hung an immense, mirrored, wall-piece, in a place where it was readily visible from just about any spot in the room. (THANK you—oh, powers that be!) I spent far too much all-too-narcissistic time—I'm certain— gazing, fondly, into the most—gratifying reflection. The image was preferable—to staring at some stupid sitcom, on "The Tube". Invigorating! Invigorating as hell!

The following day, Sunday, I drove up the Coast. As mentioned, I got my first glimpse of the hallowed Pacific—some dozen-or-so miles north of Coos Bay, Oregon.

Of course, I couldn't resist pulling off at the aforementioned, roadside, observation spot. There to gawk at—among other things—that dazzlingly-white lighthouse. I was enraptured! Spent far more time drinking in all this unimaginable beauty, than I'd ever intended.

As anxious as I had been, to see my exciting new digs—merely a few miles to the north—I'd simply remained rooted to that "hallowed" ground!

Dazzled by the panoramic, the out and out, splendor of scenery! The overwhelming magnificence of that area! My area! (Apparently!)

Eventually, though—at long last—I did arrive, in Newport! It was later, though—on that special, that glorious, Sunday evening. Much later—than I'd ever intended.

I was thrilled—electrified, all over again—as I'd pulled my poor, tired, pig-iron beauty into the parking lot The blacktopped area was the "jumping off point"—for the luxurious-appearing complex! Six four-story buildings—plus a flat, round, one-story structure, which housed the management offices. The grounds were perfectly manicured. The grass was green—and the trees vibrant—despite the nearness of that massive amount of saltwater.

This magnificent conglomeration would— undoubtedly—be my future! Probably my entire future! Of that I'd, finally, become convinced! One of those gorgeous buildings would—most certainly— contain my new residence! One of those exquisite "towers", I knew, would be my life's center-point! Now—and, probably, for always! It would be furnished with all the stuff—presumably—that the angel had promised! That "The Guys"—in their infinite charity— had, I was sure, prepared for me! For handsome me! This was all pretty heady stuff—for the former Paul Marchildon!

Needless to say, in the immense parking area, my faithful, dogged, "Iron Lady" stood out! Flagrantly!

Like the proverbial sore thumb. Unique, it was—in amongst all the Cadillacs, Town Cars, and Mercedes, (as well as one opulent dark-green Bentley). What? Not a single Rolls Royce? (How common!)

It was easy to find my condo! I hurried—to see the promised dwelling! To take it in! My new home! My from-now-on residence! I didn't bring one thing up with me! Not one item—from the poor, overworked, still-panting, Chrysler!

Sure enough, the condo's door opened—without benefit of key! Presumably to me (and me alone)! And for that one time only—as I'd been informed!

I simply stood there! In the doorway! Taking in the mind-bending interior! The splendor—of this unimaginable place! Not even what you'd call transfixed! I was out and out dumbfounded!

I can't say I'd never seen such opulence. I have seen a movie or two, don'tcha know. Have even read a few magazines. (That, you might find a little difficult to believe. But, I have!) In addition, my late mother—up in Detroit—had always subscribed to a bountiful number of House & Garden-type magazines. They were always lurking around the place.

But, I'd never dreamed—had never even dared to try and envision, not in my wildest fantasies, could never have conceived—that I'd ever actually dwell in such a posh joint! Consciously—or subconsciously—I'd been convinced (for all of my life) that I would, forever, remain a poor man! (For all of my life.)

I finally entered! And then, I just stood there! I looked—stared, actually—out the immense picture window. The massive one—which was located over the obviously-very-expensive emerald-green, quality-leather, couch. Immense? HAH! (And that's the couch—to which I refer!)

The beach, now! IT was really immense! That heavenly body of sand must've been a half-mile wide at that point! Maybe even more! The already-calling-out-to-me, almost-pure-white-sand-laden, stretch ran north and south—like "forever"!

And the water! The water—it was so blue! I could actually tell that from my own living room—despite the fact that the daylight was starting to fade into the shadows. The shadows—that foretell an invigorating nighttime. Couldn't quite see the wondrous lighthouse, from there, however. (Sigh!) But, I suppose that one simply can't expect everything. (Can one, Dah-ling?)

Unsteadily, I walked out onto the rather-small terrace—over which the picture window looked. Still couldn't see the lighthouse! (Damn!)

There were two "regulation", aluminum-piped, leisure, chairs and one of those white metal round tables—with the traditional green-and-white-striped awning protruding upward. Matched the crisscrossing plastic strips on the chairs. The "glut" of furniture gave a somewhat-crowded look to the pleasurable little retreat.

There were, probably, only 8 or 10 feet between my outdoor facility—and the one directly to the left (or to the south). A much-longer expanse between mine—and the terrace to the north of me. The architectural pattern seemed to almost "pair" the things—up and down the building. The ones that I could see—all seemed to be furnished, in about the same manner as mine. Nothing wrong with that. (Well, upon further review, it did seem a little "common".)

I was too impatient to "set a spell" out there! Had to see what the rest of the "joint" looked like! Must—immediately—inspect the posh residence! Ascertain what wonders might await me! My overheated mind could never rest! Nor, by then, was it capable of even imagining!

Well, the dinette was a little smaller than I'd expected. (See? I was spoiled—already!) The substantially-built, round, wooden table was also on the smallish size. But, it—and the four matching chairs—just reeked of class. And expensiveness! Hell, it was all I'd really needed. There was only me, after all. This nifty set would more than suffice.

Sure enough, there were the keys to the place, lying on the table. In an absolutely ornate leather case. There would be room enough to add the keys to the heroic "Iron Lady". The valiant one—out in the parking area. The one I'd so hastily—and without conscience—deserted. Had absolutely abandoned! Mercilessly!

The kitchen was also fairly small—but, exceptionally serviceable. I'd never owned a double sink before. Nor had I ever possessed a fridge with a side-freezer! One that went all the way from bottom to top! From the floor up! (Remarkable!)

I'd always had to "make do" with those stupid little compartments that held a couple or three ice cube trays—and nothing more! Well, in point of fact, I'm lying to you. The house in San Antonio was new. And it did have a fridge with a rather generous-sized freezer. But, it was atop the fridge part. Went side-to-side. (How gauche!) This magnificent piece ran almost floor-to-ceiling!

Maybe all of this opulence would not have been so spectacular, to some people. Most folks, probably. But, to me, it was anything but ordinary! I'd, truly, fallen into "Wonderland"! Without benefit of that stupid rabbit! Just "The Guys"!

It was about then—that I realized that I'd really needed to use the bathroom.

This lavish-to-me "convenience" was located between the living room and the bedroom. Had doorways to/from both rooms. And, like the kitchen (I guess), it was fairly "ordinary".

The facility wasn't especially large. There were no spectacular spigots. Just simply the necessary accoutrements. The sink (sadly?) was not carved out of marble (or ivory)—to resemble a *Shell Oil* sign. The spigot did not resemble a golden goose's neck. The hot-and-cold knobs did not look like swan's wings. None of them were even made out of gold. Were all manufactured from (can you imagine?) chromium. (Also, how gauche!) The utility certainly did fill the need, obviously. (Urgent need—in this case!)

The verdict—vis-a-vis the lavatory—was that it, simply, was not spectacular. (Really spoiled, I was. Already!)

The bedroom, now! That facility, on the other hand, was something out of someone's possibly-twisted, demented, imagination. The room was huge! Twice the size—at the very least—of Joanne's and my quarters, in San Antonio. It featured the largest dresser—and matching (what else?) chest of drawers—I'd ever seen. (In or out of some movie house—and/or any of Mother's glossy magazines.)

But the *piece d' resistance* was the bed! It was really large! And it was (I kid you not) really round! Yeah! A round bed! A perfect circle! 180 degrees—of nothing but bed! How esoteric is that?

I could never have imagined—even in my warped little mind—such an amazing hunk of eroticism! A round bed, for heaven's sakes! The diameter, of that mind-warping sucker, must have totaled nine or ten feet! Maybe more! Who could possibly have thought—could have conceived—of something like this? In his or her most perverted, highly-erotic, imagination? ("Guys"?)

A terrific bonus: I was soon to discover that I'd not need a whole new wardrobe! Would you believe—that I'd "inherited" one? An extensive collection of clothes! Fine clothes! Expensive clothes! Fashionable clothes! (A first for me! A spectacular first for me! Especially the "fashionable" part!) This more-than-generous largesse included six pairs of dress shoes—plus an assortment of "tennies"—all neatly arranged in a specially-built rack, on the floor of the massive closet!

On the shelf—up above all these really neat "threads"—were three separate sets of ornate sheets, for that "obscene" round bed! "The Guys" had thought of everything!

How could they possibly do that? Do all of this? Accomplish so much—in such a short an allotment of time? I guessed that such talent—and/or power—are all a part of being an angel. Especially, I supposed, if one or two of "Those Guys" happen to be—don't you know—an <u>archangel</u>!

Once I was able to pry my eyes off of—literally—everything in that dynamic bedroom (and closet), I kind-of-stumbled my way back out to the living room.

(My memory has me actually <u>staggering</u> out there—but, I'm <u>sure</u> that I was a <u>bit</u> more steady than that! Well, <u>reasonably</u> sure!)

Sure enough, located in the massive, built-in, bookshelves, sat a very expensive, brown-leather, wallet! (Matched—to the nth degree—with the key case, on the table in the dinette, Dahling) This opulent billfold contained the promised driver's license—complete with a picture of the "new me"! And of mighty higher quality—than the usual DMV grotesque, amusement park-type, photo. It also contained a Social Security card—along with a certified voter registration certification. How could this <u>be</u>? How could all of this <u>be</u>? How could <u>any</u> of this be?

Whatever! I truly <u>was</u> Taylor Young! Was <u>truly</u> Taylor Young! It <u>said</u> so! Right <u>there</u>! On my <u>driver's</u> license! On my Social <u>Security</u> card! Who could ever doubt <u>those</u>?

The bulging billfold <u>also</u> contained $3000.00! <u>Three thousand bucks</u>! In <u>cash</u>! Can you <u>imagine</u>! I couldn't! A thousand of the generous—of the overwhelmingly charitable—booty was in twenty-dollar bills! As had been the case, on that previous—that grotesque, that from-hell—Saturday, I'd never <u>seen</u> that much money! Let alone being in the same <u>room</u> with it!

This was absolutely incredible! This whole—this entire—from-heaven (literally) situation! How does one even begin to cope with such an unbelievable turn of events? How does one deal with them? And remain even semi-sane? How indeed! (I supposed the answer to that question—would result in a lot of "currency" changing hands, up there.)

Then, I caught sight of the envelope! It wasn't hidden or anything. The unobtrusive thing was simply lying atop two or three books to the right of the well-heeled wallet.

This was a plain, nondescript, regular-sized, white envelope. Number 10, I believe. An item you could buy in any dime store, or drug store.

I was curious—as to why the angel hadn't mentioned an innocent-looking, bland, white, envelope. That "oversight", of course, would not be for me to question. Of that, I was sure.

When I saw the contents, the out and out shock made me wonder, however! Wonder—even more! Inside were 300 one-hundred dollar bills! Dear Lord! Can you imagine? (Obviously, I could not! I still have difficulty picturing such a staggering, overwhelming, windfall! Even to this very day!)

THIRTY-THOUSAND DOLLARS! Thirty grand! I'd always been convinced that there wasn't that much money—in the whole, entire, world! Not in the whole damn universe! And there it was! There I was! Standing in the same room—with such a mind-warping amount! Standing a mere few inches from it!

How did all this happen? How could all this happen? And why? For heaven's sakes (which I'd come to believe to be totally apropos) WHY? For what <u>reason</u>? All of this <u>money</u>! As indicated before, I don't <u>believe</u> that I'd ever been in the same room as $1000—or $3000! Let alone $30,000! It didn't add up! <u>None</u> of it added up! (Well the <u>money</u> added up! I'd <u>counted</u> it—six or eight times!) But, aside from that, <u>nothing</u> added up! <u>Nothing</u> made the least <u>bit</u> of sense! In <u>spades</u>!

<u>Nothing</u> made sense! (Oh! I'd just <u>said</u> that—but, really, nothing <u>did</u> make sense! <u>Spectacularly</u>— nothing made the smallest amount of sense!)

The angel had been so painstakingly meticulous— in outlining <u>everything</u> that would be waiting for me! <u>Defining</u> it all! <u>Everything</u>! <u>Describing</u>—in the utmost detail—what I would be "inheriting"! Including my profession!

So, why, in heaven's name, would he choose to "overlook" the "mere" thirty-thou? The omission <u>had</u> to have been intentional! <u>Had</u> to have been! An angel certainly couldn't have—wouldn't have— <u>forgotten</u> such an earthshaking item! I didn't think that <u>any</u> of "The Guys" would have! Why were these overwhelming riches <u>not</u> included in the angel's "sales" pitch?

Well true, he'd <u>also</u> not mentioned the all-encompassing wardrobe. Or the "fency-schmency" bedclothes.

Well, for that matter, he'd neglected to mention the bed. Most especially the <u>shape</u> of that incredible piece of furniture. But, <u>all</u> of that was minor-league stuff. At least I'd <u>thought</u> so. Completely insignificant! Compared to—gasp!—$30,000! WHY? Why should <u>that</u> be? Why should <u>any</u> of this be?

After standing there, like some kind of pillar of salt—virtually (maybe literally) not moving the proverbial inch—for, fully, five or six (or seven or eight) long, never-ending, minutes, I discovered that the ultra-bountiful shelves (that I was, supposedly, "staring" at) had also contained a massive collection of books. (Imagine! Books, of all things—in a bookcase!) The bountiful group included the three "masterpieces" that I—myself—had (ahem) personally "written". There were a dozen copies of each one!

I picked up the three "classics"—and (most probably) staggered over to the ever—so-opulent, emerald-green, leather recliner. The one that (of course) matched—perfectly—the immense, opulent, sofa.

I placed the books upon the massive, it-would-take-a-battalion-of-Sumo-wrestlers-to-ever-lift-it, kind-of-beige, marble, square, coffee table. Then, I collapsed, into the chair! (I really did—collapse, I mean. My memory of that abandon-all procedure is indelible! Is infallible.) Well, I was conscious enough—to be aware of one additional fact. To wit: This was the most comfortable chair that the ol' fanny had ever graced! What could be next? What more? (What—what could possibly—be more? How could there—possibly—be more? There could be no such thing—as more!)

Once I'd reclined myself—and had, unexpectedly, dropped off to <u>sleep</u> (for, probably, 20 or 25 minutes)—I finally returned to the body! (More or less, anyway.)

Upon "coming back to life", I discovered that I'd, apparently, written a time-travel novel, a police/detective/crime novel—and, for good measure (I was guessing), a formula "romance" novel!

I <u>tried</u>—honestly, I <u>did</u>—to begin sifting through the time-travel "epic". But, before I got halfway through page two, I'd fallen asleep—once again—in that glorious chair! Slept for—I believe—the better part of five hours. (It could have been even longer.) I don't really recall when I'd dropped off. I, most assuredly, hadn't intended to.

That second, also-unexpected, nap turned out to be the most relaxing—most luxurious—sleep I'd experienced, in years! Maybe, even, in my entire life! On the other hand, it cannot say a lot—vis-a-vis how "compelling" my "talent" toward authorship might have been.

When I awoke, it was a little past midnight! <u>That</u> was a real shocker! I believe that, most probably, I'd come close to losing all track of time. Not unheard of—in the Marchildon DNA. Probably too—in the <u>Young</u> DNA? Well, I <u>had</u> come across three time zones—in what had felt (in a way) like only a mere few hours!

In my own behalf, let me just say that becoming, literally, a new man will—undoubtedly—do that to one.

To say nothing—of the impact that goes along with "inheriting" a brand new home! And a brand new lifestyle! Or, quite possibly, simply struggling—doing one's best, to drag one's fanny two-thirds of the way across the country. That might could do it.

Then—all of a sudden—I became aware of the fact, that I was totally ravenous! It also occurred to me—out of the well-known blue—that I'd not eaten anything since early morning. I'd had no idea as to what restaurants—if any—might be open, at that time of night. Or where they might be located. Certainly, I couldn't go knocking on the doors, of my newly-acquired neighbors—seeking advice. Asking directions—to some eatery. Not at that hour. Even I knew that.

It was at that point that I'd wound up making another "executive decision". One of the more intelligent ones, in my life: I decided to open that luxurious refrigerator. To even look into the cupboards. While I'm not going to tell you that there was enough food, in the place, to feed a regiment, you could make a pretty good-sized dent in that program—with merely the provisions on hand.

I fried myself up a huge hamburger—and stashed it in an actual hamburger bun. (Both provided by "The Guys"—obviously.) Then, I seated myself at the classy table—and scoffled down one of the most delicious meals of my life. Then? Then, I "frazzled" up another burger. And devoured it—as though I'd become some kind of buzz-saw.

My lone emotion—other than appreciating the fact that the food was wonderful—was hoping that the heroic "Iron Lady" was doing all right, out in the parking lot. I <u>had</u>, coldly, deserted her, after all. To my discredit, I had not been <u>that</u> concerned about her! Not so worried about her—that I had actually schlepped back to the parking lot.

Finally, I went to bed. To that round, "obscene" (Hee-Hee)—exceedingly comfortable—bed! And wafted off to dreamland, once again!

EIGHT

I AWOKE THE FOLLOWING MORNING—Monday—at a little past six-thirty. Look, Ma—no alarm clock. And my brand spanking hew body wasn't, yet, even on Pacific Coast time. Or, at least, I didn't think so. (At that point, though—in my young life—who actually knew? Who knew anything?)

I was exceptionally anxious to get my brand-spanking-new body out! Out—and onto that remarkable beach. Could hardly wait. All of the scenery, thus far—and, presumably, (by extension) these scenic wonders would include the beach—was world-class magnificent! Of that, I was already aware! So, I definitely knew that I needed to get to that beckoning beach! That would, more or less, complete the cycle! Quick! Like a bunny!

I found myself rifling through my new monster of a chest of drawers. Sure enough, I came upon a pair of navy-blue trunks—as well as a maroon pair, and ones of emerald green. Plus, yet, another pair—in darling canary yellow. There was even a pair of dazzling, bright-red, ditties. Plus. a bountiful number of large beach towels.

From this many years later, I look back—and I sincerely believe that I'd never before actually seen a bona fide beach towel. Not "in the flesh", anyway. Now, here I was: The sole owner of a whole boodle of the durn things! To say nothing of possessing more swimming trunks than I knew even existed— throughout all mankind. How great was that? All of that?

I trundled across to the beach—after making sure that "My One True Love" was okay. There she sat. My wondrous Chrysler! She'd never looked better— never looked more beautiful—in her life. (Or in mine.) Even she seemed to be thriving! (No more having to cope with the inferno of the Arizona dessert, for one thing!)

Spreading out a light-blue towel—with a huge image of an irritated Donald Duck taking up most of the surface (a little celestial humor there, no doubt— those "Guys" knew me pretty well)—I plopped myself down, onto my tummy.

What a truly remarkable feeling!!! What a wonderful, never-before-experienced, sensation! For the first time—the first time in, virtually, my entire life—I was not burdened by a worry in the world. Well, for the first time, I'd—literally—not had to deal with any sort of really serious worry!

The sun was getting, maybe, a little warmer than I'd anticipated—by the time that 8:45AM had rolled around. But, even that was not a worry. I'd simply lain there—languishing under the soothing, ultra-relaxing, health-giving, peaceful, gratifying, warmth. It was great!

There was no one nearby. Quite a surprise—for me, anyway. I'd expected "a ton" of humanity to be milling about. Well, in point of fact, numerous tons of humanity.

Up the beach, there was a gathering of three or four people. They were far enough away—that I was unable to determine if they were male or female, young or old, beautiful or ugly. (Not that I much cared.) I was content to simply be lying there—at peace with the world. Was afraid—a little bit, anyway—that I would, maybe, drop off to sleep. And, quite possibly, wake up, hours and hours later. Appearing akin to a lobster. On one side of me, anyway.

Still, among all this previously-unheard of tranquility, eventually there crept in (slowly—and ever so stealthily) what was becoming a rather disquieting "feeling"! Probably an inevitable—an inescapably-human—unease. Fear that a more-or-less "shadow" was, maybe, approaching. A feeling—that, something semi-frighteningly, seemed to be lurking, "just over the horizon". I cracked open one eye. That was sufficient—to determine that there was no one else around. No human being, anyway.

What—I began to wonder, as the optic quickly closed—was really behind all this? Behind all of this new-found opulence? All this heretofore-never-experienced peace? All this tranquility? All this independence? Behind, even, my mind-blowing, dynamic (for me), change in appearance?

Here I was! Happily ensconced in my new life! Reeking of totally-foreign-to-me abundance! My not having to—constantly—dodge a brigade of relentless, dedicated, bill collectors. A delightfully new way of life! Yet, there was this whole new, disquieting, specter— regrettably formulating within my suddenly-troubled, still-trying-to-deal-with-all-these-new-conditions, beginning-to-fear-the-unknown, brain!

My peaceful—my ultra-relaxing—beach stay was starting to become less and less peaceful! The "relaxing" part was beginning to unravel! Rapidly! At a, quite frankly, frightening pace! This newly-developing, more-and-more-troubled, quickly-overheating, mind of mine was—all too rapidly— reaching some kind of, totally-unexpected, emotional crossroads! And—even more troubling—the old gray matter seemed, relentlessly, to not want to let go of this multitude—this massive gaggle—of increasingly-troubling questions!

I guess that the most disconcerting aspect of the barbed-wire-ingested minefield—where my troubled psyche had begun digging—was the fact that I had convinced myself that I'd become a certified, card-carrying, schmuck! I'd assigned that status to myself—as soon, really, as I'd initially hatched my evil little plan (wrapped around that stupid C-note, at "The Truck Rental Joint")!

I'd absolutely assured myself—that I'd attained that despicable ranking! So! So, if I actually was an in-the-flesh schmuck—was this the way in which a true schmuck deserved to be treated? Should he or she be—rewarded? Favored—with all this stuff? Any schmuck? Should he/she be given—all of this? All of these luxuries! All of this ambience? This abundance? Should he/she be given any of this? Even the most minute <u>fraction</u>—of what I'd just come upon, in the past few days?

Well, the angel—the one in my beloved Chrysler's dashboard (of all places)—seemed to indicate that "The Guys" had believed otherwise. A little bit, anyway. They <u>seemed</u> to believe that I really was <u>not</u> a real, genuine, bona fide, dyed-in-the-wool, garden variety, schmuck. That was what I'd taken away from that extremely-contorted exchange. The one that had brought to a merciful end—that horrible, God-awful, "Day From Hell"! In Seguin, Texas! (Well, it was still a little <u>bit</u> "From Hell"! I didn't <u>have</u> my kids any longer! Maybe—down deep—<u>that</u> was what was troubling me. Here <u>I</u> was—amid all this splendor! And who <u>knew</u> what they were dealing with? And <u>that's</u> not even counting Joanne! Or—God help me—Elena!)

That disjointed nocturnal encounter—with the angel—had taken place, just five days previously! The events that had crossed my path, since then? The staggering happenings? They were simply overwhelming! Mind-warping! To say the least!

Ergo, there I was! Lying, on a gorgeous beach! In a <u>most</u> glorious setting! In even wondrous, freebie, form-fitting, trunks yet! (One of many sets of those dandies!) I was now a successful—yea, even a published—author! One with—<u>money</u>! More money—than I'd thought had ever been printed, in the history of the world! And I was the owner of a posh condominium! Hell, the owner of a posh body! The prideful owner—even—of a heroic, valiant, grand old lady of a Chrysler!

That antique—the glorious worrier, out in the parking area—had no business making it as far as it had. Nor as quickly as it had. Stout-hearted as the dedicated vehicle undoubtedly was, it still had no business performing in the heroic manner that it did! Not at the speeds it had been forced to have experienced, from time to time! And through sometimes-blistering heat! Yet, there she sat—gracing the landscape—on the other side of "my" building.

Was all this on the level? Or was I—in some way—being set up?

Was this going to be heaven's way of saying, "Not so fast, Man! You actually are a tried-and-true, dyed-in-the-wool, schmuck! Remember? And, you'll see! You'll see! You're fixing to get yours! Just you wait!"

Does heaven do stuff like that?

At that point, I'd found myself wishing—mightily—that, during my life, I'd become some kind of Bible scholar. So, I'd know if Heaven actually operated this way! Whether "Management" dispenses "justice"—in such a manner as my troubled, run-away, imagination seemed to be formulating!

Well, Jesus was tempted, I kept muttering to myself. And by Satan himself! (Yeah, I kept answering myself. But, Jesus didn't give in! You jolly well did!) I was positive that, at this point, my brain—what was left of it—was going up in flames! I could practically smell the wood burning!

I began doing my best to rationalize—again. Rationalize thusly: "I have lost my wife! I have lost my kids! Lost all of them . . . along with my house and my car! I've also lost the one woman . . . the one woman who I truly loved! (Oh, and—by the bye—I've also lost her kids! I've lost them all! It made up a tidy package—of losses! Of costly losses!)"

I was especially troubled—was really worried—by what Elena had said about her oldest son. Her concern—with his having to cope with the loss of both of the only father figures he'd ever known! The "abandonment" of two men—both of whom had absolutely, undeniably, deserted him.

The only "logical" answer (in this "rational" analysis, of mine) was that—now, once the die had obviously been cast (enter, one "Taylor Young")—I might as well sit back (or, in this case, lie back) and enjoy what I've got! What I've gained! What I've wound up with! Ill-gotten—or otherwise!

Bask in it . . . while you've got it, anyway.

That was the "logical" plan. The only plan that made any sense at all! To me, anyway! If that was the answer—then, why was I so damn troubled?

It is not easy to actually implement such "logic". Not in a brain that has always had a problem dealing with whatever made sense. That had no history of ever intelligently processing what is known as "horse sense". Or, at the very least, it was never easy, for me—to stay with any sort of logical thinking!

On the other hand, could it be that the sum total of human body, mind, soul, psyche (and whatever else might be involved)—the whole, entire, caboodle—is simply incapable of ever being "at total rest?" Is "true peace" totally—completely and utterly—beyond the finite, highly-limited, reach of the human element? Any part of the human element? I was beginning to think so! Beginning to be positively convinced of such a frightening "truth"!

Truth to tell, I must not have been as wrapped up in that intellectual, internal, psychological, philosophical, debate, as I'd thought/feared. For I actually did fall asleep!

Fortunately, not for the dreaded "hours and hours", however. Thankfully! Probably for only 15 or 20 minutes. Though my back and the undersides of my legs were turning quite warm, I was, fortunately, not charred to a crisp. Still, once I'd awakened, I found that I was still wondering—if I was being set up! Elaborately set up! For some kind of spectacular fall! I could not shake that dreaded specter!

You guys, up there! You sure have got me worried!

I spent, probably, another hour in my new-found, sandy, paradise. Gracing the wondrous beach. Spent the rest of the time—lying on my back. Pure logic! Hadda even things out, don'tcha know—lobster-wise. T'was only fair treatment—for the new-and-spectacularly-improved bod'.

It was not quite noon, when I'd finally decided to pack it in. There still were not that many people on the beach. Not in my area, anyway. That continued to be a bit of a shock. Actually, quite disquieting—although I, for sure, didn't know why. Part of my wondering might have been a bit of disappointment—at the lack of opportunity, to show off the new-and-improved physique! Maybe that was even a good deal of my rambling, run-amok, emotion! Well, none of my thought processes (so called) were making a helluva lot of sense. Maybe it was exposure to the sun! (I'd doubted it.)

There appeared to be a fair-sized crowd—milling about, literally hundreds of feet to the north. Maybe thousands of feet to the north. Well, there appeared to be a goodly number of apartment complexes—and, perhaps, a hotel or two—up that-a-way.

However, given the size of the glorious complex—in which I'd found myself (had literally found myself) living—the sparseness of the crowd on the beach, in my area, was a good bit disconcerting. (Was all of this "unreal" stuff some extremely-clever part of a truly-sadistic—a gates-of-hell—sinister plot? Try as I might, I absolutely could not shake that macabre specter!)

Once I'd gotten back to my condo, I showered—and put on a crisp new, bright-yellow, sport shirt, and a pair of double-knit, dark-blue, slacks. (Over my newly-"inherited", maroon-with-white-stripes, briefs, of course.)

I'd always worn boxers—till then. Did "The Guys" not know that? They seemed to know everything else! Boxers or briefs? Did that make a difference? (Well, the choice made for some political interest—a couple of decades later. Hello, Bill Clinton!)

Getting back to my own troubled, muddled, quandary, could even something as seemingly insignificant as that—boxers vs. briefs—be part of some elaborately-planned, meticulously-carried-out set-up?

I was fast becoming <u>paranoid</u>! I <u>knew</u> it! I was <u>aware</u> of that all-too-apparent fact! But, I was seemingly powerless to <u>do</u> anything about it! Was <u>that</u> the plan? To slowly (or, maybe, <u>not</u> so slowly) eat away at a schmuck's brain? Destroy his thought processes? Maybe not! But, maybe <u>so</u>! <u>None</u> of this was helping!

I seated myself on the unmade round bed—and donned a fresh pair of beyond-my-financial-ken-till-then silken socks! Then, I slipped the dainty little size-tens into a <u>very</u> expensive pair of black loafers—with leather tassels, yet.

I arose—and stood in front of the mirror! For, probably, as long as I'd stared at the thirty-thou. What was that old saying? Something about, "Death, thy name is vanity"? I think that the ancient, hackneyed, bromide went something like that. Close enough, anyway! Was that something <u>else</u> that was overtaking me?

Once I was able to tear myself away from that handsome-dog image in the mirror, I folded the envelope—the one with all that money in it. Folded it in half. Not an easy task. And I never <u>did</u> make it look truly folded. Or truly in half. After a minute or two—of futile jostling, with the outsized package—I was able to force it into my pants pocket. (Another struggle—albeit a highly-enjoyable one.)

I eagerly rejoined my broiling-inside "One Love", in the parking lot. Hadn't remembered the interior temperature of the Chrysler ever being <u>that</u> overheated. Even in and around Phoenix. Ah well. I rolled all the windows down—and set out to do a little reconnoitering. I needed to find out exactly what my new hometown actually looked like. The angel had said it was a pretty little town—in amongst all this beautiful terrain.

My highest priority: I felt that, first thing, I should find out how many banks the alluring burg might boast. Something told me not to put all that loot in one single bank. This, despite the fact that, even back then, any deposit—up to $100,000—would be covered by our handy-dandy FDIC. A strange inkling, I suppose—this mood toward diversification. I'd had no way of knowing whether this might be an intelligent—maybe even a positively brilliant— financial decision. You must remember: Handling money certainly had never been one of my strong suits, during my young life. (Not ever!)

I also needed to scope out the various restaurants—as well as what manner of stores that my new (my nifty new) hometown might have awaiting my dining/dancing, and shopping, pleasure.

Newport was—and still is—a completely charming town. Listen, it seemed especially enchanting to me. Especially on that first day of my residence, therein— in 1965.

There were, as it turned out, four banks—all within a few blocks of one another. It is interesting to note that all this new-to-me potential "high-finance" stuff would be taking place, decades before it became a "Big Brother"-type, heavily-enforced, law that financial institutions were required to report, to our benevolent, all-seeing/all-knowing, government, each and every transaction of $10,000 or more.

Still, as previously indicated, I thought it would not be advisable to stash the whole 30 grand in one bank. So (what could be fairer?) I opened savings accounts—in the amount of $7500—in all four of those financial houses.

I also opened a checking account—in the amount of $2500—in the last such institute. (It looked, to me, to be the most substantial—judging, primarily, from the ponderous building, in which the facility was located. Well, that—plus the reeking-of-money furnishings therein.)

In addition, the attractiveness of the receptionist—as well as the figure, vis-a-vis the lady who'd opened my accounts for me—were, probably, important considerations. The latter possessed an all-universe fanny! And she knew it. Her skirt was tailored to emphasize the asset.

Twenty-five hundred bucks I'd deposited. Do you realize that this meant that hokey old Paul—excuse me, handsome young Taylor Young—was actually carrying around well over $500? On his very person? To me, such a possibility—of that ever happening (as in ever)—was the stuff out of which pipe dreams are made!

These monumental, "high-finance", hurdles having been so deftly—so cleverly—cleared, I decided to hunt for a decent (well, hopefully, a better than decent) restaurant.

Now, this was well before the coast—to-coast explosion of national eatery chains. I don't recall seeing a *Chili's* or an *Applebee's* or a *Red Lobster* or a *TGI Fridays* in those days. Anywhere. *Denny's*, I guess, had gotten pretty well underway, by then. Had fairly well taken hold nationally. In fact, they'd already opened a place in San Antonio. At least one.

But, I'd never graced the joint with my presence. It was located pretty far from my former residence. (Probably a wise business decision, on their part.)

I'd seen a few of those new-fangled eateries along the route from Seguin. Also, there'd been a whole host of tried-and-true *Howard Johnson's*—but, they'd been around forever. Truth to tell, I've never been a big fan of *HoJo's*.

Besides, I'd been so anxious to see my new digs—if, indeed, they would even <u>exist</u>! As you can tell, I'd remained filled with enormous amounts of doubt, at the time, despite the new bod'/looks. Still, I was <u>so</u> "interested" in what might lie ahead—that I didn't stop very often to eat. Or to perform other essential exercises. Just ask my kidneys!

Apparently *McDonald's* and *Burger King* had started up. It <u>seems</u> to me that I'd seen a *"Mickey D's"*—somewhere in the Los Angeles area. Didn't partake of their gastric delights though. Well, their presence didn't make much of an impression. Same held true for *Burger King*.

Thankfully, in Newport, there seemed to be a plethora of Mom-and-Pop restaurants. One of them was (are you ready?) *Joe's Cafe*. (Without the obvious "essential" prop of an "Eat At Joe's" sign. No portly man walking up and down—in front of the joint—wrapped in a hokey "sandwich board". Can you even imagine?)

Joe's specialty, I quickly learned, was roast beef. And they were the most delicious—most delectable—morsels I'd ever tasted. That piquancy never changed. The lean, well-seasoned, meat was— without exception—gloriously wondrous. Each and every time! The succulent delicacy was cooked—and whatever-else-was-done-to-it—by an elderly Jewish couple, from Brooklyn. (I really don't <u>think</u> the man's name was "Joe".)

On my first, never-to-be-forgotten, foray into the eatery, I ordered a hot roast beef sandwich—on white—"with plenty of gravy". That was <u>exactly</u> what I got! <u>Plenty</u> of gravy! Well, plenty of meat, too. It was glorious!

This place—fast—became my favorite hangout. (<u>Really</u> fast!)

A contributing factor, to my continued presence at the eatery: There was this waitress, you see. This lady was a couple of years my junior. She was as neat as the restaurant itself. (Neater, actually.) Kind of a dishwater blonde—who could've stood to drop, maybe, four or five pounds. (But, then, who <u>couldn't</u>? Well, <u>me</u>! New bod', don't you see!) Listen, she was a real <u>stitch</u>! Had more jokes than anyone I'd ever met. And the great preponderance of them were actually <u>not</u> risqué. Imagine <u>that</u>!

I would've had a hard time trying to honestly tell you whether the greatest attraction to *Joe's* was that incredible roast beef—or whether it might actually have been <u>Gretchen</u>, the waitress (who, I would find out—rather <u>quickly</u>—was not married).

Once I'd gotten back to my opulent quarters, I made another world-famous "executive decision". I'd finally decided that—now that the panic-type excitement had, more or less, slacked off (to a point, anyway)—I should devote my attention to actually "taking stock" of what I now owned. (This despite the fact that I'd still felt—strongly—that I was being set up. That all of these "earthly" possessions were most likely temporary! Precariously temporary!)

Once I'd reentered the condo, I stood smack-dab in the middle of the huge living room—and did my best to, singularly, focus on each separate area. I would move my gaze—only a few feet at a time. (Sometimes, only a few inches.)

Well, that had been my resolution. Until I'd spotted a massive, floor-model, radio/phonograph/television set! This monumental appliance was positioned up against the south wall—next to the little alcove, leading to the john. I'd walked past this glorious thing, probably, a dozen times—and (stretching plausibility) had never actually noticed it. (Can you say "preoccupied"?)

The TV screen was massive! Well, it was—for that epoch, anyway. Something like 29-inches. (This is all pre-Flat Screen/HD/wall-mounted television.) And it was a color set! Practically unheard of in the mid-sixties. (Oh, they'd been around. But, I'd never met anyone who'd owned one.)

The radio? It was wonderful. Very powerful. Very powerful! Great tone. (And—look, Ma—no angel included in the speaker! Presumably.)

But, the record player! That was the unquestioned topper! The phonograph produced the highest-quality sound I'd ever heard. Anywhere! Ever! Under any circumstances! In my entire life!

I doubt that the people of *Bose*, today, would agree—but, that magnificent machine sounded to me, then, as Bose's "Wave Machine" does to me now. In the large compartment, at the very bottom of the staggeringly—massive "entertainment center" were located (would you believe?) 35 "schmaltzy" 33-rpm LP records. All in Stereophonic Sound!

This discovery was the "mother lode"! I'd only possessed a very few stereo records—in my own hokey little collection.

In addition, I'd always believed that my majestic, answer-to-an-addiction, *Olympic* machine had provided the finest of tones. But, when I decided to—hurriedly—place a Mantovani LP. to play on my newly-"inherited" stereo, it made the venerable *Olympic* sound almost "tinny"! Amazing! Made the revered old record-player sound like something out of the twenties. A crystal set, maybe. Incredible!

I'd been so bedazzled so often—and for so long—by everything else, that when I'd finally gone on to discover the beautiful, the tasteful, (I could never relate to "tasteful") wall-hangings, the newly-recognized furnishings seemed so, well, so "ordinary". Strictly by comparison. Was I becoming la-di-dah—or what?

The two table lamps—and even the floor lamp, next to the still-dazzling chair—screamed, positively-expensive, class.

Look, I was still so numbed by this overwhelming, mind-boggling, avalanche of, well, of remarkable "things"! Caught up in the never-ending avalanche—

of all these staggering, newly-acquired, possessions! (As well as the overflowing multitude of mind-numbing happenings!) I'm sure, that I hadn't come close to showing the proper amount of appreciation, for the less-critical stuff. Such as wall-hangings and lamps.

Proper ration of gratitude—at that still-stunning point—was, almost definitely, out of the question.

And yet—among all of this glorious wonder—there was always, lurking about, that disturbing unease! That haunting, if you will! That ever-present fear! That inescapable question: Was I—your friendly, neighborhood, schmuck—being painstakingly set up? How to know?

I pulled "my" well-written (by someone) time-travel novel from the massive bookshelf—and plopped myself into that huge, sinfully-comfortable—green leather chair.

Initially, I'd expected that I'd have a bit of a problem getting "in" to the tome. But—hey! I was pretty good— damn good, actually—as a writer! I was intrigued by not only the plot—but, by the style. Somehow I could picture myself as—in point of fact—having actually written the book. It just seemed to—well, to be—to simply be me!

The narrative had the protagonist—who, very easily, could've been me—being sent back to 1939. He marries a widow—a few years older than he is. The woman has a son stationed in Pearl Harbor! As you can understand, December 7, 1941, is coming! With a rush! He's got to get that kid out of there! But, he cannot tell anyone—even his new wife—that he's from the future! Posed a bit of a problem!

Strange! I'd thought—had actually fantasized (many, many times)—about actually being sent back in time. To a "kinder, gentler" era; although I don't think I'd ever heard that expression before. (This was more than 20 years before President Bush, the elder, would've used those words.)

My dream/wish—to be transferred back to such an epoch—had spectacularly blossomed, mostly, when everything (like, for instance, my whole universe—in San Antonio) had begun closing in on me. Everything had started to unravel—big time!

We're talking pure escapism, here! Pure escapism! Yet, here was this book! This very new, come-lately, book! This "classic"—that seemed to have looked (deeply) into my very psyche! Into my very soul! That is, if I'd still had one! This beautifully-written tome had encapsulated my very being! That was frightening! Scary as could be! (Another ingredient to add to the massive unease that I'd been experiencing, all along! The very real—to me—prospect, that I was being "set up"!)

According to the book—this veritable "epic" that I'd "written"—it wasn't so cut-and-dried easy to survive, in the late-thirties.

For instance, my protagonist in the narrative, is now roughly twice his mother's age. And, on the very first day in his new/old life, he thoroughly freaks her out! Intriguing concept.

Again, though, I could actually—for real—totally see myself, having written this "masterpiece". Could, in fact, visualize myself as attempting virtually all of the things—that whoever-had-written-the-work had his/her protagonist involved in. Would the wonders—

the sheer wonders—of my earthshaking new existence? Would they never cease?

After about an hour-and-a-half spent with the works of the newly-minted "Bard of Newport", I finally decided it would behoove me to revisit my "one love". That venerable "hunk of iron"—in the parking area. Sooner or later, I was going to have to begin offloading my suddenly-gauche possessions. Haul 'em inside—into my posh new residence. I was fixing to set the joint back—taste-wise! Set it back—substantially!

The unloading operation took longer—much longer, and a helluva lot more energy—than I would've expected. By the time I'd lugged the last "load" inside, I was ready for a little—a well-deserved—"cardiac arrest" break.

However, I spied the box with my precious LPs inside. There it sat—in the middle of the living room. Almost "beckoning" to me. To my utter and complete devastation, I discovered that most of my treasured records had perished! Had gone "belly-up"! Had—literally—melted, in the all-day heat. The all-day heat—of many days. I was heartbroken. My treasures! And I'd flat-out ignored them! As mentioned, some of those 10-inch LPs would be—I was positive—irreplaceable! (Back to "bitter wormwoods"!)

The God-awful inferno had claimed every one of these precious recordings! It must have been a very painful death! For each of these cherished discs! Well, the villainous heat—that had done the dastardly deed—had not only been the elements in Newport. I'd experienced a veritable furnace—almost entirely throughout the trip west.

As previously noted, the temperatures had been especially torrid—in and around Phoenix. It seemed to me, that I'd probably pulled off—somewhere in that foundry-like area—to refresh myself. Had remained in some stupid restaurant—for the better part of a damn hour. Had done that—undoubtedly—more than one time. The heat—when I'd opened the door, each time, to continue that fantastic trip to my destiny—had decked me! Like a Rocky Marciano punch, or something!

Obviously, that same overwhelming heat had not done my cherished records any good. And—most assuredly—the poor things having been forced to languish that entire Monday, under the Pacific sun, certainly hadn't helped! Rest In Peace, treasured recordings! You'd always served well! Had, forever, gone above—and beyond—the call to ever-schmaltzy duty!

Well—thank goodness—I now had this dazzling, brand-spanking-<u>new</u> collection! This already-cherished conglomeration—of pure, out and out, schmaltz! Each LP was mint-new! Was this death-knell situation something <u>else</u> that "The Guys" would've thought of? The fact that—like some kind of idiot—I'd leave my vinyl "treasures" to fend for themselves, in all that toxic heat? Hmmm!

After that lamented, melted-recordings, discovery, I decided—and probably loud enough for the neighbors to have heard—"The hell with it! The hell with <u>everything</u>! I'm <u>through</u> for the day! For the whole damn entire <u>day</u>!"

It turned out that I actually was <u>not</u> quite finished. I'd grabbed a can of root beer from the fridge—and made my way out onto my <u>terrace</u>. <u>My</u> terrace! This was my maiden "set-a-spell" voyage—out to the little cement slab.

Plopping myself down—into one of the aluminum-with-green-and-white-plastic strip chairs—I began to totally unwind. It <u>had</u> been a busy day. <u>Another</u> busy day—for this "little man". One in a seemingly long-running series! "Lot of that goin' around," I muttered—hopefully to myself.

I'd kind of stretched out on my chair. Almost as though I was lying on some kind of lounge. But, this little item was substantially harder on my back. Still, I was halfway into slumber-land—when I heard some stirring, on the terrace next to mine. The one which was really close by.

I cracked open one eye—which I'd hoped was the one nearest the new-arrival. That way, I wouldn't have to turn my head, or bother with trying to open the other eye. A daunting prospect—given my state of utter, total, complete, relaxation. (Also known as "collapse".)

What I saw—through the blur—was a rather portly gentleman. He was seating himself in his own chair. The latter was, pretty much, an identical-twin to mine.

I was judging this man to be in his mid-fifties. (A lot to take in—for just one single, semi-opened, orb.) He was wearing a pair of blue shorts—with white fish, in varying positions, plastered all over them. He was attired in nothing else—I was certain.

He spied my single open eye—and smiled broadly. He had a definite twinkle in his almost-green eyes. (Well hell, I guess I must probably have opened the other optic, by then.)

"You must be Mister Young . . . the new inmate," was his greeting. "I'm Charlie McNulty. Your neighbor. Y'see? The neighborhood was already shot . . . courtesy me. Went straight to hell. Even before you ever got here."

"Glad to meet you," I responded—as I got up, and extended my arm as much as possible, in his direction.

He made the same futile attempt. But, our fingertips fell well shy of touching. Let executing alone a bona fide handshake. Possessing minds like a pair of steel traps, we both abandoned the traditional rite—and seated ourselves once more.

"What do ya think of the joint?" he asked.

"It's gorgeous!" I was going to add that I'd never lived in such a posh place. But, I'd figured that a declaration like that would be far from the image of a successful—published—writer. "And the town," I did manage to add, "is simply gorgeous."

"Yeah," he agreed. "And so clean. Almost like, y'know, almost like they slosh the whole city out . . . every night . . . with Listerine. I love it here. Been here, y'know, for . . . I dunno . . . probably fourteen or fifteen years now. It really flies . . . time, y'know. Really flies . . . when you're having fun."

"Have you lived here . . . here in the building . . . for long?

"Naw. The place has only been here . . . a couple or three years, now. Moved in about six or eight months ago. I understand you're a writer. What do you write?"

"Oh, fiction mostly. Did a time-travel novel. Also, one about a police operation . . . in a little town in Texas. An imaginary town in Texas. But, if it reminded anyone of Austin . . . I couldn't help it. And . . . ta-DAH! . . . I also whomped up a romance novel."

I did my best to fill him in on my "creations"—and found myself glad that I'd taken the time (amid all the turbulence and tumult) to have glanced through each of the books. On the other hand, it was more than a little bit frightening—to me, anyway—that I was so adept in "filling him in" on these literary "gems". Summarizing them, fully—the way I just had. They were supposed to be strangers to my mind. (Another disquieting ingredient.)

He asked if I'd come from The Lone Star State—and I informed him that I was just in from San Antonio.

"Figgered as much. Well, y'know, the plates on that sturdy old Chrysler . . . out there, in the lot . . . they pretty much told me that." He sighed—heavily. "Had that same car, y'know. Years and years ago," he advised. "Well, mine was, y'know, a forty-seven. I'm guessing yours is a forty-eight . . . although there wasn't ever a helluva lot of difference in those models. Forty-six through forty-eight. All them . . . pretty much the same automobile, y'know. And great! Great automobiles! Great as hell!"

"Yeah. Mine is. It's a forty-eight. And I love it. Really love it."

"Well, if you ever have a problem with her, I run a really nifty auto repair shop. *Charlie's Auto Repair.* As you can see, I'm not very inventive . . . when it comes to naming stuff.

"Well, that's good to know. If anything <u>does</u> happen to the 'Old Girl'."

"Been there . . . going on twelve years now. On Main, y'know . . . out at Sixteenth Street. Don't have all the diagnostic crap . . . that they're comin' out with these days . . . sad to say. But, I've got a pretty good reputation."

"I'm sure."

"Can usually, pretty well, figger out what the hell's wrong. On the other hand, cars really <u>are</u> gettin' to be where they're so damn complicated nowadays. I figger that . . . if they keep gettin' more and more complex . . . I'm either gonna have to, y'know, start buying all that expensive crap. Or, y'know, get the hell outta the racket. Out of the business, I mean. Gonna hafta, y'know, start sellin' *Fuller Brush*, or maybe encyclopedias, or somethin'."

"Well, I'm about as mechanically . . . or electrically . . . inclined as that table, over there. But, even I can tell that they're getting more and more complex."

"Sophisticated, is what they call 'em now, y'know. All these new . . . quote/unquote . . . advances that they're making. No, really . . . if you ever <u>do</u> have a problem . . . I'd sure as hell admire to work on such a classic. One like that Chrysler of yours. And I ain't gonna be chargin' ya an arm and a leg, y'know. Merely an arm'll do."

"Well, if/as/when I ever have a problem, you'll be the first to know. I wouldn't want 'My Baby' . . . in the hands of just <u>any</u> uncaring mechanic."

"What do you think of your fellow inmates here?"

"Can't really say . . . inasmuch as you're the first one I've met."

"Most of the people, here, are good 'uns. We've got a few weirdoes, y'know. But, so would any complex this size. The management . . . over in that little round building, out there . . . they're pretty easy to get along with."

"Well, I'm glad to hear that."

"Most of the people, here, are . . . you know . . . they're just work-a-day people. The couples who live here . . . most of 'em . . . they have to both work. Need two jobs, y'know. Two incomes. Just to meet the monthly bills, I'm guessin'. So, you won't see too many of 'em around during the day. Not during the week, anyway."

"Well, that's understandable."

"Saw you out on the beach this mornin'. Most of the people, here . . . . at that hour . . . were off, y'know. On their way to work. Or gettin' ready to go. Like I was."

"Yeah. I guess I can understand that. Well, really, there isn't any guessing about it. I can fully understand . . ."

"You gotta realize, y'know, that we ain't all successful, published, authors . . . . like someone I know."

"Well, it's not all that lucrative."

"I dunno. You musta been doin' all right. Especially if you're livin' here. I assume that . . . if push came to shove . . . you could do a little better than a forty-eight model car, y'know. I'm guessin' . . . just guessin' . . . that you're mighty in love with that old bucket of bolts."

"You've got that right."

"Well . . . speakin' of the inmates . . . you'll get to where you'll, pretty much, get to meet everybody. Sooner or later. Lots more action on the weekend. Nothing spectacular, y'understand. Everybody likes to, y'know, hang out at the beach. Well, I guess, most everybody. Few . . . I don't know why the hell they're even <u>here</u>. They <u>never</u> go out on the beach. They might as well be livin' in West LA. . . . or Hackensack, or Pocatello, or some damn place."

"Yeah, <u>that</u> I can definitely understand. Well, I mean that I really <u>don't</u> understand. Can't <u>fathom</u> someone being here . . . and not taking advantage of that glorious beach. But, I can . . . most assuredly . . . see the beach, as being pretty crowded on the weekends."

"Only one inmate that I probably should warn you about: Should really give you an <u>alert</u> on her. Charlotte Klukay . . . in three-oh-two. Third floor. She's a certified, bona fide, nympho, y'know! A real-life . . . in the flesh . . . <u>nymphomaniac</u>! You may not consider this to be a real 'warning'. And maybe . . . to you . . . it's not even some kind of heads <u>up</u>! Dependin', y'know, on what you consider . . ."

"Wait a minute! You're not <u>kidding</u>? You're <u>telling</u> me that this . . . this Charlotte woman . . . that she's a true, dyed-in-the-wool, <u>nympho</u>? I mean a nympho . . . as most people understand the meaning of the word? Most people . . . including me? Us sexually-twisted individuals?"

"Yup. Only problem is that she's not a millionaire, y'know. And she doesn't own a liquor store either. Nothin' like the old joke goes."

"But, she . . . she . . . she . . . ?"

"Yeah. As I understand it, she was some kind of big-assed child star. In Hollywood, y'know. In the forties, I guess. Don't know for <u>sure</u>! That's what I've <u>heard</u>! <u>She</u> doesn't talk about it, y'know. Not at <u>all</u>. This is all accordin' to all the gossip, y'know. And there's plenty of <u>that</u> goin' around."

"Sounds logical. I mean I <u>guess</u> it does. Actually, I've never <u>met</u> a real-life nympho."

"Well, I'm sure your paths will cross! She's . . . ah . . . <u>met</u> just about every other guy in the complex. Met them, y'know, in their <u>beds</u>!"

"Sounds like <u>fun</u>! On second thought, I'm not sure that I'm . . ."

"She's supposed to have got all caught up in all that Hollywood . . . what they like to call . . . morality. Supposed to have lost her . . . ah . . . lost her amateur standing there! Lost it . . . really <u>early</u> in life, so I understand!. <u>Really</u> early! Like at age eleven . . . so they say."

"<u>Really</u>?"

"That's what they <u>say</u>. Turns out, I guess, that she got to where she <u>loved</u> it! The <u>sex</u>, y'know. Apparently, she really grooved <u>out</u> on it, y'know! Supposedly . . . right from the <u>start</u>! Well, hell . . . <u>that</u> became obvious! Real <u>quick</u>, y'know! Really <u>soon</u>. Enjoyed the hell out of it, she did. Still <u>does</u>! Let me assure you of <u>that</u>! She simply never lost the old urge to . . ."

"And she . . . and she . . . continues to . . . ah . . . to pursue those . . . ah . . . those nymphomaniac ways? To this day? I mean, here in . . . ?"

"Yup! And don't be surprised . . . don't let yourself be real shocked . . . if she wanders into your apartment, some time! Sometime soon! She's up on everything, y'know! Ain't much ever gets by her! You'll meet her . . . and probably soon! Most probably, late at night, y'know. Well, most always, late at night! And in any manner of dress! Or any manner of undress! Usually the latter, y'know! Bare-assed naked, she is! Most of the time, anyway! Yessir! In the ol' buff!"

"Aw, c'mon! How could she . . . ?"

"Has a master key, y'know," he answered—with the dirtiest laugh I'd ever heard. "Actually, master keys . . . is what she's got! Plural! Real plural . . . I guess. Nobody knows where . . . or how . . . she get's 'em. But, apparently her stock, y'know . . . her supply, of the damn things . . . I guess it's totally inexhaustible! About a year back, management went . . . and they changed every single lock! Every single lock! On every damn door, y'know! Every single door! In the whole furschlugginer complex! The entire complex! Every damn apartment!"

"They did that? They did all that? Because of her?"

He nodded. The smile got broader. "Set ol' Charlotte back . . . probably all of two or three days," he answered. "Before long, she had another 'un . . . another master key! Probably only one . . . of a whole never-ending series of the damn things! She's pretty . . . ah . . . resourceful, y'know! Very resourceful! Damn resourceful!"

"That's . . . why, that's incredible! Absolutely in-damn-credible!"

"Isn't it? Maybe to you, it's no big-assed warning. Like I said, you might . . . ah . . . warm up to such a neighborly neighbor. That type of what they call networking. Not a whole helluva lot of complaints, does she ever get, y'know."

"This is . . . this is jolly-well astounding! Astounding as hell!"

"Well, I'm maybe makin' it sound more widespread than it actually is. Of course, you have to realize, y'know, that most of the inmates here are actual couples! Some married . . . some unmarried! And I guess she, pretty well, leaves them alone. There's only ten . . . or, maybe twelve guys . . . in addition to you an' me, y'know. Really only that many . . . who're batching it, in this particular building."

"Does that mean that our paths will cross . . . often?"

"Probably not all that often. Apparently, she's enterprising enough . . . resourceful enough . . . that she's long since expanded her field of endeavor!"

"Expanded? How so? What do you mean by . . . ?"

"She's pretty willing to share, y'know! To the multitudes! She 'serves' some of the other buildings! Hell, maybe all of the other buildings! Probably all of the other buildings! Resourceful as hell, y'know!"

"Aw c'mon, Charlie. You can't be serious!"

"Never more serious in my life. M'boy. Some things you simply don't joke about! Sex, politics, religion, forty-eight Chryslers . . . and, of course, nymphomaniacs!"

"Yeah," I muttered. "I guess."

"You might want to consider laying in one of those two-by-four wooden beams. Be sure . . . and get a big one. Mount that sucker over your apartment door. Use that huge sucker . . . as, y'know, a kind of bolt, at night! Of course . . . bein' as how we're here on the ground floor, y'know . . . she might just go ahead, and still come right on in. Climb right on . . . through the damn window, y'know! She just might. Ya never know. With Charlotte? None of us never really know."

"You sound as though you've had . . . uh . . . had some . . . ah . . . real-life experiences with her."

"Yeah, well who hasn't?" He let go with another most-obscene laugh. Then, mustering a contented smile, he continued. "There were two or three times, though . . . believe it or not . . . when I just slapped her on the ol' ass, y'know! Just slapped her on the old wet ass . . . b'lieve it or not! And went and told her to just go ahead . . . and beat it! Poor choice of words, I s'pose! Just told her to get the hell on out! There were times, y'know, when I simply didn't want all the . . . ."

He let the sentence trail off. His bright-and-shiny expression showed—very clearly—that he'd not needed to elaborate.

NINE

I'D LIKE TO TELL YOU that these sorts of things just continued to dazzle me—on a daily (if not hourly)) basis. However, things had reached a point where I was <u>not</u> experiencing a whole, never-ending, sequence—of earthshaking experiences. Every day was <u>not</u> a replay of that first glorious Monday Each and every day which followed had <u>not</u> held some kind of glorious (or, maybe, even staggeringly remarkable) new adventure. It was, undoubtedly, just as well. The human psyche can handle only so much.

For the rest of that first, "highly-interesting", week—and well into the second one—things appeared to have settled in. More or less, anyway. I certainly can't say that I'd gotten into any sort of a rut. Or even into a semi-routine. Mainly because simply grappling with each aspect, of my new life, was still taking a helluva toll. Emotionally—and otherwise. A helluva lot of continuing getting-used-to.

Every morning <u>did</u> remain a continuous thrill! Just waking up—on that "adulterous", deliciously-obscene, round, bed (to simply be living in that incredible condo)—was enough to hold any normal, work-a-day, mindset at bay. Well, my without-fail morning jaunts—to that remarkable beach—was always a most comforting experience; although I'd begun to not spend hour upon hour out there.

So, I guess you could say that my life—my new life—was taking on some bit of form. And even substance. I ate a fairly late breakfast—most days—and a later lunch (every day) at *Joe's*.

I was working up a bit of a friendship with Gretchen—the waitress at the eatery. I'd discovered—on my second or third visit—that she'd had a dog. The dog's name was Fanny. The pooch was a beautiful golden retriever—who was upwards of 14-years-old. Ancient in our years.

So, "Gretch" and I had begun—almost from the very outset—a rather unusual (to say the least) routine, wherein I'd ask her if I could inquire as to how her Fanny was.

She'd always come back with something like, "The condition of my Fanny? That falls under the heading . . . of None Of Your Damn Business".

Was that great, or what? We coulda put Abbott & Costello and/or The Marx Bros. out of business. (Eat your hearts out, guys!)

We seemed to be working, rather rapidly, into something resembling a relationship. She was divorced—and had no kids. (Only her "Fanny".)

By the Wednesday of the following week—my second one in town—I'd worked up enough courage to ask her for a date. (I'd already given her an autographed copy of my time-travel novel—dedicated to "My Friend Gretchen—And Her Fanny". Was that "inspired"—or what?)

She advised me that—after having put in all that "waitress mileage", Monday through Friday—she really liked to spend weeknights at home. Enjoyed soaking her feet, among other things. The restaurant's owner's had a son and a daughter and a daughter-in-law—all in their twenties—who comprised the wait staff/salad bar attendees/coffee brewers on Saturday. (The joint was closed on Sunday—a fact which I'd discovered [to my great disappointment] on my initial weekend in Newport.)

So, our first magical date was set! "Gretch" and I would go to a movie—come the following Saturday night.

Listen, don't disparage that! The local theater was really innovative. They always seemed to have some kind of "special showing" going on. Including reviving a lot of the older film "classics", that I'd always loved. Most were genuine gems! The house would, in fact. be showing *Gone With The Wind* on that soon-to-be-wondrous (I'd hoped) Saturday.

(I'm ashamed to admit that I had never seen this epic movie before 1965. So—initially anyway—the night seemed to bode well.)

This fantastic "social life" of mine would, as noted, begin at the tag end of the second week of my "new life". There'd never been much "action" on the beach—despite the fact that there had been infinitely more people out there, during the first weekend. Ergo, mostly, I'd wound up spending most of my time lying, by myself. No matter how extensive (or brief) my stay.

Or else, you'd find me seated on the terrace—often chatting with "Good Old" Charlie McNulty, my next-door neighbor. (Hardly a thrill-a-minute existence! But, I <u>was</u> thrilled—anyway!)

Things, however, <u>did</u> get "more than a little interesting" on that second Thursday night, in my new venue! This took place—less than 48 hours before my proposed first date with Gretchen!

This epic happening had taken place—<u>well</u> after midnight! I was in bed! Naked—as usual! As previously noted, I—most always—slept in the nude. Especially when I was by myself. The last few months of Joanne's and my marriage? Not so much. Sometimes in the raw. Sometimes not. Didn't make much difference—one way or another. With either one of us. <u>That</u> portion of our lives had been deceased—for some goodly amount of time.

I don't believe that she or I could've told you—exactly when the sexual activity stopped. Not completely accurately, anyway. No one drew a circle on the calendar—and said, "As of this date . . . no more intimacy". Like just about everything else, in our marriage, the sex had simply withered away. And it eventually died. No one knows precisely when that particular "Point Of No Return" actually occurred. It came and went—purely unnoticed.

On this particular, what-turned-out-to-be-spectacular, Thursday night, in Oregon, I was caught up—in the midst of a dream! A really <u>wild</u> one! A terribly <u>turbulent</u> one! A violent whirlpool of emotional—and physical—<u>upheaval</u>! The most <u>disjointed</u> spectacle that I believe I'd ever found myself involved in! Awake—<u>or</u> sleeping!

I can't—to this day—tell you what <u>any</u> of the unending, tumultuous, scenarios were about. All I know is that I'd always seemed to be in some kind of life-or-death struggle—with some unknown (and, seemingly, shapeless) force! An unimaginable mass of <u>something</u>! Ectoplasm? Quite possibly! (Whatever <u>that</u> is!)

In any case, no matter <u>what</u> might've been at stake, during this bone-rattling, nocturnal, sequence, I—most assuredly—was <u>not</u> winning! All of a sudden, I awoke to the fact that I was <u>spurting</u> my seminal fluid! All <u>over</u> the place! Can you <u>imagine</u>? (Well, <u>I</u> couldn't!) Listen, I'd not had a "wet dream" in—literally—decades! Had never even come close! Not since high school—or. possibly, shortly thereafter! (Have always been a little retarded—in that area.)

As I, more or less, fought my way to the surface—trying, desperately, to escape from all this incredibly-raucous, life-threatening, action—I <u>thought</u> I was seeing someone!

In the midst, of this frenzied blur, there appeared to be a <u>lady</u>! Actually, a <u>naked</u> lady! And she seemed to be springing—bolting, frantically—from my <u>side</u>! From my <u>side</u>—which happened to be <u>naked</u>! (Well, <u>all</u> of me was in the old buff-o!)

And, here was this unclothed <u>woman</u>! She was <u>vaulting</u>—from my <u>bed</u>! There was a fair amount of illumination coming in, through the double window over that round dandy on which I slept! The generous amount of lighting was courtesy the many flood lights, spread across the beach!

Once I was able to focus my sleep-infested eyes—I could tell for sure! There was a woman! There could be no doubt! There had been a woman! A well-constructed woman! (I could also tell that!)

And, at that juncture, this "visitor" was making a hasty departure! The "lady"—this intruder—was dashing through the john! Speedily headed for the living room! But, in that less-than-subdued lighting, I could tell that it was a woman! And that she was unclothed! She was indeed unclothed!

Once the fog had begun to lift, the situation began to fit in! I began to recall what Charlie, next door, had advised me. His assertions about the celebrated Charlotte Klukay—our friendly neighborhood nymphomaniac!

Could that have been her? There didn't seem to be any other readily available explanation—although my still-ridiculously-clouded mind was definitely not operating on anything approaching all cylinders!

What had just happened? Hell, I couldn't have done—could never have done—could not possibly have ever gotten involved in such an unspeakable scenario! Not in such an unforgivable action! Could never have indulged in the God-awful act! Not in the brain-broiling situation—that I was afraid I'd just participated in! Could I?

As a means of pure research, you understand—I reached down into my pubic area! I most certainly had! Had, apparently, "participated"! Had "participated"—liberally! Exceptionally liberally! Zounds!

My "social life"—in this new venue—it seemed, was off and running! And propelled into a more illustrious start—than I could ever have imagined! I wondered what "Rhett" and "Scarlet" would say. I really wondered what "Gretch" would say! (If she, of course, ever found out!)

You may or not believe this—but, I did not go back to sleep! Couldn't go back to sleep! Not for that entire night! Nothing close! Not after what had just happened—to unsuspecting little old me! (Actually, despite all of these years that have evolved since that mind-warping night, I'm not sure—exactly—what I truly believe, about the erotic experience! And I was there! Was I ever!)

To say that nothing like that had ever happened to me before would not only be an understatement of colossal proportions—it would be abusing the privilege. Think the "Marie Antoinette/ Sore Throat" example, cited earlier.

Joanne, my wife, had been the only woman—with whom I'd ever been intimate. She'd also been a virgin, when we'd married. (Neither one of us knew what the hell we were doing that first night. You should-a been there. No you shouldn't have been there!) To be truthful, for months thereafter, we were still groping—so to speak—our way through that aspect of our lives.

And—kids or no kids—nothing like the tidal wave or tsunami or volcano or typhoon or cyclone (or whatever it was that had just finished bowling me over) had ever happened between my former spouse and me! Nothing even close! (I'm positive that she'd vouch for that. Tell you the same—exact—thing. Same story—coming from both directions!)

I dunno. I was in a complete and utter dither! Maybe it wasn't so much the from-out-of-nowhere sexual encounter, that had me so damn distraught. (And, then again, maybe it was! Maybe it was—in spades! Yet another "puzzlement"!)

Let me tell you: I honestly believe that the most troubling aspect involved with the whole, entire, bone-rattling (literally) adventure was this: My first concern was, "What did 'The Guys'—those sly, fun-loving, angels, up there—what did they know?"

How did they come to choose this particular condo—to which to send me? Why did they pick this particular building—in this particular complex?

Well, according to Charlie—my next-door neighbor (who, apparently had "boffed" Charlotte on more than a few occasions)—the nympho didn't really confine her endeavors to any one single "favored" building. Maybe not even to one single "favored" complex! (Hell, maybe not to one single "favored" city!)

There must have been thousands—probably tens-of-thousands—of complexes on The Left Coast. Of course, condominiums were relatively a new phenomenon in 1965. But, who had ever said that I'd have to land in a condo? I'd have been just happy (I'd guessed) living in a nice apartment complex! And just about anywhere! Anyplace—in the entire country! Especially, since "The Guys" had been so incredibly generous with the currency—and, truth to tell, all the other really neat, expensive, stuff.

Surely, they must have known that Charlotte lived in this complex—and was exceptionally—ah—liberal (really most generous), when it came to plying her (how shall I say?) "trade".

So, why me, "Guys"? Why here? Why this place? I'd never even heard of Newport, Oregon. Not till I was advised—by that goofy angel—that this was where I'd be landing!

Newport was where I would light—if I'd wanted to be a part of "The Deal"! Look—they could've sent me anywhere. An apartment in Toledo. A flat in Terre Haute. A house in St. Louis. A duplex in Dubuque. Why Newport? Why Newport—and the far-flung, highly-esoteric, "territory" of one Charlotte Klukay? Why, indeed?

It hadn't troubled me at the time—mainly because I'd had more than a few other things on my mind—but, that angel had gone out of his way, during that inspiring conversation via my blue dashboard, to assure me that neither he, nor any of the other "Guys", were going to send me anyone!

"No one," he vowed, "would ever come into my life! Not from them!" Really? Truthfully? Would that "promise" include naked, sex-crazed, ladies? In the middle of the damn night? And the fact that this spectacular upheaval had occurred less than 48 hours before my initial date with Gretchen? That fact was particularly troubling! Was this the first notice— that they'd begun to trifle with my life? Especially my "social" life?

Nothing, as you can see, was making sense! There was not the slightest bit of logic—involved in any part of the esoteric, nocturnal, goings-on! Not in <u>any</u> of them! Not from the very <u>beginning</u>! I guess that, maybe, there didn't <u>figure</u> to be. <u>Ever</u>! Part of some sadistic, angelic, <u>set</u> up?

There might've been the possibility—that I'd gotten just a little bit <u>too</u> "comfortable", over the previous few days. Perhaps <u>far</u> too "comfortable"!

Did I need something—some fresh "ingredient"—to <u>think</u> about? Should I now spend my entire <u>life</u>—in a totally <u>rattled</u> state? Again, was this—<u>all</u> of this—was it all part of some exotic "heavenly" set up? Was Charlotte Klukay part of the "Original Cast"—in what was playing out so spectacularly? Was she to be a <u>major</u> "performer"? In some kind—of warped celestial, <u>way</u>-off-Broadway, "production"?

I was reminded—and highly troubled—by a sudden memory of an old 1950s TV show. I couldn't remember the title—nor the series—but, the protagonist (I couldn't remember who <u>he</u> was, either) had died. Had <u>thought</u> that he'd gone to heaven.

And Sebastian Cabot (<u>him</u>, I'd remembered) was ushering the man through this glorious afterlife. <u>Anything</u> this fellow wanted, Mr. Cabot provided! Whenever—and wherever—the guy wanted. And in the exact quantity that the poor soul had asked for. There had been absolutely <u>no</u> challenges, for the main character to overcome. If he wanted to meet—and to bed—some beautiful woman, he'd had but to ask.

If he'd wanted to go to a casino—and win a lot of money—Mr. Cabot would ask exactly how much coin of the realm the fellow wanted to win. Then, he saw to it that this was the precise amount the gentleman would come out of the casino with.

Finally, the guy—in the midst of all this uncontested luxury—told Mr. Cabot that, maybe, he'd like to go to "The Other Place". (You couldn't say "hell" on TV in those days. Not even in the biblical sense.) Mr. Cabot then advised the man—that he was already <u>in</u> "The Other Place"!

Was I being sentenced to some kind of "Other Place"? One located on Earth? Had I already <u>been</u> damned? Is <u>this</u> the way that they deal with <u>schmucks</u>? Schmucks—such as <u>me</u>?

On Friday morning, I'd stayed away from *Joe's*. On purpose. I had really dreaded facing Gretchen! Simply by dint of the fact—of what had taken place, so erotically, on Thursday night? Probably so. Hell, <u>definitely</u> so! I <u>sure</u> didn't know what I'd say to her. Probably, <u>nothing</u>! (<u>Hopefully</u>, nothing!) Nothing would've certainly been preferable than <u>something</u>! <u>Much</u> better—than <u>anything</u> that would come close to touching upon my mind-blowing, nocturnal, encounter with Ms Klukay!

Listen—I was going to skip lunch there also. But, would <u>that</u> be a good idea? Was <u>any</u> of this a good idea? What remained of my brain was definitely <u>overheating</u>! I could just imagine that <u>everyone</u> would be able to see the smoke—churning out of my ears!

"Gretch's" shift would end before the supper crowd started to infiltrate the eatery. (The elderly couple—who'd owned the joint—had two part-time ladies that handled that meal, during the week.)

I'd had "Gretch's" phone number, of course. And the social event was firm. At least in my mind. Set for Saturday night, at seven-thirty.

Still, what would happen, if she was to not see me—on the day before this initial date? When I'd always stopped by (at least once) literally every previous day? Would that start her to thinking all kinds of things? Rotten things? Thoughts that, maybe, she shouldn't be thinking? Things that I'd prefer her to not be thinking? Nothing like a guilty conscience to further screw up one's already-muddled thought processes. (Trust me.)

So, hesitantly as hell, I showed up—for lunch. Gretchen seemed especially vibrant. Bubbly as could be. She was in a wonderful mood. She expounded with several jokes—ones I'd never heard before. She was in rare form. Even beat the by-now-slightly-ragged "Fanny" routine—to death.

And—try as I might—I couldn't "keep up with her". Was relating to her—very poorly. The problem was not for lack of effort on my part. I was striving—mightily—to hold up my end of the conversation. It was just—flat out—not working. None of it was!

Finally, once the "waitressing stuff" had reached a pronounced ebb, she sat down—across from me—and asked, "Taylor . . . what's wrong? What is it? Do you want out of our date, tomorrow?"

"No!" I'd answered quickly. Maybe too quickly. And—definitely—way too loudly. But, following that belted response, I could continue with nothing! Absolutely zero! All I could come up with—were numerous "uh"'s and a few well-chosen "ah's". (Brilliant?) I was totally wiped out!

"Something's up," she'd finally responded—in a tone that was more dejected, than I'd ever heard come from her lips. "Something's up! Big time! Now, do you wanna tell ol' 'Auntie Gretchen'? Tell her . . . what it's all about?"

"Honest, 'Gretch', there's nothing . . ."

"I thought it was pretty odd . . . well, I figured that it was damn unusual . . . that you didn't pop in for breakfast this morning. Now, here I see you . . . like this. And I'm thinking . . . I'm afraid! Scared now, of all this . . . this, this, this . . . this change! All this . . . this change . . . that has come over you! I'm afraid that it's all tied up in our date tomorrow. So . . . look! If it's going to be that big a deal to you, then we certainly don't hafta . . . ."

"NO!" Again, too much volume! "I want . . . more than anything . . . I want to go out with you! Today, tonight, tomorrow . . . whenever!"

"Well, dammit, there's definitely something wrong! Look! Taylor . . . tell me! Tell me this! Did Charlotte . . . did Charlotte Klukay . . . did she finally catch up with you? Like maybe last night? Is that what this is all . . . ?"

She didn't have to continue! Nothing had to continue. There's one thing that the angels never got around to "adjusting": The fact that I'm pretty darn transparent. The only situation—ever, in my entire life—that I can remember anyone not being able to read me like the well-known, proverbial, book—was Joanne's continual failure to believe that Elena and I had never been to bed. That had been the sole non-transparent factor—in my entire life!

Gretchen could—obviously—read my silent scream! My inept, attempt-to-cover-up, answer, to her question/accusation! Immediately! It was written all over my face—as well as, probably, every part of me that was not covered up! Well, maybe not even limited—to those exposed portions of my probably-blushing body! My undoubtedly-blushing body!

"SO," she said with—of all things—a more-or-less semi-smile. "I should-a known! Look, Taylor. I knew that she'd get to you! Get to you . . . sooner or later! One of these days! Or . . . more probably . . . one of these nights! Track you down . . . eventually. That she'd nail you . . . as we say! Sooner or later, I knew it would happen! Sooner or later . . . she gets to everyone! Screws everyone! Well, just guys! She royally screws 'em . . . as I understand it!"

"Look, Gretch . . ."

"Don't sweat it, Taylor! It was always just a matter of time! Simply a matter of time . . . before she got to you! Always! It was ever thus!"

"You . . . you . . . you mean . . . you mean you know about her?"

"Of course! Name me anyone, in town . . . any one person, in town . . . that doesn't. That doesn't know about Charlotte Klukay."

"God! I had no idea! No idea . . . that her reputation . . ."

"It's not a reputation. What we're talking about here . . . is a legend!"

"And . . . and . . . and you're not upset?"

"Well, let's just say . . . that I've had more welcome news, in my day. Am I surprised? Well, I'd certainly hoped that she'd have . . . ah . . . left you alone. But, deep down, I knew that this was an unrealistic aspiration. Especially with you living in the same building as she does, don'tcha know. But, hell, you could be living in Portland . . . probably . . . and she'd still have found you! She'd have gotten to you! Would've nailed you! Eventually. Did she . . . uh . . . how to put this? Did she . . . ah . . . have her way with you?"

"Yeah," I muttered. "But, I was asleep at the time! Asleep . . . through it all! Through the whole . . . the entire . . . performance! Honest! It was all part of a . . . part of a . . . well, part of a dream. Well, that's what I thought!"

"Must've been one helluva dream."

"Well . . . uh . . . yeah. That it was! By the time I really woke up . . . it was . . . it was . . . well, it was, you know, all over! She was out of bed, already. Was making a run for it! Gone!"

"But, you could see that it was Charlotte?"

"I'm guessing that it was Charlotte. I've never met her. Not formally, anyway. All I really saw . . . was someone's naked bottom! A naked woman's bottom! That much I could tell! Observed that . . . as she got the hell out! It was definitely a woman's bottom! And it was definitely naked! Definitely bare!"

"You should just see the look on your face," she responded—smiling broadly. "I can tell . . . that you could tell . . . that it was a woman's bare fanny!"

Her expression, at that point, turned more serious than any I'd ever experienced with her.

"Taylor, look." she continued. "I have no . . . ah . . . exclusive on you. We've never dated. We've never even held hands. You've never patted me on the fanny. Well, of course, I've never patted you on the fanny, either. We've never kissed. Nor have we ever done any of that other neat stuff. Again, I'm not thrilled . . . that you and Charlotte wound up playing Mattress Polo. But, you don't belong to me. Nor I to you. Now, if this is such an earthshaking thing . . . that you don't want to go out with me tomorrow, then all you have to do is to say so. I'm not gonna . . ."

"NO! No, I want to . . . really want to . . . to go out with you. It's just that . . . after last night . . . well, I just guess that I simply didn't know how to . . ."

"Well, if *Gone With The Wind* is all right with you . . . then, it's all right with me. There may be even some fanny-patting included in the mix. Between us! Not "Rhett" and "Scarlett"! One never knows . . . dew one?"

I don't remember—ever—being so glad to hear anything! The GWTW part, I mean! I was figuring—hoping—that the "fanny-patting" thing might take care of itself. Eventually!

Let me tell you: I didn't figure to relax—until the big "Rhett"/"Scarlett" date would have taken place. And with good reason!

Somehow, I'd managed to get through the rest of Friday. Don't ask me how. Well, a friendly few minutes spent with Charlie McNulty—on our terraces—helped. Charlotte was not a part of the conversation. (My neighbor didn't ask—and I didn't tell. And neither one of us was in the military, at that moment.)

By Saturday morning, I was feeling slightly better. Especially after having acknowledged (to myself—and with great relief) that Friday night had, thankfully, represented a "Klukay-Free Zone"! Well, I guessed, it <u>figured</u> to be—given the far-flung, the unlimited, boundaries of the woman's "territory".

First thing, on that morning, I'd hauled myself out to the magnificent beach. It was only a little after seven-thirty—rather early, apparently, for the weekend crowd to be gathering. I plopped myself down—onto my tummy! Peace and harmony descended—immediately—upon my person.

Eventually—about a half-hour later—a group of four people set up their aluminum-and-plastic-strip chairs a mere two or three feet away from me. I'd thought <u>that</u> to be completely—totally, and curiously—unusual. Given the vast amount of glorious beach at their disposal—and they chose to "set up shop" next to <u>me</u>. When there was all this glorious <u>vacant</u> beach.

Cracking open one eye (don't ask me which one), I quickly interpreted the situation: Two young men—one seated at each end—and two nubile, scantily-clad, young women (I'd noticed) between them. Why they had decided to "establish operations" so close to my personal body was, as indicated, <u>not</u> so easily determined. The reason why they would've chosen the close proximity to a semi-sleeping, prone, person—like me, for instance—was beyond any logic. (There's that "L-Word" again!)

Ah well! It wasn't that big a deal. I went back to my fairly-successful (till then) pursuit of nodding off.

I was on the precipice of realizing that lofty goal—when I felt an ungodly tug! At the back of my trunks! An ungodly—and a highly-successful—tug! A rather-violent sea breeze seemed to have—quite suddenly—churned in from the ocean! This veritable "hurricane" had—immediately—wafted in! Big time! A brisk zephyr—gyrating across my suddenly-naked rear end! I'd been "de-panted"! Successfully (and quickly) de-panted! The picture of efficiency!

Both girls giggled—loudly! The guys burst into roaring laughter—even more loudly!

I'd had presence of mind—to not have rolled over. (Such a display of wisdom! It may never fall that way again.)

Standing above me—looming over me, lurking over me—stood what had to have been the celebrated Ms Klukay! (I'd only beheld her elegant butt, don'tcha know—as she'd hastily departed some thirty-six or thirty-seven hours before! But, you can see the spirit in which my opinion was formed. Even in such haste!)

There she stood! Hands on hips! Smiling—broadly! She was a pretty lady—a very pretty lady—once a person was fortunate enough to see the entire package! The entire (would you believe?) "clothed" package! I don't know whether she was "clad", in what has come to be known—as a string bikini. I really don't know if string bikinis even existed, in 1965. But, let me assure you: There wasn't much to this revealing little number—in which she was decked out!

By comparison, the suits that the two other girls were wearing—both of which were, I'm positive, bikinis—those frocks looked almost like nuns' habits! (Well, not quite!)

"Nice roll in the hay, Taylor-Baby," this tugger-of-trunks opined. "You do remember the other night, do you not?" Ms Klukay's voice simply reeked of sex! "Helluva bed, by the bye! Helluva bed!" She patted me twice—then smacked me once (a mustard-laden lick)—on my uncovered posterior. "Who'd-a thunk it?", she'd continued. "Who'd-a-thunk that a guy like you would have that . . . such a neat-o fleet-o . . . bed? A round bed! Who'd-a thunk it?"

A guy like me? What the hell does that mean?

This "unusual"—this suddenly-uncovered-buttocks—encounter had brought forth the first words that this obvious-celebrity had ever spoken to me! (It was probably about time—given our "history".)

So saying, she bounded away. I had, pretty much, been turned into a Biblical-type "pillar of salt", by the surprising, out-of-the-blue, encounter! Totally unable to move, speak, think—or anything else. I just stared at that almost-naked—very-well-put-together—bottom, as it flounced its way up the beach! (Maybe "writhed its way up the beach" would be a good deal more accurate.)

"Uh," muttered one of the nearby girls, "you might want to think about pulling up your suit, there, Taylor-Baby."

Oh! Oh, yeah!

As it turned out, that was a capital idea. One upon which I'd immediately acted—at long last. (Mind like a steel trap, as you can see.)

Then—at even <u>longer</u> last—it occurred to me that protocol, for such an event, (if such protocol exists) would call for me to apologize. Especially to the girls.

"Uh," I mumbled, "look. Look ; . . . I'm awfully sorry that . . ."

"Don't give it a second thought," responded the man in the chair nearest the water. "Happens all the time. Kinda like a 'rite of passage', around these parts. Almost always takes place . . . after ol' Charlotte has chalked up a new person. Celebration . . . of a brand new victim."

"Besides," added the young lady, two seats away, "you've got a great <u>bum</u> there, Taylor-Baby!"

"<u>Bum</u>"! That was the word—the very word that Elena had always used—when referring to that portion of the anatomy. A <u>monumental</u> tug—this time on the old heartstrings! Why could this lady not have simply said "ass"? Like, practically, everyone else? <u>That</u> word, I would've welcomed.

I guessed that there really <u>was</u> no place to run! To get, completely, <u>away</u> from such continually-troubling utterances—and/or events. Well, I deduced, "you can run . . . but, you can't hide"! Would "The Guys" have gotten <u>their</u> finger(s) involved—in <u>her</u> use of that all-too-sensitive word?

I'd wound up engaging in a, for-the-most-part, eminently-forgettable conversation with the quartet of fellow tenants. None of them were married, I was to learn. And they'd all lived in apt. 407. I'd had no idea (still don't) as to who might've been sleeping with whom. Or if their situation might've been—ah—"Catch As Catch Can" (as we say).

As the morning had worn on, many other people began to populate that wondrous beach. Most of them appeared to be couples. (Or, hell, in some cases, quartets. Well, there were some trios—seemingly. In more than a few instances.) They all appeared to be leading a lifestyle that was identical to my original quartet of neighbors/observers from the fourth floor.

The word "swinger" may not have reached its full popularity, in the mid-sixties. But, it was "around". Even I had heard it mentioned. I even actually knew what the term meant. (An upset—of major proportions.)

Was this entire complex—except for me and good ol' Charlie—comprised, exclusively, of people who were actually devoted (devoutly devoted) to the worthy cause of "swinging"? Was this "the wave of the future"? In 1965, the concept was still rather new. (To me, anyway.)

A continuing "puzzlement": All related to most of the other tenants' lifestyles. Did that crowd, from #407, sit so close to me—because they knew that dear Charlotte was going to perform her traditional "bare the bum" act? Were they all—were every one of my fellow tenants—of one, singular, mindset? Dedicated—sincerely—to one "communal" lifestyle? Was every one of them projecting (and protecting) this monumentally "enlightened" way of life—strictly devoted to being "sexually liberated"?

And—if that actually was the case (I'm probably the least-perceptive person you'll ever meet)—then, surely "The Guys", up there, must have been aware of these rather bizarre "rituals"! (<u>Rather</u>?) They <u>had</u> to have been informed of the overwhelming "swinging" lifestyles—of so many (if not <u>all</u>) of my neighbors. Been <u>aware</u> of these staggering, overwhelming, facts! <u>Must</u> have known—of <u>all</u> of this! (<u>Mustn't</u> they?)

Well, we finally <u>made</u> it! "Gretch" and Taylor—their monumental first date! Actually, there wasn't <u>all</u> that much that was so durn-fooled earth-shaking—or even high-falutin'—about the celebrated get-together.

Don't get me wrong. The movie was <u>great</u>! There wasn't a heck of a lot of fanny-patting going on. Not between my date and me, anyway. (We <u>were</u> seated most of the time, don't you see. Makes that little worthwhile endeavor somewhat difficult.)

But, I <u>did</u> have my arm around her/ Well, during most of the long picture, anyway. (Until it fell asleep, anyway. Then, we switched—to merely a goodly amount of shameless hand-holding.)

Afterward, I suggested a small neighborhood bar/ restaurant. She advised me that she wasn't hungry. (We'd both packed away a bountiful amount of popcorn. Topped with all that "healthful", "authentic", grease, that they seriously—and expensively—continue to refer to as "butter".)

"Besides," she'd added, "I spend my whole life in a restaurant. One that does not provide the benefit of booze. I would use the alcoholic stuff . . . natch . . . for purely medicinal purposes. There are times, y'know . . . when I'm positive that I've seen a snake crawling around, out there in the parking lot."

Obviously, my date was not intrigued by my suggestion.

I ferried this nice lady home. (OH! She <u>loved</u> my "tank of a car", by the bye.) She even invited me in. She lived in a small, white-shingled, bungalow—about six blocks from the beach. Neat little place. Almost "intimate", one might say.

I took her up on the invite—and got to meet the celebrated, world-famous, Fanny. This was the nicest doggie I'd ever met. I don't recall ever having crossed paths with a Golden Retriever before. My loss. This was an old dog. Her snoot, I guess, had long lost its brownish hue. Had turned to a "dignified gray"—as Gretchen had put it. She also referred to the nifty, venerable, pooch—as "The Head of The House".

My hostess (the one with the fewest legs) was, it turned out, a very <u>interesting</u> woman. More so than I'd ever guessed—from merely our free-form give-and-take, at the eatery. The dog's name notwithstanding.

Thankfully, "Gretch" didn't ask if I'd had any further run-ins with our sainted neighborhood nympho.

I didn't feel honor-bound to give her a play-by-play description, vis-a-vis having had my trunks yanked down—"in front of God and everybody"—earlier that day.

Gretchen was more into music than she had let on. <u>My</u> kind of music, too! (Aka "Schmaltz"!) She possessed a <u>marvelous</u> collection of LP records. More than half featuring "Stereo Sound"! (Those were about as high-tech as we'd ever gotten, back in those Neanderthal days. It would be a year or two, before I'd ever <u>learn</u> of those new-fangled "miracle wonders"—known as 8-track tapes.)

Well, truth to tell, there <u>were</u> more sophisticated devices. Ways to improve a person's "listening and dancing pleasure". I'd just not known of them. For instance, an unimagined inspection—as would be advised by my date (on that very night)—had never occurred to me: Probably <u>should</u> have—but, never <u>did</u>. "Gretch" recommended that I check out the back of <u>my</u> "inherited" stereo.

"There <u>should</u> be," she explained, "a couple of openings back there. Little round holes. They can be used to hook up, for instance, a reel-to-reel tape deck. That way . . . if you were to go out and buy a tape deck . . . you could record whatever you wished, off your records. Or even off the radio. Put 'em all on a reel-to-reel tape. Then, you'd be able to listen to 'em . . . whatever you damn <u>pleased</u> . . . <u>whenever</u> you damn pleased. It'd be awfully easy to install. I could even help you . . . if you'd wish."

She'd already detected how "un-inclined" I am—both mechanically and electronically. (To me, remember, a rubber band—is a machine.)

A <u>real</u> bonus: She knew all the lyrics—to virtually every song on the Original Cast recordings of *South Pacific, Sound of Music, Oklahoma!, Carousel, Brigadoon, Annie Get Your Gun, Finian's Rainbow, My Fair Lady,* and *Fanny! Fiddler On The Roof* was still a little bit too new—to get a real handle on. So were *Hello Dolly, Funny Girl* and *Mame.*

She's the only person I've ever met—that would know the words to *I'm In Love With An Octopus.* That melodic, will-live-forever, ditty was featured in *Fanny*. ("The show named after my dog"—as she'd hastened to inform me. On more than one occasion.)

We sat up till almost three-thirty—singing virtually every song, on (literally) every one of those Broadway LPs. Let me tell you: It was great!

The fanny-patting pace also picked up! Noticeably! As the time had scampered by. *I'm In Love With An Octopus* will—trust me—do that to/for you. Well, it did for us! We were, I guess, just a couple of romantic fools!

By the time that I'd finally dragged my iron-lunged, raw-throated, well-patted, rear end out of there, we'd engaged in a long, languid, not-really-sensuous, kiss! But, it was more—much more—than a mere "peck-on-the-cheek". Don't get me wrong, I'd enjoyed it. But, relative to what I'd experienced with the lips of Elena—especially on that one magical morning in the Valiant—this buss was anything but overly earthshaking. (It was enjoyable, though.)

As indicated, the date—in total—was great! The whole evening and night turned out to be wonderful!

The only thing that I really hoped for—as I snapped my condo's door into the "lock" position, that night/early morning—was to avoid another collision, with one Charlotte Klukay! Of course it was quite late. On the other hand, I'd had no idea as to what her "store hours" would've been.

Maybe I should . . . as Charlie suggested . . . get me a two-by-four! Bolt the damn door . . . with one of those suckers!

Of course—as Charlie had also posited—she could come in through the damn window! Nothing, though, was going to shake the satisfaction—the welcomed contentment—that the evening with "Gretch" had brought about.

More untroubled than I'd been in a long time, I'd dropped off—immediately—into a deep sleep! Zonked out—as soon as I'd dropped off my clothes. I would make it through the remainder of the night— unmolested. For that, I was thankful! Truly thankful!

Sunday morning found me up and staggering about. And not a moment later than eleven o'clock. The beach was already pretty well populated. (Not a whole lot of church-goers in that crowd. A fact—of which "The Guys" also must have been aware. Was their intent—to have me convert this sinning throng of "pagans"? Boy! Did they have the wrong boy! Me? Me! A bona fide schmuck!)

I made my daily schlep out onto those wondrous sands. Plopped down (again)—on my tummy (again)—in the most sparsely populated portion of the beach possible. I was building a pretty nifty tan, by then.

As I'd lain there, images of the previous night's date kept dancing through my quite-at-peace mind. I had to acknowledge that I'd been absolutely fascinated by Gretchen. By who she was. And

why the night before had been such a surprise—
especially "Schmaltz"-wise.

This undying interest that I have always had—
this out and out obsession with hokey music—has,
continually, been something that has, without fail,
remained tremendously important to me. Critical, you
might say. To the point of—literal—addiction. And
this wrapped-up-in-schmaltz situation has been with
me—from the time I was a little kid. Seven—or eight-
years-old. Maybe younger. Probably younger.

Having been a "music nut"—literally all my life—I'd
been sorely disappointed, when it became evident
that Joanne had merely tolerated my love of, and for,
that kind of music.

Elena! Elena, I believe, had felt most of the
more tender lyrics! The way that I did. The way that
I always had. Listening to the beautiful music with
her—had comprised some of the most rewarding,
most happy, experiences of my life. I missed that! I
missed her!

I doubted, though, that I'd ever see her again.
Not in my lifetime! Never in my lifetime! Yet another
major frustration! I found myself suddenly overcome
with a vast, all-pervading, sadness! An empty, bleak,
weariness! There it went! The old contentedness!

Maybe my crossing paths with Gretchen had
provided some kind of halfway logical explanation—
pertaining to my new life! Pertaining to my new
venue!

Maybe "The Guys" knew that she was here. Well,
undoubtedly they knew! Maybe all the swingers—and
the obligatory, well-put-together, nympho—maybe
they were merely the "price" one has to pay. The

"currency"! Maybe all these esoteric goings-on—the "culture" that completely surrounded me—was the "cost" of finding my true love. (Well, the "true love"—the one, this side of Elena.)

If that's the case, "Guys" . . . then, thank you1

That neat Saturday night notwithstanding, I was not at all comfortable—not totally, anyway—when it came to the thought of a potentially serious relationship with "Gretch". And, dammit, I wasn't sure why! Why should I be so uncomfortable? Especially when a relationship such as this one would seem to be exactly "what the doctor ordered" for my fragile psyche?

Joanne was—for sure—out of my life. Way out of my life! As far as my former wife was concerned—as far as she knew—I was dead! (Even before "The Guys" would've faked my death—I was as good as dead, from an emotional standpoint, anyway.)

The saddest part of this particular, this latest, "puzzlement"—although I didn't know exactly how it would've fit into the equation (Gretchen-wise)—had to do with my kids! My four kids! For one thing, I missed them! Missed them—terribly! Thought about them! Thought of them—consistently! Pictured them! Pictured them—constantly!

There was—as you may well understand—this constantly-troubling, terribly-haunting, always-with-me, discomfort, concerning my children: THEY—sadly—also thought that I was in the grave. My own kids! And they'd all thought that I—their father—was past tense! Out of their lives—forever! Forever!

Well, hell! I guess I was! I was, most assuredly, not a part of their existence! Not anymore! I had no idea—not the slightest—as to how happy they might be. (Or how unhappy?) As you can probably imagine, this stifling burden, not knowing—having no idea—of the welfare of my children, was a tough load to lug around! The exceedingly heavy yoke—as it were—around my neck! And the problem was becoming worse—more overpowering—by the day!

The whole situation—whenever I'd devote a significant amount of time to thinking about it—was absolutely (and continually) out and out shattering, to/for me. I'd found myself struggling—to keep such disturbing thoughts away from my overheated, troubled, mind. But, seldom with much success. They are—at least, were—my own flesh-and-blood! Dear Lord!

Well, I'd concluded (and, fortunately or otherwise, that turned out to be a real help) Joanne wouldn't need to be a consideration. Still, there was a tinge of concern when it came to my wife! More than a tinge—of regret!

The problem was—that Elena shouldn't be a consideration. But, she was! She remained! In spades! And she would continue to be!

When it came to these two good women, I was, supposedly, dead to one—and I was some 1200 or 1500 miles from the other. (To Elena, I was—let's face it—as good as deceased! And that was whether or not "The Guys" had seen fit to advise her of my "demise"! That was, also, an unsettling "puzzlement"!

Another one! A troubling situation, that I probably—
that I <u>undoubtedly</u>—should've paid more attention to,
going in.)

Maybe <u>that</u> was it! <u>Probably</u> that was it! I'd reached
a point—where I'd considered Elena to be my one
true love. Was I being unfaithful to <u>her</u>? Betraying
her—in even <u>considering</u> a relationship with another
woman? <u>Any</u> other woman? Gretchen—or anyone
<u>else</u>?

<u>Come on, Taylor</u>!

That immensely-stupid line of "reasoning" went
against everything that we're all supposed to hold
holy. <u>All</u> of us! Well, if not holy—then, at least, logical.
(Of course, logic has never been my strong suit. Have
I mentioned that before?)

I finally became convinced that—beginning a
relationship with Gretchen would render me as being
unfaithful! I would be, I felt, <u>cheating</u>—on Elena!

TEN

AS THE WEEKS—AT LEAST a few of them—had gone by, I'd started to, pretty much, "settle in". As "settled" as things generally got for me.

The situation was beginning to get more than a little serious with Gretchen, I was finding. And the relationship was becoming a source of quiet unease for me. I was not destined, I'd believed, to possess the ability to handle a serious relationship—with "Gretch", or anyone else. Not "equipped" to engage in one. Not at that point, in my life. There were a whole host of reasons, I was positive, for that mindset. But, I'd have been at a complete and utter loss—if you were to have asked me to list one.

My waitress friend appeared to pose a threat, to what I was beginning to count on. That commodity is called stability. And I didn't know why Gretchen's pronounced presence, in my life, should be so disconcerting.

For one thing, I don't know why I would not have figured as much—right from the git-go—but, she was a whole lot "deeper" than I'd first envisioned. I guess

<u>that</u> fact was part of the problem. There was more to her—<u>much</u> more—than simply batting around her dog's name.

For some reason, I'd simply assumed that, on any given day—once her shift would be over—she'd just go on home, and (first thing) remove her girdle. (Right from the start, she'd continually informed—and never failed to remind—me, of this one ever-present, unassailable, Playtex fact. That vital—that critical—fact being: "The damn thing's <u>always</u> killing me".)

I'd always figured that she'd simply—hurriedly—divest herself of such an unreasonable restraint. Then, just plop herself down (in whatever manner of dress, or undress, she'd choose)—in front of the ol' Sylvania "Halo-Light" TV. (That <u>was</u> a really neat set, by the bye.) And, finally, she'd complete the picture—by putting her feet up on the coffee table. She would have—by then—placed her mind in Neutral.

Inexplicably, the uncomplicated, overly-simplified, image had always offered a certain amount of—well, of contentment—for me.

Not so! She was <u>anything</u>—but, that cut-and-dried.

For one thing, she'd had seasons tickets—to what they'd called "The Civic Light Opera". Fortunately, the organization had maintained a pretty liberal ticket policy. Especially as related to long-time subscribers, for the entire season. Gretchen had been a season's ticket holder—for years.

Once she and I had started to date, we'd always attend these wonderful productions. Never missed. The powers that be would give her full credit for her seat—then, sell us a pair of side-by-side ducats.

We'd usually wind up maybe six or eight rows behind her "normal" seat. Always good placement. Great people—with whom to deal.

We got to see—to behold—<u>glorious</u> performances of: *The Student Prince, The New Moon, The Vagabond King, Rosemarie* and *Music In The Air.* All of these—positively <u>reeking</u> of schmaltz music! The whole program was, of course, right up my alley! I <u>loved</u> each and every one of those remarkable performances!

Two weekends each month—this brilliantly-talented troupe put on these dazzling productions. They'd presented some of the most amazing live entertainment—that I'd ever beheld. These gems were presented—at the local high school auditorium. The ticket prices were a little high—but, were certainly far from being even the slightest bit unreasonable. They'd simply <u>had</u> to charge a lot. Patronage at these musical wonders were (alas!) deplorably low. (Damn!)

With "Gretch", I found myself enjoying a surprisingly-bountiful "social life". Unlike anything I'd ever experienced before. Thanks, "Guys"! (Still, there <u>was</u> this underlying—this unexplainable—degree of unease. Go figure!)

I may be fibbing just a little bit—about the <u>newness</u> of the new-found "social life". But, this situation <u>was</u> unlike anything I'd known before.

Truthfully, as pertains to the pure "enjoyment" portion, of my newly-discovered "social lion" existence, I'd actually kind of "been there/done that" before. To a point, anyway. How-ever-miniscule those scenes, from my storied past, might've been.

You see, Elena and I had "shamelessly" ventured out four whole times. "Dates", I guess you could call them—although we never did. Four entire times—in our troubled, post-Thunderbolt, lives—did we "go out steppin'".

- That first "date" found us having dinner at a *Denny's*-type restaurant, in "Beautiful Downtown San Antonio". I was certain that they were going to throw us out. The meal developed into one of those things where someone, inevitably, says something stupid. (In our case, I don't remember who performed that service. Or what was said.) But, we'd started laughing! Both of us! Uncontrollably! And, as always happens, just when we'd thought that we'd gotten the hysterics completely under control—one of us would burst out laughing again. And so, we were back to "square one"! Never had a stupid meal been that "exciting" before. Nor since! At least, not for me.
- Our second "outrageous" get-together found us venturing out, to see a movie—*It's A Mad, Mad, Mad World*. One of the funniest flicks I'd ever seen. It featured a starring cast that was overwhelming. And every one of those people performed remarkably. We'd both enjoyed the laugh-filled package. We did (shamelessly) hold hands—throughout the entire duration of the exceptional "mo'om pitcher".

- The third foray found us attending a live—an utterly <u>brilliant</u>, highly-professional—road company performance of Lionel Bart's classical, remarkable, *Oliver.* Jules Munshin's performance as "Fagan" was one of the most outstanding I've ever witnessed. The high point of the entire evening for me, however, turned out to be the heart-rending—the totally unexpected—invisible "door"! This was the magical portal that <u>I'd</u> opened wide! Opened—for <u>Elena</u>! She'd never known from such things as Broadway musicals. Hadn't been aware that they'd even existed. Joanne knew of them, of course. In spades! And, apparently, she had always been totally unimpressed. She and I had seen numerous musicals in Detroit: *My Fair Lady, Guys & Dolls, The Music Man* and *South Pacific* among others. Neither schmaltz—nor live theatre—(as previously indicated) had ever been my spouse's forte. Elena, on the other hand, had sat—in total, complete-and-utter, awe! <u>Enraptured</u>—from curtain up, to curtain down! I believe that I'd spent most of the evening watching <u>her</u>—as opposed to what was happening on the stage. The next day, she <u>bought</u> me the LP of the Original Cast offering, of the show. Obviously, we practically wore out that poor, overworked, vinyl record, over the next few weeks.
- Our fourth—and, sadly, our <u>final</u>—journey-into-the-forbidden was, by far, the most emotional. By <u>far</u>! Joanne was beginning to suspect, by then, that something was, very definitely, amiss and amuck. I'd lied to her the first few times. Told her

that I was chasing delinquent debtors—at their residences. (That had been the truth on most occasions, when I was late coming home. I had been experiencing a fairly-serious delinquency problem—and I truly was spending a goodly amount of time chasing deadbeats.). After that glorious production of *Oliver*, though—when I didn't get in till about eleven-thirty—I hadn't said anything. Neither had Joanne. Communication with each other, by then, was "fer-sure" not our "thing". On this most special night, Elena and I—and another couple (acquaintances of hers)—had wound up, at an "intimate" little bar, northwest of town. Let me tell you: For all of my life, I'd never been able to dance! Not with anyone! Not ever! Inevitably, I'd look down, and—making their appearance—would be two left feet. Without fail! Without exception! Joanne, on the other hand, had—always and forever—been a wonderful dancer. As you can imagine, I'd been a constant, major, disappointment, to/for her, on the old dance floor. With Elena—I could dance! YEAH! ME! I could dance! ("Look, Ma! I'm dancin'! I'm dancin'!) I don't maintain that I'd ever make you forget Fred Astaire—or, probably, even "Fred Mertz"—but, dammit, I was good! Really! Damn good, actually! And Elena and I—we danced our hooves off that night! Finally, as it turned out, our final dance became the "Crown Jewel", of that remarkable, "enchanted", evening. We were dancing—exquisitely, I might add—to Percy Faith's recording of *Till*. And, as Mr. Faith's male chorus was singing the beautifully-tender lyric—emanating from the juke box—I was holding Elena! Holding her tightly—<u>very</u> tightly! And I was whispering those same tender, sentimental, words into her ear. She sighed (heavily)—and clung, <u>tightly</u>, to me. We had never "melded"—not like <u>that</u>—before! <u>Ever</u>! It was (probably) a good thing that the other couple was <u>with</u> us! Because—if this wonderful woman and I were to <u>ever</u> have become intimate—<u>that</u> would've been the night. (That indescribable—that incredibly troubled, that storied—Saturday night, on her front porch, notwithstanding.)

When I'd gotten home, on that memorable night—<u>well</u> after midnight—I finally "came clean". Told Joanne about Elena—and what I'd felt for her! The overwhelming love that I'd harbored for her! The <u>overwhelming</u> love! (I probably <u>used</u> that word a dozen-or-so times!)

I don't want to say that "everything went downhill from there". Our situation had been in one manner of an over-the-cliff plunge—or another—for the better part of a couple years, at that point! The marriage had—continually, whether Joanne realized it or not—been caught up in a real, true, freefall! Into a bottomless pit! <u>This</u>—this night to end all nights—had been just the maraschino cherry! Atop the whole furschlugginer sundae!

Back to my encounters with Gretchen. Outside of that one, totally-moving, performance of *Oliver*, I don't think I'd ever enjoyed any live productions—as much as I'd reveled in those of "The Civic Light Opera", in Newport. Their consistently-wonderful work with those glorious old—schmaltzy-as-hell—operettas were a constant source of joy for me. Well, for both of us.

As mentioned, "Gretch" was a helluva lot "deeper" than I'd first thought. She'd advised me that the movie house—the one at which we'd taken in *Gone With The Wind*—had sustained a once-a-month program, where they would show an old, bona fide, silent movie. She'd also never missed one of those! They were great sport!

The first one that we'd attended together turned out to be—as the master of ceremonies had announced, to a goodly number of chuckles—"A Silent Musical". This magnificently-directed work was titled *Men Of Heidelberg*—the story from which Sigmund Romberg's remarkable *The Student Prince* was taken.

The flick starred Gene Hersholt. This distinguished gentleman went on to become a well-known personality—*Dr. Christian*—in the close-to-follow "talkies". And then, on the radio—with Rosemary DeCamp, as his costar. The silent movie was great! Much more entertaining than I would've imagined.

It wasn't long, before I found myself spending—almost literally—every evening at non-girdled Gretchen's.

The two of us would sing along with three or four (or five or six) LPs of Original Cast recordings—Broadway musicals (or, maybe, even a Hollywood sound track or six).

We also waged great Chinese Checker wars. This was the one game—at which <u>both</u> of us were pronouncedly proficient. She'd beat the pants off of me (well, not literally) in Pinochle. And I would "return the favor" in Rummy. I usually won in Scrabble—and she always did well in Canasta.

Eventually, we came to realize that those "contests" weren't much fun. Chinese Checkers was—most definitely—our game. I think I won as many as I lost—when it came to those wondrous competitions. It was close, however. Just about a win-one/lose-one situation—for both of us—every night.

I was becoming more and more taken with this woman. Which, as mentioned, had never ceased to lend a troubling degree, to the situation. For me, in any case. I don't know if my partner was picking up on these always-just-beneath-the-surface emotions or not. But, for whatever reason, it remained in the mix!

It wasn't helping that—on a few occasions—one of my hostess' LPs would pour forth a song; one that had been special to Elena and me. There were <u>not</u> that many! But, there <u>were</u> a few! And I'm <u>certain</u> that my demeanor would've changed—noticeably—when one of <u>those</u> would pour out of the speaker.

Especially troubling was the fact that, on one of those vinyl treasures of hers, was the song *Somewhere*—from *West Side Story*! Whenever that song had played—at our hokey little loan office in San Antonio—everything had <u>stopped</u>, for Elena and me! The hopeful lyric had spoken—ever so beautifully—of "A place for us". And—deep down—we <u>must</u> have known that there <u>was</u> no "place for us". <u>None</u>! None <u>whatever</u>!

The haunting song ends—with the boy singing, "Hold my hand/And I'll take you here/Hold my hand/ And we're halfway there". How I'd always <u>wished</u> that I <u>could</u> "take her hand"—and actually "take her there". <u>Very</u> frustrating! <u>Heartbreaking</u>! For <u>both</u> of us! <u>Constantly</u>! <u>Continually</u>!

For reasons—which I <u>still</u> do not understand, not altogether, anyway—It took Gretchen and me "forever" to actually become intimate. A sexual relationship simply seemed <u>not</u> to be an accepted thing between the two of us—despite what the fast-expanding "culture" would've appeared to have dictated. For what <u>ever</u> reason, we'd not been to bed! Not until five or six whole, entire, seven-day, weeks had passed. (It <u>may</u> even have been a tad longer. I <u>should</u> know! But, I <u>don't</u>!)

Our sexual hi-jinks began at <u>her</u> place, though! (That, I <u>do</u> remember!) And—once "the dam had overflowed"—it became an every-night thing! (Well, for the most part, anyway.)

I know! Listen, I've always had a pretty good head for remembering names, places, and dates. By all logic, the first time Gretchen and I would ever have had sex, should've been <u>forever</u> emblazoned in the ol' gourd. But I <u>honestly</u> don't think that either one of us recognized that we were "in the ol' sack"—until we were actually "<u>in</u> the ol' sack". (Some could—possibly <u>would</u>—maintain, "Maybe not even <u>then</u>"!)

I guess you could say that the much-delayed intimacy turned out to be a "natural progression".

That, probably, would be the most plausible—most accurate—"diagnosis". (I suppose.)

On the other hand, our relationship had taken on a weird—probably grotesque—dimension! Well before that auspicious, bona fide, premier-sexual-encounter occasion, we had seen one another in the altogether! Seen the other—buck naked! Early and often—as we say. "How could this be?" you might well ask. (Well—mightn't you?)

On this one "magical" evening—between Chinese Checkers, and the LP of *Finian's Rainbow*—she got to telling me about her "theatrical career". About her (ah) rather X-rated "career"—and about her very straight-laced parents.

Her father—who'd passed away six or eight months before I'd met "Gretch"—had been a lay-preacher, in a little church at the eastern edge of Newport.

Upon her father's death, her mother—who was every bit as morally "correct" as Gretchen's dad had been—had moved in with her maiden sister, in a suburb of Portland.

Two or three years before her father's passing, however, Gretchen had joined a "progressive" theater company, in Newport. She'd always wanted to be in "show biz". This rewarding, fulfilling, "vocation" had been, she'd explained, a lifelong "calling" for her.

Many years before, she'd been a part of two of her high school's "Broadway Shows" casts: *Oklahoma!* and *Carousel*. Her roles in both Rodgers & Hammerstein productions had been quite minor. She'd "lusted in her heart"—to have been able to play the role of "Ado Annie" (a lady of "rather questionable morals")—In *Oklahoma!*.

To her extreme distress, once she'd graduated, it seemed to her as though—tragically—those two scholastic musicals were to have been "<u>it</u>"! They, apparently, had made up her whole—her entire—"theatrical career"! For <u>life</u>! She may not have been heartbroken. But this seemingly-inescapable fact <u>was</u> extremely frustrating for her.

Then, in 1960 or 1961, she'd joined this amateur theatrical group. This "really progressive" troupe. She'd actually taken to calling it a "cult".

"Which is not to say that I didn't <u>enjoy</u> myself there," she would always add—and very quickly—"I'd always had a <u>ball</u> with them! The problem was that there were too <u>many</u> balls! Too many <u>balls</u> present . . . and too often."

"Are you meaning this . . . the way I <u>think</u> you're meaning it? I mean . . . <u>balls</u>?"

She nodded! Rather exuberantly!

The group, you see, was doing this one play—an "epic" that one of the troupe's members had penned. The "work" had to do with "a house of horizontal pleasure"—as Gretchen always described it. A house of ill-repute. Yeah! One of <u>those</u> houses! <u>This</u> one catered to <u>both</u> genders!

"Gretch" did <u>not</u> have a speaking part. She'd simply appeared. With numerous other non-speaking people—of both sexes! Hers was a "stage presence"—as she described it. That <u>presence</u>, though, was (in her words) "very dramatic"! She'd been "scantily attired"—in the first five or six group scenes. Usually, these gatherings took place in the "lobby" of the brothel. Incidental interchange—by a select few members of the cast. Mostly, with the madam. Every now and then, there'd be a snippet of conversation with one of the paying "clients"—of both genders.

"I really didn't think that my parents could've known . . . <u>ever</u> have known . . . about the thing," she'd explained. "I figured that they never would've <u>heard</u> of such a thing. But, <u>somehow</u>, they did! Somehow, they <u>had</u>! How they ever found out about it . . . is <u>still</u> beyond me. So, this one night, they were gonna surprise me, you know! Gonna surprise their virginal little girl! Their pure-as-the-driven-snow little <u>thespian</u>! It was a <u>surprise</u>, all right! For <u>everyone</u>! And <u>that's</u> putting it <u>mildly</u>!"

"I can imagine."

"No you <u>can't</u>1 Not only did <u>they</u> attend . . . my parents . . . but, they'd brought along <u>another</u> couple! The Webbs were also <u>very</u> religious! The subject matter . . . . well, and <u>plus</u> the many, many, many four-letter words . . . <u>those</u> were bad enough. But, for Mother and Dad to see their darling, innocent, <u>daughter</u> . . . their own sheltered little <u>girl</u> . . . sitting around in this diaphanous outfit, was out and out <u>galling</u>. For all <u>four</u> of 'em. That was <u>before</u> all the naked bodies!"

"You're right! I <u>can't</u> imagine."

"Yeah. Well the <u>topper</u> was . . . when the hated police wound up <u>raiding</u> the joint! In the <u>play</u>, it was! There was this dramatic scene! The finale! And it's a <u>police</u> raid! A raid . . . wherein the cops are made out to be total bastards! Turned out . . . that Mom's and Dad's little girl was totally <u>naked</u> in that scene. So were five or six other girls! Not to mention four or five guys! All of which were exceptionally well-endowed! And . . . obviously . . . excited, at the time! Obviously excited!"

"Really? You were . . . were in the ol' buff? You? In the altogether? That's something else . . . that I can't imagine! Especially your being on stage! In front of all those people! In the raw!"

She nodded—emphatically! "I think," she continued, "I'm pretty sure that the guys, like I said, I think . . . all of 'em . . . they'd all had erections! Yeah." She allowed herself a closed-eyes, exceptionally-warm, smile. "Very definite erections! Couldn't hardly miss those! There wasn't one stitch of clothes . . . that any of us were wearing! Well, of course, that was too much! Way too much!"

"I can believe that!"

"Well I'd thought that they'd have had their fill . . . way before the finale! When all the nudity came, you can bet that my parents . . . and their guests . . . they walked out! Well, they stormed out! In the well-known huff! Made quite a scene! Wanted their money back! That wasn't gonna happen! Actually, at the time, I didn't even know . . . that it was them! I didn't know any of this! Not until I got The Phone Call the next day!"

"They weren't thrilled, hah?"

That's putting it mildly. Mother said she had to really restrain my father! Just short of physically confronting him! He was going to take his old razor strop! And he was gonna come over here! And he was gonna use it on me! Use it on me . . . liberally! Was hell-bent on . . ."

"Oh, surely he wouldn't . . ."

"Hah! You've never met my father. But, there was one thing that the experience . . . the experience with the theater group, not with my parents . . . one thing that it taught me! That it really drove home to me! And that was . . . that I'd enjoyed it!"

"Well, if you'd wanted to get into show biz, all your life, that was perfectly understandable!"

"I'm not talking about being in show biz! Not exclusively! It wasn't only the stupid theatrical career. The point is, that I'd. thoroughly, enjoyed the naked part!"

"Really? Being undressed . . . meant that much to you?"

"Yep!" Another exuberant nod. "Being naked! I thoroughly enjoyed it! Especially, I liked being bare . . . in the presence of others! Especially, if there was a whole bunch of others! Especially, if they were people . . . ones that I didn't know. The fact that these people were all total strangers! Great! I guess I've probably enjoyed it . . . well, at least the thought of it . . . for, literally, all my life. Does that upset you? Did I just gross you out?"

"Well . . . as sheltered a life as I've lived . . . I've never had the pleasure of being naked, in the presence of a whole bunch of others! I believe that I'm probably poorer . . . for that lack! I can see . . . where that'd be a real thrill! Naked! At least, I figure it could be!"

From that point on, the evening became a bit of a blur. I don't know how any of this ultimately came about. Don't exactly know who said what! Or to whom! But—in some kind of goofy unison—we'd both decided to remove our clothing! <u>Completely</u>! <u>Simultaneously</u>! And <u>unanimously</u>!

We sat—in "The Old Buff-o", as we say—singing along with Ella Logan and the others in the glorious "Finian's" production. From then on, she'd always be in the altogether—whenever I'd arrive. Without fail. And, surprisingly, "Look Ma! No distracting girdle imprints"!

As you might imagine, it never took me long to match her—in the nudity factor. It wasn't even a case of playing "Strip Chinese Checkers"! We would—without fail—be in the <u>raw</u>! Right from the git-go! Without <u>fail</u>!

And all of this "action" took place—<u>well</u> before we began our sexual adventures!

You hafta admit: This <u>was</u> an unusual relationship.

And, I guess you'd also have to say this: It didn't take long—before things between "Gretch" and me got a goodly amount even <u>more</u> strange!

For openers, once we'd pretty much settled in to our patented "Nude Chinese Checkers/Sing Along With The Original Cast" routine—these goofy feats of derring-do, always "performed" at her place—we suddenly decided to transfer most of these "wholesome" operations over to my condo. Don't ask me why.

Well, I guess that the primary cause for this change of venue, was that—once she'd discovered that I was the proud possessor of a round bed—

she'd developed a hankering to continue our sexual activities atop <u>that</u> esoteric facility.

For some reason or another, I'd never mentioned the bed (the shape of same) to her—for the better part of (I'm guessing) two months. I suppose that, maybe, I didn't want to appear "too forward".

As indicated before, my expertise—in dealing with females, of the opposite gender—was (at best) nil.

The actual, truth-to-tell, reason that "Gretch" had even <u>discovered</u> that "obscene" circular bed is as follows:

She'd come over to "help" me install the reel-to-reel tape deck that I'd bought. As mentioned, I'm "all thumbs" when it comes to such things. (I <u>did</u> manage to unpack that dandy new toy—but, my guest took over from there.)

She hooked the thing up—then, showed me how to record my hokey tunes, from those magnificent, "inherited", LPs. I was presented with the undreamed-of opportunity to record what looked like an endless stream of schmaltzy music, on one of those blessed reels. The sanctified latch-up worked out! Worked out—<u>beautifully</u>!

<u>Then</u>, came her resounding discovery of that round, esoteric, piece of furniture! The one which highlighted the bedroom! The <u>resounding</u> discovery!

An even <u>more</u> outrageous "augmentation" vis-a-vis our "social" lives was added the very <u>next</u> night: Beginning with that second get-together, in our new venue, we'd added another little fillip. (I'd barely survived the first one! She'd become a literal <u>tigress</u> in bed.)

However, having ground our animal-like way through that initial occasion, we began doing skinny-dip missions! Modest human beings—that we'd always been—we never failed to wear bathrobes to the beach. (What? Did you think we were <u>weird</u> or something?)

Plus, we'd always waited till <u>well</u> after dark. And we were—in every instance—<u>very</u> "discreet"!

I offer—as proof of that truth—the fact that we <u>never</u> disrobed under the high-powered, direct, beam of any of the many flood lights out there. In addition, we'd spent just about all of our time—on these exciting little forays—actually in the <u>water</u>. So, as far as we knew, we were doing all of this "outrageous"—this esoteric—stuff "on the sly". Was <u>that</u> clever—or what? (Crafty, fun-loving, ol' us. Hee-Hee!)

However, after five or six weeks of indulging in this rather risqué conduct, we received the <u>shock</u> of our lives: On this particular celebrated Thursday evening—at about ten-thirty (a few minutes after having returned from our nightly nude romp on the beach)—Gretchen and I were sitting there. Simply sitting there—minding our own business—and, of course, deeply involved in one of our patented, in-the-old-buff-o, hotly-contested, Chinese Checkers competitions.

Suddenly, this solace-laden, highly-peaceful, not-bothering-anyone, episode was noticeably disrupted! Noticeably! And somewhat violently!

The front door (well, the only door into or out of my humble little abode) exploded open! ("Exploded" is not an exaggeration! Well, not much of one.) And—seconds later—this lady burst into the room! This naked lady! Of course, it was none other than (who else?) the infamous Charlotte Klukay! (You'd guessed that, maybe?)

"OH!" she exclaimed. "I didn't know that you weren't alone, Taylor!"

That was strange! She seemed to know about everything else! Appeared to know everything—always! Everything about everyone else!

"Hi," she said. Listen, she never ceased advancing—relentlessly (and swiftly)—toward the two of us "poor civilians"! She thrust out her hand—to Gretchen. "Hi," she repeated. "I'm Charlotte."

"I know," answered my original guest. "Your reputation has preceded you. By . . . oh . . . by about four or five years. I'm Gretchen."

Was I the only one—in the whole damn room (in the whole damn complex, in the whole damn universe) who was totally uncomfortable? Completely nonplussed? Apparently! That seemed to be the unmistakable situation! Because "Gretch" invited our "added starter" to close the door—and to join us in our sans-clothing Chinese Checker endeavor. Of course,—from a strictly sartorial standpoint—she, sure as hell, was qualified.

I don't remember—ever—playing three-way Chinese Checkers. Certainly, not with two unclothed ladies. (I've, of course, played many games with four participants. Each one, however, had—stalwartly—left his/her clothes on. Killjoys all! Some kind of fanatics!)

Even after the three of us had "settled in"—to our first actual contest—there would be (of course) much more going on! More mind-bending events—than simply board game strategies! Boodles of additional stuff! Completely-unsettling happenings! Most-troubling things! Ones—that were totally unassociated with my highly-uncomfortable experiences in the currently-underway, three-sided, game! All of this, I guess, would've taken place—whether we'd been clothed or unclothed!

I'd never really gotten a look—a really close look—at our nude interloper! Not a really close, inventory-taking, look! Until she'd joined "Gretch" and me! Till she'd, demurely, seated herself there! She was—flat-out—beautiful! From head to toe! As well as all points between! Especially all points between! She appeared to be in her mid-thirties. Maybe late-thirties. Guessing women's ages—again, clothed or unclothed—has never been a particular talent of mine. Of course. there'd never been all that many opportunities to attempt to ply that desirable "talent". Especially, if the subject female was sans her clothes.

The silence—during the first game (and well into the second) was (as we say) deafening. (The winner of that initial contest, by the bye, was Charlotte. Gretchen and I had merely thought that we were unbeatable.)

Midway through our second "heated" contest, though, Gretchen asked the winner of the first one,

"How did you get your start, Charlotte? When did you begin . . . you know . . . how did you become a . . . a . . . a nymphomaniac?"

The query was a real barn-burner! At least for me! But, I'd remained the well-known pillar-of-salt—especially when it came to trying to speak—ever since our unclothed intruder had invaded the joint! It was, of course, a straight-forward question. One that had me almost ready to dive under the table.

"I dunno," came the frank, unemotional, answer. "Well, maybe, I do. I guess I do. You see, I was brought up . . . in a little town, in North Carolina. I believe that the main culture, there . . . among all the mothers of that day, at least in that town . . . was for the mothers, to scare the living shit out of their poor, innocent, daughters!"

"Scare their daughters?" I'd finally collected myself enough to ask what I'd hoped was a halfway-intelligent question. "Their poor, innocent, daughters? How would . . . ?"

"It's true! Scare the hell out of them! Terrorize them . . . as far as sex was concerned. My mother always told me . . . from the time I was eight or nine years old . . . what a horrible experience it was. How I should always be on my guard! Avoid it . . . at all costs! She couldn't even bring herself to actually say the word. It was, of course, a dirty word. The ultimate four-letter word . . . although there were only three letters! Not . . . ever . . . used, in the best of regulated families."

"Word? What word?" I wasn't doing too well—intelligent-wise.

"Why, <u>sex</u> of course! <u>Forbidden</u> word! Not <u>used</u> . . . like I said . . . in the best of regulated families. Of course, you only 'did it' . . . <u>did</u> this terrible, this <u>despicable</u> thing . . . whenever your husband would absolutely <u>insist</u>! <u>Never</u> . . . unless he positively <u>demanded</u> it! Then, you'd have to close your eyes . . . and grit your teeth . . . and prepare for the inevitable <u>onslaught</u>! Do your best, to <u>endure</u> the horrible . . . the God-awful . . . thing! 'Just lie there . . . till he'd had his <u>pleasure</u>'! Till he was, finally, <u>through</u> with you. You were nothing more than a damn <u>receptacle</u>! A receptacle . . . for his <u>lust</u>!"

"Gosh," muttered Gretchen. "That's a horrible thing! But, I can sort of understand. I kind of know . . . where you're coming from! <u>My</u> mother never brought the subject up either. Like, <u>ever</u>! When I got my first period, it scared the bejeebers out of me! Couldn't <u>imagine</u> what was happening to me! I thought . . . I seriously <u>believed</u> . . . that I was <u>bleeding</u> to death! Was <u>sure</u> . . . lead-pipe <u>certain</u> . . . that I was gonna <u>die</u>! Kick the <u>bucket</u>! Then and <u>there</u>! <u>Gone</u>! I was a <u>goner</u>!"

"Yep, I can relate," related Charlotte. "Can <u>totally</u> relate!"

"Mother," continued "Gretch". "finally gave me a few of the 'dirty' facts. Darn few! She simply told me that it was 'natural' . . . for a woman to <u>bleed</u> like that. And that I could expect it . . . every month, from then on. She also took the occasion to warn me . . . to not let <u>any</u> boy <u>ever</u> touch me! <u>Ever</u>! Something like that . . . should <u>never</u> happen! I had no idea . . . back then . . . as to what, in heaven's name, she was even <u>talking</u> about!"

"Really?" I was back among the present. "I can't believe that!"

"Believe it," responded "Gretch"—in a tone I'd never heard her use before! "I honestly think that . . . to this day . . . I really think that she believes that I'm still a virgin. Firmly believes that. Wants to, anyway. Fervently! Despite the fact she'd seen me . . . that one time . . . naked! Naked . . . on stage! With a bunch of other naked people. Boys and girls! But, despite that, I believe that she still holds on to the virgin thing!"

"Yeah," responded Charlotte—with a semi-smile. "All of that is familiar ground to me too. Familiar . . . over and over! Non-stop! But then, there was this one night! I was fifteen-years-old! And David Piper . . . he got to me! Really got to me! Got to me . . . but, good! In the back seat . . . of his father's brand new Oldsmobile! I still recall the new-car smell. I also recall a lot of other things! A whole lot of other things!"

An oh-so-quick, reminiscent, smile took over her gorgeous features. She was, obviously, savoring the memory.

"I put up a pretty good fight," she continued. "At first, anyway! Then, all of a sudden, it occurred to me that . . . this might not so bad after all! It was like I was having some kind of a . . . well, I having this huge awakening! This overwhelming awakening! Started asking myself why am I fighting like this? Why am I fighting at all?"

"Don't tell me," interjected Gretchen. "Let me guess."

Charlotte smiled—broadly. "'Hey,' I thought. 'This might not be such bad duty, <u>after</u> all! So, I went ahead . . . and let 'er rip! Well, what I did . . . was I allowed <u>David</u> to let 'er rip! I still didn't have all that much of an idea . . . really hadn't the foggiest clue . . . as to how to proceed, y'know. Not at that point, anyway. So, I just simply laid back . . . and let <u>him</u> show me the way! And, of course, I <u>enjoyed</u> it! Enjoyed the <u>hell</u> out of it! Like they say you're <u>supposed</u> to do . . . if it's inevitable! That's what the situation seemed like! To <u>me</u>, anyway! Inevitable as hell! And, I guess, the die was cast! And a <u>glorious</u> die it was! <u>Has</u> been . . . ever since! <u>Glorious</u>!"

"Purely understandable." That was Gretchen. I—the humble host—was back to being incapable of anything. Except to sit there—utterly stupefied.

"If I were to tell you that I'd merely enjoyed it . . . that'd be one hell of an understatement," expanded our guest.

"What does <u>that</u> mean?" I didn't realize that I was capable of asking <u>any</u> question—till I asked <u>that</u> question.

"It translates out to . . . I <u>loved</u> it! Like they say . . . 'Love it, <u>Love</u> it! Can't get enough <u>of</u> it'!"

I guessed that I should've been able to have figured out the meaning of her statement. And went back to shutting up.

"So, from that humble beginning," expanded Charlotte, "I became one of those raging, snarling, bitch-beasts that you hear about. I practically <u>destroyed</u> poor David! Not only that night . . . although he <u>did</u> 'go to bat' three times! He was <u>incredible</u>! I didn't quite <u>realize</u> how phenomenal he was that night. Not in the rather-cramped back seat of that Oldsmobile."

"I can understand <u>that</u>," sympathized Gretchen.

"Yeah," responded our local nympho. "Let me tell you: In the years that followed, I was able to realize exactly <u>how</u> incredible David was! I was <u>anxious</u> . . . anxious as <u>hell</u> . . . to <u>continue</u> the thing with him! <u>More</u> than anxious! And then, when it reached a point, where <u>he</u> couldn't . . . ah . . . keep up with my requirements, I just went on ahead . . . and expanded my field of battle, so to speak!"

"Expanded it?" This was still Gretchen speaking. She was practically <u>squealing</u>! I'd continued to be *hors d' combat.* "Went on the prowl, did you?"

"Yeah," confided Charlotte. "I <u>really</u> expanded it! There wasn't one boy . . . not <u>one</u>, in the whole damn high school . . . who was safe. Not by then. I don't know that I actually screwed my way through the <u>entire</u> student body. But, there were very few boys there . . . damn few . . . who wound up graduating <u>unscathed</u>, as they say. Not many, who completed their high school curriculum . . . and did so, <u>unsullied</u>, by yours truly. I'd become a genuine <u>legend</u> by then. A legend . . . and in my own <u>time</u>!"

"That's . . . that's <u>amazing</u>," observed the other female in the room. "Absolutely amazing!" The synopsis may have amazed her—but, she didn't seem all <u>that</u> taken aback. She was, heroically, <u>dealing</u> with the ribald details. <u>Coping</u> with them—one helluva lot better than I was. Not all that remarkable an accomplishment.

"It gets better," assured the latecomer. "It was later determined that I have a tilted womb! Otherwise, I'd have brought forth <u>dozens</u> of kids . . . over the years! There would've been <u>many</u> of my offspring . . . all in swaddling clothes! 'That Time Of The Month' truly <u>was</u> a curse! For <u>me</u>, anyway. Back then . . . at least in our town . . . <u>no</u> boy would <u>ever</u> go to bed with a girl! Not when she's menstruating! Wouldn't come <u>near</u> you! Fortunately, my periods didn't last very long. They still <u>don't</u>!"

That last sentence was accompanied by the most obscene leer I'd ever seen. And directed—at <u>me</u>!

Gretchen, as indicated, wasn't <u>nearly</u> as blown away as I was. "And you've just continued," she probed, "to go ahead and do . . . and do what it is, that you do?"

"Yup! Like the saying goes: 'Can't get enough <u>of</u> it!' Over the past few years, I guess it's become more like a game! More a battle of wits . . . than anything else! <u>Love</u> to catch my subjects . . . when they least <u>expect</u> it!" She added an obscene laugh. "Like I say . . . battle of wits!"

"A . . . a game?" I managed to ask. (Weakly.) "A battle? Of wits?"

"Yeah. Kind of like some kind of sport! Seeing what unit I can break into next! And when! And then, getting myself screwed! Getting screwed . . . by the inhabitant. The poor . . . the innocent, unsuspecting . . . inhabitant! Getting thoroughly <u>screwed</u>!"

"I'm sorry now . . . that I asked," I rasped.

"Listen," she explained. Obviously, she'd felt that I'd required further clarification. "It's <u>always</u> been about the sex! I <u>love</u> it . . . in case you haven't been paying attention. I <u>love</u> . . . absolutely <u>love</u> . . . love being screwed! Have always . . . have always and always . . . loved it! Ever since I'd crossed paths with the 'Boy Wonder' . . . David Piper. Thank you, David! I always try and stay away from a guy, though . . . if he's already got a partner. That's a critical demographic, for me. A really important consideration . . . for the likes of me anyway. Well, that resolution . . . it changes from time to time. Of course, there have been a few times . . . when the ethic changes a bit! Sometimes, it changes radically! And without much advance warning."

"I can understand that too," acknowledged Gretchen. (I had returned to my natural state! Being unable to speak.) "The way things are around here . . . nowadays," she continued, "I can sure understand that."

I finally managed to fire off what I'd hoped would be an innocent question: "I understand that you used to be a child star. A veritable Shirley Temple. In Hollywood."

"Naw. Don't know where that would've got started. I was a starlet, all right. But, in a different idiom. Back then, I was, though, the most famous girl in town! For a good while, anyway. A good long while!"

"Hmmm," muttered Gretchen. "That Hollywood angle . . . I'd have thought that that would've explained your sexual . . . ah . . . proclivities."

"Nah! I've been a free agent . . . all my life. Look," offered our Friendly Neighborhood Nympho, "if the two or you would like to, maybe, get into a few threesomes, I could . . ."

"NO!" I was finally able to say something. Well, at least to say something—emphatically!

"Uh . . . I don't think so," was Gretchen's more diplomatic reply. I was really unable to gauge the sincerity—or lack of same—my mind being so numbed, at that juncture.

"Well, if you guys ever want to . . . ah . . . double dip," advised Charlotte, "I think I could probably get old Charlie . . . old Charlie, next door . . . to participate. He's a little on the elderly side. But . . . let me tell you . . . he's hung like some kind of a stallion! And he's pretty good! Hell, he's <u>damn</u> good! In the old sack-a-roo, y'know! Not David Piper, maybe. But, close! Even after all these <u>years</u>!"

"Look," I managed to say, "this is all just a bit much."

"I dunno," contended Gretchen. "I've been finding it all . . . pretty interesting. Damn interesting!"

In summation, there was no "damage"—no <u>physical</u> damage, anyway—done that night. Charlotte finally left—after the fifth game. Let me assure you that—once she'd departed—"Gretch" and I did not delay our footrace to the bedroom. No more Chinese Checkers! Not for <u>that</u> night! And the Original Cast LP of *My Fair Lady*? <u>FIE</u>! It, also, would have to wait.

My relationship with "Gretch" was becoming more and more (how shall I say?) "intriguing". Still—truth to tell—sadly, a <u>little</u> of the luster was beginning to wear off. I guess that a goodly amount of the blame should probably have been shouldered by me.

For one thing, that "progressive" theatrical group—the one to which Gretchen had belonged, when she'd made her nude stage debut—had, all of a sudden, resurfaced!

I guess they'd been pretty well drummed out of the local "culture"—a few weeks after having closed the "work of art" that had so upset her parents

From what I understood, the company had produced yet another sparkling "gem"—shortly thereafter. A "classic"—which featured a couple performing a simulated sex act, right on stage. (Some people, apparently, believed it to not be that all-fired simulated! Those rehearsals must have been a real hoot!)

After the second or third public performance, the local authorities had—at long last (in the opinions of many)—shut the thing down! The "drastic action" had actually led to a couple locally-high-profile court cases.

It all seemed to boil down to a question of whether the troupe's "cherished" first amendment rights had been violated. I guess that—whatever might've happened on the stage—must have proved to be too much, even for the somewhat-liberal Western Oregon environs. The group of thespians was put out of business—for a second time!

However, four of the erstwhile group had, at long last, reorganized. This "second coming" occurred during the span of our nude Chinese Checker "tournaments". The theatrical players had begun to produce their deathless "gems" once again.

Eventually, they'd contacted Gretchen—among other people. Not only that, but she'd actually persuaded me to join her—in the rebirth of this celebrated group. The troupe was able to expand—

rather rapidly. Despite the many, and varied, legal difficulties of the past.

The "masterpiece"—which the intrepid group had concocted—to lead off their "new lease on life"— had to do with just one single mission: To glorify the homosexual lifestyle. If not glorification of the lifestyle, at least a very definite preachment—of, at the very least, toleration.

This had become a massive "cutting edge" subject by 1966. And anyone branded as being intolerant—in this "classic" was pilloried! Ridiculed—mercilessly! Obscenely! Constantly! I still have no idea why I'd consented to join! To my way of thinking, the "work" was terribly slanted—and the dialogue (what there was of it) highly stilted! Highly stilted!

The production featured (what else?) a whole bunch of nudity. In my "artistic" role, yes—I'd appeared in the raw! But, the number of my stage-presence "opportunities" were the least—of the other eight or nine people. Gretchen—to her great pleasure and satisfaction—was completely naked, most of the time. An abundant amount of this nude time was spent—be still her heart—on stage!

I don't think I'd wanted to admit it, at the time—even to myself—but, I was probably more than a little bit upset, by the entire situation. Maybe it was jealousy. It probably was. But, I'd hated to see "my girl" appearing in the altogether—in front of so many others. (The exciting "discussion" with Charlotte Klukay notwithstanding. That had occurred in an entirely different category.)

Fortunately—to my mind, anyway—I would find that the audiences, once the production had actually opened, would turn out to be exceptionally sparse!

Gretchen—on the other hand—seemed to have absolutely no reservations about the "gathering multitude" (whether few or many) gazing upon my nakedness. In fact, I'm convinced that this aspect had excited her—even further!

Ultimately, the whole project was beginning to leave me with a goodly amount of trepidation. Even before The Grand Opening! The discomfort, in fact, increased—noticeably—as the never-ending rehearsals had continued to grind, relentlessly, on.

When we'd finally opened, I believe that I was probably at the height of my discontent. This despite the fact that there were not that many spectators. Not that many "patrons"—to gaze upon the nudity. The nakedness—of either one of us. Of any one of us.

The production actually consisted of two separate plays. Gretchen was in both. I was merely included in the opening one-act scenario. It was—thankfully—much shorter, than the second "opus!

I don't know if the subject matter (with which I've never been comfortable) hurt—or helped—my jaded attitude. I did go through with it, though1 ("The Show Must Go On"—and all that!)

On three occasions, in this "epic", I was required to appear—unclothed—with another unclothed young man, about my age. Just the two of us! Seldom were we not in the nude! In merely two or three settings, were we "decent"! These "gem" settings took place, in the presence of the couple—also clothed—who were playing his parents.

This other man and I were supposed to be lovers—a situation which had plainly dismayed the characters who were the "parents". This entire "masterpiece" revolved around their terrible sex life. By comparison, my "lover" and I were portrayed to have been "so much more fulfilled" in our relationship!

This older couple was—in real life—married to one another. And they were wonderful. They were the two "stars" of the show (although they were, in truth, only a few years older than me, and my "lover").

In my portion of the production, they'd carried most of the dialogue—arguing, vociferously, whether I might "be a fairy", or not. The word "gay"—while not completely unheard of—was not that commonly used to depict homosexuals, in those days. "Fairy" was heard early and often in the play.

I wasn't bothered—not really—by the close association with another naked man. We weren't required to actually embrace—or to engage in anything beyond some fairly-salty dialogue. Nothing close to actual, physical, contact! We mostly spoke of our erotic—highly-esoteric—sexual meanderings.

What mostly upset me was the close proximity of "Gretch"—my supposed "sister", in the production—with her unclothed partner.

Their interaction did require a good deal of physical interchange. Mostly kissing. But, there was a generous amount of caressing-of-breasts. Gretchen did not share my discomfort—at their many intimate exchanges. She, in fact, seemed to have gotten the proverbial "large charge" from the role-playing. What, I guess, really upset me—was the fact that "Gretch" was, continually, patting her naked "lover's" bottom. (Virtually all of that was "ad-libbed"! Of that, I was positive!)

I'd hated to admit it—but, I did have to concede that there was a certain "rush" that appearing, sans my clothing, in front of the crowds (however sparse) provided for me! At first, anyway. But, nothing like the out and out joy (and obvious fulfillment) that my Chinese Checker partner was experiencing. Her partner's fanny had, quickly, become an old chum!

This grand and glorious production lasted the better part of two months. Toward the end, we'd drawn a few better-than-expected numbers of patrons. However, even the people who were devoted to our "cause" eventually tired of the show, and—pretty much unexpectedly—attendance dropped off, to next-to-nothing. So, tearfully, the enterprise closed shop.

I'd opted out of the follow-up enterprise, by the group. Another bit of a wedge between Gretchen and me. The nude Chinese Checker games had—over the course of our thespian pursuits—well, they had diminished to practically nothingness.

Even our love-making had seen a precipitous drop-off—the round bed notwithstanding. The same held for our nude romps on the beach. Things had reached a point—where we'd seldom ever ventured out.

On the other hand, there remained—in my emotional make-up—a goodly amount of affection for this woman. There <u>was</u> more to life than playing Chinese Checkers while we were naked. Even more to life than frenetically coupling on the circular "facility". Or schlepping around the beach—in nothing. <u>Essentially</u> more to our relationship—than romping around, in the altogether, on stage, In front of perfect strangers.

There <u>still</u> were breakfasts and lunches—virtually every day—at *Joe's*. And we <u>still</u> discussed schmaltzy music. And listened to Original Cast albums—even those, from the latest shows to hit "The Great White Way".

So, that part of our lives remained rewarding. To a point, anyway. "Gretch" was still one of the most interesting people I'd ever met. Certainly one of the most liberated! (<u>Certainly</u>!) And, definitely, one of the most adventurous. The perfect example of "still water—running deep".

I guess things were going <u>too</u> smoothly. As time had gone by, I'd found myself having <u>dismissed</u>—pretty much out of hand—the "Old Conspiracy Theory". The one that had "The Guys"—up there—setting me up—for a precipitous fall!

I'd rationalized, pure and simple, that there <u>is</u> evil! <u>Much</u> evil! Just about everywhere in the country! (Hell, in the world!). Ergo, that being the case, I would have—inevitably—encountered the likes of Charlotte Klukay and/or all the swingers in the complex! No matter <u>where</u> "The Guys" had set me down! Undoubtedly pure <u>rationalization</u>! This sort of thing—these brands of people—do exist! Literally, everywhere! So, my location-related suspicions were abating! Slowly—but, steadily. Thankfully!

And Newport was beautiful! (One had to wonder—when one got down to it—exactly how many Charlotte Klukays actually were running about in other parts of the country. Truth to tell, though, I'd, long since, stopped contemplating all those filled-with-wonders mathematics.)

Something else—of, probably, even more significance: I wasn't so quick to call myself a schmuck any longer. I don't guess that the idea had vanished altogether. I found myself wishing that it had! But, I had succeeded in kind of putting the disquieting, self-depreciating, theory on "Hold". Pretty much, anyway.

I was still seeing "Gretch"—just about every night, although the get-togethers were not quite so "adventurous" any longer. In point of fact, not nearly as "adventurous"! We'd reached a point—where we were watching more and more inane sitcoms on TV. I suppose that it was a "logical" progression. (I suppose!)

I usually had breakfast and lunch at Joe's. Those occasions seemed as rewarding as ever. There must be a moral there—somewhere!

As indicated, at the beginning of this chapter, I was pretty well settling in. Things were definitely "calming down". Events were turning out to be much less frenetic. It was probably—it was undoubtedly—just as well.

Had even started a brand new novel on my own. How 'bout <u>that</u>? (It was exceptionally autobiographical—so, who knew how it would sell? Or <u>if</u> it would sell?) But, what <u>else</u> did I know to write about?

ELEVEN

THE *I SUPPOSE I SHOULD Have Known Dept*: It kicked in! Things actually <u>were</u> going too smoothly. Unaccustomed as I was—to all this symmetry, to all this "smoothness"—I'd still managed to reach a point, where I'd stopped questioning it. I was simply blundering on—blissfully—with my seemingly-uneventful, everyday, life.

Then, it <u>happened</u>! I was on my way back from lunch—at *Joe's* (natch)—when I was "T-Boned"! A lady—who was applying 17 pounds of makeup at the time—ran a stop sign! Crashed into the passenger side of my beloved Chrysler! Smashed into it—smack-dab in the center! Both right-side doors wound up totally <u>crushed</u>! The post, in the middle, had held up pretty good—thank heaven!

If this woman would have clobbered me—on <u>my</u> side—you'd not be reading this tome! As it was, I was not expected to live. "The Kid", here, was in a "coma-like state"—for, literally, six-and-a-half weeks. Can you <u>imagine</u>? (I couldn't! Still <u>can't</u>!) I was fed intravenously! (Trust me—you don't want to <u>know</u>

from all the rest of what they'd had to do to/for me—to simply keep me alive! I'd certainly not wanted to know! I don't think the expression, "Too Much Information", had been coined back then—but, it was TMI!)

I, of course, knew nothing—of any of this! It was just as well!

When my eyes kind of winced open, I was in a totally unfamiliar place! Obviously, I was located—in a hospital room! Certainly obviously, when I'd, shockingly, discovered all manner of tubes—plus a whole bunch of other stuff. which (to this day) I cannot identify—running into and out of various parts of me!

I'd had no idea as to what had happened! I'd—for certain—not seen that humongous battlewagon, of a Buick Electra, coming at me.

Miraculously, I'd not suffered any broken bones. Another "Can you imagine?" portion, of the frightening, obviously-life-threatening, situation! The rest of the diagnosis—vis-a-vis my condition—wasn't quite so sunny. Liver damage! All kinds of internal bleeding! I guess they'd debated—as to whether they should remove a kidney! (Fortunately, they'd decided against that little, still-rattles-me, probably-life-altering, procedure.)

There was a lot of other medical gobbledygook—pertaining to my precarious medical state! None of which I understood! Still don't!

As things were explained to me, it was all that internal stuff—that had kept me in the stupid coma (or whatever it was). And for such a distressingly long time. As you can imagine, I'd been in no position to be the least bit concerned—at the time! (I was unconscious, y'know!) Apparently the powers that be—at the hospital—were worried enough, for all of us!

When I'd finally "come out of it", I was almost pain free. Almost! Every now and then, something would send a blizzard of pain—through my entire body! Fortunately, the out and out agony didn't last all that long! And, thankfully, it didn't happen all that often! But, when it did, it was a real bear to contend with! Always left me totally drained! And, as you can also imagine, I'd not had all that much strength and/or energy, to begin with!

What I've just relayed to you—in a few short paragraphs—took me three long days to learn. And in mere bits and pieces. A snatch of a conversation here—and a doctor's admonition there. Every now and then—a sobering bulletin from a concerned nurse. Even then—with all that—I'd not been filled in. Not totally.

Loyal, devoted, Gretchen had maintained a "vigil" at my bedside for—literally—days, I was advised. When the elderly couple who'd owned Joe's, insisted that she return to work (and I didn't seem to be making any progress), she'd been forced to abandon "the watch".

She did so—ever so reluctantly. Still, as soon as her shift would be over, she was always back, at my bedside. Sometimes, the nurses would even bring in a cot—plus a blanket and pillow—so that she could spend the night. (I'd known none of this, of course. However, it was, I think, the first iron-clad fact, of which I'd been advised—by numerous members of the hospital's staff—once I'd "rejoined the living".)

Three or four days after I'd regained consciousness, I was visited by a second highly-concerned guest. Good ol' Charlie McNulty!

After, relentlessly, cutting through massive amounts of red tape—and piles of paperwork—he had managed to have the Chrysler towed to his place.

"Can it be saved?" I'd asked. My voice, believe it or not, was coming back. I'd been able to speak to the doctors (three of them) as well as the multitude of nurses. Of course, "Gretch" was there every evening and night. Even got to speak with a couple officers from the Police Dept. "I've grown to love that old car," I'd added, not surprising Charlie one whit.

"Listen," my neighbor had replied, "if you'd have been in any <u>other</u> car . . . <u>any</u> other car . . . you wouldn't be here. I don't know if I can save her or not. Frame is badly bent! Bent into shit. I'd have to have it towed to this place . . . an outfit, out in Portland. Listen, they're good people . . . and, if anyone can straighten the damn thing out, it'd be them. But, also listen! Listen to Ol' Charlie. It's gonna be expensive. Expensive as hell. I was surprised to see . . . that you didn't have any <u>insurance</u> on her."

<u>THAT</u> had been the one thing that I'd <u>not</u> thought of. I <u>certainly</u> could have/should have insured that venerable old bus. What an idiot I was! It simply never <u>occurred</u> to me.

Once all those celestial-generated things had stopped being hurled at me—one after another—<u>something</u> ought to have commanded me to get insurance on the "lady". But, it <u>didn't</u>! And <u>I</u> didn't! Idiot!

"If you can save her," I'd advised, "please save her . . . no matter <u>how</u> much it costs."

"Fortunately, the old broad that ran you down <u>has</u> insurance! Insurance up the ass! Oodles of it. With old Cliff Fletcher . . . who's been in that office, over on Fifth Street, since the year of the flood. He said that he'd . . . <u>personally</u> . . . see that you'll get every penny you've got coming to you!

"Well, <u>that's</u> comforting."

"It <u>ought</u> to be. Your hospital bill, here, <u>must</u> have reached war-debt proportions by now. <u>All</u> being taken care of! Well, <u>to</u> be taken care of! The car, though . . . that's the old horse of another color."

"I can <u>imagine</u>! Or, maybe I <u>can't</u>."

"*Blue Book* says she's worth, maybe, three—or four-hundred bucks. And <u>that's</u> the high side. Listen, <u>they</u> don't give a rat's ass . . . about <u>how</u> much you may love that old tub. They <u>ain't</u> gonna pay to have it repaired. Certainly not the kind of money we're talkin' about, here. Well, hell, they're simply not gonna have it <u>fixed</u> . . . period! As far as they're concerned, it's totaled! A piece of iron! A piece of iron shit! They don't want to <u>hear</u> anything else!"

"The . . . this 'old broad'? Who <u>is</u> she? <u>How</u> is she? It never occurred to me . . . to even ask about her. Is <u>she</u> . . . ?"

"Oh, she's all right. No really bad injuries. As I hear it, she wound up with a broken nose . . . and a couple of fractured ribs."

"I'm sorry to hear that."

"We all are. She's really a nice lady. Been the old Pillar of The Community for years! Decades! I think she's really concerned . . . well, I know she's greatly concerned . . . about what she might've done to you! About what she did do to you. Came up to see you a couple or three times . . . as I understand it. But, you were still out of it, y'know. Inconsiderate bastard that you are."

"What's her name? Do I know her?"

"Gladys Grimshaw. Naw . . . I don't think you know her. Lives in that big old house . . . humongous old house . . . out at the far end of Maple Street. The 'Old Grimshaw Place', y'know. I think it was her grandfather, was the one . . . the one who built the place. In the late-eighteen hundreds. Before you or I was ever a gleam, in anyone's eye. But, Mrs. Grimshaw . . . she is concerned about you. At least she was."

Happily—if anything about this episode could be classified as "happily"—Mrs. Grimshaw did come to see me! The very next day, as a matter of fact.

Her visit came—about twenty minutes after Gretchen had arrived. I'd expected this stranger to be a much older lady. To listen to Charlie, a person would've pictured a doddering, exceptionally-frail, old woman. One in her nineties. On crutches, maybe. Possibly in a wheelchair. Or, at the very least, requiring a walker.

I'm guessing that this lady was probably in her mid-sixties. And she certainly was anything but frail-appearing. Even with her broken nose. (Well, the old proboscis had healed—substantially—by then.)

She was dressed in a tasteful, beige, suit. (I'd pictured her in a black velvet dress—one that went all the way to the floor—and featured a white-lace bonnet. Maybe accompanied by an even-lacier shawl around her shoulders.)

Dear lady that she is, she couldn't apologize enough—for having crashed into me. Told me that she'd been—stupidly—slathering makeup on. (I couldn't understand why she'd ever thought that she would've needed all that much cosmetic "assistance".)

"Gretch" knew her well—as, I guess, did everyone else in town. And she assured the distressed woman that I'd forgiven her. Which, I guess, I had. Yeah, hell, I really had. She was a very nice lady. And she promised me—faithfully—that she'd "do whatever it takes" to "make things right" with me. She would prove—over the next few years—to be a woman of her word!

"I just cannot shake this horrible sense . . . this terrible feeling, I have . . . of this overwhelming guilt. This God-awful guilt, that I feel," she'd lamented—continually. "I just cannot seem to shake it. I assure you, Mister Young, I've never done anything like this before. Never in my life! Nothing even close!"

I think I finally managed to convince her that I'd forgiven her—but, it took some real doing. And much backing by Gretchen. After about fifteen minutes, she'd decided to leave. But—before making her exit—she bent over the bed, so that I could give her a kiss on her cheek. To me, it was a little unusual. But,

I believe that, to her—the "ritual" was simply a normal part of her life. Nothing out of the ordinary. Something to be expected. And—more importantly—I think it solidified the fact that I <u>had</u> forgiven her.

It was about ten days after I'd regained consciousness, when negotiations began—to <u>free</u> me from the depressing confines, of the hospital. I still couldn't walk to the bathroom. Well, I <u>could</u>—but, not without becoming totally exhausted. It was too much like work to stand—while I urinated. So, I simply sat down.

Gretchen never ceased to kid me about it. "The Spectacle"—as she'd <u>always</u> referred to it. <u>Endlessly</u>. She kept telling me—that I was merely "identifying . . . with my feminine side". I'm sorry—but, I didn't think it was so damn funny. (I still don't! I know—no sense of humor!)

The hospital would not release me! Absolutely <u>refused</u>—unless someone would be there, <u>with</u> me! The requirement was that there should be a professional nurse present—at all times! To care for me—24/7! Well, I got the impression that the <u>full</u>-time part of the decree might've been negotiable—to a point, anyway. But, living alone—staying <u>anywhere</u>, by myself—was <u>out</u>! <u>Verboten</u>—according to the medical "authorities". <u>Irrevocably</u> out!

Even "Gretch" got involved. She'd be glad to even move in with me. (She had already checked—beforehand—and was assured, by the complex's management, that she'd be allowed to bring "her Fanny" with her.)

On the other hand, she'd <u>sorely</u> wanted to—simultaneously—keep her job at the restaurant. And <u>that</u> wound up being a non-starter—with the medical community. For starters, she'd be gone all day—every day—Monday through Friday. And I would be (gasp!) <u>alone</u>—far too often, and for far too long! So—<u>rejected</u>!

Finally, the wonderful Mrs. Grimshaw entered the arena. There was a company in town—that provided professional help. At the "patient's" home. 24/7—if required. And, of course, it was left unsaid that those services were only available—if the recipient was able to afford them. My elderly benefactor assured me that—if her insurance wouldn't cover such care—<u>she</u> would pick up the tab. "And for as long as it takes."

It came to pass that the insurance company—how-ever-reluctantly—paid for the service. Her longtime insurance broker, I was told, had issued the ultimatum, steeped in a goodly amount of venom—and the giant firm had, ultimately, agreed to go along!

The far-too-complicated arrangements were, finally, solidified—to where a professional nurse would stay at my condo, with me, from 7:00AM till 3:00PM. That person—presumably a woman—would be relieved in the afternoon.

The second "pro"—another nurse—would take over, at that time. She would remain till 11:00PM. This care-giver would only leave at that time—once she'd determined that I was, safely, in bed for the night. (A bedpan was even, thoughtfully, provided. I shouldn't have to cope with having to get up—during the night—to heed "nature's call". Had they thought of everything—or what?)

The "Morning Nurse" turned out to be a slight Hispanic lady—about three or four years my junior. Her name was Magdalena. (That—alone—presented a bit of discomfort for me.) Magdalena Longoria!

The consistent unease was difficult for me to understand—for the first few days. I'd finally realized, of course, that her name was so eerily similar—to that of Elena. I believe that some subliminal part of me—was doing its best to block out that cryptic association!

And, damn! In a way, this woman looked a little too much like my former "girlfriend". Her personality, however—while still quite charming—seemed much different. But, then, no one was—ever—going to be like Elena! No one could—ever—be like her! Close wouldn't even be possible!

Magdalena's relief was an enormous Anglo woman—named Shirley!

If ever you'd wanted to make a movie about World War II—and needed an overbearing Gestapo officer (male or female)—Central Casting would have sent you Shirley.

She and "Gretch" did not get along well. Actually, they didn't get along—at all! For one thing, Gretchen was constantly at my place. She'd always arrive an hour or so after Shirley had "filled up the joint"—with her overwhelming presence.

And—no matter how many times (or how fervently) my Chinese Checkers partner would have assured her, that I would be in the best of hands—Shirley simply <u>refused</u> to "abandon her post". (Which, sadly, meant that there would, positively, be no nudity—during our tense checkers bouts. And singing along with the OC of *Annie Get Your Gun*—while sans our clothing—wound up as being also "out".) Somehow, it just ain't the same—clothed or unclothed—when you're indulging in such cornball things, in front of some hostile, almost-snorting, Sumo Wrestler.

And, unfailingly, Shirley always threw Gretchen out—promptly—at 10:45PM. (A couple of times, I'd been afraid that the evacuation edict was actually going to lead to something <u>physical</u>! <u>Extremely physical</u>!)

My devoted nurse <u>always</u> insisted that she'd needed the fifteen "professional" minutes—to, properly, get me ready to retire. (Regrettably, I was forced to start sleeping—clad in the massive selection of tasteful, silken, pajamas that "The Guys" had (so thoughtfully) provided for me. But, Shirley had to—always—assist me out of my slacks (or jeans) and drivvies, and then into my PJs. (Something <u>else</u> that didn't sit well, with the constantly-fuming "Gretch". <u>That</u>, I couldn't understand. She'd had no <u>problem</u> with my appearing in the altogether—during the hokey run, of that stupid, "work of art", play!)

I'd had not the foggiest idea—as to <u>how</u> long this entire, difficult-to-say-the-least, arrangement was going to last.

I only knew, down deep, that—once home from the hospital—I was <u>not</u> progressing! Not as well—health-wise—as I'd expected. Certainly not as well as I'd hoped

And Charlie wasn't much help—telling me, two or three times each week (sometimes, two or three times a <u>day</u>) how "crappy" I'd looked. (But, he <u>was</u> on his way to realizing his number-one mission in life: Fixing my beloved Chrysler. One out of two ain't bad. At least <u>one</u> of us—the "Iron Lady" and me—was doing all right.)

As the days continued to drag by, everything seemed to be, once again, closing in on me! Some of the same feelings—hell, some of the same damn <u>fears</u>—that I'd so horribly experienced, during my last months as Paul Marchildon, were beginning to be reborn!

But, how could <u>that</u> be? How <u>can</u> that be? I was a new <u>man</u>! With a new <u>life</u>! Even with a new <u>body</u>! In a totally new <u>locale</u>! In a new <u>lifestyle</u>! (I now had <u>money</u> and even <u>good looks</u>—not necessarily in that order—to mention a bountiful number, of unheard of items. Those constituted a whole bunch of <u>major</u> items! Not to be taken lightly! Obviously!)

I'd <u>tried</u> to remedy the situation—by attempting to get back into my writing. But, nothing was coming. Man! You talk about writer's block. No matter <u>what</u> I would try to get down on paper—the effort ended up being a "dry hole". <u>Always</u>! The Muse was, definitely, missing in action!

Then, something—a terribly-hard-to-identify reality—was ever so slowly beginning to make itself evident! Even to imperceptive little old me.

That totally disquieting taste of reality turned out to be solidly, undeniably, embodied in—Magdalena!

She was becoming—indeed, had become—the, unfailing, high point of my day. Every day! Imperceptibly, she—her very presence—had crept into, practically, my every thought, word, and deed. Any day! Hell—like I'd said—every day! How could this happen? And why?

Indisputably, the fact that "Oxen Shirley" had always been so—well, so—so damn overwhelming, so completely domineering, in contrast, was a very definite factor. Of that I'm positive.

In addition, all the never-ending tension—between "The Gestapo Lady" and Gretchen—wasn't helping the PM portion, of my daily living. Well, it wasn't helping anything! In addition, the electricity between that pair was growing! Seemingly, by the minute! Not good!

None of that tension was present—thankfully—during the earlier portion of the day! The part—where Magdalena, without fail, "brightened up the joint"! (Continually!) The vast difference was, unquestionably, visibly, palpable! But, mostly, the stark difference was simply wrapped up in the Latina woman's seemingly-trouble-free demeanor! Her very personality! Her consistently-pleasant presence! Her devotion to my, not-improving, physical condition!

Something else, about which to think: Magdalena had a child! "Only" one kid! But, who knew—if that might not have been "one too many"?

This offspring was a young boy—12-years old. Pretty much the age of my own older son, Steve! Listen, he'd already turned 11, by then. My care-giver's son was, in point of fact, a good bit closer to the age of Alton—Elena's child! The unfortunate kid! The one who had already lost two father figures!

This lad's name was (could you believe?) Bonifacio!! That was the name of the valued service agent at the truck-rental place, in San Antonio.

That Bonifacio and I had always gotten along extremely well. Always! Mainly, due to the fact that we'd shared a genuine, distilled, lusty, hatred—toward our (hearty laugh) "Dear Friend"! That would be Red, the sainted, gifted, manager of the place.

So many troubling "close associations"—in all of this! I couldn't tell how many of the exceedingly-disturbing similarities were conscious—and/or how many might've been subconscious. Some of them might even have been some sort of a "reach"! A distinct "reach"! Possibly many of those psychological "reaches"! Probably many of them.

I knew, though, that a goodly amount of something was boiling! In some kind of psychiatric cauldron! Just under the surface! The old "tangled web" thing! And I was betting—that it was never going to let me out of its relentless, damnably-troubling, clutches!

Magdalena—and Elena. Such disturbingly similar names. To add to the rather frightening similarities, both had sons about the same age. Even more troubling—Magdalena's kid had to be named Bonifacio. Some kind of celestial "link" there? A celestial hearken—back to my last job? The one where I'd stolen a thousand bucks? Was there more to "The Guys" having replaced that G-Note? Something much more devious—than merely an angelic "show of good faith"?

I was—obviously—back to wondering if "The Guys" were playing with my head! Was this another tour-of-duty through the emotional hell—the mental/psychological inferno—into which <u>all</u> schmucks, apparently, <u>must</u> be cast? Often times, I found myself believing that I wasn't very far from "going over the edge"! The old psyche—fragile, at best—seemed to be giving out! Totally <u>unraveling</u>! I felt myself—on the precipice of becoming a certified, bona fide, whacko! Schmuckdom (yes, I was back to <u>that</u>) was bad enough! But, to be a schmuck—and an emotional basket case—was a bit <u>too</u> much! <u>Way</u> too much!

Magdalena, as it turned out, <u>also</u> knew <u>nothing</u>—about the Broadway stage. <u>Another</u> troubling similarity—vis-a-vis Elena. My care-giver and I got to where <u>we</u>—she and I—were beginning to listen to *My Fair Lady*, and *West Side Story*, and *South Pacific* and *Finian's* Rainbow and *Camelot*. And <u>yes</u>—dammit—listening to *Oliver*. ("The Guys" had, thoughtfully, included <u>that</u> Original Cast recording—in my wondrous collection of LPs! The very same album—that Elena had, so thoughtfully, bought me almost a year before. <u>Frightening</u>!)

This gentle Oregon woman was in absolute <u>awe</u>—as I'd do my best to explain the mostly-hokey plot of each of these (and many other) musicals. I was even able to sing enough of the more romantic songs—in my own, patented, "rusty file-like" baritone—that I could sometime bring her to actual tears!

Her rapt attention made me more and more cognizant of that glorious "door that I'd once opened"—for Elena! Had opened that emotional portal, for her—the better part of a year before! On that magical night—when we'd taken in the unforgettable *Oliver!*.

Magdalena was <u>amazed</u> that I knew the lyrics to virtually <u>all</u> the songs on the many LP albums. (Yes, even *I'm In Love With An Octopus*.) I didn't go out of my way to inform her that Gretchen could also sing the words to each of those tunes. And <u>her</u> voice was much more melodic than mine.

Amazingly—to me, anyway—my morning/early afternoon companion seemed in awe of <u>everything</u>! <u>Everything</u>! <u>Anything</u>—that I might ever have "accomplished". There hadn't been all that much "accomplishment", of course. But, to her, each of my hokey little experiences seemed to hold some kind of special meaning for her. To Magdalena, these were all "adventures"! And I'd—without fail—"mastered" <u>all</u> of them! (Let's face it: We <u>all</u> love to have our egos massaged—intentionally or unintentionally.)

I would later—<u>much</u> later—learn of the harsh life <u>she</u> had lived! <u>Her</u> real-life experiences would make <u>mine</u> seem like something out of *Boys Life* magazine! Or from something written by Hans Christian Anderson!

Along the way, during Magdalena's stay, I'd sorta/ kinda phonied up my background. Made a number of very significant—ah—"adjustments" to my life's story.

Obviously, the main missing ingredient had to do with the fact that I'd, at one time, <u>been</u> named Paul

Marchildon. I'd also "fudged" the thing with Joanne. Told Magdalena simply that she'd "merely" divorced me. On the other hand, I had owned up to the fact that she was living—along with my four kids—in Brownsville. That could've proved to be a fatal move!

"Why would you leave them? Desert them? And come all the way up here?" I could see her tense up—just this side of violently—as she'd asked the question! This was something I'd—definitely—not counted on!

"Uh, well, I'd . . . my wife had . . . actually, she'd turned everyone against me! Especially down there! Everyone! And . . . after we'd parted . . . I guess that it was that I couldn't deal with having to leave my kids . . . whenever my visitation time was up. I couldn't really hack holding my kids . . . especially my little girls . . . and then, you know, having to go ahead and then just leave them! Just having to go away. Even if it was just for a stupid-assed week or so. Damn . . . I don't really know. I really don't! Honestly, Magdalena! I don't! Everything was just so . . . so damn mixed up! So totally screwed up!"

"I guess . . . I guess that I can, maybe, understand your feelings," she had responded—a tear forming at the corner of each of those ravishing, almond-colored, eyes.

"Look," I'd expanded—not knowing exactly where I was going, with any of this. "My father-in-law . . . he's a big noise, down there! Down there . . . in Brownsville. And do you know? He'd had me jolly well blackballed!"

"Blackballed? He did that to you? Could he do that to you? Does that mean that he'd blocked you from . . . from even holding a job?"

"Yep," I nodded. "No way . . . would I ever begin to get a job down there. No way could I ever get a job down there. Listen Magdalena, it was a six-hundred-and-fifty or seven-hundred mile drive . . . a fanny-dragging round trip . . . from San Antone, down to Brownsville! And for what? Well, I did get to hold my little girls . . . Cynthia and Mary Jane. For a damn little while, anyway. Too damn little awhile! Then, I'd have to drag my butt . . . and my heavy heart . . . back on up to San Antone."

"I had no idea, Mister Young, of all those problems."

"Well . . . and I wasn't happy at my job. Probably . . . mostly, anyway . . . due to my mental state! The thing with losing the kids. Hell, I probably wouldn't have been happy anywhere."

"Probably not."

"And . . . quite honestly . . . I was not doing a really good job. For . . . and I'm positive, of this . . . for the same damn reason. For all those reasons! So, I guess, I simply decided to try and . . . you know . . . try to escape. And that escape . . . for whatever it wound up being worth . . . was into writing!"

"I didn't know that you were a writer. That you wrote books. Not until lately, anyway. I can see where such a thing would be an escape."

"Listen. Once I'd sold a book or two . . . then, I wanted to really escape! So, I moved up here. Hoping, I guess, to just . . . to just, you know . . . to just get <u>away</u>! Get away . . . from <u>everything</u>! And, probably, from <u>everyone</u>! I don't know. I simply do not <u>know</u>!"

"Yes, Mister Taylor," she sighed. "I can . . . I can most certainly . . . understand how you'd feel." She wiped away more than a few tears. "How you must've felt."

Even more tears cascaded down her wrinkle-free cheeks! Her outpouring of sympathy was simply incredible! To <u>think</u> that she could be—that <u>anyone</u> could be—<u>that</u> empathetic, was practically beyond belief. I was <u>touched</u>! <u>Deeply</u>!

In addition, at that point, I felt <u>really</u> bad! Felt <u>horrible</u>—for the unforgivable amount of deceit I was laying on her! Was <u>every</u> road going to lead to— every road I would <u>travel</u>—would it lead to <u>this</u>? To out and out <u>deceiving</u> everybody? Or <u>attempting</u> to? <u>Deceiving</u> people! <u>Lying</u>—through my teeth! Was this the new <u>me</u>?

I guess, the topper—the thing that made me realize what, exactly, was happening—was when she'd said, on another occasion (a few days later), "Mister Taylor, I've never heard anyone talk as beautifully as you talk." We'd been discussing something entirely different. (I don't remember now exactly <u>what</u>. But, as you can imagine, I'll never <u>forget</u> the remark!)

Her accent was just the nth degree more pronounced than that of Elena. And I'd been bowled over when <u>she</u>—when <u>Elena</u>—had told me that I'd always talked so beautifully. And now—to hear the exact same sentiment—from <u>Magdalena</u>! In virtually the same exact dialect! It was almost too much! All these similarities! This whole situation was practically beyond belief. Except that there were all these likenesses. All of this out-of-the-blue (or was it?) familiarity! The whole thing defied credibility— except, of course, for the fact that I was actually living these things! These incredulous "adventures"! Living them, in what was—undoubtedly—an over-sensitized fashion! It was as though I'd entered into some kind of bizarre "fourth dimension".

One strange aspect of our relationship— Magdalena's and mine—was the fact that I'd had the darndest time, trying to deter her from calling me "Mister". I'd realized that I was her "patient". And that, of course, meant that the formal "Mister" was, probably, a professional requirement.

It took some doing—but, eventually, I found myself trying to convince myself that it had been a "giant step forward"—the fact she'd, at long last, stopped calling me "Mister Young". How-ever reluctantly that had been.

It had taken long enough—and we'd already engaged in many deep-seated conversations, before the transformation had taken place. Many of them!

Now, an important part of the arrangement had always been that she (and Shirley) would each possess a key to my apartment. I was—invariably— still in bed, whenever Magdalena would arrive in the morning.

She would help me out of bed and make a discreet retreat—when I "went potty". Then, she'd always helped me take a shower. Someone had even bought me a stool for the shower. I think it was Gretchen—although it could have been Mrs. Grimshaw. In any case—thanks to this very necessary piece of "furniture'—I'd not been required to stand through "the entire performance"—shower-wise. For that, I was—always—most grateful.

Those morning showers were always great! Always! A big help! Once I'd washed the rest of me (while standing)—I'd plop myself down, on that stupid stool. And have Magdalena wash my back (and the upper portion of my bottom)! Pure heaven!

Then, to have her dry me off—once I'd step out of the shower—was almost as glorious!. (Well, she would dry everything, on the old bod'—except, of course, for "my private".) One immense difference—when referring to the similarities of my relationships with Elena and Magdalena: Elena had never seen me naked! Ever! Not even close!

You'd have thought that, the reality, of a beautiful woman—one who was seeing you unclothed every day—would've produced a relationship much more erotic! Substantially more esoteric—than the heavily-platonic arrangement, that was taking place between this beautiful Latina lady and myself. (Well, in most cases, you'd think that, anyway.) Not so! Flagrantly not so! Not in our situation!

She was—at all times—strictly the ultimate professional! The truly "intimate" part of our time together was taken up—with my doing my best, to sing all those hokey lyrics from all those hokey Broadway musicals. (My voice could only be described—as noted above—sounding, mostly, like a "rusty file".)

Well, upon reflection, I guess that we might've been just as close—just as "intimate", if you will—on those occasions, where I would be relating one of my "glorious" life's experiences (one of my "epic adventures") to her. Or even simply describing the plot of some schmaltzy old *MGM* musical.

This was a relationship—unlike any I could ever have <u>imagined</u>! And I didn't even <u>realize</u>—that our undoubted friendship was <u>developing</u> into what I'd always pictured as a wonderful relationship! Her continued use of "Mister Taylor"—for such a bastardly long time—I guess, would tend to put, somewhat, a pair of blinders on such a situation. For awhile, anyway.

The question of her seeing me—daily—in the buff, or not, seemed to not cast the slightest influence on our situation. My continued nakedness—and on a daily basis—didn't seem to be any sort of consideration! It added not the slightest ingredient to the relationship. Nor did it detract from it. At least, that was my impression. Imperceptive ol' me.

There was never to <u>be</u> a "lightning bolt"! I suppose <u>that</u> would've given me, at least, some sort of <u>clue</u>—as to what was happening.

The hackneyed old saying is so <u>true</u>—when it comes to my sense of perception: "I don't need a house and a lot to fall on me. Just a house." Sadly, nothing ever came close to <u>that</u>! Not a <u>hint</u> of the old "lightning bolt"! Undoubtedly, such a bone-rattling phenomenon is a once-in-a-lifetime event! (Undoubtedly! To me, anyway.)

Then, there was this one morning—probably six or seven weeks after I'd become her patient—when she'd called and asked if she could bring her son with her.

Usually, young Bonifacio had been cared for by her mother. But the boy's grandmother had been under the weather, for a day or two. At twelve, Magdalena guessed that the kid would probably be all right—if left to his own devices. But, she sure would feel better, if she could simply bring the lad with her—for just that one day.

Of course, I'd advised her that I'd be happy to have her child come along.

Listen—this turned out to be a <u>great</u> kid! He was quite <u>in</u> to sports—especially football. The boy seemed enraptured, when I'd regaled him, in story and song, of some of the many athletic contests that I'd attended in Detroit! Was able to give him an almost-play-by-play description of <u>many</u> differing situations—in baseball, football and hockey! The many events that I'd attended—during my youth, and young manhood. He seemed saddened—when I'd advised him that I was not much of a basketball fan.

He'd not been at <u>all</u> familiar with hockey—and had never heard of Gordie Howe, who was, in the mid-sixties, still playing for the Red Wings. (Part of his 25-year career in Detroit.)

This amazing man would—in the mid—and late-seventies—play for the old Houston Aeros and then the New England Whalers, of the *World Hockey Association*. This iconic figure would be in his fifties by then.

And he was privileged—in the seventies—to be able to play with Mark and Marty, two of his three sons. They were their dad's teammates in the late, lamented, *WHA*. The setup had been a source of great pride—and unparalleled accomplishment—for this great athlete.)

In any case, that day, with Bonafacio, was simply remarkable! For me, anyway! I thoroughly enjoyed my time with the boy. Here he was: Another youth—one without a father figure! How complicated some things can be. How regrettably complicated!

Some days later, I would learn that Magdalena and her husband—along with their young son—had come to the United States, in 1958. They were in this country illegally! I don't know as I'd ever heard the term "coyote" applied to people who smuggled other people into the United States, back then. But, that was what had happened to this family! And, fortunately, successfully!

This "yote" had, apparently, been an honest man! (Unheard of—in this day and age! The "occupation" has, of course, since deteriorated! Immensely! Demonstrably!)

This honorable "crook" had even secured—for the father—a moderately-well-paying job. In Portland. As an apprentice car mechanic.

Magdalena had, she'd advised me, just finished a rather-advanced nursing course, in Mexico. And—since, years before, the coyote had smuggled her mother up to that city—the young woman had gone to work at a Portland hospital.

Alas, eighteen months later, Bonifacio's father had run off—with an Anglo lady.

Neither his wife—nor his child—had known to where he'd "escaped".

Adding insult to injury: A year later, the schmuck had—somehow—obtained a divorce decree from some court in Manitoba, Canada. (To that very day—weeks after she'd brought the kid "to work" with her—she'd not known whether that "obscene piece of paper" was valid in the U.S. or not. Her illegal status—rightly or wrongly—had prevented her from inquiring of the proper authorities. And—with my limited knowledge, pertaining to any manner of immigration law—I was of absolutely no help.)

Once all of this turbulent, matrimonial, turmoil had come down, the woman could no longer stand to remain in Portland. Somehow, she'd made contact with the home health firm, in Newport. The one that, at that point, was employing her. A friend of hers ("whom," she advised, "speaks a little better English than I do") had sent out a raft of job-seeking letters, to those sorts of businesses—up and down the West Coast. And she'd scored—and had latched onto this one! Fortunate—for me!

She'd, eventually, persuaded her mother to move down to Newport, some months later. She was relieved to find that Bonifacio's grandmother would take care of the boy while Magdalena worked. Day Care had "cost a fortune"!

There had been all this intrigue in her life—and there she was! Enraptured with mine! With whatever stupid little "adventures" (all of which were true—to a point, anyway) I would lay on her.

Bonifacio had, of course, been horribly <u>devastated</u> at his father's abandonment. (A <u>lot</u> of that going around!)

On the day that I'd met him, it had <u>appeared</u> that he'd been handling the loss pretty well. His mother would later inform me that the lad would—often—awaken, in the middle of the night, in cold sweats. Apparently, these traumatic experiences were occurring quite often. And the condition—the frequency of it—was <u>not</u> improving. On the contrary, Magdalena believed the malady was, if anything, getting worse!

As things "progressed"—vis-a-vis the happier and happier time I was spending with Magdalena—I was becoming more and more uncomfortable with <u>Shirley</u>! Not difficult to imagine.

It should be fairly easy to understand my disenchantment. She <u>was</u> awfully overbearing—threatening, on one occasion, to "turn me across her knee . . . and spank" me. (Obviously, I <u>was</u> getting better—health-wise—if she thought I'd be able to survive <u>that</u> onslaught!) More and more, I was getting the feeling that I could get along—very well—without her.

But, more significantly (<u>much</u> more significantly) was the totally-unexpected—and ever-increasing—problem, concerning my relationship with "Gretch".

She was not happy! Especially, it was developing, when it came to my morning nurse!

In my warped little mind, what was happening—with regard to my arrangement with Magdalena—was reaching Joanne/Elena proportions! Not good! I didn't believe that I'd needed another complication, at that point!

But, why should that be? Why should any of this be? I had been in the midst of a most rewarding relationship with Gretchen! Much more rewarding—much more fulfilling—than anything I'd ever experienced with Joanne. Especially so—before colliding with Mrs. Grimshaw's Buick!

At that point, though, I was experiencing this really "creepy" feeling! This frightening image—that the time that I was spending with Magdalena had turned into some sort of cheating! No matter how platonic the thing with Magdalena might've been (look, Ma, no lightning bolt, nor, even, pats on the "bum"), I'd had this image of cheating! Cheating—on "Gretch"! What the hell kind of thinking was that? (Well, I guess, for me, it was probably quite to be expected. Quite to be expected. Normal as hell!)

There were all these mental/psychological/emotional problems going on! On so many fronts! Certainly for me! Well, and for Gretchen, apparently. I was lead-pipe certain that Magdalena was experiencing a terribly rocky road. Although her concerns were, for the most part, wrapped up in her son's wellbeing. That was my "perceptive" assessment, anyway.

And, as far as my relationship with "Gretch" was concerned, there didn't seem to be any logical way out! No escape—from the difficulties that were fast developing between us. Certainly no easy way out. And I could see her becoming more and more distant—as time was going on!

I didn't know whether the frigidness was coming from her difficulties with Shirley. I'd thought not! Could she be reading something into my so-called relationship with Magdalena? (Hell, at that point, I didn't know if I'd even had a relationship with Magdalena! A relationship—of any sort!)

Given my propensity for not wanting to confront such situations—especially when they're mired in details as complicated as those which were constantly staring me down—these mind-blowing circumstances did not figure to change! Not dramatically! Not any time soon!

TWELVE

ALMOST TWO-AND-A-HALF MONTHS AFTER MY accident, things—events—were, at last, beginning to "move right along". As you might expect, I was unable to determine whether that was going to be a good thing—or not.

First of all, I got my beloved Chrysler back. It wasn't <u>quite</u> like it had been. But, as my neighbor, Charlie, specified, "You'll hafta look damn close to really see any <u>real</u> difference". Most of that "difference" was probably in my overripe imagination. I was, as you can well imagine, glad to have her returned—even though the extensive repairs had set me back $6667-and-change!

Not much, I guess, in today's dollars. But, in the mid-sixties, that was a tidy amount! The repairs cost a little more than <u>twice</u> what she'd cost the initial buyer—in 1948—brand new. But, she was <u>most</u> welcomed back. Not only by me. A couple of my neighbors told me that they were glad to see her back. If I'd have gotten around more, I'm sure that a goodly number of other tenants would've expressed that same sentiment.

Not that I'd actually <u>needed</u> my revered old "Bucket Of Bolts". I still wasn't driving anywhere—although I <u>was</u> progressing pretty well by then.

To complicate matters a little further (a <u>little</u>?) my suddenly-obscenity-laced confrontations with Shirley were increasing—each and every day! I'd finally reached a point where I'd, unfailingly, <u>insist</u> that Gretchen remain—till <u>well</u> after the Shirley-imposed 10:45PM "curfew".

The overbearing "professional", of course, was anything but thrilled with the "unappreciative turn of events". And, predictably, she'd always storm out of the place! Noting—for the immediate world to hear—what an ungrateful malcontent of a patient I'd become. And how under-appreciated <u>she</u> had always been. (And had remained—to that very minute!)

Immediately, the nude Chinese Checker games <u>did</u> renew. But, somehow, they were never the same. Not really approaching the rewarding closeness that they had promoted, in the past. I guess they didn't figure to be.

The ambitious campaign to resume these once-almost-divine, naked, "contests" <u>had</u>, at least, served one noble purpose. That quest being: To get the Gestapo Lady to drag her abundant butt the hell off the premises, each night—BN (Before Nudity). She was, at long last, "out of there"—each night—and (Gasp!) without my having been securely "tucked in" for the night. The bedpan had long since ceased to be a major consideration.

Another complication: Surprisingly, "Gretch" and I didn't even bother resuming the Original Cast Sing-Alongs. We just never seemed to have "gotten around" to them. Again, everything was different. Most disquieting! And we both knew it! Nothing—except for the traditional nude Chinese Checkers—was, in the slightest, the same. Would it ever be? (Sigh!)

I'd reached a point, in fact—where I was seeing everything in varying shades of gray. Everything! Well, I was feeling better—physically. But, fat lot of good that was doing for me—emotionally. My entire life seemed to be—in some degree or another—slowly (but, definitely) unraveling. And I couldn't (or, maybe, I wouldn't) put my finger on it. My existence—except for those precious few gratifying hours that I was spending with Magdalena—was turning into one giant, blah! A never-ending, malaise! And this was taking place—amid all this "worldly splendor"! ("Guys"?)

Nine or ten days after my "liberation" from Shirley's nightly "last rite" ministrations, I'd had this overwhelming team of medical "experts" descend upon my unsuspecting bailiwick. They pinched, probed, pinched again, listened, pinched again, observed, pinched again—and decided that I was disgustingly healthy!

Their unexpected verdict—their learned diagnosis? I was to be discharged from "The Program"! Like immediately! The suddenness of their action came as a substantial shock! To me, anyway!

This august group operated like the heroes of all those westerns—in the thirties and forties. At the end of those horse operas, the hero would say to his sidekick ("Smiley" or "Gabby" or "Fuzzy" or "Tonto" or whoever) "Our work is finished (dramatic pause) here". And—having so said (in real life)—this medical crowd simply "rode off into the sunset". "The End"!

I'd pleaded with them to let Magdalena continue her healing efforts in future mornings. (Who the hell really needed Shirley at night?) But my pleas—undoubtedly overdramatic—fell on, predictably, deaf ears! They had spoken! Period! Paragraph! It was over! All of it! A gut-shot, to me!

I was, obviously, devastated! I'd not wanted to admit—even to myself—the emotions that I had been experiencing toward this dear Latin Lady. And for a good while longer—than I'd wanted to admit. (Even to myself.)

In my more honest moments, I would acknowledge (yes, to myself) that I'd invariably spent a whole lot of time—most usually, after she would've just left for the day—trying to come up with some way to date her.

Maybe this tragic turn of events, for me, might turn out to be fortuitous! Perhaps now—since we no longer had a professional relationship—I could wheedle myself into a (Hoo-Hah) personal situation!

More or less as a sinister byproduct, of this nefarious mind game—I would seek to act as a sort of surrogate father to Bonifacio. To, at least, make a sincere attempt at the role. My own four kids, I'm sure, figured into my paternal mindset. As well as my concern for Elena's two sons. All of them—all six of those kids, in Texas—were now fatherless!

That to the side, I'd honestly been completely taken with Magdalena's kid—on the one day that his mother had brought him "to work" with her. I'd asked her—dozens of times—to let him accompany her, when she came! Bring the lad—anytime! But, she'd always declared that such a situation would simply be "unprofessional". That one-time visit had simply been "an emergency". Not likely to happen again. (Damn!)

There was very little I could do, for mother or son—from a social (or even a sports) standpoint—in Newport. I was aware of Magdalena's newly-acquired interest in the Broadway stage. But—outside of "Gretch's" naked little theater troupe—there was not all that much live-stage stuff going on, in town.

The "Light Opera" season had ended. I wasn't absolutely positive that their great performances would've been the answer. But, they sure would've been worth the shot—Gretchen's anticipated, continuous, presence notwithstanding.

Of course, anything interesting at the nifty movie house—would, obviously, be attended by the aforementioned Gretchen. Lord only knew what would happen if/when our paths would ever cross at the theater. All of these potential, very real, conflicts in my life—I did not need!

Another probably-impossible ingredient: In my overheated little mind, I'd, for weeks, been trying to plot some kind of a trip—which could/would include

Bonafacio. To Portland? Or, maybe, up to Seattle. Possibly even down to San Francisco. Or—if it should come to that—even as far away as Los Angeles. But, my "openings" turned out to be extremely limited. Especially from a sports event point of view.

For one thing, the Portland Trailblazers would not enter the *National Basketball Association* till 1970. As indicated, I'd wanted to include—and maybe even cater a little bit to—Bonifacio.

Priority One, though—was the fact that I'd wanted to treat his <u>mother</u> to some real-live theatrics. Maybe wind up staring at her—more than at the activity, on stage—as had been the case on that magical night with Elena. Not much chance of accomplishing <u>both</u> goals—to fulfill mother <u>or</u> son! Not in any fairly-close-by city, anyway.

A little more research: Sports-wise, Seattle was also no help. The Supersonics would not join the *NBA* till 1967. I guess they must have been a gleam in <u>someone's</u> eye—during the time that I was going through all these mental/emotional gymnastics. But, I'd been completely unaware of such a planned franchise.

The Seattle Pilots—the city's first major league baseball team—would not enter the *American League* till 1969. (They would last only one year, in the Pacific Northwest—then, be moved to Milwaukee; to become the Brewers.)

The *Major League Baseball* Seattle Mariners were still <u>years</u> away. So were the Seattle Seahawks, who would join the *National Football League* in 1976. So, <u>none</u> of these avenues were available. (Also damn!)

Hockey? <u>That</u> was out, too. The *National Hockey League* would not expand—and include Oakland (the Golden Seals) and Los Angeles (the Kings)—till 1967.

The Seals turned out to be not so "golden". Due to lagging attendance, they became the Cleveland Barons—in 1976. The Barons lasted until 1978.

Through some extremely-complicated arrangement—that I never <u>did</u> understand—the team was "merged" with the Minnesota North Stars, but the latter didn't retain all that many of the Barons' players. I'm <u>sure</u> the arrangement made sense to <u>someone</u>! But, they would've been <u>much</u> smarter than me. (Oh, and the North Stars ultimately moved. They became the Dallas Stars—in 1993. Even won a Stanley Cup—in 1999!)

In any case, from a sporting standpoint, the San Francisco 49'ers seemed to be "it"! Tickets, I was to find, were at a premium—if available at all. And, given the present circumstances, scheduling such a trip would be "iffy"—at best. The 1966 Giants baseball season opener was still a few <u>months</u> away.

As you can see, I was immersed—non-stop—in quite a quandary. For one thing, how could I even be sure that Magdalena would <u>ever</u> consent to go <u>anywhere</u> with me? Even to the movies? With or without her son? In the back of my devious little mind, I <u>knew</u> that such a scenario—<u>any</u> similar scenario—was, undoubtedly, nothing more than some far-fetched, extremely-wishful, probably-not-in-the-cards, reach. Frustrating, it was! Frustrating as hell!

All of this planning—so called! And for what? It was quite possible that this woman could be/would be walking out of my life—forever! Could it be—that she'd simply feigned all that "keen" interest in all that schmaltzy "culture"? All the hokeyness—that I had been laying on her?

Maybe she'd simply figured that such faux "attention"—to those things, which were of such major interest to her patient—was all just "part of the job". Possibly that was the tenor of the training that she'd received, in Mexico. Or some "refresher course"—in Oregon. Maybe even the primary aspect of any such indoctrination!. Who knew? Who the hell knew?

To no one's surprise, Gretchen was—quite visibly—relieved to see Magdalena out of my life. (Supposedly out of my life! I'd sincerely hoped that she was temporarily out of my life! I was praying for such an arrangement! "Guys"?)

For the longest while, I'd had no idea that this remarkable Latin lady had—apparently anxiously—wanted the highly-rewarding nurse/patient thing to come to a screeching halt! That was a heartbreaker! To my utter dejection, even I could detect the out and out relief she seemed to be exhibiting, over the final few days. And, sadly, not too suavely. (Like I said—even I was able to pick up on it!)

All things considered, it seemed that "Gretch" and I would never return to our former relationship!

Probably to nothing even close! What is it that they always say? "You can never go back"? Probably the truth. Almost definitely the truth. At least, in this case.

At the height of my despair, she'd apparently gotten a wild hair—you-know-where—vis-a-vis our relationship! She began trying to resurrect it! But, I really couldn't get the least bit comfortable, with the situation! Everything seemed so phony! Well, if not phony, then stilted!

Adding to the problem, was the inescapable fact—that I was getting even more restless, than she! Nothing was making sense!

Amidst all this, I continued trying to contact my former nurse. Maybe—as at least some sort of show of interest—I could finally get her to drop calling me "Mister". She'd re-inaugurated that formality—once the medical people advised her that her Taylor Young project was history!

Maybe, I remember thinking, I could even take her out! Even merely for dinner! (At some restaurant—other than Joe's, of course!) Then again, maybe I could not! The more I'd thought about it, the more I was convinced that she'd never accompany me. Certainly not on an overnight! Not out of town! With or without Bonifacio. (With or without even separate rooms.)

At long last, I got to speak with her—on two different occasions.

She'd been unable to continue to dodge me! And, both times—after I'd caught up with her—her end of the conversation turned out to be awfully stilted. It all-too-quickly became evident that—whatever the circumstances, in which she'd found herself, during those two forced conversations—she was terribly, noticeably, uncomfortable!

Was her discomfort merely a temporary thing? The result of some "temporary" situation? An untenable position—in which she might've been immersed at that moment? Possibly, her current patient (whoever he or she might be) had presented some kind of staggering problem for her.

Would her present, distant, demeanor represent a permanent—an impenetrable—wall? One I could never hope to scale—or to break through?

Something had to be done! So, depend on ol' Taylor—to muddle things further!

I came up with what probably sounds to you like the most cockamamie plan in the history of the world. There's a distinct possibility, y'know, that you might be right! But—for better or for worse—I'd made an "executive" decision! At that troubled time, it was a decision—that I would stick to! Stick with! Come the proverbial "hell or high water"!

The project—no matter how far out—had to portend a better set of circumstances for me! What was forming in my warped little brain, had to present more potential—for a realization, of a modicum of happiness and even satisfaction—than the clueless, restless, unrewarding situation, in which I'd been mired for, literally, weeks! Probably months!

No matter what I'd found myself doing, during that dizzying period—no matter what project I might be undertaking—that old "Everything Is Closing In On You" feeling prevailed! In overwhelming quantities!

Not only did the exceptionally-bleak outlook prevail, it was pervasive! Completely bowling me over! Continually! This unending blackness-of-spirit! It filled every room in my opulent condo. Constantly! Consumed every hour of every day! Without let up! There was absolutely no escape!

Obviously, I was having a God-awful problem! And simply trying to contact Magdalena—unsuccessfully, virtually, every time—was positively not helping! Gretchen—equally ás obviously—was becoming more and more impatient with me! Less and less tolerant—of the way I was acting (or not acting) toward her. Who could blame her?

I'd found myself wishing—sometimes praying—on a daily basis, that I could feel for Gretchen, the emotions that I'd continued to experience, vis-a-vis Elena! Or even Magdalena! For whatever reason, though, it was out of the question!

But, every bit as complicated—and disquieting—as was the current situation in Newport, the desolate state of affairs paled! Paled, big time—compared the gut-wrenching worry that had been developing for, literally, months.

The inescapable black cloud had developed—mostly since my accident! Since I'd learned that I'd so narrowly escaped death! After that frightening realization had finally set in, I'd become ever more and more concerned—about my own kids! I missed them—terribly! And, hell, worried about Elena. I found myself totally wrapped up—emotionally and psychologically (and every other way)—with questions of their wellbeing! I was even worried about Joanne! That was a bit of a surprise! But, it should not have been!

I'd begun having really-troubling dreams—especially about my two daughters.

There has always—since the beginning of time—been something special between daddies and daughters. At least in my mind and heart, that has been so.

And these constant—these tormenting—dreams were most disquieting! I didn't recall the angel saying anything about "The Guys" controlling dreams. Could it be that they had their fingers in some of my, without let-up, nocturnal unrest? Maybe this was an important ingredient—in the way they dealt with schmuckdom! If so, that is "hitting awfully close to home"! Again—who knew?

I believe I would've almost welcomed a late-night "visit" from Ms Klukay. But, apparently, she'd considered me "taken"—and had dropped me from her delights-of-the-flesh "route".

In any case, the culmination of all this obviously-unhinged hodge-podge—this mish-mosh, that had, so completely, taken over what is laughingly referred to as my life—was this aforementioned decision! The decision! This highly-emotional, quite-possibly-cockamamie—certainly-troubled—conclusion that, for better or for worse, I'd reached. This—fervently—hoped-for solution!

If I'd had any sort of reason to question my judgment—and, of course, I did—the logic of that decision was really put to the test! Was raked over the coals—when I'd advised "Gretch" of what I'd hatched in my overheated, twisted, little mind!

It was the occasion of what turned out to be our final Nude Checker Game (for the nonce anyway)— when I'd, so undiplomatically "sprung" this vast idea on her. (I'm reminded of the old saying: "Some people say that my ideas are vast. Others say that they're half-vast".)

"Do you know what I'm thinking?" I queried—after what turned out to be our final game.

"I never know what you're thinking, Taylor. Especially lately," she'd responded—rather testily.

"I'm going away!"

"Going away? Going away? Now what the hell's gotten into you?"

"Well, 'Gretch' . . . look. Look, I'm worried about my kids, and . . ."

"You've . . . Taylor, you've never seemed worried about them before. Listen, my good man. I've never gone into your past with you. Storied or otherwise! I've never questioned you about your past. Never inquired. All I know is that you're divorced. Divorced from some girl . . . some woman . . . some woman named Joanne. And . . . as you've mentioned more than a few times . . . you've got four kids. They're all down in Texas somewhere."

"Yeah. Down in Brownsville. Southern-most tip of the state."

"So you've said. Look, I never <u>could</u> figure why you'd <u>ever</u> leave them," she groused. "Why you'd <u>ever</u> . . . well . . . why you would've <u>abandoned</u> them!"

"Listen, Gretchen! I didn't just . . ."

"Why you would've <u>deserted</u> them," she continued, undeterred. "<u>How</u> you could've left them . . . in the first damn place? How could you ever <u>leave</u> your kids, for God's sake? I mean . . . <u>leave</u> them? Leave your <u>kids</u>? Leave those <u>kids</u>? Leave 'em . . . <u>way</u> down there? Down there . . . in <u>Texas</u>? And then, go ahead . . . go ahead . . . and move your fanny all the way up <u>here</u>? But, listen! I <u>never</u> wanted to pry! I never <u>would</u> pry! Never <u>did</u> pry! I simply always figured . . . well, I just figured . . . that, hell, it's your own, private, <u>business</u>! None of my own."

"Well, I was really kinda mixed up, at the time. Was <u>damn</u> mixed up! In a real <u>snit</u> . . . most of the time. Especially those last few months. You talk about anguish! The whole thing . . . the whole damn situation . . . it really hit me! Flattened me . . . like a ton of bricks!"

"I suppose." She sighed—heavily. "Yeah, I can imagine that it probably <u>did</u>. That it <u>undoubtedly</u> did. But, now . . . <u>here</u> you come! Here you <u>come</u>! From out of left damn <u>field</u>! Now . . . all of a damn sudden . . . you're gravely <u>concerned</u> about your kids! Taylor . . . I really don't <u>understand</u> you! Well, to be honest, I guess I've <u>never</u> understood you! Never came <u>close</u> . . . to understanding you! But, <u>now</u>? Now I <u>really</u> can't even . . . cannot <u>imagine</u> why, all of a sudden . . ."

"Look, 'Gretch'. There've been a <u>lot</u> of things that have been eating at me, lately. And I . . ."

"<u>That's</u> true! If nothing <u>else</u> is true . . . <u>that's</u> true! I could <u>tell</u>!"

"And especially since the accident. When I figure I could've been killed, you know. Since then, well, I've begun to <u>see</u> things in a . . . well, in a . . . in an altogether different <u>light</u>."

"Yeah," she muttered. "But, I'd always thought that the <u>light</u> . . . the big-assed illumination, that you're talking about . . . I always thought it was that morning <u>nurse</u>! That <u>Magdalena</u> . . . or whatever in hell her name was. Whatever in hell her name <u>is</u>." I'd never heard such <u>venom</u> in this woman's voice before. Nothing close!

"Well, I <u>do</u> have to admit," I responded in an almost-inaudible tone: "I <u>do</u> have special . . . ah . . . special feelings toward Magdalena. But, that's really not the . . ."

"Yeah." Her voice was showing even more irritation. To an even <u>greater</u> degree, than before—something I'd thought not possible! "I <u>thought</u> you had 'special feelings' for her. And how did <u>she</u> feel? How <u>did</u> she feel? And don't tell me that you didn't feel her <u>up</u>! At the very <u>least</u>! You <u>must've</u> . . . at the least . . . felt her up! Hell, she was . . . all the time . . . <u>seeing</u> you! Seeing <u>you</u>! Looking at you . . . bare-assed <u>naked</u>! Every damn day! Seeing you . . . with no goddam <u>clothes</u> on!"

"<u>Gretchen</u>! Magdalena and I have <u>never</u> . . ."

"Yeah. Sure. Right. A likely story." Why was Gretchen, suddenly, sounding so much like Joanne?

"Well," I was trying—valiantly—to rally, "whether you choose to believe it or not . . ."

"And you could care less . . . whether I do believe it or not! Here we sit! Naked as jaybirds! And you don't give a rat's ass! Could care less . . . what I believe! Couldn't give a shit . . . what I think!" Tears were beginning to form in her suddenly-faded blue eyes. "Could care fucking less! Bare-assed naked . . . or not! No biggie . . . one way or another!"

I'd never heard her use the "F-Word" before. "Ass" was even a bit of a surprise—despite her numerous in-the-nude stage appearances, and her associations with various cast members. I don't believe I'd ever heard her use language that was gamier than "hell" or "damn". Obviously, I was striking a nerve! Hurting her! Hurting her—deeply! And I'd, honestly, not wanted to! So help me!

"Of course I care," I responded—probably too weakly. And far too late.

"No you don't!" She was next to tears! "You could care less! You've had me! Screwed me . . . numerous times! Numerous times! You've even had Charlotte! Probably screwed her . . . more often, than you're willing to admit! If you haven't had that goddam nurse . . . then, it's because she's being smarter than I ever was! Wouldn't let you into her panties?"

"Gretchen, Look! Listen to me!"

"She doesn't want to let you screw her? Is that your problem, Bunky? So, now . . . what? You're looking for new worlds to conquer? Is that what this is all about? New babes to boff? Is that it?"

"NO! Of <u>course</u> not! No . . . <u>that's</u> not it! Not it . . . at <u>all</u>! Look, she wasn't . . .! We didn't . . . Not <u>once</u> did we ever . . . Magdalena and I . . ."

"Taylor, I don't <u>believe</u> you. You've never been yourself . . . not even close! Not since that goddam accident. And . . . even <u>before</u> the stupid accident . . . I never <u>understood</u> you! Not <u>really</u>! Now? Now . . . you've <u>completely</u> thrown me off my feed! Set me back . . . set me back years . . . in my goddam toilet training!"

"Look, Gretchen. You've <u>got</u> to believe that I'm . . ."

"I don't <u>got</u> to believe <u>anything</u>! I don't got to . . . to . . . don't <u>got</u> to believe . . . believe <u>shit</u>!"

This whole episode was covering all-too-familiar ground. The names had changed—but, this was the Joanne/Elena conflict! All <u>over</u> again!

"Well," I rasped, "I'm sorry you feel that way!" I was surprised at my tone of voice. The firmness therein. "But," I stated, more forcefully than I could've imagined, "I <u>am</u> going away! Whether you choose to believe it or not . . . I <u>am</u> interested in my kids! Especially my <u>daughters</u>! My little <u>girls</u>! And I <u>never</u> . . . as in <u>ever</u> . . . I <u>never</u> laid a glove on Magdalena! Not <u>once</u>! Not one <u>time</u>! Nothing even <u>close</u>!"

"Then, <u>go</u>," she sobbed. "<u>Go</u> . . . and be <u>damned</u>!"

So! I <u>went</u>! Whether I would be damned? <u>That</u> remained to be seen!

But, I <u>did</u> wind up showing, I'd felt, a generous amount of mercy—at least, in <u>some</u> areas. Well, all right—in <u>one</u> area. I certainly was <u>not</u> going to depend on my trusted, freshly-repaired. "Old Girl" for a trip of that length. She'd already given the well-known "above and beyond" efforts. <u>Well</u> above! And <u>really</u> beyond! And, for her valiant service, I'll <u>always</u> be grateful!

There was a really great song—right at the beginning—of the Broadway production of *Damn Yankees*. In the live production, "Old Joe"—who's about to become "Young Joe", courtesy "Mr. Applegate", the Devil—sings (to his wife, who is upstairs, asleep) "Goodbye old girl" He winds up proclaiming, in the song, that he'll "come back to you one day". I <u>hoped</u> that I'd be able to behold <u>my</u> made-of-iron "Old Girl" again! But, again, who <u>knew</u>?

So, as bountifully merciful as I'd become, I bought—in my charity—a brand spanking new 1965 Dodge Polara 4-door sedan. A blue one. They'd not had many choices of colors, by then. Well, they'd not had many choices of anything, by then. Craftily, Ol' Taylor had waited till <u>well</u> after the introduction of the 1966 models. (My old penurious ways coming to the fore again.) I figured that, if my angel wanted to talk to me, he'd know which dashboard I'd be sitting in front of.

Can you believe this? I upset the dope—and did the (gasp!) <u>logical</u> thing. I got a good night's sleep! A <u>surprisingly</u> good night's sleep! (Look, Ma—no

Charlotte Klukay!) Can you also believe—I left the next morning?

I'd headed for Texas (natch)—and San Antonio in particular. (Don't know how "natch" <u>that</u> was. Didn't really know how "natch" <u>anything</u> could have been, at that point!) Still—rightly or wrongly—my first concern seemed to center around <u>Elena</u>. Think of me what you will!

My primary, highly-troubled, thoughts <u>probably</u> should have been of my kids. And—most assuredly— they were (had constantly been) a consistent worry. Especially, as mentioned, since the accident. I was <u>certainly</u> going to do everything—within my power— to catch up with them. Hopefully, to even find some way to relate to/with them. It was—of course—merely a <u>hope</u>. Hell, it was, I was certain, a far-fetched dream.

But, the tads <u>were</u> 350 miles further away from Oregon, than old "San Antone". Besides, the more I would think of Elena, the more troubled I'd become. And I didn't know exactly <u>why</u>! Not <u>exactly</u>! Listen, by then, I'd given up any <u>thought</u> of out and out dismissing her from the smoldering shambles of my mind! (By that time, I'd reached a point—where I was not prone to even try and guess. At <u>anything</u>!)

"The Alamo City"! The supposedly <u>hated</u> (by me) town of San Antonio! Still, the outskirts had never looked so good to me. On the other hand, as I'd progressed toward "Beautiful Downtown San Antonio", the feeling of pending doom was beginning to—more and more—overtake me. Something bad would soon—I was positive—catch up with me! My prayer was that it didn't involve Elena! Or my kids! Or her kids! Or—for that matter—me!

It was shortly after one-thirty in the afternoon, on that memorable Wednesday, when I pulled into the small, gravel-covered, lot—where I'd once rented a parking spot, by the month. (Think "lightning bolt"!)

The attendant—a tall, slender, Latino chap, named Eduardo,—could not, possibly, have recognized his treasured former customer. Paul Marchildon was, after all, deceased. You should have heard the problems the lad had always had—trying to pronounce my former last name. This was a neat guy—and, though he could not have known my feelings, it was nice to see him again.

Walking to the storefront of my former employer seemed to take, at least, three times as long—as it ever had before.

I was, scarily, beginning to suffer actual heart palpitations! I could feel the old ticker pound more rapidly—and much more loudly—as my extreme, rubbery-legged, unease was, all of a sudden, zooming into the stratosphere!

I'd not had the foggiest Idea—at what might (or might not) await me! Just say that these tremors—reaction from the overheated, overworked, heart—continued to increase! Measurably! And rapidly!

And then! And then? When I got there—reached the front of my old place of employment—everything seemed to close in on me. I'd become—physically (and visibly)—dizzy. I could not breathe! Well, actually, I was experiencing great difficulty—in merely trying to inhale and exhale! I sort of staggered into the tiny facility! (Must have been a million laughs!)

I grabbed onto the front part of that stupid counter—which I, myself, had (so majestically) built.

"Can I . . . can I help you, Sir?" This was a strange—and highly-alarmed—woman who was greeting me. "Are you . . . are you all right?"

"Is . . . uh . . . where is . . . that is . . . is there a girl . . . a . . . a lady here? A lady named Elena?"

"I'm sorry, Sir. She doesn't work here anymore. Can I help you?"

"Uh . . . no thanks." I was beginning to rally. But, only slightly. "Look . . . can you tell me where I might . . . where I might . . . ah . . . might find her?"

"No, Sir. My name is Mary Rose. Elena hasn't been here . . . in, oh, about . . . in a couple or three months I guess. Maybe a little longer."

"And you don't know where she went? Where she could've gone to?"

"No, Sir. I really didn't know her. Don't know her, at all. Have never met her. She left, as I understand it, a few weeks before I came to work here. A couple or three weeks . . . before I got here. There was another girl . . . another lady . . . here, temporarily. I never met her either. Not even aware that I knew her name. I'm sorry . . . but, I have no idea as to how you'd be able to contact Elena."

"Is . . . is Tony here? He's the manager . . . isn't he?

"No, Sir. Not anymore. He was . . . I guess he left some time before Elena did. A few days before . . . as I understand it. I've never met either one of them. Our manager now is Richard Billingsley. But, he's at lunch, at present. Is there any way I can help you? Do you need . . . did you want to . . . did you want to apply for . . . for a, you know . . . for a loan?"

"No, I . . . look, Miss! Look, Mary Rose! It's important . . . it's urgent, it's critical . . . that I find Elena." I'd not realized exactly how urgent or critical— or how panic-stricken I'd become—until I'd uttered those words! As well as those which followed.! "Anything . . . anything . . . you can do to . . . to . . . to help me, I'd appreciate."

"I'm awfully sorry, Mister . . . ?"

"Uh . . . Young. Taylor Young."

"Well, I'm just as sorry as I can be, Mister Young. But, I really have no way of helping you. I would . . . I really and truly would! I would . . . if I could. I can see how urgent it is, for you. And, I'm sorry. So terribly sorry. But, I can't make even the slightest . . . not a halfway intelligent . . . suggestion. I have no idea . . . as to the circumstances of her leaving. Or of Tony . . . the former manager . . . for that matter. Of his reason for leaving. No inkling of reasoning . . . behind his leaving. None! Why he did. Why he would've . . ."

She let the sentence drift off—and shrugged. I'd never seen such a frustrated—such a helpless—look on anyone's face. Before or since. What a wonderful young lady. And she had not known me from Adam.

"I'm sorry," I rasped. "I don't mean to pry. I certainly don't mean to upset you."

"There's no problem there," she answered—with a forced smile. Then, her pretty face took on an expression of strict confidentiality. "Between us," she advised, in a husky tone, "the people in Tyler have been <u>awfully</u> quiet . . . awfully <u>circumvent</u> . . . about the . . . ah . . . departures of both Tony <u>and</u> Elena. I don't know that I should be <u>saying</u> any of this to you. <u>Telling</u> you any of this. I might . . . I could be . . . could be <u>alarming</u> you. <u>Needlessly</u> alarming you . . . and for no good reason. Mister Taylor? Would you like to sit down? There are those reasonably-comfortable chairs over there."

She indicated the six chairs—three on each side of the door—in the tiny "lobby" area. None of which came close to "reasonably-comfortable". I know. I was the one who'd <u>bought</u> the damn things.

I thanked her—profusely—for all of her "help", then kind of semi-staggered back out, onto Main Street. I made my way down two doors—to another loan office. (There were four of them—all small loan establishments—in just that one block. And another half-dozen-or-so within a two—or three-block radius. In the mid-sixties, the area was <u>crawling</u> with 'em. Most Texas towns—and cities—were.)

Entering the two-doors-down "store"—which was about three times the size of the one I'd just left—I looked around. There she <u>was</u>! <u>Dolly</u>! The manager. I don't know <u>what</u> I'd have done, had <u>she</u> no longer been employed there.

I guess there'd not been much chance of that. This fifty-ish woman had run that same office for 16 or 17 years. Maybe longer. Over the years, she'd become, more or less, "a cornerstone" for that entire block—whether she knew it or not. (Undoubtedly, she did.) <u>Everybody</u> knew her. Everybody—with very few exceptions—<u>loved</u> her.

This great lady was a theatrical nut—and almost as "in" to schmaltzy music as I'd always been. Over the too-few months, when I'd been her "commercial neighbor"—as she'd always referred to me—we'd had a lot of really neat discussions. Usually at the lunch counter—at the drug store that separated our places of business. Most of the chatter between us, had to do with my kind of music. (Well, Dolly's and mine.)

She was the only one who also knew who Axel Stordahl was. (He was Frank Sinatra's first arranger/ conductor—after "The Voice" had left Tommy Dorsey's band, in 1942. I'll go to my grave believing Mr. Stordahl was the most gifted A/C in the history of the world.)

Dolly believed that such a distinction should've gone to Paul Weston, who, along with his talented wife—Jo Stafford—had left the Dorsey aggregation a few months before Frank had departed. I'd always considered Mr. Weston as Number 1-A. That must've been some <u>kind</u> of arrangers' staff that Tommy had employed.

I'd spoken of Axel Stordahl—many times—to Joanne. I <u>still</u> don't believe she really knew—or much cared—who he was. When this genius had, tragically, <u>died</u> of cancer—<u>way</u> prematurely, in 1962—I'd been <u>devastated</u>. Joanne—to this day, I'm sure—could <u>never</u> understand why!

Dolly, of course, could not have recognized the "new" me. Obviously, I couldn't hit her—with all the "olde tyme" Stordahl/Weston stuff. She'd think I was a total idiot. (Now, <u>who</u> could possibly think <u>that</u>—of a nice boy like me?)

"May I help you?" It was one of three female clerks who worked there. I'd not remembered seeing her before. Well, I didn't really recognize the other two, either. "Did you want to apply for a loan, Sir?"

"Uh . . . no. Could I speak to that lady there? The manager? Could I talk to <u>her</u>?"

The young woman seemed ill at ease. But—after a noticeable, palpable, hesitation—she did call out, "Mrs. Raffenberger? This gentleman, here . . . he'd like to speak to you."

Dolly got up—and made her way to the counter. I'd <u>forgotten</u> her patented "waddle". Her behind had always been rather (how shall I say?) "generous"— but, she'd always added a highly-provocative wriggle to it. (<u>Highly</u> provocative! She knew <u>that</u> too!)

"Yes, Sir?" Her tone was always so bright-and-shiny. "Can I help you?"

"Uh . . . well, I'm a good buddy of . . . of Paul Marchildon. He said that you were his friend. His close friend."

I'd not come close to anticipating her reaction!

"Did . . . did something <u>happen</u> to him?" Her face was—all of a sudden—terribly contorted! In abject horror! (Helluva compliment, there, I guess.) "I'd heard . . . there was this rumor, you see . . . that he'd . . . that he'd <u>died</u>! I'd always thought that it was probably more than a rumor. Can <u>you</u> tell me? <u>Could</u> you tell me . . . ?"

"Uh . . . well, you see . . . yes, he <u>did</u> pass away. About a year ago, I think. We all <u>miss</u> him. I'd known him for quite a long time. He'd told me a <u>lot</u> about San Antonio. Especially, you know, about his time . . . when he was working for *L And M*, a couple of doors down. He spoke of you . . . quite often."

"<u>Me</u>? He spoke of <u>me</u>? <u>Often</u>? <u>Really</u>? What did he have to say?"

"Well, for one thing, he told me . . . especially . . . of some of the all-encompassing conversations you two used to have. At lunchtime, as I understand it. He said you guys used to gab . . . about music, mostly, I guess. Especially about music. He said you two had . . . ah . . . differing opinions, when it came to Axel Stordahl and Paul Weston. He positively <u>adored</u> Mister Stordahl. And, you know, he <u>loved</u> those . . . ah . . . those spirited discussions. Those brisk little conversations, he'd had with you. He was so 'in' to that kind of music. More so than anyone <u>I've</u> ever met."

She seemed to relax—noticeably. Thank God for <u>that</u>.

"Yes," she acknowledged, laughing softly. "We used to have some fairly interesting tete-a-tetes. Some of them, I guess, went pretty far afield. But, we always had a good time with them. You're right. He <u>was</u> in to 'schmaltz' . . . as he'd always called it. But then, so was I. So <u>am</u> I."

"I'd always threatened to come down to San Antone. I'm from Detroit, originally. That's where Paul used to live."

"I know. He spoke about the city . . . many times. I'm positive that he'd hated to <u>leave</u> there. What brings you down here?"

"Well, business mostly. But, he told me that, if I ever got down here . . . down to this part of the country . . . I should look you up."

"Well," she replied, "I don't know if I'm the bearer of some measure of bad news, myself."

"Bad news? You?"

"Yes. I'd kind of . . . you know . . . heard that he'd . . . well, that he and his wife had had a bit of a falling out. Had, sadly, broken up."

"Yeah." I sighed—heavily. "It happened . . . just before the accident. He died . . . not far from here! On Interstate Ten! Just the other side of Seguin, as I understand it. I'm pretty sure that it was only a day or two . . . maybe even just hours . . . after they'd gone and separated."

"I can't tell you how sorry I was to hear that. Like I'd said, there'd been this God-awful rumble . . . about the breakup. That . . . I heard that rumor . . . well before I'd gotten rocked by the second rumor! The rumble about his dying! Then again, I'm probably not telling you anything that you don't already know. About his marital situation."

"Yeah. We were all sorry to hear about them splitting up! And especially about his being killed! I was going to try and look up Joanne . . . and his kids. I guess they're down in Brownsville, though. Don't know if I'll be able to make it that far down."

"Look, maybe I'm speaking out of turn . . . inescapable habit of mine . . . but, did he ever mention the lady? The one . . . with whom he'd worked? Over at L And M?"

"Yes. Yes, he did. Quite a few times, as a matter of fact. In fact, I'd really wanted to look her up. Her name was Elena. Elena Barrientos."

"I know. Again, I might be telling tales out of school, but, I think that his . . . ah . . . relationship with Elena . . . that their sort-of-arrangement . . . that . . . well . . . that his marriage might've broken up, because of that. Did you ever know Elena?"

"No. Not really. I'd not ever met her. But . . . through Paul . . . I felt as though I actually knew her. Really wanted to meet her. To talk to her, y'know. But, damn, I just found out . . . found out just a minute or two ago . . . that she doesn't work at L and M anymore. I was hoping, maybe, that you could tell me where I could . . ."

"You're . . . you're looking for Elena?" She was withdrawing! I could feel the tension. It was as though I'd just been hit by an iceberg! "Look, Mister. I really don't know who you are! But, don't be asking me about Elena. Or about her, and her . . . ah . . . relationship with Paul, for that matter. You can just . . ."

"It's nothing," I tried to reassure her. "Look! Paul knew that I'd be coming here . . . eventually. Coming here to San Antonio. And he simply asked me to look in on her."

"Come now! Why would he ever ask you . . . to do a thing like that? To . . . ah . . . ah . . . look in on her? On Elena? Her . . . of all people?"

"Look. I really think he'd had this . . . well, this feeling! This kind of feeling of . . . feeling of . . . well, of foreboding! The last time I'd ever talked with him . . . this was a day or two before his accident . . . he'd sounded so . . . well, so strange!"

"Strange? How so?"

"Well, it was really frightening! Almost as though he'd divined . . . was lead-pipe certain . . . that something was going to happen to him. Something bad! It was really kind of . . . well, of chilling."

"I can understand that." She seemed to be softening. "At least, I think I can understand it. I guess . . ."

"So, I'd especially wanted to look up Elena. More or less as fulfilling a wish! A sort of quest! For him . . . for Paul . . . if you can believe it! For Paul! Honoring a sort of unspoken request . . . I sincerely believe. Don't mean to sound macabre or anything . . . but, I'd judged it as almost a death wish! That's all! All this thing is about! Nothing . . . uh . . . sinister about it! Nothing like that! Nothing even close!"

"Well . . . now you look! I don't know you from Adam. But, I'd be doing you a disservice . . . if I didn't tell you that there was a big upheaval at that office! Big upheaval!"

"Yeah. I'd always had that feeling."

"I don't really know exactly what happened. And I'm not lying about that! Have no idea! Paul left. And, look! I knew how he felt about Elena. How she felt about him. We all did! We could . . . all of us here on the block . . . we could all walk by L And M. And we'd look in. And you could tell! Could tell just how much in love they were! You'd have to be an out and out idiot . . . not to recognize it! Fanny-over-teakettle, they were! Deeply, in love! With one another! Deeply!"

"You knew that? You could tell that? Even from here?" I was hoping that my tone of voice was not coming out, as being totally rattled! As I'd feared it was!

"Well," she said, "I don't think they knew what we were all thinking. And saying. I doubt that they knew . . . either one of them . . . how we'd always referred to them." She lowered her eyes—and her voice reeked of confidentiality. Then, she continued. "We all called them 'The Lovers'. Not in front of their faces, of course. But . . . look, I don't know why I'm telling you all this. It's . . . I guess . . . it must be from your reactions. If you could've seen the look on your face a few seconds ago!"

"I'm sorry . . . if I've upset you at all."

"No, you didn't upset me. Well, you did . . . at first. But, I can tell . . . you're upset. Very upset. I'm sorry. Sorry for your . . . ah . . . discomfort."

"Oh," I groused. "I'll get over it. We all do."

"Well, I'm not so sure that Paul ever did! Get over his feelings . . . his love . . . for Elena! He left!"

"Yeah. Went to work at some truck-rental place. He'd hated it there."

"Well, he'd have hated anywhere . . . if he couldn't be with Elena! I guess he was fired . . . over at L and M. And it . . . the dismissal . . . seemed to have devastated Elena. You could just look at her . . . poor thing . . . and see the terrible hurt in her eyes! The damnable hurt! We . . . all of us . . . could tell that it was all downhill for her! From then on! A veritable disaster for her . . . ever since Paul left. Then . . ."

Dolly had, obviously, begun to say something—and was, quite probably, thinking twice about relating the thought to me. She seemed to be, in fact, reevaluating our entire conversation!

"Yes?" I probed. "And then?"

"Then . . . and I don't, for the life of me, know what happened . . . but, there was this big . . . like I said . . . this big to-do, over at that office. The bigwigs from the home office . . . Tyler, I think . . . they came in! Descended on that office! And then, all hell broke loose!

"All hell?"

She nodded—emphatically! "They tied the can to Tony's fanny! Then, a couple of days later, it was Elena! She was gone. I don't know why! The suits had all gone back up to Tyler. And Richard had . . . out of the blue . . . had taken over as manager. Then, a day or two went by. And . . . all of a sudden . . . Elena was history! Haven't seen . . . or heard . . . from her, since! And this was . . . you know . . . a good while back! Weeks! Months, maybe! Months . . . I'm sure!"

This was all too much for me. I felt myself getting dizzy once again.

"Look," I pleaded. "Do you mind if I sit down? I really don't want a loan, or anything. I just . . ."

"That's obvious," she responded. She was—I could tell—having a whole bunch of additional second thoughts! Probably third and fourth thoughts, as well! All, undoubtedly, pertaining to how much she'd told me.

She indicated a bank of chairs—next to the front full-length window. She turned—apparently to return to her desk. Then, obviously, she'd changed her mind.

"Listen," she began—as she seated that storied posterior in the chair next to mine, "I'm really worried . . . over what I've just told you. Won't you, at least, tell me who you are? Other than you're a good friend of Paul's . . . from Detroit?"

"Yeah," I mumbled—totally deflated. "I'm sorry. My name is Taylor Young. I don't know if Paul ever mentioned me, but . . ."

"No . . . he never did. Not to my recollection, at least."

"Well, it's obvious . . . obvious, that I'm not telling you anything, when I say this. But, he had these many . . . ah . . . great feelings! <u>Really</u> great feelings . . . toward <u>Elena</u>! Again, I'm not telling you anything you evidently don't know. I guess . . . one way or another . . . the two of them decided that it just . . . that it'd never . . . you know . . . never work <u>out</u>! And then, his wife, you know . . . she went and <u>left</u> him. Left him . . . and took the <u>kids</u>. Took ;em <u>away</u>! Took 'em . . . down to <u>Brownsville</u>!

"Plus," she advised, "he'd had all these goodly number . . . goodly number, you know, of <u>financial</u> problems! <u>Lots</u> of problems . . . money-wise. <u>Lots</u>!"

"He . . . he told you <u>that</u>?"

"No," she answered, laughing softly. "He didn't <u>have</u> to. Everyone <u>knew</u> it! Something <u>else</u> . . . that was no big secret! Everyone around <u>here</u>, anyway . . . we were <u>all</u> well aware of it. Just for kicks and giggles, I ran the credit bureau on him . . . when I gave him that loan.'

"He had a <u>loan</u> with you?" I'd, of course, been completely aware of that fact—and all the other similar goings on. But, it surprised me, more than slightly, that she'd advise <u>me</u>—the well-known "perfect stranger"—of that highly-personal fact. Especially since she'd appeared so fond of Paul.

"Oh look," she added. "He'd had a loan with <u>everyone</u>. One of my cherished competitors . . . Howard Leslie, the guy that owns the company, at the other end of the block . . . <u>he</u> has never quit bitching about it. <u>I</u> gave Paul a seventy-five dollar loan . . . knowing that I'd <u>never</u> get it back. But, hell. He <u>was</u> a good guy. And, you know . . . what are friends <u>for</u>? And so, I just figured . . ."

"You thought that Paul was a <u>good</u> guy?"

"Well, of <u>course</u>!" She <u>sounded</u> mortally wounded. "Of <u>course</u> I did. Of course I <u>do</u>!"

"Not a <u>schmuck</u>? You don't consider him a <u>schmuck</u>? You didn't <u>ever</u> consider him a <u>schmuck</u>?"

"What would <u>ever</u> give you a thought like <u>that</u>? <u>You</u> are supposed to <u>know</u> him. <u>Supposed</u> to be his friend! A <u>schmuck</u>? I don't . . ."

"Well, look. Paul has always imagined that people would, you know, look down on him! And <u>that</u> train of thought was bucked up . . . by the fact that his wife left him. Plus, his kids were gone. And, listen, people frown on guys being married . . . and having girlfriends. There were also those many financial problems. He just felt that . . ."

"Look. I don't know what they were paying him . . . at *L and M*. But, I'm <u>sure</u> it was less . . . <u>much</u> less . . . than what he'd put on his application for the stupid damn loan. The one I gave him."

"Yeah," I muttered. "I'm sure he did."

"He'd had a record for being delinquent with the <u>big</u> finance company . . . the one over on Elizabeth Street. He'd had to refinance his car . . . two or three times . . . over there. The bank said he was struggling to pay his loan there."

"You <u>knew</u> all this? You <u>know</u> all this?"

"Certainly. And I'm absolutely <u>convinced</u> that the bank would not have even <u>given</u> him the damn loan . . . had he not been branch manager, of one of their better <u>customers</u>. Their <u>larger</u> customers.

Then . . . one way or another . . . he'd lost his job! Listen, he probably made some mistakes. He undoubtedly made some mistakes. I don't know how horrible any of them might've been. But, I could tell . . . he was a good guy. I really liked him!"

"Really? He wasn't some kind of . . . some kind of schmuck?"

"Of course not! Why he should ever think that any of us . . . except for that asshole, on the other end of the block . . . would ever consider him a schmuck, well it's passed me."

"Not a schmuck, huh?"

"No. Hell no. I don't know where he'd ever get that idea."

"Well, he's probably a little too oversensitive. That is, he was a little too oversensitive. Probably."

"Then he was a lot oversensitive! Listen, I don't know what might've gone on between Paul and Elena. I really don't want to know what went on with them. But, I don't think that they were out doing all kinds of, you know, rotten things! Really bad things! I know both of them pretty well, and . . ."

"But, you can't tell me . . . what might've happened to Elena?"

"Taylor . . . you sound a little too anxious to know what's going on with her. Not a just-asking-for-a-friend kind of a thing, y'know. Doesn't sound that way to me, anyway. Now, why . . . exactly why . . . are you all this hepped up? This deeply involved . . . over finding Elena? Or learning about her, anyway! Why? Come . . . and tell ol' Dolly why! And don't try bullshitting a bullshitter! It'll never work! What's behind all this interest in Elena?"

"Dolly, you've got to believe me. I'm just . . ."

"Wait a minute! How'd you know my name was Dolly?"

"Well, for one thing, you just told me."

"Yeah. That's right, I guess I did. I guess I must have."

"But, I knew your name anyway. Paul . . . like I said . . . he's told me a lot about you. He had a special . . . a special affection . . . for you. Remember? He really liked talking to you. And he loved those the great conversations you'd had. I think he went to his grave, believing . . . in his heart of hearts . . . that Axel Stordahl was a greater genius. Greater than your Paul Weston."

Without particularly meaning to, I'd hit her right between her emotional eyes! It defied logic! I couldn't imagine why it would've taken that long—but, at that point, her physical eyes filled with tears.

"Listen," she sniffled, "Axel couldn't hold Paul Weston's baton!"

That one remark made me feel better! Better— than I'd felt in a long time. Don't ask me why!

THIRTEEN

I WASN'T QUITE SO PANIC-STRICKEN—FOR some unknown reason—as I'd made my way back to pick up my car. Dolly's remark about "Paul Weston's baton" seemed to have had a bit of a soothing effect on me.

And yet, there was something—some unidentifiable "force" just under the surface—that had been more than merely a little disquieting, about even <u>that</u> statement. Innocuous as the observation had been, it was the source of some unease. And— guess what? I couldn't put my finger on <u>that</u>, either. A tradition.

I drove—at speeds well in excess of the limit— out Bandera Road. Once I'd reached this small strip-shopping center, I wheeled off a much-too-dangerous left-hand turn onto the next side street. Elena's house was on yet another—albeit much-shorter—side street. One that paralleled, directly, behind the strip-plaza. Second bungalow on the left.

I parked the Dodge (some <u>might</u> say— "abandoned" the Dodge) across the street from her residence! I hurried up onto her front porch. Even then, I could tell that something was definitely amiss and amuck! (Especially the latter.) I was, once again, experiencing this God-awful bleak, terribly-foreboding, feeling. (We'd become old friends, by then.)

In a near-panic, I knocked! And, of course, I heard the inevitable (the dreaded) <u>hollow</u> sound! My frantic rapping had reverberated around—and through—the entire interior of the small house. It was <u>empty</u>! I <u>knew</u> it! There could be no doubt!

But, "just in case", I went around and peered in through the living room window! Then, the dinette, the kitchen—and (yes) even the bedroom windows! <u>Nothing</u>! Not one damn <u>thing</u>—in the whole furschlugginer place!

Had she left something I could've identified—something personal of hers—I do not, to this day, know if I'd have been able to have resisted the temptation: The totally overwhelming—highly-enticing—inducement! The mind-clouding temptation! To break the hell <u>in</u>! Burglarize the joint—and <u>take</u> whatever I could find! But, alas (as they say) there was <u>nothing</u>! Not one damn <u>thing</u>! The place was totally <u>empty</u>!

Hoo! You talk about <u>foreboding</u>! <u>Spooky</u>! Not only <u>that</u>—but, terribly <u>heart</u>-<u>breaking</u>! <u>Now</u> what do I do? <u>Think</u>, Man! <u>Think</u>!

You'd be surprised (or maybe you wouldn't) at the stupid things that unceasingly <u>slam</u> their way into your mind, in a situation such as the one in which I'd so sadly found myself! Found myself immersed in a God-awful, extremely-perplexing, dilemma! "Fanny-deep", as Dolly would've said!

I'd remembered that Elena had, most always, gotten her hair done every Wednesday. I'd always lamented the fact that—given the "generous" stipend that the company was bestowing upon her—she really couldn't afford it. I'd usually wound up paying for it. Which, of course, was one of the reasons for all those damnable small loans (including the one that had unleashed the unbridled wrath of Howard Leslie—who'd owned the office on the far corner from Dolly's little "loan emporium")! And, of course, it had done nothing—to help with the inescapable foreclosure on the house! Or with the height-of-futility car repo situation!

Let's face it: I'd really not been able to afford the stupid dinner—where she and I couldn't control our laughing—or, for that matter, *Mad, Mad, Mad World*. Couldn't really afford that one night—in the little bar northwest of town, when we danced the night away. (Most especially, we'd been so close—so tightly clinging to one another—while dancing to Percy Faith's recording of Till.) I certainly could never have afforded the third-row tickets—to that magical live production of *Oliver*. But, obviously, none of those cautions had stood in my way!

In my mind—and to this day—I "knew" that I could never have afforded to have not gone ahead, with all those rewarding "jaunts"! I'd simply had to have "invested"—in those glorious, warm-and-fuzzy, memorable, certainly-unforgettable, "adventures"!

A sudden realization: This was Wednesday! Maybe she was having her hair done! When she'd begun working with me, she'd found a little beauty shop, just a couple of blocks from the office—down near St. Ferdinand's Cathedral. That was a long way from her residence. Well, sadly for me, her former residence.

Logically, she'd not be going way back there. (I was thinking logically? All of a sudden—I was thinking logically?) She should have—again, logically—patronized some beauty salon out in her neighborhood.

There was such a beauty parlor in the strip-center, just a block away. I ran around the block—to inquire therein! One of the four ladies inside said that she knew Elena. "But, I haven't seen her in . . . in God . . . not in months. In ages!" Not good! The other beautician had never heard of her.

There was a drycleaners and a hobby shop in the mostly-vacant plaza. No one—in either establishment—had ever known Elena. Also not good!

Well, maybe she would travel all the way downtown to have her hair done. Despite the fact that—as far as I knew—she'd had no car. And—even had she scored some "wheels"—where would she park? Still, maybe—just maybe—she still patronized that beauty joint. (Logic be damned!)

As long as we're discussing goofy thoughts, I knew that she used to get her dad to drive her—in his 1957 Chevy Nomad station wagon—out to the *Montgomery Ward's* store, in a fairly large shopping center, where Bandera meets Loop 410. Also, a fair amount of mileage from where I was standing. (Actually, back standing—in the middle of her side street—by then.)

Her father! Of course! He might be able to lead me somewhere in this highly-frustrating, God-awful-so-far, lamentably-dead end, quest.

Elena's folks lived three or four blocks away—on a parallel side street. It was, though, a corner house. And the family's garage faced out onto busy Gen. McMullen Road. Her father had, for years, owned and run a small sales/service business out of the garage. He dealt in power, rotary, lawnmowers. (The use of those dandies, back then, was not as nationally widespread—as we may all be imagining.)

I hurried over to where the old man's shop was located! In his late-sixties (easily)—he was still purveying his lawnmower wares and expertise. He was busily sharpening one of four blades, attached to a wheel-type mowing device, when I walked in.

"Can I help you, Sir?" His smile was broad. I'd only met him two or three times—when he'd come to pick up "his little girl", in that classic "Dusty Rose" Nomad. His smile was infectious. Everything about him simply reeked of class. Of true character.

"Yessir, Mister Salazar," I'd answered. "Look. You don't know me . . . but, I was trying to . . . ah . . . trying to, trying to . . . to reach . . . to contact . . . your daughter. Your daughter, Elena."

With one master brushstroke, the smile disappeared! Not only disappeared—but, was instantly replaced with an icy, exceedingly-grim, clench-jawed, stare! Immediately, I felt two fast-rising burn holes seer into my forehead! It was as devastating a reaction as I'd ever encountered!

"Who are you?" he hissed. "And what do you want of my daughter?"

"Well, you see, I used to know her. And . . ."

"Know her? Know her . . . from <u>where</u>?"

"Well, I . . . uh . . . you see, I used to work with her."

"<u>Where</u>? At that piece-of-shit loan company . . . downtown?"

"No, Sir. I was . . ."

"Then . . . from <u>where</u>?"

My mind—what was left of it—was <u>churning</u>! <u>Madly</u>! <u>Frantically</u>! Try as I might, I could not remember <u>one</u> thing from the application for employment that she'd filled out—so long in the past!

Of course, <u>that</u> had been over a year before. Almost a year-and-a-half. And <u>who</u> could ever have <u>thought</u> that I <u>should</u> have placed such heavy value on some of that data? At <u>this</u> vitally-critical moment in my life?

"Well?" he persisted. "<u>Where</u> did you work with my daughter? Where <u>could</u> you have worked with her? Other than at that shit-assed loan company. Weren't a hell of a lot of Anglos that have <u>ever</u> worked with her! Other than those rotten bastards . . . those pieces of shit, those sons of bitches . . . from downtown!"

<u>Man</u>! He really had it <u>in</u> for "those sons of bitches"!

"Well, I didn't actually work <u>with</u> her, you see."

"<u>HAH</u>! I thought so."

"No, you see . . . I worked at that little drugstore next door to the loan company." As you might have remembered, there <u>was</u> such a place. <u>Really</u>! The cozy little store was located between my former employer's bailiwick—and Dolly's little den of iniquity.

That had been where our paths had most often crossed.

"You're all . . . all of you . . . you're all goddam Anglos! You're all pieces of shit . . . from downtown! You're all sons of bitches! I will tell you nothing! Will tell you nothing of . . . or about . . . my daughter! Nothing . . . will I tell you!"

I got the distinct feeling that he wasn't going to tell me one thing about Elena. But, amidst all this tumult, I found myself wondering why he was so reluctant—so hesitant—to simply use her name! He continued:

"I must ask you, Sir, to leave!" Not only was he not going to be a fount of information—but, he was throwing my "goddam Anglo" butt out!

Well, I could take a hint. I left. (There was this one, very-troubling, thought—bouncing around, helter-skelter, throughout my already-fragile psyche: The very real possibility—that my "host" was on the verge of turning violent! Even deadly violent! He'd been that upset! That rattled!)

I was "hiding out"—if that term can adequately apply to parking my Polara three cars behind his Nomad, on the side street. I figured that, maybe (just maybe) the obviously-irate father might decide to drive out—to wherever Elena might be. If he'd been unhinged enough, by my presence, he just might do that. (Of course, whether or not he'd been upset at my queries, he could simply have called her—on the stupid telephone.) But, when you're grasping at straws—as I definitely <u>was</u> (my life's work)—being sensible is not an easy call.

About three endless hours later—as the sun was beginning to set (and I was on the verge of giving up)—Mr. Salazar emerged from the front door of his house, and climbed into his '57 wagon. Ah HAH!

I couldn't tell if he'd seen me. I didn't <u>think</u> he'd seen my car—when I'd "visited" him earlier. There was no parking permitted—on Gen. McMullen. So, I'd pulled around the corner. Had left the Dodge on the side street—across from his house—while I'd "visited" him. Obviously, I'd since moved the vehicle—deployed it—to my present, oh-so-clever, "observation point".

Amateur detective that I am, I followed him. To what they call—in Texas—an "ice house". Those revered sanctuaries are merely small-sized beer joints. About the size of a convenience store. Usually with a bunch of garage-type, roll-up, doors across the entire front. And <u>no</u> air conditioning! They're places—where "Good Ol' Boys" usually hang out! A gathering place for "red necks"! Despite our "spirited" confrontation of that afternoon, I could—most assuredly—see Elena's father as being one of <u>those</u>! Fitted the definition—to a tee!

On the other hand, that image had never fit my first impression of the man. Not before I'd had my totally-unexpected—expletive-laden—run-in with him, that afternoon.

His daughter—my fellow employee at the time—was always writing him notes. (She'd mail 'em—tapping into the roll of corporate postage stamps. Yet <u>another</u> glaring example—of my gross misfeasance.

Or is it malfeasance?) But, what this loving exercise, of hers, had always struck in sentimental, schmaltzy, old me—was the fact that she'd never fail to begin each of those tender little letters, with the cherished words, "Estimado Papa".

The English translation is "My Esteemed Father". How I found myself wishing that—one day—just one of my kids would refer to me as his/her esteemed father.

Fat chance! For one thing, officially, I was dead! Plus, the tads were all in Brownsville! And, soon—all too soon—they would absolutely forget me! Forget all about me! There would come a time—in the not-too-distant future, I knew—when they wouldn't even know who I was! I shuddered—from head to toe—at that disheartening prospect! That chilling prospect! Certainly, there could never be any way—for them to know who I am!

Not unless I would be able—to pull off something! Something spectacular! Some incredible, brilliant, feat of legerdemain—to radically change all of that! Yeah. Right. But, what? And how? What could that ever be? How would I ever be able to accomplish some kind of wild-hair scheme like that? And when? But, mostly, how? How, indeed? It was a most-frustrating—most disappointing—brain-warper!

I sat there—for over an hour—across the street, from the raucous beer joint. It finally became evident—even to imperceptive little old me—that my quarry was thoroughly enjoying himself! He was far too contented! And with a bunch of Anglo guys, yet! Can you imagine? (That revelation was—most definitely—a surprise! Yet another shocker—in this day filled with the damn things!) He was—definitely—not in any sort of panic mode, as pertained to his daughter. Or anyone/anything else! My thought was—that he'd probably remain immersed—in his brew-directed activities—for the foreseeable future.

It would be hours before he would—in my uninformed view—drive himself home. (He'd have to drive. Just from the number of beers I'd already watched him slosh down, he'd be in no condition to walk.)

So, I left!

I say that I left. Well, in point of fact, I did. But, I'd had not the slightest idea as to where I should be headed. You'd have thought that I'd have—cleverly—mapped out my next move, during the seemingly-endless "vigil" that I'd maintained outside that dive. You'd have been wrong!

It was far too late—to even begin to consider the long schlep to Brownsville. Logically (that word again) I should simply check in to a motel—and then leave, early in the morning, for The Rio Grande Valley.

Yeah. I should—definitely—head on down to Brownsville. (Sigh—why the hell not?) On the other hand, my heart was so weighted down—with not knowing where (or how) the lovely Elena was—that it would be a major undertaking, for worried old me to actually leave San Antonio. (Think pulling teeth!) How could I abandon my more-urgent-than-ever quest? How could I possibly <u>leave</u>? <u>Abandon</u> my mission? Beset by that damnable—that frustrated, highly-troubled—state of mind?

As I'd pulled out onto Commerce Street—headed in the direction of our ill-fated home in the *Valley Hi* subdivision, across Loop 410 from *Lackland Air Force Base*—it suddenly occurred to me: I became aware of the fact—that I was hungry! Ravenous! Starved! I'd not eaten anything all day long!

It seemed to me that there had been a fair number of respectable fast-food joints in that shopping center that Elena had so often frequented. So, I turned onto The Loop—and headed north, toward Bandera Road. There was always that one-in-seven-trillion chance that I just might blunder <u>in</u> to this wonderful woman! Our paths <u>might</u> cross—at one of those eateries! One never <u>knew</u>! Yeah, I was reduced to <u>that</u>!

There weren't nearly as many restaurants in that facility as my "memory" had led me to believe. I'd looked through three of them—scoped them out thoroughly—and, finally (out of sheer frustration) settled into the fourth. Those were the only eateries I was able to stumble across. Once ensconced in the joint that I'd decided to grace with my presence, I'd watched the eatery's entrance—incessantly! Hoping, of course, against hope!

After about 40 minutes, I'd gotten this <u>one</u> flickering! A glimmering of <u>hope</u>—no matter <u>how</u> remote! The prospect that—maybe, just <u>maybe</u>—the prayed-for-albeit-far-fetched good fortune might smile upon me!

The lady who'd lived across the street from Elena—and the lady's husband—entered the place. I'd—immediately—left my seat at the counter, and approached the pair, in their booth, at the far end of the restaurant.

"Excuse me," I'd said to the woman. (I'd never seen the man before.) "You don't know me, but I'm a friend of Elena's. The lady who used to live across the street from you. At number 93. I'd tried to look her up today . . . but, found she'd moved. Could you tell me how I might reach her? And . . . and is she all right?"

As soon as I'd spoken that last line, I wished that I'd had it back. I believe that I was doing all right—till then. But, apparently, my asking—inquiring about her well-being—made me come across as being <u>way</u> "too interested".

"No," she answered—quickly and in a tone that was far harsher than I'd thought would've been called for. "She moved away! Far, far away! Way last summer sometime. I don't <u>know</u> where! No idea <u>where</u>! Have never <u>heard</u> from her since. Now . . . if you'll <u>excuse</u> me?"

It was obvious that <u>she</u>—also—was going to be anything but a fount of information. Lot of that going around. I couldn't help but be upset—yes, even <u>more</u> upset—at her tone of voice, and her <u>very</u> brusque manner. After all, I'd never done anything to her. Had never even spoken with her before. Further, she'd never laid eyes on Taylor Young. Why should she be so <u>upset</u>? So <u>dismissive</u>? And so <u>quickly</u>? And so <u>definitively</u>?

Even <u>I</u> know when I'm licked! I finally checked in at a hotel—close by, on The Loop. But, as you might imagine, it was impossible to sleep. The day's happenings—all, of course, revolving around Elena—just wouldn't let up! Never ceased their relentless churning through what we laughingly refer to as my mind. (You could probably smell the wood burning from there!) As you can also imagine, morning broke—with no solution in sight.

Back in the mid-sixties, you usually had a legitimate shot at finding a local phone book—no matter <u>where</u> you might've been. Hotels—even then—were especially good, when it came to this long-forgotten phase of hosting the public.

At breakfast, Thursday morning, I brought the copy that had been assigned to my room with me, as I headed for the hotel's coffee shop—hoping all the while that I'd discover that Elena would, magically, appear! She might even materialize—as my "server". (Or "waitress"—as they were called, in those Neanderthal times.)

Of course, she did <u>not</u>! Was <u>not</u>! Didn't <u>figure</u> to be! Elena, of course, was nowhere to be seen. It wasn't as though not discovering her presence was some out-of-the-blue, unexpected phenomenon. The whole "thought process" had been a totally out-of-the-blue scenario! Still, I <u>was</u> experiencing further heartbreak.

The blessed Yellow Pages! They were filled,
with private detectives. I picked one out of the
overwhelming pack—because of his name. "Sam
Peck"! (Now, there was a "private eye"—if ever I'd
heard of one!) Except that—when I got back to my
room—I found his phone had been disconnected. So
had the next two "dicks"—with less-likely monikers—
that I'd sought out.

I figured that I'd wind up with some guy named
"Oglethorpe"—who'd look like *Mr. Peepers*. But—for
better or for worse—I hooked up with a guy named
Adam Browning. He sounded quite efficient—over
the phone.

I made my way downtown to his office—on the
11th floor, of a fairly-impressive building on St. Mary's
Street. (He looked more like Carl Reiner—of the
early-fifties *Show Of Shows*—than anyone else.)

I made a deal with him. Gave him a check
for $2000! Told him he didn't have to start his
investigation until the check had cleared—but, I
wanted him to "move heaven and earth", to find the
lovely Elena!

He was pretty forthright. Told me that he could
not guarantee any positive results—especially
considering the dearth of information I was able to
provide. On the other hand, there wasn't much else I
could do—again, logically—but accept his deal. The
current day field of PIs seemed awfully fallow.

Having, hopefully, unloaded the wearing-me-down
"burden" on Mr. Browning, I—at long last—headed for
The Rio Grande Valley. It was almost eleven o'clock.
I'd hoped to have begun my journey, to South Texas,
earlier—much earlier—than that.

FOURTEEN

I GOT TO BROWNSVILLE SHORTLY AFTER five o'clock that evening. That might have seemed like a long time to today's travelers—those familiar with the highway system of today's Texas. But, the rural routes—in 1966—were far less efficient back then. Numerous small towns—and they were not bypassed, back then. But, eventually, I did make it to The Tip of Texas.

The first item, on my list—the top of the ol' agenda—was, of course, to drive past my parents-in-law's house. I was totally unprepared for the out and out tsunami of emotion that I would experience! Outside the cheery bungalow—in the middle of the front lawn—was Mary Jane (now four-years-old)! My Little Girl!

You're so beautiful, Baby! So very beautiful!

She was digging around a short-but-wide, circular shrub—with what looked like a tablespoon. There was no one else around.

I pulled up across the street—and watched! Watched My Little Girl! She seemed happy! I was glad for that! Ever so glad! Still, it was terribly heartbreaking to look at your daughter (or your son)—and know that, even if they saw you, they'd never recognize you. Mary Jane had probably forgotten about me, by then, anyway. She'd lived—roughly—a quarter of her life, and had not seen her father, during that period! Dear Lord! Can you imagine? Tragic!

I must've sat there for 20 or 25 minutes. There'd still been no one else who'd wandered outside. Only one car had driven by. Someone I'd never laid eyes on, had been behind the wheel. But, no one from inside the house ever made an appearance! I'd thought that awfully unusual—but, like they say, "Mine not to wonder why".

I drove into "Beautiful Downtown Brownsville"—and pulled into a Denny's-type restaurant. One that had caught my eye—on the way through to Joanne's parent's abode. I'd never seen that one before—and we'd made numerous trips from San Antonio (during my "other life").

Surprisingly, the joint did not have a counter. I found myself ensconced in a booth—in one of the far corners. I was halfway through my hamburger—when I was totally shaken! Shocked, I was!

Stupefied—to see my mother-in-law enter the eatery. The hostess seated her three booths from me. Pretty close. Quite disconcerting! At least, at first. I'd had to—constantly—keep reassuring myself that Paul Marchildon really was dead, as far as "The War

Horse" knew! She'd <u>never</u> recognize Taylor Young. <u>Really</u>! She <u>wouldn't</u>!

The woman was alone. <u>That</u> was something <u>else</u>—that was totally unexpected. She and I had—seemingly, always—had our problems. But, she'd always been extremely close to her only grandkids. I would have <u>thought</u> that she'd have one of my tads with her. At the very <u>least</u>! But, no! There she was! Solo! And she'd looked particularly <u>haggard</u>! As though she'd been dragged through some kind of an emotional meat-grinder! I'd never seen her looking so <u>bedraggled</u>! Nothing <u>close</u>!

I watched her—intently—as she'd ordered either a ham or corned beef sandwich, and a cup of coffee! During her short stay, she nibbled at her sandwich—but, went through a <u>barrel</u> of coffee (or so it seemed).

She spent, probably, 30 or 35 minutes in the cafe—during which time she'd never stopped fidgeting. I discovered myself almost feeling <u>sorry</u> for "The Old War Horse"! (<u>Almost</u>!)

Once she'd left, I looked down—and found that I'd not <u>touched</u> my own burger! Not once! Not during my mother-in-law's entire stay!

<u>Why should that be</u>? I found myself wondering. Old debbil logic kept trying to make its presence known, once again. <u>You can't be concerning yourself with her</u>, Taylor. <u>When has SHE ever shown YOU anything</u> . . . <u>but the back of her hand</u>? <u>You've got your own worries</u>! <u>Have you EVER got your own worries</u>! <u>Your own problems</u>! Yeah. Right. I know. But, still . . .

That evening-into-night, I drove by the home of Joanne's parents four different times. Not once did I see a <u>soul</u>—although, once darkness had set in, I'd not figured to see any of the kids. But, my former wife, maybe.

Possibly, my father-in-law would be sitting on the front porch—smoking his cigarette. I wondered if he still smoked *Chesterfields*. I wondered if they still <u>made</u> *Chesterfields*. (On the other hand, it finally occurred to me—on my third pass—that, at no time, did I ever see his celebrated, "fabulous", Park Lane, in the driveway. Just his wife's six-year-old, badly-faded, washed-out-blue, Plymouth Fury.)

At <u>no</u> time did I see <u>anyone</u>! That one, all-too-brief, sighting of Mary Jane—had been <u>it</u>! For some reason—possibly logical (who could tell?)—the lack of activity, at the place was <u>terribly</u> disquieting! The continued absence of the old man's station wagon was <u>not</u> helping!

I checked in—to a small, locally-owned, motel. To the surprise of no one (particularly me), I found, for the second night in a row, that it was practically impossible to sleep. There were so many troubling, barely-visible—out and out spooky—specters flitting about! The room was <u>filled</u> with them! Evil spirits! <u>Undoubtedly</u> evil! It seemed as though I was <u>surrounded</u> by them! For want of a better name—snarling, eerie, <u>gremlins</u>!

The following morning, I got up early—before six o'clock. It was about 6:45AM—when I made my first pass! When I initially drove by the home of Joanne's parents. Her father's Park Lane was in the driveway. But, strangely enough—to me, anyway—her mother's old Plymouth was missing. Why should that be? This whole "atmosphere" was terribly troubling!

I headed back into town. If the fact of my mother-in-law's Plymouth's absence from the family's bungalow was surprising—and it was—it was a positive shocker, to see it (once again) in the parking lot of that same restaurant. The one that we'd both patronized the evening before. Naturally (I suppose), I gave the steering wheel a hard yank to the right! And—after cutting off some pour soul, in a ratty old Chevy—I pulled into the eatery's lot.

"The Old War Horse" was seated, once again, in the far reaches of the beginning-to-rapidly-fill eatery. Don't ask me why—but, something told me that it was urgent (if not critical) that I speak with her.

This sudden "need" was—sort of—a bolt out of the blue! (No! Not that kind of a thunderbolt!) The fact that I was aware that my impulses are usually not very reliable notwithstanding, I found myself experiencing this tremendous "pull"—to make some kind of contact with her! I didn't know what manner of ruse I would use. But, it was vital—that I make some sort of contact with her! Part of it, I guess, was the fact that she was looking even more haggard than she had the night before—something I'd have thought impossible!

Now, how does one go about injecting himself—into a situation, about which one knows absolutely nothing? Hell, I'd never let such a teensy item as that stand in my way before. Still, this would take some doing! Some serious thinking! The plan, most certainly, could not be some kind of damn-the-torpedoes move! (Probably, the most intelligent plan of all, I found myself thinking—would've been to drag my butt out of there. But, you knew that such a reasonable course would be out of the question.)

Damning the torpedoes, I made straight for her booth! I rapped—lightly—on her table, startling the poor woman! Two years' growth—shot to hell!

"Excuse me," I said—in a more articulate, non-panic-filled, voice than I could ever have expected. "You don't know me. And . . . if you wish . . . I'll just move on. But . . ."

"Who . . . who are you?" Her voice was weaker than I'd ever heard before. Measurably weaker! And reeking of sadness! "What did you want?" Her voice was growing even more troubled. More subdued. "What do you . . . do you want . . . do you want, of me?"

"Listen, Ma'am. I don't mean to frighten you . . . or cause you any undue problems. But, my name is Taylor Young. I'm from a little town, in the Pacific Northwest. State of Oregon. I'm a psychologist . . . and I saw you in here last night. You were sitting over there." I pointed to her venue of the night before.

"Yes?"

"Well, you'll excuse me for saying this . . . I hope you will, anyway . . . but, you'd looked so very troubled. Extremely troubled. I have friends . . . in San Antonio . . . and I'd come down to visit them."

"You're a considerable way from San Antonio," she responded. "I'd have to say," she added with the merest flicker of a smile, "that you've overshot your mark. By a considerable amount."

I was happy—thrilled—at even the lame reach for humor, such as it was, that she'd displayed, although the stalwart action did nothing to change her obviously-troubled countenance!

"Oh, I've already been there," I answered. "Spent a goodly amount of time with them, as a matter of fact. I'd come down here, to Brownsville . . . in the hopes of being able to look up some old friends from Oregon."

"And . . . how would I fit in to all of that?" The haggard look remained.

"Well, the point I'm trying to make . . . and doing it very badly . . . is that I'm, forever, in contact with people. Various people! A lot of people. Literally hundreds. Wide variety of people. Every day, I see . . . literally . . . dozens of people. In my practice, you see. And I take note . . . probably professionally . . . of so many other people. Folks . . . in all manner of emotional levels."

"That's all well and good. But, I don't see . . ."

"Well, I have to tell you, that it's been a long time. An awfully long time . . . since I've ever observed anyone who'd looked as positively distressed as you did last night. And now, I see you this morning. And, if you don't mind my saying so, you seem every bit as troubled . . . even as we speak . . . as you did last night. Maybe even a little bit more disturbed. I was just wondering. Wondering if it might not do you some good . . . to simply be able to speak to someone. To talk with another human being . . . and, of course, in the strictest of <u>confidence</u>. And . . . don't worry. I won't be sending you a bill. It <u>might</u> be advantageous for you to . . . well, to . . . to, just maybe, <u>unload</u>! Talk it out . . . with a perfect stranger! You'd be surprised. Such things have been known to work <u>wonders</u> . . . in my profession. I can't <u>possibly</u> know . . . by just looking at you . . . what it is that you'd be telling me."

Until that last sentence, I'd gotten the feeling that I'd been talking to a brick wall—or a cement barrier or something. But, the "can't possibly know" remark elicited a smattering of a smile—for the second time.

"What did you say your name was?" Her question was yet another surprise. Not the logic (again, that stupid word) of it. But, the fact that she didn't tell me to get lost—almost caught me off guard. The fact that she didn't call the cops—or, at least, the manager— was even <u>more</u> shocking! Maybe the fact, that she didn't have me on the carpet—in a step-over <u>toe</u>-hold—was the <u>biggest</u> surprise of all! The lack of all of these "venues" was gratifying! And more than a little <u>encouraging</u>!

"Taylor, is my name. Taylor Young," I was answering her question. "From Newport, Oregon."

"Well, look . . . Doctor Young . . ."

"Please! Please . . . just call me Taylor. <u>May</u> I sit down?" That request from—anything-but-forward, little old me—was, probably an even <u>bigger</u> shock, than any of that other stuff, listed above. Such an aggressive maneuver simply wasn't my "style". Ever!

She nodded—more vigorously than I'd had any right to expect. And much more quickly! I slid in across the table from her.

"Now," I began, "if you don't want to give me your name . . . or even your right name . . . that's fine with me."

Again, I got a smile out of her. This one even a little broader than before. And it lasted, maybe, a second or two longer.

"I'm Eva York . . . is my real name. And . . . and I'm married. My husband . . . his name is Luther York."

That was more information than I'd expected to have gotten out of her—in the proverbial month of Sundays.

"Down here," I asked, "do they call you 'Evita'?"

"Oh, a few people do. Some have. But, not many. You see, we've only been down here, in Texas, for something like eight years. Came from Michigan, you see. Little town northwest of Detroit."

"Farmington?"

"Close. Novi. Next town up."

"Know it well. My parents lived in Detroit. Finally moved out to Milford . . . the next town up from Novi."

"That's remarkable."

"Not really. They're retired now. Moved to Oregon. Bought a house in Portland . . . so I just kind of landed out there. I'm located . . . right on the Pacific Ocean. Beautiful country up there! Really gorgeous!"

I was hoping (praying, actually—"Guys"?) that all this information that I was dropping on her—false as it might have been—would make her feel a little more at ease with me. Apparently, it was beginning to work. It seemed that way, anyhow.

"You say," she queried, "that I looked so . . . so, so heartbroken . . . that I . . . that I stood out? Stood out . . . from, literally, hundreds of people? Is that true? Could it be true? Did I actually stick out that much?"

"I hate to tell you this . . . but, yes. Like the proverbial sore thumb."

Another smile. Was the ol' charm working—or what?

"Well," she responded, "I feel kind of silly. Kind of stupid, actually. If I was that much of a . . ."

"I really don't know that it was so much that you were looking totally troubled. Or if there was, maybe, just something about you. Some sort of thing . . . that made me want to . . . want to . . . ."

Bad move! I could see her begin to stiffen! The old iceberg was already in an advanced state of manufacture!

"I'm married," she said, flatly. Whatever positive emotion I'd stirred before was now MIA.

"I didn't mean it that way," I hastened to reassure her. "Look, I really don't know what made me want to . . . well, want to . . . want to see if I could . . . could maybe . . . could, possibly, figure out a way to help you. I simply can't tell you the exact reason. And I'm a damn shrink! Supposed to be one, anyway! On the other hand . . . four fingers and a thumb . . . we don't know everything! Us head doctors. There are some . . . who'll tell you we don't know anything. I've encountered a few of those kind of doctors . . . along the way . . . too."

I'd had her smiling again! Not quite big-time! But, close! (Whew!)

"Look, Doctor," she said—more warmly than I'd had any reason to hope for, "I'm just going through a lot of . . . well, a lot of . . . a lot of . . . of, you know . . . a lot of anxiety! I guess you'd call it that. A whole lot of that . . . of out and out anxiety . . . in my life, these days."

"Can I . . . may I . . . pry into the reason? The cause . . . for all this anxiety?"

"Well, quite frankly, it's my . . . my daughter. Among other things."

I'd hoped that my reaction—as quickly passing as it had (thankfully) been—to her unexpected response hadn't frightened her. I couldn't imagine that she and Joanne could—ever—be at loggerheads. I'd fully expected the answer to center around her uncaring, overbearing, husband.

"Your . . . your daughter?" I'd managed to respond. "You . . . you're having a problem . . . a problem with your . . . with your daughter?"

"Well, the problem is that . . . well, I . . . I just don't know where she is, right now! Geographically! Have no idea!"

That answer really buffaloed me! Came—totally—out of left field!

"Your . . . your daughter? She's . . . she's missing? Have you . . . have you . . . contacted the police? I mean, if she's . . ."

"No. Well, yes. I've talked to them. But, they're not going to do anything to . . . anything to . . . to, you know, bring her back." Eva was on the verge of tears.

"What do you mean? Look! If she's been abducted, or something . . . why, they'd have to do something to . . ."

"Joanne wasn't abducted. At least, she wasn't . . . not in the definition that the authorities always want to use for the term. You see, she . . . she, ah . . . she went and . . . and . . . well, she ran off!"

"Ran off?"

I was really beginning to unravel. Was that the reason that only Mary Jane had been visible the day before? On the other hand, why would Joanne have left—and would've taken only three of the children?

"She ran off," expanded Eva—apparently not noticing that I was positively disintegrating, across the table from her. "She ran off with a goddam . . . excuse the expression . . . but, with a goddam cult member!"

"Cult member?" I was flabbergasted!

"She's with him now," she answered—with a withering sigh. "God only knows where! Oh, they're out in Arizona . . . or Nevada! Or Utah, maybe! Out there . . . someplace! But, he's got Joanne . . . exactly where he wants her! I don't even want to think . . ."

"Why would she . . . ? I mean was there trouble? Trouble . . . in the family? With your husband, maybe? Or her husband?"

"Well, Luther sure wasn't a help. Has not been any help! Any sort of help! You see, Joanne . . . my daughter . . . she left her husband. Up in San Antonio. His name was Paul Marchildon. A day or two after they'd split up . . . and Luther had brought Joanne and the children down here . . . Paul turned up dead. Car accident . . . on the Interstate highway. The one . . . just east of Seguin."

"I'm sorry to hear that. Children? How many children?"

"Four. Four of 'em. Two little boys. Well, they're not so little anymore. And two really little girls."

"And you have the kids . . . all the children . . . now? They're with you?"

"Yes. And, listen, the boys are not happy. Well, Luther's not happy either! He's on the kids! On their butts! All the time! Well, mostly with the boys! The girls . . . they pretty much, get a pass! But, he's on the boys' rear ends! All the damn time! To the point that one of 'em even ran away! Ran away! Just last week! Ran straight away!"

"Ran away? Really? Last week? Which one?"

"The nine-year-old. His name is Randy. He turned up two days ago. In Laredo. I guess he'd hitchhiked out there. I can't even imagine a kid . . . especially a kid of that age, can't imagine a kid that young . . . can't imagine him doing that! Hitchhiking that far! I really can't imagine a kid . . . that age . . . hitchhiking anywhere! Even into town, here."

"Dear Lord! Neither can I!"

"He took . . . this kid, he took . . . took a hundred-and-forty dollars, out of his grandfather's wallet! All that my husband had in it! And then, he took another sixteen or seventeen bucks . . . from my purse. All the money I'd had. I guess he'd gone to Nueva Laredo. And, when he came back into Texas, from Mexico, the border authorities . . . well, they had him detained. Questioned him . . . extensively! Finally got the kid to break down . . . and tell them where he lived. And that he was a runaway."

"Dear Lord! Like you, I could never imagine such a . . ."

"Well, they called us. And my husband . . . he drove up to Laredo yesterday. Picked the kid up. Brought him home. Now the kid's in worse condition . . . from a mental standpoint! From a psychological standpoint! Worse than he ever was! He's the one . . . that could probably use a shrink. I'm sure Luther had gone and raised all kinds of hell with him . . . probably all the way back from Laredo. He isn't talking . . . my husband. Not to anyone! Me or the kids . . . or anyone else! Which some may consider a blessing."

"Dear Lord! I had no idea!"

Well, I don't think Randy is the worst off."

"You don't? I mean, the kid ran away! That's pretty serious stuff!"

"I know. And I'm not making light of it. But, you see? My husband . . . well, Luther . . . you see, he doesn't like kids."

That, pretty well, comported with what the angel had advised me—in Seguin.

"That's why the nine-year-old . . . why Randy . . . why he ran off? Because your husband doesn't like kids?"

"Yeah. Like I said, Luther is always on their rear ends! The boys, anyway. But . . . in truth . . . he's not real thrilled with the girls, either. Steve . . . the oldest, he's . . . a little better able to take all the . . . all the, you know . . . all the crap . . . from his grandfather. But, the problems between my husband . . . and Steve's siblings . . . are, fast, wearing even that kid down! Fast wearing him down! I'm afraid that . . . one of these days . . . Steve is gonna explode! You can just see the pressure mounting! The pressure . . . building!"

"Explode? What do you mean? What do you mean . . . explode?"

"Actually, I don't really know! I don't have any idea! I may not even know what the hell I'm talking about! I just . . . you see . . . I can't . . . !"

She broke down! Convulsive sobs! Her entire body was caught up—in one spasm after another. The manager hurried over—and asked if she could be of any assistance. I told her no—that it would be best, if we'd just let Eva "cry it out"! It took about five never-ending, consistently-spasmodic, minutes!

When—at long last—my mother-in-law (yeah, "The Old War Horse") was able to compose herself, she apologized, profusely, to me. The last thing I'd felt entitled to—at that moment—was a stupid apology! I couldn't believe what was happening to my kids! My own kids! What a terrible—what a horrible—damn situation they'd found themselves in! MY kids!

I also had a good deal of trouble believing that Joanne would leave the children! Abandon them! Desert them! And then it occurred to me: I had come this close to doing the same damn thing! Schmuckdom reigns! Especially in the Marchildon household!

Once I'd felt that Eva was ready to halfway converse, once again, I asked her: "You say that your daughter . . . your daughter, Joanne . . . that she ran off with some . . . with some . . . some kind of . . . some kind of cult member?"

"Yes! The son of a bitch . . . excuse the expression . . . he took her away. Swept her away!

Bulldozed her right out of here! I halfway blame my late son-in-law . . . rest in peace."

Somehow those last three words made me feel a tad better. (A tad!)

"Why is that?" I asked—hopefully not letting her see the massive (and continuing) interior wince I was experiencing.

"Well, I guess he . . . Paul probably meant well. I mean, he was good to the kids, and all. But, damn him, he never had two nickels . . . never two damn nickels . . . to rub together. They were losing their house. I guess his car was fixing to be repossessed. But, he was always buying phonograph albums. Whenever Frank Sinatra . . . or Bing Crosby, or someone . . . would come out with a new album, there was old Paul! Paying money for it! Money he didn't have! Plus . . . Joanne found out . . . he was cheating on her! He had a girlfriend, and he was . . . well, he was goddam cheating on her!"

How I'd wanted to deny that to her! But, I knew that I could not! I did try and get some little bit of justification in, though:

"Are you sure . . . are you positive . . . that he was cheating?"

"Aw, you guys! You guys are all the same! You'll always stick up for one another!" The tears were gone! She was out and out mad now! "YES," she half-shouted. "Yes, I'm goddam sure! Positive . . . that he was cheating! He was laying his secretary . . . or the girl he worked with! Whatever she was! But, he was screwing her! Royally . . . to hear Joanne talk! Early and often . . . as they say in those commercials for the Post Office."

"All right," I was conceding—although it was a dagger through my heart! "If you say he was cheating . . . then, dammit, I guess that he <u>was</u> cheating."

"Anyway, he had this wild hair . . . you know where! Wanted to move! Move the whole damn family, move 'em all! Move 'em all . . . up to New York, for God's sake! Listen, he didn't have a pot to pee in! But, by God, he was going to move everybody! Lock, stock, and barrel! Move 'em . . . all the way, up to New-Damn-York! There wasn't much Joanne could <u>do</u>! He was <u>that</u> hell-bent . . . on being a total horse's ass! So, what could she <u>do</u>? What <u>could</u> she do? She jolly well <u>left</u> him! Took the kids. Brought 'em on down <u>here</u>! Moved in with <u>us</u>! And then Paul . . . well, he got <u>killed</u>! In some kind of an automobile accident . . . somewhere east of San Antonio. But . . . you can <u>bet</u> . . . he was on his <u>way</u>! On his way . . . up to 'The Big <u>Apple</u>'!"

"I'm sorry. I had no idea that . . ."

"Now, aren't you <u>sorry</u>? Sorry that you <u>ever</u> sat down here?"

"<u>No</u>! No . . . I'm <u>not</u>! I'm . . . genuinely . . . <u>not</u> sorry that I engaged you in this conversation. Listen, for one thing . . . and, of this, I'm <u>sure</u> . . . you really <u>needed</u> to get rid, of all of this! Get it off your chest! You'd <u>needed</u> the catharsis! Whether you choose to believe it or not . . . you <u>had</u> to unload!"

"Yeah," she nodded, wiping away a late-arriving tear. "I guess I did."

"How did your daughter . . . how did Joanne . . . how did she ever get hooked up with this . . . with this . . . this <u>cult</u> guy?"

"Well, it was the old 'on the rebound' thing, I guess. She was <u>really</u> vulnerable. As vulnerable as she could <u>be</u>! And he picked <u>up</u> on that, I guess. He <u>took</u> her places! <u>Lots</u> of places! Spent a <u>lot</u> of money on her! A <u>hell</u> of a lot of money! Listen, there are a <u>lot</u> of neat nightclubs, across in Matamoros. In Mexico. Right across the river. Right across the Rio Grande. I guess he could dance. Dance . . . really well. Something <u>else</u> that Paul couldn't do. Or <u>wouldn't</u> do. And . . . I guess I'd have to say . . . dancing was probably as important to Joanne, as Paul's stupid music was to him. His stupid music . . . and all those damn Broadway shows. So, this guy . . . this <u>cult</u> guy, his name was Bart, short for Bartholomew, I guess . . . he hit all her <u>weak</u> spots! <u>All</u> her weak spots! Every damn <u>one</u> of 'em! Bowled poor Joanne over!"

"I guess he <u>must</u> have," I groused. "He sure <u>must</u> have."

"I'm not sure <u>how</u> he did it . . . or exactly <u>what</u> he did . . . but, he got her to where she was taking a damn <u>drug</u>! Taking this <u>drug</u>!"

"A . . . a <u>drug</u>? Dear Lord!"

"Well, it wasn't <u>cocaine</u> . . . or even <u>marijuana</u>. <u>Nothing</u> like that. This was something. Something you can <u>buy</u>! You can get it . . . at any <u>drugstore</u>. It's called <u>Niacin</u>. I <u>think</u> that's the name of it. As I understand it, it'll give you a . . . well, a sort of a . . . a kind of a rush!"

"A . . . a <u>rush</u>?" Very few times had I ever heard that word back then.

"Oh, it won't get you <u>intoxicated</u> . . . or anything like that. But, it <u>does</u> make your body . . . starting at the top of your head, so I understand . . . this stuff makes your entire body <u>hot</u>! Really <u>hot</u>! Makes it get entirely wrapped up . . . in some sort of <u>fever</u>! Starts at the top of your head . . . and goes all the way to your toes. Lasts . . . I guess it lasts . . . fifteen or, maybe, twenty minutes. Enough to worry anybody! At least, enough to worry somebody . . . who doesn't know what's happening to her."

"I've never heard of that drug. That <u>Niacin</u>. Never <u>heard</u> of it. And <u>I'm</u> supposed to be a small part of the medical community. Small . . . and distant. I just never realized <u>how</u> distant!"

"Well," she continued, "he'd wind up taking her to his hotel room!" I was experiencing that internal <u>wince</u>, once again. "Went to his room . . . a lot. He'd rub her down. Rub down her whole, entire body! She'd have to have been <u>naked</u>, you know! All her clothes . . . <u>off</u>! But, he'd rub her down . . . with some secret kind of cream or lotion or something. Always made her feel better. But, they tell me that the fever would've left <u>anyway</u>! Of its own <u>volition</u>! She didn't <u>know</u> that, of course! I've, since, done a little studying on the subject. Well, <u>more</u> than a little."

"I can tell."

"Push finally came to shove, of course. And the inevitable happened! She ran <u>off</u> with him! Took <u>off</u> with him! With the bastard! We found the note on the front seat . . . of Luther's station wagon. She didn't say <u>where</u> she was going, of course! She'd only mentioned the cult's national headquarters, once or twice. And it's somewhere out <u>west</u>! <u>Way</u> out west! It <u>could</u> be Oregon . . . where <u>you</u> come from . . . for all I know. But, I don't think so. Utah, maybe. Or, possibly, Arizona. New Mexico, maybe. Hell, I don't know!"

"Well, I can't tell you . . ."

"Look, Doctor Young. I've told you far more than I'd ever intended to. In fact, I'd intended to tell you nothing! I didn't intend . . . to tell anybody anything! A half-an-hour ago, I didn't even know who you were. Who you are! I was never going to tell anybody! Tell anybody . . . tell 'em . . . tell 'em anything! Wasn't gonna do it! Not one damn thing . . . to anybody! And now, here I am . . ."

"Well, like I said, you needed the catharsis. Needed to let loose . . . with somebody!"

"Yes. I think you're probably right. I do feel better now. Somewhat, anyway! Little bit better! Not that I feel the weight of the world has been lifted off my shoulders, you know. Not by a long shot! But, I guess that . . . the fact that I've finally been able to share the whole damnable thing . . . share it with, at least, someone . . . I think that's been a bit of a help."

I waited about five long, silence-filled, staring-at-one-another, minutes—before I made a suggestion: I offered to "let her" bring the children to me! For a "professional evaluation". Offered to rent the conference room at my hotel. (I'd fervently hoped that the joint had such a room.) Eva, of course, would be more than welcome to sit in. I'd encouraged her to join the proposed pow-wow! She'd be free—to make whatever contribution, she would deem worthwhile.

She smiled, softly—and told me that she'd consider it. Would call me at the hotel—"in a day or two"! She would, at that time, let me know!

Look, this was—hopefully—a bit of an "opening"! A possible one, anyway! One that I'd felt—in my heart—I didn't really deserve.

And I'd found myself wishing that my mother-in-law hadn't sounded quite so cavalier about it.

FIFTEEN

I WAS, OF COURSE, ON THE well-known "pins and needles"—for two whole, everlovin', blue-eyed, days, after my encounter with Eva York.

I'd not heard <u>anything</u>—not one word—from my mother-in-law! I was <u>deathly</u> afraid to leave my room, at the hotel. Kept pestering the poor employees, at the front desk—constantly asking if they might've missed notifying me of a call. Each one of those neat, considerate, people kept—patiently—responding, in the negative!

I really didn't know <u>what</u> to do. I was <u>supposed</u> to know not where Eva lived—so, a visit out there might raise too many eyebrows.

<u>Then</u>, it finally occurred to me to (duh) look into that ever-faithful phone book. Sure <u>enough</u>—there was a "York, Luther" listed. In fact, it gave his office number (and address)—<u>and</u> his home number. The most important item (to me, anyway) on the page— as you can well imagine—was the listing of his home address. So, <u>anyone</u> could've determined the

location. A perfectly plausible explanation—should I decide to go out there.

That, obviously, was THE question" Should I decide to go out there?

I waited till mid-afternoon of the third day. Monday! I figured that the weekend—the fact of the weekend—might've put a "hitch in the giddyap" of my mother-in-law.

Her illustrious husband—doubtlessly—would've been lurking about. The kids would be in and out. On Monday, Luther would—presumably—be in his office (God also being in His heaven and all that). I presumed that the kids would be in school. Surely, I would hear from her—on that hopefully-magical Monday.

But, when it got to be three o'clock—and still not a peep from her—I picked up the phone, and rang the number so generously supplied to me, by that sainted phone book.

A woman—with a distinct Spanish accent—answered. It was—I was able to figure (and correctly, for a change)—the maid. "Wetback" help, down there, was still amazingly low-wage—and illegal maids were almost a-dime-a-dozen. This maid's name turned out to be "Lupe" (short for Guadalupe).

It didn't take long for her to realize that I'd wanted to speak with Mrs. York. When Eva came on the line, I asked her if she'd made a decision—as to whether she was going to let me speak to the children. To my children.

"I don't know, Doctor," she'd replied. "I've been wrestling with this thing! Jacking with it . . . for over the weekend.

<u>That</u>, I could believe. Three or four times, I'd driven past that cafe—and her ratty old Plymouth had, each time, been conspicuous by its absence. Much to my dismay!

"Things have been <u>so</u> tense," she advised—after a long, heart-palpitating (on my part) delay. "There's practically no <u>living</u> with my husband, right now. And the atmosphere . . . between him and the <u>kids</u> . . . I don't <u>know</u>! I was <u>scared</u> . . . scared to <u>death</u> . . . that Randy was going to run <u>away</u>! Run away . . . <u>again</u>! And, listen, I've just . . ."

"Then," I interrupted, "I don't see what could hurt . . . if I was, maybe, able to talk to them. To kind of . . . you know . . . assess the situation a little. The hotel here . . . they don't have a conference room. Not as such. But, they've got a couple of suites here . . . which have what you might call a bit of an office-like set up. I'm sure I could rent one of those . . . most any time."

"But . . . but, <u>why</u>? <u>Why</u> would you want to do <u>that</u>? Don't get me wrong, I think it's extremely <u>generous</u>, on your part. But, why would you go to all that <u>bother</u>? And to all that <u>expense</u>? I mean, it's just so . . ."

"Look, Mrs. York . . . Eva . . . I really can't explain it. The very first time I saw you . . . at the diner . . . <u>something</u> made my heart go out to you. I <u>realize</u> that you're married. I'm <u>certainly</u> not trying to put a move on you . . . as they say, nowadays. It's just that you seemed so . . . seemed so . . . well, so terribly <u>troubled</u>. <u>Something</u> made me want to see if there was . . . was any way that I could help. And then . . . when you told me about your daughter being caught up in the clutches of this guy from a cult, for heaven's sake . . . I was caught up, even more!"

"That's nice of you. But . . ."

"And then your grandson," I interrupted. "Him upping and running away! Dear Lord! Why, I felt as though I just had to do something! And, damn me, I don't know what that is! And I'm supposed to be a professional . . . in this sort of thing! I should have some really neat way out, for you! For all of you! You, the kids . . . even your husband! But, what could that be? Quite frankly, I'm damned if I know! If I know . . . for sure! I thought that, if I could just see . . . could maybe talk to . . . the kids, I thought that something brilliant might suddenly occur to me. God knows, it sure hasn't yet."

"I appreciate it, Doctor. Appreciate it . . . more than I can ever tell you. But, I just don't know if . . ."

"Look, Mrs. York. Let's just see if we can get together . . . with the kids. Your husband doesn't have to know! I'm certainly not going to tell him."

"Well . . . uh . . . maybe. Look. Listen . . . this may sound off-the-wall to you . . . but, do you think we could get together, at this . . . this pizza joint? There's this pizza place . . . out near 'Five Corners' . . . where the kids like to go. I don't think that it's ever all that crowded . . . I'm talking around four o'clock, in the afternoon. Place is usually pretty empty . . . around then. Do you suppose that . . . that we could get together there? It's not too far from our place. And the kids . . . well, they always enjoy going there. Would that be all right?"

"Yes!" I was trying to control my enthusiasm. "That'd be fine. I'm sure that four o'clock would give me time enough to get out there. I'll need directions, of course . . . but, four o'clock would be great! I'll be there!"

She advised me as to where the pizza restaurant was—and how to get there. (I'd, of course, been past the place dozens of times—but, there was no need for her to know that.)

Once the connection had been broken, I raised both arms in the air—and hollered "GREAT"! (That was before "YESSSS!" became so popular, for such occasions!)

I might not have broken any speed records getting to the pizza parlor—but, I must have come close! I arrived at 3:50PM. Not more than four or five minutes later, I saw my mother-in-law's old Plymouth pull into the lot!

And—HALLALUJAH!—she'd had the kids with her! All four of them! I—literally—felt faint! My heart resembled one of Gene Krupa's more spirited drum solos! I—and I'm being truthful, here—I actually imagined myself suffering a real-life heart attack!

Ever so slowly—ever so deliberately—Eva walked into the eatery. Well, she'd ushered the tads in first. Once inside, though, it took practically no time—before she spotted me. (How could she miss? I was waving—frantically!)

The children didn't seem all that enthused. But, how-ever-reluctantly—along with their grandmother—they joined me, in the large, circular, booth, in the far corner of the joint.

I shook hands with the boys—as Eva introduced us. (I'd <u>hoped</u> for a firmer clasp from each of them.) The girls looked <u>particularly</u> reticent—to show any emotion at all. They seemed to be looking into the depths of the booth—maybe through the entire restaurant—for some place to <u>hide</u>! <u>None</u> of the children was even close to being thrilled by the meeting!

All of this was a complete and utter shock to me! A <u>devastating</u> turn of events! It only <u>added</u>—to the still-continuing accelerated heart-palpitation!

These didn't <u>seem</u> like my "tads"! Not at <u>all</u>! Good <u>heavens</u>! How they'd <u>changed</u>! And in so <u>short</u> a time! Dear <u>Lord</u>! It all seemed so <u>tragic</u>! Steve—my 11-year-old first-born—appeared especially ill at ease. And more nervous—than I ever could've imagined! It was heartbreaking!

"Well," I enthused—once everyone was seated, and the introductions were out of the way, "let's get acquainted! Shall we?"

Let me tell you: Kids can spot a phony—from <u>miles</u> away! And I was coming off—like unto the proverbial "three-dollar bill"! My children were showing an immediate <u>distrust</u>! And, at that point, I'd not had the faintest idea—as to how to dispel that image! I was—obviously—goofing! How to "set things right"? I couldn't <u>conceive</u> of the extent of the tragic results— were I to go ahead and <u>blow</u> this first meeting! (This <u>last</u> meeting?)

"You never get a second chance . . . at a first impression"—as they say. That adage kept ricocheting through my head!

I asked Steve to tell me the name of his favorite sports team. He answered—that he didn't <u>have</u> one!

<u>That</u> was a danger. San Antonio had no major league sports franchises, at that time. But the city <u>was</u> home—to a really competent minor league baseball team. The "Bullets" franchise had been the "Missions"—dating back to the late 1800s. But, in 1963, they'd become a farm team for the Houston Astros—and adopted the "Bullets" name. And Steve had <u>always</u> been a fan of theirs.

I <u>might</u> have been more frightened than I should've been: At the end of the 1965 season, the team had been moved to <u>Amarillo</u>! I'd not been aware of that fact! Their disappearance from The Alamo City, had <u>soured</u> poor Steve on professional sports franchises.

Sadly, he'd never <u>missed</u> *NBC's Game Of The Week*, on Saturday afternoon. Not till <u>then</u>, anyway. True, Brownsville was certainly not what you'd consider a sports Mecca. But, still, my son's interest in sports <u>never</u> should've so definitely diminished—despite the "Bullets" being moved! Not to <u>that</u>—critical, to me—point, anyway!

Of course, his grandmother had advised me that he'd been terribly concerned about the wellbeing of his siblings. "That's all he <u>thinks</u> about," she'd advised me, at one point in our previous discussions. His nervous demeanor was an obvious testament to the accuracy of that statement. The boy's seeming total lack of interest in sports—only added a <u>frightening</u> ingredient to the already-toxic formula!

Randy would say <u>nothing</u>! I was <u>never</u> able to get more than a grunted, awfully-surly, "yes" or "no"—in answer to <u>any</u> of my questions. (And there were <u>many</u>

of those!) I was "all over the lot" with him. Most of the stupid inquiries, I cannot remember. To this day, I still draw a blank. But, no matter what I did—what I said, what I tried—I could not get through to that kid! Totally unable to get a rise out of him!

He'd never been the most gregarious child you'd ever want to meet. But, on his worst days, he'd been nothing like the way he was acting at the pizza place! It was incredible—how he'd turned inward.

To look at him, anyone would've thought that he was "afraid of his own shadow". That had never been the case! Ever! On the other hand, he had hitchhiked to Laredo. He had run away! In a way, his current demeanor was more scary than that of his older brother! Dear Lord!

Then, there were my two daughters! My little girls! Don't get me wrong, I've always loved the boys— every bit as much as the girls. Every bit! But, I've always felt that there was something absolutely special—between daddies and daughters. And there they were! (Here they are!) Sitting a mere few feet from me! My own daughters! And they hadn't the foggiest idea—as to who the hell I was! That fact— that dark knowledge—was a knife! Right through my heart!

Happily, though, they didn't seem to have changed! Well, not nearly as much as their older brothers. Thankfully, they each seemed to have retained that what-I'd-always-called a special "sparkle"! Not only in their eyes! But, in their whole—their entire— personalities! Little girls, of that age, are always such little busybodies. Always so adorably fussy.

Cynthia! She was now <u>six</u>! And she seemed to have grown a <u>yard</u>! But, basically, she was still the same! <u>Thank</u> God! Thank <u>God</u>!

How I was tempted to holler out, to her, "Are you a good dog?" That had been our "fraternal" greeting. She'd <u>always</u> answer, "No . . . I'm a good Cynthia".

I'd <u>always</u> loved that name. Joanne and I must've gone 15 rounds of "free-style grab-ass" over the name—when this glorious little girl had come into the world. Surprisingly, I'd <u>prevailed</u>! I used to advise My Little Girl—to always use her full name. "Don't let <u>anyone</u> call you Cindy," I'd instructed her—continually. In her short life, thus far, I'd done a <u>lot</u> of glorious things with her. Apparently, those very-tender moments were—tragically—all in the <u>past</u>! Confined to the God-awful <u>past</u>! The <u>regrettable</u> past! The past—from which I'd been totally <u>expelled</u>! <u>Heartbreaking</u>!

And Mary Jane! My little "Mary <u>Jane</u>"! Now four! I'd watched her spooning sand in the front yard of her grandparents' place, that one night—but, not up close. Not close enough! <u>Never</u> close enough! She'd always had that special smile.

There'd been so <u>many</u> times—so many <u>heartwarming</u> times—when, at age two and three, she'd climb up into my lap, and put <u>curlers</u> in my hair. Told me she was going to make me "look sexy". <u>Also</u> history! Tear-producing <u>history</u>! <u>Agonizing</u> history!

Eva jumped in—exactly when I'd needed her most: "Doctor Young, here, has taken a special interest in youse guys," she announced. "He'd like to . . . well, he'd like to . . . to talk to you. Talk <u>with</u> you."

Now, there was an understatement—if ever there was one! I most assuredly did want to talk to them. But, now what? What do I say?

"Look," I began—very shakily. "Uh . . . youse guys, as your grandma calls you . . . are you happy where you are? With Grandma and Grandpa York?"

There was much looking—frantic gazing—at one another! Amongst all four of them. None of them seemed to know what to say, Finally, Steve spoke up:

"Well," he began—sounding more gown up than I could ever have imagined, "it's not like . . . well, not like when we lived in San Antonio, you know. It sure is different down here. And . . . you know . . . our father, he died! And now, our mother . . . she . . . she's . . . well, she's gone and . . . uh . . . well, she's not . . . she's not with us anymore. Not with us now, anyway."

"We keep looking for her . . . for Mama . . . for her, to come back!" added Cynthia. "Any day now . . . we hope! Every day . . . we keep looking for her!"

"Yeah," spoke up Randy. (A bit of a surprise.) "And . . . well . . . Grandma's okay. We get along with her. Get along pretty well. But, I don't think Grandpa . . . I don't think he likes us."

His three siblings all nodded! All at once! And—all except Mary Jane—they nodded vigorously.

"Would you . . . do you think . . . I mean, since your father has . . . ah . . . passed away, and your mother, she's not around . . . at this time, anyway . . . do you think that you could possibly be happy someplace else? Someplace . . . different? Someplace . . . other than with your grandparents?"

<u>No</u> one was more surprised at that question—than I was! And it was <u>me</u>—who'd asked it. I was scared that I'd <u>grossly</u> overplayed my hand!

Actually, <u>Eva</u> was more taken aback by the inquiry—than any of the four children!

"Uh . . . Doctor," she asked—her voice trembling, badly, "why would you . . . why would you <u>ask</u> a question? A question . . . like <u>that</u>?"

"Well," I answered—far more strongly than I'd expected, "I just wanted to show them . . . show them that I was interested in them. That I <u>am</u> interested in them. I was <u>hoping</u> to get a frank . . . a frank and honest . . . answer from them."

"Yes, but . . ."

"It's been my experience," I blundered forward, "that children are, basically, the most honest creatures . . . on the face of the earth. I was <u>hoping</u> to get rid of that six-hundred-pound elephant in the room. Whether or not they'd be . . . well, be happier. Happier in some other place. To get it out of the way. Right from the git-go. Hopefully! <u>Please</u> try and see the logic in that."

"<u>I'd</u> sure like to go somewheres else," volunteered Randy. (<u>Not</u> all that much of a surprise! Not to <u>me</u>! Not at that <u>point</u>!)

"He ran away," advised Steve. "Ran away . . . just a few days ago. Grandpa had to go up . . . and get him. Go get him . . . get him out of Laredo. I just think that it's . . . that it's all maybe too <u>much</u>! Just too much for <u>Grandpa</u>! I mean, he's an old <u>man</u> . . . and I think that we kinda get on his <u>nerves</u>! Get on his nerves . . . a <u>lot</u>! We don't <u>mean</u> to. But, we <u>do</u>! And Mother . . . she . . . well, she . . . she went away! And I think Grandpa . . . I don't think . . . well, since Mother's gone and left . . . well, Grandpa's been awfully . . . ah . . . he's been awfully . . . you know . . . really up-tight! Really up-tight!"

I turned to face Eva. "What do you think, Grandma?"

"I . . . I don't know what to think! Not right at this moment! What Steve says is true! Too true! Unfortunately, what Randy says is also true! My husband has never had a . . . well, he's never had a thing . . . a thing, for kids. Never led any crusades . . . to see that youth be served, and all that."

"Somehow, I got that impression. And I've never met the man," I lied.

"Actually, I really don't know what to say about Luther," she explained. Her voice seemed to be getting stronger. "In a way, he's . . . in truth, Luther . . . has gone above and beyond the call of duty. Here he is. Kind of . . . in his mind, anyway . . . saddled with four kids. He'd already raised his own kid, y'know. And . . . truth be told . . . he's not, at all, happy with the situation! With the situation the way it is! I . . . personally . . . think he's been too strict on the children! Too demanding! Too harsh with 'em . . . from time to time. Well, more often than just simply 'from time to time'."

"Are we going away?" asked Mary Jane—her eyes seeming to glow. (Or, hell, maybe it was just my imagination.) "Is this man . . . is he going to take us away? To someplace else?"

"Well," I answered—much more weakly than I'd have imagined, "I suppose that that could be a possibility. I guess it could, maybe, be a . . . you know . . . a <u>possibility</u>!"

Eva folded her arms—across her bosom—in a display of disgust! Or anger! Or distrust! Or something! In truth, she appeared more confused than anything else. As the next three or four minutes inched, uncomfortably, past, she appeared—if anything—to be becoming more and more rattled!

I really didn't know what to say—as a follow-up to my little bombshell! Well, eventually, I began to realize that it was up to <u>me</u>—to say <u>something</u>!

"Look," I finally advised. "It'd be a whole complicated thing. <u>I'd</u>, of course, be willing! <u>More</u> than willing! Willing to . . . ah . . . look after the children. Do my <u>best</u>, you know . . . to make 'em <u>happy</u>! But, there's a whole <u>mountain</u> of legal stuff. A whole boodle of stuff . . . that we'd have to overcome. For instance, I'm not married. I have no wife. Courts frown on that sort of thing. So, it <u>could</u> get really <u>complicated</u>!"

"You're <u>not</u>?" My mother-in-law was—suddenly—outraged. "How could you <u>possibly</u> lead the children on? Lead us <u>all</u> on? Tell them . . . tell the <u>children</u> . . . tell them that <u>going</u> with you . . . that it would be a <u>possibility</u>? And you're not even <u>married</u>? How ridiculous can you <u>get</u>? Children, I think we'd just better go ahead and <u>leave</u>! Obviously, the doctor . . . he has no <u>idea</u> . . . has no idea, as to <u>what</u> he's talking about."

As you can imagine, I was totally <u>flummoxed</u>, by her flare-up! By her out and out <u>anger</u>! Her out and out <u>rage</u>! Though I was trying—frantically—I could not come up with any sort of even-halfway-intelligent response.

Thankfully, Randy spoke out:

"Wait, Grandma." His voice was showing a good deal of emotion. More than usual, anyway! Way more than normal! "Let's hear what he . . . hear what the doctor . . . what he has to say."

"Yeah," agreed Steve. That was another surprise. Normally, he is more reserved—much more laid-back—than his brother. "He might be a complete whack-o, Grandma! But, maybe he can think of something."

"Well," I'd had to admit, "I don't know what it would be. I probably never should've said anything like that! Started anything like that! About your coming with me! About it being a possibility, and all. It just kind of . . . well, it just kind of . . . you know . . . it just sort of slipped out!"

"Probably?" Eva was, once again, back to being "The Old War Horse". "Probably?" she repeated. "You probably shouldn't have said that?"

"Like I said . . . it just kind of slipped out. But, they are wonderful kids. Anybody would be thrilled to have 'em."

"Not my grandpa," muttered Randy. "Sure as hell . . . not my grandpa."

"Randolph," his grandmother half-shouted. "Watch your language."

"Well, it is true," noted Steve. Another surprise. "He is right!"

"I don't know who this guy is," maintained Randy. "But . . . even so . . . I think that, maybe, I'd be happier with him! I don't think he'd, you know . . . I don't think he'd be like Grandpa!"

"Oh," sighed Eva—heavily! "This is so . . . so damn confusing."

"How 'bout you girls?" I asked. "Are you, Cynthia . . . and you, Mary Jane . . . are you guys happy now? Happy at your grandma's and your grandpa's? Tell me! What do you guys think?"

"I miss my mommy and my daddy," rasped Mary Jane.

"Yeah," affirmed Cynthia. "I do too. I don't know why I don't have them anymore. Grandma and Grandpa are fine. I don't think that anyplace else would be . . . would be . . . would be . . ."

"She means," explained Steve, "that . . . well, we've been kind of moved around a lot. More than the girls can deal with, I think. My mother and father . . . they split up! Pop died! Mom's gone! I don't think any of us can understand that. I know that I don't. And . . . here we are. Down here . . . where we've never lived before. Grandma has knocked herself out! But, our grandpa? He's a different story. He's definitely not happy! Not with us being here. He sure lets us know that. A lot!"

"That's for sure," echoed Randy. "He always lets us know! Always!"

"I don't know who you are," resumed Steve. "And I don't know what you can do . . . what you will do . . . to change things for us. I don't know if you . . . or anyone else . . . should do anything for us. I . . . I just don't know!"

He broke down. Tears flowed down his face. He wasn't sobbing—and he was doing his best to stem the tide. (Not macho, y'know, for boys to be crying, and all that.) But, of each of the kids, Steve had appeared to be a rock! The most solid of all! And I believe that he must've felt embarrassed—to be (in his mind) "falling short". He was the big brother, after all. The titular head of the family, as it were!

Randy's expression was embedded in stone. He'd—most assuredly—wanted out! I think that I could have been Jack The Ripper—and, I believe, he'd have been willing to give me (or anyone else) a shot.

The girls—both of them—were the pictures of abject confusion! And—in a manner of speaking—of soul-twisting heartbreak. My own heart was reaching out to them! Reaching out for them! And I really didn't know what to do! What to say!

"Would you be our daddy?" Cynthia asked—after a few moments of the, so-called, deafening silence.

It was almost too much for me. I felt a tear or two begin to trickle down each cheek. Listen! I had to do something!

"Look," I suggested—locking my gaze in on Eva. "Maybe I could rent an apartment! Right here in town! A three-bedroom apartment. And the kids could, maybe, move in with me! On a temporary basis, of course. Just to see how it'd work out. How it would . . . possibly . . . work out. You would be welcome . . . welcome to come see them, of course . . . Mrs. York. Whenever you choose! Stay as long as you'd want. Your husband too . . . if he was of a mind to. It's pretty radical . . . this whole thing. I admit that. But I can't . . . I really can't . . . I can't think of anything else. If you've got another suggestion, I'd be more than happy to . . ."

"I can't think of another suggestion," she muttered. "Which is a problem! Because I don't think it'd be a good idea. For one thing, I don't really know you. I'm still uncomfortable with the way . . . with the reason . . . that you even approached me, at the restaurant."

"I tried to explain . . . explain to you, Eva . . ."

"Why would it be . . . why should it be . . . that you'd pick me out? Pick me out . . . to . . . to help? Especially since your path crosses with hundreds of other people? Hundreds of other people! All kinds of people! All of the time! Part of this whole thing . . . most of this whole cockamamie thing . . . it just doesn't pass the smell test. Yet, I look at the children . . . all of the children . . . and I can see how discontented they are. How . . . well, how . . . how upset they are. And it never ends! That's the way they are . . . all the time! The way things are! All the time! It's obvious . . . obvious that they're not happy. That something . . . something must be done! And yet . . ."

Randy actually grinned—and nodded, vigorously. His expression fairly shouted, "You've got that right!".

"Look," I responded. "If we were to set up some sort of a trial thing . . . a period of, maybe, a month or so . . . and then, we could all see how things were going. I could even hire a maid . . . would hire a maid . . . if you're uncomfortable with the little girls being in a living quarters with the likes of me."

"Well," she answered—sighing, heavily, again, "rightly or wrongly, that part doesn't really worry me.

Not that <u>much</u>, anyway. I'd be <u>more</u> worried about you just . . . well, just up and . . . and, well, <u>absconding</u>! Absconding . . . with the <u>children</u>! <u>That</u> would be my <u>main</u> concern!"

"I can understand that. And I'm highly <u>complimented</u> by the fact that the girls being with me isn't that big a worry. <u>Highly</u> complimented. As for my absconding with the kids . . . what would be my motive? Seeking a <u>ransom</u> . . . for their return? I can think of . . . if you'll excuse my frankness . . . think of many <u>other</u> people to approach for a ransom. <u>Many</u> others . . . beside your husband. I can't see much lucrative <u>potential</u> there. And I <u>would</u> have to lay out a few bucks for rent . . . and, I'd imagine, a security deposit . . . for an apartment. Not much profit potential there either, you know."

"I think <u>that's</u> what bothers me more than anything," she replied—herself on the verge of tears. "Why would you <u>bother</u>? Why <u>is</u> it . . . that you're so <u>interested</u>? That you're so <u>concerned</u>? So hung up on <u>their</u> well-being? Why should you be <u>worrying</u> . . . about these children? Why <u>you</u>? And why <u>these</u> specific children? These <u>particular</u> children? Do you not have children of your <u>own</u>?"

"Uh . . . well, look. I <u>used</u> to," I managed to respond. It was a question that I—undoubtedly—should've expected. But, the query caught me <u>totally</u> off guard. "I . . . uh . . . lost them. Look . . . I'd prefer not to go into it. If it . . . if my answer . . . if it causes you to <u>refuse</u> to even consider my offer, well then I . . . well, I apologize. I <u>guess</u> I'd understand. I <u>guess</u>."

"I think," she rasped, "I believe I can understand. Sort of understand, anyway. Just from the look you've got! The look you have, right this minute! The expression . . . on your face."

"Would you be our daddy?" Cynthia pressed.

"I would be proud . . . to be your daddy, Baby," I answered—I was becoming less and less successful in holding back the tears,

"Our daddy," chimed in Mary Jane, "he used to call us 'Baby'. Cynthia and me. He always called us 'Baby'."

I didn't know whether I'd been highly "un-politic" in calling the little girl "Baby". It had simply "come out"! I'd said it—before I'd ever realized it. I probably would not have been the least bit aware of using that "sacred" word—had my youngest daughter not brought it out. It was that natural.

"Do you," I managed to ask, "did you . . . did you like to be called 'Baby'?"

"Oh, yes," she said. And Cynthia nodded—with great enthusiasm.

"I don't know," sighed my mother-in-law. "I really don't know."

"Listen," I suggested. "Why don't you talk it over . . . run it by your husband? In fact, why don't you discuss it . . . discuss it, in depth . . . with the kids themselves? I think they'd probably be more inclined to open up to you . . . especially with my not being here. And in a less public place. You can, maybe, call me . . . tomorrow! Or, heck, I can call you! Whatever you wish. It's not like we have to come to some kind of agreement . . . tonight! Or even tomorrow!"

I could see Randy wince.

Both little girls gave me identical (loving—I found myself fervently hoping) expressions. In fact, I'd thought that I'd detected an almost-recognition— in the eyes of Mary Jane. I didn't know if that was a good thing—or a bad thing. Probably, it was an inaccurate thing!

I could not read Steve's expression. His face was not unlike a blank page. Could it possibly be that— eventually—I might be able to write on that sadly-empty parchment?

Was all of this—was any of this—too much to hope for?

Eva—after waiting about six-and-a-half eternities— allowed as how my suggestion(s) probably made as much sense "as anything else . . . the way things have been going". We wound up agreeing that she'd discuss the issue—at length—with the kids. And then, broach the subject to her husband.

She promised—that she would contact me. "Probably", she'd allowed, on the following day.

Once they'd departed, I'd slumped over in the booth! Rested my head—which could've weighed no more than the proverbial 16 Tons—in my hands!

Guys? You've GOT to let this thing work out for me! You've simply GOT to!

Why should this be? It suddenly occurred to me— at that very moment—that we'd not ordered anything. Not Eva. Not I. Not one thing. That seemed to have been fine with the kids.

Surprisingly—or, maybe, not surprisingly. The waitress—a beautiful Hispanic young lady—had, apparently, heard enough of our conversation, to cause her to, courteously, back off. Obviously, she hadn't wanted to "intrude". What a fine young woman. Would that everybody could be that sensitive! Her attitude gave me a much-needed warm feeling. Best I'd felt in—I couldn't remember when! Sometimes, simple gestures can be a form of therapy—for complicated situations!

I dropped a ten-dollar bill on the table—and left.

Two days went by—Tuesday and Wednesday—and I'd not heard from Eva York. I was going nuts! (You may find that difficult to believe. Just kidding.) So was the poor lady, at the front desk! Going nuts—I was sure. She must have decidedly wearied of my continually asking if I'd missed any phone calls. Decidedly wearied!

Still, I'd dared not call my parents-in-law's house. I was scared—bountifully afraid—that I'd already come on as far too anxious! Had acted like some kind of snake-oil salesman! In just that short meeting—at the pizza parlor! On the other hand, how can one possibly gauge the pathway one takes—or should take—in such a staggeringly-implausible situation?

In the increasingly-tense meantime—on Wednesday—I checked with Adam Browning, my friend, the crack detective, in San Antonio. He was apparently satisfied that my check had cleared—and had started working on my behalf, that very morning. He went on to inform me that he'd not gotten very far. Well, obviously, he hadn't figured to.

I spent those unending days—staying close to the hotel. I shouldn't miss a call. There, frankly, wasn't much to do, in town.

The big shopping malls were not yet a "gleam" in anyone's eyes. *Amigo-Land* would not open till 1974—and *Sunrise Mall* would not put in an appearance until 1979. There was a fairly new *Sears* store, on Elizabeth Street—along with a few specialty shops. Three or four restaurants, a couple of drugstores lined—and, of course, the main theater in town—populated that "main drag". But, that was, pretty much, it.

I did take in a movie—at *The Majestic*—the theater across from the post office, on Elizabeth Street. But, I have no idea, as to what flick I'd been treated to—or how good (or bad) it might've been.

I bought a book. Should have brought one of my own. (But, that would've made too much sense.) Tried to read. Nothing! Could not concentrate! I was—for all practical purposes—locked in a state of suspended animation! Not a comfortable dimension, in which to find yourself!

Thursday morning, there was this highly-unanticipated (and scary) knock on my door. I opened my portal—and was face to face with both of Joanne's parents. That was a shocker! A real eye-crosser!

I bade them enter. Luther plopped himself into the one-and-only comfortable chair in the room. I pulled out one of those common hotel-model plastic numbers, and seated myself thereupon. Eva eased herself down upon one of the beds—and fidgeted nervously. (She remained in that mode—for the entire time that she and her husband were "visiting".)

"Doctor Young," began my father-in-law, "I don't know what the hell you may be up to."

Neither did I! But—whatever it was—I'd figured, the jig was up. This creepy—this eerie—feeling, coming from just those very few words, out of his never-more-abrasive mouth. He'd always appeared to me, as having an exceptionally harsh tone of voice— even in his happier moments (which, I'd always felt, had been "damn few"). But, his modulation—on that fateful day—abused the expected, grinding-stone-like, privilege!

"I couldn't believe it," he went on, "when Eva told me about you . . . and this horse's ass idea of yours! About your confronting her in the restaurant, and . . ."

"Excuse me, Mister York . . . but, I did not confront her. I merely told her that . . ."

"I know what you told her. And I know about your little confab . . . with the kids . . . at the stupid-assed pizza joint. I couldn't figure out . . . not for the life of me . . . why, in hell's name, you'd want to insert yourself! Insert yourself . . . where my grandkids are concerned! That's totally idiotic!"

"I thought I'd told Mrs. York . . . told Eva . . . what my concern was."

"As I said, I know what you told her. But, quite frankly, I thought you were up to something! Are up to something! Have to be up to something!"

"Look, Mister York. I'm just . . ."

"No one would just . . . out of the goddam blue . . . no one would get himself all caught up in four kids.! Not with four strange . . . unknown . . . kids!" It was as though I'd not spoken at all. "Not with four kids . . . that he'd never even seen before. Didn't make sense! So, I wasn't going to do anything! Not going to let my wife do anything! Not until I'd had you checked out! Thoroughly checked out! Hell, anyone can claim to be a doctor! Claim to be a shrink!"

Oh-oh, I'd thought. Here it comes!

I found out, though, that you are a psychologist. Apparently, a well-qualified one. I can't understand why you'd have given up your practice. Unless there just simply are not that many nut cases up there . . . in Oregon. If you're fixing to start up a new practice, Brownsville'd probably be fertile ground for you. Fertile as hell! Lots of nut jobs down here!"

I was—obviously—taken aback (taken way aback), at what my guest had just told me. Then, it occurred to me: If "The Guys" could return that stupid $1000 bill, set me up in a complicated (highly-complicated) new lifestyle—and phony up a whole series of documents (not to mention three entire fiction novels)—they most certainly could dummy up some sort of false resume for me! That had to have been the case! Had to have been!

Thanks, "Guys"!

"Well," Luther pressed on. "Don't you have anything to say?"

"Uh, well, this is . . . this whole thing is . . . well, it's all a little bit out of left field. I mean, I'd never met you before. I certainly didn't expect you to . . . you know . . . turn up at my doorstep, so to speak. So, it's just . . ."

I'm out of left field? You're not out of left field? This whole thing . . . you getting involved with the kids . . . or wanting to . . . that's not out of left field? What're you . . . ?"

"I realize that it is kind of far out, Sir. It's just that I . . ."

"Look, Doctor. I've talked with the kids. With my grandchildren. And . . . to a kid . . . they all want to give your idea, a try! Your asshole idea! This bullshit, you've come up with! About your taking an apartment! Here in town! They'd like to give the damn thing a try, for God's sakes!"

I think the walls must've expanded—noticeably— from the gust of wind that I'd expelled. I'd never been so happy to hear anything! In my entire life!

"Well, Mister York," I'd rallied enough to reply, "thank you, Sir. You can bet that I'll . . ."

"Yeah," he snarled. "We'll just see how well it all goes. I do want you to take an apartment . . . here in town, though. Not up in Harlingen or anywhere else! Port Isabel . . . nix! Has to be here . . . here in Brownsville!

"Yes, Sir! I'll be glad to . . ."

"And I do want you to hire a maid. Plenty of 'em around, to be hired! And cheap as hell, they are! After . . . oh . . . say a month or two, we'll see how things are going."

"That's fine with me, Mister York."

"If this whole thing is to be permanent (I could hear my mother-in-law gasp—audibly) then, I think we can, maybe, get around that whole 'No Woman In My House' thing. I'm not without a little bit of influence at City Hall! And with the county! I believe I could, quite possibly, get some judge . . . from whatever court . . . to, you know, sign all the necessary documents."

"That would be a relief . . . a big relief . . . Sir. I'd . . ."

"Well . . . understand me, now . . . all this would be after a bona fide trial situation. Of at least a month or two. I'd have to talk to the kids. See how they're doing! See how they act! See how they look! That sort of thing.

"I'm perfectly willing to . . ."

"I'm sure that it's no secret . . . that they're not very happy at our place. Not happy at all. Especially . . . they're not happy with me! And the younger boy . . . Randy . . . he's really unhappy with me! He's been a problem . . . ever since he came to live with us! And . . . just between us girls . . . I'd kind of welcome it! Would welcome . . . being out from under the responsibility of having to raise four kids. Four kids . . . who're not my own."

"I believe I can understand that, Sir. Although . . ."

"Listen Young. I love my daughter! Despite what anyone may have told you! And I really don't know what that piece of shit of a husband of hers ever did . . . but, he's ka-PUT! As for my daughter, I don't expect for her to come back. Not anytime soon, anyway. She's completely lost her goddam way! To the point that . . . well, I'm afraid . . . afraid she's not ever going to find it again. At least . . . like I say . . . not anytime soon!"

"I . . . I don't know what to say, Sir. I'm just . . ."

"You don't have to say anything! You don't have to say shit! You just have to act! Act responsibly! And be a good parent . . . or guardian, or whatever the hell it is, that you'll want to call yourself. Show me that you'll be good to the kids. Be good for them."

"You have my assurance, Mister York, that I'll be . . ."

"I'd have a hard time convincing them . . . convincing the kids . . . but, I do love 'em. Do care for 'em! I'm certainly not the type that'd just simply throw 'em out! Throw 'em out . . . on their little asses!"

"I realize that, Sir."

"I don't know if you do . . . or don't. But, being honest about it, this whole thing . . . for whatever reason you might've gotten yourself involved . . . this whole, entire, thing . . . this could, maybe, be the answer to a few problems. More than one really hairy problem."

"I believe I can understand that, Sir."

"But, let me assure you, Doctor Young! You're going to have to prove . . . prove to me, and prove to my wife . . . prove, to us, that you are, indeed, the answer. Let me tell you, Doctor: I'll be watching! Watching . . . closely! If you don't know anything about me, know that I'll be goddam watching! And goddam closely!"

"This whole thing," rasped Eva, "is all almost too much for me! Way too much for me! I've never gotten myself caught up in a situation . . . in anything like this." She swept away a tear. "I love my grandchildren, Doctor! But . . . and I'm forced to admit this, to myself . . . the situation, at home, is deteriorating!

It's _fast_ deteriorating! I'm _deathly_ afraid . . . scared _stiff_ . . . that Randy's going to run away again. So, maybe this _is_ the solution! The answer . . . to a _lot_ of problems! I never thought I'd _ever_ hear myself saying that! Can't even _imagine_ . . . myself, even _thinking_ such a thing! Such a . . . well, such a _ghastly_ . . . such a ghastly _thing_! Goes against _everything_ that I . . ."

"Well," I'd finally responded—my voice much huskier than I'd ever remembered hearing it, "let me assure you . . . assure the _both_ of you . . . that I'll treat those kids, as if they were my _own_! Exactly . . . as if they were my _own_! You can _count_ on it!"

Now, really I don't know _why_ I'd said that! I could feel a tug—a definite yank (a lusty one)—at my heart. Though it _was_ the truth, I was afraid that I'd just "queered the do", as they say in England! (As it turned out, thankfully, I had _not_!)

Once Luther arose, to leave, Eva joined him. We said our goodbyes. I promised the two of them that I would rent a suitable apartment in the next day or two. They would be welcome to inspect the place— and would have veto power, should they decide that the quarters would not be suitable.

My father-in-law advised me that he would be able to procure a maid for me—and informed me as to what I would be required to pay her. (The amount was incredibly _cheap_!)

The pair departed! I immediately plopped into the chair—the one that Luther had just evacuated! Time for a little coronary break! I didn't stop _shaking_— _wouldn't_ stop shaking—for, literally, ten or fifteen minutes. I'd _heard_ of "The Nine Day Trembles"—and was positive, by then, that I was caught up, in that head-to-toe malady!

The next few days—hell, the next few weeks, the next few months—would be Verrrrrrry Interesting!

SIXTEEN

THURSDAY AFTERNOON, I BEGAN WHAT I thought would become a spectacular search, for housing—for me and the kids. Well, maybe it wasn't that spectacular. Maybe that's because I was totally unable to come up with a satisfactory apartment. A distinct surprise! (Are you detecting a pattern here?)

Brownsville was just beginning to semi-boom. Lyndon Baines Johnson had been president for, roughly, a-year-and-a-half—and his considerable influence, vis-a-vis political and financial sources, were just beginning to take effect.

Fat lot of good that all this new-found Washington money was doing me. Six months later might've found me a little better off, in my hunt. There seemed to be numerous construction projects already underway—but, completion, in every case, appeared to be a good way down the road. And who knew how many apartment complexes were included—in all this expansion?

I was able to blunder upon—during that depressing Thursday afternoon and evening—only two three-bedroom apartments. As far as I could tell, they were the only ones in town! And neither was acceptable.

There was no need to attempt to obtain the approval of Luther and/or Eva. I knew—from the well-known seat of my pants—that neither one would ever pass muster. Hell, they didn't pass muster with me. And I felt as though I'd probably be substantially less demanding than my parents-in-law. Substantially!

Friday turned out to be a much better situation. I don't remember how I'd managed it—but, I blundered in to a medium-sized bungalow, on Palm Boulevard.

This was a really nice neighborhood—and the house sported three bedrooms. One of these rooms was located on an undersized second floor. The bedroom—and a small john—were the only facilities up there.

A minor consideration—but, nonetheless, a consideration: It didn't cost me the traditional arm-and-a-leg. I did have to sign a year's lease, though. It was too late, on Friday, to get any of the paperwork done. The formalities could not take place till Monday. I left $200—as "earnest money"—and thanked my lucky stars (and maybe "The Guys") that I'd found the house.

I was, as mentioned, thrilled to have found such a venue—and I hoped (two-hundred dollars worth) that the Yorks would be equally impressed.

I brought them by—on Saturday. Well, they came on their own. But, the main hurdle did wind up cleared. They both approved of the joint. Eva, in fact, told me that she loved the place.

"Why would you go to all the trouble . . . and expense . . . to rent a damn <u>house</u>?" asked the ever-cynical Luther. "A damn <u>house</u> . . . for God's sake!"

"Mainly because I couldn't find a suitable apartment," I'd answered—with <u>considerably</u> more authority than I could've expected.

He <u>appeared</u> to accept the explanation. But—down deep—who <u>knew</u>? Who <u>could</u> know? He gave me some sort of an indescribable "look"—as he and his wife were leaving. I spent—literally—hours, futilely trying to decipher the drive-you-nuts expression. Without <u>any</u> success.

After completing the paperwork, on Monday, I went furniture shopping. The house was unfurnished. I found myself glad that Gretchen had conned me in to applying for a couple of credit cards. Not with all that much success, I might add. I'd felt really fortunate—that I'd finally managed to secure a *BankAmericard*—as *Visa* was then called, back then.

I'd wound up being "declined"—by three other cards. (Thanks a helluva <u>lot</u>!) Didn't have enough credit history—despite what my father-in-law was able to dredge up, about my professional history.

I <u>was</u>, however, able to obtain a welcome line of credit—at one of Brownsville's largest banks (through my most-frequently-used bank in Oregon). Listen, it was most convenient to be able to go through three or four stores, buy the necessary furniture and appliances, and just have the merchants give the old plastic a whack!

By Tuesday afternoon, I'd had the nifty (if I <u>do</u> say so, myself) housing unit ready for occupancy. I summoned the Yorks—to get the final seal of approval. <u>She</u> loved it! <u>He</u> approved—albeit grudgingly!

The big adventure was all <u>set</u>! HUZZAH! The kids would move in—on <u>Wednesday</u>! Was this <u>great</u>—or what?

I busied myself for the rest of Tuesday—by transferring my stuff, from the hotel—to my new residence. Also did a little shopping—mostly for whatever clothing I felt I might need for the nonce.

Somewhere in there, I'd found time to check with my detective friend, in San Antonio. Sadly, he'd turned up absolutely <u>nothing</u>—vis-a-vis the whereabouts of Elena. (<u>Really</u> sadly!)

Wednesday afternoon, Luther hired two Mexican laborers to move the kids' stuff in. He and Eva (mostly the latter, I was convinced) had bought their grandchildren a whole <u>lot</u> of stuff. Mostly clothes.

As you might imagine, there were numerous toys in the mix! Virtually all of those little treasures would have been <u>far</u> beyond the ability of Paul Marchildon to have provided. Especially the for-the-time-high-tech stuff that the boys had.

This, of course, was all taking place—before the massive breakout of video games. Still, some of the things that my sons had come into—the lavishness and sophistication of them—made me think that the situation, relationship-wise, in the York household must have been quite horrendous! Horribly bad—for Randy to have undertaken his overwhelming run-away adventure! Leaving all this behind!

There were a few complications. For instance, I was aware of the fact that I would be required to drive my new charges to school—and pick them up—each and every day. They were now living in a different school's area. But, I didn't want to add to the upheaval! The turbulence—that the kids were already undergoing. So, I opted to have them continue in their present classrooms.

Part of that plan came under question—somewhat, anyway—when I found that Cynthia was not called by her beautiful name, when she was at school. Apparently, once she'd gotten to the first grade, she'd stood up to the class bully—another little girl. It was, as I understood it, more a stare-down—than a slap-down—situation. But, her classmates began calling her "Butch"! That was much more troubling, for me, than it should have been. I finally reached an "executive decision"—that the moniker was not sufficient grounds to have three kids change schools.

An added fillip: The fourth child—Mary Jane—had been enrolled in a pre-kindergarten facility, near the Yorks' house.

It was in the evening—on Wednesday—when Eva brought my kids over.

I was thrilled, of course, to get them. But, the tearful farewell that took place—when their grandmother was about to leave (even including Randy) really tugged at the old heartstrings. I was substantially more moved—than I'd ever thought would be the case. No more "Old War Horse" designation!

We'd, obviously, had our many differences— over the years, during my marriage to Joanne. And it troubled me—deeply—the image she'd still maintained! The idea that Paul Marchildon had cheated on her daughter was highly-disconcerting! But, I kept trying to convince myself that her opinion— while wrong—was completely understandable. As noted above, I most assuredly did not consider her to be "The Old War Horse"! Not any longer.

My mother-in-law advised me that she and Luther had engaged a Latina, as a maid/cook—and, more or less, as a nanny. This turned out to be a woman named Maria—who'd lived fairly close by. She could easily get to and from our house. The bus line ran within a block-or-so of each of our residences. She was living with her parents—and a couple of younger siblings—at the time.

Maria would work from 11:00AM till 7:00PM. She would cost me $60.00 per week. (That, apparently, was a fairly good-sized stipend, for the times. And for the area. Again, this was before the total effect of LBJ's presidency had set in.)

The children were fed their lunch at school— and that arrangement would continue. I would be responsible for the children's breakfasts. But, if I'd wanted to stop, with them, at a restaurant—on our way to school—that was acceptable, to my parents-in-law.

It was decreed, at that point, that their grandmother would <u>deliver</u> them home! Every afternoon!

<u>That</u>, my mother-in-law advised me, had turned out to be a hard-fought concession—from her husband. But, she <u>had</u> wanted to spend as much time as possible with her grandchildren.

Maria would cook dinner—for the lot of us (herself included)—at about five o'clock. She would give me shopping lists. For groceries, mostly. And I was advised—by my mother-in-law—to "pretty much abide by it". (I <u>had</u> my orders!)

That first night, the kids and I—for the most part—watched television together. They'd all had their favorite TV shows. I'd not thought of it, but I figured that it would probably behoove me to get sets for the bedrooms. For the boys' bunker—upstairs—anyway.

I was <u>honored</u>—<u>spectacularly</u> honored—that, for the most part, <u>both</u> girls sat in my lap, during our "quality time", viewing the tube.

Fortunately, one of the local stations was playing *Pride Of The Yankees*—the pretty-much-factual life story of New York's famous first-baseman, Lou Gehrig. Gary Cooper, of course, played Mr. Gehrig. But, Bill Dickey—the Yankees catcher in those days—and Babe Ruth played themselves. Randy was intrigued with the movie—and was fairly wrapped up in the situation. Especially once I'd explained to him who Dickey and Ruth were. (Well, he—and Steve—had both known who "The Babe" was.)

On the other hand, Steve was kind of "once removed". Again, I'd not—ever—remembered him being as serious as he'd seemed to have become. Not continually as grave—and, sadly, unsmiling—

anyway His high-priority concern was—it was obvious—the wellbeing of his younger siblings. And I found myself doubting that he was absolutely convinced that moving in with me was the real answer to his younger brother's—and his little sisters'—best interests.

Mary Jane fell asleep in my lap—about two-thirds of the way through the movie. I carried her into her bedroom—and simply laid her on top of the bedspread. When I returned to the living room, Cynthia crawled back up into my lap. Two or three times, she asked, "Are you going to be our new daddy?". I could detect—thought I could, anyway—an almost-imperceptible "wince", on the part of Steve!

Thursday morning, I got the kids up—and off to school—via a stop at that very same restaurant. The diner—where I'd "confronted" Eva York. It had been a real worry for me—but, the girls had gotten themselves dressed. I have the feeling that Mary Jane might have needed a little assistance from Cynthia—but, the end result was very satisfying! Most satisfying! And quite a relief!

Promptly—at 10:55AM—Maria appeared! She was a slender, attractive, Latin lady. My mother-in-law had advised me of the fact that she did live with her parents—and one or two younger siblings. I thought that to be quite unusual. Especially when I'd expected a much younger woman.

This lady appeared to be in her late-thirties. Maybe even early-forties. For her to be living "at home" seemed—to me, anyway—to be a trifle outlandish. But, what did I know? On the other hand, I'd been less than overly familiar with the Mexican culture. Much less!

I'd thought that both Elena and Magdalena had given me, at least, a peek into the customs—and even a few of the traditional folkways—of their people. Apparently not!

My new employee spoke perfect (as perfect as any of us do) English. That struck me as a little bit odd. Both Elena and Magdalena were totally fluent in the language—but, both had retained slight accents. The latter slightly more than the former. Maria was a mere stone's throw from Mexico—and spoke better English than one woman who'd lived 350 miles from her native land. And another—who was located a couple thousand miles away.

The very competent Maria immediately took over. She inventoried the sparse contents of the fridge, the cupboards—and the multitude of stuff I'd "stored" (liberally) on the two counter tops in the kitchen. In a matter of minutes—after she'd, efficiently, cleared away the counters—she was, very industriously, whomping up a shopping list.

I, of course, followed orders—and went straight to the neighborhood *H.E.B.* food store. I wound up buying out half the joint. And—lest you worry—I did manage to procure every item that I'd been instructed to lay in. I do remember working up a bit of a sweat—lugging all that stuff into the house.

Maria immediately stored the multitude of items. Ever-so-efficiently. Then, she returned to the project in which she'd been engaged, while I'd been away. She was a positive whirlwind—with what few cleaning tools my landlord had provided me. Well, they'd been—liberally—augmented by the many chemicals I'd been ordered to buy. She put <u>everything</u> to good use. To <u>wondrous</u> use. Before I knew it, the house was "tidied up" (her term). Or "clean as hell" (mine).

When Eva brought the kids in from school, she took one slow-motion look around the place—and nodded, contentedly.

Maria got the girls into their play clothes—after slapping Randy on the bottom, and sending the boys upstairs to get out of their "good clothes".

My mother-in-law hung around for ten or fifteen minutes—without saying anything of import to me—then, left.

By five o'clock, my new housekeeper had prepared a <u>wonderful</u> dinner for us—and participated in imbibing the glorious repast. Once she'd done the dishes—and laid out my daughters' school outfits for the following day—she left.

She was amazing! What struck me as strange: I don't think we'd spoken more than a dozen-or-so words to one another—including during our "quality time" at the dinner table. I didn't know whether I should be troubled by the lack of communication or not. It <u>certainly</u> hadn't impeded her—in "making her rounds".

I'd <u>forgotten</u> about buying new televisions for the bedrooms. We'd had to "make do", once again, with the one black-and-white set in the living room. And, listen—it was great fun. Again, the girls sat in my lap—for most of the evening, anyway—and, this time, both remained awake. I think the comedy fare was a little more to their liking. As opposed to the life and times of Lou Gehrig.

Friday went pretty much the same. The lone exception being that the phone company came— and installed my new instrument. I now had all the comforts of home. I didn't feel as though it was vital— that I should put one of their instruments in any of the bedrooms.

I called Adam—my detective friend up in San Antonio. I got his answering machine. Not too many of <u>those</u> in use, in 1966. Not that <u>I'd</u> ever encountered, anyway. I left my new number on the tape. It bothered me—more than a little—that I'd been unable to converse with him. Was <u>he</u> going out of business too?

Again, Maria and I seldom indulged in any conversation. This was something else—building on the lack of communication the day before—that was beginning to raise a good bit of concern. I was getting the feeling that she didn't approve of me. Or that she viewed my arrangement with the kids—especially as it affected my daughters—with great disdain. I was sure that either Eva or Luther would've filled her in on all the details.

I certainly was not looking to enter into any sort of relationship—outside of our professional one. But, I really was getting upset—how-ever-mildly—that she was being so, well, so formal. So closed-mouth—with me. Her attitude—toward me—was quite troubling.

The weekend would prove to be even a little <u>more</u> frightening. I would be on my own. Maria would return—on Monday—and, she assured me, she'd clean up, "as necessary". (Oh! And I <u>did</u> hasten to purchase three TV sets for the bedrooms. All rather small "Glorious Black-And-White" units. But, they each produced quality picture and sound.)

Saturday morning, I got a rather alarming call—from San Antonio. It was Adam. He'd been staking out Elena's parents' house—and had followed the father, a number of times. (Many trails had led to that same, "world-famous", ice house.)

But, he <u>had</u> discovered that Elena's two sons were now <u>living</u> there—in the care of their grandparents! (Sound familiar?) He was afraid that something might have <u>happened</u> to my former fellow-employee! He said he'd need another thousand bucks to stay on the case! I told him I'd send him a check!

The call's aftermath worked out pretty well. There was a really neat picture playing at *The Majestic*—and the theater was right across from the post office. So, I was able to get off a check that afternoon. And then, to herd the tads into the movie house.

We ate at. for the most part, fast food joints over the weekend. Watched a few movies on TV. I took them shopping—mostly at "the five-and-dime". The kids—mostly Randy and Cynthia—seemed interested in jigsaw puzzles, so we laid in six or eight of those (in varying stages of complexity). Even bought a card table—on which to set them up.

I was really very pleased—the way the weekend turned out. Even Monday morning went well. Maria had already laid out the kids' go-to-school clothing—on Friday. So, the many fears that I'd harbored—the many fears—all seemed to have been unfounded. (Key word there is "seemed".) The main thing—the most critical priority—throughout the entire weekend, had been not only that I'd "get along" with the kids. There really needed to have been a "productive" relationship begun (if not, hopefully, firmly established).

We'd "done good"! Not only had we apparently "gotten along" with one another—but, we'd appeared to have bonded, about as well as anyone could've expected. The satisfying degree of closeness was more, quite frankly, than I'd expected! Much more! (And the girls—at one time or another—continued to ask if I was going to be their "new daddy"! I can't tell you the warm-fuzzies that produced!)

Maria! Now that was—she was—another deeply-felt concern. As stated previously, I'd never expected any kind of romantic involvement. Certainly, I'd not pictured her as "rushing into my arms". But, by the same token, I didn't expect her to be treating me as coldly as she had. And the frigidness was apparent! And it continued—unbroken! As I eventually came to understand it, she had already experienced some kind of relationship with my parents-in-law—for more than a few months. Of course, I'd not <u>known</u> that till a few days after that icicle-laden morning.

When she'd arrived, on Monday morning, she had busied herself—"cleaning up" from our family weekend. (I'd not thought that we'd made a deplorable mess. I'd <u>really</u> not thought we'd made a mess at all. But, what did <u>I</u> know?)

That afternoon, I'd finally approached her—in the boys' bedroom, upstairs.

She took one look at me—and even <u>I</u> could tell that she felt absolutely "trapped"! I could <u>never</u> have anticipated the look of abject <u>terror</u> on her lovely face!

"Maria," I said—tentatively, "please sit down. We've got to talk."

"Yes, Sir."

"Please!" I was surprised at the overwhelming amount of pleading, in my voice. "Please . . . don't call me 'Sir'. Your calling me 'Mister Young' is bad enough. I really wish you'd call me 'Taylor'. Or . . . at the very least . . . <u>Mister</u> Taylor'. Anything but '<u>Sir</u>'!"

"I'll . . . I'll try," she replied—softly—settling in on one of the boys' beds. She sat there—so demurely. With her hands folded in her lap. "I'll try and do my best to . . ."

"You don't have to do your best at <u>anything</u>." I found myself—fervently—wishing my tone hadn't been so filled with admonishment. "What I mean is . . . look, Maria . . . you've done <u>everything</u>! <u>Everything</u> I could reasonably expect! That I could <u>possibly</u> expect! And you've done it <u>wonderfully</u>! Beautifully! I have no <u>complaints</u>! <u>None</u>! None <u>whatever</u>!"

I can't begin to describe the look of abject <u>relief</u> that her expression showed. But, she still said <u>nothing</u>. And her physical position didn't change. It almost reminded me of a turtle pulling its head into its shell. Maybe poking it out—slightly—from time to time. She was—clearly—in a <u>protective</u> mode. I can't exaggerate the feeling of unease that had swept over me.

"Listen, Maria," I resumed. "You act as though you're frightened of me." She shuddered. It wasn't a head-to-toe thing—but, it was, definitely, a healthy tremor. "Either that," I continued, "or you're afraid that I'm going to <u>demand</u> that you approve of me. That I <u>require</u> you . . . to approve of my living here. Living alone . . . and with two little girls in the house. Girls that are not my daughters." (That last sentence was just another knife through my heart.)

"It is not mine to judge. How you choose to live your life . . . it is not my concern."

"Well, tell me. Are you upset . . . is the fact that I'm here with the children . . . is that upsetting to you? Especially given the ages of the girls?"

"No, Sir. I'm not. It doesn't . . . well, I've never seen . . . I mean, it <u>is</u> kind of strange. I've never known of such a relationship. Never in the past."

"Let me assure you . . . or, at least, let me <u>try</u> to assure you . . . that my intentions are purely honorable. I'm here . . . <u>they're</u> here . . . for no other reason than I'm <u>terribly</u> concerned about their welfare. Really. Nothing more . . . nothing less."

"It's not mine to question, Mister Young."

"Look, Maria. I'm <u>not</u> getting through to you. And I don't know <u>why</u>. I'm at a total <u>loss</u>. Why is it that you . . . constantly . . . seem so . . . well, so . . . so concerned. Tell me . . . true. Are you really upset with me? With the circumstances? What? What is it? Please . . . tell me what!"

She burst into tears! Frantic spasm upon spasm of full-bodied sobs!

"Maria! What is it?"

"It's . . . I can't . . . I'm afraid! Afraid you're going to tell me to leave! That you won't like me. That you don't like me! If you tell me that I'm through here . . . it would . . . I've tried to be good. I've tried to . . ."

"Maria? How many times do I have to tell you? You've been good! You are good! You're great! You've done wonders around here. Why would you ever . . . what would ever cause you to think . . . to be afraid that I'm going to fire you? That is what you're talking about, is it not? You're afraid I'm going to let you go?"

She nodded—almost imperceptibly. She was crying softly, by then. One almost could describe it as silently weeping. I didn't know what else to say! I'd completely "run dry". I'd had no idea as to how I could better confirm to her—that she'd had absolutely nothing to worry about, when it came to continued employment. Finally, she spoke:

"It's my father, you see," she finally explained. "Papa, he doesn't . . . well, it's been a while since I've had a job. One that pays me money. And you see . . ."

"Wait a minute. What does your father . . . what does he have to do . . . why should your father be a part of this conversation? What does your father . . . what does he have to do with whether you work here or not. Work <u>anywhere</u>, or not? I don't understand it."

"It's been a long time, you see, since I've had a job. I haven't . . . how should I say? . . . I haven't <u>contributed</u> to the . . . to the income, at the house. In fact, I've been a . . . been a drain . . . an awful drain on the . . ."

"Maria? Please excuse the question. It's one that people . . . especially men . . . are not supposed to ask a lady. But, how <u>old</u> are you?"

"I'm thirty-three. I'll be thirty-four . . . in June."

<u>That</u> was a <u>real</u> shocker! (Yeah! <u>Another</u> one!) I'd pictured her as being eight—maybe ten—years <u>older</u> than that. I'd <u>tried</u>, valiantly, to hide my reaction—but, I don't believe I was the least bit successful. In fact I'm sure of it.

"I know," she said, softly. "I <u>look</u> older. Much . . . much, much <u>older</u>."

"It's not that, you know. It's just . . ."

"Look, Mister Young. My father . . . he is very . . . well, he is very, very demanding. He has, you see . . . he's had a drinking problem. Has had this problem . . . this problem with the bottle . . . he's had it for many years. My poor mother, she worked her fingers to the <u>bone</u> . . . I think you could say! Worked very <u>hard</u>! For many <u>years</u>! Many, <u>many</u> years! To <u>support</u> him! And my little <u>brothers</u>! Papa . . . <u>he</u> would not work! Today, he <u>cannot</u> work! No one will <u>hire</u> him! To do even odd jobs! Because <u>everybody</u> . . . everyone in our <u>community</u> . . . they all <u>know</u>! They are all <u>aware</u> . . . that he is an <u>alcoholic</u>!"

"I didn't . . . I had no idea . . . that . . ."

"It even affects my two brothers," she continued. The emotional dam appeared to have burst. "Well, Santos . . . he sometimes drinks a little too much. But, not very often. Pedro . . . he doesn't drink at <u>all</u>! Won't even <u>look</u> at beer . . . or whisky. You've met them. Mister York hired them to move the children's stuff in here, and . . ."

"<u>Those</u>? Those were your <u>brothers</u>?"

"Yes. They are good men. Sometimes, though, it is awfully difficult for <u>them</u> to find work . . . because of my <u>father</u>. Because of his <u>reputation</u>. Our house . . . such as it is . . . it is all <u>paid</u> for. My mother . . . how she was <u>ever</u> able to <u>do</u> that, I'll never know. To bring in money . . . and to see that the house . . . that it got paid for . . . it was <u>amazing</u>! And, for her to raise us . . . , and to put up with Papa's <u>behavior</u> . . . I don't really know <u>how</u> she did it. But, you <u>see</u>? No <u>longer</u> can she work. Her health is . . . well, she's rather <u>sickly</u> now. I think that Mrs. York . . . I think she sometimes gives Mama some <u>money</u>. Helps her out . . . a <u>lot</u>!"

Hmmm. <u>The 'Old War Horse' strikes again</u>.

"So, your father . . . he becomes <u>angry</u>? Becomes angry . . . with <u>you</u>? When you don't have a stupid <u>job</u>?"

"Yes, Sir. He <u>needs</u> money, you see. Needs it. For, as you know, whisky . . . well, whisky . . . whiskey does not come <u>cheaply</u>."

"And so, he expects you . . . uh . . . you kids, to pay for his <u>booze</u>?"

"Well, and the electric bill. Our phone . . . the phone company cut us off, years ago. I don't think they'll reconnect us any longer. And then, there's the taxes. It seems as though they get <u>higher</u> . . . year after year after year! <u>That's</u> where . . . I think . . . Mrs. York helps out! I don't think that <u>Mister</u> York is aware of her giving! So, it's kind of . . ."

"This is <u>incredible</u>! <u>Maria</u>! Why don't you move out? Move <u>away</u>? After all, you <u>are</u> in your thirties."

"Oh, I couldn't do <u>that</u>! He <u>is</u>, after all, my father. And, if I were to move away . . . or if my brothers were to move away . . . it would <u>destroy</u> Papa. And I cannot bear to think of what such a thing would be for my <u>mother</u>! It would be <u>horrible</u>! For Papa would not take it <u>kindly</u> . . . if his children were to 'desert' him. It would go that much <u>worse</u> for Mama."

"I'm not <u>believing</u> this! You mean your father rules . . . rules with an iron <u>hand</u>, so to speak?"

"Yes, Sir. He even spanks me . . . every once in awhile."

"Wait a minute! He . . . he <u>spanks</u> you?"

"Yes, Sir. And, always, I have to take down my panties. And he . . ."

"This is . . . this is <u>incredible</u>! There are <u>authorities</u>, you know! <u>Authorities</u>, that could put the kibosh on . . . put the <u>kibosh</u> on . . . on this kind of outrageousness!"

"But, Mister Young! He is my <u>father</u>! My <u>Papa</u>!"

"I don't care if he's the <u>Pope</u>! He has no right to . . ."

"I don't <u>mind</u>! I really <u>don't</u>! I just . . . I just need to be working. Need to be working . . . to <u>continue</u> to be working . . . so that I can help out. Help out . . . at home."

"Maria, look. Would you want to move in <u>here</u>? You could have my bedroom. I could bunk in up here . . . with Steve and Randy."

A look of stark—undiluted—<u>horror</u> came over her! "Oh, <u>no</u>! <u>No</u>, Mister Young! <u>NO</u>! I could never even <u>think</u> of . . ."

"Listen, I'm not attaching any <u>strings</u>. I'm not angling for you to . . . for you to . . . for you to, you know, to <u>sleep</u> with me. It's just that I'm <u>horrified</u> . . . at the way you have to . . . the way you have to . . ."

"I understand, Mister Young. I understand . . . understand that you're not . . . how shall I say? . . . that you're not <u>propositioning</u> me. It's just that I cannot . . . cannot 'desert' Papa! Cannot 'desert' him!"

"I <u>still</u> don't understand. But, I want <u>you</u> to understand. Understand that this is an open-ended <u>invitation</u>. The offer has no <u>expiration</u> date. Open-ended offer . . . . that anytime you want to <u>escape</u> that horrible situation . . . you have a <u>home</u>! A home . . . right <u>here</u>! <u>Waiting</u> for you. And again, no <u>strings</u> attached. No <u>proposition</u>."

"I understand that, Mister Young. And I'm most <u>grateful</u>."

I'd not really noticed it—I was far too outraged for it to have registered—but, as this incredible conversation had unfolded, this woman had <u>relaxed</u>! <u>Measurably</u>! (It just takes me a little longer to fathom these things—than it does for most people.)

I felt as though we'd gotten significantly <u>closer</u>. <u>Significantly</u>! The horrendous iceberg <u>seemed</u> to have melted! Somewhat, anyway. Still, her home situation was proving to be more and more <u>troubling</u>

to me. Very troubling! I couldn't imagine living under those conditions! Could not conceive of anyone having to cope—day after day—with a situation like that of Maria's!

Something else that was fast becoming an additional worry: I was beginning to become concerned about the pace at which I was spending money. I'd realized that I'd "started off" my "new life"—with an unheard-of amount of cash. Unheard-of in the history of Paul Marchildon, anyway. Had been well aware of that fact. Never far from the ol' consciousness!

$30,000 went a helluva lot further in the mid-sixties than today. For instance, a Buick Lucerne or a Chrysler 300 would cost you in excess of "thirty thou" today. Forty-five or forty-six years ago, the equivalent would've set you back little more than six or seven grand.

In San Antonio—a few months before everything had blown up, in my face—one of my neighbors bought a 1965 Ford Galaxy four-door sedan. It cost him a few bucks north of $4000. I was astounded! How could anyone—ever—afford to pay that much for a damn car? Especially for a Ford, Chevy, or Plymouth? It had only been three years prior, that Ford had introduced its legendary Mustang—for less than two-thousand bucks.

Our house payment, in San Antonio—whenever we managed to come up with it—was something like $77.50 a month.

We'd paid about $14,500 for the joint. So, though I was not close to being rich—even in my present "Taylor Young" circumstance—I was far from being broke. (Which had been my natural habitat, throughout my life).

Still, I knew that I was going to have to do something—to begin to bring in a few bucks. My newspaper column had gone out the window with those extended, life-threatening, health problems—that my accident had brought on.

I was supposed to be a writer! An author! That was the way "The Guys" had set things up. And, the more I would ponder it, the more I felt as though I was perfectly capable of actually writing a novel or six. Each of the books—the ones that had my new name attached to them—all seemed, to me, as though I, in point of fact, could have created them.

One of those books had been a "time travel" opus—wherein a man, sick of the "downward spiral" of the sixties' culture, gets sent back to what he'd always considered to be a "kinder, gentler" epoch. It had been a good read. And I felt as though I could actually write that type of novel myself.

So, I bought me one of those new-fangled IBM Selectric typewriters. How "sophisticated" they were. This "incredible" machine was introduced in 1961—and they were expensive as hell. Or at least I thought so. I spent something like $1100 for the thing. (But still, it was pretty neat!)

Writing, as it turns out, is not as easy as I'd pictured. I worked, mostly, in the mornings—after the children were in school, (and before Maria would arrive). I was alone—"with my thoughts". And, truth to tell, I was doing pretty well with the in-the-works "masterpiece". It's just that The Muse was a little more elusive than I'd figured.

Once this amazing Latin lady would arrive, however, I found that more and more of my attention would center around her. Her home life still bothered me.

Another aspect of her situation—that had not truly occurred to me at first—was her accelerated aging. If she looked 43—when she was actually 33—what would she look like at 63? Even 53? Would she even make it that far?

I had to get her out of that impossible environment. I'd seriously considered petitioning "The Guys". Maybe they could facilitate "a slight—oh, say fatal— heart attack", for the old man???? Didn't know if that would've been heavenly (ah) "protocol" or not. Still, there seemed to be nothing—nothing of the human element, anyway—that could/would rescue this woman from her frightening, God-awful, existence.

Whatever solace I was able to find—in the fact that Maria was not upset with (or disapproving of) me— always seemed to be countered by my overwhelming concern for Elena. Completely obliterated—by the constant, fear-of-the-unknown, worry, related to this special woman!

It had been well over a week since I'd heard from my detective contact in San Antonio. "I should call him," I kept admonishing myself.

But, something inside me was keeping me from making the stupid phone call. Looking back, I'm rationalizing that I'd been afraid—petrified of considering any answers he might give me. Also looking back, I'm not so sure that it was rationalization at all.

So, I was worried about Maria—and the hell she appeared to be living through at home. I was worried about Elena—and what my gumshoe buddy might tell me. And—to add to that tidy little mix—I was beginning to be worried about the money!

Fortunately, the kids <u>seemed</u> to love me. <u>Seemed</u> to be happy with me. <u>Seemed</u> to be content with their circumstances.

However, there was <u>always</u> Luther York! He continually seemed to be looming—to be lurking—in the background.

As noted, I'd <u>never</u> been the least bit perceptive—under the best of circumstances! So, whatever sorts of thoughts my father-in-law might be harboring—well, that constituted yet <u>another</u> worry!

I couldn't get over this feeling—that he could spring! At any <u>time</u>! At <u>any</u> time!

SEVENTEEN

THE WORRIES CONTINUED! EVER PRESENT, they were! Especially so—over the following ten or twelve days. I <u>was</u>, of course, more than a little concerned about Maria—and her God-awful home life. But, I was <u>more</u> worried about Elena! <u>Considerably</u> more worried! I don't know how understandable that might seem. Whatever! I <u>was</u>, though, pretty well wrapped up in my former coworker's wellbeing. (I'd left two or three messages on ol' Adam's answer machine! And, dammit, had gotten no response!)

Thankfully, I was beginning to be slightly less anxious about the kids. Concerns about my relationship with them were—again, thankfully—diminishing! Slowly—but, surely (as they say). There remained some small-but-significant worry—one that I really couldn't specifically <u>identify</u>—as far as how the girls were relating to me. But, even <u>that</u> phase seemed to be going well! (As far as I could tell, anyway.)

Baseball season had kicked off—and the boys and I had started watching *NBC's Game of The Week*, on Saturdays. If I'm remembering correctly, Curt Gowdy and Pee Wee Reese did the play-by-play. This was before veteran play-by-play man, Vin Scully—and former Major League catcher, Joe Garagiola—had begun their celebrated, long-term, run. Sometimes, the girls would sit in my lap, during the telecasts. An important bonus! But, mostly, they usually wound up doing little girls stuff. By themselves. In their room. They <u>seemed</u> contented. (I could only <u>hope</u>!)

Maria was becoming—more and more—a big help. This was (possibly?) a gift from heaven. Something <u>else</u> that had come to <u>seem</u> that way, anyway. This nice woman had decided—for some reason or another—to get deeply involved with Cynthia and Mary Jane. From the time they'd get home from school, she was with them. Almost exclusively.

There were times when I'd wondered if dinner was actually going to get served, on a particular day. (It always <u>was</u>.)

In any case, her attention to my daughters was a big help—and was an important factor in my becoming less and less concerned about their wellbeing.

Oh! I'd started my "next" time-travel novel. As mentioned previously, the words—let alone the paragraphs and pages—were not coming as easily as I'd envisioned. After four or five days—in front of the ol' Selectric—I don't think I'd put more than four or five sentences on paper. Certainly, my new "toy" was not being overworked. And it sure wasn't lending any sort of inspiration.

At the time I'd bought the amazing typewriter, I decided to take the clerk's advice: I went ahead—and subscribed to *Writers Digest*. My first issue arrived—more promptly than I'd figured (thankfully)—and one of the first articles, in that initial month's edition, had to do with the illusiveness of The Muse. (Also thankfully.)

A highly-successful, multi-published, writer advised all of us great unwashed to "write down . . . whatever pops in your mind, no matter how dopey you may deem it to be". His position was that—even successful authors don't use most of what they initially put on paper. "If you, ultimately, wind up throwing out 90% of what you've written . . . so be it. Who'll ever know? That ratio will decrease as time goes by . . . and you begin to expand upon your original train of thought."

It was beginning to work! I was starting to keep as much as 30% of the stuff I was writing. Subscribing to that magazine would turn out to be one of the more intelligent decisions I would ever make.

Then, came the call! The call! It came about two-and-a-half weeks into my newly-found, gloriously-welcomed, solace. The call (from hell) was from my "private eye" buddy, in San Antonio.

He was—finally—able to discover that Elena had been committed! She was actually confined! Was being held—against her will! In a facility that he'd called (wince!) "a loony bin"! I don't remember—

ever—having experienced such a dark feeling! I'd never been confronted with a situation—that was any more bleak than this one was!

"The Looney Bin" turned out to be a government-run mental hospital! An "institute for the mentally unbalanced"! This was where the woman I'd loved had been forcibly confined!

Elena, apparently, had suffered a severe nervous breakdown! Adam had been unable to learn—with any accuracy—exactly how badly she might be doing. How serious—how dangerous—the breakdown might've been! Well—obviously—they're all serious! Listen! To my way of thinking—they're all dangerous! But, was Elena in (for want of a better term) critical condition? Or whatever damnable classification the psychologists might use for such an earthshaking evaluation?

Her situation had to be desolate! No matter how one might choose to define it, she was confined! Dear Lord! She was not free to leave! That fact alone, would seem to indicate that her status was more serious—than merely a simple, basic, "just raising an eyebrow" classification. To me, she was in a damn cage! Probably held prisoner—in some kind of dungeon!

Adam (bless his heart) had even tried to get in—to see her! But, try as he might, my detective friend had been unable to negotiate his way into what I was positive would've been "a house of horrors"!

"Rebuffed at every goddam turn," as he'd put it. "No matter what I tried, I got shot down! Every time! Every damn time!" Frustration fairly oozed out of his labored tone of voice.

"Where's the facility, Adam? Where is she? Where is Elena?" I was hoping to keep the overwhelming, heart-wrenching, anxiety out of my questions! (Not altogether successfully, I'm afraid.)

"Well . . . for one thing . . . she's not in San Antone. It's . . . this place . . . it's in a little town, a good way north of here. Probably fifty-five or sixty miles north of here. Don't know why they . . . whoever it was . . . would've sent her up there. The hospital isn't all that snooty. But, it's certainly not cheap. Nothing is, these days, y'know. But, this is not one of the places . . . not one that's rated as the best one in the whole damn area. I'd never heard of it, to tell you the truth. Listen, this place is kind of secluded! It's located . . . in a little berg, Small town . . . called Lockhart."

He gave me the name and address—even the phone number—of the tiny, out of the way, hospital to which she'd been sent. I couldn't understand why who-ever-it-was would've shipped her off to such a remote spot! Certainly, there were competent facilities in "The Alamo City". There had to be! This place—this probable dungeon—according to Adam, was quite small. What kind of professional equipment would they have up there? How sophisticated? How up-to-date? How (gasp!) antiquated might all that stuff be? (Or—worse yet—how sadistic? Could this be a modern-day "Bedlam"?) Again—dear Lord!

"Any indication," I pressed, "as to why she'd had one? Would've had a breakdown? A breakdown, for heaven sakes? Why she would've had . . . had a . . . had a goddam nervous breakdown, for God's sakes?" I could barely hold the receiver in my hand!

It was shaking that badly! "A nervous breakdown! That's . . . that's . . ."

"Negative. Well, that's not true. I was able to get a bit of a glimmering. This whole thing . . . her going all to pieces . . . it had to do with her job! With the one . . . at that loan office place, that she worked in. The one . . . downtown."

"I suppose I should've known!" I don't know why I let that gem go.

"Apparently," he continued—as though I'd not interrupted, "the guy who she'd worked with . . . his name was Paul Marchildon, the guy who'd managed the place . . . apparently, she was sleeping with him."

Another knife through the old heart! It was becoming a veritable pin cushion! But, how could I even attempt to argue with the guy? It always took a good deal of emotional calisthenics—for me to remember that Paul Marchildon was "dead"! And, sadly, so many people were under the regrettable— the horribly mistaken—impression that he, Paul, and Elena had been intimate! Totally intimate! Consistently—in the minds of many!

"What about him?" I managed to—at long last— ask. "What about this Paul? The guy she worked with?"

"Well, as it turned out, he was married, don'tcha know. And, I guess, he'd upped and left! Left her . . . his wife . . . and his kids! Just pulled out! I understand he was working . . . at the time . . . for some truck rental outfit. Went from the finance company to the truck place. In South San Antone. He worked there . . . a couple or three miles from downtown . . . the last three or four months, I guess.

Before he split! Elena was upset enough, of course. She'd . . . apparently . . . gotten over the fact. The fact . . . that he wasn't working with her any longer. The fact that they were no longer together. Then, a couple days after he split . . . ba-da-<u>boom</u>! He turned up . . . <u>dead</u>! Deader'n <u>hell</u>!"

"And <u>that</u> . . . this guy's death . . . <u>that</u> was what put her over the edge?"

"Yeah. Well, <u>apparently</u> it was! Actually, I guess it . . . his being killed in a car crash . . . <u>that</u> was the topper! That was the <u>crusher</u> . . . from what I've been able to learn. Kinda the maraschino cherry, don'tcha know . . . on top of the whole damn sundae! First the company . . . the finance company . . . they <u>fired</u> her lover. And then . . . as I understand it . . . he was considering <u>moving</u>! I guess it <u>sounded</u> pretty definite. To <u>her</u> . . . to Elena . . . anyway. He was supposed to be <u>moving</u>!"

"<u>Moving</u>? Moving . . . <u>where</u>?"

"Moving away . . . as I understand it . . . with his <u>family</u>! With his <u>wife</u> . . . and his kids! Moving somewhere out of <u>town</u>! Don't really know <u>where</u> . . . or how <u>far</u>! I'd <u>heard</u> they were, maybe, gonna go all the way up to New <u>York</u>, for God's sakes! But, I don't think <u>that's</u> the straight dope! I mean . . . <u>why</u> would he . . . ?"

"Up to New York? Adam, that doesn't sound possible. Certainly, it doesn't sound <u>feasible</u>."

"Look, Taylor. I talked to seven million of her neighbors . . . of Elena's neighbors. As well as a few dozen of the people who lived across the street, and down the block, from where her parents' house is located. The consensus seemed to be that this asshole was going to move to Houston. Either way . . . the son of a bitch was gonna be gone! Houston or New York . . . or possibly, hell, somewhere in between. Don't really know. Nobody seems to know. Not for sure!"

Asshole! Here he was! Calling me an asshole! Another knife through the old heart! And what am I going to use for a snappy rejoinder?

"So," I managed to respond, "this guy . . . his deciding to leave, and then she learned of his death . . . that is what sent her around the bend?"

"Apparently so. At least, I'd have to think so. I mean, I can't see any other way! Any other reason! That had to be like . . . like some kind of emotional trapdoor for her! And, I think, she . . . you know . . . just kind of fell through it! So many sons of bitches out there, y'know. They're married! But, they've always got to have some bimbo . . . some strange stuff . . . on the side. Gotta be banging some other broad! Getting some strange stuff!"

I was more upset at "bimbo" and "broad"—than I was at the "son of a bitch" reference. None of the names were heartwarming!

And here I was! Helpless—totally helpless—to try and set the detective straight. To set anyone—anyone, anywhere—straight! The frustration was presenting as much an emotional train wreck—as anything else—for me.

Obviously, what had appeared to have been a simple, uncomplicated, "way out"—as offered by "The Guys"—was anything but simplistic. The consequences had turned out to be far more complicated! Much more complex—than I could, possibly, have ever imagined! I could never have conceived of such a tangled web! In the wake of my "simplified" decision! I'd given absolutely no thought—not the slightest consideration—.to those human beings! The people—who I'd *left behind*!! None whatever!

"Could you," I finally asked, more huskily than I'd intended, "could you find out a little more . . . about what actually happened, down at the finance company?" Suddenly, it had become a tremendously-draining effort for me—to even speak.

"What do you want to know, Taylor? What do you have to know? He worked there, for God's sakes. She also worked there. They were . . . hell, they were shacked up! Then, he wasn't there anymore! He wound up leaving her! Leaving her . . . in the goddam lurch! Then, he bloody-well turned up dead! That was just simply . . . it was too much for her! Pure and simple! She just went off the deep damn end! What's to learn?"

"Well, I was wondering . . . for the most part . . . what happened with the thing about company firing her. I mean, maybe that could be part of her . . . ah . . . part of her . . . uh . . . her difficulties."

"Nah. I doubt it. But, if you want me to look in to that end of the thing . . . I'll do it. But, I'm gonna have to need another thousand bucks."

"All right," I replied—my voice overflowing with resignation. "I'll put a check in the mail. Today . . . if possible. If not this afternoon, then tomorrow, for sure."

"Taylor? Listen? Why are you so wrapped up in this thing? In this whole dismal situation? As I understand it, you didn't really <u>know</u> this broad. Not all that well. In fact, you <u>seemed</u> to indicate . . . when we first spoke . . . that you hardly knew her at <u>all</u>. And it's set you back . . . well, it's set you back a goodly amount of <u>money</u>! Don't get me wrong, I <u>need</u> the dough! I can <u>always</u> use the extra revenue. <u>Always</u>! Not that many people breaking down my door, these days . . . to hire me, y'know. I just don't . . . I simply can't understand <u>why</u>! <u>Why</u> you should be <u>that</u> interested. That wrapped <u>up</u> in this thing."

"Falls under the heading of none of your goddam business," I snarled.

I don't have to explain to you, dear reader—that I was more than a <u>trifle</u> upset. What was left of my <u>soul</u>—was twisted into a <u>knot</u>! A highly <u>complex</u> knot!

"I'm sorry," I hastened to say. "I . . . I didn't <u>mean</u> that, Adam. Not the way it came <u>out</u>, anyway. Look, Adam. Listen. It's a private . . . a really <u>private</u> . . . matter. I <u>apologize</u> . . . for biting your head off. But, this is . . . well, it's <u>important</u> to me. Really <u>important</u>! I'd really <u>appreciate</u> your looking in to it. Finding out everything you <u>can</u>! About her <u>situation</u>! Her situation . . . as pertains to the finance company! Why they would've gone and <u>fired</u> her! The reason that they'd have let her <u>go</u>! Was it actually <u>before</u> . . . or <u>after</u> . . . she'd learned of this guy's <u>passing</u>? Anything you can <u>glean</u> . . . about her situation there, at the <u>office</u>!"

"My guess would be that her life . . . and her performance, at work . . . that they were, probably, all going to hell. Probably pretty rapidly. The old 'in a hand-basket' trick, y'know."

"Key word there . . . is that it's your guess! Don't get me wrong . . . it's logical. Logical as hell, I'll admit. But, I would like to know more about . . ."

"Well, you shoot me that check. I'll get right on the thing. I'm not going to wait for the money to get here, Taylor. I trust ya. I'll start on it now. Well, probably, tomorrow. You've always shot fair with me."

We wound up the conversation. I was more than slightly interested in Elena's final few days—maybe (I shuddered) her final few hours—with *L&M*.

Whatever the management's role—presumably in her termination, but possibly not limited to that phase of her relationship with the firm—it certainly had her father grossly upset! Probably understandably.

But, I couldn't imagine why her being let go would've been the ultimate breaking point. The undeniable fact was: Something had thrown her father into a rage! I was guessing her being fired—was what had turned the trick! But, as I'd stated to Adam, this was all just a guess! Everything was! Nothing more!

Maybe it had been my "death"! Dear Lord! Maybe that had been the tragic "point of no return". Who knew? Who the hell knew? But, I was certainly wanting to get a clearer picture—of what might've happened. At least, I thought that I was wanting some sort of clarification. On the other hand, that old "Be Careful What You Wish For" adage kept ricocheting through my badly-overheated brain!

In the meantime, my budding writing career had come to a complete and utter screeching halt! I could think of nothing—other than Elena! Other than Elena—"wasting away"! Locked up—in some horrible "Bedlam", someplace. Well, some "Bedlam"—in Lockhart, Texas.

Why, in the world, would they—why would anyone—send her up there? How were her kids? Were they getting along as badly at their grandparents' home—as my children had fared at my parents-in-law's place?

Was any of this—was all of this—due to my "deal" with "The Guys"? I kept reminding myself—that I'd given absolutely no thought to *those who I would've left behind*! Those who I did leave behind! Listen, those "reminders" had to have been coming from somewhere!

The debilitating miasma all boiled down—inevitably—to what could I do? What I would be capable of doing! At this time! And in these circumstances! How could I help her? How could I help this dear, sweet, woman? Maybe spring her? Help her escape—from what (in my mind, anyway) had to be a God-awful situation?

My first inclination—was to attempt to travel up there! To get in to actually see her! From what Adam had told me, though, that would take a good bit of doing! He had been unable to gain entrance to her room (or quarters or dorm—or whatever-in-hell it might be). Presumably, he was, more or less, a pro at such things. And he couldn't come close to accomplishing such a far-flung, far-fetched, feat. Why should I, possibly, think that it would be any easier for amateur old me?

I was even entertaining thoughts of breaking in to the place! Climbing through some window! Some window—somewhere! In some place—wherever (or whenever) the "guard" (or whoever) would not be paying attention! But, then, I began picturing all the windows being barred! Big, thick, virtually-impenetrable, steel! How, in heaven's name, would I—how could I—ever hope to get through them?

Even if the external barriers were simply (simply?) comprised of a matter of bales (and bales and bales) of barbed wire? (Or of even chicken wire?) How would I EVER get through even that? Through all of that?

And—even if I did get through! Even if I were to make it through all of those obstacles—then what? What do I do then? Paul Marchildon is dead! That fact alone—could've been what pushed her over the deep end!

The result of "his death"—meant that she would never recognize Taylor Young! Would I be able to convince her of what had actually taken place? I know that I'd never believe such a cockamamie story. Besides, would "The Guys" even permit me to explain who I actually was? I didn't recall them swearing me to secrecy. On the other hand, the angel never told me about the 30-G's, either. (Or about the celebrated Ms. Klukay.)

Might the sight of a complete and utter stranger—just one more stranger—might that not be enough to send this woman I loved? Send her completely over the cliff? Totally undo any perceived "progress" that might've been made? Providing any progress had actually been attained?

Then—hopefully not as <u>secondarily</u> as I'm making it sound, here—there were my <u>own</u> children to consider. How could I—how <u>would</u> I—be able to, ever, get away with some "wild hair" scheme? Manage some outlandish plan—without jeopardizing <u>their</u> security? And without wiping out what I'd perceived as unmistakable progress in <u>their</u> states of mind?

How could I <u>possibly</u> get away, from my present "locked in" situation? And <u>pursue</u> whatever hare-brained scheme that might be hatching in my twisted little brain—vis-a-vis Elena? It would take me seven or eight hours—just to <u>get</u> to Lockhart and back! <u>That</u> would merely be the travel time!

And who <u>knows</u> what difficulties (to put it mildly) I might encounter up <u>there</u>? <u>Jail</u> time, perhaps? <u>Probably</u>! The whole idiotic scheme was too <u>fraught</u> with dangers—known and unknown! With all manner of <u>uncertainties</u>! And <u>that</u> would be a best-case scenario!

I could <u>never</u> leave the tads alone. Under <u>any</u> circumstances! It would be <u>impossible</u>! The whole thing was patently <u>ridiculous</u>!

Even if—in some way—I could, perhaps, get <u>in</u> to see Elena, what would be the <u>result</u>? As you can see, I'd <u>not</u> stopped "thinking about it"!

As previously noted, she wouldn't even <u>know</u> me! Would have absolutely <u>no</u> idea—as to who the hell I am! Might set back any <u>progress</u> they might've made with her! (Also previously mentioned. <u>That</u> stumbling block, alone, should've been enough to cause me to drop such dippy thinking—<u>immediately</u>!)

Then, again, who says they've made any PROGRESS? Well, who says that they HAVEN'T? Holy DAMN!

The whole thing was so—so God-forsakenly troubling! And reeking with abject confusion! For yours truly!

A whirling dervish of thoughts continued to swirl through the twisted, overheated, ruins of my mind. In amongst it all, there was this flash of a thought: A crazy scenario—that had me taking the kids with me! All the way—up to Lockhart.

But, then what would I do? Put 'em in a movie? I didn't even know if there was an actual theater in that town. And—should there be a movie house available—they'd probably be showing some stupid "R" rated flick! And—if I did wind up in police custody—the kids would wander out of the movie, and wonder what the hell happened to their trusted, devoted, guardian! Their "New Daddy"! If there were to be no handy-dandy movie—in which to "dump" them—then, there loomed the very real chance that they'd see me marched off to the paddy wagon—in handcuffs! Or chains! Or whatever!

There would be—there could be—absolutely no upside, to any of these imbecilic thoughts/plans/dreams/visions/scenarios! Absolutely none!

So, what was I to do? Could I do anything? Seemingly, not! But, there still remained this never-ending, gnawing, stomach-churning, feeling! An inescapable, overwhelming, thought process—that I ought to do something! That I had to do something! But, what?

This feeling of total helplessness—complete frustration—continued! Day after bleak day after bleak day, I would just sit there! In a consistently-dazed condition! Like some kind of lump or something! Or something! Completely drained!

If nothing else, I began to realize that there is never a simple solution. Not to really complex problems, anyway. I'd thought that—if Paul Marchildon had simply disappeared, and had begun this brand new (and wonderful) life—that everything would be hunky-dory. In all areas. Or, at least, things would work themselves out—eventually.

I'd been caught up—almost totally—in wondering whether I'd be thought a schmuck! Whether I actually was a schmuck!

I'd simply not given sufficient thought—to *those we leave behind*! Truth to tell, I'd had to admit that I'd given no thought at all to those people. So, what had happened? Well, let's see:

My wife—my "widow"—had run off with (according to my mother-in-aw) some "snake oil salesman", and had gotten herself, fanny-deep, into some sort of outrageous cult. Some manner of cult—somewhere. One could only imagine the results of that matchup! (No! One couldn't!)

The woman I'd truly loved was in a mental institution! I couldn't even imagine such a situation! Such a circumstance was totally beyond comprehension! I'd not had the foggiest notion—as to her wellbeing (or her non-wellbeing)! In addition, I'd had no idea as to how her two boys might be coping with that potentially-devastating state of affairs! (Potentially? Potentially devastating?)

Then—not incidentally—there were my own four kids. They were—make no mistake—still struggling! Dealing with the "death" of their father! And the desertion (what else could you call it?) of their mother! To say nothing of a grandfather who (at the very least) considered them a pain-you-know-where. At present, they seemed to be doing pretty well— trying to adjust to their new "guardian" (i.e. me). But, I knew, they were still mighty fragile! All of them! I knew it!

Basically, I believed that things seemed to be going fairly smoothly—vis-a-vis my relationship with the tads. My latest, seemingly-eternal, funk, of course, was not helping. In fact, it either touched me deeply—or broke my heart—when, on the day after I'd received that horrendous phone call, Mary Jane had asked me, "Daddy, is there something I can do . . . to make you happy?".

What was making me happy—if anything—was the fact that the girls had begun to call me "Daddy". The boys, however, still called me "Taylor". And my being down in the dumps so regularly seemed to be affecting Steve—my oldest—more than any of the others. On the other hand, who actually knew—what Randy was thinking? Ever?

Then, of course, there were even "those I'd left behind" in Newport. Gretchen was heartbroken—or, at least, that was my perception—at the way our relationship had gone. Was that relationship past tense? Was she past tense? Hell, was Oregon even past tense?

More of an enigma than anything else—in my mind, anyway—was the situation with Magdalena. Hell, I didn't even know—hadn't the slightest inkling—whether it was a for-real situation! I'd had not the faintest grasp—as far as what her feelings, toward me, might be. Didn't know if there were any feelings! I wasn't completely sure—how I'd even felt about her! Was there—could there be—a genuine love there? Or did she merely remind me of Elena? Well, there was nothing "merely" about my emotional entanglement with her. I just had no earthly idea—as to exactly what it was. (What it had been?)

I was—plainly—worried about her son, however. Probably more so than I was concerned about Elena's boys. Did that not make sense—or what?

It would be another 35 or 40 years before I would ever see Jimmy Stewart—in the motion picture, *It's A Wonderful Life*. But, "George Bailey"—in that hallowed flick—had not realized how many lives his life had touched. Or the horrible consequences—when his "I wish I'd never been born" statement was made to come true! I could—most certainly—relate.

All these emotions—this veritable whirlpool of God-awful, terrible, disruptive, emotion—kept me in a constant state of out and out miasma! Even Maria had noticed. She'd asked me—three or four times—the same question that Mary Jane had posed: "Is there something I can do . . . to make you happy . . . Mister Young?" (Well, for one thing it wasn't helping that she was still calling me "Mister Young".)

Finally, Adam called. He had discovered the reason why the powers that be—those wonderful folks from the home office, up in Tyler—had descended upon their San Antonio branch. (Apparently, en mass.)

They had fired Elena! And for what I knew to be a false reasoning!

Howard Leslie—the bastard, who'd owned the neighboring small-loan company (at the other end of the block from Dolly's)—was so upset that I'd flown the coop (owing him $50 or $75—probably the latter), that he had phoned the *L&M's* home office! He had "advised" the head poobah that Elena and I were sleeping with one another! (Dolly had informed me that we'd been referred to—by everyone on the block—as "The Lovers". Apparently—obviously—everyone had thought that!)

This guy—this real schmuck, this Howard Leslie—had also accused Elena (and me) of phonying up all kinds of fake loan documents! And pocketing all the money—from that multitude of false loans. We'd never done that! Ever!

It was, evidently, three or four days later—when Elena had suffered her apparently-disabling emotional breakdown!

The information didn't make me feel any better. But, at least (at last) I finally knew! I also knew why this poor woman's father had harbored such hatred for the gringos from the company.

To this day, I wonder whether "those gringos" had ever sent bona fide auditors down to San Antonio—to establish whether Elena and I had done such a dastardly deed! If they had—and the numbers-crunchers had established that Ol' Howard was a damned liar—I wonder what their feelings (if any) might've been!

The data, provided by Adam, was a help, I guess. (I guess!) But, it was not enough to pull me out of the really serious doldrums. In fact, just when I'd thought that I might be being logical (for once in my life)—I began churning up additional plots (fresh schemes), in my demented mind! Just-as-wildly-impossible scenarios—as to how I could gain entrance to wherever Elena was confined. As you can determine, my life definitely remained considerably unsettled! (Considerably.)

My being wasn't in enough of an upheaval! About three weeks after I'd first learned the genesis of Elena's God-awful situation, I found out that Joanne was back in town!

Luther York was a very enterprising man! And a most determined one! I'd been aware of that little piece of information—for years. But, this time, he'd outdone himself! At least, in my humble opinion.

He had managed to track down the SOB—who'd lured his daughter out to the Arizona desert!

He headed his glorious Park Lane west—and had found the cult's compound. The character who'd absconded with Joanne was paired up with her—along with another man and another woman! The four of them lived their enriching, rewarding, devoted, lives—in a little cabin-like structure, located just inside the group's headquarters. There was no fence! No gate! No guard house! Nor any uniformed gun-toting militia-types! I think Luther had, pretty well, determined that there wasn't much in the way of sanitation—in the entire compound!

My father-in-law had pulled out his trusty "thirty-ought-six"—and had entered the sprawled-out, intensely-furnace-like, enclave. This was at mid-afternoon. He'd pointed his weapon at some poor, unclothed, lady—the first person he'd encountered! He was seeking directions! The frightened woman had gladly "finked"—as to where he could locate his daughter!

Whenever Mr. York had ever set his sights on someone/something, you did not want to hamper him! Not in the slightest! He'd marched into the hut! Both women were inside! Both were completely naked! Neither of the men were to be seen!

Luther commanded his daughter—to "get decent"! Then—allowing her just the simple cotton dress, that she'd always worn, when not in the buff (she'd no longer owned such "symbols of the outside world" as a bra or panties)—he herded her into the station wagon!

She'd experienced the overwhelmingly-frigid sensation of cold steel—the firearm—pressed into the small of her back! The gesture was a big "help"! It surely hastened the pair's departure! Once inside the Park Lane, her father headed for The Rio Grande Valley. He'd encountered no resistance—from anyone, in the compound! (Well, except for his own daughter's highly-traumatized condition! She was plainly upset! Plainly!)

There were, easily, 12 or 15 members—men and women—who'd watched the father marching their fellow commune member off, the sacred grounds! At gunpoint! As the old Lorenz Hart lyric says, "Not a single word was spoken".

Three days after they'd returned—and I'd been unaware of the fact that my former wife was back (despite that many visits from my mother-in-law)— she showed up at my domicile! (As stated, things were not unsettled enough! There has to—always— be "something else"! So, of course, there stood Joanne—along side her father! At least there was no 30.06 in evidence!)

The kids were all home. Maria had, minutes before, finished the dishes—and had just left. Five or six minutes after her departure, enter Joanne and Luther!

The girls, of course, rushed into their mother's arms. They were clearly happy to see her—which was yet probably going to be another complication for me. Randy, though, did not get up from the couch. Steven hugged his mother—but, I'd thought, without a whole lot of enthusiasm. He seemed more than a little concerned about the turn of events! (Didn't we all?)

My former wife, for her part, did not appear to reflect the out and out affection—in whatever dimension—from the tads. Not to the degree that I'd expected. Joanne had always been the most altruistic person I'd ever known. Whatever she'd felt, she'd always felt it very deeply. Anything she ever thought—or did—came completely from the heart.

Yet, here she was—appearing more reserved than I'd ever seen her. I didn't know if that was good or bad. (What else was new?)

Luther stood—with his arms folded, and the steel-like stare that we'd all come to know and love. His daughter—finally—spoke! I hardly recognized her voice. She'd acquired some sort of throaty quality.

"Would you kids want to come home with me?" she asked. "Come back home . . . to Grandma's and Grandpa's house? Come back with me?"

To my utter surprise—and amazement—the question had totally befuddled the girls. You could see the internal warfare taking place inside their troubled little heads! They really didn't know what to say. It was some helluva complicated question—in which to be putting to two highly-confused little girls! Helluva complicated question!

Steven looked even more perplexed than usual. But, it was Randy—who spoke up:

"No!" You could barely hear him. But, he repeated it—a little more loudly. Then, he expanded upon his answer. "I don't want to go back! I don't want to go back! Not ever! Grampa and I . . . we don't get along! If you take me back, I'll just run away again! And this time . . . this time, you'll never find me."

I could never have imagined such a response! From Randy—or any of the other kids! (Of course, I'd always been pretty good at not imagining things!)

His grandfather's expression changed not one whit! His mother was plainly crushed! Although, for some reason, she didn't seem quite as destroyed, as I would've imagined.

Then, Cynthia spoke up: "I . . . I think I'd rather stay here! Daddy has been good to me. He loves me. He doesn't say it much. (That comment floored me!) But, I know that he does!" (The last statement warmed me more than I could ever tell you! I made an immediate resolution—to rectify that situation!)

Out of the mouths of babes!!!

"Oh, Baby!" I was in tears! They were cascading down both cheeks! Liberally! "I do love you, Baby! You and Mary Jane . . . and the boys! I love you all! I love . . . all of you! Love you guys . . . so much! How much . . . you'll never know! And I will say it more often! I promise you I will! You'll probably get so tired of me saying it!"

Mary Jane rushed up to me! I picked her up—and held her close! "I love you, Baby! I really do! I love you so much!"

"You . . . you want to stay," asked Joanne—her eyes narrowed on the still-shaken little girl. My "widow" was absolutely stunned! But, again, not quite as shocked—as I'd have imagined. "You . . . you want to stay here? With him?" She repeated the question—three more times! Looking—in turn—at each one of the children! Looking at her children. And continued asking them—that same damned question!

The two girls nodded—immediately! And in unison! And more vigorously—than I'd ever dared to hope. Randy had already made his decision known. Most emphatically! All eyes, now, turned to Steve. Even the softened gaze of his grandfather. (Yeah—softened! That's Luther we're referring to! Amazing!)

"I'd . . . I'd like to stay too, Mother." Stephen's voice was barely audible. But, it was there. "I'm sorry . . . but, you did desert us."

"Yeah," hissed his younger brother. "You ran out on us! You picked up . . . and you screwed! Screwed . . . right on out of here!"

The remark seemed to register more with his little sisters—than with anyone else (including his mother). I was scared—deathly afraid—that whatever ground I might've gained, was being lost! The girls—plainly—did not want to hear their mother talked to, in that fashion!

I doubt that they were aware of the definition of the key word their brother had used! Whether or not that was true, they were plainly troubled!

I was in the highly-troubled midst, of a couple of the longest—most tense, most slow-moving, most apprehensive—minutes of my entire life! I'd had not the slightest idea—as to where this heart-rendering exchange was all heading! (I felt that it couldn't be good!)

The unwavering, fill-the-room, silence had become an impenetrable fog! A deadly smog! An unrelenting cloud—of terrifying emotional pollution! A stifling haze—that was engulfing every one of us, in that room! Including (surprisingly—shockingly) my father-in-law!

Finally, Mary Jane began to sob—violently! But, she clung on to me! To me! And solidly! Desperately!

"I want to stay," she fairly screamed! I want to stay! Stay . . . with Daddy," she cried. "I'm sorry, Mommy. But, I want to stay! I want to stay . . . with Daddy!

The smothering mist evaporated! Instantly! POOF!!!!!

"C'mon, Joanne." It was Luther York. His voice was huskier than I'd ever known it! "C'mon," he repeated. "We'd best be going."

EIGHTEEN

YOU KNOW? LOOKING BACK, I don't think that we give our kids enough credit. In some areas, anyway. After the unimaginably-poignant, heart-rending, confrontation with their mother, my kids seemed to "settle in". To accept their situation with me—with more enthusiasm, than I could ever have thought possible.

Prior to that emotionally-draining moment, Randy had tried—in a few minor instances—to play the old "Poor Me" card. The "I'm The Product Of A Broken Home" thing, don'tcha know, But—though Steve was worried about the situation (somewhat—I could tell) he'd never play that game, along with his younger brother.

Once Luther York—and my one-time wife—had left, I was hearing less and less of that scenario. I believe that Stephen was, maybe, more relieved, about the situation, than I was. (Well, that probably would've been damn nigh impossible!)

The girls—to my surprise—had caused me fewer problems than the boys. I'd gotten the feeling—and had never stopped believing—that they were both in search of some measure of stability. A goodly measure of security. That—I firmly believe—had been their top priority. Thank God, they'd seemed to have found it—with me.

So, while the presence of their mother—for even just that brief moment in time—had been a highly-emotional circumstance, they had come away from the confrontation more settled than, even, their brothers.

Things were beginning to level off. I was—believe it or not—even back in to my writing career. In fact, things—The Muse—seemed to be more readily available to me; from a day or two after Joanne's from-out-of-nowhere appearance (and subsequent—tragic-for-her—exit).

Even Maria was becoming more and more comfortable—during the expanded number of hours, that she would (voluntarily) spend at our house. She would stay overtime—virtually every night. Sometimes two or three hours past her quitting time. Most usually, she'd remain "merely" an extra 30 or 40 minutes. Listen, her added presence was a stronger-than-I-could-have-expected contribution to the enriching, peaceful, environment that had—so thankfully—descended upon us.

By then, thankfully, my only real worry was Elena! Her condition—both emotional, and confinement-wise—was a consistent cause of distress! I'd thought that I'd begun to come to grips with her situation. Obviously, everything related to this wonderful woman's dreadful situation—every possible thing—was far beyond my control. After time, I'd finally realized this regrettably-indisputable fact, I guess. (I guess.)

There was even an added—an equally disquieting—dimension to this whole situation with Elena. My detective friend—Adam, from San Antonio—had done a little extra (gratis) work on my behalf. Just when I'd figured that I'd not be hearing from him again, he called me—one early, unsuspecting, Tuesday afternoon:

"Thought you might be interested, Taylor," he'd announced—his voice a study in unsteadiness. "I was able to inveigle an ounce or two out of one of the sainted administrators . . . up there in Lockhart! As I'd told you, I'd worked my ass off . . . to try and get in to see Elena. Struck out! Struck out . . . but good! Thought that <u>everybody</u> . . . everybody on the whole damn <u>staff</u> . . . was <u>sure</u> that they were <u>all</u> against me. But, this one lady . . . her name's Dorothy Swanson . . . she <u>called</u> me! Can you <u>believe</u> that? Called me . . . just a few <u>hours</u> ago. But, I wasn't able to return her call . . . not till about a half-an-hour ago."

"What'd . . . what'd she tell you, Adam?"

"That Elena is getting along 'passably well'. Her words . . . 'passably well'. She has no idea, though, <u>when</u> they would ever release Elena."

"Dear Lord," I muttered. <u>Another</u> knife through the old ticker. "I'm . . . I'm . . . I can't <u>tell</u> you, Adam. I can't . . ."

"From her tone of voice," he interrupted, "it didn't sound like it was gonna be anytime soon. She wouldn't go into it . . . Dorothy wouldn't. Would <u>not</u> go in to things . . . any more than that. <u>None</u>

of the particulars! I didn't want to pump her. Well, not too hard, anyway. Figured, what the hell. I <u>knew</u> I wasn't gonna get anything more out of her. Why screw up a possible future connection? You never know when something's gonna work out with her. With this Dorothy bird. Anyway, that's the latest bulletin . . . from out of the dynamic municipality of Lockhart."

It—obviously—wasn't much of a help. I was grateful to the gumshoe—for his devotion to duty. Especially since it was "pro bono".

And I was glad (I guessed) that Elena was doing 'passably well'—whatever-in-hell <u>that</u> meant. But, there <u>was</u> a dimension to his call that was reconstructing all of my previous frustrations! Started me, even, thinking—once more—about possible ways of getting in to see this wonderful woman! Or of even <u>springing</u> her! (Where have you heard <u>that</u> before?)

But, of course, the more I'd rehashed (once again) the woeful—the dreadful—circumstances, the more (once again) frustrating the situation became. Or "re-became"—if there's such a word. As before, the "news" wound up putting a definite crimp in my writing pursuits. A "hitch-in-my-giddyap"—literary-wise! Well, temporarily anyway.

Still, by and large, things <u>had</u> "leveled off"—and we all seemed to be doing well. The kids, Maria—and me. The thing with Elena was beginning—thank heavens (I was guessing)—to fade ever-so-slightly every day. It was good to know that Elena <u>was</u> (I was also guessing) progressing!

A month passed. Then, two months. Not much "action" seemed to be in the offing. As mentioned above, everyone seemed to have "settled in". In June, the kids got "liberated" (Steve's far-from-original term) from school, for the summer.

We were able to take numerous side trips. Mostly over to Matamoros—the Mexican town, which borders Brownsville. Also, we took in a copious number of movies. The *Majestic* almost became our second home. And—thanks to Maria's bountiful food preparations—we also indulged ourselves, with an abundant number of picnics. (All of which included our culinary benefactor. She seemed to enjoy the outings as much as the kids. Well, so did I.)

The boys and I were watching the major league baseball games—whenever we could. Once or twice a week, it seemed. And—unexpectedly (but, happily)—the girls would sit in my lap for most (if not all) of those contests. I'd laid in <u>tons</u> of the old *Jiffy Pop* popcorn. That wondrous stuff—that you'd had to "skitter" atop the burner, on the kitchen stove. And we'd always managed to consume a bountiful amount of that delicacy. Most times, under the disapproving-but-indulging eye of Maria.

We saw the Yorks fewer and fewer times. Their grandmother no longer delivered the tads from school. Their mother, Joanne, virtually <u>never</u> came to see them. I figured <u>that</u> was probably just as well.

So, things appeared to be going pretty well—for the lot of us. And, as July 4th had come and gone, I'd begun thinking about moving the kids up to Oregon with me. Well—truth to tell—I'd not ever not thought about that glowing possibility. But, I was scared to death of the consequences. (You see, I have this "back trouble". This yellow streak.)

But, along about the middle of July, there took place a "happening"! A huge "happening"! Joanne "ran away"! Again! Snuck out of her parents' house! In the middle of the night! And (are you ready for this?) she stole her father's opulent Park Lane! And headed for points unknown!

Oh, and she'd emptied out the old guy's wallet. (Hee Hee!) I was positive that he'd always carried at least $200 or $300 with him—at all times. At least! Those amounts were considerably more substantial in 1966 than they are now. But, even so!

My "widow" had even left an extended, expletive-filled, note—glued (substantially) to the mirror in the bathroom! Well, actually, The one-page, typewritten, missive was more like a letter—assuring her parents that, this time, they'd never find her!

Luther, as you might expect, immediately, reported the station wagon as having been stolen! A serious crime, obviously! One perpetrated, by his own flesh-and-blood daughter! Damn the consequences!

I have the feeling that he was planning to get into his brand new, blue Chrysler New Yorker (a considerably different-looking vehicle than my old '48)—and head for Arizona. As far as I know, he never did set forth on that quest—which was probably best for all concerned.

As September approached, I was getting more and more "itchy" to relocate my newly-acquired family to Newport! The Yorks were less and less a part of the kids' lives. I'd had no idea—as to whether Eva would continue to transport them home from school—in the upcoming semester.

There was still the never-ending concern about Elena! I guess my continued stress—wondering, on a daily basis, (actually, on an hourly basis) how she was doing—was what was keeping me in the Rio Grande Valley area.

I'd heard <u>nothing</u> about her—since that one, out-of-the-blue, phone call from Adam. I'd tried calling him back—sometime in August. But, his phone had been disconnected.

He'd, apparently, gone out of business. He'd indicated to me—in numerous incidental remarks, during some of our conversations—that being a "private dick", in San Antonio, was not the easiest profession, in which to carve out a living.

I'd even <u>called</u> the facility, up in Lockhart! Three or four times! They'd steadfastly refused to confirm that Elena had ever <u>been</u> there. Dorothy Swanson, as it turned out, was no longer employed at the facility!

I <u>did</u> manage to get hold of some lady—in late August—who'd acknowledged that Elena <u>was</u>, at that point, still a "patient"! But, she'd resolutely, consistently, <u>refused</u> to comment on the woman's condition. <u>Very</u> disconcerting! Very <u>frustrating</u>! The ever-present totally-helpless feeling continued! Unabated! And it seemed as though there was no end in sight. (And, in point of fact, there <u>wasn't</u>!)

The word "end" was tough! I'd shuttered at the thought that—as long as she'd been so damnably incarcerated in that institution—I'd had no idea as to whether this beautiful woman might be <u>near</u> to "the end" (in the most horrible—the most feared, most God-awful—sense of the word).

I'd mentioned, to Maria, the possibility—the "wild hair"—pertaining to removing the children, from Brownsville. I didn't know whether there'd be a potential mother figure "warming up in the bullpen", up in Newport. And as my absence from Oregon had become more and more pronounced, I was less and less sure—of what might be awaiting me, if/as/when I was ever able to return.

Gretchen and I had certainly not parted on the best of terms. In addition, I'd had not the slightest clue—as to where (or how) Magdalena might have been faring! Had no idea—as to whether she'd be interested in even a light-dating situation. Let alone something/anything serious.

Still, I'd not put together any sort of concrete plan—to actually <u>move</u> the tads up to The Pacific Northwest. There was Elena—always <u>Elena</u>! A further consideration—and quite possibly a considerable complication—was the always-looming, totally-unknown, factor! Said factor: How my parents-in-law might react. I'd still had a few months left on my lease of the house—but, that was minor-league stuff.

There was so much to take into consideration. I'd reflected before (and often) on how many lives had been so drastically changed—since Paul Marchildon had "died". Mostly those of my children. But—more than peripherally—it had affected my parents-in-law. They'd not asked to become custodians of four kids. And it was Joanne—who had "inflicted" the tads on them. I'm positive that she'd believed the "young 'uns" would be in a better place, at her parents' home. A more beneficial situation—away from me and the always-present, attendant, poverty!

Joanne! I'd, quite possibly, not reflected nearly enough upon Joanne!

When I'd first met her—and all throughout our relationship, from childhood on—she'd been the most loving person I'd ever met. Certainly, the most altruistic. She'd never thought badly—of anybody. Ever! Well, until the "thing" with Elena had, so groaningly, come up.

And—try as I might—I could never convince her that nothing intimate had ever happened between us. (Well, I guess you could say that the numerous kisses—and my consistently patting her on her "bum"—was intimate.) But, we never had been to bed. And, if the fact that Adam was convinced otherwise was terribly upsetting to me (and it was), you can imagine how frustrating it continued to be—that Joanne had come to the unshakable belief that we'd gotten deeply involved sexually!

Joanne! Things could have been so much different! Probably should have been so much different! Undoubtedly should have been so much different!

I guess that it all redounded to my lack of ability to handle money! Hell, to even earn any damn money!

She'd <u>had</u> to do without! Without so many <u>things</u>! For our <u>entire</u> married life!

I firmly believe that—had I not, personally, gone out and bought her a dress or two, from time to time—she'd have walked around naked. She'd always believed that those clothes—or shoes, or any non-esoteric undergarments, or whatever—had, for all practical purposes, <u>taken</u> <u>food out of the mouths of the kids</u>! And she'd always been dead set <u>against</u> anything that would further deprive the children! The message <u>there</u> was that they'd been terribly deprived—throughout their lives! I cannot deny the <u>truthfulness</u> of that line of thinking!

She'd always <u>seemed</u> content with things, though. Our being unable to talk to one another very much, and her <u>indulging</u> me in attending the occasional Broadway shows notwithstanding! <u>That</u> had all changed—once we'd gotten to San Marcos. It was <u>there</u> that her mother (formerly known as "The Old War Horse") became an overbearing influence in her life.

Whatever warm and/or charitable feelings I might've since harvested toward my mother-in-law, things <u>did</u> go downhill from San Marcos on!

Of course, I'd not been aware of so many things. Circumstances—as they'd pertained to Eva York. I'd not known of Luther's hostility toward her—for her having "tricked" him, when Joanne had come upon the scene. Had not known that the move from Michigan, to Texas, had been against her wishes. Had not known that her husband had harbored such a low tolerance for kids. Kids, in general. If not an out and out dislike for them.

I probably would still not be aware of those things—had not the angel in the dashboard divulged them to me, on that far-reaching night in Seguin.

Joanne! She had never had the two proverbial "nickels to rub together". Had continually been broke! For all of her life!

And—as long as she'd have stayed married to me—she'd have had very little prospect of the financial outlook improving! In the near—or even distant—future!

That really fell upon me! Upon my failure! I was back to considering myself a schmuck again. (Would that never end? Should it never end?)

Well, the argument did have some merit. Because of my failings in that area—for, virtually, her entire adult life—she'd been (apparently) swept off her feet, once she'd gotten to Brownsville! By some true schmuck! Some real bastard! One who was able to give her a multitude of things. Material goods—that I could never have come close to providing.

Due to her father's life-long (apparent) hostility toward kids—even his own child (obviously)—it had to have been terribly embarrassing for her, when Luther had shown up at the cult's headquarters, in Arizona! She'd been unclothed! And her father had hauled her away—literally—at gunpoint!

And now, there she was! Legally, a bona fide "fugitive from justice". Her father (most likely) didn't care if she was caught! Or even killed! Dear Lord! It was not his concern, I'd supposed! No "skin off his nose"—if she were to suffer a fatal accident—in his cherished, beloved, "hot", Park Lane.

All of this turmoil—every <u>bit</u> of this God-awful tumult—could've been avoided! Had I been a little more intelligent (and a <u>lot</u> more productive) when it came to monetary stuff—then, <u>none</u> of this would have to have happened!

I was doing my best to rationalize! To assure myself that "She's a big girl, now . . . and can make her <u>own</u> decisions". Still, I was, most certainly, experiencing a good deal of guilt—for having let her down. What was to—ever—<u>become</u> of her? What would—what <u>could</u>—the future hold for her? Would I—ever—<u>know</u>? (Did I <u>want</u> to know? Yeah—yeah, I <u>did</u>!)

Something I'd <u>not</u> counted on was Maria's reaction to my proposed relocation. The manner in which she would "take" the news that I was considering a move up to the Pacific Northwest. Stupidly, I'd not even <u>considered</u> it.

I'd reached the inevitable point, where I was—more and more—getting caught up in the idea of <u>leaving</u> the State of Texas. It had—seemingly—brought me nothing, but grief! More rationalization, of course.

There was this one emotional asset that I'd <u>always</u> hold onto—for the rest of my life: My move from Detroit—to (as it turned out) San Marcos—<u>was</u> made out of the purest of intentions! I'd <u>honestly</u> wanted to give my marriage a much-needed "rebirth". And I <u>did</u> do my best! Obviously, it was none too good. Especially monetarily.

Our relationship was to have been glorious from then on. Joanne was in a place—where she would be near to her parents. Further, she was far away—from a city where four-million people all hated her. She was ensconced in a small, ultra-friendly, town—as opposed to that big, hostile, city. This was perfect! Everything was going to be simply wonderful—no?

Then why did everything—simply everything—turn into (forgive the language) shit?

So, getting away from the source, the location, of all this—this, this, this—damnable excrement, well it had to be playing a more and more significant part in my thinking. Especially, when I'd had that beautiful condo—on that beautiful beach—in that beautiful town, up in Oregon. Just sitting there! Waiting—patiently—for me!

But, inevitably, came the occasion—when I was simply "thinking out loud"! And, in the process, I broached the intention (well, the thought) to Maria! I was afraid she was going to go off the deep end! (And there'd been more than enough of that!) Fortunately, we'd been alone, in the house.

"Mister Young!" She'd been seated on the couch across the room—but, she'd bolted up, and hurried across the room. She was almost looming over me! "Why . . . why would you want to do that? Why would you want to leave? You have everything . . . everything . . . down here! The children . . . why, they all love you. And . . ."

"Maybe you didn't understand. I was going to take them with me. I have a lovely condominium up there. It's beautiful country, Maria. Right on the ocean. The Pacific Ocean. My condo is right there!

I mean . . . right on the <u>beach</u>! It's a really glorious place!"

"Oh?" I could practically see the ice cubes cascading out of her mouth. "And is there a <u>lady</u>? Do you have a <u>woman</u> up there? One who would <u>care</u> for your children?"

"I don't really know. Not for sure. I'd <u>like</u> to think so."

"You . . . you'd like to <u>think</u> so? You don't <u>know</u>?"

I was treading on terrain—that was <u>loaded</u> with landmines and barbed wire. I <u>knew</u> it! Imperceptive little old me! I was <u>positive</u> that I was going to (what else?) put my foot in my mouth! But, I honestly didn't know <u>how</u> I was going to deal with the suddenly-volatile, totally-unexpected, situation!

"Look, Maria," I'd responded—most hesitantly. "There was one woman up there . . . a lady that I'd been dating. We did <u>not</u> part on the best of terms. In fact, when I left . . . well, I can't tell you the word she used. The words she used. Can't say them . . . in mixed company."

"Well. <u>that</u> doesn't sound . . . how do you say? . . . real encouraging."

"Well, she may <u>miss</u> me. Of course, she may not. Hell, she might've gone ahead . . . and <u>married</u> someone else by now. She <u>could</u> be <u>dead</u> . . . for all I know." I <u>wished</u>—fervently—I'd not uttered that last cryptic sentence.

"Mister Young . . . Taylor . . . listen! Listen to me!"

To the best of my recollection, that was the first time she'd ever called me by my first name. <u>That</u> little factoid was of some significance.

"Taylor," she repeated. "Listen. I'm being very selfish. I realize that. But, please! I don't want you to go!"

"Oh, Maria. Come on! Listen, you'll find . . . that there'll be other families who'll . . . ."

"It's not that!"

"Well then, what is it? Surely, your father'll understand. I'm sure he'll give you sufficient opportunity . . . to find another job. You said that he even spanks you, from time to time. But, listen, I'm sure he's not going to . . ."

"The job means nothing! Not to him! Maybe you haven't noticed . . . but, I've even had a problem sitting down today!"

"He's . . . he . . . he . . . ?"

She nodded. "You see, Taylor. Like I think I've told you before, my father is . . . Papa is . . . well, he's an alcoholic. He ran out of liquor last night, and . . . when he sent me out to get some more . . . I took too long! Just a few stinking minutes! But, it was too long! So? So, I have a problem sitting down."

"That's positively ridiculous! Outrageous! You can't have him going around, and all the time . . . ! Look! Look here, Maria! Why don't you . . . what would be wrong with . . . why don't you come up there, with us? Come with us . . . up to Oregon?"

Suddenly, I was having second thoughts! Gretchen! My relationship with her (as up-in-the-air as it might've been) was not something about which I could just say "Pish-tosh"! Could not simply blow it off!

And, damn me, there was Magdalena! Magdalena! I really didn't know exactly what I felt toward her! Well, there were times—many times—when I was positive, as to my emotions! And, of course, I'd had not the foggiest idea—as to what she thought of me! If she thought of me at all!

And here I've gone and just added even more confusion to the mix! I've invited, yet, another lady into what could become the well-known "Chinese Fire Drill"!

Plus, I really didn't know what I'd felt—or not felt—toward Maria! It had always bugged me—just a little—that she'd never called me by my first name! And now? Now she'd begun—to call me "Taylor".

Every time—I suppose, that each time, throughout my entire life—that I'd think things can't possibly become any more confused, I'd find that I was patently wrong! The situation would become even more mixed up! Hell, it had become a tradition by then.

"I . . . I don't think I could do that, Mister Young."

So, we were back—to where she was calling me "Mister"! Things were—obviously—not going swimmingly!

"Why not? Look, we could find adequate sleeping quarters."

"It's not that. I can't . . ."

"I've only got one bedroom, as it is," I interrupted. "I'm sure that I'm going to have to find another place. Someplace . . . that's got three or four bedrooms. But, that can be worked out. We'd all get separate rooms . . . on the way up there! Well, the boys would probably bunk in with me. The girls . . . if you came . . . they could, maybe, bed down in your room. That's not . . ."

"It's not the sleeping arrangements I'm speaking about, Taylor."

That was a relief! The fact that I was back to being on a first-name basis with her.

"Look," she continued, "I've never been married! And I certainly have never slept around . . . although Papa thinks I'm a whore! That fact alone . . . has gotten me more than just a few sore bottoms. But, I've been very particular about any times that I would've ever slept with a man! Any man! And you can count 'em on one hand! And even have finger or two left over!"

"Uh . . . Maria. I didn't intend to . . ."

"I don't have . . . I haven't had . . . didn't have the backbone to tell you this: But, I've grown so fond of the children. Since there's never been a . . . how shall I say? . . . never been a lady of the house, so to speak, the children . . . they've become almost like my own. And I've loved . . . absolutely loved . . . coming here. Coming here . . . every day. In truth, I miss you . . . miss all of you . . . on the weekends. That's why, on some of those Saturdays, I'd just pick up . . . and come on over. I miss you . . . and the kids. I don't know if you're aware of it . . . but, I do miss you! You . . . yourself. You've been so kind to me. I enjoy being in your company. In your presence!"

That struck a nerve! That was exactly how I felt— when Elena and I were "together". (As "together"—as we ever got.)

"Well, I have to say: I'm highly complimented. I couldn't . . ."

"Have I not shown it to you . . . in my daily care? In my daily chores, around here? That was the only way

I'd had . . . of showing you how much I care! I couldn't imagine what else I could do! Well, I could imagine, but . . ."

"Uh . . . well, having you call me 'Mister Young" . . . that hasn't made me feel especially close! Not all that close to you! I could see how much you love the kids, though. Anybody could. I'd have to be blind . . . not to see all the love and care that you've shown them. Ever since you've been here."

I guess that I had made a decision—of sorts. It would all depend upon Maria, of course! I say "of course". But, she was a sure thing. (I didn't mean that to come out—as insensitive as it probably sounds.)

Let me try and explain: I'd had no idea—as to who I could get to care for the tads, up in The Pacific Northwest! I couldn't visualize my ever marrying Gretchen. Who knew about Magdalena? And—when one comes down to considering it—the kids were the most critical items in my life. And Maria had been just wonderful with/for them. Her accompanying us would be so damn logical—once I'd put that thought into motion!

So, as our conversation so laboriously proceeded, I found myself hoping—more and more—that she'd accept my offer! In fact, her acceptance was—all of a sudden—becoming the most important thing in my life! At that moment, anyway. (Probably had been—for all of 80 or 90 seconds.)

"I have this unease," she was saying.

"Unease? Unease . . . over what? You're a fully-grown woman . . . and a very nice lady. You're perfectly entitled to make your own decisions. And . . . I assure you . . . you wouldn't have to worry about any sexual demands on you. I promise you that I wouldn't . . ."

"That doesn't worry me! Not at all! I've said that before! A number of times, I think. Did you not understand that?"

"Then, why should you hesitate? Why would you hesitate? Unless you like carting around a sore fanny."

"No! I hate it! It's not the fact of the spankings, themselves. It's just that I hate the fact of . . . of being under Papa's thumb. Of his treating me like a little girl. Well, I guess, more like a whore! Feeling he can do whatever he wants with me. Whatever he wants . . . to me."

"Then . . . for God's sakes . . . pick the hell up! And leave him! Leave there! Leave the whole damn environment! I'm certainly not going to treat you like some little girl! Certainly not like a whore! And I'm . . . for sure . . . not going to be spanking you."

"It's just that . . . that he is my father. And he's so . . . so dependent on me. He can't . . . he really can't . . . can't look after himself. And Mama . . . after her hard life . . . she really can't do anything for him. Can't do much for herself, either. They . . . both of them . . . are so dependent on me."

"Look, Maria. There are programs . . . for people like your parents."

"Oh, Papa . . . he could never take charity. It would . . ."

"How much of your money does he take?"

"That's different! We're family! He's my father!"

"Does the fact that you're his daughter not mean anything? The fact that he treats you like . . . as you, yourself, have said . . . like a little girl? In more ways than one? And . . . worse yet . . . like a damn whore?"

"You don't understand our culture."

"I'm sure I don't. But, I do know fairness . . . and injustice . . . when I see it. Or when I hear it. And you've been . . . for far too long . . . way too submissive to him! You have given him all kinds of indulgence! Frankly, it's indulgence that he damn well doesn't deserve. I hate to say it . . . but, he doesn't deserve a daughter as indulgent as you are. As devoted as you are. As loving . . . and as caring . . . as you are."

"I think you place me too high. He is my father, after all. I don't know . . . I don't think . . . that it would work out. Me going all the way up there! Thousands of miles . . . and my poor parents . . . they'd be . . . they'd be . . . be devastated! They can't . . . either one of them . . . fend for themselves!"

"Look, I'm not made of money . . . and I haven't the foggiest idea as to how much cash it's going to take to get me out of my one-bedroom condo . . . and into a bigger one. Or whatever kind of lodging I can find. But, I'm sure we could help your father out . . . from time to time, anyway. Help him out . . . financially. I just can't make any kind of monetary promise. Not right now. Not at this time. Can't tell you . . . not honestly . . . how much, or how often. How much . . . or how often . . . I'd be able to contribute. Not right at this moment in time."

"I just . . . ! Taylor, look! I can't do it! Couldn't possibly think of leaving my poor parents. Not now. Probably, not ever. They do depend on me."

Well, I'd guessed. That took care of that! Another one of my genius-type schemes—shot down. And—though it took me forever to realize it—this one actually had made sense! So, naturally, it was not going to work out!

The whole exchange, however, left me with still more unanswered questions. Pointedly significant ones. Probably critical ones!

For instance, there were my feelings toward Maria to consider. And how she felt toward me—given our conversation.

But mostly, I guess, there was this terribly bleak—this terribly black—feeling. Not unlike the vast, terribly bleak, unending, frustration that had seemed to be my constant companion—during my relationship with Elena. Only this situation, with Maria, was—so far anyway—bereft of any kissing. Or any pats on the "bum".

Well, once I'd locked in to my decision to relocate, there really wasn't much to do—except to try and put things together.

I don't know why—but, one of the first items on my agenda, was to send a letter to my detective friend, in San Antonio. As previously noted, his phone had been disconnected. But, I'd written "Please Forward" on the envelope. I'd enclosed a check for $250—and gave him my address and phone number, up in Oregon, Asked him to—please—if he was able to turn up any new info on Elena, to (again, please) keep me advised.

Of much more significance, I went to see Eva York. I'd driven by the home of my parents-in-law a few times—and waited till Luther's new Chrysler was gone, and Eva's old Plymouth was parked in front. I didn't especially want to deal with the old man. (Actually, I especially wanted not to deal with him.)

I advised my mother-in-law that I was probably going to move the kids up to The Pacific Northwest. She was a good deal less rattled than I'd feared. She told me that—while losing the grandkids was a sad situation for her—she'd "perfectly" understood my position. (Perfectly?)

"I've got a pretty good plateful," is how she put it. "I have no idea where my daughter is. I have no idea how my daughter is. My husband has disinherited her. He even hopes that she gets in trouble . . . gets in bad trouble . . . for having stolen his damn station wagon."

I didn't know what to say. How to respond. How to—possibly—comfort her.

"And," she sighed, "let's face it . . . I'm not getting any younger. I just simply can't cope, anymore! Can not cope with all the . . . with all the crap, the out and out crap . . . that seems to keep coming my way,"

She certainly was not "The Old Warhorse" anymore. I guess that she probably never was! My bad! (No one said that, back then.)

Last of all—realizing that an intelligent list of priorities was never my strong suit—I'd had to bounce the relocation off the kids. It was something that I was looking forward to! The move, itself! But, <u>not</u> looking forward to trying to convince the tads that it would be a good—a <u>wonderful</u>—move!. (I was <u>petrified</u>—as you can imagine—over what the kids' reaction might be.)

Strangely—or maybe not—they were all <u>excited</u> about leaving Texas (in general) and Brownsville (in particular)! Each <u>one</u> of them! Without <u>exception</u>!

Randy, especially, wanted to "get out"! Steve did too—but, he was <u>much</u> more reserved in his enthusiasm.

I'd worried more about the reaction of my daughters—more than anything else. But, surprisingly (to <u>me</u>, anyway) the girls were <u>more</u> than willing to leave. I can't quite quote—not directly, anyway—what Cynthia had to say. But, it translated out (I believe) to something like: I was the only person in the world—besides Maria—who really and truly <u>cared</u> about her! About <u>all</u> of them! So, <u>naturally</u> she'd want to go with me. Especially, if the new venue was as beautiful as I'd described.

There would be further words with Maria, over the following few days. They weren't exactly uncomfortable—but, our actions (vocal and physical) could best be described as "stilted". And the move was seldom brought up.

Just as I'd thought that my plans had pretty well solidified—the last Thursday in August (I was planning to leave early Saturday morning)—I got word, from Eva, that Joanne had been <u>arrested</u>!

"Apprehended"—two days previously! In some little town—in Missouri!

Luther was going to go forward, and press charges—much to my mother-in-law's travail! They were going to extradite my former wife, since the theft had occurred in Brownsville's Cameron County. She was, Eva advised me, expected to be back in Brownsville on Monday or Tuesday.

It turned out that—though she'd arrived on Monday—I'd not be able to see her till the following Friday.

Why should I go visit her? She didn't "know" me. In truth, probably, the only thing she knew—for sure—about me, was the fact that I had custody of her children. I'd had no clue as to how critical my removal of those kids would be in her current state of mind.

But, I'd been so hung up, of late, on *Those We Leave Behind*. And Joanne was definitely one of them! She was, after all—whether she knew it or not—the mother of my children.

When I finally got to see her—over one of those latch-ups that looked like a whole bunch of ping-pong tables strung from side to side (with little wire mesh separators between prisoner and visitor), and an armed guard seated (actually lurking) at each end—her expression was one of incredibility. She did recognize me, though.

"What are you doing here?" she asked—after numerous uncomfortable seconds.

"I . . . I came to tell you that I think I'm going to take the kids home with me. Take them up to my home. Up in The Pacific Northwest. State of Oregon. It's beautiful country up there. I figure that . . . in addition to my being a little bit on the homesick side . . . it'd probably be a good thing for the children. Kind of a fresh start . . . with a new coat of paint . . . sort of thing."

"And?"

"And I thought I should let you know."

"You need to clear <u>that</u>? With <u>me</u>? I thought it was all pretty well set <u>up</u> to where . . ."

"Since they're <u>your</u> children, I thought that . . ."

"Listen, Taylor . . . or Young, or whatever your name is . . . for the past year or two, my life has been nothing but <u>shit</u>! <u>Nothing</u> but shit! The only time I've <u>ever</u> been happy . . . <u>ever</u> . . . was when I was out in <u>Arizona</u>! Didn't have all that much money, out there. Well, actually, I've <u>never</u> had all that much money. But, out there, I didn't <u>need</u> hardly any money. Anything I've ever needed . . . all I've ever wanted . . . was <u>there</u>! It was all out <u>there</u>!"

"Joanne, look. This hasn't been . . ."

"I <u>know</u> that the thing . . . running out to Arizona . . . made me look like some kind of a shitty parent. That's really something . . . something that I'd have to <u>agree</u> with."

"From what I know of you . . . of your life . . . I can't <u>imagine</u> you being a shitty parent."

"You don't know me." Her laugh was almost cryptic. "You . . . sure as hell . . . don't <u>know</u> me."

(Another—albeit smaller—dagger through my heart! You never get <u>used</u> to those!)

"I may know you better than you think I do," I offered.

"How can that be?" Another cryptic laugh. "My mother loves me. My father hates me. I suppose that . . . like they say . . . one out of two ain't bad. But, how are you ever going to get a . . . a, well a . . . an objective story of who I am? Or how I am? It's impossible for you to have the faintest idea . . . as to who I am."

"I'd like to think that I'm a pretty good judge of character."

"I don't care what you think. Or what you think you know. You don't know shit about me. Here I sit! In goddam jail! I've deserted my own children! I've stolen my father's car! He's not only gonna press charges for the goddam car . . . but, I stole something like three-hundred and eighty dollars from his pissy-assed wallet. I know I'm going to remain in jail . . . for, I'm sure, years and years and goddam years!"

"You've never been in trouble . . . in legal trouble . . . before. Have you?"

"No. But, you figure out . . . figure how some kind of jury is gonna look at me! At a woman . . . who deserts her kids! And rips off her parents! They'll look on me . . . as who and what I probably am. They'll look at me . . . as a piece of shit! And, I guess, they'd maybe be right!"

"Joanne! Joanne, Joanne, Joanne. Don't talk that way. You're not a piece of shit. Have never been a piece of shit!"

"Yeah? Well, you're probably the only one . . . in the whole goddam county . . . who thinks I'm not! And I'd say that's pretty damn stupid of you!"

At that point, she broke down and cried! Loud—convulsive—sobs! Her body wracked—from top to bottom! Violently! And from side to side! To the point that both guards rushed to her side! (Man! They were quick!)

"What the hell's goin' on here?" hissed one of them—staring two burn-holes in my eyes.

"Leave him alone," wailed Joanne. "He didn't do anything! He was just trying to . . . to . . . to buck me up! It's all on me! Just like everything else!"

"Joanne," I began—my voice steeped in pleading. "Don't go thinking that . . ."

"I know that you mean well, Mister! But, just leave me the hell alone! Take the kids! Take 'em! Take 'em . . . wherever! They'll be a helluva lot better off with you! Better off with you . . . than with their irresponsible, jailbird, piece-of-shit, mother!"

"You'd better leave," advised the second guard. "Please, Mister. You'd really better go."

I left! Another helping of whatever—piled high, on my plate!

After the indescribable session with my former wife, I was totally unprepared for what awaited me at home.

It was slightly after four o'clock—when I'd arrived. The boys were out in the backyard—playing catch. The girls were in their room—watching television.

I'd entered into a deserted living room, and plopped my emotionally-drained body into the old recliner—there to close my eyes, and try to reflect on what had, so horribly, just taken place fifteen or twenty minutes before. I'd dared not try to analyze the confrontation, on my way home. Had I pursued that avenue, I'd have caused, I'm sure, an accident!

To say that the remnants of my mind were caught up in a tornado would probably rank with one of the all-time understatements, that our civilization has ever known. And, as you may have figured, I was highly unprepared to face any further "irregularities".

Then, came a soft holler (if there is such an animal) from my bedroom. It was Maria. I'd managed to drag myself out of the chair—and kind of shuffled back to see what might await me now! I couldn't imagine what it would be!

And for good reason! When I opened the door—and entered the room—Maria had her back to me. Her dress was pulled up around her waist—and her underpants were at mid-thigh! Her backside was grotesquely swollen—and badly bruised!

"What . . . what's . . . what's going . . . going on?" I managed to stammer.

"I wanted you to see what Papa did to me. Well, the results of what Papa did. He has this special paddle, you see. He doesn't use it on me very often. Just usually Mama's hairbrush. But, last night, he became very upset! He's decided that we've been sleeping together! You and me! And . . . for some reason or another . . . he's convinced that I'm now pregnant! He . . . he hit me so hard that, I think . . . I think he was trying to make me miscarry!"

"Look, Maria! For one thing, I can't handle this! Not right at this particular minute! Not right now! Why do you show me your fanny? I mean . . . there's nothing

I can do! I've <u>offered</u> you a way out! Apparently, you don't want to take it. Don't want to avail yourself of any kind of <u>escape</u>! Any kind of <u>remedy</u>! Any kind of way <u>out</u>! Is <u>this</u> your way of saying . . . of <u>showing</u> me . . . that you're going to <u>come</u> with us? Going to move up to <u>Oregon</u> with us?"

"No. No . . . it's just a way of, I guess, of saying that . . . as long as I have the name, I might as well have the game."

"Now, what the hell do you mean by <u>that</u>?" (Imperceptive little old me.)

"Do you not want to have <u>sex</u> with me? Has it never been your desire to . . . ?"

"<u>Maria</u>!" All of a sudden, all the emotion left me! "Look," I rasped. "For one thing, I can't <u>handle</u> this right now. Yeah, I guess I've wondered what you might've <u>looked</u> like . . . with no <u>clothes</u> on. I certainly <u>never</u> pictured a fanny like yours! Not the way it is right <u>now</u>. I don't <u>think</u> I'd thought about taking you to bed . . . because I'd always <u>thought</u> that it would be out of . . . out of the . . . well, out of the realm of possibility. I couldn't <u>imagine</u> . . . <u>can't</u> imagine . . . that you'd ever want to be <u>intimate</u> with me."

"Oh, Taylor! You're so <u>naive</u>! Of <u>course</u> I've thought about it! On the other hand, showing you my bottom wasn't just . . . just to, you know . . . just to <u>lure</u> you into bed."

"Now I <u>completely</u> don't understand!"

"Well, I just don't want you to <u>leave</u>! <u>Ever</u>! Not <u>ever</u>! I don't know . . . not <u>exactly</u> . . . what I feel for you. I don't <u>know</u> if I . . . whether I might love you or not. I just don't want you to <u>leave</u>! I want to be <u>with</u>

you . . . and in more ways that I'd ever thought I'd ever be comfortable! I really don't know. Don't know if showing you my bottom was to lure you to bed . . . or make you feel sorry for me! Or what! Maybe I could make you feel really sorry for me! And then, maybe you'd not leave!"

"Oh, Maria! You can't know how impossible that statement is! Especially in my present state of mind!"

"Or . . . perhaps . . . maybe I'd have excited you! And we'd go ahead . . . and make love! And then, you wouldn't want to leave me! I'm . . . Taylor, I'm so mixed up."

"You? You're mixed up? Listen, I wrote the book! In any case, I'm honored! You do me great honor! I just . . . Maria, I just can't . . . can't handle all of this! Not right now, anyway!"

"I'm . . . I'm sorry . . . I apologize if I've given you any grief! Especially with my trying to excite you . . . or exploit you."

I could never have imagined her using the word "exploit"! That only added to the mish-mosh!

"Look," I responded, "I'm sure that, in another time . . . perhaps in another place . . . I'd jump at the chance! Just leap . . . at the opportunity to make love to you! But, after the afternoon I've just been through, I'm not emotionally up to it! Not remotely capable of it! Even if I was, I don't think that . . . physically . . . I'd even be able to perform! You know what I'm talking about."

"Oh, Taylor. There are ways to, you know . . ."

"Maria, look"! I'd reached a point, where I could barely speak. "Maria . . . believe me . . . I just simply can't! Like I said, you do me great honor! But, please! Pull up your panties! If the kids were to come in . . . and find us like this . . ."

"Yes," she said—as she complied with my request. "You're right! It <u>was</u>! It was <u>stupid</u> of me! Stupid, to even <u>think</u> . . ."

"I suppose that . . . in a way . . . it <u>was</u> stupid." I was having maximum difficulty, in choosing my words. "But, you <u>did</u> do me great <u>honor</u>! I mean that . . . <u>sincerely</u>! Meant it <u>then</u>! Mean it <u>now</u>! It's just that . . ."

"<u>No</u>! It was completely <u>stupid</u>! To <u>think</u> that I could . . ."

"Look, Maria. There's an <u>answer</u>! An <u>answer</u>! A <u>remedy</u> . . . for <u>all</u> of this! Come <u>with</u> us! Up to <u>Oregon</u>!"

"I <u>can't</u>, Taylor! I can't . . . just cannot! Cannot leave Papa."

"You <u>say</u> that? You talk about not <u>deserting</u> 'Papa'? With a fanny . . . that's as torn up as <u>yours</u> is? It doesn't make <u>sense</u>!"

"No . . . you're <u>right</u>! It <u>doesn't</u> make sense. But . . . but, I <u>can</u> not. I cannot <u>go</u> with you. I'm sorry for the trouble I've caused."

I took her in my arms—and <u>stifled</u> the overwhelming inclination to pat her on her devastated derriere!

"Maria, listen to me! You've caused me absolutely <u>no</u> trouble! <u>Ever</u>! Believe me . . . you've been such a <u>blessing</u> to me. <u>I'm</u> the one who's sorry. I'm such an emotional <u>basket</u> case, at this point! <u>I'm</u> not the coherent one. You, I think, probably <u>need</u> a much more stable person . . . a far more <u>stable</u> man . . . than I am. At present, anyway. If you were to move to Oregon with me . . . move up there with us . . . why, it could turn out to be most satisfactory! For both of us! For all of us!"

"I . . . I think, Taylor . . . I think that we're just going to have to leave things as they are." Her voice was barely audible.

"And you? You're satisfied to have your fanny torn up . . . from time to time . . . have it torn up, the way it is now?"

"Oh," she answered—emitting a room-filling sigh. "It's usually not this bad. Maybe once or twice a year, I'll get the paddle. This one . . . his special paddle . . . it has holes in it! And it's very thick! Otherwise, it's just usually the hairbrush. And I can most always handle that!"

"Then, you're a better man than I, Gunga Din!"

NINETEEN

OFF TO OREGON! I'D REMAINED in Brownsville—about two-and-a-half weeks longer than I'd intended. I, undoubtedly, should have put the kids back in school. But, I was always going to "leave tomorrow". Things—and my mindset—just didn't permit it work out that way. I was, forever, staying that "just one more day". Those "one day" extensions? They added up.

Mainly, I really needed to wait—and see how Joanne would fare. As it turned out, the authorities—in their infinite charity—let her cop a plea. As I understand it, she could have gotten up to twenty years in jail—for "Grand Theft Auto".

The benevolent, sanctified, prosecution could also have charged her with a second theft count. For the money that she'd lifted from her sainted father's wallet. "Kind hearted" old Luther York, as I understand it, was pushing for such an indictment! But, loving-and-caring souls that they were, the authorities had, generously, dropped that charge.

My once-wife agreed to serve a ten-year sentence. Dear Lord! Ten years! Ten whole years—out of her still-young life! Ten blue-eyed years! She'd gone from a form of "debtor's prison" (i.e. life with me)—to the real thing!

Of course, Grand Jury proceedings are, supposedly, highly-secret proceedings. (Yeah, right!) Well, at least they're supposed to be. But, don'tcha know, things do leak out. The continual, constant, "word" was that the gracious, the lovable, Luther York really slammed his daughter before that august board! Repeatedly! Somehow, I do not have the slightest doubt—that this is true!

I could do nothing for my former wife, of course. Can't even say that I "could merely stand on the sidelines". I'd never come close to having a sideline seat! A thousand times removed!

I suppose that—from a purely-objective, strictly-legal, standpoint—the sentence was not that outrageous. (I suppose!) I really imagine that someone—simply reading the blurb, in the newspaper—would nod, and move on to the comics page.

But, given the onerous life that this dear woman had been forced to live, it was a gross miscarriage of justice! To me, anyway! And the one person who could have helped—her glorious father—had, like some kind of python or something, turned on her! In an ever so vicious manner! That, most assuredly, could not have helped her mental condition at that time.

So, now she—and Elena—were both behind bars! Swell!

I cannot tell you—even these many years later—what a knife through the heart Joanne's situation was/is to me! (Sound familiar?) Why should it be that I was the one who came up with all the money? Along with the nifty condo—in a beautiful setting? Even a more lithe body (can you imagine?) and some pretty handsome "looks"? Clothes and furnishings up the you-know-what? And she wound up in freaking jail! Where was the fairness in that? Where is the fairness in that?

I'd rented a *U-Haul* trailer—and packed it full. Mostly of the kids' clothes and toys. I'd accumulated a few clothes, a couple pairs of shoes—and, of course, more than a dozen LP albums. They all went into the trailer. The operation left a fair amount of room for us, in the car. Well, I'd put the two TV sets that I'd bought for the tads, on the floor—in the backseat portion of the Dodge.

I'd advised my landlord that I'd leave everything in the house—including the furniture, and the few appliances I'd bought. (I did take my phonograph, though. You'd had any doubts? The record player had set me back more than a few bucks.)

I'd asked the owner to try and find a new lessee, as soon as possible. Asked him to let me "off the hook"—for as many months rent as possible. (I did not come away with a really good feeling—vis-a-vis his intentions, however. He'd been—more that slightly—on the upset side.)

I'd really wanted to make the long jaunt as palatable as I could—for the tads. They were, I'll always believe, most assuredly, ready to leave Brownsville. And San Antonio held no real attraction for them. I'd found myself hoping that I'd not painted too beautiful a picture of Newport in general—and my condo in particular. (Especially since there'd not be enough room in my housing up there—to accommodate my new family!)

There would, obviously, have to be major "adjustments" in my living quarters. All of us could never fit—into a one-bedroom facility. And I'd had no idea as to how much cash I'd have to lay out for a two-bedroom (or, more aptly, a three-bedroom) venue. I didn't even know whether they'd have a larger condo available. (I really didn't know if they'd had any accommodation—larger than the one, in which I'd been living.) All of that was way up in the air! Certainly, it was of more than passing interest to me. I'd been bleeding money pretty good over the previous few months. (Story of my life!)

Financial concerns aside (well aside) I'd decided to journey a good bit out of our way. For openers, we stopped in Houston. *The Astrodome* had been opened for about a-year-and-a-half. "The Eighth Wonder of The World", as it was billed! I wanted the kids—well, Steve and Randy especially—to be able to attend a major league baseball game. (And we/they did! The Astros were thumped—mightily—by the Cardinals. But, at least it was a Big-League game.)

After a couple of days in Houston, we headed west. I negotiated my way around San Antonio. No sense in rattling cages for the children. Ones that didn't <u>need</u> to be rattled!

I <u>did</u>, however, swing up through Lockhart. (How could I <u>not</u>?) The institution—where Elena had been "imprisoned"—didn't seem all <u>that</u> formidable. A fair-sized, two-story, red-bricked, building. About the size of an average big-city art museum or something.

Of course, it featured thick, black, iron bars on the windows—on the ground floor. But, none on the top floor's windows. I'd had to wonder at the logic in <u>that</u>! If the "inmates" were all supposed to be "loonies", wouldn't, at least, a <u>few</u> of them seem to entertain—altogether unrealistic—thoughts of escape? By, maybe, exiting through one of those unbarred windows, on the second floor? Just wondering.

There was an added "impediment"! A six-foot-high cyclone fence surrounded the place! Look, Ma! No barbed wire on top! Or lethal razor-sharp strips! And it didn't <u>look</u> to be electrified! There was an immense in-and-out gate—with two separate lanes. And, of course, the to-be-expected guard house. I couldn't see a guard—behind the dark-tinted windows. But, surely, there <u>must</u> have been one. (At least.)

The whole scene had gotten me to (what else?) toying with the idea—of trying to get in to see Elena. Truth to tell, more than <u>toying</u> with it. There <u>had</u> been a movie theater, in "Beautiful Downtown Lockhart". (I'd <u>looked</u>!) I don't remember which picture was playing—but, it would even have been appropriate for the kids! So, I <u>could</u> have schluffed them off for a couple of hours.

But, what sense would <u>that</u> make? We were back to <u>logic</u>! If Adam couldn't get in to see her—providing he was being truthful (and I'd had no reason to believe that he had not been faithful in his reporting)—how could <u>I</u> (a literal "civilian") expect them to let <u>me</u> in?

And—even should I be able to surmount the insurmountable odds—<u>then</u>, what would I <u>do</u>? What would I <u>say</u> to her? What <u>could</u> I say to her? I would be a perfect <u>stranger</u>! Paul Marchildon was <u>dead</u>! (Remember?)

What would my presence <u>mean</u> to her? Probably nothing! Almost <u>certainly</u> nothing! But, suppose there'd be something <u>there</u>? In my manner of speech (which she'd always thought to be "beautiful")? Or my inimitable physical mannerisms? Some <u>thing</u>—that would <u>remind</u> her of Paul? What <u>then</u>? Would <u>that</u> be enough—to drive her "off the <u>cliff</u>"? Truth to tell, It's hard to imagine such a scenario being any sort of <u>benefit</u> to her!

There appeared to be no good <u>answer</u>! There could <u>be</u> no good answer! And (who knew?) such a "visit" could very well turn violent. I could, very well, wind up—in <u>jail</u>! <u>Then</u>, what would happen to the kids?

Somewhere during those unrealistic, tortured, mental calisthenics, I'd even hatched an evil little scheme! One which had me scaling the fence, and (somehow) breaking in! <u>That</u> would—undoubtedly—mean my being detained, by the local constabulary! For who-knew-how-<u>long</u>? Not good! Only <u>problems</u>—especially for my children—could arise, from all (or any) of these flea-brained thought processes! Only <u>problems</u>!

How-ever-reluctantly, we, logically, moved on!

Our little group wound up that night—in El Paso. We even stayed in the very same hotel—where Paul Marchildon became Taylor Young. (I couldn't resist!)

The next evening, we'd reached the Los Angeles area. Ever since *Disneyland* had opened—11 years before—I'd had this wild-eyed vision of, somehow, taking my children to that wondrous entertainment park! (Obviously, I'd never come <u>close</u> to realizing that far-fetched plan. But, at this point here I <u>was</u>! Close by the glorious gate—with my <u>children</u>!)

I checked us into a hotel, in Anaheim! The next day, <u>we all went to *Disneyland*</u>!

What an <u>adventure</u>! What a neat <u>place</u>! I'm sure that the admission prices are <u>vastly</u> different today—but, back then, they let both of my daughters in <u>for free</u>! Tickets for the boys were a little over five bucks, each! And I <u>think</u> I got in for less than ten bucks! And our ticket booklets contained admissions to <u>many</u> of those exciting rides and highly-intriguing exhibitions! It was <u>wonderful</u>!

There were so <u>many</u> things to do! The boys were <u>thrilled</u>—hell, they were <u>enraptured</u>—by "The Matterhorn"! This <u>had</u> to be absolutely the wildest rollercoaster in the history of the world. I was <u>never</u> a big rollercoaster fan. In fact, I'd never <u>been</u> on one—till that magical day. (Against my religion, don't you see! I'm a devout coward!) But, all five of us took one ride. (The girls did a helluva lot better than I.) The boys spent, I think, all the rest of their tickets—riding the thing! Most of 'em, anyway!

I took my daughters on, pretty much, a tour of the rest of the park. We went on rides—that took us through the glorious worlds of *Snow White & The Seven Dwarfs* and *Peter Pan*. "Flew" around in *Dumbo*-shaped ships. Took a tour down a river—through a jungle (where the driver of the boat pulled a pistol—and shot a hippo! One that had burst up out of the water! The stupid thing had scared <u>me</u>—if not the girls)! But, the pilot of the boat <u>plugged</u> him—"in the tonsil"!

We'd set it up to where the boys would meet us at the *Mickey Mouse* restaurant every two hours! And things went splendidly! The whole entire day was <u>glorious</u>! (I'd had to spring for a few more tickets for the guys to do the Matterhorn thing again—and again and again. I think Cynthia, Mary Jane and I had just barely used up our supply of tickets—by eight-thirty that night. At that point, we all headed back to the hotel! I don't think that <u>any</u> of us had eaten since two-thirty or three o'clock, that afternoon. But, we'd all "conked out"—within minutes of hitting our rooms.

The following day, we took in a Saturday afternoon American League contest at the Angels' ballpark—next to *Disneyland*. Was <u>that</u> apropos—or what? <u>This</u> was a really close game. The Red Sox won—but, it took 11 or 12 innings! Even the girls were <u>thrilled</u>!

Okay, it seemed like <u>forever</u>—but, we <u>finally</u> made it up to Newport! On Sunday evening. I'd pulled in to that observation point, on the highway. And—I swear—each one of the kids was completely dazzled by the (well) dazzling beauty that they'd beheld! I found myself hoping—and praying, and everything in between—that they were going to love this place! Be more than happy—where-ever we might wind up living! These dear children—after everything they'd been through—deserved nothing less!

Once we'd gotten to my condo—which had never looked so good—the tads were overjoyed! I tried to explain to them—that, eventually (and, probably, sooner than eventually) we'd have to move! Relocate—to larger, more accommodating, quarters! That didn't diminish the fact that they fell in love with that remarkable beach! I made a solemn promise that—"first thing, on the morrow"—we'd all go swimming. (I was more than mildly surprised—that they'd all had swimsuits. That most-fortunate "inheritance"—turned out to be Maria's doing! Nice lady!)

Sleeping arrangements presented a bit of a problem. Took a little bit of brainpower. We finally ended up with my sleeping in the bed—with the two boys. (The shape of the bed drew a few comments. I'd have given a cookie to have known exactly what Steve—the "Deep One"—was thinking.)

Amazingly—or maybe not—the girls fit on the couch; if their heads were at opposite ends. And, fortunately, "The Guys"—up there—had blest me with an abundance of blankets.

So, things seemed to be working out. At first anyway. Meals—with four chairs—would simply mean

I'd have to buy a fifth chair. Or, maybe, a stool—which would be perfect for Mary Jane.

The following day—before anybody had entertained thoughts of breakfast—we'd all made our way out onto the beach. The kids were absolutely thrilled! We spent the entire morning out there! There'd been numerous waves—big ones, high ones—for the tads to dive through! The boys—especially—were in their glory!

My neighbor, Charlie, had seen us out there, and—before heading off for his garage—he'd come out to renew acquaintances. He looked—most inquiringly—at the tads. I told him that it was a long story—and I'd fill him in later. The explanation was semi-satisfactory. (I could never adequately describe his many-faceted expressions—as the short conversation had progressed. And had—finally—ended.)

It was—as you can imagine—good to be home! The condo was exactly as I'd left it—so many months before. Well, a sizable coat of dust had come to rest, in a few places. But, for the most part, the joint was the same as ever. (The same held true for the "dearest" Chrysler ever built!)

We spent the forenoon and early afternoon—us "boys"—emptying the U-Haul and the Dodge. All that closet space—and floor and shelf space—that I'd thought I'd had? Gone! All gone! Vanished! I figured that—for the nonce—we'd just go ahead and put the TVs on the floor in the bedroom. Simply use the big one in the living room. The kids had never seen one like it. One with such a huge screen—and in color, yet!

Obviously an encounter—or meeting, or confrontation, or whatever—with Gretchen was inevitable! A situation that had to be faced—sooner or later! I figured I might as well get it into the past—as soon as possible.

So, although we were all "starving", I'd waited till the lunch crowd would've cleared out, at *Joe's*. Then we—the entire horde of us—descended upon the unsuspecting eatery! And "Gretch"!

If Charlie had been taken aback (and, clearly, that had been the case), my waitress friend was absolutely floored! You've seen those cartoons—where the wolf's jaw drops (literally) to the ground. Well, those images are not that far removed from reality. Not when it pertained to Gretchen's reaction—when we converged upon the innocent restaurant!

"Taylor!" she managed to gasp. "What is . . . ? Who are . . . ? Are these your children? What about their mother? How long have you been back? Are they . . . these kids . . . are they going to be staying with you? Living with you?" The questions abounded! Were unending! Were nonstop!

"We'll pull into that booth, there . . . in the far corner. When you can get a break, come join us. But, short answer to your question: Yeah . . . they're my kids. Well, not biologically! Long story. But, yes . . . they are staying with me. I've kind of . . . ah . . . inherited them."

I herded the tads into the designated booth—and did my best to explain that this was a woman that "Daddy" used to date. To the best of my recollection, that was the first time I'd ever referred to myself as "Daddy". At least, to all four kids—all at once. Since I'd become Taylor Young, I'd not taken advantage of that missed opportunity. For some reason or another.

No matter <u>how</u> I'd referred to myself, I was easily able to determine that they could all see that I was troubled. Every one of them!

It was Stephen who asked, "Is she upset with you? Are you in trouble . . . over <u>us</u>?"

"Naw," I'd answered—with as much bravado as I could muster. I don't think I was able to bring it off very well. "We just . . . well, when I left town, we . . . we, you see . . . we weren't exactly on the best of terms. She's really a very <u>nice</u> lady. You'll <u>like</u> her. Really."

There happened to be an uptick in business about then. Gretchen brought over a chocolate milkshake for each of the kids (they <u>loved</u> her already)—and a cup of coffee for me. It would be close to 45 minutes—into the terribly-troubled future—before she could actually join us.

I introduced each of the tads to her—and she, graciously, shook hands with every one of them.

I did my best to "explain" to her—how I'd "happened" to get involved with the children. By way of their grandmother. I "explained" that their father had died—in a horrible automobile accident—and that their mother had come upon a multitude of "legal problems".

How could I (or anyone else—<u>any</u> responsible person) <u>not</u> want to take them under his/her wing?

I was hoping (probably against hope) that "Gretch" would see the logic in that.

Though I could tell that my waitress friend had extreme skepticism written all over her continually-stiffened countenance, I found myself wondering if the kids were picking up on it. Children—as you probably know—are, almost without exception, incredibly perceptive. Especially when adults, in their presence, are attempting to deal with some difficulty. (Especially one originating in one of the adult's imagination!)

We'd—eventually—wound up exchanging a lot of meaningless small talk. Don't ask me how I'd managed to transport the woman out of her filled-with-doubt inquisition mode. But, after 12 or 15 difficult, never-ending, minutes, Gretchen got up—in the midst of all the minutia—and fetched us all hamburgers, fries, and refills for the shakes and coffee.

Once we'd—at long last—eaten, "Gretch" got each of the tads yet another milkshake. (I could picture each of them gaining 38 pounds—before we'd ever get out of there.)

Then, she asked if they'd mind if their "father" (heavy emphasis on that word) and she would repair—to one of the booths across the restaurant.

"Your father (again, she'd hammered that word) and I have a few things we'd like to . . . ah . . . to talk over. If youse guys wouldn't mind."

Steve looked quite troubled—but, the other three seemed not to care. (Especially if those nifty milkshakes were to continue to abound.)

My waitress friend and I seated ourselves in the booth nearest the counter. It was the furthest—

geographically—from where the kids were busily attacking their unexpected riches-in-confection.

"Now," she practically hissed, "suppose you tell me what this is all about. You leave here . . . without any notice! Hell-bent on finding out how <u>your</u> kids are! Two boys and two girls! Now, you come back with <u>these</u> four kids . . . two boys and two girls! <u>Helluva</u> coincidence! And here you <u>go</u>! You claim that they're <u>not</u> your biological children!"

"They're <u>not</u>! <u>Look</u>, Gretchen! If you'd just let . . ."

"Then," she continued—totally undaunted, "I get this cockamamie story . . . about your <u>blundering</u> upon <u>these</u> four kids! Through their grandmother, yet! Their grandmother? Whom you'd never met? Are you <u>sure</u> . . . it wasn't their fairy godmother? Or 'Bernadette of Lourdes'? I don't know <u>how</u> you'd <u>ever</u> expect me to believe such a . . . such a . . . such a totally-cockamamie story."

"Look, 'Gretch'. This is . . ."

"No! <u>You</u> look, Taylor! <u>You</u> listen! All <u>along</u> . . . since, just about, the first time we <u>ever</u> got together . . . there's been something about you that just didn't . . . just didn't . . . well, there was something that just didn't seem <u>right</u>! Didn't <u>fit</u>! Didn't <u>register</u>! Didn't <u>compute</u>! I don't know <u>what</u> that was. Or what it even <u>is</u>. You'd had <u>some</u> sort of logic, I guess, going for you. Back then, at least. Pretty much, away. But, <u>now</u>?"

"Gretchen . . . you're going off half-cocked! You're completely . . ."

"The sheer <u>coincidence</u> . . . of your blundering onto four kids?" My words were not having the <u>slightest</u> effect! "<u>Blundering</u> onto them? Four kids . . . who just happen to be of the exact same gender as your own kids? And . . . as near as I can tell . . . pretty much close to the exact ages of your own kids? But, these are someone else's kids! Kids? Some unfortunate kids . . . whose father had just happened to have died? In some kind of a damn car accident? Whose mother . . . for God's sake . . . is in jail? And then . . . on a pure chance meeting, with these kids' grandmother . . . you just happen to wind up with custody of them? I could vomit! I could puke!"

"Look, Gretchen. It's . . ."

"No! You look, Taylor! You go running off, to Brownsville . . . or some damn place in Texas . . . to look in on your four kids! Two boys and two girls! And now you come back with four kids! Two boys and two girls. Like I said . . . helluva coincidence! And they are from Brownsville! And they're the exact same sexes . . . as your own kids! And about the same ages! But, biologically, they're someone else's kids! There's that old saw, y'know: About 'I may have been born at night . . . but, I wasn't born last night'. Taylor . . . for heaven's sakes . . ."

She began to weep. Ever so slightly—but, tears were dribbling out of both of her eyes! That, of course, simply added to my emotional plight!

I know! I should have thought all of this through! Grappled with it—well beforehand! Solved the damn dilemma! Even before it would've begun! But, I don't know! I just don't know! I guess I was probably afraid! Scared—to, thoroughly, play it out in my mind! There'd been enough turbulence in my life, I'm guessing—without creating more of it, in the warped recesses of my overheated mind. That must have been what I'd been underline. (If I'd been thinking—at all!) This was probably the "logic"—behind which I'd been so stupidly hiding. (But, who knows?)

There had always been the chance, I guess I'd figured—no matter how remote, or far-fetched—that "Gretch" would actually buy the story. In my warped thinking, there seemed to have been a part of her that would believe anything I'd tell her. Obviously, that was far from being a fact. The code word—in her, rather violent, reaction—was "cockamamie".

Still, the one inescapable fact was, that—sooner or later—I would have to have had this "discussion", with this woman. First of all, in a town the size of Newport, it would be inevitable that our paths would, once again, cross. That was, obviously, inevitable. Plus "unusual" news travels fast—in any locale! And "inheriting" four kids is pretty unusual!

More importantly, I did harbor feelings—a goodly number of feelings (most of which I was having a problem identifying)—for Gretchen. There was this gigantic need inside me. To put what was now happening—to put it behind me! Get it the hell out of the way! And the sooner the better. ("The sooner . . . the quicker", as my maternal grandmother—now in heaven—used to say. In heaven—and probably shuddering!)

"Look, Gretchen." It had taken me forever—to simply come up with those two brilliant words. "I really can't help what you think. But, things like this have been happening to me all my life. I once ordered a new hot water heater . . . this was years ago . . . and it got installed across the street. Anyone else could order it . . . and it'd get installed, and signed-for. No problem. But, not <u>me</u>! With <u>me</u> . . . <u>for</u> me . . . <u>everything</u> has to be complicated! <u>Hopelessly</u> complicated . . . in some cases. Either that, or . . ."

"Taylor? What was your wife's name? What <u>is</u> her name . . . where <u>ever</u> she might be?"

"Uh . . . why . . . uh, it's Beverly. It was Beverly."

I was <u>hoping</u> that I'd never mentioned Joanne's name before—to my waitress friend. I'm surprised that I'd had enough snap to realize that—before too many minutes would've passed—Gretchen would—undoubtedly—ask the tads the name of <u>their</u> mother. (Whew! Well, I'd <u>hoped</u> "Whew!".)

"Look, Taylor," she muttered.

And from those two words, I could <u>not</u> tell—was unable to ascertain whether—I'd <u>ever</u> divulged Joanne's name before! Could not determine— whether she'd just caught me in the old bald-faced lie.

"Listen," she continued, her voice a few crescendos lower. "You don't owe me <u>anything</u>! Any <u>sort</u> of explanation. I have no <u>call</u> on you. You have no <u>responsibility</u> toward me. But, I just want you to know: I think your story <u>stinks</u>! I think you're <u>lying</u> to me! Lying through your <u>teeth</u>! I can't put my hands . . . put my finger . . . on anything <u>concrete</u>! But . . . like I said . . . the whole thing does <u>not</u> pass the smell test! To me, it's all a bunch of <u>crap</u>! Pure, unrefined, <u>bullshit</u>! And . . . damn me . . . I don't know <u>why</u>! Cannot figure <u>why</u> you'd go to all this trouble! To all this <u>bother</u> . . . to concoct such a stinking <u>lie</u>! Such a <u>bunch</u> of stinking lies!"

"I suppose that means you don't want to <u>see</u> me anymore. I already <u>had</u> the feeling . . . had this inkling . . . that the naked Chinese Checker games were a thing of the past. But, I'm assuming that you're not interested in seeing me . . . at all . . . anymore. Would it be all right, though, if I brought the kids in here? From time to time? This is a nice place to eat. The kids . . . I can tell . . . love it! On the other hand, if you don't want to . . ."

"Taylor? Those kids are . . . all of them . . . just the sweetest things in the world. The sweetest things imaginable. You can bring them in . . . any time you wish. I'll be glad to see them. Genuinely glad to see them. They are all . . . each and every one of them . . . as delightful as they can be. As for you and me? I dunno. I really don't know! I don't know! I simply don't know! It's not every day, you know, that a man . . . or anyone else . . . who's been near and dear to me, springs four kids on me! Four kids . . . and a far-fetched story! A stupid story that's, that's positively . . . that's absolutely, positively . . . that is totally ape-shit! So, I . . . I really . . . I really need some time! Some time to . . . as they say . . . think it over! To 'review the situation'!"

I felt a particular "arrow" when she'd made that last statement! *I'm Reviewing The Situation* was one of the wonderful songs—that "Fagan" had sung in Lionel Bart's *Oliver.* That was, you'll remember, the glorious Broadway musical—the one which, unforgettably, I'd attended with Elena! On that incredible—that magical—evening!

"You'll . . . you'll let me know?" I realize how stupid—how inept—my response must've sounded. But, I was unable to come up with something more articulate. More scintillating.

"Taylor? <u>Listen!</u> <u>Listen</u> to me! There's something terribly . . . terribly . . . terribly <u>wrong</u> here! Something <u>terribly</u> wrong! And I don't know <u>what</u> it is! Don't know <u>precisely!</u> Well, in fact, I have no <u>idea</u> . . . as to what it <u>is!</u> But it <u>stinks!</u> This whole stupid-assed <u>story</u> of yours! It absolutely <u>stinks!</u> Stinks . . . to high <u>heaven."</u>

"I'm . . . I'm truly sorry that you feel that way. I'd kind of hoped . . ."

"I'd <u>also</u> kind of hoped. Hoped we could . . . that we would . . . would get back together. The naked Chinese Checker games were, I guess . . . I guess they were <u>always</u> going to be a thing of the past. I'd held out <u>hope</u>, though! Hope that we might breathe life back into . . . for instance . . . the naked romps on the <u>beach</u>. To say nothing of romping . . . on that round bed!"

"Gretchen, look. This is . . ."

"But, <u>now?</u>" She was undeterred. "Now . . . with all this cockamamie <u>BS</u>, you've come up with? I just don't <u>know</u>, Taylor. I don't <u>know</u>. It's not a question of my letting you <u>know!</u> Like I said before, I have no <u>hold</u> on you. But, <u>you've</u> got no hold on <u>me</u>. I have so much to . . . so damn much to . . . to try and sort <u>through!</u> More than just simply a spoonful, y'know. I just . . . I just . . . I simply don't <u>know</u>, Taylor. I just fare-thee-well don't <u>know!</u>"

She went back to work, and—eventually—brought us all additional burgers and fries. Each of us—had remained quite hungry. I got coffee—and, of course, the kids all got another milkshake. The only one to finish his entire allotment was Randy. He'd had to struggle—to achieve that lofty accomplishment. He always was the most competitive of all the children.

From time to time, Gretchen would slide in beside the two boys—across the table from me—and make small talk with all of the kids.

Me? She'd had nothing to say to me. I'd kept waiting—hoping, desperately, that I'd not wince, when she'd ask the tads the "inevitable" question: "What was your mother's name?"

I was still unable to remember if I'd used Joanne's first name in any of our many conversations. As many exchanges as we'd had, it was probably an inescapable fact that I had! Of course, there was always the remote possibility—that she'd have forgotten it. But, that would've been very un-Gretchen-like. Remote as hell! The whole thing was such a muddle!

To my utter surprise—and extreme relief—the feared question never got asked! Then, that made me wonder if she was hatching some kind of deep—just-this-side-of-evil—scheme! Was creating some kind of really hurtful campaign—in her inquiring little mind. One to "bring me down"!

Finally, we left! It was just after three o'clock in the afternoon. I was extremely happy to be able to vacate the eatery. And even more glad—that this confrontation was behind us. Behind me. For better—or for worse—I seemed to have survived. (Key word is "seemed".) I'd hurdled a definite barrier! Time would tell how effectively! (Of course, maybe I'd not hurdled it at all!)

I don't think the tads wanted to look at another milkshake. Not at that particular moment, anyway.

On the way back from our "confab" with Gretchen—a confrontation which had left me still rattled—we stopped at The *A&P*, to do some grocery shopping.

My best friend, in the Navy—circa 1951/1952—and I never simply went to "The A&P". We had always patronized *"The Great Atlantic And Pacific Tea Company"*—their official name. We loaded up at the market. (I had a little freer hand—with "the sugary stuff"—than had been the case with our Brownsville "House Mother".)

I think that we were all glad to be "home"! Each one of us five took a nap! About two-and-a-half hours' worth. Stephen—for some reason or another required well in excess of three hours "in the land of nod". Hmmm.

I'd whomped up hamburgers for din. (Yeah, even more hamburgers. My "favorite fruit"—and so easy to fry. Don't require all that much creativeness.) The simple dish was apropos. I think that we were all still pretty well dragging. On the other hand, I got into a more-serious-than-I'd-intended conversation with the children during the meal:

"Look, kids," I began. "I'm going to ask you a favor. A big favor. A gigantic favor, in fact. If Miss Gretchen ever asks you what your mother's name is, please . . . please . . . tell her it's Beverly!"

"Beverly?" I'd never seen Steve look more exasperated. He'd looked almost cross-eyed! "Why? Why Beverly, for God sakes?"

"Well, it's something I really don't want to go into. Not with youse guys. Look, it's a long story. And kind of a private thing . . . between Miss Gretchen, and me. It's just important to me . . . very important to me . . . that you indulge me, this one time. Please go along with me on this."

"What does indulge mean?" asked Cynthia.

"It means we should keep our mouths shut . . . and help him with the lie." Randy—ever the diplomat.

"Ordinarily, I frown on anyone lying." I was hoping to rally. "Or with anyone even helping with a lie. But . . . and I realize that I'm rationalizing here . . . but, this one is really important to me. And for reasons I really can't tell you."

"What does rationalizing mean?" queried Cynthia.

"Don't ask," muttered Randy.

There was a long—extremely pregnant—pause! Finally, Stephen spoke up:

"All right, Pop," he said—even smiling somewhat. "We'll go along."

This was the first time he'd ever called Taylor Young "Pop". For years—most of his life—he'd always called Paul Marchildon "Pop". Randy had gotten to where he'd always called the former me "Dad".

The two girls had always used "Daddy"—and had resumed that gloriously wonderful, heartwarming, tradition a few days after I'd "taken custody" of them, in Brownsville. Believe me, it was great to hear "Pop"—coming from my firstborn!

"If it's <u>that</u> important to you," he'd continued, "we'll go along. It's not that big of a thing. We don't have to know <u>everything</u>."

I got varying nods of confirmation from his siblings. The last—and least emphatic—signal of assent came from Randy. I'd had this worrisome feeling that his reticence might lead to trouble! Somehow! Somewhere down the road!

The following day—after a somewhat less extensive collection of festivities on the beach—I fixed the tads some "brunch". Hotcakes and sausage. Can't go wrong with "Basic Breakfast".

Then, I made my way to the condo's management office—to deal with one of my <u>other</u> major problems. (I'd had the distinct impression that there would be a <u>multitude</u> of them—lying in wait for me, in the weeds!)

As far as I knew, finding suitable quarters was—or should've been—my highest priority. I'd had no <u>idea</u>—as to what might be available to me, in one of the complex's larger units. (I only <u>knew</u> that—when I'd find out—I'd probably not be able to afford it! Whatever "it" would turn out to be. Lifelong habits—and thought processes—die hard, don'tcha know!)

"We <u>do</u> have such an animal as a three-bedroom condo," the manager cheerfully advised me. "But, none are available at this time."

Then, <u>why</u> the cheerfulness?

"When we'd first planned out this community," he went on, "we actually believed that there'd be . . . literally . . . no market for a unit that large. We were so wrong! We'd put six . . . on the top floor of each building. And we were worried . . . that we'd never come close to selling them. But, they got snapped up! Bought . . . so fast it made our corporate head swim."

They did have a few two-bedroom units available! But—as expected—they were way out of my price category. (A situation that the manager could not begin to comprehend.) They would give me a dollar amount—for my present quarters—as a "trade-in", on a larger place. But, to me, the offer was way too niggardly!

I kind of staggered out of the man's office! I guess I wasn't so much stunned—as I was overwhelmed! By the out and out enormity of my situation!

I'd more or less considered having to deal with the people at the management office—even before I'd gotten custody of the kids. But, I'd had no idea—as to the amounts that would be involved. The little get-together with the complex's manager removed any doubt—that I'd not had the foggiest idea! That I was in—way over my head!

I kind of blundered my way back to my digs! The first thing—once I'd kind-of-staggered-in—Mary Jane asked me what was wrong. Cynthia wanted to know if it had anything to do with "the Beverly thing". Kids! The two girls kind of snuggled into my lap—and things didn't look quite so bad!

I <u>did</u> have to work <u>something</u> out, however. And I finally got some <u>expert</u> advice! From Stephen.

He'd wanted to know what was "ailing" me. I explained it to him—and to Randy—as best I could.

"Don't you have any connections up here?" asked Steve. "It seems to me . . . like you should know someone at the bank, or something."

<u>That</u> did it! I phoned <u>Gladys Grimshaw</u>! The lady who'd plowed into me—a good many months back! <u>She</u> knew <u>everybody</u> in town! She advised me that she'd be <u>pleased</u> to "receive" me—that very afternoon. What a neat lady!

I knew that I could trust the tads enough to leave them to their own devices—and, 45 minutes later, I found myself seated in the ornately-furnished living room of her humongous, charming, old house!

I explained my dilemma. And went on to say, "I thought that, maybe, you might have an 'in' for me. The more I think about it, I'd probably be better off . . . just going ahead and buying a house. I <u>hate</u> the thought of leaving the beach, though. But . . ."

"Well, my insurance agent . . . the one who went to bat for you, those many times, with regard to the accident . . . he also happens to be the biggest real estate broker in town. I'll put you in touch with him. I'm sure that he can find something totally suitable for you. For you and your children. Maybe even something . . . really close to the beach. And he can get you more . . . <u>much</u> more . . . for your condo. <u>Many</u> more dollars . . . than those bozos over there would ever <u>dream</u> of offering you. I wouldn't be surprised if he couldn't come up with someone who'd be glad to pay half-again as much as they'd offered for the place."

"Mrs. Grimshaw, I can't thank you enough. You've been . . ."

"My pleasure, Dear Boy. And here's something else. Something that might be worth your while considering: Maybe you'd be better off simply renting a house. That'd free up a whole lot of cash . . . from the sale of your condo, don't you see. Horace . . . my agent . . . is up to his prosperous fanny, in rental properties, too. I wouldn't dream of trying to advise you . . . one way or another. Horace probably will, though. He's always got some nefarious scheme or two . . . bubbling over in his evil little brain. Let me tell you: Most of 'em . . . are jolly well worth listening to."

Major Horace Crowe USMC (ret)! Hmmm! I was expecting some doddering old man—sporting one of those old fashioned, highly-bulky, hearing aids, on his paunchy belly! I mean—with a name like "Horace"?

Turns out, this was Horace Crowe 4th. He'd served 20 years in the Marine Corps. Saw a goodly amount of combat action in Korea—while that "police action" was in full-swing. He'd retired, from "The Corps." in 1963.

The man had inherited the insurance agency from his father (who may, very well, have inherited it from his father). But, this Horace was a human dynamo! He'd—greatly—expanded his base of operations. Had lost no time—in getting his real estate license! That factor alone—had doubled his business revenue.

Then, he got into rental properties. Along the way, he'd also acquired the hardware store across the street from his agency. (Rumor had it that he was in the process of taking over the Chevy/Buick/Cadillac agency down the block.)

In the late-forties and early-fifties, he'd become a devout fan of the old television show *Kukla, Fran & Ollie*. (As was I.) There'd been a special character flitting in and out of the cast. Her name was "Clara Crow". (She was an old flame of Ollie's—if you can imagine a dragon and a bird ever hooking up.) Lieutenant (at the time) Crowe had been so enamored with "Clara"—that he enticed his son into naming his granddaughter "Clara". (No, the son was not Horace 5th. He wound up being named George.)

Just to sit and listen to this amazing man was to be staggered by the sheer energy—in every word, motion (and, undoubtedly, thought).

And he did advise me! Recommended that I rent this really nifty three-bedroom bungalow (which he just happened to have available). The abode was located a mere three blocks from the beach.

The rent was $350 a month—which was quite extravagant for the mid-sixties (but, not outrageous). Plus, the place was only a block-and-a-half from a K-12 school—which enjoyed a brilliant scholastic reputation. A more than trivial consideration. (The Major had thought of everything!)

He'd also assured me that he could get an "almost outrageous" price for my condo. This way, he explained, I would have a "pretty good cash cushion . . . for whatever may come along". (He added, "And, these days, you never know what <u>that'll</u> be".)

I signed on the dotted line! Well, I signed on <u>many</u> of them, actually.

<u>Another</u> wonderful surprise: Gladys Grimshaw picked up the tab for the movers.

Not only that! She came to see us—an hour or two after we'd called ourselves "settling in". She inspected the joint—and determined that we would need four beds, and an assortment of chests of drawers and dressers. Plus a vanity—with a huge mirror—for the girls. She asked if I'd mind—if <u>she'd</u> pick them out—and pay for them. (You can, I'm sure, <u>guess</u> my answer.)

The stuff all got delivered—and professionally set up—that very evening, at a little after seven-thirty!

The tads were <u>overjoyed</u> with the new living quarters! Especially since our new "pad" was so close to the beach!

I suppose that I <u>should</u> have thought of something—like getting go-karts or something—so that the boys could chauffeur the girls there, and I wouldn't have to "bother". (Of course I did not.)

Listen, having bought me a lawn chair to take along—I regaled in sitting on the beach, and watching my children! (<u>MY</u> children!) I was positively <u>thrilled</u>—

to see them frolic on the gorgeous sand. And flailing around—in the always-refreshing surf!

Soon, that would all have to end! The following Monday, I would enroll them in that wonder-of-wonders school that The Major had spoken so highly of. (Old Killjoy, "Daddy"!)

TWENTY

THINGS WERE SEEMING TO SETTLE in for us. Key word is "seeming". (Sound familiar?) I was simply incapable of not looking over my shoulder. Constantly! Surely, something bad will overtake me! But, well into June, of 1967, things were going awfully smoothly!

The Major had succeeded in selling my condo. He'd gotten me almost $70,000—cash—once all the taxes/commissions/six-million other things had finally cleared away. Needless to say, my swag, from the deal, turned out to be far more than I'd ever begun to hope for!

The kids were loving the school, which they were attending. A real upset—when it came to Randy. (Only mildly so in the case of Stephen.) Both of my daughters did really well. By June, though, they were all ready for the cherished summer vacation.

Whether in school season—or out for the summer—we seldom missed a few hours in the sand. Whenever the weather would permit, we'd romp around on the beach—early in the morning, whether school would come later, or if it was the sanctified weekend. I can't tell you what a high it was for me— to watch my till-then-poverty-stricken kids frolic about, on that blessed beach!

The kids also <u>loved</u> my Chrysler! At least once each week—most usually two or three times—we'd take a ride around town (and, from time to time, the surrounding countryside) in "The Old Girl".

I did my best to fairly administer "the rotation program". I believe I was pretty fair. Each <u>one</u> of the tads <u>always</u> wanted to "ride shotgun"—<u>lusted</u> to "ride shotgun"—on these many and varied trips. They <u>all</u> loved that "cool" blue dashboard. Seldom stopped talking about how beautiful it was. They were flat-out <u>thrilled</u> by the car—and the usually-lengthy excursions.

Some of our most "fun times" were spent in that old iron vehicle.

Happily—luckily—the children had all found playmates, as the weeks and months had passed. I was content to let them go about their way—within reason—once they'd come home from school (and had gotten out of their "good clothes").

There was a vacant lot, across the street— and down four houses. It wasn't wide enough to accommodate baseball games. But, it was ideal to use as a football gridiron. My sons—and, usually, eight or ten other boys, of varying ages, in the neighborhood—would play a game, virtually every evening. The contests usually broke up around six-thirty. (A little later—as summer was arriving.)

The girls usually spent time with the girl-type twins, from across the street—playing jacks and hopscotch and jumping rope. Doing all the girl stuff that I'd forgotten even existed. They seemed satisfied too.

The tads didn't mind all the late dinners. And, amazingly, through the winter/spring, I'd become a passable chef. (We did order in pizza from time to time. Like, maybe, twice a week. And—every now and then—Mexican.)

I'd given modest thought to taking in another "House Mother". But, I had never crossed paths with anyone who'd even come close (in my humble opinion) to what Maria had contributed. Truth to tell, I'd never really hotly pursued anyone though. (I probably could have found someone—had I alerted Mrs. Grimshaw.) Things, though, were running so well. Didn't want to louse it up.

Speaking of Maria, I'd sent her a Christmas card. But I'd never received one from her. Or any sort of acknowledgement.

I'd have cherished a "Merry Christmas" from her—in just about any fashion. T'was not to be, I'd reckoned.

Speaking of Christmas, it was wonderful! Not spectacular! Just simply magnificent! And totally simple! I didn't go overboard with presents. Charlie—my former next-door-neighbor? This guy bought more frivolous stuff for the kids—than I'd ever thought existed. Somehow, that didn't surprise me. I enjoyed that 1967 Christmas—the whole <u>season</u>—more than any other I could remember. I think the tads did too.

On Christmas Eve, we <u>all</u> went to bed early—so that Santa Claus could come. The girls still believed in Santa! (Actually, so did I! So <u>do</u> I!)

I'd <u>even</u> finished my novel—in late April! And, as June became July, of 1968, the publishing house, in New York, was working its magic. A few <u>more</u> dollars coming in! A not-insignificant occurrence! The agent up there told me that—while he didn't believe I'd had a genuine blockbuster—he thought the "work of art" <u>should</u> sell well! <u>Wonderful</u> news! (As it turned out, he was <u>prophetic</u>! The work <u>did</u> sell well!)

Gretchen and I had, over the months, dated three or four times—mostly flings at the local movie house. But, <u>nothing</u> was happening! "It"—whatever chemistry that had previously existed between us— had pretty well evaporated. In a way, the situation was <u>particularly</u> saddening!

I guess that each of us hoped that the mist— the naked Chinese Checker vapor—of what we'd had between us, would return to the really nifty full head of romantic steam, that we'd once known. But, at the closing of each of these dates, nothing more happened, than a more-or-less peck of a kiss goodnight—and, possibly, a few coeducational pats on the fanny.

Seldom, in fact, did "us Youngs" venture back into *Joe's*. There just seemed to be an increasing futility, as to the lack of attraction—one for the other—between their star waitress and me. So sad!

For one thing, "Gretch" loved the kids. (Didn't everyone?) As far as I'd been able to determine, she'd never (thank heaven) popped the feared question! She'd, apparently, not invoked that most-disturbing situation! The one—where she'd ultimately ask the tads their mother's name!

As you might imagine, that always-present possibility had continued to frighten me! (Probably another of the reasons that we didn't patronize the eatery all that often: My out and out fear—of her posing that heavily-troubling question.)

Another consideration: "Gretch" appeared to be going off—in all different directions! It was worrisome! For reasons—other than the possible concern—vis-a-vis the identity of the kids' mother!

She'd gotten herself involved, once again, with that stupid "progressive" theatrical troupe. I guess that—in their umpteenth reincarnation—they'd really decided to be "razor's edge"! (I don't think anyone "pushed the envelope" in those days.)

The authorities weren't quite that enthused! They closed the enterprising troupe down—on opening night! About two-thirds of the way through the production! Apparently, there was much "simulated sex" in the "performance". Some said that—for the most part—very little of it was actually simulated! Ergo, the shut-down!

I don't think Gretchen wound up with any real legal difficulties—but, suffice to say that, if I'd changed, over the time we'd spent apart, she'd changed a helluva lot more! And whatever we'd had working for us—was, obviously, no longer employed.

In any case, all five of us—in the Young family—plodded along. And—to all appearances—we were doing pretty well.

I'd even reached a point where I wasn't constantly thinking of "The Guys"—and/or about their motives toward me. I'd even decided that I was—finally—emerging from "schmuckdom". (Hopefully, anyway.)

It was, probably, the second week back in Newport, when I'd looked up Magdalena. Even contacted her. Possibly as many as eight or ten times. On each occasion—without fail—she did her best to cut the "conversation" short. (They were, mostly, one-sided. Guess which way.) It was as though she'd always needed a shot of Novocain to speak to me.

She <u>assured</u> me that her boy was "doing well". I'd gotten the distinct impression—on more than one occasion—that, despite her statements to the opposite, the kid was far from <u>thriving</u>! <u>That</u> really worried me! Worried the hell out of me—although, I guessed, there was really no valid reason why it <u>should</u> be all that disconcerting. There'd been nothing—on which I could "hang my hat". Still, there remained this very-disturbing "inkling"! Something not Kosher, in Denmark—and all that. So, it <u>was</u> very unsettling!

I'd even discussed it with Charlie McNulty—on one of his many earlier visits. I <u>still</u> have the distinct feeling that he was coming to see the kids—as much as to swap lies with me. They all called him "Uncle Charlie"—which, I could tell, delighted him. Surprisingly he was the one, who'd brought up the subject of Magdalena:

"Do you ever see that girl?" he'd asked. "The Latin girl. y'know. The one who was your nurse . . . while you were in rehabilitation? You seemed attracted to her. At least a little bitty. More, actually . . . than a little bitty."

"Yeah. Well, I was. Attracted to her, I mean. I guess I still am. To a point, anyway. She'd brought her son . . . a really neat kid, about Steve's age. Brought him with her . . . to work, this one day. But, dammit, these days, whenever I try to talk to her . . . over the phone, you know . . . she seems, well, almost scared! That's my impression, anyway. I have no idea what could be so frightening to her. I'm really quite worried about her. Not because she doesn't seem to want to give me a tumble! I really don't think that's part of it! It just sounds like there's something radically wrong! Significantly wrong! I'm worried about her! And the boy!"

"I'll look into it." He'd had the damndest—most indescribable expression, on his craggy face, when he'd said that.

"Look into it? What can you do?"

"Oh . . . you might be surprised."

I hadn't the foggiest idea—what that meant!

During July, we made a trip up to Seattle. Took the boat rides around Puget Sound. We even did *The*

Space Needle Restaurant. Built in 1962—for the city's World's Fair—it was still as fresh and new, as could be! And a <u>real</u> adventure! The spectacular scenic vista—the vast panorama—was simply breathtaking! It was quite expensive—to my way of thinking—but, worth every penny. The children were <u>aghast</u> at the wide-sweeping view!

We'd also made a few day/night trips to Portland. Got to see a live production of *Damn Yankees*—and a few weeks later—*Guys & Dolls*.

I was enjoying myself—enjoying <u>life</u>—more than I ever <u>had</u>! In my entire life! <u>Some</u> of it was pure escapism! But, <u>most</u> of it was my <u>kids</u>!

The day after we'd gotten back from our latest trip to Portland, I got a call! Strangely enough, it was from <u>Magdalena</u>! Yeah! <u>Magdalena</u>!

"I'm sorry," she'd said—before we'd really finished our hellos. "Sorry that I'd put you off . . . all those times . . . like I did. You see, I was in a . . . well, in a . . . in a sort of unpleasant situation! But, it's been resolved, you see. And I . . ."

"What <u>sort</u> of unpleasant situation?"

"It doesn't do any good . . . for me to go into it. Let's just say that it finally . . . eventually . . . got <u>resolved</u>. Look, Mister Young . . ."

"<u>Please</u>! <u>Please</u> don't call me 'Mister Young.'"

"All right . . . Taylor. As I say, there's really no reason to go into things. Things that have been . . . since . . . straightened out. But, I <u>did</u> get the distinct impression that you were wanting to . . . were at least <u>open</u> to . . . a bit of a . . . well, a relationship. I don't know how serious you were. How serious you might've been. And . . . at this point . . . I don't think I'm capable of anything really <u>deep</u>! But, if you'd care to . . . say . . . go to a movie, or something, why I'd be amenable."

"This has all kind of come out of left field. But, <u>yes</u>! I'd <u>certainly</u> like to see you. Could maybe even . . . from time to time . . . work out something where we could go someplace with Bonifacio and my kids."

"You'd include <u>him</u>? Include my <u>son</u>? In with whatever you'd do, with <u>your</u> kids?"

I was <u>most</u> gratified the way that almost <u>everybody</u> was referring to them as <u>my</u> kids! I'd brought them—the <u>fact</u> of them—up, to Magdalena, in numerous phone conversations before. She'd never seemed all that interested. Appeared mostly <u>dismissive</u>! Of <u>everything</u>!

"Of <u>course</u>," I'd answered. "Of <u>course</u> I would! He's a fine boy."

"OH! Oh . . . that would be <u>wonderful</u>!"

"Don't act like I'm doing you such a big favor. He's a great <u>kid</u> . . . and I'd <u>love</u> to include him in. Anytime."

"I can't <u>tell</u> you how wonderful it makes me feel . . . to hear you <u>say</u> that."

Handily enough, our local movie house was in the midst of a one-week run of the motion picture version of Rodgers & Hammerstein's *South Pacific*—which starred Mitzi Gaynor, Rossano Brazzi, John Kerr and Juanita Hall (the "Bloody Mary" from the Original Broadway Cast)

Magdalena agreed to meet me at the theater—as opposed to my picking her up at her residence. The modest request produced some degree of unease, for me! But, I went along with it.

It was almost unbelievable! Well, it was <u>totally</u> unbelievable! Watching the movie, *South Pacific*, was <u>far</u> different than watching the same show on stage. Yet, Magdalena was almost as captivated by the film—as had been the case with Elena, a few years before. <u>Almost!</u>

Like Elena, she'd not—<u>ever</u>—been exposed to <u>anything</u> like a musical production. Oh, I guess she'd seen a hokey *MGM* musical or two. Some flick with Fred Astaire or Gene Kelly and/or Ann Miller. I've always <u>loved</u> them—but, they're an entirely different breed of cat, than what *South Pacific* presented. Even in movie form. In a way, I'd opened a bit of "a door" for Magdalena also. Sort of, anyway. For this, I was <u>most</u> grateful!

There's a part—in the movie (and in every live production I've ever seen, before or since) where "Nellie Forbush" discovers that "Emile" has gone on a reconnaissance mission with "Joe Cable". A dangerous undertaking—on an island swarming with Jap soldiers!

She rushes down to the island shore's edge—and pleads "<u>Live</u>, Emile! Please . . . <u>live</u>, Emile" <u>That</u> has always been a three-handkerchief scene for me. I looked at Magdalena—and tears were streaming down <u>her</u> cheeks. The fact that the action on the screen had touched her—touched her so deeply—well, it touched me! Deeply!

After we got out, I wanted to take her home. But, she insisted on taking the bus! This, I—really and truly—could not understand. There wasn't much I could do—but, agree. She walked across the street—and down a half-block—to the bus stop.

Now, I'd had enough snap to know that—at that late hour—the buses run "every other day:" (which is, of course, an exaggeration—but, not by a helluva lot). I could not fathom why she'd subject herself to that kind of irritation—when the alternative had been close at hand.

So—sneaky old me—I drove a few blocks away, and then, came on back! I shut off my headlights (almost no traffic at that hour)—and parked behind the bank's drive-thru, located across from the bus stop!

Eventually, the bus did materialize—and she got aboard. It was a long ride! Almost four-and-a-half miles—before she disembarked! At a side street! In a really strange—awfully seedy—neighborhood! One in which I'd never been! A completely run-down section that—in my, I guess, naivety—I, truthfully, didn't know existed! Not in Newport!

Magdalena walked two blocks, and turned onto a second side street. When she'd gotten to the sixth house, she walked up the driveway—and entered the garage! The damn garage!

I'd had my lights off—ever since I'd seen her arise from her seat on the bus. I pulled up across the street from the house. Once she'd disappeared into the stupid garage, I followed in her footsteps. As I approached the flimsy structure, I could hear voices inside.

I paused outside. She was talking with a kid—presumably her son. I was unable to decipher anything they might've been saying.

Unlike the Taylor Young you've come to know and love, I acted with some authority. (It might well have turned out to have been with a good deal of stupidity—but, there was a generous amount of authority!)

I pulled open the door! Yeah, it opened outwardly!

Magdalena barely stifled a scream! I think that the boy might have recognized me. But, more than likely, he would've welcomed any intruder! Especially if he thought the late comer could/would improve his existence!

There was absolutely no furniture in the cold, drafty, place. They'd had a couple more-or-less "mats"—which they'd used as beds. No stove. No refrigerator! No toilet! Dear Lord! This was beyond belief!

"TAYLOR!" she semi-hollered. "What are you doing here?"

"More to the point, what are you doing here? You and Bonafacio! What the hell is this? What mannerism of crap is this?"

"Oh . . . we're all right."

"Yeah. I can see that! What the hell are you guys doing? Doing here, for God's sake? Living in this shit hole?"

"We're all right!" I couldn't tell if she was mad at me—or trying to establish some form of faux outrage!

"Yeah," I muttered. "You said that! It didn't make any more sense then . . . than it does now. Now tell me! What the hell has happened? How is it . . . that you evidently live here? And don't give me some kind of cock-and-bull story! I want the truth! The goddam truth!" I couldn't believe that this was me—issuing all these commands!

"Grandma died." It was the lad, who spoke up. "Since Grandma died, it's been really bad! The landlord threw us out. Well, Mom had had to quit her job! Almost a year ago, now. She had to, you know care for Grandma! And so, we didn't have any money! So, we got thrown out!"

"How long ago was this?" I asked his mother. "A year, for God's sake?"

"I don't know," she rasped—on the verge of tears. And not from some damn movie. "Four or five months! It wasn't nearly a year! Although it must feel like that . . . to him!"

"Longer than that," corrected the boy. "More like six or eight months."

"Well," contradicted his mother, "it's not been as bad as this! Not this bad . . . for anywhere near that long."

"Just about," groused the lad.

"Look," I pleaded. "Someone . . . please . . . tell me! What the hell happened?

"Well, like Bonifacio said, I'd had to quit work . . . and take care of my mother," explained the still-distraught woman. "And we wound up pretty poor! Had to depend on some welfare program . . . just to bury Mother."

"Aren't there programs? Unemployment compensation? Food stamps? All kinds of stuff?"

"I couldn't get unemployment. The company contested it. Said that I'd resigned! Well, I did! I asked for a leave of absence . . . but, they refused that. We did get food stamps . . . and, I guess, it's enough for us to live on."

"Mom tried for welfare," advised Bonifacio. "But, where we were living at the time . . ."

"Look, Mister Young," interrupted his mother. (We were back to "Mr. Young".) "I might as well tell you. I was . . . well, we were . . . living with this man! This lawyer! Harvey Holt! Very influential man! In fact, he's the one who'd advised me . . . about getting a leave of absence."

"I've heard of him," I grumped. "He's got a lot of money! What the hell are you two doing . . . living here?"

"He . . . well, he threw us out!" She was back to sobbing!

"He used to beat Mom," expanded the lad. "And . . . this one time . . . I happened to walk in on them! Mom's nose was bleeding! She wound up with a broken jaw! I hit him! I hit the sonofabitch! Picked up a kitchen chair . . . and I damn well hit him with it!" He smiled—broadly—for the first time. "I knocked him . . . knocked him into the middle of next week! I don't think I broke anything! But, it wasn't because I didn't try!"

"So, he threw us out," sniffed Magdalena. "He's got a lot of pull . . . down at City Hall. And at Police Headquarters! I couldn't get the police to arrest him! Though . . . God knows . . . I looked a mess! A complete <u>mess</u>! And I couldn't <u>get</u> anywhere . . . when I tried to <u>sue</u> him!"

"He's turned everybody in <u>town</u> against us," interjected her son. "<u>Everybody</u>! It even went down . . . to a bunch of guys giving me a hard time, at school. So, I haven't gone <u>back</u>! Not in a month or two!"

"Why haven't <u>I</u> heard about any of this? If he's turned everybody in <u>town</u> against you?"

"Well," responded the woman, "not <u>everybody</u>! Just . . . well, every time I tried to get somewhere . . . tried to get ahead . . . he had me blocked at every turn! Kept getting knocked <u>down</u> . . . everything I tried!"

"Why the hell didn't you call <u>me</u>? You know . . . you <u>ought</u> to know . . . that I'd <u>never</u> let you live like this! Live in all this squalor. You don't even have a toilet! Where do you . . . ?

"You don't want to <u>know</u>," blurted Bonifacio. "You damn well don't want to <u>know</u>!"

"How did you wind up in this . . . this . . . this . . . ?" I began.

"This shit hole?" finished the kid.

"The people who live in the house here," explained his mother. "I used to have the woman's father . . . as a patient. He died . . . a couple of years ago. They consented . . . the guy's daughter and son-in-law . . . they <u>allowed</u> us to live here."

"This is no place to even <u>loosely</u> call 'living'. Do you have any luggage? Clothes and stuff?"

"No. Harvey sealed it all up," she said.

"Stole it," expanded her son. "We don't know where! Don't know where any of our stuff went. Where he's hiding it!"

"Well," I asked—totally astounded, "how is it that . . . when I was with you tonight . . . well, to be quite frank, you didn't stink? I don't mean that . . . not the way it sounds! But, if you've not had any . . . uh . . . facilities, in all this time . . . ?"

"Well," she answered, "to be quite frank, we bathed this afternoon. Both of us. In the yard! We've done that a number of times! Usually two or three or four times a week! Must be a million laughs . . . for the neighbors, I mean! To see a naked woman . . . and a naked boy . . . out in the backyard! Using the damn garden hose . . . and all that icy-cold water . . . to clean ourselves!"

"Doesn't someone . . . one of them . . . don't they offer you their shower or bathtub?"

"Nah," responded the lad. "I think they enjoy seeing us bare-assed naked . . . screwing around in the backyard."

"This isn't the best neighborhood in the world," explained Magdalena. "Lots of drug dealers here. And people into all kinds of stuff."

"Well, dammit," I muttered, "I don't know why in hell you didn't call me. You should've known that I'd never . . . ."

"The few times that you called," she declared, "Harvey was right there! I suppose that I could've called you . . ."

"You suppose? You damn well should've called me!"

"I know. But, things were . . . how do you say? . . . really <u>precarious</u> at that point. And . . . after he'd thrown us out, and we'd had so much trouble . . . I was afraid that you'd be <u>mad</u> at me! <u>Upset</u> with me! I was so <u>short</u> with you . . . all that many times! So, I guess we . . ."

"I don't know what kind of <u>creep</u> you think I am!" I was totally exasperated. "I would <u>never</u> . . . I mean, how could you <u>think</u> that I'd . . . ?

"I know," she said, softly.

That sounded so <u>much</u> like Elena! All I'd needed was her two fingers on my lips.

"Listen, dammit," I snarled, "you're coming home with me! <u>Both</u> of you . . . are coming home with me."

"Oh," spouted Magdalena, "we couldn't do <u>that</u>! We couldn't . . ."

"God <u>damn</u> it! I don't want to <u>hear</u> it! What kind of animal . . . what kind of sub-human . . . do you think I <u>am</u>? You're <u>coming</u> with me! <u>Both</u> of you! And I don't want to <u>hear</u> any more of this stupid . . . stupid, stupid . . ."

"Stupid <u>crap</u>?" supplied the youngster.

"Yeah," I answered—proud of the lad. "This stupid <u>crap</u>! Now, get your fannies the hell <u>out</u> of this vulgar . . . this crappy . . . place. I'm parked across the street! And I don't want to hear any more static!"

And I did <u>not</u> hear any further objections. Obediently, the two of them followed me down the drive, across the deserted street, and into the car!

When we got home, it was well after midnight. The kids were all asleep, of course. I rousted poor Mary Jane out of her bed—and put her in with Cynthia. After a most welcomed hot shower, Magdalena had a bed in which to sleep—for the first time since God-only-knew-when. I gave her one of my shirts, for the night. The one I could find—with the longest tail. Best I could do.

Once his mother had gotten out of the shower—it had been a long wait for the kid—it was Bonifacio's turn. I gave him a pair of Steven's pajamas—and set him up on the couch, in the living room.

I sat there—in my recliner—and watched him drop off (immediately). And with a satisfying (to me, anyway) smile on his face.

It wasn't till after three o'clock that I finally dragged myself off to bed. I'd sat there—in the living room—doing my best to sort things out. I don't think that Bonifacio moved one inch—in that entire time.

What was I going to do now? I'd had to see that the boy and his mother would come upon better times. How could I not? How could anyone not?

Money would seem to not be a worry. I'd had my windfall—from the sale of my condo. Presumably, there would be a substantial amount of money coming in—from the publication of my celebrated novel. I'd never had to pour over such high-falutin' money problems before. Mainly, because I'd never had any money before.

I'd had no idea—as to what Magdalena would or would not go along with—as far as accepting any help from me. Obviously, she was in no position to be able to pick and choose. But, her feelings—her wants, her needs—were of primary importance to me. No matter _what_ circumstances may apply!

I finally pulled my exhausted self from the stupid chair—and looked in on "the girls". My two daughters were fast asleep—oblivious of any upheaval, at that point. Our guest was also "sawing wood". Apparently, she was at peace. For the nonce, anyway.

When I finally conked out, it was well past four o'clock.

At shortly before nine o'clock, that morning, I was awakened by the smell of bacon cooking. I got up, donned a robe, and more or less staggered out to the living room.

Magdalena had found the bacon and eggs—and was whomping up what appeared to be an epic breakfast. (Can't go wrong with the old basics.) She was still clad in my shirt. It managed to cover "enough". She was decent. (But, just barely. Very little bending over—when others were present.)

Bonifacio had long since arisen. Well, all the kids we up and about. Some more bright-eyed and bushy-tailed than others. Stephen had, I was to discover, wandered out in his briefs—and was _shocked_ to be seen, in his drivvies, by a strange _woman_! I'm _positive_ that he'd have to have wondered—long and hard—as to which _bed_ she'd spent the night.

By the time I'd come upon the scene, all five kids were seated at the table. Magdalena continued to churn out "eatin's"—and I just stared, slack-jawed, at the highly-proficient procedure.

As the children's needs seemed to have slacked off, our guest chef piled enough bacon, toast, and eggs, onto a pair of plates. Enough—for the two of us—to have satisfied an army's needs.

We repaired to the living room—and seated ourselves on the couch by the far wall. It wouldn't do—we both felt—for the tads to be listening to what it would be that we'd be discussing. We balanced our platefuls on our laps—as best we could. (She was much more talented at such things than I could ever hope to be. She'd had to be. She was still ensconced in my shirt—and it was almost unable to meet the modesty need.)

"I can never thank you enough," she began, "for rescuing us last night."

"Yeah, well I still don't understand why it had to be last night! Why you'd never let me know . . . well before last night . . . that you were in that God-awful situation! That deplorable situation. I ought to put you across my knee!"

"I couldn't! I beg you . . . beg you to try and . . . to try and understand. I just simply could not!"

"I'm trying to understand. Still trying! But, so far, it ain't making much sense. Look! You had . . . you have . . . your son to think of! If not your-own-damn-self!"

"Oh, he was doing all right."

"Yeah," I responded, sardonically. "I could tell. Could see . . . just how well he was doing."

"Listen, it's hard to . . . well, to . . . to ask, to depend on . . ."

"Look, Magdalena. There ain't none of us can be completely . . . totally . . . independent. Not forever . . . and always. We all need a helping hand . . . from time to time."

"Yes, but . . ."

"But, nothing! Now, we're going to have to figure out where we go from here."

"Oh, Mister Young . . . Taylor . . . I couldn't . . ."

"Dammit! Maybe I will put you across my knee! We've got to come up with something! Something for you and the boy. Now, you're both welcome to stay here . . . for as long as need be. Sleeping arrangements may not be ideal. But, they're not that terrible. And one thing I don't want you thinking . . . is that I'm going to require you to share my bed with me. I'm not going to demand that. I'm not even going to ask that. The girls are all right, I'm sure, with sharing a bed. Not either one of 'em . . . take up that much space. So, that's one thing . . . you don't have to worry about."

"I never was worried about that. It's just that . . . the general imposition I'd be bringing. My son and I. We couldn't . . ."

Dammit! Will you stop that? It's no imposition . . . general or otherwise! And, look. If the shoe had been on the other foot . . ."

"Oh, I'm sure you'd never get yourself caught up in what Bonifacio and I were involved in. Get to where you were that low. At the end of your rope."

"Don't count on it. Look, this is gonna take some thinking. On both our parts. Now, I don't want you take this the wrong way . . . but, if you'd like to stay here . . . stay with us . . . I'm sure I could get Major Crowe to find us a bigger house. One more suitable. And the lack of requirement . . . to sleep with me . . . that remains. You'll not be required to share my bed. We'd find adequate . . ."

"Oh! I couldn't ask you to do anything like that! Getting a larger . . . and, without a doubt, a more expensive . . . place!"

"Did you ask? Have you ever asked? You never have . . . which is why I'm pissed off! I'm the one doing all the talking around here. At least all the halfway-intelligent talking! One thing is final! For sure final! And that is . . . you sure as hell are not going back to that goddam, stupid-assed, crappy, garage! Period! Paragraph! Now, unless you can come up with a more logical situation . . . for you and the boy . . . then, I'll be glad to listen. But . . . if, off the seat of your pants . . . if you can not, then, dammit, you're stuck with us!"

"Listen. The easiest thing in the world for me is to . . . would be to . . . to say yes! But, you have to . . ."

"Then, for God's sakes, say 'yes'! It won't hurt! I assure you. Maybe you'd like a shot of Novocain!"

Magdalena actually laughed! For the first time— in, I'm certain, ages. (Although, I have to admit— am proud to say—that South Pacific had extracted a number of smiles, from her, that glorious night before.)

Then, quite surprisingly, she put her plate of unfinished vittles on the coffee table. She arose—and put my own half-emptied plate beside hers. I couldn't imagine what she was up to.

What she was up to—was seating herself on my lap! The shirt had slipped up to the top of her bottom—a fact I'd immediately become aware of! My own robe had parted slightly—well, more than merely "slightly"—and it was flesh-to-flesh. Her behind—and my right thigh!

She put her arms around my neck, and purred, "Listen, Taylor. If you want to take me to bed, you can. This might not be the ideal time . . . the kids all being around. But, I want you to <u>know</u>: Any time you want me to accompany you to bed . . . you merely have to say the <u>word</u>!"

"Get <u>up</u>! Get <u>up</u>, Magdalena!"

"So <u>soon</u>?"

"Stand right <u>there</u>," I'd ordered—as soon as she'd arisen.

She'd had her back to me! I raised her shirt tail—and smacked her, smartly across her bottom! I probably <u>should</u> have left the fabric between her rear end—and my palm! When it landed, it caused a smack—that <u>must</u> have hit nearly a five, on the *Richter Scale*, out at the University! All activity, in the kitchen, came to a complete and utter halt!

Hastily, I jerked her shirt tail down—and yanked my robe closed! Then, I pulled her down onto the couch! She wound up in a semi-seated position! Respectable enough—that when Steven and Bonafacio walked out of the kitchen, they both smiled! And returned to their serious eating!

"Now, you listen to me," I hissed, once the coast was, again, clear. "Don't you ever do that again! Or you might get more than that!"

"I might enjoy . . . more than that."

"Will you . . . for God's sake . . . listen? For one thing, I don't know how I feel about you. Not exactly! But, I damn well do not want you cheapening yourself! I care enough about you . . . that I don't want that!"

"I'm touched by that, Taylor." All traces of levity vanished! Immediately! "I'm honestly and truly touched! If you could know some of the stuff . . . the out and out crap . . . that Harvey Holt had me doing . . ."

"I don't want to know! One way or another . . . that's a closed chapter in your life! We need to set up . . . or try to set up . . . what the future holds for you! Holds for . . . maybe . . . for us! Short term and long term."

"I didn't know that you had any feelings for me," she responded. "But, I definitely do now." She rubbed her derriere. "Definitely do now."

"Of course I have feelings for you. Have had . . . from practically the first time I ever laid eyes on you. Why do you think I kept calling . . . during your little adventure? Your damnable adventure . . . with Harvey?"

"Yes," she replied, even more serious than I'd seen her—since we'd repaired to the living room. "There is that. But . . . don't you see? I was so screwed up back then, that I . . ."

"But, you weren't screwed up . . . when I asked you to the movie."

"Don't bet on it. I was faced . . . first thing . . . with the prospect of taking a shower! Naked! In the damn backyard! Not your <u>normal</u> preparation for a date. And to get my clothing to where it was . . ."

"That's <u>another</u> thing! We've got to get you some clothes."

"I would like to have <u>you</u> pick some out for me. That is . . . assuming you're thinking of buying me some clothes. I'll give you my sizes. For one thing, I can't very well go shopping in this shirt . . . although I'm grateful for it. And I don't <u>want</u> to wear that damn dress <u>again</u>! <u>Ever</u>!"

"Well, I don't know how good I'll be at . . ."

"You'll be <u>fine</u>! Will you take Bonifacio too? He's . . . well, he's gone through a <u>lot</u>! Especially for a young <u>kid</u>!"

"Of <u>course</u> I will. I should probably take <u>all</u> the kids. Give you a chance to be alone, and . . ."

"I don't really <u>want</u> to be alone! Maybe you could leave the <u>girls</u>. They are <u>delightful</u>! The little one . . . Mary Jane . . . told me that I should know that her mother's name is 'Beverly'. Is that <u>important</u>?"

I had to laugh out loud! (No one <u>knew</u> from "LOL", back then.)

TWENTY ONE

WELL, I TOOK ALL THREE boys shopping. This was shortly before noon. They were all getting along quite well. All five of the tads had seemed to have "jelled" during—and after—breakfast. The meal had been extremely rewarding to both Magdalena and me. To have <u>hoped</u> to have my children interact with Bonafacio the way they did was something I think we'd both avoided pondering. The result of the "cast of thousands'" first meeting—and meal together—was <u>most</u> fulfilling.

On our hokey little shopping expedition, my sons and Bonifacio appeared to have a good many interests in common. I was thrilled—that they had <u>that</u> going for them. Most of the conversations were sports related.

On the other hand, their new acquaintance had, pretty much, filled in my two boys—as to his, and his mother's, previous, God-awful, situation. He got a little more into detail than I'd have preferred. Describing things like their lack of clothing and backyard "showers" and the like! All of this—held

Steve and Randy in rapt attention—all the way to *Sears*.

Once he'd become aware of the amount of clothing, and the variety of footwear, that he'd be allowed to pick out—and take "home"—Bonifacio's attention became riveted to his newly-found "sartorial splendor".

Sears did not provide shopping carts—at least not in Newport (at least not in mid-1968)—and it took all four of us to haul Bonifacio's new duds to the car. And then, cart them into the house.

Magdalena was still clad in that stupid shirt. I'd not imagined her wearing it—well into the afternoon of the following day. On the other hand, there wasn't a helluva lot else for her to wear—especially since she'd foresworn <u>ever</u> getting back into "that damn dress" again.

She had given me a list of her sizes—dress, blouse, slacks, panties, bra, etc. etc. etc—and told me that she would "love" for me to pick out her new wardrobe.

"In fact," she'd added, "if you would pick out what you'd want me to wear . . . it would be a <u>blessing</u> for me." To me, that was pretty strong stuff.

I headed—not back to *Sears*—but, to a rather stylish ladies clothing store. And, promptly, went <u>nuts</u>! I've always been partial—and will <u>remain</u> partial—to women wearing shirt-waist, full-skirted, dresses. I guess they're all pretty well out of style nowadays—but, apparently, such a woman's garment wasn't totally "out to lunch", style-wise in the late-sixties. Because this outlet had a large number of them available. (Judging by the number I brought home, a person would, undoubtedly, conclude that the store had stocked an astronomical number of those items.)

I also bought her a few slacks—and a number of blouses, sweaters, and skirts. As well as a vast selection of bras and panties. (Those were the most fun!) Some were even "serviceable"! But many were on the esoteric side! Hee Hee!) I only bought her a pair of ordinary, common, garden-variety, loafers. They would be sufficient for her to get around in—at least, on a temporary basis. (I was a little afraid of shoes. They do have to fit comfortably.)

I even bought her a couple pairs of pajamas and two or three "non-erotic" nightgowns. Some of the sexier numbers—well, it would've been, I'd felt, too much, to be stocking up on those items. At least, for the nonce.

I wouldn't have thought of slips. But, the ladies at the store were most helpful. Full slips and half-slips. They were all in there.

I don't remember now, if pantyhose had "come in" by then. But, if they were available, the concerned saleswomen had hastened to pick out an assortment. If the collection had wound up including merely "regulation" hosiery, I don't recall them picking out a garter belt. (I'd have remembered.)

Magdalena was thrilled—when I'd lugged the "cargo" into the house. All three boys were wrapped up—participating in a spirited football game, in the vacant lot across the street. The girls were in the backyard—playing in the sandbox. The one—which I'd bought for them, on the third or fourth day after we'd moved in. I'd managed to snarf the newly-bought clothing into my bedroom. (Hmmm!)

"Good heavens," she'd emoted—smiling broadly, and taking in the display from the ladies shop, which had, literally, covered the bed, Yeah! That bed! That huge—that epic—that round bed! There were few isolated inches of the spread showing.

"I know," she cautioned, her voice turning much more serious "that you'd thought I was being a little bit too 'kittenish' this morning. Maybe way too kittenish. On the couch, you know. And I'd sure earned that slap on the fanny! And I really should never have said what I did . . . about enjoying more of the same."

"Well, It did kind of take me back . . . truth be told."

"Look," she observed, "I'm not usually prone to be saying outrageous stuff like that. Far from it. In fact, I've been told . . . by more than one person . . . that I'm a bit of a prude. But . . . as sleazy as this sounds . . . I'd like to have you remove this shirt!"

To say that I was taken aback—by the suggestion (which, to my mind, had come "out of the blue")—would be yet another understatement of unbounded measure!

"Remove it, from me," she repeated. "And then, I want you to dress me. I've seen you naked . . . literally dozens of times. Or do you not remember all those showers?"

"I remember them . . . of course. Of course I do! But . . ."

"Then, I want <u>you</u> to be the one . . . to remove this shirt! And I want you to then <u>dress</u> me! To cover me . . . in whatever <u>you</u> choose! Put my panties on me! My brassiere! The ones that <u>you'd</u> select . . . from this vast array! Then, place me . . . in my slip and my dress. And . . . judging from this overwhelming selection . . . I'd have to say, that you'd prefer me in a dress."

"Well, I . . . uh . . . yeah."

"I thought so. Listen, Taylor. Before . . . when I was your nurse . . . well, there <u>are</u> professional rules. And . . . though I figured that you were 'interested' . . . I was <u>forbidden</u> to try and pursue anything personal. Or romantic. Or anything <u>else</u>! Would've been unethical. Then . . . when you came back from your trip to Texas . . . I was in an <u>impossible</u> situation. It was <u>untenable</u>. The whole <u>thing</u> was . . . was simply <u>impossible</u>!"

"Where'd you ever get a word like <u>that</u>? like 'untenable'?"

"I'm not as dumb as you might <u>think</u>." Another remark—that had come from "out of left field. "Listen," she explained, "to keep a 'safe' distance . . . between me and my patients . . . I'd always kind of overstated my accent. And I'd always tried not to use any multi-syllable words. No more than necessary."

She could tell—that, by then, I was completely dumbfounded!

"Look," she elaborated, "I've worked with some <u>very</u> intelligent men. Patients mostly. I've <u>learned</u> a lot from them. From <u>each</u> of them. Kept my eyes open . . . and my mouth shut."

"I don't understand . . ." I began.

"I had this one man," she continued. "He was chairman of the board of a really good-sized company. And he . . . he talked . . . well, he talked so beautifully. I've always wanted . . . to be able to talk. To talk . . . like he did."

She was bringing back a whole flood of memories. Elena had once told me—that I'd "talked so beautifully". I'd, obviously been deeply moved!

"That schmuck of an attorney," Magdalena continued. "That bastard . . . Harvey Holt . . . I thought that he was the first person that I could talk to, like that. I felt that I could converse with him . . . on an equally intelligent basis. That did not work out well. When I met you . . . to see *South Pacific* . . . I was afraid to come 'out of character' with you. Because of dear old Harvey. So, I tried to stay 'in character'."

"This is all so . . . all so surprising . . . to me."

"I'm sure. I'd, of course, heard of *South Pacific*. Knew, pretty much, what it was about. But . . . I swear to this . . . I could never have conceived what seeing it was actually like. I'd love to see a live production, of that show. In fact, I'd love to see a live production of just about anything. Except, maybe *Hair*. I hear that it has a lot of nudity in it. I say that . . . just as I'm asking you to remove the only piece of clothing I'm wearing! Which brings me to ask . . . why are you not removing the only piece of clothing that I'm wearing?"

This was all coming so fast! I can just imagine how stupid that must sound—coming from a man in his late-thirties. But this—well, it was different! Vastly different! This was Magdalena! The closest I'd ever come to relating to anyone—even remotely like my cherished Elena! This was a much deeper situation than Chinese Checkers In The Nude—followed by a romp in the hay! And she'd—this remarkable woman—had just invited me to see her naked! No—I shouldn't say "naked". That's too crude—when spoken in connection with Magdalena. She was inviting me to see her unclothed!

You'll be gratified to know that I did manage to pull myself together—to the point that I began to unbutton that silly-assed shirt. The first time that the backs of my fingers came in contact with her breasts—even through the fabric—I'd just about required an iron lung. That old saw about, "Two aspirin . . . and an ambulance . . . and I'll be fine"!

Then, when I beheld her—without her clothing—I was absolutely petrified! I pulled her close to me. In my mind, I was caressing her! Caressing every portion of her magnificent body. In truth, I was probably ravaging her pretty good! I was, don't you see, highly excited!

On the other hand, she appeared to be as ravenous as I was—the way things were progressing. Still, when (after a frenzied minute or two) we "came up for breath", she pushed me away!

That gesture positively devastated me! What do I do now? We've come this far!

She read what was left of my mind! She put two fingers over my lips—just as Elena had done on too few occasions—and whispered, "Wait! Wait . . . just one moment!"

She hurried to hang her dresses in the closet—my closet! Then, she pushed her undergarments, slacks, etc. etc. etc—pushed them all to the floor! Thus clearing the bed! The <u>entire</u> bed! <u>Nothing</u> atop it! For the moment, anyway! Finally, before returning to me, she closed the bedroom door! Closed it <u>firmly</u>!

Then, she led me to the bed!

Three hours later, it was on the shakiest of legs that I went off to *Sears*—to buy a couple more stools (or something) to accommodate the two extra, additional, fannies at the kitchen table.

I was still having a problem trying to <u>connect</u> with what had gone on—that short a time before. Our lovemaking had been <u>wonderful</u>! <u>Glorious</u>! I cannot say that I'd pictured it in any other way. That's because I'd never visualized it at <u>all</u>! Not before it actually <u>happened</u>!

Oh, my overheated mind <u>had</u> dabbled—countless times—with the, shall we say, <u>possibilities</u> pertaining to such a situation. But, I'd really never gotten into calling up exacting, clear-cut, images of the actual <u>coupling</u>! Those thoughts had always, pretty much, remained in the "Wouldn't It Be Nice?" category.

And <u>now</u>? Now—having not merely "talked the talk", but having, most definitely, "walked the walk"— my poor little, defenseless, mind was just this side of being totally numbed!

The physical side of the equation had turned out to be far <u>beyond</u> anything I could've imagined. I could never conceive of <u>anyone</u> being capable of actually <u>picturing</u> the true <u>reality</u>—of what had just, so miraculously, happened.

You hear of those people (most refer to them as sexual maniacs, I believe) who—once being overwhelmingly gratified by ("a trip to paradise", as Cole Porter had once referred to it, in *Love For Sale*) throw everything else aside! Their good sense? Gone! Morality? Hah! Only their sense of principle prevailed! Everything else seemed to get thrown to the side—all in complete and utter adoration of the sexual adventure(s)!

Was that going to be me? Could that possibly already be me?

There was so much to consider! Four kids! Well, five kids, actually. Four of them, I'd fought so incredibly hard to acquire! The fifth was kind of "dropped into my lap"! But, I'd had paternal feelings for Bonifacio—since I'd first laid eyes on the lad! So many questions:

What do I tell the kids? Any of them? All of them? Do I tell them anything? Where would Magdalena sleep tonight? Still bunked in—in the girls' room? Or. possibly, with me? On that round bed? If that should become the plan, what do we—what could we—tell the kids?

Bonifacio seemed a little more worldly than either Steve or Randy. Well, as pertained to Randy, that might be the slightest bit disputable. I couldn't imagine any other kid his age—running away, and making it all the way as far as Laredo.

And how about the girls? They were too young to know all that much about anything that was clouding my alleged mind at that moment! (Presumably, anyway.) Rightly or wrongly, it had always been important to me—critical, actually—that daughters not think badly of their daddies. It was vital that the same would hold true for boys and their fathers. But, the daddies/daughters thing always seemed to be primary, among all those considerations.

The most frustrating ingredient in the whole shebang—was the fact that, as long as the sex was available, I could never visualize myself as being strong enough to forego the—well, the—"trip to paradise"!

I found myself so caught up in the fearful, mind-warping, situation—that I'd temporarily forgotten what the hell I'd come to the stupid store for!

I'd finally managed to fight my way through the miasma—and came home with two of those rather-high, red-and-white—metal stools. The ones that have those little ladders enclosed—in the lower portion. I'd figured that the girls could sit on the kind-of-weird gismos. And the ladders would assist them in getting up upon them.

To this day, I have no idea as to the intelligence (or lack thereof) related to the purchase. I was fortunate to have gotten to the stupid store and back—with something, that was, at least, workable. (Given where my alleged mind had been luxuriating!)

When we'd all sat down to eat that evening—Cynthia and Mary Jane safely (I'd hoped) atop their new dining venues—Magdalena pulled a real rabbit out of the proverbial old top hat!

"Dad?" she began—her gaze shifting from kid to kid, then settling on me, "Dad . . . I had quite a chat with the young ones today. Didn't I, kids? Didn't we have a pretty good chat?"

All the tads nodded their heads. Not in unison, maybe—but, close. I did my best to try and assess the expression on each little face. And <u>failed</u>—100% of the time! Randy presented the most puzzling of these youthful countenances. But, hell! I couldn't tell what <u>any</u> of them might be thinking.

"What we spoke of," continued Magdalena, "is the fact that Mary Jane can now have her <u>bed</u> back. I'll be sleeping in <u>Daddy's</u> bed. Now, I'm sure that every one of us <u>knows</u> that this is a little . . . ah . . . <u>unusual!</u>"

In the late-sixties—despite the loosening of morals that seemed to have begun sweeping the nation—such (ah) sleeping arrangements <u>were</u> still somewhat unusual. Possibly even more than <u>somewhat</u>.

"Your father and I will be getting married," this remarkable woman continued—looking, mostly, at the girls. "Right now, it's not possible. Well, actually, we don't <u>know</u> if it's possible . . . or not. I'd gotten a letter . . . or maybe it was a telegram . . . <u>something</u> from some supposed court, up in Canada. British Columbia, I believe. I believe it <u>said</u> that I was <u>divorced</u> . . . from Bonifacio's father. I don't know . . . have no idea . . . if it's authentic or what. It could just be that the man was trying to . . . ah . . . 'get off the hook', as it were."

"What did it say?" asked Steve. A perfectly logical question.

"Like I explained earlier, I'm not <u>sure</u>. Not absolutely <u>positive</u>. I'm pretty <u>sure</u> it said I was <u>divorced</u> from him. I don't really know if I can find the letter or telegram . . . or whatever it was. The whole thing . . . could've been a fake. Like I said . . . a man 'getting off the hook'."

"Really?" I interrupted. "You can't find it? Don't know from exactly where it came?"

"No. It wasn't that big a deal then. Down deep, I was glad to be rid of him. I wasn't planning on any sort of relationship . . . with any man. Hoo! Was that ever wrong!"

She turned back—especially seemed to lock in on my daughters—and continued:

"Then, I met your father. And now, it's desperately important to me . . . and, hopefully, to all of us . . . that I find my exact marital status! Determine exactly what that is! And that is going to take time! Possibly a good bit of time! And . . . I'm fairly certain . . . a lot of money!"

She'd turned back toward me—while making those last two declarations. I nodded—enough that she was able to determine the affirmative assent. She looked much relieved. And so was I!

"So," advised my newly-minted intended— turning back to face the tads. "Even though it is my fault . . . and I accept the blame . . . it's not fair for us to be denied the fact that . . . in our minds . . . your father and I are truly married."

I cannot tell you! In one "swelled foop"—as the comedians say—I was off the well-known (and previously referred to) "hook"! As to how to relate to the children—sleeping arrangements-wise.

Plus—though I was the last (of seven) people to learn of the fact—I was now betrowed! And happily so!

Not only that, but the kids had had a couple hours to have "chewed upon"—and "digested"—what I'd been laboring over, for all of those emotionally-draining hours. They all seemed to be going along with the program! So far, anyway. (Key word in all this is "seemed"!)

This woman was—truly—remarkable! Truly!

The following morning, I engaged an attorney! Mrs. Grimshaw's lawyer, natch. His name was William Beck. We met at his office—and he questioned Magdalena! Extensively!

About five minutes into the interview, he gave us both a bit of a news bulletin! One of staggering importance:

"It seems, Mrs. Longoria," he intoned—narrowing his steel-like stare at Magdalena, "that this might come as a bit of a shock to you. As quite a shock, as a matter of fact. I understand, you see, that you were . . . at one time, anyway . . . affiliated with one of my colleagues. A man I'd always considered a close friend. Mister Harvey Holt! Were you not a . . . well, a . . . a friend of his? An intimate friend of his? Did you not have a close . . . a very close . . . relationship with him?"

"Well," she answered, I knew him . . . yes."

"Hmm. I was given to understand that it was a good bit more than . . . than just . . . ah . . . knowing him."

"Well, there for awhile, we did have a rather close . . . uh . . . a fairly close relationship. But,

I've not <u>seen</u> him in a good <u>while</u>! It's been many months!"

"Oh. Then, I thought you might be interested! He suffered a brutal <u>beating</u>! A terribly-bloody, life-threatening, beating! Night before last! He's in the Intensive Care Unit . . . over at the hospital! Both arms . . . <u>broken</u>! One leg . . . <u>broken</u>! The other? Merely a couple of hairline fractures! They're <u>still</u> trying to untangle the scrambled discs in his back! And . . . as the *coupe d'grace* . . . <u>someone</u> shoved a cucumber up his anus! Would you <u>know</u> of <u>anyone</u> . . . who could <u>possibly</u> want to inflict such <u>devastating</u> injuries on Harvey? Devastating . . . and <u>degrading</u>!"

Magdalena <u>shuddered</u>—from head to toe—at the bulletin! Well, so did <u>I</u>!

"No," she replied—in a hoarse, barely audible, voice. "No, Sir. I have absolutely no <u>idea</u>! Have no <u>clue</u> . . . none in the world . . . as who would, possibly, want to <u>do</u> such a thing! Not necessarily only to . . . only to Mister Holt! But, good Lord! To <u>anybody</u>! Why <u>anybody</u> would do such a thing . . . to <u>anybody</u> . . . is beyond me!"

She was still shivering—as attorney Beck—continued his (what <u>seemed</u> like) cross examination. He was becoming more and more vindictive! Or so it seemed. I simply couldn't <u>imagine</u> why! The whole consultation had taken on a spine-shivering dimension! One which had been unimaginable to me—when we'd entered his plush office!

Once he'd finished his veritable third-degree, he advised us that—from his standpoint—he'd had pitifully little to go on. Initially anyway.

"It's going to take a lot of research . . . a lot of gumshoe stuff . . . to get anywhere on this thing," he'd half-growled. "Especially, since we don't know the city or town . . . or, for sure, even the province . . . from which this thing came. Not even the type of document . . . or letter or wire or whatever."

He promised us that he'd "get on it" right away.

That was good enough for me. My fiancée looked somewhat worried! Her expression of concern had deepened—noticeably—as the brow-beating interview had gone on.

I could not understand why! Hopefully, we were in the beginning throes of what should be the process of getting a formidable legal hurdle out of her life! Out of our lives! Forever! What could be wrong with that? The attorney certainly could have been a little more diplomatic. (A little?) But—if he could just get this thing resolved—his brusqueness would've been small price to pay.

On our way back home, I asked my intended why she was—all of a sudden—so sullen.

"Look, Taylor," she'd responded. "I don't have much confidence in Mister Beck."

"What're you worried about, Magdalena? It's just going to take some time . . . a little time . . . to get this thing, about the stupid divorce, straightened out. That's all. We weren't able to give him a whole helluva lot of data, y'know. Not much for him to work on. We knew that . . . going in. But, you were perfectly bright-eyed and bushy-tailed, when we went into the attorney's office. Damn, though, I could see you getting more and more upset . . . as things proceeded."

"Listen, Taylor, he was very close to Harvey . . . Mister Beck was! I'd heard Harvey talk about Mister Beck! Often!"

"Well, he . . . Mister Beck . . . he couldn't have known about what went on between you and Harvey. Could he?"

"God only knows what Harvey would've told him. Harvey had this . . . ah . . . this talent! For over-blowing things! In great detail! He was capable of really elaborate, detailed, descriptions! I can only imagine . . . or maybe I can't imagine . . . what Harvey may have told him! Especially when it came to our sex life! Obviously, he's terribly upset . . . Mister Beck is . . . at what happened to Harvey! God . . . I'm upset at what happened to Harvey! And I, flat-out, hated the sonofabitch!"

"Well, I think that Mister Beck'll do his best for you. Do his best for us. Mrs. Grimshaw's been his client . . . for years!"

"I . . . I really hope so. I hope he's going to have our best interests at heart."

"Is that all that's worrying you? All that's on your mind?"

"Look, Taylor, I'm scared! Scared to death . . . about what I might be doing to you!"

"To me? I don't understand."

"Well, I was acting too uppity . . . or suggestive or something . . . yesterday morning. I could cut out my tongue . . . for being so flip. For that stupid comment . . . about it might be that I'd enjoy more."

"Oh, come on! I thought it was rather clever. But, you know? You've always conveyed a different . . . well, a different . . . a different image before. It was a bit of a shock . . . that your accent is completely gone! And . . . not only do you speak better than most people I know . . . your vocabulary is most extensive."

"Me? You speak so beautifully. You're the one who talks so beautifully!"

As previously noted, that was not the first time I'd been told that—by a beautiful Hispanic lady.

"As to the accent," she informed, "I'd way overdone that. I'd have thought that you would've gotten onto me . . . and a long time ago."

"I like getting onto you."

"Now who's being flip? Look, I'd had trouble with male patients . . . almost since I got into the nurse business. Lots of problems . . . with many of them! I realize that I'm fairly good-looking, and . . ."

"Fairly?"

"Thank you, Sir. But, there must be something . . . something about a nice-looking woman seeing them bare naked . . . that sets off a lot of guys. I don't think you noticed, the first few days . . . you were in pretty tough shape . . . but, I was wearing my wedding ring. After that, I . . . somehow . . . figured that you were different from the others. And so, I ditched the stupid ring."

"You're right. I never noticed . . . any sort of ring."

"Listen, aside from you, I'd always talk up the fact that my husband and I . . . and the four kids . . . that we'd all gone out to the pizza place the night before. In our station wagon, for God's sakes. We were always gonna take the four kids . . . I always emphasized the number . . . and drive up to the zoo, in Portland, or something. Of course, there were times when I overdid it. The phony accent got so thick . . . that, sometimes, they couldn't understand me. For you . . . in your situation . . . I didn't lay it on all that thick. Don't ask me why. I guess I must've known something. Something about you! Your manner . . . and such. Your attitude. I guess that I always knew . . . that I didn't have to be quite so careful with you."

"Well, I'm honored. But, still . . . thick layer of accent or not . . . you had me fooled. In fact, I really don't think the accent . . . or lack of it . . . played all that significantly, in my image of you. It's your vocabulary. You'd always spoken in more . . . how shall I say? . . . in more basic terms back then. And now? And now? Here I sit . . . looking at a virtual encyclopedia. That, I'm having a bit of a problem with."

"Don't dangle your participle."

"I'll dangle my participle . . . whenever I damn please! And wherever I please! Don't you be telling me . . . what to do with my participle. Actually, I'm not having a problem with your vernacular . . . or your vocabulary . . . so much as it is my amazement! My out and out amazement . . . in how you managed, so successfully, to hide it. I'd have thought that . . . somewhere in the mix, somewhere during our time together . . . you'd have slipped! And out would've popped a fifty-cent word or two. I just can't imagine . . ."

"Well, down in Mexico, I'd had to take a really brutal curriculum. Well, they called it an 'extensive' curriculum. To become a licensed nurse. At that time, I spoke hardly any English at all. A critical part of the program required that I do learn the language. Well, I'd had this professor. He came from California. And he taught me English. But . . . and you're probably not going to want to hear this . . . but, we struck up a personal relationship. I was already married! But, at that time, Bonifacio wasn't even a gleam in anyone's eye."

"A . . . a personal relationship?" (She was right! I didn't want to hear it.)

"Oh," she exclaimed. "There wasn't any sex involved. Well, no real sex."

"No real sex?" (I couldn't believe how upset the conversation was making me. And against my will. I think against my will.) "What does 'no real sex' mean?"

"Well, he had this little kind-of-an-apartment. Upstairs over someone's garage. And we got together every Monday, Wednesday, and Friday night. And he'd give me a homework assignment . . . a really difficult one . . . every time we'd do one of these things."

"'One of these things,'" I groused.

"And, if I didn't get it right . . . proper pronunciation and inflection . . . which happened virtually every time, I'd have to remove my clothes. Looking back, I guess I'd have to admit that it happened . . . literally every time."

"Oh, dandy!"

"Well, we never had <u>intercourse</u>! He would <u>tie</u> me up! Sometimes to the bed . . . but, most often, to a chair. And I would have to repeat . . . and repeat and repeat and repeat . . . the page-and-a-half-or-so of what that particular lesson consisted of."

"<u>Now</u>, whose participle is dangling?"

"I claim equal rights with you . . . dangling-wise. But, <u>that</u> was one of the things that Cary was surefire death on! In any case, by the time I'd graduated, he was calling himself 'Professor Henry Higgins' . . . and me 'Eliza Doolittle'. From *My Fair Lady*, don't you see? I'd <u>really</u> like to see a live production of <u>that</u>!"

"I <u>get</u> it! But, you mean to say that . . . while you were naked . . . that's <u>all</u> he did? Was to merely tie you <u>up</u>?"

"Yes. Let me tell you! He had a formidable knowledge of knots . . . and numerous bondage techniques. There <u>were</u> a few exceptions . . . to the chair being my base of operation! A couple of times, he bound me . . . hands <u>well</u> over my head . . . to a clothes rack that was fastened to his closet door. Another time . . . to the shower rail, in the bathroom. One time, he bound me . . . on my tummy . . . on the porcelain table, that was his dining table. On the very <u>cold</u> porcelain table!"

"I don't think I like this."

"As I <u>told</u> you . . . that as far as anything <u>ever</u> went! When he'd tied me to the table, I guess I was surprised! Well, I <u>know</u> I was surprised! And . . . I guess, for that reason . . . I botched the lesson, that night! Royally screwed it up! Early and often . . . as they say! He <u>said</u> he was going to take his belt to me. But, he never <u>did</u>! And . . . I confess! <u>That</u>

experience . . . or lack thereof . . . was what made me floor you, with that 'might enjoy it' line, yesterday."

"But, he never did? Never did use the belt? As a . . . as a strap?"

"Nope! But, I want you to know that . . . when all was said and done . . . I'd probably mastered that lesson, far better than any other one. That was his intent. I guess so, anyway. It was a vital lesson! He said that it was the most important of all the lessons. Looking back, I think he was right! Definitely right! In any event, whatever proclivities I have in the English language, I owe to Professor Cary Kaleta."

"An amazing story."

"But, a true one. Look, Taylor. The only reason I'd ever leveled with you . . . and am now telling you, probably, more than you want to hear . . . is because I want to spend the rest of my life with you. I've never felt that way before. About anyone! Including my husband! Or my ex-husband . . . whatever-in-hell he is! The bastard!"

"I don't think I want to know what he might've done to you."

"You . . . for certain . . . do not! Not everything, anyway. But, look, I think I might have had a tinge of romantic . . . even sexual . . . feelings! Back when I was nurse . . . and you were my patient. But, to have pursued anything with you . . . to have gotten involved, in any way . . . would not have been professional. And I was a professional! Above anything else . . . in this world . . . I was determined to be a really true professional!"

"Yeah. I can tell. And you were! Totally professional. Look, Magdalena. This is a whole lot of stuff, to have to . . . to have to . . . have to, you know, digest."

"And with which to cope? Note the correct non-dangling of participle.'"

"I . . . well, I guess so."

"My sweet Taylor. Maybe I should never have thrown all of this at you. Not all at once, anyway. Not all in the same spiffy episode. But, I did want to level with you . . . about everything! And to explain the probably-out-of-bounds remark . . . of yesterday morning."

"I'd never really thought that much about the remark. But, the rest of it . . . has me just slightly taken aback."

"Just slightly?"

"Well, it's not so much this guy's tying you up,,, that has me so buffaloed. Actually, I guess it's part of it. A fairly significant part of it . . . truth to tell. But, the whole thing! Like . . . how you don't speak with an accent! How your vocabulary would stop a stampede! And . . . I guess . . . how you got there! But, also that you want to spend your life with me! That declaration . . . in and of itself . . . is a real barn-burner! To me, it's . . . well, it's . . . it's quite astounding!"

"It shouldn't be. I told you: I'd pretty well had some of those feelings . . . ever since I was your day nurse."

"Yeah! That . . . in a way . . . is even more astounding! You . . . Magdalena, you hide . . . you hide everything! In a way . . . in a fashion . . . that almost defies logic! Or description!"

"Almost?"

"Yeah. Look . . . I've led a rather strange life myself. There's not a helluva lot that I'd really like to get into, with you. But . . ."

"That's fine! I'll never question you about your past. I've chosen to relate mine! It's something I felt as though I had to do! You are under no such obligation to me."

"And you, honestly . . . you honestly do . . . want to spend the rest of your life with me? Lock, stock and barrel? Whatever the package might contain?"

"The lock and stock, yes! I'm not that sure about the barrel, though," she responded—laughing mightily.

TWENTY-TWO

THE REST OF THE RIDE home—was spent in total silence. I have no idea as to what Magdalena might've been thinking. I have no idea as to what I'd been thinking about. Fortunately, we were only three or four blocks from home—when what had been a troubling conversation (to me, anyway) had petered out.

Once we'd trudged back into the house, one thought popped into my pretty-much-drained, certainly-overheated, brain: The apparently-very-severe beating of Harvey Holt. I'm pretty sure I knew what drove me to pick up the phone—and make a call. But, I'm not really positive.

"Hullo?" came the answer on the other end. "McNulty's Garage."

"Charlie? This is Taylor. What do you know about Harvey Holt getting himself beaten up?"

"Well," he responded—with the most obscene chuckle I'd ever heard, "he didn't really get himself beat up! He had a little help, y'know."

"Were you one of those that might have . . . ah . . . assisted in that little service?"

"Well . . . between us girls . . . yeah. It took us a good while to catch on to some of the things that were happening. Happening with the girl . . . that Magdalena. By the time we ever put the whole damn thing together, it was too late for us to do anything to help her. Too damn <u>late</u>! She was already out of his clutches. But, when we finally got wind of what had happened to her . . . this was a couple of days ago . . . we decided to pay him a little call. Don't know <u>what</u> happened to the girl. Not yet, anyway."

"She's here with me. But, who's this 'we' you're talking about?"

"A few of my Irish gentlemen friends. We're known around here . . . as "The Murphia". There <u>is</u> no actual Mafia in town. Just us . . . and a few Jewish guys that hang out at *Cohen's Deli*, over on the east side. They call themselves "The Cosa Nussbaum".

"So, you guys . . . you and the Jewish guys . . . you take the law in your own <u>hands</u>? You go ahead, and . . . ?"

"Well, let's just say that our official police force . . . here in Newport . . . they have <u>their</u> hands full. And there are times, when we feel that the court dockets are too . . . ahem . . . overloaded. So, rather than inconveniencing the local constabulary . . . or further clogging the judicial system, by having to present all kinds of irrefutable evidence . . . we just go ahead, y'know, and . . . ah . . . facilitate the way of correct . . . and fair . . . justice! It's just your basic 'Truth, Justice . . . and the American Way, y'know."

"Charlie? If I didn't know better, I'd say that you'd had that last blurb . . . the one about 'Truth, Justice, and the American Way' . . . all rehearsed."

"Not quite rehearsed. Let's just say that I've had to repeat it, y'know. Repeat it quite often. Of course, none of this conversation . . . the one we're havin' now . . . ever took place!"

"Agreed! Never happened! But, Charlie . . ."

"Look, Taylor. Holt has never been one of my all-time favorite citizens. And, when we finally got to where we were able to determine . . . most of it . . . to figure out what he'd done to that girl . . . that girl, and her boy . . . it wasn't so much the well-known public service. I took great delight . . . in what happened to the dear boy. Great delight! Anytime I can be of service . . . and all that, y'know . . . why I'm always glad to do muh duty."

"But, I don't understand."

"Listen. One of the Jewish boys is . . . is himself . . . is a cop. There's just some things . . . not a helluva lot, but just some things . . . that need to be handled on a . . . let's just say on a . . . on a different level. Our dear friend, Mister Holt . . . he presented just such a case. I'm glad we could be of service."

"Charlie! I'd never suspected . . ."

"Well, you're one of the very, very few people in town that have never suspected. I'm sure everyone . . . in the law community . . . knows."

"Yeah. Maybe. Look, Charlie. Magdalena and I went to see William Beck, this morning. We were referred to him by Mrs. Grimshaw. Anyway, Mister Beck is the one who'd told us about what happened to his esteemed cohort. He was <u>quite</u> upset! Pissed off . . . is what he was."

"I can imagine. They're pretty close buddies. I'm <u>sure</u> he knows who was behind Mister Holt's unfortunate happening. I've been watching my back. We <u>all</u> have. But, if <u>you</u> were there . . . at his office . . . with Magdalena, you might want to keep an eye out, over <u>your</u> shoulder. Beck, undoubtedly, <u>knows</u> that what happened to his fellow attorney had its roots . . . in the way the sonofabitch treated the girl. So, if . . . on one the following days . . . you and she show up at his office? You can <u>see</u> . . . where he might be making some sort of parallel. I'd be on my toes, y'know."

"Jeez! I never <u>thought</u> of that! It would never occur to me that . . ."

"You and the girl were <u>there</u>, hah? At Beck's <u>office</u>? What . . . if I might be so bold to ask . . . are you sly, fun-loving, folks up to?"

"Trying to straighten out a legal matter. Has to do with whether Magdalena is actually divorced. Some time ago . . . good while ago . . . she got some sort of paper from some hick-assed town or county or something. Someplace . . . up in Canada.

"From <u>Canada</u>?"

"Yeah. The thing told her that she was now <u>divorced</u> from her asshole husband! He'd run off, and deserted her . . . some years ago."

"Hmm. Divorce deal, hah? Does this mean that the two of you are gonna get . . . ? Should I get my bridesmaid dress out of mothballs?"

Yes. No. Hell . . . I don't know. For the present, she's staying with me. She and the boy."

"Golly-Gee, Batman! Does that mean that you're . . . dare I say? . . . you're living in sin?"

"That, Sir, falls under the heading of none of your goddam business!"

"My! Touchy, touchy, touchy, aren't we. Well, look old buddy. I <u>hope</u> everything goes well with you. She's a neat lady. <u>Deserves</u> to have something nice happen to her. And the boy? He's a neat kid, y'know. I really <u>wish</u> you guys all the best. But, with your ass in mind? I'd do my best . . . if'n I were you . . . to keep it covered."

The next three or four days seemed <u>filled</u> with adventure. Some were major. Some were minor. But, they were <u>all</u> adventures.

First of all, I spoke with The Major. Not much of an adventure there. Except that he'd advised me that there was "not a helluva lot of housing available . . . that'll accommodate you and the lady and five kids". But, it was an adventure—all the same. I'd planned a smooth transference—and this was presenting a bit of a problem.

More complicated was the fact that school would be starting in a matter of a few weeks.

I was positively <u>overwhelmed</u> to learn that Bonifacio did <u>not</u> attend school. His <u>mother</u> had homeschooled him! Between the day job—as a nurse—that she'd held for so many years, and educating her son, when could she <u>possibly</u> have had any time for herself? The fact that her husband was such a schmuck, I'm sure, didn't help.

They didn't know much about homeschooling back then. Magdalena taught her boy—magnificently—using whatever books she was able to locate. (Remember—no internet, Ma! The ability to research virtually anything, and everything—something that we all take for granted these days—was nowhere being nearly a whisper, of what's available now.)

I'm absolutely convinced that a lot of this obviously-well-educated lad's education came from his mother's vast amount of dedication—and knowledge. (Knowledge come by, I guess, for the most part—while she was naked and tied to a chair. Or a cold porcelain table.)

There turned out to be much discussion—between Magdalena and me—as to the school situation. Ultimately, we both decided that this remarkable woman would homeschool all five of the children.

There were no educational programs—none that I was aware of, anyway—to help us along. On the other hand, I was able to track down a fair number of textbooks—mostly used, but seemingly up-to-date—in each subject that my intended and I could think of. It cost the proverbial pretty penny—but, I felt that we'd pretty well covered our educational fannies. It was simply a matter of waiting for most of them to get to our seemingly-more-permanent-than-we'd-intended residence.

Once I'd had a chance to reflect, I'd determined—in my own warped little mind—that the reason that Bonifacio got along so well with my own kids was due to the fact that, not having attended school, he was hungry for companionship. He and Steven were reaching a point where they were almost inseparable. Was that great—or what?

I found myself ruminating about not having enough snap to realize that—on the one day Magdalena had brought him "to work" with her—that her son was not attending school. And I'm positive that this had taken place—on a Tuesday or a Wednesday. Definitely on a school day.

Then, trouble really broke! A Newport Police car pulled up in front of the house! This was before all law enforcement entities had gone to the red-and-blue lights. But that "bubble gum machine" atop that cruiser was rotating its red light with great enthusiasm! Throughout the neighborhood!

But, not nearly as emphatically, as the two uniformed police officers—each one a burly six-foot-two specimen of manhood—who'd herded Magdalena, and her son, into that damnable Black Maria!

We're all familiar (or, at least, we should be) with ICE—Immigration Customs Enforcement. Back in the sixties—and, I believe, for years thereafter—there was never the public focus on ICS's predecessor, INS, the International Naturalization Service.

I'm sure that there'd been a problem—maybe a major one—with illegal immigrants. There must have been! But, never—back then—was it as "Center Stage", as the issue has become in the last decade or two! If there were such entities as "Sanctuary Cities", I'd never heard of them.

So, I guess you could say that—when "they raided the joint"—and absconded with Magdalena and Bonifacio, it was, pretty much, a "strictly business" situation! And—totally—out of the <u>blue</u>!

I'd had <u>one</u> thought—after trying to cope with the safety of my intended, and her son! <u>How</u> did this happen? <u>Who</u> had "called the law"?

It finally <u>occurred</u> to me! Of <u>course</u>! <u>William Beck</u>! Our esteemed—our <u>sainted</u>—attorney! He <u>must</u> have come back with some feedback—from <u>somewhere</u>, in Canada. He'd been retained to straighten out Magdalena's marital status! And his research had—most probably—turned up <u>something</u>! Something <u>devastating</u>!

Magdalena was—undoubtedly—<u>right</u>, in her intuitive opinion, relating to Mr. Beck. He—<u>also</u> undoubtedly—believed that I/we had had something to do with the beating of his dear friend, and colleague, Harvey Holt! And—undoubtedly—he was getting <u>back</u> at us!

And he had <u>scored</u>! <u>Big</u> time!

At first, I didn't know what to <u>do</u>! Then, I obeyed the only impulse that had entered into my overwrought mind! I called Charlie McNulty.

After I'd explained my situation—and Magdalena's and Bonifacio's plight—his first words were, "That sonofabitch, Beck!"

"Look, Charlie," I'd responded. "I don't want 'The Murphia' taking him out! Leastways . . . not till I can get this thing straightened out! I <u>say</u> that . . . and I don't have the foggiest idea as to <u>how</u> I'm gonna straighten it out! Get <u>anything</u> straightened out! Or <u>if</u> I can <u>get</u> any of it straightened out!"

"Okay, Taylor. I'll keep the wolfs at bay. For the time bein', anyway. My only suggestion would be to call Mrs. Grimshaw. Beck, the bastard, was . . . I guess, he probably still <u>is</u> . . . her attorney. But, <u>she</u> knows everyone in <u>town</u>. And probably everyone who has the least amount of <u>pull</u> . . . in the whole furschlugginer state! <u>She</u> can . . . I'm sure . . . come up with a <u>much</u> more intelligent plan of attack than either you or I can. Although kicking Beck's ass . . . might be a good start!"

"<u>That's</u> the most intelligent thing I've heard . . . from <u>anyone</u> . . . since lightning struck the shithouse, a few minutes ago."

Dear Mrs. Grimshaw! After I'd phoned her—and had given her a play-by-play description as to what had happened to Magdalena and her boy, and had also filled in a little background, pertaining to Harvey Holt's beating—she had <u>called</u> William Beck!

Apparently, there'd been quite a "heated exchange" between the pair, over the phone. (I'd <u>never</u> want to get caught in <u>that</u> crossfire!)

This dynamic woman called me back—not quite a half-hour after our initial conversation. She had abruptly <u>fired</u> the sanctified Mr. Beck.

"Well, I'm glad to hear that," I'd responded. "But, dear Lord! It doesn't help me with my problem.

Or . . . more accurately . . . with Magdalena's. Or with Bonifacio's."

"Let me see what I can do, Dear Boy. Listen! Before he retired . . . about six or eight years ago . . . my attorney was my very close friend, Alonzo Strathcona. I'll give <u>him</u> a call. Tell him to get his too-well-comforted fanny out of his easy chair. Get to work . . . and see what <u>he</u> can do to help out. We'll come up with <u>something</u>, Dear Boy!"

"Oh, <u>thank</u> you, Mrs. Grimshaw. I'm <u>most</u> grateful!"

"In the meantime, I would imagine that the pair of 'em are being held in the county jail . . . till the feds can deal with 'em. I've got a little pull . . . with a few people . . . down there! And there's a judge or two that owe me a favor or six! I really don't know what may be possible . . . coming at it, from the influence angle! Have to see! But, don't worry, Dear Boy! We'll <u>resolve</u> it! One way or <u>another!</u> It <u>will</u> get resolved!"

Her tone would've scared even the strongest of men. Me? I was surprised that it didn't turn my "flaxen" hair to gray! Or even pure <u>white!</u>

It was about two-thirty, in the afternoon, when Mr. Strathcona called. Clearly, a no-nonsense type, he got right to the point.

"Look, Mister Young. I think that, if you'll sign a few-dozen papers, that state that you're <u>engaged</u> to Miss Longoria . . . and intend to <u>marry</u> her, once this divorced-or-not thing is resolved . . . . I <u>believe</u> that we can get the government to go along. By the way, that <u>divorce paper</u> was . . . we think . . . an <u>official</u> document. It was . . . again, we <u>believe</u> . . . issued by an official arm of the provincial government, up in Manitoba. I firmly <u>believe</u> that Miss Longoria <u>is</u> divorced! That she <u>is</u> . . . a <u>single</u> woman! It'll take a few days, I'm pretty certain . . . to get all of that <u>established</u>. Established . . . for <u>sure</u>. In the meantime, I'm working on getting her . . . and the boy . . . <u>home</u>, in time for supper."

One could <u>never</u> have heard more encouraging—more pleasant, more welcome—news.

As it turned out, Mrs. Grimshaw—wonderful lady that she was—wound up posting bond for my intended, and her son. Obviously, she <u>did</u> have sufficient "pull" with at least <u>one</u> of the judges down there! The illegal woman and the lad got home—at a little past six-thirty! (Who <u>cared</u> about supper?) Incredible! Flat-out <u>incredible</u>!

<u>Man</u>—was I glad to <u>see</u> them! The feeling was mutual. (Quite frankly, I don't <u>remember</u> if we actually <u>ate</u> dinner)!

All seven of us just simply <u>sat</u>—in the living room. Not much was said. My two sons and two daughters seemed just as drained as us two adults. Bonifacio seemed to be the most animated. But, the rest of us were simply too dragged out—to, satisfactorily, relate to him.

When Magdalena and I finally got to bed—about 20 minutes after the kids were all ensconced—we <u>still</u> didn't talk much. Well, we didn't do hardly anything. Just laid there—like a couple nebbishes. We both—eventually—drifted off to sleep. I don't remember who'd gotten to dreamland first. And, I imagine that her dreams were just as disconcerting—and as troubling—as mine.

In the days that followed, things seemed to settle down, pretty well. In fact, Magdalena was preparing to begin homeschooling the kids. There were two books that she felt she'd still need. After an exhaustive search, we found one of them—two copies of it, actually—at a tiny used-book store, downtown. I'd not known of its existence. But, my self-accomplished teacher mate had dealt with the little leprechaun-looking owner many times before. He felt sure that he could snag a copy or two of the missing tome.

Monday—the Monday of the following week— Mr. Strathcona called! The contact had been much-anticipated, of course. In fact, the lack of any information—as to Magdalena's legal married status—had made for a rather tense weekend. For all of us.

It was good news! The document—advising my intended that she was indeed a legitimately-divorced woman—caused a tremendous sigh! Simultaneously! By all seven of us! Why the walls of the entire house did not contract—and then expand, to the bursting point—is beyond me!

Back then, there was a delightful—and very expensive—steakhouse located on the highway north of town. Mr. Strathcona's news deserved nothing but the best—celebration-wise! So, we'd all piled into the Chrysler—which was only called upon to serve, on special occasions! And nothing could be more special than learning that Magdalena was legally "available"!

I'm sure that ninety-five-point-six percent of the conversation between us "two crazy-kid lovebirds" had to do with our upcoming wedding's details.

I don't think I'd won any points from my lady love—when I'd described the nuptials as "A Twelve-Gauge Affair". And on numerous occasions.

See? There's this same reference—cited here in the past: Things were going just too good! Running just too well!

Magdalena and I had had a bit of a problem—getting everything into line for the upcoming wedding. For one thing, neither one of us had a "church home". Which surprised me the slightest bit—about my prospective bride.

Yet and still, we'd wanted a church wedding. It was going to take some doing. First of all, Magdalena—who had grown up Catholic—wanted to "test the waters" in that "persuasion". But, the pastor advised us—well, he confirmed to us what, down deep, we'd already known: That—because she'd been divorced—marriage in the Catholic Church was out of the question. We'd be—in the eyes of the Church—"living in sin". Besides, he couldn't believe that—with four kids—I'd not been divorced. Could still be married—many times over—in his eyes!

Three other pastors—from three different denominations—told me that I could not provide adequate documentation that I was not currently married. (Those four kids again—for the most part, anyway.)

Finally, I really don't know <u>how</u> we'd managed it, but the pastor of a small nondenominational church—in the far-east part of town—consented to marry us. He was <u>another</u> leprechaun look-alike. (I found myself wondering if there might not be a whole colony of the little dickens up there.) I think that the fact that he was a more-or-less friend of Charlie McNulty might've been a help.

It also took some doing—but, not as much as I'd feared—to get all the licensing paperwork taken care of. Magdalena did most of <u>that</u> navigating—and, literally, <u>all</u> of the talking.

When all was said and done, we found that it would take almost <u>four</u> weeks before we'd be able to get all the blinkity-blankity details taken care of! <u>Clear</u> all of the (expletive deleted) hurdles! The blessed service would take place on the second Saturday of October, 1968!

<u>Whoo! Finally!</u>

The day that the you-know-<u>what</u> hit the fan—happened three days before "The Big Day"!

The kids were busy with their studies. The boys at the table, and the girls lying on the floor—both studying a rather large book. Cynthia was doing her best to explain something—probably something that I'd have trouble understanding—to Mary Jane.

All <u>five</u> were not only doing well under the expert tutelage of Magdalena. They <u>seemed</u> to be <u>thriving</u>! Hell, they <u>were</u> thriving!

The Bride-To-Be had piled into the Dodge—a longer while before, than I'd expected. She was off and running—to do some grocery shopping at *The Great Atlantic & Pacific Tea Company*. (She was a quick learner.)

I'd actually expected her return to take place an hour or so before. I'd, of course, already alerted the three boys—to carry in the groceries. When two—then, two-and-a-half—hours had, slowly, ground themselves by, I'd begun to get a little uneasy.

It was shortly thereafter, when she rolled in. She was sans groceries. Not an *A&P* sack in sight. And she looked extremely <u>troubled</u>!

<u>Now</u>, <u>what</u>?

"Taylor," she rasped. "We need to talk. Can we go down to *The Arrow*?"

The Arrow? *The Arrow* was a fair-sized coffee shop, on the highway—near all the motels. I couldn't understand why she'd want to go <u>there</u>! As opposed to *Joe's*. (As it happened, we'd reached a point—where we'd seldom gone to the latter eatery. I <u>believe</u> that Magdalena had always been a little ill-at-ease—by the presence of Gretchen. God knows, I was too! Constantly scared out of my skin, actually—when she was around.)

We drove the few blocks to the hamburger joint—and, fortunately (or maybe <u>unfortunately</u>), ensconced ourselves in an oversized booth. It was located in the furthest rear corner.

Once we'd settled in—to a point—I'd looked into her exceptionally-troubled, doe-like, brown eyes, and asked, "Now, what's this all about?"

"I ran into Gretchen today," she responded. "Actually, she ran into me! I have this creepy feeling that she'd followed me! At least a good bit of the way . . . to *The A and P*! I really have the feeling that she'd been watching our place . . . watching our house . . . for a number of days." She shuddered— head to toe. "Weeks, perhaps."

"Days? Weeks? She was watching us? Following you? But . . . but, why? Why would she . . . ?"

"Well, to me, it was obvious! Obvious . . . that she wanted to catch me. Get me alone! Away from you! And today? Today, she caught me! Caught me, all right."

"I have no idea what you're talking about," I lied. I was afraid that I already was aware of—knew, all too well—what she was talking about. "Calm down, I continued, "and tell Ol' Dad . . . tell me . . . tell me what this big to-do is all about."

"She . . . this is Gretchen, now . . . she told me that she was positive that I was in some kind of danger! Maybe really serious danger!"

"In danger? In serious danger? What the hell are you . . . what the hell is she . . . is she talking about."

"She says that you're not . . . that you're not who you say you are."

"C'mon! What the hell is she talking about? Look! She and I . . . we used to be . . . well, we used to be a . . . used to be a thing! You know . . . we'd become quite . . . ah . . . intimate. She's, I think, maybe a little bit jealous. You know, we'd never gotten anywhere near talking about marriage. Not ever! But, we were . . . you know . . . we were . . . ah . . . we were in a situation where we were more than just necking, y'know."

"I know! I knew that, anyway! Well, I really didn't know about the stupid . . . the naked . . . those Chinese Checker games!"

"She told you? She told you about that? About those?"

"Yes. And she recapped the naked romps on the beach. Even filled me in . . . about Charlotte Klukay bursting in on you! Well, on you . . . then, on the two of you!"

"Look, Magdalena. If my previous sex life is going to upset you . . ."

"It's not your previous sex life. It's your previous life! Period! Sex . . . or no sex!"

"What're you talking about? What the hell are you talking about?"

"Gretchen is sure . . . she's absolutely positive . . . that you're not who you say you are! That you're not Taylor Young!"

"Not who I say . . . ? That's nonsense! Total nincompoopery!"

"She doesn't think so! She's even gone ahead and hired a private detective! Well, she hired some law firm . . . and they hired a PI! To look into you. To look . . . into your past life."

"Aw, come on, Charo'!"

I'd begun to call her that—ever since we'd seen the singer/classic guitar-player pop up on late-night

TV. She'd quite surprised me. I'd seen her wiggle her glorious bottom—plenty of times—when she'd been the featured vocalist, fronting with the Xavier Cugat orchestra. I'd rather enjoyed the provocative undulating. (I am human, after all.) The woman had a more-than-passable voice—and her "style" of delivering a song (or anything else) was (how shall I say?) "unique". Highly unique!

But, on that particular *Tonight Show*, she'd played the guitar—the classical guitar. It was strange: Once she'd gotten into the guitar piece, her entire manner had changed. She'd become, almost, a different person—Instead of that well-known flighty, semi-naughty, ditzy, blonde, she became an artist! A true artist!

Her demeanor reminded me of that of Harpo Marx. This incredibly talented man was, arguably, the zaniest of all the Marx Brothers. But, once he'd begun to play the harp, his entire image had always changed! He was no longer a nut! He'd become a true artist! For that short a time, anyway. Same with Charo. She was showing me a side of her—one that I could never have imagined. (Well, she'd already shown me—had shown everybody—a copious lot of her.)

After that, I would begin calling Magdalena "Charo"—from time to time. Usually while patting her on the fanny. It had become a tradition—of sorts. She'd never seemed to have minded. Either the new nickname—or the not-so-new pat.

"Don't come on with that 'Charo' stuff, Taylor," she responded, while we were deep in conversation, at *The Arrow*. Her voice reminded one of the largest glacier on earth. "This is <u>serious</u>," she muttered. "<u>Damn</u> serious!"

"Yeah," I muttered. "I can tell."

"Listen! The first thing . . . when your kids first laid eyes on me . . . one of the girls asked me a <u>really</u> strange question. She asked me . . . if she should tell me that her mother's name was <u>Beverly</u>! The question didn't <u>mean</u> anything to me. Not at the <u>time</u>. Never <u>thought</u> much about it. One way or <u>another</u>. Pretty much <u>forgot</u> about it. <u>Until this afternoon</u>."

I could've "lip-synced" those last three words with her! I <u>knew</u> that there was trouble ahead!

"What <u>was</u> your wife's name, Taylor? It was <u>not</u> Beverly . . . was it?"

"Look! This is a long . . . long and <u>complicated</u> . . . situation."

"Gretchen said that your former wife's name was Joanne. I'm wondering why . . . when one of your daughters asks whether she should tell a perfect stranger that her mother's name is <u>Beverly</u> . . . I wonder what she's been <u>prepped</u> for! Is <u>their</u> mother's name . . . is it really <u>Beverly</u>? Or could it be <u>Joanne</u>? You'd told me, one time . . . if I'm not mistaken . . . that <u>your</u> wife's name was <u>Joanne</u>! Told me that your former wife's name . . . the woman that divorced you . . . you, was <u>Joanne</u>! I'm <u>sure</u> you told me her name was Joanne! The mother of your children . . . and I'm <u>positive</u> you'd called her <u>Joanne</u>!"

"Listen, Magdalena! There are <u>some</u> things, that . . ."

"I <u>should</u> have been more leery of . . . more suspicious of . . . that! Of the '<u>Beverly</u>' thing!

Should've been <u>really</u> suspicious of a lot of things! For instance, it never occurred to me before . . . but, it <u>seems</u> to me, that you <u>told</u> me, <u>way</u> back, that your daughters' names were <u>Cynthia</u> and <u>Mary Jane</u>! I can't <u>remember</u>! Not for <u>sure</u>! A <u>lot</u> . . . one <u>hell</u> of a lot . . . has gone on in my life, since you would've told me that. <u>If</u> you would've told me that. <u>Any</u> of that!"

<u>THAT</u> seemed to be my only way off the hook! She seemed <u>unsure</u>! Of, at least, that <u>one</u> particular phase! The tads' <u>names</u>! That one <u>flimsy</u> particle! Not much to grab onto!

"I don't remember <u>ever</u> discussing my kids with you."

"I do! <u>That</u> part, I remember! You told me about how your father-in-law had had you <u>blackballed</u> in Brownsville. That you were living . . . had been living . . . in San Antonio. And how you couldn't put up with having to tear yourself away from your <u>kids</u>. That you picked up . . . and moved up <u>here</u>! Bailed <u>out</u> . . . from down there! To <u>escape</u>! And, I'm <u>sure</u> . . . well, truth to tell, I can't be <u>positive</u> . . . but, I'm <u>pretty</u> certain that you'd told me the names of your two daughters! During that long, drawn-out, conversation! I remember . . . being awfully <u>troubled</u>! Being <u>really</u> troubled . . . by the horrible situation that you were describing! <u>That</u>, I remember . . . <u>clearly</u>!"

"Look, Magdalena. This isn't . . ."

"Taylor? Taylor . . . who <u>are</u> you?"

"Magdalena . . . there are just some things I can't <u>explain</u>. Can't <u>tell</u> you! Simply can <u>not</u>!"

"Why <u>not</u>, Taylor? Why <u>can't</u> you explain? What are you <u>hiding</u>?"

"I'm not . . . I'm not hiding <u>anything</u>! That is to say . . ."

"To say <u>what</u>, Taylor? To say <u>what</u>?"

"Look . . . Magdalena! There are a <u>lot</u> of things here! Things that you'd <u>never</u> believe! Things that <u>I'm</u> having a problem believing! <u>Still</u> having a problem believing! Things that are <u>way</u> above any . . . any, any . . . any <u>mortal</u> understanding!"

"Any <u>mortal</u>? Any <u>mortal</u>? Now let <u>me</u> ask: What the hell are <u>you</u> talking about?"

"Magdalena, there are some thing that . . . well, some things that . . . that you're simply going to have to <u>accept</u>! Gonna have to accept . . . on <u>faith</u>! On <u>sheer</u> faith! On faith <u>alone</u>!"

"On . . . on <u>faith</u>? On faith <u>alone</u>? I should <u>accept</u> this whole . . . accept this whole <u>outlandish</u>, this whole <u>cockamamie</u> . . . <u>thing</u>? I should accept it . . . . go <u>ahead</u> and accept it? Just <u>accept</u> it . . . accept it, on pure, unadulterated, <u>faith</u>? On nothing <u>else</u> . . . but, but, <u>faith</u>? What . . . Taylor, what . . . what do you think I <u>am</u>? <u>Who</u> do you think I am? <u>Bernadette</u>? At <u>Lourdes</u>? I'm not <u>that</u> saintly!"

"I think you're the woman I <u>love</u>! The woman that I love . . . more than any <u>other</u> woman. And <u>that</u> is saying something!"

"Any <u>other</u> woman? You mean . . . like, maybe, Joanne?"

"<u>No</u>!" I was probably too emphatic—with that one-word denial. "No. You've got this all wrong! And there's no way that I can . . . can <u>possibly</u> . . . fully explain it. Again, you're simply going to have to accept it . . . on pure, blind, <u>faith</u>! But, the woman's name . . . the <u>one</u> woman I <u>truly</u> loved was <u>not</u>

Joanne! I believe I can tell you this much: Her name was Elena!"

"Elena? Latina?"

"Yes! And we were not . . . were never . . . intimate! Not in a sexual way! There are a lot of other forms of intimacy . . . other than sexual! When you let a person into your deepest . . . most cherished . . . thoughts, that is an intimacy! When the two of you are brought to tears . . . by some line, in a schmaltzy lyric . . . that is an intimacy! When you share some private situation . . . something deeply personal . . . from your past, that is an intimacy! In that way, Elena and I were very intimate. Were positively intimate! But, we never went to bed! Not even any nude Chinese Checker games! Or romps on the beach! Well, there was no beach!"

That brought a smile from Magdalena. (In spite of herself, I'm sure.)

"Look, Charo," I began to continue—then, brought myself up short, because she'd seemed to "indicate" that she was not receptive to my using that name for her. For the nonce, anyway.

"No," she replied—softly. "It's all right."

That startled me! "It's all right?" I could hardly speak. "It's all right?"

"Listen, Taylor. What you just said . . . what you've just told me, about Elena . . . just the way you spoke of her, I could tell that you were sincere! Probably tragically sincere! I've always . . . for as long as I've known you . . . felt you were a sincere man. I think that started . . . the first time I ever helped you take your shower. You didn't want to let on, but . . . I could tell . . . you were embarrassed. You'd tried to hide your privates! This was the <u>first</u> time I would've seen you unclothed! But, you didn't pull the thing off very well. Listen, a lot of guys . . . more than you could possibly imagine . . . think that <u>any</u> woman wants to drop her panties, whenever she sees a naked man! Wants to climb right into bed with him! <u>You</u> were never <u>like</u> that. Not even close."

"I never dreamed that so many mental calisthenics were going on . . . when I was removing my clothes."

"I <u>think</u> you were in the bedroom . . . when you were removing your clothes. With the door closed . . . as I remember."

"Look, Magdalena. I'm not very good at reading people . . ."

"I've noticed that."

"Well, I <u>think</u> I've detected a . . . well, a . . . a <u>softening</u>, in your manner."

"Taylor? There was <u>something</u> . . . something in your talking about <u>Elena</u> . . . that brought back to me. That brought back to me . . . made me realize, all over again . . . that I've always been <u>moved</u> by your sincerity. I know that you <u>must</u> have loved Elena! Must have <u>loved</u> her . . . very <u>much</u>. I have no way of knowing if <u>she</u> loved <u>you</u>, but . . ."

"She <u>did</u>!"

"I'm sure that she <u>must</u> have. If you were <u>that</u> much in love with her . . . she'd <u>have</u> to have loved you back. And, when you spoke of her . . . spoke so <u>lovingly</u> of her . . . that was the <u>same</u> tone, the same inflection, as when you said that you love <u>me</u>! The two were the self-<u>same</u>! Totally <u>identical</u>! I don't know Elena . . . but, she must've been a <u>wonderful</u> woman."

"A great lady! Great lady!"

"I'm sure of it! Am I a great lady?"

"Of course you are! You have to ask? Of course you are!"

"Taylor? Taylor, I think I'm going to need a time out. Well, maybe a semi-time out. What you've had to say to me . . . most especially about Elena . . . has touched me. Has touched me . . . deeply. But, I'm still troubled by what Gretchen has told me. And what you've not been able to tell me. Not as deeply disturbed . . . as when we first got here."

It was at that point that the waitress—finally—approached the table, and took our order. We both ordered the obligatory burger & fries—along with coffee. I was somewhat relieved by the "intrusion".

And, I would discover, at least Magdalena wasn't so upset that she was refusing to eat. Another consideration: She didn't order a full meal—which meant that we'd not be spending a great deal of time, at the restaurant. I really didn't know if that was good—or bad!

During the span—the time between the waitress taking our order, and delivering our food—my (hopefully) intended sat, in strark silence. In pure, unadulterated silence! You remember that old saw—about silence being deafening? It's true!

"As I was saying, Taylor," Magdalena began, once the waitress had deposited our vittles, in front of us—and had, gracefully, departed, "I kind of need time . . . and a lot of room . . . to think! It'd be easy for me to say, 'All right, Taylor, I'll accept everything you say! Accept it all on blind faith . . . because I love you! And I know that you love me. And that's halfway true!

At least, at this point! But this is a big pill . . . a helluva big pill . . . for me to swallow. At least in one taking! I know you're being sincere. I just can't imagine! Can't imagine why! Why you can't tell me the full story."

"It's . . . it's not really . . . it's anything but a story. It's a real-life experience! And, for reasons that I cannot divulge . . . you're going to have to trust me on this . . . I can not tell you any more. I simply can't, Magdalena." (I figured I'd be well-advised to use the "safe" name.)

"All right," she answered with a gargantuan sigh. "Let me chew on this monster of a cud. We won't say anything to the kids. But, I do want to have the right to back out! Even if it's at the last minute!" She'd said that last—with just the slightest trace of a shudder.

That was where we'd left it. Obviously, I could see where she "was coming from". That was a pretty hackneyed cliché—even back then. Despite the fact that I'd fared better than I'd feared—better than I'd had any right to expect—it was a real worry!

Was I to lose the only other woman that I'd ever really loved?

TWENTY-THREE

WELL, WE FINALLY GOT HITCHED! (A 12-guage affair. The old ones don't die easily.) We had three Best Men and two Maidens of Honor. (Guess whom. Guess the entire party.) The bride was given away by Charlie McNulty—who kept making remarks about not wanting to <u>give</u> her away.

"I might be persuaded to <u>sell</u> her . . . providing the price is right," he'd muttered—countless times. "Otherwise, you're gonna have to get through all the barbed wire and landmines . . . outside the church . . . to get to her."

The preacher was more than a little confused by the situation. Well, "bewildered" might be more accurate. Not the most pleased cleric you'll ever encounter. I could almost <u>see</u> him staring daggers at his pastor!

Even in the late-sixties, wedding procedures had remained pretty well standardized. Still pretty much cast in iron. (Pretty much.) The actual ceremonies may have varied from denomination to denomination. Even from church to church—in those houses of nondenominational persuasion. So, having that many "attendants"—as the preacher had referred to them (constantly)—turned out to be a bit of a trial for him. But, he seemed to be rallying. Well, most of the time, anyway.

On the other hand, he was especially perplexed—when I'd burst out laughing, shortly after he'd advised me that I could kiss the bride. As our lips were about to meet, Magdalena whispered, "Thank you . . . for making an honest woman of me."

It wasn't so much the words themselves. I'm positive they'd been said before—many, many times. In church! It was the way this particular declaration was stated. Maybe it was simply the fact that—with the "Husband and Wife" pronouncement—a monumental amount of pressure had been lifted from a copious number of shoulders. (Not the least of which were mine!)

But, I positively broke up! And so did she! Followed closely by Charlie—and, eventually, all of the kids! Not exactly what the poor man-of-the-cloth had expected. Nothing even close. (Well, considering "the cast", maybe it was not that surprising.)

All in all, it was a wonderful ceremony! One for the ages—the preacher's view of the festivities notwithstanding.

We'd decided to remain in our current living quarters. The boys' bedroom was big enough to stash another bed inside! And—with the additional piece of furniture—came Bonifacio. Steve and Randy seemed not to mind. The new roommate was—undoubtedly—happy to be free of the cursed sofa.

Closet space would, eventually, become a problem. So—while it made the room look somewhat cluttered (well, really cluttered)—we bought a rather ponderous, wooden, "wardrobe" (as my bride called it), which pretty well answered the problem (in a less-than-artful way).

Speaking of my bride, "Charo" was—once again—a "safe word"!

When all was said and done, we'd all grown to love the place—and no one seemed anxious to move away. That was the primary factor!

Royalties began rolling in—for my latest book. And, over the four or five months following the nuptials, I'd churned out yet another time-travel "masterpiece". The "masterpiece" was on its way to the publisher.

The kids were thriving—scholastically—thanks to my new wife.

There was one well-known "fly in the ointment", however. We discovered that we were having a problem with the local school board. They were loath to accept the remarkable results of our family's wonderful homeschooling projects.

The remedy: I don't know what this man did—how he'd ever accomplished it—but, the never-to-be-denied Mr. Strathcona convinced the denizens of the board to go along with our really-productive program!

Somehow, the sainted Mr. Beck wound up getting beaten up—pretty thoroughly—by some unknown band of muscular men. Charlie McNulty seemed to be sporting an evil grim—more evil than usual—along about then. Magdalena and I managed to control our grief.

So, obviously, things were going far <u>too</u> well—once again. Almost a year of tranquil, peaceful, coexistence in our little "Love Nest". As stated, I'd even begun calling my bride "Charo" once again. And she continued to not mind. You <u>know</u> things are progressing too well, when <u>that</u> happens.

So, of course, lightning <u>had</u> to strike the outhouse! What else?

The "torn asunder" factor appeared—out of the well-known blue—in late September, of 1969! In the form of—of all people—<u>Joanne</u>!

Her father had died—suddenly and unexpectedly—from a massive heart attack. Her mother—on the day after the funeral—had appealed to the Cameron County court system. She'd, obviously, wanted her daughter freed.

It worked. A number of judges—to say nothing of a copious number of local politicians—no longer had Luther York to fear! To a man, or woman, most thought that the punishment—for Joanne's theft of her father's stupid station wagon—had been <u>far</u> too harsh!

Within a matter of three or four <u>hours</u>, Joanne wound up being freed! Her sentence was—quickly—

commuted to Time Served. A copious number of legal shortcuts were—I'm sure—involved. She was, at long last, a <u>free</u> woman! A free <u>agent</u>!

She'd, of course, known that I'd moved "her kids" up to Newport. Two days after her release from prison, she was on an airplane—heading for Portland. She'd landed, rented a car—and had, immediately, headed to Newport!

The driven woman had checked into a motel—barely a mile-and-a-half from where my little clan was living. ("Little"?) We were, as you can imagine, listed in the phone book—and they were still quite plentiful, in those days. There had, of course, been one of those "gems" in her hotel room. Well, hers—and everyone <u>else's</u>. So, it didn't take all that much research—to find where I was living.

Within <u>minutes</u>, she was headed our <u>way</u>!

Us unsuspecting Youngs were, of course, completely wrapped up in our "normal", work-a-day, activities—when came the fateful knock on the door!

Jane Ace—the supposedly dim-witted star of the popular old radio show, *The Easy Aces*—used to have a rather humorous saying: "You could've knocked me over . . . with a <u>fender</u>!". I'd always thought that this was a rather funny line—till it happened to <u>me</u>! It lost a helluva lot of the humor—on that fateful day!

I was the one who'd opened the door—and there she <u>was</u>!

I don't know that I was staggered! Just the opposite! It was almost as though roots had— instantly—grown out of the soles of my shoes! I was planted—securely planted—into the floorboards!

"Mister Young?" Her voice seemed about three octaves deeper than I'd ever remembered. "Do you remember me? Do you know who I am?"

I groped for an answer! But, nothing was coming! I was—literally—unable to speak! Struck totally dumb!

Magdalena—seeing (but, certainly not understanding) my plight, (not completely, anyway)— stepped up. Came to my rescue—more or less.

"Can I help you?" she asked.

"No! Well, yes! Quite possibly! I'm . . . look! My name is . . . is Joanne Marchildon! Does that name mean anything to you?"

"Yes. Yes, of course! Of course it does! You're the mother of . . . of Taylor's . . . of Taylor's children!"

My children, at that moment, were gathered in the living room—along with their new brother. My "widow" had broken in on one of Magdalena's better home-schooling sessions. Even I was learning something.

"Only," snapped our visitor—loudly enough to have caused both Cynthia and Mary Jane to, literally, cringe! To cling to one another—on the couch, snug against the far living room wall. "Only," our irate visitor repeated, "they're not Taylor's children."

I'd finally came out of my stupor—when that exclamation finally hit home—and asked, "What do you mean . . . not my children? What the hell do you mean by that?"

"What did I just say? Do I have an impediment of speech or something? They are not your children!

They are my children! Mine . . . not yours! And I'm here to claim them."

She was employing the old "looking-daggers" glare—directed directly at me! Till then, I'd been unaware of the facts that real knives could be involved in such stares! Actual steel!

"To take them home!" she snarled. "Take them home . . . where they should be! Where they belong!"

"What're you talking about?" I half-hollered. I'd really come out of my shell! "They should be . . . be right here! Right damn here . . . is where they damn well belong! And right here . . . is where they're goddam staying!"

A lot of Paul Marchildon's old, pent-up, animosity had begun to come to the surface! I'd never really unloaded on Joanne! Not during our marriage! Not really unloaded! Not like I was about to cut loose, on her! A whole lot of anger—fury that I'd been positive was far behind me—was about to explode! The dam was about to burst! Big time!

Magdalena could see this! Anyone could have! My spouse, at that point, made a most intelligent—most logical—remark: "Won't you come in?" she suggested.

Her invitation appeared to have cut through everything! I seemed to have reentered my stupor, once more, as I pushed open the screen door.

I can't say that Joanne "stormed in". A good deal of the wind seemed to have also vanished—from her sails! I couldn't imagine why! Why the sudden change—on her part? The sudden display of seeming civility? (Key word there could be "seeming".) Could it be possible that she'd been (somewhat, anyway) disarmed by Magdalena? That didn't seem to make sense! Of course, nothing—at that juncture—was making sense!

"Are you Elena?" asked my "widow"—as she seated herself on the edge of my recliner. That little inquiry had, also, come out of the well-known left field!

That totally off-the-wall question had—also—made absolutely no sense! To me, anyway! Joanne and Elena had met two or three times—over the course of my "joyful" employment at the sainted loan outfit! The two Latin ladies looked nothing alike.

"No," answered my bride. "I'm Magdalena. I'm Taylor's wife. He's in the process of adopting Bonifacio . . . my son. Well, the son . . . to both of us, now."

"Look," I was beginning to rebound again. "Look, Mrs. Marchildon! Why should you believe that Magdalena . . . my wife . . . would ever be this . . . this, this, this . . . this Elena? I don't even know this Elena."

That statement hit Magdalena—right between those beautiful eyes! I had disclosed to her—the name of the one woman I'd truly loved! Until "Charo" had come along, of course!

"I . . . I don't know," admitted the late-comer. The answer was barely audible. She seemed even more subdued. Most un-Joanne-like! "I just saw her here," she muttered, "and . . . ! You see, my husband . . . my late husband . . . he was out screwing around, you know! He was screwing some Latin American broad! Some Hispanic bitch . . . named Elena!"

I was really steamed, at that could-hear-a-pin-drop point! (I'd only thought I'd been completely outraged before!) Listen! I was about to really let go—with an expletive-laden outburst, the like of which neither woman had ever heard! Not coming from my lips, anyway! But, Magdalena—quickly (and deftly)—headed me off!

"What does that have to do with my husband? Or even me? Most of all, what does that have to do . . . with the children? You'll have to excuse me, Mrs. Marchildon . . . but, you're coming across, as completely unwound! As totally unhinged! And it's not doing any of us any good!"

"Well, I've been without my children . . . long enough," she seethed. She was beginning to return to character! "My children were taken from me! I want them back! It's only natural that . . ."

"Only natural . . . that you would've abandoned them?" interrupted my wife. "Only natural . . . that you outright deserted them? For you . . . that's natural?"

"I . . . I didn't desert them!"

"Oh?" This was still Magdalena—and pressing our visitor, with a great exuberance! "And who, pray tell, wound up in the Arizona desert? With some yahoo? From some stupid cult? Was that Mary Poppins?"

I was shocked! I'd never dreamed that I'd spoken so extensively—to anyone—about my "widow's" conduct, post the sudden "demise" of Paul Marchildon!

"Well," responded our guest, weakly, "that was just . . ."

"And," posed Magdalena, "how about the years . . . that you were in prison? You did steal your dad's station wagon, you know! Cleaned out his wallet, pretty good, I'm told! How would you have attended to those . . . to your maternal duties? How would you have accomplished those . . . when you were in jail?"

This—to me—was incredible! Mind-warping! I'd been unaware that I'd even spoken to my spouse about any of Joanne's legal difficulties. And yet, here she was! Even aware that the vehicle involved had been a station wagon! Her knowledge of the "wallet-cleaning" was also a bone-rattling shock!

"Listen, Mrs. Marchildon," insisted my wife. "I can understand your being upset. I'd be upset . . . more than upset . . . had I lost my four kids. But, as you can see, the children are happy here. Very happy!"

In truth, the girls had bounced back—noticeably! My sons had seemed to have taken the "spirited" exchange—the entire "discussion"—in good spirits! Had viewed the encounter—well in stride! (Yet, another in-depth shock!)

"But," persisted Magdalena, "if you want to ask them . . . petition them! Ask them as to whether they'd choose to remain here! Stay here . . . or to go back to Texas, with you! If you'd care to put it to a vote . . . I'd be content to abide by their decision! Whichever way they'd decide!"

I didn't know that I'd be prepared to go that far! I didn't know whether I'd have been able to handle any of this! But, before I could even begin to speak, my youngest daughter stepped forth:

"I . . . I want to stay here! Stay here," emphasized Mary Jane, "with Daddy! And with my new mommy!"

That was a crusher for Joanne! I almost felt <u>sorry</u> for her! (Hell, I <u>did</u> feel sorry for her!) I'd <u>never</u> seen such a massive amount of <u>life</u>—so much <u>spirit</u>— drain. so swiftly (and so completely) out of someone! Nothing even close—to the way that every ounce of energy was seeping from my "widow"! Well, "seeping" doesn't quite cover the process! It was as though you'd taken a bucket of water—a bucket of <u>dirty</u> water—and thrown it up against that chair! The resultant puddle would've accurately described Joanne—at that moment!

"Look," pushed the also-sorrowful Magdalena. "I'd have no objection to your moving here to Newport. Setting up residence here."

Well <u>I</u> did! But, fortunately, I'd kept my big mouth shut. An upset of major proportions!

"Of course," continued my wife, "there wouldn't be much I could do about it, <u>anyway</u>. Nothing I could really <u>do</u> . . . to <u>stop</u> you!"

Touché!

"But, Mrs. Marchildon," expanded my esposa, "I'm a nurse. A bona fide nurse . . . by profession. And I've seen more of these kinds of things . . . more than you can possibly <u>imagine</u>! It's not a question of us <u>winning</u> . . . or you <u>losing</u>! That is a fallacious concept! You're pretty well going to have to <u>accept</u> the facts! The <u>facts</u> . . . in this situation. <u>Accept</u> them! With good grace . . . <u>or</u> with ill will. But . . . either way . . . the facts <u>are</u> the facts."

"Listen, Mrs. Young." This was the first sign of life, from Joanne—in what had seemed an eternity. "You'll have to <u>understand</u> that . . ."

"I <u>do</u> understand, Mrs. Marchildon. I <u>do</u> understand! More than you could ever <u>know</u>! But, I'm <u>telling</u> you this: You can leave here . . . go back to Texas . . . as a <u>beaten</u> young woman! One <u>filled</u> with outrage . . . and vengeance! <u>Or</u> you can see this whole situation . . . as a new beginning!"

"A new <u>beginning</u>? What're you . . . what the hell are you <u>talking</u> about?" Joanne was back to sitting up—more erectly than I could've imagined.

"You are a beautiful young <u>woman</u>," responded Magdalena. "A <u>beautiful</u> young woman! A beautiful <u>young</u> woman! One whose horizons are incredibly <u>broad</u>! You have your <u>whole</u> life ahead of you. I'm sure that you still have child-bearing capabilities. But, the secret ingredient is <u>this</u>: You've also lived a whole <u>life</u>! Virtually, a <u>full</u> life! One full of <u>experiences</u>! <u>Unique</u> experiences! Good <u>and</u> bad! You have a <u>much</u> better . . . much more <u>mature</u> handle . . . on what you <u>require</u> in your life. That you <u>choose</u> . . . at your age, and in your situation . . . to require! And <u>those</u> things are what you should <u>pursue</u>! <u>Rescue</u> the rest of your life, Mrs. Marchildon!"

"I'm . . . I can't imagine . . ." Joanne found herself muttering.

"Look," explained Magdalena, "I'm assuming that you are not as financially <u>troubled</u> . . . things are not <u>nearly</u> as critical . . . as they were during your marriage to your late husband. And . . . let's face it . . . financial horrors can make up a substantial <u>portion</u> of married life! Of <u>your</u> married life, I'm sure! A <u>substantial</u> portion! Those conditions . . . as I understand it . . . no longer <u>exist</u>! Quite probably, would <u>not</u> exist . . . in your future relationships."

My spouse was bursting—fearlessly—into waters that were shocking to <u>both</u> Joanne and me! <u>Extremely</u> troubling—in <u>my</u> case!

"I'm given to believe," she continued to push forward, "that your father was <u>extremely</u> well-off. Surely, <u>some</u> of that money . . . a goodly portion of it, I would imagine . . . would, or could, come your way. Either as a direct bequest . . . or through your mother. So, you don't have to fall for some despicable snake-oil salesman . . . who could dazzle you with a few trinkets!"

Joanne seemed to be almost <u>shrinking</u>! She was—at least from my viewpoint—virtually <u>cowering</u>! Literally pressing back—and into the chair.

"You don't <u>have</u> to assure some guy that you share his <u>interests</u>! Especially, if they're deep-seated interests! Situations . . . in which you'd have to invest <u>way</u> too much emotional currency, in sharing them. In other words, you're in <u>perfect</u> shape . . . to pick and <u>choose</u>!"

From where was she <u>getting</u> all of this? Joanne was just as bewildered as I!

But—bewilderment to the side—my wife <u>was</u> getting through to my "widow". (Apparently, I knew my former spouse—better than I'd ever <u>thought</u>!) Well, I didn't know her well enough—that I wasn't totally surprised, when she sat straight <u>upright</u>! And began to <u>weep</u>—softly!

"You . . . you're talking about my late husband? That 'sharing things' remark? That 'sharing things' . . . stuff in which I was never all that interested? Why would you say something like that?"

"Well, is it . . . or is it not . . . true? Did you have to try and fake interest . . . in things that didn't really interest you? And did you try to fake it? And . . . after a while . . . did it became too much like work? A real bother . . . to try and feign interest, in those same things?"

"Yeah," Joanne responded—sighing deeply. "Yeah, I guess so. He was always in to his dopey music, you know. And Broadway shows . . . and that sort of stuff. To the point that it was . . . all the time, all the time . . . Bing Crosby. Or Frank Sinatra. Or Rosemary Clooney. Or somebody. Somebody like that! Percy Faith! Mantovani! Axel Stordahl! And we went to see more stupid musicals! All the damn time! But, that's true . . . with everyone! You always have to . . . well, to adapt! Adapt to their tastes!"

"Well," responded Magdalena, "how did that work out . . . for you? Listen . . . it doesn't have to be true! At least . . . not in your case. You can kick back. I realize that sounds terribly insensitive, but you can kick back . . . without any financial worries, I'm guessing. Not many anyway."

"No," responded Joanne. "Not those anymore."

"And, certainly without any physical or emotional responsibilities," added my wife. "A little emotional baggage . . . maybe. But, you get to pick and choose . . . at this point in your life. More or less, anyway. Certainly more than most people. I believe you'd do well . . . to look on the, maybe-unexpected, positive side of your situation. There's a huge positive side . . . whether you realize it or not!"

"That's fine . . . for you to say. You didn't lose your kids."

Believe it or not, I was thrilled to hear Joanne say that! To say it just like that.

She'd seemed to be indicating that she'd accepted the fact! The reality—that she'd already lost her children. A purely selfish feeling on my part! But,— admirable or not—I was happy to hear her say it. And just like that! Most happy!

"That's true," agreed Magdalena. "But, you have to understand: We've . . . all of us . . . we've all had different life experiences. Not all of mine have been that pleasant. Not until I met . . . and married . . . Taylor. This environment was certainly not . . . ah . . . 'Happy Valley' for me. There've been some pretty hairy situations . . . in my life. Whether you choose to believe it or not, Bonifacio . . . my son, our son . . . has had it anything but easy. We've all had some God-awful things to overcome. That's true . . . of everyone! You, me . . . everyone!"

Joanne began to, once again, weep—silently.

Obeying an almost-invisible gesture from his mother, Bonifacio headed, hurriedly, for the bathroom—and fetched a huge box of tissues from the back of the commode. He presented the package to our guest—who gratefully accepted it. (I'd not seen that look of pure tenderness in—literally—years.)

"Look," suggested Magdalena, why don't we all go out? Go to a nice place . . . a nice restaurant . . . and celebrate? I'd certainly like to celebrate having met Joanne! I believe she's a nice lady! A wonderful woman. And I'd like to celebrate the fact that . . . in all of our lives . . . we seem to have turned a corner! I believe . . . I'm sincerely convinced . . . that nothing but <u>good</u> can come from our having gotten together, on this day! From having <u>come</u> together this day!"

All eyes—I mean <u>all</u> eyes—zeroed in on my "widow"!

She seemed to gulp—hard—a couple of times. Then, she seemed to blink away a multitude of tears. Finally she nodded her head—ever so slightly—and even halfway smiled. She'd <u>agreed</u>!

Magdalena never ceased to amaze me! She'd known of this tiny—and very expensive—restaurant, almost hidden in the many trees on the east side of the highway, about 15 miles north of town.

We'd not only arrived at the posh eatery, we took <u>over</u> the joint! The Maitre d' was <u>not</u> thrilled—when he saw five kids approaching his station. Five dreaded <u>kids</u>!

As the meal went on, though, he seemed content that his chances of surviving the onslaught were not all that devastating.

I, myself, was marveling at how well the "event" was going. I was especially overjoyed when Mary Jane began to speak—in earnest—to her mother. She'd begun by advising Joanne that <u>this</u> daddy "plays the same kind of music . . . all the time . . . as my other daddy."

Joanne responded by saying she couldn't believe <u>anyone</u> could "play that stuff as often . . . as your daddy did."

Mostly, the conversation revolved around our guest apologizing to her kids—to <u>our</u> kids—for "not staying with them".

"I didn't realize . . . never expected . . . that Grandpa would be acting as he did. To <u>you</u> . . . or to <u>me</u>," she elaborated.

The kids seemed to be concerned—more than slightly—about the results of her adversarial relationship with her father. Steve pretty well summarized the situation by advising his biological mother—that her life ought to be better "with Grandpa out of the way".

"And," added Magdalena, "I think . . . I truly believe . . . that your mother could probably <u>use</u> a little love and attention. A <u>lot</u> of love and attention. I'm sure that the past few years could <u>not</u> have been easy for her."

Where did she keep coming <u>up</u> with these things?

Joanne allowed that her hostess was probably right.

All in all, the dining adventure proved to be <u>well</u> advised! <u>Extremely</u> well-advised! Thanks to Magdalena, Joanne seemed to have gotten a <u>much</u> better handle on things—on her life! And aware of the possibilities that the future might hold for her! <u>Far</u> better—than I could <u>ever</u> have figured! It—this entire encounter—was simply <u>amazing</u>!

Once we'd arrived back at our residence, Joanne kissed each of the kids goodbye—and patted the girls on their fannies. Then, she left—directly—for her hotel.

The following morning, she called to say goodbye. She appeared <u>exceptionally</u> grateful—to Magdalena—for "setting her straight". That was the last contact—direct-in-person contact—that any of us would have with Joanne Marchildon."

That night, while lying in our round bed (we'd long since stopped being aware of its esoteric shape), I'd asked Magdalena, "How could you . . . <u>possibly</u> . . . have <u>known</u>? Known so much? About <u>me</u>? About <u>me</u> . . . and my <u>past</u>? How could you have <u>known</u> so <u>much</u>? We'd never spoken about <u>half</u> of those things. Those things you spoke about . . . with so much passion . . . to Joanne. How could you have <u>known</u>?"

"You forget," she responded—sounding much more sleepy than the occasion would've called for, "that you were an awfully sick <u>man</u>! A <u>really</u> sick man! For an awfully long <u>time</u>". <u>Exceptionally</u> sick . . . when I first came to care for you. You <u>talked</u> a lot! A <u>whole</u> lot! Mostly when you were asleep!"

"<u>Really</u>? I <u>did</u>?"

"You have to remember: The doctors had you on some pretty strong meds! At first, anyway. There wasn't much for me to do . . . but, to simply let you ramble on. No big sacrifice on my part. Your story was <u>very</u> interesting! I kind of got a little bit wrapped up in it. Well, <u>more</u> than <u>kind</u> of. More than a <u>little</u> bit. I think that <u>part</u> of me . . . must've started falling in love with you then. But, I could never <u>admit</u> that! Not even to <u>myself</u>."

"How . . . how many years did I go <u>back</u>? I mean, did I . . . ?"

"Did you reveal too much of your dim, dark, past? No. I don't think so."

Her words "dim" and "dark"—didn't set well with me. And her statement that she didn't "think" I'd "revealed too much" was also troubling.

But, having so said, she'd dropped off—immediately—into a seemingly deep sleep.

And I guess that I was, at last, realizing <u>why</u> she'd not taken Gretchen's "advice"—and <u>dumped</u> me then! It had been a struggle for her then.

On the other hand, I could only wonder <u>exactly</u> how much about me—the <u>real</u> me—that she actually knew!

THE END

EPILOGUE

THINGS HAVE LEVELED OFF—CONSIDERABLY—since that "Round Table Discussion", at that posh restaurant. The one which included all of my family—along with my angel-manufactured "widow".

For one thing, Joanne left—for Brownsville, Texas—the very next morning. And, surprisingly, she's kept in touch with us—with all of us—over the years. Pretty much, anyway.

Thankfully, she's made out well! Really, really, well!

Her mother had been in desperate need of moral—and, mostly, emotional—"back up". Joanne did not discover Eva's need—until she'd returned from her trip to The Pacific Northwest. Well, truth to tell, she'd not truly recognized it—until she'd gotten back home. I attribute that better-late-than-never realization—to the bountiful, logical (and highly emotional) amount of wisdom, which had been laid upon her by Magdalena.

Joanne—basically good woman that she's always been—more or less devoted a goodly portion of her life to attending to her mother's abject need for happiness, and even for some sort of satisfaction.

The older woman had, of course, been under the dictatorial thumb of Luther—for (literally) decades. And, of course, there'd been the attendant problems with her daughter (and with me)—as well as the situation with her husband's out and out disenchantment with (among other things) his grandchildren.

Eva had been on the brink of a nervous breakdown. Her daughter had advised us—in one of her many missives—that, had she spent any further time, in Oregon, the older woman might have "gone over the edge". (In those pre-internet days, it's hard to imagine, today, all the thought and effort that went in to all those many postal exchanges.)

When Eva finally had to be committed to an "assisted living" facility, Joanne met the man she ultimately married. The man who has, by now, sired three children with her. (Joanne maintained that just about every casual observer had thought the youngsters were her grandchildren. She'd handled the situation quite well.)

So, the mother of my children turned out to be very happy! And, for that, I'm eternally grateful!

My own children turned out exceptionally well! Exceptionally well!

Bonifacio and Steven went into business for themselves—when both were only 24-years-of age. The enterprise was a (hiss/boo) collection agency. It has proven to be exceptionally lucrative!

Both had run—and delivered—what turned out to be the largest paper route (at least in our part of town). They'd started that ambitious project—when they'd been barely 14-years-old. Once they'd turned 18, Charlie McNulty hired Steve to work at his garage. A month later, he also hired Bonifacio.

It fell to Randy—to take over the massive paper delivery operation. And he handled it beautifully—something he'd not let his older brothers forget.

When Steven turned 20, he realized that Charlie was—heroically—struggling to retain both of my sons. So, he went to work for a small collection agency—and took to the business, like the proverbial fish to water. Six months later—when Charlie was getting ready to retire—Bonifacio joined his brother, at the agency.

They picked up on the collections field—very nicely. Not only the collection end, but the marketing end. (You do have to find "clients"—who will place delinquent debtors accounts with your agency.)

Practically immediately—after having undertaken to buy the business from the rather discouraged owner—they'd landed two of the banks, where I'd been doing business, for years (thanks to "The Guys"). That was a great start! Shortly thereafter, they'd signed up the largest medical clinic, in the area. Then, came the hospital—and the phone company.

Eventually, they'd had additional banks, auto supply stores, furniture stores, appliance stores—even ladies clothing stores—placing their "paper" with their thriving, fast-growing, enterprise. Clients from as far away as Portland. After almost 9 years, they'd purchased a large agency, in Seattle! The acquisition more than <u>tripled</u> their revenue—and, at least, <u>doubled</u> their management responsibilities.

A little over a year ago, they sold the entire—the immense—corporation! Both are now <u>millionaires</u>!

Randy came <u>close</u> to earning numbers like that! He chose sales. For awhile, he sold highly-overpriced waterless cookware—then, highly-overpriced vacuum cleaners. With the latter company, he moved up into management. He finally became a vice president of the organization. He's still with 'em—and taking home a six-figure income.

The girls, now! They're a whole 'nother thing! From just about the git-go, I was worried—massively worried—about them. I'd not been perceptive enough to have spotted it (not at the time) but, looking back, I believe that—from the time we'd gotten to Newport—they were apprehensive over the possibility of their mother "coming to get them".

I think that—when Joanne had finally arrived—Cynthia and Mary Jane had, both, figured that "doomsday is here". When things had—wonderfully—worked out the way they had, it had still taken my daughters a heartbreaking long time, to actually buy into the fact that their situation was <u>not</u> going to change!

Again, as imperceptive as I've always been, I didn't pick up on their apprehension. But—as always—my wife did. About a week after Joanne's departure, Magdalena made a big production—out of taking them to a very exclusive store, in the center of town. There, she encouraged the girls to pick out whatever doll they would like—no matter the expense.

Both girls chose the most beautiful dolls I'd ever seen. What's more, they <u>cared</u> for those china masterpieces! <u>Mothered</u> them! For <u>years</u>! <u>Well</u> into their late-teens!

Cynthia—even before attaining her high school equivalence diploma (Magdalena had homeschooled them through all those years)—got into social work.

She volunteered—then, after "graduating", interned—at the orphanage, run by the Catholic diocese. She ultimately became one of the attendants there. After almost 17 years, she wound up running the joint.

With the financial help of Steven and Bonifacio—and the administrative aid of Randy—she opened a whole <u>new</u> facility, equipped with "state of the art everything". But, the <u>love</u>! The <u>loving</u>? And the <u>caring</u>? <u>That</u> all came from Cynthia! Still <u>does</u>! My oldest daughter—to this day—spends 16 or 18 hours each day, at the facility. She has never married. She's <u>that</u> devoted to her cause—and "all those wonderful kids".

She put together—on her own—a marketing campaign, to <u>get</u> these kids adopted. A highly-<u>successful</u> campaign! She's been so successful in this undertaking that the archbishop of Portland came out to—personally—take note of how she was achieving these magnificent results!

Mary Jane went "the other way". When she was 16, she met Robert (not "Bob")—who had, for years, planned to become a Catholic priest. But, once the powers that be—for some reason—decided that he was <u>not</u> fodder for their seminary, he "took up" with Mary Jane. Two years later, they were married.

They are the proud parents of seven kids! Four boys and three girls! The latter trio are—of course—the apples of their grandfather's eye.

And there is Magdalena! What can I say—about my wonderful wife? (The old "What Can I Tell You?" classic.) She's been a truly remarkable woman. (Still is!)

A most important ingredient—vis-a-vis our marriage: She was devoted—completely devoted—to me. That sounds so anti-feminist—but, it is not! Was not! Never has been!

She became dedicated to seeing that everyone in the family—with the possible exception of herself—was continually happy! Happy and contented! Happy and contented—and successful!

My wife homeschooled each one of our children! Our children! And I would stack any of them—all of them—against any other group you'd ever want to trot out! And it wasn't just the "book-larnin'" phase of her far-flung contributions. She taught them character! She taught them moxie! It's no accident that they've all been highly-successful—in their various, multi-faceted life's calling.

She was of immeasurable help—when I'd get hung up in some phase (in any phase) of any one of my books.

As a family, we've made many trips to Portland and Seattle—to take in a multitude of Broadway musicals. Even two or three trips down to San Francisco—to take in a few concerts. Once, all the way to Los Angeles.

An answer to a prayer: A fervent prayer! I'd opened that same door to Magdalena—as had been the case with Elena! Well, our having taken in *South Pacific*—the movie—on that fateful night, had pushed the door ajar! But, I'm <u>convinced</u> that it was at a small theater, in Tacoma, that we'd "kicked the sonofabitch in"—As Houston Oilers Coach, Bum Phillips, had once described it. And <u>that</u> show was (would you believe?) *Oliver*!

As time had gone by—and our responsibilities, toward the kids, had slowly diminished—she and I had come more and more closely attuned to one another.

We'd never approached the sort of thing where we'd sit up till all hours—and sing along with the Original Cast of *Finian's Rainbow*, as had been the case with Gretchen and me. It was an altogether different situation.

We'd curl up on our newly-bought—our <u>immense</u>, our very-<u>expensive</u>—curved couch, and listen to schmaltzy music. Mostly stuff by Mantovani or Percy Faith or Paul Weston.

I would (ahem) "sing" the lyrics—in my own inimitable eight-octave-crack, rusty-file, voice—to her. Sometimes, we'd curl up in our round bed (yes, we still had <u>that</u>)—and I'd sing to her there. (Part of my scorched-earth policy, y'know! I showed no <u>mercy</u>!)

There was <u>one</u> deep disappointment! There was no getting around it! A major <u>disappointment</u>! A sometimes overwhelming <u>frustration</u>! I was <u>never</u> able to determine what happened to Elena.

Three or four times, I engaged my old contact, in San Antonio—Adam Browning. He was never able to get a handle on Elena's fate. Apparently, her father had passed away—shortly after the kids and I had settled in, in Newport. Her mother had moved away—almost immediately thereafter.

From that point on, it was as though she—and Elena and her kids—had disappeared off the face of the earth.

To say that Elena had not had a definite effect on my life would be sheer folly.

There was always a slight ghost of my having sung the lyric to *Till*—while dancing with her, at that little bar northwest of San Antonio. A specter of it had always remained—while singing to Magdalena!

I've <u>always</u> steered clear of sharing the singing of *Till*, with my wife. But, I've always had the feeling that she was aware of the fact—that there was "The Ghost Of <u>Something</u>" present, during those exceptionally pleasant interludes. She also knew—peripherally—of my <u>search</u> for "Someone Unknown", during our years together. I'm positive that she was aware of the fact that that "Someone" would've been Elena! <u>Never</u> did she question <u>any</u> of those fruitless quests! <u>Ever</u>!

Through the years—ever since that angel took over the speaker, in my beloved 1948 Chrysler (which I still <u>have</u>, by the bye)—I'd always spent a <u>lot</u> of time, wrapped up in the fate/the wellbeing of *Those We Leave Behind*.

For the most part, those that <u>I've</u> left behind have fared pretty well—with one notable exception. (Where <u>ever</u> you are, Elena, God bless!)

But, for the most part, each of those "success stories" was due to <u>Magdalena</u>!

She was a glowing influence on my children—all five of them. And—in a great measure—on the complete and utter turning-around of Joanne.

And—through my "widow"—she'd had a good deal of influence on the well-being of Eva, my mother-in-law! I thank God for my wonderful, loving, caring—and perceptive—wife!

I hate to say "on the other hand", but, that angel—on that incredible night, in Seguin—had promised me that neither he (nor would any of the other "guys") would ever send "anyone special" to me. On the other hand, my remarkable wife was "special". Always will be!

Now, maybe I did do all that talking—to Magdalena—when I was under her care. But, would that have meant that "The Guys" had divined that accident? Mrs. Grimshaw had never done anything like running a stop sign before! And—through the years—she'd been a tremendous help to me! In so many ways!

In any case, I cannot imagine what life for me would've been like—had I not taken the "deal" from "The Angel In The Dashboard"! The same holds true—when pondering what would've happened to Joanne and the kids (as well as Magdalena and Bonifacio)!

And, thankfully, I've gotten—completely—over wondering about "schmuckdom"!

To this day, I've always wondered how she could've known so much about me. Could she have had a direct line to "The Guys"? On the other hand, she did know that her husband loved a lady named Elena. And so did Joanne's.